BRODIE COLE

On the Line

First edition

ISBN (paperback): 979-8-9903851-5-3
ISBN (hardcover): 979-8-9903851-6-0

Editing by Gayle Wardenski

This book was professionally typeset on Reedsy.
Find out more at reedsy.com

I cannot express enough how thankful I am to have the people in my life who have waited and helped me in this journey.

A huge, astronomical shout-out to my lovely and sweet Gayle. Who worked so hard to help my dream become a reality and help me so much on this journey. She has gone above and beyond, and I couldn't have done this without her.

"If there's something you want in life, don't find time for it, make time for it."

BRODIE COLE

Contents

1

Master

"To the future!" the strong voice of a powerful man roared above the hundreds of newly inspired soldiers cheering down below. Each warrior swung their weapon high in the air as they whooped and rallied together. Not one could tear their eyes away from their wise and fierce leader who stood at his lofty podium, smiling with confidence.

The dark-eyed man held one fist high to the sky, as he boldly scrutinized his army. The echoes of their voices rattled from the walls of the coliseum-sized room. Their leader, whose confident grin crept to the corners of his jaw, turned to leave the ledge and head back to his quarters. He marched through the long tunnel with his two right-hand men, Ogan and Kenji, following alongside.

"Sir, the troops seem really fired up today, even after that incident we had a few weeks ago. How do you do it? How do you inspire them all so easily?" Kenji asked, still hearing the cheering behind them.

Their leader did not reply; he kept his eyes forward, seemingly unimpressed. As they looked at him more closely, they could see that his eyes were locked forward with ferocity, and the musk of rage flowed behind him. His footsteps boomed loudly through the hall; the stomping sound was nerve-racking. He pushed back his mostly silver hair and his hand grazed over the last few remaining strands of black. His mouth was closed in a grim line, and the rough beard that followed his jagged jaw was almost as bushy as his furrowed eyebrows.

The two young men glanced at one another. They didn't understand why he was like this. His speech had been inspiring and all-out empowering to his cause, so what could possibly be the matter?

They reached the end of the tunnel and hurried ahead to open the doors for their leader, who stormed in. A gust of wind blew past them as chills ran down their spine. They caught a glimpse of his cold, dissatisfied black eyes.

"Shut the door!" he yelled.

The two quickly did as commanded and watched as he marched inside, the sound of his name still thundering out from beyond the closing doors.

Their leader walked behind his desk, slumped down in the chair and put his head in his hands, elbows propped on the desktop. His fingernails dug into his skull, and the veins on his arms could be seen bulging through his crepey skin. The wooden desk creaked when he leaned forward, and small clouds of cold breath puffed through his arms as he stared down.

Once again, the two young men looked at one another, alarmed at this sudden change of mood. The air felt thick with a cold pressure, like a demon was festering inside the walls of the room. They heard the echoing voices from outside the room grow quieter, and noticed the angered huffing of their master intensify. Whatever they did next could make him snap as if they'd taunted a bear who hadn't eaten in years.

It was Kenji who finally asked, "Is everything alright, sir?"

He abruptly slammed his fist on the table, splitting the wood. Kenji and Ogan flinched in fear as they stared into the eyes of a monster. Their leader stood up slowly with his head dropped to his chest and jaw clenched, as he huffed out a breath through gritted teeth. Splinters of wood fell from his hands to the floor as the desk was barely holding together.

The two young men were absolutely terrified of their master at this moment. They had seen him like this before, but never under these circumstances. Neither had any idea why the boss's emotions had changed so quickly. Their hearts raced as the only move they could make was to try to stop the uncontrollable shaking of their hands.

Seeing their fear, the old man scoffed aggressively at them, then carefully sat back down in his chair. He rubbed his aging eyes and slowly calmed himself. "Have a seat, boys," he commanded in a low voice. Kenji and Ogan fearfully walked over to the chairs opposite him and sat quietly before their leader, nervously awaiting what was next. They moved cautiously, trying to calm themselves as the nerves inside their bodies still rattled.

Their master sat up and leaned forward to them. "What do you two think I'm upset about?"

They turned to one another and paused before either of them spoke. What *was* there to be upset about? He had just given an inspirational speech to his army; they were fully motivated and ready to fight for his cause. They had successfully conquered another location and spread the will of the world in the past few days. None of this made sense.

The smaller of them, Ogan, finally built up the confidence to speak, and asked in a small voice, "Is it because of what happened a month ago?"

"What about it?" The grim man's tone was ominous.

The two were silent once more. They stared at their leader whose eyes were now filled with even more rage than before. His clenched fists began to shake with each second that passed without a response, the veins ready to burst out of his aging skin.

"Maybe... It's because we probably lost a key stronghold in that incident—because *you two* couldn't do a simple task!" he shouted as he shot to his feet. His chair flew backward, crashing into the wall. The books on the shelf behind him fell to the ground as his chair knocked into them, then he slapped his hands down hard on the desk once more.

Kenji and Ogan flinched with fear as their boss glared at them with frustration blazing from his very core.

"Hundreds and hundreds of our men, so utterly pitiful and weak! That base is useless now, you know! A crucial chunk of our army, beaten in a matter of *minutes!*" he raged on, louder now, as he stomped around to the front of his desk. The walls rattled with each word he shouted and both of them sank deeper into their chairs.

3

"How come three pathetic weaklings, and *that* brat, all got past our army and were able to defeat so many of our men, and so *easily?*" he fumed and pressed even closer to them.

"Please, sir, we had no idea. You knew that the one guy was capable of great power; it was all just a miscalculation, a fluke even," Ogan explained. The older man turned to his lieutenant, then abruptly grabbed him by the collar, lifting him into the air. Ogan's tangled black hair fell over his face, covering his wide blue eyes. Their master's blood boiled so furiously that a kind of psychic tremor rumbled through Ogan which made his teeth chatter.

"I don't want to hear an *excuse!* I want to know why you two couldn't *kill* him!" their irate master shouted, as he tossed the boy back into the chair. The boss's eyes next focused on Kenji, who tried to keep up a confident appearance even as sweat dripped down his face. Kenji sneaked a glance to his right and made eye contact with his master. It had been a while since he had seen him quite like this.

"Maybe, if it wasn't for *you* demanding that we needed to retreat from *our* base—where we outnumbered them by the hundreds—then we might have killed them!" their leader bellowed.

Kenji lowered his head and took the discipline like a helpless dog being cowed and beaten.

"I raised you two for years and years. I trained you to be warriors for the cause. Day after day I used my time, effort, and skills to mold you into the perfect vessel, the perfect example of what a truly powerful man could be. Now, all I can see are those pathetic young boys I once took in—small, weak, and helpless!" Their leader shook his head, then stomped off and left the room, slamming the door on his way out.

The walls shook as the door closed with a sudden echoing boom. Even as they heard his footsteps move farther from the door, their tense bodies could barely move. The two young men just sat quietly, letting their heart rates lower slowly, though the fear remained. The terror they had felt as they'd looked into their master's eyes was immense. They knew he was a strict and powerful man, but never once had they seen him quite this angry over something.

"You okay, Ogan?"

"Yeah, yeah I'll be fine. Thanks."

The two of them stood up and took a slow deep breath, then exited through the opposite door. They walked on with no words to speak as they headed to their quarters for the night.

The dark halls were only lit by the faintest of lanterns. There was no window or any opening to the outside world. The base they resided in was completely hidden from the sun, and impossible to get into without entering through a hidden entrance. Their footsteps echoed down the rocky, human-made corridors and the sound clattered across every wall.

After they got to their room, they sat on their beds in silence. The sound of that silence was louder than ever. They felt the echoes of their master's words burning in their ears. The pits of their stomachs ached as fear overtook all other emotions. The silence magnified their fear and left them to imagine what fresh hell awaited them. The few minutes that they had been in that room with their master had felt like hours. They tried to shake off what they had witnessed.

Many quiet minutes had passed when Kenji said, "Ogan, what do you think about the master?"

In response, Ogan flopped on his bed, and then stared at the blank ceiling above him with his arms behind his head and his feet propped up on the footboard. His eyes closed briefly before he replied, "That man took us in when we were no one, Kenji. He trained us like we were his sons and provided us with a future. We never knew our families because this harsh world we live in had cast us out. We were taught how to fight and become stronger to help this world in our master's vision. He will be the one to fix this still-broken world, and I want to be there to see it through."

All of this was quite true, they were nothing before he came along and saved them ...

Many years ago...

5

"Alright children, pack it up!" a grumpy old man shouted down a long hallway lined with many doors.

Each child jumped when the sound of his crackly voice hit their ears. They all ran to poke their heads out from their sad little rooms and saw their aged caretaker standing next to a stranger.

This stranger was old, tall, muscular, and scary-looking. He had muscles as big as boulders, and towered far over their caretaker, who was, admittedly, on the shorter side. The thin, salt and pepper beard on his face traversed his still-firm jawline underneath a slight smile. His nearly coal-black eyes stared boldly down the hallway at the sixteen children peeking from the doorways. The stranger's long, jet black hair was finely streaked with white and was slicked back from his forehead, forming a slight widow's peak. His dark eyebrows, which seemed to want to meet in the middle, always made him appear angered. The children peered at him shyly.

"This man is takin' alla' youse home!" the round-bellied caretaker announced. The mysterious stranger beside him smiled and gave a little wave to all of the nervous children.

"No way."

"Is he for real?"

"*All* of us?" they whispered to one another. Being adopted was a rare occasion in these parts of the world, and for someone to adopt sixteen children all at once, well, that was unheard of.

The stranger knelt to be on level with the children—boys and girls who appeared to be no more than eight to nine years old. "Hello, I will be your new caretaker. I hope we can all get to know each other better in our new home. You all can think of me as your teacher, but just call me 'master' for now," he said with the slightest of smirks.

Some of the children's faces began to light up as they could see that this was not a joke; they were really going to have a home.

"Did you hear that, Kenji? He's gonna take *all* of us in! We don't have to go hungry anymore," Ogan whispered, his kind eyes glowing with anticipation.

"You and I are *really* like brothers now!" Kenji whispered back.

Both had black hair, as brothers may, though Kenji's was parted in the middle, falling to chin-level, and Ogan's tousled black mop seemed to have a life of it's own, accentuating his luminous, bright blue eyes. Kenji was taller, and his clear, but hollow-looking, hazel eyes glowed above dark circles; Kenji even worried as he slept, and he slept less than most. Both were thin and malnourished.

Most of the children ran straight back into their rooms and began to collect the meager items they'd had with them when they were first dropped off in this miserable place many years ago. One by one, they all ran back to their new caretaker with no fear in their minds anymore. Homebound they were, with a new life to start; it began that day.

"Do you have everything, Ogan?" Kenji asked.

"Yep! I'm all ready!" The two giggled to one another as they held tightly onto their sparse belongings and rushed to join the others. Lining up one by one, the giddy kids could hardly stand still.

"You sure you want to take them all? Just sayin', that seems too good to be true." the old caretaker said, and hiccuped. This stranger had interrupted him mid-ale.

"Absolutely. These children deserve a good life, and I plan to set their futures the right way," the man replied as he called for the children to follow him home.

The last two in the line, Kenji and Ogan, watched their friends follow along behind their new master. Together they walked through the rickety orphanage, then out of the large wooden doors. The sunlight beamed down on them from above the clouds as they marched on like one big family.

"Where do you think the master lives?" Ogan asked.

"I don't know but I hope it's better than the orphanage, with enough food and water for all of us to eat till our bellies burst!" Kenji cheered. The two laughed as they followed along at the back of the line through the big city of Cannon-Gulf.

"Here we are, children." the man finally called out to all sixteen of them as he stopped in front of quite a large house. The long walk through the city was over, and with sore legs and eager anticipation, they were home. Everyone's eyes widened as they gazed at the beautiful house before them. Their mouths gaped, no words able to exit their lips.

"Why don't we go inside?" the master suggested as he walked up to open the front door.

Like a pack of wild animals, they rushed after him to scramble inside. As soon as they'd all surged through the doorway, they saw that it opened up into a big foyer with a long stairwell leading up to the second floor. The ample downstairs was remarkably open. There was a spacious kitchen and an immense living area, with a large outdoor yard for play accessed by double doors in the back.

"You may all place your things upstairs in your rooms. You will have to share a room with someone else, but I will let you decide who that will be. Then please put on the new clothes that I've put in your rooms, and meet me back downstairs in a few minutes," the master instructed as he headed towards a chair in the living area.

With a burst of energy, they all charged noisily upstairs to claim their rooms. Left and right, they zig-zagged across the second floor to pick out the best room for themselves. "Hurry! This one Ogan!" Kenji called out, as he found one that was just right for the two of them. In only a few minutes, everyone was able to find a partner and settle into their new rooms.

The two boys jumped on their beds and felt the warmth of soft sheets on their skin. They sighed, finally feeling comfort. "These are *so* much better than the beds at the orphanage! These are actually comfy and have fluffy pillows!" Ogan shouted.

Then they ran around the room checking out every nook and cranny to be found. It wasn't until they opened up the closet that they saw the many options of clothes available for them to wear. "Oh right! Master said we should hurry up and change so we can meet him on the first floor," said Kenji. So the two of them quickly got out of their dirty clothes and put on their fresh-looking new ones.

"Wow, these are so *nice*! I feel all warm and clean now!" Kenji posed jauntily as he looked at himself in a mirror.

The stomping sounds of the other kids hurrying down the stairs began to echo through the house, so the two quickly joined the others heading downstairs.

"Ah, there you are boys and girls," the master mumbled as he moved to sit forward in his chair. He rolled up the paper that he was reading and called for the children to have a seat in front of him.

Rushing to be the first and closest, they huddled together in front of him, all sitting cross-legged on the floor. Their eyes and ears were wide open, as they waited with excitement to see and hear what would be next. It hadn't even been a full hour since their arrival, and these children were already having the time of their lives, revelling in this unexpected new beginning.

"I assume you all are enjoying your new home?" he asked.

That question turned out to be a bad choice of words, because the result was a clamor of children's voices all interrupting one another as they tried to loudly articulate just how happy they were indeed.

The master raised his hand and silenced the young ones so that he could collect himself before speaking. "I am pleased to hear that you are all comfortably settling in with your new home. Now, if you are going to be living here, I have a few rules that I will be going over. Do I make myself clear?" he began.

"Yes!" they all shouted eagerly.

He smiled softly as he sat in front of all of these grinning children, who did seem to be listening carefully.

"Rule one, you will all address me as your master and reply with 'sir' after each question. Does that make sense?" The master then tilted his head waiting to hear them say it.

"Yes, sir!" all exclaimed.

"Good, you all seem to get the hang of it. Now, as your teacher, I will be showing you how to protect yourself in this world. As each of you has experienced firsthand, this world is not as it was many years ago. In order to survive and create a place of order, you must be powerful and create said order," he preached sternly.

The children all began chattering to one another, growing excited at the fact that not only would they get a home to live in, but they would learn to fight just like those heroes in the legends that they told to one another. Their little feet began to wiggle uncontrollably at the idea that they could become like those strong warriors.

"Settle down, I am not one to wait and repeat myself," the master said firmly, as his pleasant face now showed an underlying hardness and impatience.

The children quickly quieted themselves and sat still, some even held their breath, but not one of them made a sound.

"Each morning, you will wake up early to begin training, and you must not be late, no excuses. Time waits for no man and I intend to do the same. Your training will not be easy, and I will be holding you to a standard no lower than that of perfection. You can always go back to that hell-hole of an orphanage if you please, but if you stay, I will make you warriors of this world," he promised with a smug smile.

The kids kept their mouths closed as instructed, but began to look around at one another. Some seemed eager about this new life, while others appeared a little nervous.

"More rules will come along as you live under my teachings but for now, I leave you with only one last order. You must never, and I mean *not ever*, go into the basement. Do I make myself clear?" He leaned forward as he pointed to the door across the room.

"Yes, sir," they replied, with a tinge of fear creeping into their voices.

"Good! Now, dinner has been cooked for you and placed in your rooms. Please go eat and prepare yourself for a long day tomorrow." The master stood up from his seat and headed for the front door.

The children wasted no time when they heard the word "food" and rushed back upstairs to their rooms. Who knew how long it had been since they had had a full meal to eat? They scarfed down every last crumb on their plates, and left not a single drop of water in their pitchers.

This place seemed like a paradise to them. Not even an hour ago they'd been rotting away in that awful orphanage run by a grumpy old sot who could barely provide for them.

"We did it Kenji, we got out," Ogan whispered as he plopped on his bed.

"We promised each other that we'd leave that place one day and become real brothers. Now, it's like we actually are!" Kenji said, cheering silently to himself, not wanting to upset the master.

The two giggled softly as they realized their childhood dreams were coming true. A new home, a life together as a family, and someone to teach them how to fight and protect one another—everything they would ever need was now within their grasp.

The setting sun shone through their window, changing the lighting to a bright orange and yellow glow. Even though this day wasn't over, all of the children were entirely tuckered out from their journey, along with all of the food that they'd eaten. They lay in their beds, drifting into a comfortable slumber. As one by one they fell asleep in their rooms, the joy of a new home brought them so much happiness that the smiles on their faces remained.

"Hey, Kenji ..." Ogan mumbled, as his eyes could barely stay open.

"Wha... what?" Kenji asked softly, as he too was a few seconds from falling asleep.

"You'll always be there for me, right?"

"What do you mean? Of course, I will. No matter what, I will be there to protect you. We're brothers after all, aren't we?" Kenji assured his friend as his eyes finally fell shut. He was out.

Ogan smiled one last time, and a little tear ran down his cheek. His mind was now cleared, and he could rest easy knowing that his friend would be right by his side to the very end.

2

Student

"Get up Ogan, this is pathetic!" the master roared, as he stood above the young boy on the ground who was clenching his stomach in pain.

Kenji ran over to Ogan's side, trying to help his friend up, but was roughly swatted away.

"If he wants to survive in this world, he will get himself up!" the master shouted.

Ogan planted one foot on the ground, and wiped the tears away from his face. As he got up and tried to straighten his back, his knees buckled, and he struggled to stay standing.

"Come on kid, do you want to die?! You have to push past all of those weak thoughts, and focus on the will to overpower, to win!"

Ogan's frail, tired body could barely keep itself upright as he charged right back in at his master. The children surrounding him all just sat there bruised, bloody, and exhausted from training.

Ogan threw punch after punch at his master but couldn't land a single one. He was too tired to focus, and was running solely off of his muscles moving of their own accord.

"Not good enough!" the man grunted, as a swift uppercut pounded into the young boy's chest, knocking him out.

"Ogan!" Kenji yelled as he ran to his friend. He immediately lifted him off the ground and lugged him over to the side of the yard, searching for his pulse.

"He will be fine; he's still too weak right now. That goes for all of you. I've trained you all for a whole year now, and you are all still pathetic weaklings. I need to see improvement or else I will strip all of you of any food for a week!" he shouted as he stormed off to the house.

"Keep training until the sunlight is bare of the sky!" the master bellowed, then slammed the back doors shut.

The boys and girls all jumped at the sound of the doors abruptly closing.

Sitting on the grassy earth, some cried, some panted, others couldn't even move. One whole year had passed since he had taken them in. Day and night the kids trained in hand-to-hand combat, sparring against one another, and even their master. They had no choice but to listen to him; he promised them such a glorious future, one where they would become unstoppable warriors of the world. His words could be both inspiring and terrifying all at once.

They couldn't even go back to that old orphanage now; rumor was that it had burnt down a few months after they'd gone.

"Let's go everyone, we have to keep training, or else the master will get mad," one of the kids called out, as he stood up from the ground. The rest of them slowly got to their feet to work on their combat skills again.

Kenji looked down at Ogan and saw that he was still unconscious. He lifted him carefully off the ground and began to carry him inside to get him out of the hot sun.

"Where are you going?" one of the girls asked.

"He won't be able to do anything now, I have to take him inside before he overheats," Kenji told her, as he struggled to open the back door. Once he managed to get it partly open, he stealthily peeked inside and saw his master opening the forbidden door to the basement. He watched as the master closed it behind him, then heard his footsteps grow softer as he went down the stairs.

Kenji opened the back door all the way, then hurried upstairs with Ogan to their room, trying not to get caught by anyone. He placed Ogan in his bed and made sure he was still breathing. The bloody blotches on his friend's body were still wet, and his bruises were growing and getting even darker.

"Damn it! Hang in there Ogan, it'll be alright." Kenji whispered. With his own back muscles cramping from carrying his friend the whole way, he stretched, then began to rush back outside before he got in trouble.

As he ran downstairs he noticed that the basement door wasn't quite shut; it was cracked open just a little bit. He hastily walked past it and reached for the handle of the back door, but then stopped and slowly looked behind him. No one was around, everyone was outside, and the master was in the basement.

I wonder... Kenji thought, his abundant curiosity kicking in. He slowly crept over to the slit in the door and listened carefully for the sound of footsteps, just in case the master was returning from wherever he was down there. All he could hear was the sounds from the kids practicing outside and the wind lightly breezing in through the windows. There Kenji stood, right outside the door, pausing in front of it with his heartbeat throbbing in his ears.

He grasped the handle of the door ever so gently and peeked in. Kenji stared down the empty stairwell, only able to see roughly ten steps that led to a left turn at the bottom. It was rather anticlimactic, but it left him thinking, *What's around the corner?*

The boy *needed* to know what was down there, so he broke the one most important rule that the master had commanded of them, and put his foot softly down on the first step toward the basement. Nothing happened. Like a little mouse sneaking away from a cat, he continued, taking every step slowly and carefully, doing his best not to make a single sound. He could feel and hear his heart beating even more quickly now, as the faintly lit stairwell engulfed him. The door behind him felt ever so far away as he approached those last few steps below.

He was almost at the bottom step where he would finally be able to peep around the corner to witness what was so forbidden to see. Taking that last step felt the most difficult. He gripped the wall and silently glanced

14

back up the stairs to see that the door was still ajar. He took in a quiet deep breath and held it as he peeked around the corner with just one eye.

"What the...?" he whispered, as he gazed down into the longest stairwell he had ever seen. Hundreds of steps descended downward, with lanterns lit beside every third step, leading to a tarnished-looking door far down at the very bottom.

The boy was very confused as to why the master would have such an odd stairwell leading into the depths of the underground. It was a very strange thing to have in any house, so why was it in his?

His master never told them anything about where he was going all those times he'd left, nor had he even told them his name as of yet. This man, who was their master, mentor, and even a father figure for the past year, was really a total stranger to them. He was their caretaker and yet a complete mystery. Never once did he share anything about himself. Even when they asked, he never really gave an answer.

Kenji was snapped back into reality by the echoing sound of that metal door at the bottom creaking open.

"Crap!" He ducked his head back around the corner and scurried back upstairs in a panic before he could be seen. He felt that his life would surely be over if he were caught. His feet flashed quickly up the stairs as he tried not to make a single sound.

When he made it to the top of the stairs, he put the door back exactly where it had been before, then ran for the backyard to join the others. He exited the house huffing and puffing, and fell to his knees near his companions.

"What's wrong, Kenji?" one of them asked.

"Nothing. I just had a hard time bringing Ogan upstairs," he gasped.

They all believed him without a second thought, then kept on training before the master caught them taking a break. Kenji wiped the sweat from his face and hustled to his feet to keep practicing, while he thought to himself, *What is down there?*

"What happened?" Ogan groaned later, as he tried sitting up in his bed. He realized he wasn't outside training anymore, and it appeared to be nighttime now. Looking across the room he saw Kenji lying on his bed throwing a ball up into the air and catching it as it fell.

Ogan thought back to the last thing he remembered doing. He had a glimpse of a fist striking him in the chest, and then everything had gone white. Ogan realized he'd been knocked out at training, and must have been brought back to his room while he was unconscious.

Slowly, he sat up in his bed and glanced across the room to his friend.

"Are *you* doing alright?" he asked.

Kenji didn't reply and kept throwing the ball up into the air, not turning his head. Shadowy silence filled the air, and the two sore, tired boys had only moonlight to softly illuminate their room.

"Who do you think the master really is?" Kenji asked.

"What do you mean?" replied Ogan.

"I mean, he obviously cares about us since he's teaching us to become warriors of the world. He was the only one there for us a year ago. He gave us a home and food to live on. He works us hard so we can be as strong as him someday, but we are all still too young and weak." Kenji observed.

Ogan stood up from his bed, slowly stumbling to the open window.

"Master just has a harsh way of teaching. I know he can see something in all of us, and one day we will make him proud. He definitely cares for us; we just have to work harder. Just like he said before, this world isn't one to give out an easy life. We have to work for it." Ogan declared.

Kenji caught the ball he was tossing and held it tightly in his hands. Even though his friend had just been badly beaten and bruised, he still had the loyalty and courage to say these things. Ogan wasn't the most physically strong, but he was the strongest mentally, and steadfast almost to a fault.

"Tomorrow is gonna be another hard day of training, you think you'll be alright?" Kenji asked.

"Of course, and if not, you'll be right by my side and I'll be next to yours." Ogan smiled.

Kenji let out a little chuckle as he rolled to his side and closed his eyes for the night. One whole year had passed since they were adopted from that run-down orphanage. Yet, it still felt like they were on their own surviving in this world. Their master was working them extremely hard every single day until they could prove to him that they were capable fighters who could survive anything.

Little did either of them know that, soon enough, they would come to terms with this way of living, and fall into a false sense of security. That is when the real master that they were following would show his true power.

Another painful year later...

"Very good! You all seem to be working well with your new abilities. I'm actually impressed," the master said, smirking as he looked out at his children sparring with one another.

All of their hand-to-hand combat skills had improved far better this year than last. A lucky handful of the children began to slowly show signs of particularly rare talents forming only now thanks to their master's unorthodox teachings. Out of the sixteen children, only seven of them had started truly utilizing a special power that was all their own. Those who showed such promise were given extra time for training and conditioning, so that their bodies could develop those talents powerfully enough to turn them into unstoppable warriors. Lately, the master had cranked up their training even more. Some of these special skills allowed them to infect their opponent with poison or even to paralyze them. Any powers like these would be essential if they were to be effective fighters against a stronger opponent.

Kenji and Ogan were lucky enough to be in that special group. Kenji was able to create little clouds of smoke from within himself, both toxic and nontoxic. Ogan had an extremely unique ability which allowed him to make his opponent drowsy and fall asleep if they stared into his magnetic deep blue eyes for long enough. He even started developing a new way to make anyone fall asleep—with just his touch.

For now, the two boys could only use a small fraction of their special abilities since they were still so young. But their bodies were adapting to the extreme training by their master, and as a result, they continued to become stronger and more adept at using them.

Today, as the children all huffed and puffed in the backyard, their master stood by the back door with his arms folded, smiling with satisfaction. The time was now, the time for these children to take what might be their final test.

"Children, follow me," he instructed sternly.

They all paused whatever they were doing and seemed to be a bit confused, but then quickly made their way inside. As they entered, they saw their master standing by the very door that they had always been forbidden from entering—the basement door!

Kenji's heart sank in his chest, he had been wondering for all these months what was down there. He hadn't told anyone what he'd seen, or that he even had been down there. He was planning to take that little secret to his grave no matter what.

"You will stay completely quiet and follow me. You will speak no words and do exactly as I say, understand?" he demanded sternly, his face grim.

They all nodded gravely, and watched him slowly open the door that led to the basement. One by one, the children solemnly followed their master down each step of the shadowy stairwell. Kenji and Ogan were the tenth and eleventh in the line, right in the middle of their group.

Once downstairs, they turned left and began walking down the much longer set of stairs to a dull grayish door far at the end. Kenji stared down the corridor once again. Finally, he would be able to answer the burning questions in his head.

The stairs seemed to go on endlessly, and each of the silent children felt their hearts beat faster as the damp walls of the passageway crept in closer to them. The pitter-patter sounds of their steps came to a halt all at once, when at last they reached the dingy steel door at the very bottom.

"We're here," their master gripped the heavy metal door's handle with both hands.

The children all took in a deep, quiet breath and exhaled slowly. They could see a dim flickering light shining through as he pushed the door fully open. Then, something unheard of was revealed, and their amazed gasps echoed back up the stairwell. They walked through the door, bunched together, and stared mutely out onto the huge underground city that lay secret and dormant beneath the city of Cannon-gulf.

It was dark and cold there, with only torches lighting the entire place, and it seemed to go on for miles in each direction. There were huge pillars of stone, some fortified with steel, reaching up to the ceiling, which would be the earth beneath the surface. Abundant bridges, stairwells, and ladders connected stone platforms to other stone platforms. People were walking around everywhere on the stony bridges and man-made walkways.

As the boys and girls looked below the walkways, they saw that the dark abyss went even farther down into nothingness. Some large stalagmites rose sturdily from the bottom of the abyss, and they saw stalactites high above their heads. Small buildings and rooms were built into the walls and platforms of stone. It was a giant underground city, and the faint smell of death was unmistakable.

"Let's go." Their master's voice echoed through the giant underground.

The children all followed quietly, frightened out of their minds. They briefly stood on the smallish stone platform right outside of the door, then stepped onto a long wooden bridge connecting it to a big pillar, where people were walking. While crossing the bridge, they held on tightly to the handrails and refused to look down into the black depths below. Looking up, they saw even more walkways crossing paths to other parts of this hidden city. The young ones were both astonished and terrified.

After finally getting across the first bridge, they noticed that all eyes were on them. Along this pillar's open streets an abundance of scary strangers sat on benches and ambled in and out of the many doorways. Whispering voices intermingled, as the strangers, all adults, darted eyes at the kids and at their master in front of them, glaring at them as they watched them tunnel through the crowd of people. Not one moment of their pointed gazes was pleasant. The stench of a foul and dark energy was growing as thick as fog. It was like a nightmare real enough to feel brushing your skin.

"Oh. I'm sorry..." one of the children apologized as she bumped into one of the strangers.

The large man barely moved as she ran into him. All he did was slowly turn his brawny shoulders and stare down at her. His face was covered with a black mask so that all she could see was two dark eyes boring into her. She squealed and backed into the others to get away.

When the hairy-armed masked man looked toward their master, he caught the master's cold gaze coming at him sideways, a gaze which meant nothing good. The stranger hurriedly looked away and went on with his business. The young girl's racing heart settled down as she quickly caught up to join the others.

This pattern continued again and again—crossing a bridge, moving through a crowd of people, all eyes watching them. Everyone in here seemed to be tough, menacing, and ready to strike out at any moment.

The kids all squeezed closer and closer to one another as they rounded one last bend to see yet another bridge which led to the lowest part of this underground city. It was a giant stalagmite that must have been hollowed out and made to walk into. It appeared that many other bridges connected to this part of the city, but why?

What was down there?

Why did the master seem so used to this place?

Their master spoke without turning around as they passed the halfway point of the long stairway downwards, "You have all trained day and night since I took you in. Some of you have made me proud, and have reached a point in their training that I could call progress. Others still have yet to show me if I made a good choice in teaching them. Today, for those who have shown me they are working hard, do not disappoint me. Those who have not, prove me wrong." He stomped down the steps.

Each child worried that they were one who had displeased the master, that through these last months they had not even learned a fraction of his teachings. Day after day they'd worked themselves to the bone until they could barely move. Some days their master would be laughing with delight, a sign that they had finally improved. On other days he would scowl at their weaknesses and seem to grow tired of the futility of his efforts. He told them that his harshness was only to toughen them up, and that one day they would thank him for it. They hoped that day would come sooner rather than later. Maybe it had…

"Ogan, you doing alright?" Kenji whispered. He looked back and saw Ogan staring straight up at the blackness above them, which was completely made up of stone and stalactites.

Ogan's face was masked in fear, and his mind was racing as their whole world was being turned upside down. Never in their lives was this a place they'd expect to be in. This was like a scene in the legends and fairytales that people would talk about to scare one another. It felt like a human-made hell.

"We're here," the master announced, as he opened the two large metal doors at the bottom of the stairs. The groan of the creaking doors echoed loudly, drowning out the distant roar of voices.

Slowly entering, the children were taken down a hallway with a smallish room at the end. As the doors closed behind them, they huddled together. The hallway and room that had echoed with the sounds of their passage went silent. The white noise turned into a void, a terrifying absence of all sound.

They saw benches and chairs circling most of the room, where they hoped they could relax and rest their legs after the long trek across this strange new world.

"Sit down and don't move; I will return shortly. For now, prepare yourself for your usual training, and do not leave this room," the master demanded brusquely. He left the room and they heard his footsteps pace back down the hallway.

They seated themselves, then sat quietly, having no knowledge of where they were or why they were here. Some sat on their hands, others tapped their feet on the floor. It was like a hospital waiting room, except no one could leave, and what was waiting for them next?

Torches burned brightly across the jagged walls of this windowless room. Droplets of water splashed to the ground and the soft splatting sound echoed in the silence. The only other thing to see here was one large double door. It was as big as the entrance had been, with a thick wooden bar keeping whatever was outside, out.

Finally, someone whispered, "What is this place?"

"I have no idea, why has he brought us here?"

"How long has this place been under our house? Why does our house connect to it?"

All of the children began rambling on fearfully about this underground city. They were not on a pleasant journey with their master, this was more of a nightmare.

Glancing around the empty room, the sixteen boys and girls walked around in it to see if there was any clue as to what was about to happen. They discovered nothing, no hints at all, except for that there was no way of leaving but where they had entered, or going through into whatever was behind those big, barred doors.

"Do you all hear that?" Kenji whispered.

They all went silent, then listened carefully as they heard footsteps coming from the entrance door. The master must have gotten what he needed and was coming back to get them. Even though he seemed a little scarier than usual, they felt safer down here when with him.

The door groaned again and opened slowly.

Two tall, muscular men dressed all in black, each with a mask covering their nose and mouth, came inside. The children were caught completely off guard, and they backed away in fear. The men paid no attention to their observers and, without even a glance at any of them, went straight toward the big barred double door. They stopped in front of it, and together lifted the immense wooden plank that kept the doors from opening.

The kids' hearts dropped; was something going to come out from behind those doors?

Each man then grabbed one of the large door handles and began pulling the heavy doors inward. The creaking, rusty, metal hinges slowly gave way, revealing only darkness. The children trembled in fear, as they awaited whatever was to come next from this horrible place. As the doors opened fully, they could see only an endless inky blackness.

"Enter," both men commanded in unison, gesturing as they stood holding the large doors open.

The children stared in disbelief. They were too scared to move.

"We have to go in *there*?"

"But the master said not to go anywhere."

"What is *in* there?" They began to panic even more, as they guessed and then second-guessed each possible option.

Finally, one of the masked men spoke. "Master requested that we bring you into this room," he said flatly.

The children paused, had they heard him correctly? This man called him "master" just as the children did, but he certainly wasn't a child.

At last, one of the boys stood up from his seat and walked towards the doorway. He walked hesitantly as he faced the dark void ahead of him. Then, one by one, all of the terrified children traipsed soberly into this next dark room, which also showed no windows or light breaking through the walls of pitch black.

They funneled in, trying their best to look around and find some sort of light source, anything at all to be able to see. The only light available was from the torchlight burning through the doorway from the room where they had just been. That was, until they heard the metal hinges creaking again as the doors shifted and started to swing closed behind them. The already deep sinking feeling in their chests worsened as they watched their only way out being eliminated.

"Wait, what is going on!" one of them shouted, just as the doors went completely shut. Then came the sound of the huge wooden bar being lowered, keeping them in for good.

Some of the kids ran back to the door and began banging on it to be let out. Others remained on guard, and surveyed their dark surroundings trying to prepare for what would be next. Was this a test, or just some twisted way of punishing them?

"The time has come!" a familiar voice boomed.

The boys and girls all looked up to the ceiling of the room, following the sound of that voice. It was indeed their master, calling to them from somewhere above. Just then, all around them, torches ignited one by one, in a bright circle. Overhead, steel doors slid open to the sides, revealing the high-domed, cylindrical room in which they could now see that they were trapped. And farther above, there he was, their master, calling down to them from a large balcony filled with many strangers.

The kids cheered and hollered as the room became clearer by the second. Then, they looked around and saw that the cold ground was covered in old bloodstains and bits of torn clothing. The sickly stench of death wafted up to their noses. They felt uneasy being watched by all of those shrewd menacing eyes, and now that they could actually see their surroundings, they felt even more terrified.

"Silence!" the master yelled.

The crowd became quiet, and all eyes were on him. He stood confidently, with his hands held lightly behind his back, his dark eyes staring down at his young students.

"You all have trained under me for more than a year now. Some have exceeded my expectations, others have failed me. Right now you are in the heart of my domain, my empire. As I told you years ago, the weak are the ones who fall by the mighty and the strong-willed. Show me, your master, that *you* are the strongest. Show me that you will stop at nothing, until you have proven to me, yourself, and the world, that *you* are the mightiest warrior! Only *one* of you can remain!" he bellowed down to them.

The crowd erupted in cheers, jumping up and down, shaking their fists in the air.

The terrified children watched in horror as weaponry was dropped from above their heads down into the pit. Then realization kicked in, this was a test. They were no longer just sparring with one another, they had to *kill* each other….

All of them scrambled to get something to protect themselves with; no one knew who would strike first. The cheering from above masked their screams for help, as several of the children were again banging on the door, bawling to be let out.

Kenji and Ogan were separated from one another and had no chance to reunite; one wrong move and someone might attack.

"This is insane! We can't kill each other!" Kenji yelled, his heart raced in his chest as his eyes darted around quickly, keeping his guard up.

We all have to stop this, we don't have to kill each other. If we refuse, we can all get out of this alive. Kenji thought, as he gripped the two daggers he had hastily picked up even more tightly. He took a deep breath in, wanting to rally his brothers and sisters-in-training to stop this before madness took over.

"Everyone listen, we have to—" he yelled. But something cut off his words. A loud and blood-curdling scream reverberated throughout the pit.

As all heads turned to see what was going on, they saw that a taller boy had just taken a knife straight to the chest. The children's eyes widened and they shivered in terror as they watched their friend, bleeding out and crying, fall to his knees and crumple to the ground.

Chaos erupted.

In the following minutes, weapons and bodies flew in a frenzy, as former young brothers and sisters-in-arms attacked and slew one another. Kenji was kept very busy just defending himself.

One fell.

Then another.

And another.

They just kept dropping as their fight or flight instincts kept them going. For those who ran, they were faced with death. Those who fought were faced with pain. For those who just couldn't strike another, they faced a tougher choice.

Gradually, the pit became eerily quiet.

Kenji, seeing all of those familiar bodies now lying quite still on the floor, felt horribly sick to his stomach. He at last saw who alone, other than himself, had survived, and he felt even sicker.

"No, no way! I can't do it to you, you're the only one I have in this world!" Ogan cried out when their eyes met.

Kenji gritted his teeth and tried his best to hold back his own tears. Seeing his friend here like this, the only other survivor, filled him with even more dread and sorrow. He watched as Ogan lowered his sword to the ground, disarming himself.

"We are the only ones left. Let us end this as brothers in death, you and me." Ogan proposed, as he raised his fists.

Kenji couldn't believe what his friend was babbling about; he couldn't agree to that. His arms shook and tears now rolled down his face, mixing with the blood.

Ogan began to stumble closer to his friend, his face flooded with even more tears.

Kenji had no choice in the matter; he knew that they would both end up being killed if they refused to fight. So, he put up his fists and exhaled a largish cloud of dark maroon smoke around himself, then watched as his friend shrieked and ran full speed at him.

Ogan ran right into the murky red-brown smoke, and started swinging. Punches between the two started flying, striking each other's ribs, stomach, and faces. One would fall, but then rise back up to continue this awful battle.

Their knuckles became painted with a deeper shade of red as their blood stained the very hands that had united them as brothers. Overflowing adrenaline took over as the pain they felt fueled their bodies to keep going.

They both stopped for a moment, and stared into one another's eyes.

This was the final match between brothers.

One must win.

One must perish.

Kenji could feel himself getting drowsy from looking into Ogan's sapphire-blue eyes for too long, while Kenji's noxious smoke-cloud, which fully surrounded Ogan, was slowly poisoning him. They both were at their limits and would fall into an endless slumber at any second.

"Kenji!" "Ogan!" The boys cried out in unison, running towards each other. They each grabbed the nearest blade and thrust it into the other.

Once both blades pierced directly into the other's abdomen, all fighting ceased.

The crowd above went silent.

As the boys' vision began to fade, each saw their friend, their brother, drop to the ground. Their minds held one last thought: would either of them see the light of day again?

* * *

"Kenji! Kenji wake up!" A voice called out. Kenji could feel his body being lightly shaken and pushed, as he painfully opened his eyes. When his vision finally cleared, he could see a familiar ceiling; he was in his room again. A single lamp burned brightly.

"What... I'm home... I'm alive?" he groaned, turning his head to the right to see Ogan, standing right there by his side, crying tears of joy.

"Ogan!" He yelled as he sat up quickly and held tightly onto his friend.

They both bawled their eyes out, as they both had indeed survived the nightmarish hell of that underworld. Bandaged and bloody, they couldn't part from their embrace, for each had feared that they had killed their best friend.

"I'm so sorry Kenji! I never wanted to hurt you!" Ogan cried out. His words tumbled out of his mouth, his face covered in tears.

"It's not your fault, I tried to hurt you too!" Kenji blubbered. His lips quivered, remembering the vision of that hell once more.

They finally let go of one another long enough to dry their eyes and faces. The sniffling boys looked at one another and noticed the many bandages wrapped around each of their bodies. It hurt badly if they moved too much, so they took everything very slowly.

Feeling the cool breeze on their skin, they turned their heads to the window, the sky was black and coated with stars. The house felt empty; no sounds at all could be heard coming from outside their door.

"Wait, how did we get back to the house?" Kenji spoke as he felt more tears building up.

"I don't know. I woke up and had no idea myself. I saw you lying in your bed and was so happy to see that I didn't... kill you." Ogan choked up. Just then, the boys heard a door downstairs open.

Their hearts skipped a beat.

The soft sound was easy to hear since the whole house was completely quiet. Heavy footsteps thumped up the stairs and into the hallway, getting closer to their room. The two shuffled away from the door until their backs were against the far wall, and they grabbed onto each other in fear. Traumatized from having watched their brothers and sisters fall in a frenzy of bloodshed, they listened numbly as certain doom approached.

The footsteps stopped directly at their door and the knob began to turn. Tears welled in their eyes; no one was there for them anymore, and they had no way left to go on.

The door abruptly opened wide to reveal the man who had taken them in almost two years ago, their master.

"Oh no..." The boys gasped, remembering him watching from above the pit with a displeased look on his face. Now, he stood before them with that same cold look.

Their bodies would not stop trembling. Their hands quivered and their feet felt as if they weighed hundreds of pounds. They believed that this would be their final moment together before he would punish them and finish them off for good.

Then the man abruptly knelt in the doorway, and lowered his head to the floor. Kenji and Ogan were extremely confused as to why he did this, and could not conjure up a single word.

"You two—you were wonderful in there. You both have shown me that I can call you my worthy apprentices," the master said softly as he raised his head.

The boys were stopped in their tracks.

Praise? He was praising them? After all that had happened, this was not at all what they expected to hear.

"This was the final test I had intended for you children. It was a test to see which of you were willing to put your lives on the line for the cause, to win by any means necessary. Both of you have incredible powers that I know can vanquish any foe that would stand in your way." He appeared to be wearing a genuine smile.

The boy's bodies stopped shaking, their muscles loosened, and their clenched jaws began relaxing. Every horrible thing that had happened in the underground city was now being blotted out by the master's surprising words of commendation.

"I want you both to become my right-hand men, my disciples. I will train you even harder, and I'll make sure that you two can help create the future this world needs. Please, trust me, and I will make you unstoppable legends of Perlaria," he promised passionately.

The master's words struck the boys deep in their hearts. His fervor, his intensity— Kenji and Ogan had never heard him praise *anyone* like this before; they felt extremely honored.

"Now that you have passed this part of your journey, allow me to give you my full trust. I am the leader of a close-knit clan who forges ahead together to create order. We are a group of rebels who intend to recover the lost power of this land. We will take down the City of Light and all of its people by our own means. They are slowly bringing our world into a time of weakness, but we can change that. We must inspire others for the cause, and save this soft, failing world. Please, are you with me, boys?" the master requested earnestly, clenching his fist to his chest and smiling into their eyes with hope.

The two friends quietly watched him deliver his message, and paused in thought. Pain, struggle, death, and murder—these children had gone through a real nightmare, and had just been forced at each other's throats. Yet somehow, this clever man was convincing Kenji and Ogan, even after he had plunged them mercilessly into a hell-hole of death, that they could have the warrior's future they wanted if they followed at his side.

"Yes, sir!" they shouted with no hesitation.

"Excellent! Remember, I will not accept anything less than perfection, so work hard! I will let you two rest up for the next few days, then back to training." He nodded, looked intently at each of them, then smiled again before he stood up and turned to leave.

"Right!" they yelled in unison.

The master carefully closed the door behind him and headed back down the foyer stairs.

"Did they agree?" a tall, masked man asked from the bottom of the stairway.

"Of course they did," the master replied coldly.

The two masked men then left by the front door and strode down the walkway from the house.

"You seem a bit upset, master, shouldn't this be a moment to enjoy? You have two students who passed this time around instead of one. You should be happy," the underling suggested.

"It doesn't matter how many pass the test, these boys mean nothing to me unless they can show me they are worthy of living another day. They are merely pawns for me to mold into the ideal warriors I need for my cause. At the end of the day, dead or alive, they are still those helpless little kids," the master replied bluntly.

3

Pawns

"I still remember how deserted that house felt when we looked into all those empty rooms that used to be the other kids'..." Ogan shivered, as the memories of their recovery in the old house came flooding back to him. Their wounds had healed nicely in time. Training had resumed, and they'd relocated to this new place, which was totally underground.

"I don't know Ogan. Yes, he did make us what we are today. But, I get this weird feeling that we really aren't like sons to him anymore. We're just disposable puppets for his mission." Kenji said with a sigh.

Ogan quickly got up and shushed his friend, then glanced quickly outside their room. Luckily, he saw no one around to hear them, and he rushed back over to Kenji.

"Kenji! You can't go around saying that! We know how really scary he can be, but he's the man who saw something in us. Without him, we would be dead." Ogan whispered fiercely.

Kenji scoffed before he lay back on his bed, arms crossed, and stared at the ceiling in aggravation.

Ogan signed as he saw the annoyed look on his closest friend's face. "Everything will be fine. You and I will always be there to protect one another, no matter what happens. Master is just going through a lot right now, and we need to be the ones to help him the most," he claimed.

31

Keeping his own spirits high, he tried his best to motivate his friend.

"I guess you're right, we got this far. He must have seen *something* in us." Kenji replied. As they both sat in their room waiting for the next orders from the master, a thunderous explosion shook the whole room.

"What the hell was that!?!" Kenji yelled, as he jumped up from his bed.

The whole place was shaking as if an earthquake was rumbling through it. A few seconds later, the shaking paused and their door swung open.

"You two! They're back, we need to hurry before they take over this stronghold too!" A foot soldier shouted, as he immediately headed in the direction of the rumbling.

Grabbing their weapons the two boys hurried down the halls toward the action.

"Come on Kenji, we have to find the master!" Ogan shouted.

4

Alone

T he sound of a log splitting cleanly in two echoed sharply through the street, and bounced across the facades of broken-down homes. Another whack followed shortly after, then another, with a soft grunt heard after each sharp crack. The only sound in the shattered village was this strong young man's ax as he split wood. He worked with unwavering focus. He held tightly to the wooden handle and swung the ax fiercely with a heavy blow, hitting his target perfectly every time. The sun's rays beamed down relentlessly from the all-blue sky, causing sweat to drip from his lean face, not that he noticed it. He was a solitary figure in a landscape of ruin.

As the young man finished chopping the wood, he gathered the pieces into a large pile then headed inside his home. Strolling up to the rickety door, he stopped in the doorway and turned to look back at the village once more. The sight of it now was exactly the same as the day he had stumbled here, empty and broken. This tiny village of no more than fifteen run-down and abandoned houses sat by the edge of a small thick forest, and he lived totally alone here.

The young man took some of his split wood inside and placed it by the fireplace, then brushed off the sap and dirt sticking to his hands. Still wet with sweat from all of the time spent under the sun, he decided to cool off inside for a while. He headed for the dilapidated icebox and opened it up, only to notice that he had almost run out of food, and there wasn't any left in his inventory.

"Crap." Letting out a sigh of agitation, he grabbed the last apple in the box and closed the lid.

He walked through this dusty and desolate living room, filled with the memories of whoever had lived there before. The crumbling walls seemed to become weaker each day, and showed no sign of surviving even into the next year. He brushed his hands along them feeling splinters of wood that poked out from the holes in the wall. The room was coated with the thick dust of the past, unable to break free from its foregone days.

The young man took a seat in the sole wobbly chair in the room, just inches away from a shattered window. The view was neither clear nor pleasant, but it was something to look out at while he ate. As he chewed a bite of the apple, he heard the slight rustle of scurrying small feet coming from just outside. His eyes darted to the front doorway, and he saw a tiny nose poking out from around the corner. *Oh,* he thought, *it's just a wollopi.*

The little critter was as fluffy as a sheep, with the body of a miniature bunny. It cautiously hopped into the house, saw the man sitting in his chair, and immediately froze in place. Slowly, the man stood up from his chair and crept closer to the little animal. He took what little bit of fruit he had left, stooped down slowly, and held it out to the creature. Its wee nose wiggled eagerly and it sniffed ever-closer to his hand until it softly bit down on the apple, then nimbly hopped off.

The young man watched as it ran through the front doorway and hurried off into the forest. He stood back up and glanced over at the shattered mirror on the wall. No matter how many times he looked at himself there, all he could ever see was the reflection of a horribly cursed person.

"Five years…" Lotus whispered to himself. He had spent most of those years here in this destroyed village without anyone else's company. When he had stumbled upon it, it was completely deserted and in ruins, with no signs of life. So he'd decided to camp out here for a bit, but that short "bit" had turned into months and even more months.

Lotus tied his headband tightly to his head, grabbed his sword, and

34

headed out of the decaying town. He needed to find some food. Striding through the overgrown weeds and brush that was found everywhere in the village, he walked the path of a cursed man. He was still being hunted, and had been since he was only twelve years old.

Through these past five years, Lotus had secluded himself from the world. Whenever he went into villages, he was either told to leave or they would force him out, or, he was simply hunted down and forcibly removed. A few times he had slipped away from both bounty hunters and the capital guards, but each time he ran, it hurt him even more to hear the way they shouted his name with such scorn and contempt. He spoke little or not at all to anyone, even himself, and refused to seek out or make any more connections.

As for his special power, the sacred ability his master had taught him all those years ago, he hadn't used it for a very long time. Lotus had been physically training his body every day since that fateful morning when he'd left his dear friend in that village, but his unique master-taught power had remained dormant, unpracticed yet undiminished, through the years. Lotus had only been training himself to survive in this world. He refused to become the man they all claimed him to be. However, it would be only a matter of time until they, the City of Light, which was Perlaria's controlling authority, found him, and forced him to either fight for his life, or to simply give it up.

With his food supply running low, Lotus made his way to a town some distance away to restock his resources. He had not yet visited this particular place, but knowing how the villages across this world usually reacted to the sight of him, he felt that this would go the same as it always did.

He kept his distance from the large towering structures that lay scattered across the land of Perlaria. These outposts, called guardian spires, were remote military stations where the City of Light guards were stationed. They were spread out here over Prosper Valley as well. He'd had his fair share of close calls but now knew to stay far away from them.

Found it. He crested the small hill and looked out over a small town. He headed down the grassy slope and marched towards the main entrance to hopefully get in, get his supplies, and get out unscathed.

As he passed through the main gate, all seemed to be casual and business as usual. The day was a scorcher, and even though the sun was blazing, people were buzzing about their normal lives, with others who looked just like him going in and out. Today seemed to be an average day in this small town for its people. Lotus hoped to keep it that way and get out as soon as he finished what he needed.

Lotus's stomach growled as he saw the many booths displaying different breads, meats, and other tempting foods. He reached into his pocket, retrieved what money he had, and then placed the pitifully meager amount back into that same pocket, sighing. He checked around the market and saw a small tavern just across the road.

"I guess I can at least eat today," he mused to himself as he headed over to it.

Lotus opened the door carefully, so that the entry bell made no sound, and quietly stepped into the moderately busy tavern. He took a seat in the most far-off corner, away from view. The young man scanned the menu, and began picking out possible options using what scant amount of money he had. If he spent as little as possible here and was very careful, he could still pick up a few small items from the market on his way home.

"Excuse me, sir, what can I get for you?" A pleasant-looking female voice asked.

Lotus lifted his once-bright blue eyes from the menu, and politely asked the young waitress, "Could I just have a small bowl of beef stew with a bit of bread?"

"Of course, is that all?" Seeing Lotus nod his head, she left at once to place his order. He put down the menu and poured himself a glass of water as he waited. He was staring down at his hands, when he heard footsteps approaching.

"Here you are, sir." Now a man's low voice spoke. Lotus looked back up and saw that it wasn't the nice young waitress this time.

"Oh, thank you—" Lotus started to say, somewhat confused, but before he could complete his sentence he was interrupted.

"As soon as you finish, you need to leave—*immediately*," the large man demanded. His voice was quiet but stern, and he stared intently into the boy's eyes.

Lotus's heart sank. He looked around and saw all of the tavern's customers staring at him with both fear and disgust. He could hear them whispering to each other, all talking about him, as he sat there in his seat. Lotus noticed that behind the stocky tavern-owner, the young waitress was poking her head out of a doorway, watching with fear.

"Yes sir," Lotus whispered, dropping his head. He slowly began to eat his food, not able to enjoy a single bite. The man was leaving him alone for the time being, but would come back shortly to make sure he was gone.

It was always the same. Lotus would come into a town, then eventually be driven out by nasty looks or threats. Never did he have any kind of peaceful experience in a town that wasn't already abandoned or destroyed.

He finished every bit of his food, and then placed some money on the table. Without another word to anyone, he gripped his sword in its saya and left the tavern, loudly ringing the bell above the door as he went out.

Lotus's dragged his feet as he walked back through the streets hearing the mingled sounds of people living their normal lives. He heard families, friends, and even strangers all connecting with each other, sharing their lives in this quaint little town that he could never be a part of. With each step he took, he felt the eyes of others focus on him more and more.

Word spread quickly, and he could feel his body burning from the glares of contempt and disgust directed at him. There was fear too, on some faces. This was a fairly usual experience for Lotus, except one thing felt off. He sensed a kind of heavy pressure around him, as if he wasn't being looked at as a threat. *More like a target*, ran through his mind. It was an uneasy feeling, but he shook it off as he headed for the main gates to exit the town. Lotus had to completely disregard the market as an option anymore; he would have to find another place to get food now. As he neared the town gates, that uncomfortable feeling returned, and actually increased.

Something was definitely off.

"I *found* you!" bellowed a deep voice. Out of nowhere, a mountain of a man came crashing down from above. He slammed onto the ground, shaking the street beneath his feet. The whole section of town shuddered with incredible force as if an earthquake was rumbling through.

Lotus didn't flinch at any of it, not the shouting, and not even the booming tremors created by this giant who had just landed on his feet, slightly crouched and off to his left. He just slowly turned and stared at this mystery man.

"There you are." The immense man straightened up and glared at the wanted criminal before him. He wore a steel helmet with pointy horns following along the jawline of it; there were slits in the front and either side, giving him a small but good visual. The sword on his back was enormous, and almost as tall as the man himself. The muscles on his body were huge and pulsed with power; he was a wall of flesh and muscle.

"So, this is the 'Murderer of a Grand Sage,' 'Perlaria's Wandering Curse', 'Ronin the Banished'. The picture on the wanted poster makes you look a lot tougher, y'know," the huge man scoffed, and then held up the newest wanted poster of him.

An uneasy feeling flooded Lotus once more. He placed his hand on his saya, reassured by its presence.

The man rolled up the paper and placed it in his rucksack. Then he pointed to himself with great pride, saying boastfully, "I am the bounty hunter, Thalrok, the titan in human form. It took a bit of my time, but I have finally found you, and now, I'm gonna take you in and collect your bounty." He dropped the rucksack, then reached back for his sword. Without a moment's notice, he lunged full speed, directly at Lotus, swinging that giant sword right at his head.

Lotus swiftly ducked out of the way, feeling the air pressure of the swinging blade zip past him. The wanted man then barraged the bounty hunter's chest with several quick punches, followed by a swift hard kick in the side. As his heel connected with the massive man's ribs, he felt a shock jolt through his leg.

Damn, it's like hitting a tree. Lotus winced and prepared to throw another strike. As he cocked back his fist, Thalrok released one hand from his sword and grabbed Lotus's fisted hand in his, just as Lotus was starting to swing it forward. With his fist trapped, Lotus wiggled and punched at the bounty hunter's beefy arm to release his tenacious grip. Then he saw Thalrok reeling back his sword arm, preparing to swing straight down. The hefty metal blade ripped through the air.

Not good! Lotus panicked, as he grappled onto Thalrok's arm with his whole body to avoid the strike. The sword struck the ground, cutting through the dirt and stone easily, and shaking the earth beneath them. Even the townspeople watching from afar felt the powerful thud beneath their feet.

Coiling his legs, Lotus pressed both of his heels on the bounty hunter's metal helmet. This move loosened his foe's grip and let him worm his way out, so that he could leap from Thalrok's arm and land behind him. Unable to be seen there, Lotus jumped quickly onto his back and wrapped one arm around the bounty hunter's neck and locked it in with his other, planning to choke him out.

Thalrok immediately let go of his sword and grabbed for the wanted man's arm, trying to pry it off. "You think this'll work, you little pest?" he gasped. Using his burly arms, he pulled and pulled but couldn't seem to loosen Lotus's grip.

"Don't let go buddy, I got an idea," the bounty hunter chuckled with a faint wheeze. He turned his body slightly, then ran full speed backward until he crashed into a wall, sandwiching Lotus between himself and the wall.

As soon as he felt the tightness around his neck release, he grabbed Lotus's arm and threw him over his shoulder. The young man's back was slammed hard onto the ground immediately after he'd been crushed against a wall. Lotus was now totally vulnerable.

Thalrok punched him three times square in the chest as he lay on the street in pain.

I... can't breathe... Lotus couldn't take it any longer, so he held his hands in front of his face and rolled to avoid the fourth punch.

As Thalrok's fist hit the street, the ground cracked below his hand and sent stony debris everywhere. Lotus rolled to his feet and shuffled as far away as he could to keep some distance from this beast of a man.

All that power from just one punch?! Lotus thought as he huffed with exhaustion.

The bounty hunter stood up slowly, then walked back over to his sword. He lifted the monstrous blade from the ground and stared at Lotus again.

"This will be over soon." Thalrok chuckled softly.

Somewhat recovered, Lotus dug his feet into the ground and charged full speed at the now armed man. He thought he'd have the upper hand and could strike while the titan wasn't protecting himself. But, as Lotus closed the gap, he lifted his head and saw that terrifying sword dropping to meet him.

"Got you, Ronin!" Thalrok yelled, pushing with all of his power into this strike. The sword rapidly lowered as Lotus came flying in at the bounty hunter with his back exposed and open to attack.

There was no way of dodging this; all he had left was a last-second idea, one final option. He reached for his hip, smoothly removed his sword from its saya, and twisted so that his body was now facing upwards. As the mighty blade came crashing down, he firmly held up the fragment of steel left on his master's broken sword to block it. The blades clashed and Lotus's flying body was brought thundering down.

Dirt and rocks flew around them as his body hit the ground. Once again the earth shook below their feet; the quaking of this fight rattled the nearby homes in the village.

"Gotcha," Thalrok muttered victoriously. He watched as the dust began to settle, expecting to see his prey lying helpless and defeated beneath his mighty blade. However, as the view of his target cleared, Thalrok's smug expression quickly faded.

"What?!" As the final dust settled, he saw that Lotus had kept his enormous blade from striking him by using what little bit of blade was left on that puny broken sword.

Thalrok's blood began to boil; this little rodent was being a bit too pesky. So he pressed down harder and harder to slice right through that feeble-looking fragment of a blade, but Lotus's arms didn't budge.

"Putting up a fight are ya? Why not just give up now!" the bounty hunter hissed.

Lotus gritted his teeth and felt a great anger swelling up inside him. As he stared at this beast of a warrior standing above him, pressing down with his mighty blade, he could feel the pressure of impending death running through him. A flow of deep anger began to build up inside him like a raging inferno. The muscles in his arms felt stronger, and the beating of his heart went faster, as Lotus gripped his broken sword even more firmly.

Thalrok could feel his arms buckling as his own sword was being pushed back from the ground. *What the hell?* He thought, struggling to press his blade down. But then with one quick swipe upwards, Lotus knocked the bounty hunter's sword back over his head, freeing himself to quickly stand up. Thalrok stumbled backward from the force of Lotus's slash, and planted his sword into the ground to get his balance. He watched uneasily as this murderer stood there in the street, staring directly at him like evil incarnate.

Then Lotus took his master's damaged sword and placed it carefully back in its saya.

"Oh, is that how we're gonna do it? A good ole hand-to-hand brawl, huh? Fine then, let's go!" Thalrok yelled, as he thrust his sword into the ground and held up his hands. The muscular foe placed his fists in front of his face, clenching them tightly with veins bulging.

Lotus's patience was fading. He began to grow tired of this man. His body had been bruised and beaten in this fight; it too was painful to bear any more of it. Lotus could feel that flood of anger and malice inside him permeate every cell, creating an untapped, deep pressure of power. His heart rate climbed as he tried his best to drown out this bothersome man's words.

I need to calm down. I need to just... Lotus tried to relax himself, so he closed his eyes for a split second, which was a big mistake. He heard a loud stomp in front of him and his eyes flashed open. Thalrok stood right in front of him now, and he was staring up at a monster, with great pain and suffering surely to follow.

How did he—?! Lotus flinched as Thalrok's barrage of punches came flying in. One blow after another struck the young man in quick succession, not letting him catch his bearings for even a moment.

Nearby townspeople could hear the crashing of the titan's great fists against his body. Whether they struck his arms, blocking them, or his body, taking the hard impact, it rattled through the village.

Lotus was trying his best to keep up with these attacks but couldn't manage to keep his cool and properly focus on them at the same time. Each time he was struck, it only fueled the dark energy inside him more. The veins of his arms began to bulge and blacken, and his head started to throb with rushing blood. Thalrok wouldn't stop punching for a moment; he wasn't about to risk any chance of letting Lotus get away from him.

"What's wrong ya murderer? Can't take it?!" Thalrok yelled with contempt.

"Enough!" Lotus shouted, as he held out his palm and stopped the next punch's movement with a single hand. The recoil shook Thalrok's body. He glared at this criminal who was now radiating a dark, malevolent aura. The pressure of power surrounding Lotus was so intense and frightening that Thalrok felt like he was looking straight into the eyes of a real-life demon.

With a slight push of his palm, Lotus sent Thalrok's hand flying back at him. The titan of a man stumbled backward once more from that one subtle motion.

Where did he generate all that power from? The bounty hunter had brought in plenty of people before. Usually, they would have the same reaction as this one. They would have a last-minute fight or flight instinct until they either gave up, or died trying.

"No matter," he smirked. Slowly, he lifted his leg into the air and stomped down as hard as he could. As the impact of his foot hit the ground, another shockwave rumbled like an earthquake across the street.

How can he make this whole ground shake with just one little stomp? Lotus lost his balance and realized he was falling into a trap.

Thalrok rushed back in, immediately throwing punch after punch. Lotus wasn't planning on taking another one of those hammering blows, so he let the dark energy inside flow just enough. As the bounty hunter bombarded him with punches, Lotus stopped most of them, and retaliated with his own. They battled through the streets of the town, continuing their feud, grunting and shouting. The two brawlers in full combat mode noisily proclaimed their presence to the whole alarmed town, and rallied quite an audience.

Face, chest, legs—each part of both of their bodies was wracked with pain. Blood dripped from cuts and bruised skin as they pushed back from one another one last time. Gasping for breath, the two adversaries stood and stared at each other, wheezing out the last remaining bit of air inside them and gulping for more.

"How are they both still standing? That bounty hunter is one scary guy, but he has to be exhausted from all those hits," a townsman whispered.

"Yeah, and that wanted man, is taking all those hits so hard, how is he not dead yet?!" another replied. The whole town had gathered, and now watched as both fighters stood hunched over and sweating from their battle and the blazing sun.

Lotus could only feel his anger swelling up more as he faced this enemy. He knew he would surely be fully consumed if the fight went on any longer. He had to find a way out. He had his sword still on him, he just had to find a way out. The wanted man began to reach toward his hip to hold onto his saya before he darted off...

Lotus's heart seemed to stop beating and sank deep into his chest. The pupils of his eyes dilated wildly, and his ears went deaf. Feeling for the saya that was no longer resting on his hip, he locked his eyes across the way on those of that titan of a bounty hunter, who was picking it up from the ground.

"This yours?" Thalrok asked sarcastically, dangling the fragmented sword in its worn saya towards him.

Lotus sprang at him even faster than before, but Thalrok swerved out of the way just before he could hit him. As Lotus flew by and was nearly out of reach, the bounty hunter grabbed his ankle and hurled him down to the ground like a hammer on a nail.

The young man's body smacked into the stones below, and Thalrok moved in to punch straight down onto Lotus's back. His fist crashed down heavily, sending more debris flying up into the air. The titan growled out in anger when he felt only rough dirt beneath his knuckles, and not the bones of a man's spine. Thalrok was then blindsided by the swift kick of a roundhouse whip flying through the air and into his abdomen. He reflexively hunched over and stumbled to his knees. Clenching his stomach tightly, Thalrok pushed himself to his feet, a guttural growl building. He shot his helmeted head up and roared to the sky, *"Ronin!"*

"That's *not* my name anymore!" Lotus bellowed back, as both again charged full-speed into one another.

Thalrok held Lotus's saya just out of reach, clasped in one giant fist off to the side, and punched viciously at the young man with the other. Lotus weaved in and out of each jab, moving faster and faster, his body a blur of motion. With every opening, he punched even harder and faster than before. With a quick twist, Lotus swung his leg hard, striking the back of the bounty hunter's heel which knocked the big man flat on his back. As Thalrok's body collided solidly with the ground, Lotus slammed a knee down on his chest, grabbed the titan's helmet tightly with one hand, and cocked back his other fist, ready to crush the bounty hunter's exposed throat.

Without a second thought, Thalrok immediately latched onto Lotus's throat with one hand and, still gripping Lotus's sword awkwardly in the other, tightened it into a fist around it, which he too pulled back, ready to strike.

The two were at a stalemate, huffing from exhaustion, and staring intensely at one another.

"Let go of the helmet," Thalrok demanded.

"Let go… of the sword." Lotus wheezed angrily as the grip on his throat got tighter.

The deadlock continued. Each was focused only on winning this battle. Lotus could see through the slits in the bounty hunter's helmet, right into his furious amber eyes.

The townspeople were witnessing this final press of the fight, watching in fear from afar. The two brawlers seemed frozen there in the center of the broken street.

Suddenly, and simultaneously, they each released their grip on the other. Lotus removed his knee from Thalrok's chest and stood up, brushing himself off. Lotus then held out his hand, offering to help him up.

What? Thalrok thought in confusion. But, he grabbed the wanted man's hand and hoisted himself up from the shattered earth beneath him. The townsfolk began to whisper, which grew quickly into noisy chatter as they watched the two clean themselves of debris and dirt. Thalrok handed Lotus his sword, which was no more or less damaged than before the fight.

"Buy you a drink?" Lotus asked.

"Ehh… why not?" Thalrok responded.

* * *

The bell above the tavern door rang once again, and all eyes locked on the two customers entering the place—one, who had been seen and expelled from here not many minutes ago, and the second, who had come in out of nowhere, claiming that he would kill the first. Bruised, bloodied, and dirty, Lotus and Thalrok took seats at a somewhat secluded table and quietly waited to order something.

The whole tavern-full of people, in truth, the entire village, was utterly baffled at the fact that these two had just been at one another's throats in a deathmatch, yet now, here they were dining together? The townsfolk had seen firsthand how strong both of them really were; it would be a suicide attempt to do anything offensive or ask them to leave. Conversations ceased as the customers gaped at this unlikely pair.

"Um, excuse me, sir... as I mentioned before, it would be best—" the stout owner stuttered.

"I think I'll have your best ale, please." Thalrok broke in cordially as he lowered his menu. The interrupted owner paused, not knowing how to respond. He watched as the wanted criminal sat staring down at the table, while the bounty hunter stretched his arms languidly up in the air.

"I... I think it's best that this man— " stammered the proprietor, looking at Lotus.

"Yeah yeah, I know, he's a wanted criminal, and I plan to take him in after we get a quick drink. Now please, I'm parched over here and would *love* a big mug of cold ale, sir." Thalrok said politely, now gently clasping his hands together in front of him, his helmeted face turned up expectantly towards the confused man.

The tavern owner looked over at Lotus. Lotus looked back at him. The wanted man just shrugged his shoulders.

Staring in puzzled wonder, the owner headed off to get the big man his drink.

The two sat in silence as outside of the front windows spectators gathered, trying to take a peek at what was going on inside.

The chatter in the tavern began to rise again as folks slowly went back to their meal, while still keeping a side-eye on the two of them.

The owner brought over Thalrok's drink and asked,"W-will that be all, sir?"

Thalrok happily rubbed his hands together, overjoyed as he looked at the quart-sized mug of alcohol he'd awaited with such longing. "Yep, this will do." he replied. He carefully lifted his helmet so that only his mouth was barely visible and gulped down nearly all of that huge mugful of ale. Lotus, watching, was surprised at how quickly he could knock one back, yet still keep his face concealed from the world. *I wonder why he does that?*

Thalrok slammed the mug on the table and let out a pleased sigh. "That hits the spot!" he said with great satisfaction.

The two weren't fazed by any stares or chatter from the townspeople.

They just sat by themselves, relaxing together after fighting each other to what should have been the bitter end for one or even both of them.

Lotus sat up in his seat and scratched his chin as he asked the bounty hunter, "So, why did you stop trying to kill me?"

"I could ask you the same question," Thalrok said.

"I asked first." Lotus quickly replied.

Thalrok chuckled to himself as he sat back in his seat and folded his arms over his chest. He paused, then said, "I've hunted and even had to kill people for a good part of my life. They all gave off this kind of energy and had the same look about 'em, like they had 'wanted' written all over 'em. The guilt and shame in their eyes was too easy to see. I guess when I fought you, it felt different. I could see in your eyes that you've been through hell, something I know all too well. Maybe you just got a raw deal. So, I stopped." Thalrok responded.

It was clear to Lotus that he was telling the truth. When he had gotten that glimpse into the slits of the giant man's helmet, in a way, it was like looking into a mirror of himself.

Thalrok picked his mug back up, chugged the last little bit of his beer, then burped loudly.

"Boy, this is the best thing to have after a fight. It's like a reward." Thalrok laughed to himself. Lotus reached into his pocket, then placed the last bit of money he had left on the table before he stood up from his seat.

"Wait, why are *you* paying?" Thalrok asked.

"I did ask if you wanted a drink, so this one's on me," Lotus replied as he began to head for the door. Thalrok picked up his immense sword which was propped against the table and followed after him. The two left the tavern with all eyes still riveted on them.

They walked right past the crowd of people still gawking at the rubble of their fight as if nothing had happened. The townsfolk all turned and watched warily, as the two former enemies now strolled together through the streets.

"So, what's next for you?" Thalrok asked.

Lotus stopped moving. He touched the saya at his hip, a reassuring gesture. "I still have no clue." Lotus sighed and began walking again. Souder, Petalbrooke—all of those places had activity, vitality, and people connecting to other people in them. Though not everyone knew each other, there was a feeling of community, fellowship, and togetherness. Having only the wildlife that ran around his abandoned village for company really wasn't the same.

"Haven't you heard about that little inn… ugh, what's the name of it? It's a place that takes in criminals like you?" Thalrok asked.

"I'm *not* a criminal," Lotus murmured.

"That's just it, It's this refugee place for criminals who have been falsely accused. Trust me, I have never been there before but I think it could be a start. Maybe that could be your new home?" Thalrok suggested.

Lotus looked up into the clear sky and thought to himself. Five years had passed since he left the last town he'd stayed in. Was there really any hope left for him? Who says the refugee village-folks wouldn't try to hunt him down, or that he'd end up bringing strife and conflict to them just like had happened before? Lotus took a deep breath, and realized there was no other option at this point. It was either a life of solitude until death, or to take one more chance at a life connecting with others.

"Where is this village?" Lotus asked.

5

Mellowtin

"The town of Mellowtin, huh. Looks pretty nice, I must say." Thalrok stretched his arms up in the air. He hopped out of the carriage and moved his stiff legs around from the long and very bumpy ride across Prosper Valley.

I still don't think this is a good idea, Lotus thought, still sitting in the carriage and staring out at the village. He readied himself for the reality of things, then stepped out. Foot to ground, it felt good to finally be able to stand after a day-long carriage ride.

"Thank you, we are truly grateful," Lotus said courteously to the man who had taken them both all the way across Prosper Valley.

"It was no trouble at all, boys," the driver replied, as Thalrok handed him a small pouch of money in payment. With a grateful smile, the man turned around and shoved off for home. The two waved goodbye, then turned to face the booming town of Mellowtin. Here was a traveler's paradise, where people from all around could grab a bite to eat, shop, or restock on weaponry on their journey. Markets lined the streets, and countless shop owners called to people walking by to stop and check out their goods. Not only were there numerous thriving merchants, but Mellowtin was chock-full of families and folks of all ages living together in harmony, just like they would in any other small town.

"This is quite the hotspot huh?" Thalrok laughed, as he headed in past the gates. After taking a few steps he noticed Lotus wasn't following. He glanced back and saw him still standing motionless in front of the town, staring up at the sign that read "Mellowtin."

Lotus couldn't get this crushing feeling off his chest. He kept telling himself that this wasn't the right choice, it would go just as always, they would notice him just like everyone else did. Or he would somehow cause these innocent people pain they didn't deserve, all because of him.

"Hey, let's go, cursed man! I'm hungry." Thalrok called out, then chuckled as he headed into town.

Lotus snapped out of his daze and watched this man, who just met him only a day ago, call for him to follow along. Lotus took his first step into the town and could feel the rush of life brushing past him. One step after another, he hurried along to follow the bounty hunter.

"Geez, I'm starving, we have got to find a place to eat." Thalrok groaned. They had only been in the town for a few seconds, but the titan's stomach was already growling for food.

They turned the first corner and saw a big eatery with a sign over it saying, "Fork and Sword Canteen." It appeared to be quite popular, with many people going in and out of its large, worn doorway.

"Now *that* just screams, 'I have good food here!' Let's go!" Thalrok rubbed his meaty hands together, pleased to find the source of his next food and drink. Lotus hesitated, the more people in the building, the more people that could recognize him.

"You coming?" Thalrok asked as he was already halfway up the dozen stairs to the canteen.

"Yeah, one second." The young man took the painful first step and braced himself for the usual outcome of these situations. As they opened the doors, the roar of jumbled voices boomed from within. Each table had different conversations battling to be the loudest. Drinks were raised high into the air and laughter seemed to be coming from all corners of the busy canteen. Waitresses and waiters zipped around the floor holding trays of food, mugs of ale, and occasionally cleaning up some drunk's mess. Cramped was one way to describe this place, but it seemed inviting and indeed homey and pleasant.

Thalrok and a hesitant Lotus made their way inside, and found two seats at a table. They checked out the place as they waited, and saw craziness unfolding in the most organized way possible. At both sides of the bar was an entrance and exit for the many servers to funnel smoothly through, balancing overfull trays of food, drink, or dirty dishes. At the same time, several bartenders bounced around briskly to serve each customer lined up at the long wooden bar. Wherever seated, once their food and drink were bestowed upon them by the energetic and skilled waitstaff, the customers seemed to enjoy their meals heartily. It was quite a sight to see.

"Hey, check this out, they have a resting nook for weaponry to stand." Thalrok pointed out. On the edge of their table were several different-sized grooves so that customers could remove their weapons and rest them securely against the table.

"I like this place already!" Thalrok hoisted the huge sword from his back and propped it up against the table. He let out a soft sigh once relieved of the sword's weight.

Lotus looked down at his sword, and then the large number of people around him. Was it safe to take his saya off in here? Trying to calm his nerves, he removed it from his waist and placed it carefully against the side of the table.

"Hello boys!" greeted a friendly woman, "What can I get you two?" She took out a pen and paper, then looked at them expectantly.

"Oh… I'll have two of your 'Roasted Hogio Legs' with a side of 'Mellowtin Style Baked Potatoes'. Also, I would love to try some of your best fish from this part of Prosper. Whatever kind you have works for me. Oh, and please I gotta have some of your home-brewed ale!" Thalrok requested, eagerly anticipating a large, tasty mug of beer.

The waitress began writing down his order and then turned to Lotus.

"Can I just have the 'West Perlarian Stew' with a bowl of apples, please? Lotus asked. The waitress cheerfully finished writing down their order.

"Absolutely! Your orders will be right out! And one of our carriers will be around shortly." She smiled and swiftly headed off to the kitchen to place their order. The two looked at one another, altogether confused about what she meant by "carriers." To their surprise, after a few moments of waiting, a tall, muscular and grease-stained man came over to their table.

"Two legs and stew, right?" He pointed at the two of them. They were truly confused and hesitant to respond, but finally both nodded their heads.

"Righty, I'll be back with these real quick." He reached over to grab Thalrok's giant sword. As he started to pick it up, his arm was halted by its incredible weight.

"Jeez, this thing's a beast," he grunted. After a bit of a struggle, he was able to get it onto his shoulder. Then he reached out to grab Lotus's broken sword. The young man's eyes widened and he immediately grabbed the carrier's arm, stopping him before he could touch it.

"Sorry, but this stays with me," Lotus said firmly. The man took no offense, and pulled back his hand.

"Why are you taking our swords anyway?" Thalrok asked.

"Oh geez, sorry, are y'all new here?" the man asked. The two nodded their heads, wondering what was going on.

"I apologize, boys, I should have told ya. Here at the Fork and Sword, we offer to take y'all's weapons to sharpen 'em and clean 'em up after your journey. It's free of charge as long as you pay for somethin' to eat." The carrier, burdened by the weight of Thalrok's sword, turned to trudge away and headed down a set of stairs to presumably go to work on it.

The bounty hunter turned back to Lotus and said, "Did you hear that?! They fix up your swords while you eat, that's fantastic!" he crowed, and he slammed his big fist on the table.

Lotus finally let go of his own sword, nestled safely in its saya, and poured himself a glass of water to cool his head. Not shortly after, the waitress came back out and placed steaming hot plates of food in front of them.

"Enjoy!" she grinned, as she rushed over to another table.

Thalrok rubbed his hands together and began to dig right in, while somehow still keeping his helmet on. Lotus joined in more slowly, and took this time to relax and refresh himself after the long ride to get here.

"So, what's your story?" Thalrok asked, his voice garbled as he chewed on the large piece of meat still in his mouth.

"Hm?" Lotus replied.

"Well for starters, ya got that scar on your face and a broken sword that no one can touch. Plus, you have the eyes of a broken man and you're hunted by the entire world. You've gotta have *some* story." Thalrok said, once he'd swallowed. He chomped down again with gusto on the hefty leg of savory Hogio meat, which had a taste similar to pork.

Lotus looked over at his sword. He could remember each second of his life, play by play; it tormented and consumed his mind. His friends, and his family, his master— he remembered every one of the horrible things that had happened, all from just his very existence in their lives. Every time he would think of a happy memory, another cursed one came right after to ruin it.

Lotus snapped out of it, when the sudden slam of Thalrok's beefy hand on the table made him jump in his chair.

"How about this? Maybe it's rude for me to ask about you, without telling you my story first, so, I'll start." Brushing off his hands, he shuffled the remains of his food to one side to focus, and dove right into his story.

"You know about the titans, right?" Thalrok asked.

"Yes, I heard from my master that they used to roam the lands, that both they and their homes towered above everyone and everything in Perlaria, but now they take refuge in the western mountains."

"Right you are. *I* was raised by them." Thalrok boasted, pointing to his chest. Lotus's blue eyes widened, surprised to hear that any human being could have possibly been raised by actual titans.

"So, I was told," Thalrok continued, " was that when I was about three years old I was found by my foster mother, Roheva. They say that she found me rolled up in a ball, crying. I was hiding in some big rocks far from any village. She was the kindest, sweetest titan in the whole village. To be honest, she was the sweetest person alive, and she had recently lost her own son to some terrible illness. Even though I was a human, she still took me in and raised me as her own. This went against the titan code, but such an adoption was allowed up until the child reached a certain age."

"She loved me dearly and raised me up the titan way, living under their teachings and forms of law. It was the best part of my life." Thalrok's eyes took on a faraway look, as if he were seeing a past that he could no longer return to. "I was trained under the strongest of them, and learned to channel the energy of a titan, even though I was a human. On my thirteenth birthday, Roheva gifted me with the sword that I wield today. A year after that, when I was fourteen, by law my time with the titans was over. The elders of the village sent out an order to have me killed if I didn't leave the village; I was never to return."

"My mother tried to convince them to let me stay, but the titans were a powerful race who always complied with their age-old rules, this one in particular. As a tradition, when a titan is eighteen years old, their parents gift them with a unique helmet, one that they specially handcraft themselves. This helmet was to be worn at all times to show power and dominance on the battlefield, as opponents could never see the warrior's emotions. Even though I was only fourteen, she gave me my helmet, and one last hug, before I left the titan's village. I have not returned since I left all those years ago… though I do wish to see my mother again someday." Thalrok stopped talking, head slightly lowered.

Lotus was surprised that this was the hidden story behind Thalrok's helmet. He'd never expected to meet *anyone* who had been raised by the titans!

"From then on, I was homeless again, and I needed to find a way to survive in the world." Thalrok continued, "I wandered the plains for a while, then found that I could make a decent living being a bounty hunter and collecting reward money. I could live wherever there was a bed and take any job that made me some money. That about sums up my whole life, without going off into the deep of it." Thalrok then lifted his mug and chugged down the last bit left in it.

"What about your real family?" Lotus asked.

Thalrok slowly placed down his mug, slid it off to one side, and signalled for another. He said, "I wonder about them every single day. Not a moment goes by that I don't ask myself, What are they doing, and do they know that their boy is still alive. Or, are *they* even alive?"

It was quite an interesting tale he told, of a life so familiar and yet so different. Two boys split apart from their homes who had both drifted into a new life in the harsh world. One cursed and the other living off the dirty labor of hunting the hunted.

"Alrighty, I guess it's your turn now, pal." Thalrok pointed at Lotus.

For some reason, the younger man felt no uncertainty, though he had never once shared his story with anyone since that awful day. Yet, as he stared at the steel helmet of this man who tried to kill him less than a day ago, he felt as if he was talking to a kindred soul, one who appeared to be someone he could trust and talk to with no regrets.

Lotus sighed and settled himself in for the journey back into the hell of his broken past.

"Souder, the small and peaceful town I used to live in, had a tradition." Lotus began. "When children were eight years old and had finished all of their basic studies, they would all gather at the center of the village and meet with the Oracle. He was the elder of our village and had the power to glimpse into our future and help set us on that path early. Everyone in my group was excited, and maybe just a little nervous. When it was my turn, as the Oracle lifted his hand from my head, he instantly backed away from me in a panic. The future he saw... was of me in the center of Souder, eyes red like the blood dripping from my body. The town lay crumbled around me, and the people that once lived, were scattered lifeless on the ground amid the rubble." Lotus paused, clenching his fists on the table, as he remembered how the faces of the townspeople had quickly shifted from eager anticipation to great fear. Their terrified whispers were so loud, and that face his mother made...

"So, he continued, "they decided to cast me out. I was tied up and blindfolded, and then they carted me out to the middle of nowhere to let me die alone. It wasn't until two days after I was banished, that I woke up in a forest and saw an older-looking man standing over me. I was really scared at first, but he told me he could offer me a place to stay and food to eat, so, having no other real choice, I decided to trust him. Later on, I learned he was the founder of his village, Petalbrooke, and was the master of the dojo he ran in town. This man raised me like a son and taught me everything I know about how to fight." Lotus paused once more. He couldn't shake off one moment of remembering that last terrible morning. It didn't matter how far in life he went, he would still remember that horrifying experience as though it happened yesterday.

"It wasn't until a few years later, that I came home from an early morning run and saw my master lying in the backyard, bleeding and deathly still on the ground. An evil man had snuck into our town and attacked him while the village slept. The thug was still there by him, so I fought him. I did what I could, but in the end, even after I hit him hard and even harder, that coward of a monster who took my master's life, used some cursed power. As he lay on the ground in defeat, he used some strange ability and then totally disappeared in a puff of grey smoke. What he did leave me with was this awful scar on my face, forever reminding me of that day. The villagers had heard the ruckus and arrived to find me, bloody and wounded, standing over my slain master. The faces of the people I had come to love were painted with horror. They saw me, an outcast who had been brought in by this man, standing above his dead body, crying in pain. They assumed it was me who killed him, no matter what I said. So, they tried to kill me then and there, but, I got away." He could feel that particular trauma still inside him swell up and seep through his body even more as time went on.

"I didn't think there was much left for me. I was cursed to never live a life of peace. My master was a Grand Sage. The wanted posters came out with my face and name all over 'em, and I knew that life there was over."

In this loud, busy eatery, not a single person actually heard their conversation, and yet to Lotus, it felt like the whole world had stopped in its tracks to listen.

"Dang, that's harsh… That explains the scar, and the pain still in your eyes." Thalrok paused, then asked, "So, this sword was your master's huh? What about that saya? It looks kinda special with those lotus flowers and 'Our Hero' on it."

Lotus glanced over at his sword for a moment.

Do you like it? A familiar soft voice echoed in Lotus's head.

"That was a gift from a good friend…" Lotus softly murmured. The day he received that saya was another memory he could play back in his head a thousand times; it was one of a very few that he wanted to last forever.

"So your master taught you some unique power, right? I've never seen someone fight with that kind of power. *Never.*" Thalrok emphasized. He nodded to the server as his fresh mugful of ale materialized by his hand.

Lotus looked down at his arms and could see the still-blackened veins across his arms. Each time he became consumed with rage, his arms would begin to stain with the dark energy that flowed and surged inside.

The young man remembered when his master had first taught him this power years ago, and how he had sworn to keep it a secret from the world, as he'd been instructed. Yet somehow, for some reason, he felt no harm in telling this man. It was as if he would be telling an old friend who had known about this for years now. Why was that?

"My power is called 'Lotus,'" he continued. "It's a forbidden power that my master's master created many years ago that can be completely overpowering and very dangerous. Unlike other special abilities, this one is almost impossible to harness, due to its incredible amount of potential energy. Only one who is of pure intent and heart, with the drive and determination earned through years of meditation, can wield this power. With it, I can control dark energy and light energy. This capability gives me a power beyond the comprehension of this world. The creation of dark and light energy can flow through me equally. Unfortunately, it has been, uh, years, since I have been able to control any light energy…" Lotus's voice trailed off.

Thalrok leaned forward and propped his elbow on the table. He looked intently through the slits in his helmet at Lotus. "Wow! You've only been able to control *half* your power? That means that you can get even

stronger than when we first fought? Damn, I messed with the wrong guy!"
Thalrok said, and then chuckled, leaning back in his seat.

Lotus found comfort in that humor. He felt himself drawn into the
cheerful and relaxed atmosphere that Thalrok so effortlessly created. A
genuine smile spread across his face.

"So, your master must have entrusted you with this power, then, right?"
Thalrok asked.

"Yes. He wanted to train me to one day help him heal the world from
its broken, lost, and forgotten peace." Lotus replied.

The bounty hunter looked around the restaurant to make sure no one
was listening and shuffled his seat a little closer to the table, leaning in.
"Don't worry Ronin, you can trust me. I won't be spreading this around;
your story is safe with me. Plus, this world could still use someone like
you to help it." Thalrok whispered as he leaned back, lifting his ale to take
a big sip.

"Oh and about my name." Lotus said, "I go by 'Lotus' now, please. I
can't, and I don't want to, go by *that* name anymore." As what Lotus said
registered, Thalrok froze in place with his mug halfway to his lips. He
lowered it slowly, placing it softly down onto the wooden table.

"Sorry pal, I ain't calling a tough guy like you some *flower* name." Thalrok
snorted with laughter, threw back his mug of ale, then burped loudly with
great satisfaction.

Lotus didn't fight him on this, even though hearing that name brought
back years of pain. But Thalrok didn't say "Ronin" with any hatred or
disgust, and it had been quite some time since he'd heard anyone call him
by that name in such a normal way.

"Since we're talking about special abilities, I'm curious about what
abilities *you* have. I mean, you were raised by titans after all, and have an
extreme amount of strength." Lotus asked, taking a bite from an apple.

"Right! Through my years of training with the titans, even though they
were towering above me, they didn't go easy on me, which made me
what I am today. The titans are strong enough to punch holes through
solid earth and create massive earthquakes beneath their feet. I was lucky

enough to adapt an ability similar to theirs, so now I can create these shockwaves when I strike. Trust me, I don't know how a human could learn the ways of a titan either, but I guess since I was around them for so long, I became kinda like one. Long story short, the harder I strike, the larger the shockwave." Thalrok answered.

That explains the crazy force he made when he struck the ground. Lotus thought to himself, biting down on the apple again.

While the two young men chatted a bit more with one another and the tavern rumbled with conversation and laughter, the waitress returned.

"Excuse me, boys. I was requested by the blacksmith downstairs to bring you two down to the shop with me," she said politely.

The two looked at one another, concerned about what could possibly be the matter.

"Is everything alright? Did something happen to my sword?" Thalrok asked.

"Nothing of the sort. The head blacksmith just wanted to see the man who used that sword," she said, and she gestured for the two of them to follow her.

Shrugging, Lotus and Thalrok got up from their seats and trailed her through the crowds of people to the broad stairway leading down to the smithy. Even though the dining area was loud, the room they entered next was even louder.

Once through some double doors, they could hear many workers shouting out to one another, as the sound of metal on metal rang throughout the room and fires blazed into the air.

This spacious room had all types of different stations for repairing and building various types of weaponry. In addition to blacksmiths, there were knifemakers and bladesmiths hard at work. The restaurant patrons were certainly not their only customers. Due to a small rise that the canteen stood on, one of the smithy walls opened onto a bustling backstreet just outside, and people often gathered to watch the work going on there as though it was an open theater.

It's crazy to think that they have a restaurant on the second floor and a smithy on the first.

When they reached the bottom of the stairs, the waitress pointed them in the direction of one of the blacksmiths. He was toweling off his greasy hands and directing the others like he was in charge of it all. She began to go back up the stairs to work, and the two ambled over toward the person who must have asked for them.

"Excuse me, sir. Were you the one—" Thalrok began.

"So that big thing is *your* sword?!" the burly blacksmith interrupted. "She is a beauty, let me tell you! Our head blacksmith had a field day tending to your sword, son," he continued earnestly.

Thalrok felt flattered, but was puzzled by something the man just said. However, before he could ask, Lotus, who had noticed the same thing, said, "Pardon me, sir—you're *not* the head blacksmith?"

"Pssh! 'Course I'm not, my boy over there is! I'm Hedric," the blacksmith chuckled and pointed over to the youngest person in the room. Lotus and Thalrok peered over the large man's shoulder to see a boy, no older than 13 years old, hammering away at Thalrok's sword. He wore a helmet with a face shield to protect him from the flying sparks as he lifted and swung his hammer down hard on it.

"Stritan! Ya got visitors!" Hedric called out. The boy quickly glanced over as soon as he heard his father's voice. He tossed his headgear to the ground and dropped his hammer on the floor with little concern for either. Then, like a bolt of lightning, he was suddenly standing in front of them.

"This is *your* sword?! This is the first and only time I've seen see a sword forged from materials found in the mountains of what I assume is the titan's domain! It has such a solid design, and these rugged features are *so* distinctive— how in the world did you get your hands on this?" the boy asked incredulously.

Thalrok paused. He had to collect himself from this sudden burst of admiration for his sword. "Uhh, I was gifted it by my mother, who was in fact a titan. I know it's hard to believe but—"

"*This* was made by the *titans*?!" Stritan exclaimed, his excited voice a mixture of awe and elation. As the kid got even closer to him, Thalrok was a little spooked, and he'd actually flinched when the kid's loud shout startled him.

"You're telling me that this sword was handcrafted by actual titans? It all makes sense now, the heft, balance, and its texture—all so unique. It's a real honor to be able to work with something this amazing. Thank you *so* much!" Stritan smiled broadly in appreciation.

Thalrok had no idea what to say, so with a bemused grin he just replied with a simple, "You're welcome."

"Sorry, I know I can go on long rants. I'm Stritan McGibbon. It's a pleasure to meet you!" He held out his left hand to the bounty hunter, which seemed very odd, until Thalrok noticed why. The boy's right arm was made out of all metal, from his shoulder to his fingertips; it was an artificial limb, a fake arm.

"I'm Thalrok…" he replied.

"That's my kid for ya, always striving to be the best." Hedric laughed with pleasure, as he tousled his boy's hair.

"You're the head blacksmith, right?" Thalrok asked.

"Yep!" Stritan posed triumphantly. Hedric's smile grew even wider, as he saw his son answer that question and beam proudly with delight. Lotus couldn't look away from Stritan's metal arm. From the marks on his shoulder where the last bit of flesh was, it appeared to have been an injury.

Stritan noticed him staring and asked, "You're probably confused about the arm, right?"

Lotus nodded his head as he apologized for staring.

"It's a long story. I don't know how to describe it, but as I got farther into training to become a blacksmith, I learned and developed this very useful ability." Stritan stated simply.

"My boy has the best ability in the world." Hedric began. "Basically, Stritan can take any material and reshape it however he wants. He can use it to repair, fix, or create any kind of weaponry. It's a true miracle."

It was not common to hear that someone in this world had the special ability to shape and re-form materials at will. And at this young of an age, to be able to control and use a power like that, well that was just unreal. Through all of his years, Lotus had never met someone with a power so specific to a cause. He was incredibly intrigued, and wanted to know more. He adjusted his own sword on his hip, the lotus-flower shaped hilt sticking out of the saya.

"No *way!*" Stritan whooped, as he rushed over to stand right next to Lotus.

"Is that a white-bladed sage katana?!" the boy asked with eager excitement. He bent over a little so that his eyes got closer and closer to the sword, staring like a starving dog who was seeing his first meal in weeks.

"Please! It would be such an honor to work on a sword as sacred as this. I've never even seen a sage katana before." Stritan begged, as he held his hands together, metal and flesh, as if praying, and looked up at Lotus with pleading eyes.

Lotus could tell that this would mean a lot to him, but even though he knew that Stritan was a highly skilled blacksmith, he didn't want to risk anything happening to his sword.

"I apologize, but I'll have to pass," Lotus replied.

Stritan dropped his head to his chest, groaning with sorrow. Then he lifted his chin and shuffled back over to the workshop to grab Thalrok's sword to return it to him. Even with the aid of his metal arm, he struggled to keep his legs from shaking or even collapsing under the weight of this mighty blade. He managed to present it with great dignity to Thalrok. As the bounty hunter took hold of his sword, his eyes sparkled with amazement.

"Wow! You did a fantastic job! It looks like it did the day my mother gave it to me!" he commended, as he inspected every inch of his refurbished sword. Stritan lifted his head, placed his hands on his hips, and standing there in a boastful stance, threw back his head and whooped with delight. Thalrok looked back over at the boy and his shiny arm, and couldn't help himself.

"Please forgive me, but how *did* you get the metal arm?" he asked. Stritan paused for a second, he looked at his arm and heard the metal rub together as he lifted his metal hand.

Hedric took up the story. "It happened a while ago when he was really young," he began. "My boy here wanted to be a blacksmith more than anything in the world. I trained him every day until he learned enough skills to work under me in the shop. After about a week of working in the shop, the town came under attack. A large group of raiders came through and took a lot of lives. They left the town in shambles. Unfortunately, in that chaos, Stritan lost his arm. Luckily it wasn't his life, and he is still here with us today." Hedric pulled his son closely to his side as he spoke.

"When the attack was over and we were finally recovering from the attack, I went to visit him where he'd been recovering but he wasn't there." Hedric went on. "Later, I found him back at the shop, all bandaged up, and working on his blacksmith skills. It was crazy to see such drive in my son, even though he had only one arm. Years went by, and he began developing that amazing ability, all on his own. Then, he made himself a metal arm, and using his special power, he could control it like a normal arm. It's incredible that such a miracle could happen after that tragedy."

The two young men listened to Hedric's tale quietly and watched as Stritan lifted his metal arm and wiggled his fingers.

"Listen here kid, it's decided! You will now be my personal blacksmith! I'm not lettin' a single person touch my sword but you." Thalrok pointed right at the glowing young blacksmith and smiled.

"Thank you *so* much, sir!" Stritan smiled back, now jumping up and down, overjoyed. That little gesture had meant so much to the boy. People always saw his age as a sign of immaturity and lack of skill, so to have Thalrok's full trust was quite an honor for Stritan.

"Stritan, we got another batch coming down," a waitress called down from upstairs. Without a second's pause, Stritan rushed over to his station to get working. He threw on his helmet and was back on the job in a flash.

"Thanks again, boys. You don't know how hard he works, day and night, to become the best blacksmith in the world." Hedric stated. He bowed his head before he went back to his own work, and patted each of their shoulders as he walked past them.

Lotus and Thalrok made their way back upstairs to the dining area. Lotus stopped at the top of the stairs and glanced back down at the young boy working with a big smile on his face.

"He will do great things for this world." Thalrok declared, as he walked past Lotus.

"Yes, he certainly will." Lotus followed right behind. They finished up their food, paid for their meals, and headed out. As the two of them walked back down the front steps of the canteen they checked in each direction to find what they had really come here for. They poked around everywhere, exploring building after building until…

"This must be it." Thalrok pointed. The refugee hideaway was there in plain sight, "The Lie-Inn." Reportedly, fugitives and outcasts, like Lotus, could stay here. In that way, it was like some kind of orphanage. Other paying visitors came and went.

Thalrok and Lotus stood outside briefly inspecting the gigantic building, which was covered in windows and had vines crawling up the sides of the walls. The porch out front had chairs for the guests to relax in as they enjoyed their stay. But, Lotus wondered, would he really be safe here?

"You done draggin' your feet?" Thalrok called out, as he approached the inn but saw Lotus still standing in the street looking dazed. The young man snapped out of it at once, and hustled over to the bounty hunter, who stood there holding the door open. As it closed behind them, a little bell above their heads rang ever so lightly, announcing their entrance.

"How can we help you boys?" two kind-looking ladies asked in unison from behind the reception counter. Lotus followed quietly behind Thalrok, as they walked straight ahead into the lobby.

Is this gonna work? If I decide to stay here, will my past just repeat itself? Lotus began to worry. The reopening of old wounds is never easy. He felt like he was bracing for impact without even knowing if he would crash. His chest sank and his heart ached in anticipation. It wasn't natural for him to feel this way anymore. It had been so very long since he'd even toyed with the thought of him rejoining society in any way, and now here he was, about to get a place to stay in this town of Mellowtin.

Once they got to the front desk, they were greeted with pleasant smiles by, upon closer investigation, twin innkeepers. The women appeared to be maybe fifty years old, lively, and even though small in stature, still forces to be reckoned with.

"Hello, we would like two rooms, please," Thalrok asked respectfully.

"One moment, please." Immediately, the two keen-eyed ladies began rummaging around searching for something, maybe their room keys, or some paperwork to fill out. Then the woman on the right pulled out a large stack of papers and abruptly slammed it down on the counter.

The sound startled the two waiting young men, and their eyes scanned the tall pile of papers from the bottom to the top. They had no clue what it was, until Lotus noticed what was on the papers.

The innkeepers' fingers ran lightly across the edges of the papers, taking a brief peek at every sheet. "What do we have here Layla?" one of the innkeepers asked, stopping at one of the pages.

"I don't know Leyla. It appears that our young friend here with the bandana is wanted for, am I reading this right... murder?" Layla replied, as she placed Lotus's wanted poster on the table in front of them. She looked up at Lotus, eyebrows raised.

Thalrok glanced over at Lotus and saw the guilt washing over him and his thousand-yard stare into some far-off hell as his mind began battling itself in a civil war of pain.

Lotus's fists were clenched at his side, his head down. He hated himself more with each second that they all stared at him.

"Hmm... and not to mention that it was a Grand Sage who died. This is a big deal. Five years running yet here he is standing right in front of us, and with quite the bounty on his head." Leyla commented. She tilted her head and looked expectantly at Lotus.

It was inevitable, everywhere he went, people knew of his name and how he was this "murderer." Even after all those years of hiding, here was yet another reminder that he was not destined for a life of joy or peace.

All he ever brought to others was ruin.

"Look at me, child," Leyla said firmly, as Lotus would not meet their gaze. He finally lifted his head somberly and stared into the hazel eyes of this small but dignified woman. Leyla's piercing green-amber gaze seemed to judge every inch of him.

This was it, he would be asked to leave yet another village, just as fate always had it. The burn of hate towards one's self was a burn that a human could never go numb to or escape.

"Did you do it?" she asked.

Lotus stood still, motionless. His throat was too tight to speak; it was just too painful to even try to produce any words.

After several seconds of silence, he was finally able to respond to her in a soft, quiet voice, "No ma'am."

Even though he'd given this same answer for many years, it had never changed anyone's mind. Lotus didn't want to take another moment of their time, and wanted to spare himself from the response that he knew was to come. He started to turn and take his first step away from the desk to leave this village for good, when he heard the sound of paper ripping. He lifted his head and saw Leyla tearing that damning paper into pieces right before his eyes.

"You poor thing, you've been running for so long, haven't you?" she asked, with true caring in her voice.

All Lotus could do was admire the kind lady's sympathetic eyes as he watched the torn pieces of paper fall to the floor. Leyla's face was filled with concern even though she had just met him.

Everyone, in every single village he had gone to, had seen his face and had immediately cast him out, or had even tried to kill him. Yet, for once, these two innkeepers looked at him as a human, an innocent person.

"You two can stay here as long as you like. Folks here will know that you're staying with us, so you'll be perfectly safe." Layla reassured them and held out two keys.

"Thank you so much," Thalrok replied as he took the keys. Lotus still could only stand mutely in shock for a moment.

"You alright, Ronin?" Thalrok asked. The young man again snapped back into reality and then took one of the keys from Thalrok's outstretched hand.

"You two have rooms at the end of the left hall on the second floor. Feel free to use the lounge area that connects those four rooms." Leyla then indicated the stairs on their left. There were twin stairs, one on each side of the counter. The eyes of both young men followed her outstretched arm signaling the left stairwell.

They walked up to the second floor. At the top, halls led in multiple directions with doors scattered along the walls. Turning the corner to the left at the top, they could see a small space at the end of that hall with couches and a big window facing out onto the village. On either side of that small lounge, they found four numbered doors, two of which matched the numbers on their keys.

"I don't know about you but I think that bed in there is calling my name. Knock if you need anything." Thalrok offered, as he walked into his room.

Lotus watched the bounty hunter close his door, then turned his head to stare at his own. He heard the lock release from inside as he turned the key, and pushed the wooden door forward, peering inside the room. It was dark, and appeared to be very small from what little light came in.

The young man walked inside and closed the door behind him. He entered the darkened room and headed over to the window that had a just bit of daylight leaking through a small gap in the loosely-closed curtains. As he pushed them aside, the whole room became aglow with sunlight. It was just as small as his room back in Petalbrooke, except it was emptier. There was a small bed for one with a desk right across from it. Down the narrow path in between was the window through which light now brushed across the worn wooden floor. A few landscape paintings decorated the walls with what appeared to be local scenery.

Not much to unpack. Lotus rubbed his hands as he sat down on his bed.

With the sunlight changing from a warm yellow to a deeper orange, dusk was coming to the town of Mellowtin. Thalrok and Lotus both stretched out and sank into their beds. For one, it was just as it always was, just another town, another bed. For the other it was, at last, a place to sleep among others once again. Though the comfort of a real bed felt so pleasant, something unsettling still brewed in his mind, and Lotus fell back into his melancholy thoughts once more before he slept.

The next day...

The birds chirp the same. Lotus sat up in bed. The bedsprings shifted and squeaked as he planted both feet on the floor. He rubbed his eyes to clear his vision, then stretched his arms over his head as he looked outside to a fully wide awake and busy town.

"I haven't gotten up this late in a while." Lotus realized, feeling rested now after finally sleeping in a real bed. It had been such a very long time since he had.

He stood up to take a closer look out of the window and saw people walking by, just going about their normal lives. He pushed the window open and took a deep breath of the fresh morning air. Lotus then turned his head to check his reflection in the mirror above the desk. Each time he looked at himself, he only saw his young self, tarnished from his tormented past. His lean, scarred face was marked with sorrow, and so little joy. Joy had been stripped from him after all these solitary years of running and hiding.

Guess I'll go for a run. Lotus decided, as he got dressed and left his room. He locked the door behind him and was about to go downstairs, when he stopped to look over at Thalrok's door. *I wonder if he's up?*

After several knocks there was no response. Lotus assumed that the bounty hunter was still sleeping, not to mention that he heard rhythmic waves of coarse heavy breathing, which definitely sounded like snoring. So, he turned and went down the hall and headed down the stairs to go out.

"Good morning, dear," the twin innkeepers greeted him as he passed through the lobby. Lotus gave them both a gentle wave as he left the Lie-Inn.

68

Sunlight poked through the clouds and he could hear the sounds of bustling activities carrying through the streets. Awakening once again to a town full of life and activity gave the young man a deeply satisfying feeling in his chest. Each day he'd lived alone in that old ruin of a village had pushed him further and further from reality. He had been simply existing there; just waiting for death. Now, he took his first step, then the next, until he was in full motion, jogging openly through the town.

Lotus took his time, as he wanted to see and experience all that lay before him. A steady stream of travelers from both near and far poured in from the various entrances to the town and filled the plaza. It was a wondrous sight to see, this flow of people moving like a river. How hard it was to keep going and not to just stop and take a good look around.

Mellowtin was a town that had everything one could need—food markets, clothing and leather stores, shops for weaponry, livestock and produce sales, a good variety of other types of businesses, and homes. All of these thrived together, side by side. *This place really is incredible*, he thought. Seeing everyone so awake, energetic, and meshed together in their society reminded him of his time in Petalbrooke. That town had been so socially connected, and quite grand, even if it was hidden past the deep forests. People walked the streets of Petalbrooke with smiles on their faces and families close by. It was home.

It was home...

Lotus, deep in thought now, stopped running. He remembered those once-happy Petalbrooke faces looking at him with such... hate. The scornful, hostile words that they had spoken years ago never left his head.

"Monster!" they'd yelled. His heart began to beat faster. Nervous sweat beaded on his face.

"Murderer!" they'd screamed. The trembling of his hands worsened as his breath thickened.

"Hey!" a voice called out from close by.

Lotus looked up and snapped out of his daze. He glanced over toward the source of the voice and saw the Fork and Sword sign up across the way. Right below it, Stritan was waving his metal hand high.

It's the blacksmith boy, Lotus remembered. He walked over to the teen to greet him.

"Good morning. Stritan is it?" Lotus asked. The boy nodded his head and smiled as he wiped his greasy hands on his blacksmith's apron. Even though he'd seen it yesterday, watching the boy be able to move his metal arm and hand at will, and so deftly, was most incredible.

"I don't mean to pry, but I didn't catch your name, sir. I got the titan man's name but not yours." Stritan said.

"Oh—my name is Lotus," he replied.

"Easy enough to remember," the boy replied.

Stritan then asked Lotus what he was doing running around the town. He simply told the boy that he was just trying to get some fresh air and maybe find a place to eat.

Lotus was in luck; Stritan told him of a great diner just a few streets over to the east. It was a smaller place, but served excellent food every morning. Lotus thanked him, then began an easy run going east.

"Don't forget, if you ever want your sword cleaned up, let me know!" Stritan yelled as he waved goodbye. Lotus waved back, and pressed onward to the diner that the boy had recommended.

Going through the town once more, he took in as much of this wonderfully interdependent life as he could. He still couldn't come to peace with the idea of him fitting in anywhere. Sooner or later he knew that he'd end up right back in that broken village, just like always. Once they all found out who he was, he'd always be doomed, anywhere he went.

"Hello there, is it just you today?" the hostess asked. Lotus nodded, and was seated quickly by a large window, where a waitress promptly took his order. He then gazed out of the window and watched the people passing by.

Mom, Dad, what should I do?

It was so hard to see his parents' faces anymore, as it had been over 10 years since he last saw them. Yet in his mind, his mother's voice never changed. Her soft voice as she'd call out for her son always sounded so... sad.

"Thalrok?" Lotus whispered, as he saw a familiar helmeted giant of a man walking toward the diner. Their eyes met through the window, and Thalrok headed for the diner's entrance. He walked in and took a seat across from Lotus.

"Looks like you slept well." Lotus commented.

The bounty hunter stretched his arms high in the air and yawned lazily from inside his helmet. "It's been a while since I got to sleep in a bed, so I took as much time as I could sleeping. Pardon my bed head though, I know it's atrocious." Thalrok apologized, as he rubbed the helmet which surrounded his entire head. As he dropped his hands he immediately picked up a menu and began choosing what he wanted to eat.

Lotus chuckled, shaking his own head at the ridiculous joke. While the two talked and settled into the morning, their food arrived. They both began to eat and wake themselves up, preparing for a day of the unknown.

"So, what's your plan?" Thalrok asked.

"What do you mean?" Lotus replied.

"What's next for the man, hunted across the world. Are you planning on settling down in Mellowtin, or do you have other ideas?" The bounty hunter inquired.

Lotus looked outside at all the people, just living their normal lives, happy and healthy, together as one community. He knew not of what the future held. If fate were to repeat as it always had, he would be putting these people in danger. Or the time would come when they would most likely cast him out. It was hard to bear, but what else could he do?

"I've been on the run for so long, there isn't much I can do now. Each town looks at me in fear and horror, then chases me out. There is nowhere I am seen as a human being. The City of Light almost caught me once before, and I don't intend to go through that again," he replied.

Now in a silent and dreary mood, the two young men finished their meals and started walking back to the inn. Once comfortable, each in their own room, they still sat quietly, awaiting some solution or purpose to appear.

Master, I don't know what to do. Is there still hope for me? Can I still be the student you trained so hard to help you on your journey? I wanted to help this world but... what can I do? Lotus brooded. He sat there on his bed and looking down at the floor, listless and still. Even though he was surrounded by people, he still felt alone.

* * *

"What's going on?" Lotus mumbled, rubbing his eyes as he sat up from his bed early in the morning. Still half asleep, he kicked his feet off the bed and looked outside to see what time it might be.

The muffled sounds of a woman wailing in distress came echoing up from the first floor of the inn, followed by even louder cries of pure anguish.

Lotus poked his head out of his door. As he looked around, he noticed that Thalrok was out to investigate the noise too. The bounty hunter shrugged his shoulders, not knowing anything about what was happening downstairs. "Good morning I guess." Thalrok groaned, still half asleep as well.

The two made their way to the top of the stairs where their eyes went naturally towards the front desk. There she was, a woman in the arms of a man who was probably her husband, crying her eyes out and wiping endless tears from her red and swollen face.

"Please! Have either of you seen our son Fedris?" she bawled hysterically.

"I'm so sorry, but we haven't seen any children like you've described here recently." Leyla and Layla were trying their hardest to comfort this woman by ensuring her that their boy was all right, wherever he was. "I wish we could help a little more, but we just haven't seen any children walking about looking lost," Layla told her.

The woman instantly burst into tears again, clinging tightly to her husband and trying to hold onto what little reason she had left.

"Please, our village has had three children go missing in the last two days, and now Fedris! Please, has anyone, anyone at all, mentioned or seen some unfamiliar children running around?" her husband begged.

The twins turned to one another, their faces a mirror image of sorrow and helplessness, upset that they had no more information. They felt terrible that they could not help this family.

The pain in the woman's reddened eyes was so deep; she must have been like this for days, exhausted with grief by the loss of her child. The husband too, showed great frustration and strain. He was just barely keeping it together to help comfort his wife.

"Their child has gone missing? That's awful..." Thalrok whispered, "They look so worn out, if only . . . " he paused as he noticed that Lotus's face was masked with horror. The wanted man was staring at her, as if he had seen this sight before. A mother, crying for her child as the father comforts her.

What can I do? These words rattled around in his head over and over again like a broken record.

What can I do? It echoed in his mind endlessly. For some reason, his heart rate began to jump, he could feel it pulsing throughout his whole being.

What can... I do?

Feeling cursed and burdened to a life of pain, he still could not tear his attention away from these two grieving parents. Lotus began to feel a sensation building in his chest. It felt as if he was reopening an old box filled with things that he had long ago found most precious, a box that had been locked away for years. The lid creaked open and its contents were free again, allowing him to reclaim those invaluable parts of himself that he thought were lost forever.

What... can... I do?

This young man, no matter how many years had passed, was still the same student he was when he'd been first rescued and taken in. He had told his master then what he wanted to do in this world. Even through all of those tough years, Lotus was still that very same Ronin, deep in his very core.

"Oh, I'm so sorry for the noise," Leyla said regretfully, as she saw Lotus coming down the stairwell. The young man lifted his hand, dismissing her apology. When he reached the bottom of the stairs, he strode briskly over to the distraught parents. He looked gently at the mother, who was still tightly clutching her husband, sobbing.

What CAN I do?! flashed in his mind.

"Where is your hometown, ma'am?" Lotus asked softly.

The woman stared at him, frozen in place for just a moment. Then she perked up a bit, trying to dry her wet face and grasp what he'd just said.

"Pardon?" she whispered.

"Your village, where is it?" he asked her in a kind voice.

Her husband stuttered, then finally explained that they were Marak and Valla from Linbud, which was about twenty miles east of Mellowtin.

Those words, "what can I do", continued to echo in Lotus's head over and over, getting louder each time. He then took a deep breath, straightened his back, and held his head up high.

"Please, take me there. I'm going to help you find your child." Lotus said firmly. And just like that, the decision was made.

The parents couldn't seem to move. They stood motionless, wearing identical blank looks. Then, as they realized what the young man had just said, Lotus's sincere promise released the tension from their bodies. All at once both of them dropped to their knees, broke down into fresh tears, and thanked him over and over again. The innkeepers rushed around the counter to help them up, patting their backs in support.

As for Lotus, he immediately headed back upstairs to prepare for this upcoming venture. Thalrok watched the young man stride past him and noticed a new aura of confidence, self-assurance, and intention, none of which he had ever shown before.

Lotus really didn't have much to pack apart from the sword and saya at his hip and the clothes on his back. He stood in the middle of his room facing the window and stared out into the town. Then he took one last deep breath in and heard the words in his mind one final time, *What can I do?*

With Lotus's room looking exactly the way it was when he first arrived, he patted the saya at his hip and turned to leave. When he did so, he spotted Thalrok leaning comfortably on the doorjamb.

"You know I'm coming, right?" Thalrok said.

"You are?" Lotus was not *totally* surprised.

"Of course I am. I respect you, and I trust your decision to help them out. Plus, I have nowhere else to go and nothing else to do. So, this will be something to do for now." Thalrok chuckled, then went to his room to pack up his things too.

Lotus couldn't help but wear a little smile as he went downstairs, waiting for Thalrok to finish up.

"You're doing a wonderful thing you know," Leyla told him, standing behind the counter with her sister.

Lotus turned around to see the twin innkeepers smiling with delight, as they watched this scarred and tormented young man going out of his way to help a family in need.

"It's nothing really," Lotus replied, scratching his head.

"You may say that, but those two seemed to have regained their hope after you offered to help them. You saw it too, it looked like they hadn't slept a wink in days. For you to make a special effort to do something like this, well, it shows great honor, courage, and character." Leyla commented.

This feeling Lotus felt in his chest was warmer than usual. It was that feeling of joy, purpose, and decency, the sense that he was helping someone in need. It had been a long time since he had known this feeling.

"Your rooms will be ready for you wherever you return." The two innkeepers then bowed their heads.

"Really?"

"Of course. We told you that you can stay as long as you'd like. Until you tell us you don't need those rooms anymore, they are yours," the innkeepers replied.

Lotus was grateful for their kindness, and bowed right back to them.

"You ready to go?" Thalrok asked as he reached the bottom of the stairs.

Lotus looked at him, took a deep breath in, and then exhaled slowly. "Absolutely."

6

What can I do?

"We're here, boys," the coachman announced, as Lotus and Thalrok lifted their sleeping heads to behold the small town just ahead getting closer. Marak and Valla, who traveled with them, looked up hopefully, thinking that perhaps Fedris had come home in their absence.

From here, nothing unique stood out; Linbud appeared to be just like any other very small town you'd stumble across in Perlaria. That was, until they actually entered the village and witnessed firsthand just how dismal things were on the inside. The townspeople walked around with their heads down. They spoke not a single word to one another, not in a spirit of hate, but of sadness and despair. The weight of gloom had settled over everything.

"This town is really taking it hard after losing those children. The whole place is in a depressed state." Thalrok whispered to Lotus.

Lotus glanced ahead where a group of people were gathering. The carriage began to slow down and the horses came to a halt.

Fedris's parents, Marak and Valla, climbed out first. They were immediately surrounded by other townsfolk who wished to offer comfort for the absence of their son, who was still nowhere to be seen. The young men also stepped out of the carriage, and began to stretch their legs after the long ride here. They looked farther down the street where they saw a second crowd forming around another man and woman who looked anguished and distressed.

"Was another child taken?" Lotus asked.

"It appears so," Thalrok responded quietly. They walked closer to the crowd around Fedris's parents to see what was going on.

"So, the Casabans lost their daughter yesterday?" Marak asked the townspeople, who had all now come to gather around the recent arrivals. They nodded their heads, sharing the unfortunate news. Clenching his fists tightly, he held in his anger at the curse this town was bearing.

"Why?" he murmured through his teeth. His wife, Valla, placed her hand softly on his shoulder to calm him. Everyone wondered just how and to where these kids were disappearing. Marak needed to remain composed; hope had been set before them, and he must inform the town.

"Please, everyone listen! These gentlemen have said they would help us find our children!" Marak proclaimed, pointing at the newcomers.

All eyes turned towards Thalrok and Lotus, looking at them as if they were the light at the end of a very long tunnel. No one had yet responded to their many calls for aid, but here were these two who had actually gone out of their way to travel to their small town just to help them.

The crowd of people surrounded the visitors, babbling excitedly about how thankful they were, and what joy they felt in their hearts at having any possible chance to see their children again.

"Please, please, settle down. We need to hear from everyone about what's been happening so we can get a better understanding of the situation." Thalrok announced.

The crowd calmed down and quieted. They gave the two young men some space, as they waited for someone to step up, speak out, and relive the ordeal.

Finally, a burly man stepped forward, removed his hat, and wiped the sweat from his forehead. "My name is Brittel. So, two days ago, it was just like any other day." he began quietly. "A bit of rain was falling, and the crops were getting just enough to replenish them. The kids were doing as they always did—running around in the streets, splashing and playing in the puddles. As the light rain turned into a heavy downpour, we heard thunder crashing in the distance and it was getting dark. So, our workday was over and we all started going home. We called for our children but…" the soft-spoken man paused in his story. Dangling by his side, his rough hands shook noticeably.

Doing his best to stay in control, he continued, "Not all of the children returned. We scoured all of our town, looked *everywhere*, and called out their names until we were hoarse. Three children were nowhere to be found, including my son, Orvis. They are all between the ages of six and nine years old. We have seen no trace of them. That makes five of them missing altogether, three boys and two girls. Day and night they're always here, and suddenly in one second they're just… gone." He lowered his head.

Some of the townspeople standing next to him rubbed his back, trying to comfort this grieving father.

Lotus scanned the crowd and saw that they all felt the same; everyone was miserable and suffering because of the loss some of them were experiencing personally. Community and connection were evidently deeply rooted in Linbud. The young man stepped forward, took a knee in front of the man who had spoken, and looked up at him.

"You have my word, I will find your boy. I'll make sure he gets back here safely." Lotus promised.

Orvis's father couldn't hold in his emotions any longer; the tears he had held in for so long streamed down his face as he collapsed there in the street, thanking Lotus over and over. The young man helped him up, then rose to his full height and stood amidst the crowd.

"Have any of you seen anyone or anything strange in the last few days? Anything at all out of the ordinary?" Lotus appealed.

The townspeople murmured softly as they looked at one another for answers. All of them maintained that they hadn't seen anything or anyone strange in the past few days, or even weeks, before the children were taken. Nothing useful surfaced.

"Please, folks, there must be something that caught you by surprise or was a little off. Anything at all?" Thalrok added.

Still, no one spoke up.

Damn, not a single lead. He began to feel that his promise might be harder to keep than he realized. How could he find these five missing kids if no one knew anything that might help him?

"I might have something," a young voice called out timidly from the crowd. Lotus and Thalrok turned around and saw a boy, who looked to be about fourteen years old, step slowly forward. He seemed very tense, and almost too apprehensive to speak at all.

"I'm Baxion," he began tentatively. "My little brother, Nethel, was taken… I remember him mentioning hearing a weird sound coming from the hills to the north. Every time he went outside and looked in that direction, he and his buddies would say they all heard it. That's all I know though…" the nervous boy offered, shrugging slowly.

Lotus walked over and patted his shoulder in thanks. Baxion lifted his head, quietly noticing the scar on Lotus's face. He wondered how *that* could have happened.

"That's the kind of lead we needed. We can start there!" Lotus exclaimed as turned to Thalrok. The bounty hunter nodded his head, knowing exactly what needed to be done next. Without speaking another word, they immediately readied their gear to go northward and investigate where the odd sound was coming from.

The townsfolk followed them through the streets as Lotus and Thalrok left through Linbud's northern gates. Behind them they heard the roar of their shouts, wishing them good luck and thanking them, as they marched into the unknown. Lotus could hear the pain in their voices. There was gratitude there to be sure, but it only thinly masked the misery and heartache that they felt from long days without closure.

"Let's get those kids back," Lotus said with determination.

"Right," Thalrok replied.

* * *

After hours of walking, they had entered the northern woodlands, the place Baxion had spoken of. A choir of the tall trees' rustling sighs permeated the forest. The smell of rain filled the air, and casual raindrops slid their way down any leaf in their path to soak the earth below. Random bursts of skittering sounds could be heard as wildlife scurried unseen in the undergrowth. They pushed on as the rain began to fall harder.

"Anything?" Thalrok asked.

"Nothing," Lotus replied, covering his face from the rain.

They had been in the forest for a while now, and had found no trace of any missing children. No structures, hideouts, or people were around to create any sound that would be considered unusual. Once again they found themselves at a dead end.

"Damn." Lotus shook his head, kneeling down to investigate the ground for any noticeable clues. He brushed the weeds away and found nothing of any help. Branches on the trees creaked in the wind and drooped under the weight of the rain. Soaked from head to toe, he stood up slowly and surveyed the area, watching Thalrok do the same. Saturated, both of them stood there, watchful, in the steady rain.

Guess we should move on to the next spot. As he began to tell Thalrok that, he stopped. He felt a chill, an odd cold feeling inside. The hairs on his arm stood up, and he could sense a dark presence somewhere.

"Thalrok..." he whispered.

"Yeah, I feel it too." Thalrok slowly reached for his sword and released the latches keeping it on his back.

Quietly standing in place, Lotus discreetly placed his left hand on his saya and looked around the darkened woods. A deep indigo hue painted the spots between the trees, as the forest was quite dark. All sounds of the wildlife had stopped. The only noise to be heard was the white noise of raindrops pattering on the leaves.

The two held their breaths, glancing around in all directions, with an uneasy feeling under their skin.

"Duck!" Lotus yelled suddenly, as three metal needles suddenly flew right past them, piercing into nearby tree trunks with three solid thunks.

The two of them jumped backwards, as quickly as cats, and faced the direction of the attack. They held their weapons tightly. There was still no one in sight, but someone was definitely there. Whoever it was had kept themself hidden and could strike from the shadows again at any time.

Lotus and Thalrok stood side by side, on high alert and keeping their eyes peeled for any movement. A crash of thunder rumbled through the trees and the panting of their breaths joined with the chorus of wind and rain.

"So, they finally decided to get someone to come looking for these cryin' kids, huh? Took 'em long enough," a cynical voice from afar called out.

The two had no idea where the sarcastic voice was coming from. The wooded terrain was too thick and dark to see much of anything.

"Where are they hiding?" Thalrok whispered.

The two shuffled around cautiously, checking all around themselves for some sign, anything, to show from where they were being watched.

"Hey, boss, isn't that guy with the bandana a wanted man?" another gruff voice spoke out from a different direction.

"Well, waddya you know, you're right! I saw somewhere he had a big bounty on him for killin' a Grand Sage. Guess we'll get some money for him *and* those kids," the boss cackled.

Thalrok's hands gripped his sword tighter as he snarled in disgust. He wanted to shout back, but Lotus quickly stopped him.

"There's no point in talking to them, we'd just play into their trap even more. If we let ourselves get off guard again, they will surely try another sneak attack," he hissed.

The bounty hunter calmed himself, then focused on the task at hand, which was getting back those five kids. Lotus may have appeared to be calm, collected and ready to go, but mentally, he was distracted.

Please, am I still able to do it? He squeezed his eyes shut, concentrating. Lotus slowed his breathing, deepened his stance, and lowered his blade to the ground. He inhaled very slowly, deeply, and focused on everything around him. He could feel the raindrops softly pelting his skin and sliding down his body to the dirt below. He both heard and felt the trees rustling above his head, along with the bushes and vegetation near his legs. Breath by breath, he searched for some faint light in the distance. He closed his eyes even more tightly, pleading to sense something, anything.

"There," Lotus whispered, and he zipped forward like a bolt of lightning. Swinging his fragmented sword horizontally, he sliced the medium-sized tree that was in his path in half with a single slash. Bark flew through the air as the shattered tree cracked and fell to the ground with a thud.

Directly above Lotus's head, a shadowy figure dropped down from the downed tree to pounce on him. The young man already knew that this was coming. Darting his eyes upward, he leaped up to meet the quickly descending figure.

No way! The bandit panicked, not expecting his sneak attack to be foiled so easily.

Lotus rocketed straight for him, and grabbed firmly onto the bandit's collar. As they landed, Lotus slammed the unknown thug face-up on the ground, pinned him down and pointed his broken sword right between the surprised man's eyes.

"Where are they?" Lotus spoke with unwavering firmness as he glared at his opponent.

A mask covered some of the thug's dirty face, but the grin of a dangerous enemy still showed. Lotus suddenly heard a noise coming from his left. He turned his head sharply and saw another set of needles flying right at him.

Gotta brace for these!

Lotus cringed as two of them pierced his shoulder. He gasped in pain, but continued to stare grimly down at his pinned foe. The thug grabbed a handful of mud and threw it at Lotus's eyes. Blinded now, and with two needles stuck in his left shoulder, Lotus released his hold and was momentarily helpless against any attack to come next. The thug quickly pulled his dagger from its sheath, and rising, brought his arm back for a forward slash.

Thalrok saw what was happening and shouted, "Jump back, Ronin!"

Without hesitation, Lotus jumped as far back as he could. Even though

82

he could see nothing, he fully trusted Thalrok.

The thug missed his target by a hair, and the follow-through left him open to attack. What came shortly after that was a giant fist, the fist of a man trained by the titans, crushing him squarely in the jaw. As his knuckles connected, Thalrok felt a crack, definitely enough to wipe that smile off the bandit's face. Thalrok's hard hit sent him flying off into the woods. The distant thwack of some flying object crashing into a tree rattled the air. The bounty hunter quickly looked over at Lotus.

"You alright, Ro—" Thalrok began, but as he took the first step towards him, he was suddenly jumped by another bandit who was hiding in the bushes. This thug pounced on Thalrok's back, wrapping strong arms around his thick neck. Thalrok felt his back arching, as he was being pulled backwards and farther away from Lotus, but he only laughed.

"So you want to wrestle, huh? I don't know why, but this feels familiar." He was being throttled more and more, but the bounty hunter squatted down as low as he could go and pulled his arms back.

"Here we go, you annoying baggage." Thalrok released all of his power into the ground and swung his arms up in the air, launching himself several feet off the ground. He grinned through the discomfort of being strangled as he turned his back toward the ground and began descending very quickly.

The thug turned his head, and glancing below, realized too late that he had put himself in a painful situation. The titan crashed to the forest floor and crushed the thug between himself and the ground. The grip on Thalrok's neck immediately released as the thug's breath whooshed out of his lungs.

Thalrok rolled over, grabbed him by the face and picked him up. Then he slammed the wretched man against a nearby tree so hard that the bark cracked and roots began to poke out of the dirt from beneath the now-leaning tree .

"Drop him!" another voice shouted, as a sword swung towards the bounty hunter.

Thalrok, using his other arm, raised his own immense sword to block the puny bandit's small one. The titan of a man hadn't even looked away from the tree. All the third bandit could see was the blinding reflection of a bolt of lightning bouncing off that metal helmet.

Thalrok chuckled to himself, as he took the man he still held tightly in his grasp, turned, and threw him straight at the other. The flying thug caught his ally full-on, and he stumbled backward from the impact.

Now the rain began to fall faster and clouds covered more and more of the sky. It was getting even darker and harder to see in this forest. Lotus was able to clean his face off somewhat and hurried over to Thalrok. "You doing alright?" Lotus asked.

"I should be asking you that. How's your shoulder doin'?" Thalrok replied.

"It'll be fine for now, don't worry about it." Lotus wiped the remaining dirt from his face, then looked over at the thugs they'd fought standing off in the distance. They all appeared spent, wounded, and beaten from what little bit of combat that they'd just experienced.

A short distance away, three more shadowy figures came out from the bushes. "This is a lot more than I expected, I didn't think they would send people like *this* to find their children. We should retreat and let *him* handle it." the boss proposed sourly. The others agreed without hesitation, then they all took off running through the woods like a bunch of cowards.

"Get back here!" Thalrok shouted, as he and Lotus started to chase after them.

Their feet splashed with each step as the rain now poured in torrents from the heavens down onto the forest. A crash of thunder rolled through and reverberated among the trees. It was impossible to see much of anything, even with the occasional lightning flash. Bobbing and weaving through the woods, the group of thugs were soon out of sight. Lotus and Thalrok stopped their headlong pursuit; their targets had outrun them. This was familiar territory to those thugs, and they had taken full advantage of that knowledge.

"Damn it!" Thalrok shouted angrily as he punched a tree.

There they were, standing in the pouring rain panting and gasping for breath. Thalrok started to pace back and forth in anger. Lotus stood staring off into the forest. The constant drumming sound of rain completely canceled out any other noises in the forest. All footfalls, all wildlife sounds, everything, was drowned out by the cloudburst of rain falling from the sky.

"What do we do now?" Thalrok asked.

He heard no response.

"Ronin," he called out again, "Ronin, do you hear me?"

Still, there was no response. The bounty hunter walked over to him, asking what was wrong, but was immediately shushed. Lotus kept his eyes locked ahead. Thalrok looked off in the distance toward where he was staring.

"You hear that?" Lotus asked.

The two of them stood still, gazing off in one direction. A foggy haze enveloped them as the rain poured down. Lightning flashed and thunder rumbled all around them, yet they could still hear this faint… stomping?

Whatever was ahead of them seemed to be getting closer. The stomping sound got louder with every second, now accompanied by the crack and feel of the very earth buckling. Mesmerized, their bodies couldn't move, not even an inch. Lotus could feel some unholy sort of pressure building up just ahead of them.

Finally, after one last loud thud, the stomping ended.

The two stood silently.

Lotus glanced up, and his eyes widened in horror. "Thalrok—run!" he suddenly shouted, as some beast the size of a huge tree came crashing right in front of them, shattering the ground beneath its root-like feet like it was a thin sheet of ice.

"What the hell *is* that thing!?" Thalrok yelled, as his feet stumbled across the sodden ground. The beast's shriek of satisfaction echoed across the whole forest; it had caught its prey totally off guard.

"Ronin watch out!" Thalrok bellowed.

Lotus peeked over his shoulder and saw a hammering tree-like fist swinging straight down at his head. He was still unbalanced from the ground breaking up beneath his feet and had no choice but to take a direct hit. He lifted his forearms above his head and felt the crush of that hard, wooden fist slam down on him. His legs buckled from the pressure of this giant creature's powerful blow. It screeched again, as it reeled back a second arm to strike.

Lotus could feel the dark energy inside him begin to flow through him like water exploding through a bursting dam. With a quick surge of energy, he pushed away the monster's branch-like arm, then dashed away from another as it came swiping wildly through the air. Lotus watched its arm slice easily through tree after tree like they were made of paper.

This monster was a terrifying beast like no other. It was the living embodiment of a moving forest with a torso made completely of wood that looked like the trunk of a massive tree. The monster's two sturdy tree-trunk legs lifted it high into the air. Its two even longer tree-like arms could support it on the ground in a gorilla-like stance. One woody arm ended in what looked like a large rectangular fist made of strong branches. Other smaller branches and twigs grew out from its limbs, sprouting leaves. A giant rock atop gave it the overall look of a hunchback. Three bright red eyes glowed menacingly in its long, barked face.

"That was way too close." Lotus huffed as he watched it turn towards him.

The two of them had never seen a tree-monster like this before. It was terrifying just to be in its presence. Even without a visible mouth, it screeched loud enough for half the world to hear.

That must have been the sound the boy was talking about hearing in the village. Whether or not those kids are here somewhere, this definitely is something to worry about.

The creature was looking right down at him, growling as it targeted its prey. Lotus glanced over to see Thalrok standing behind it with his gigantic sword pulled backward over his shoulder, feet planted wide apart and firmly on the ground.

"Just stay right there, you scary piece of— " he breathed, and with one swift swing, he chopped straight through the monster's leg.

86

It howled out in pain and kicked the stub that remained of its severed leg backwards like a horse, hitting the bounty hunter solidly in the chest.

"Thalrok!" Lotus cried out.

Thalrok, still holding his sword, was sent soaring backward, where he crashed awkwardly into a tree.

"Damn, this thing is powerful." Thalrok groaned, as he watched the beast turn in his direction. Even with one of its legs lopped off and shorter, it still loomed over them.

"Kill them both, Timerackil! I don't want a single trace of them left!" one of the thugs shouted from a short distance away.

Both of the young men's heads turned in the direction of the voice, as they realized that these thugs had somehow managed to make this beast listen to them.

"Thalrok, are ya good!" Lotus called out.

"Of course! This is actually the best I've felt in a long time." he replied cheekily, as he picked himself up off the ground.

Thunder erupted around them and lightning flashed as they waited for an opening. The two of them engaged the monster, the Timerackil, from either side, gripping their weapons tightly as the rain sluiced across their bodies. Lifting its front-fisted arm, the Timerackil first made a quick swipe at Lotus.

Moving quickly, Lotus weaved and dodged around each swing the monster threw at him. Even though the beast towered over the two young men, it found itself struggling to hit any of its targets. Lotus and Thalrok both weaved in and out of cover, eluding the beast's frenzied rampage. With each strike that missed, the Timerackil's anger and frustration grew as it failed to crush its bold and elusive prey.

Thalrok saw another opportunity to strike and lifted his sword high into the air, forcing it with all his might into the earth. The tremor from his weapon caused the ground to quake, rattling the whole forest. The Timerackil found itself unbalanced, and turned its three baleful red eyes back to Thalrok. As it shifted its stance, it saw the bounty hunter below pulling back his sword again, this time next to its uninjured leg. With a quick slam from the side of Thalrok's giant blade, the monster's remaining leg buckled. As the Timerackil fell forward onto its front limbs, Thalrok didn't waste a second. He pivoted his foot, swinging his sword in the other direction. He dragged it lightly through the dirt as he spun all the way around until he faced the beast head-on. Using the momentum from this rotation, he followed through, swung upward, and punched hard into the jaw of this woodland monster. It stumbled backward, writhing in pain. The beast's high-pitched screaming resonated through the forest as it thrashed in agony.

"We gotta finish this right here and now," Thalrok yelled. He lifted his sword back up, then charged right back at the creature.

As tough as the Timerackil was, it seemed pretty defenseless to the bounty hunter's attacks. At least that's what he thought, until one of its injured legs swung across and hit him in the ribs. Surprised, Thalrok absorbed that blow, then found himself being pushed across the ground in the follow-through. The bounty hunter planted his feet against a large rock anchored deep in the earth, and grabbed the monster's leg. As the mud and water kicked up from the ground, he was barely able to stop its momentum as he held on for dear life.

"Damn it, that hurt!" Thalrok howled, but he refused to give up his hold on the tree-like leg.

The beast twisted and pulled, but was not able to free itself from the tenacious grip of this titan of a man. Screeching at its prey, the Timerackil now felt a weird feeling of weight on its back. It turned its head to look over its shoulder, where, through the corner of one red eye, it saw a man standing there.

In the same style that his master had used many years ago, Lotus planted his feet and took in a deep breath. He held his sword tightly and slashed multiple times into the air at great speed without seeming to hit any target. Then he jumped clear of the surprised beast, and watched as its arms and legs crumbled into pieces right before their eyes.

"Now that's what I'm talkin' about. Good stuff, Ronin!" Thalrok cheered, as he approached the fallen beast.

The Timerackil flailed helplessly with its limbs all shortened to stumps. Thalrok stood by one of the longer stubs, drew back his arm and dropped his elbow down on it, breaking a small bit clean off. At that, weakened and in pain, the monster collapsed all the way to the ground, splashing into the mud. As its body hit the earth a loud crash of thunder erupted in the distance. Their deed was done; this monster's berserk fit of rage was over.

Thalrok dropped the piece of wood he was holding and hurried over to Lotus.

"You alright, Ronin?" he called out as he walked around the large monster's twitching body.

"Yeah, I'm fine, just a little banged up," Lotus replied, as he saw his friend come from around the side of the downed beast.

The two took a moment to stare at it and catch their breath. Thalrok looked up into the sky of dark clouds and watched the pouring rain continue to fall.

"Those thugs should still be nearby if they were watching us fight," he stated, as he turned toward the last direction he'd heard their voices.

Lotus agreed, hoping he'd be able to sense their presence again. He stooped down and closed his eyes like before, breathing in and out slowly, deeply. Trying to be calm and to free himself from the dark energy that still lingered, he focused intensely on every bit of life around him. Nothing showed up at all, maybe he wasn't able to do it again.

I'm losing touch, I can't sense any light. That was, until he felt… something. His eyes lit up as he concentrated on the one faint source of light he detected. The tiny bit of light he sensed was coming from right behind them. Then Lotus realized just what he was sensing, but by the time he turned around, he saw that it was too late.

"Thalrok—look out!" Lotus shouted, but it really *was* too late. Thalrok was hammered in the back by a punch from the Timerackil's broken wooden leg. With no warning, he was sent soaring through the wet forest and was soon out of sight.

"Thalrok!" Lotus yelled out once more. Fog and rain blocked his vision.

Lightning flashed from the sky, revealing a terrifying, moving shadow on the ground. Lotus watched as the crumpled Timerackil gathered itself and slowly stood back up. Vines stretched from and around its broken body, pulling the once severed limbs securely back in place. Once again, the Timerackil was whole and at full strength.

"You are kidding me!" Lotus panted, as he put his broken sword back inside its saya. He felt his inner wrath trying to release its malignancy through his body for a second time. Lotus tried to calm himself, he felt some of the darkness seeping through the cracks. His hands and forearms began to stain darker with malice, and a thick aura of dark energy radiated out of him.

Just as fast as it was before, the Timerackil swung its arm, trying with all of its power to dispose of this last pest. Like a fly avoiding being swatted, Lotus zipped and jumped through and among the trees, hoping to be allowed some time to think. Each time this thing attacked, it only drew out more dark energy from inside of him.

As Lotus leaped to avoid another strike from this rampaging creature, he jumped backward and thunked right into a tree. The beast took this chance and thrust its thick stump of an arm at the young man with all its might.

Instead of being crushed against the large tree, once again Lotus held out his hands and bore that attack, just barely holding it back. He could feel the Timerackil pushing harder as it stepped forward. Its screech rattled in his ears, enraging him more with each moment he felt this thing push. With his hands firmly in contact with the wooden leg, his dark energy began to decay and rot the treelike limb as he pushed back. Both foes were focused solely on the battle in front of them, until Lotus was snapped out of it by a familiar voice.

"Ronin! Get out!" Thalrok shouted.

Lotus did not question those words for one instant. He pushed off from his left foot, which was set solidly against a smallish rock, ducked and dodged off suddenly to the right, causing the monster's leg to crash into the tree that had been at his back.

After its initial shriek of rage, the Timerackil heard a great growling roar coming from behind. The creature turned, just in time to see a titan-man dropping down from above like a meteor, his hands locked together high above his head. With a savage yell, Thalrok came crashing down to the ground and slammed his clasped hands into the dirt. The forest exploded and shook as if a bomb had gone off. The beast struggled to get its bearings and worked to stay upright as its legs buckled and wobbled.

"Now!" Thalrok shouted, seeing that the Timerackil was off-balance and disoriented from the quaking earth.

Lotus dropped down on top of its head. The young man screamed out, thrusting both of his palms downward. The potent dark power held inside Lotus burst out of him in one all-out blast which instantly incinerated the head of the monster into a fine black ash. The Timerackil's headless body crumpled to the ground like a dead tree, motionless there in the forest.

Rain, thunder, and the sound of the two huffing and puffing were the only sounds left to hear in these woods."You alright?" Thalrok asked.

"Deja vu," Lotus replied as he looked down at his arms and saw the dark stains getting worse. Neither they nor the blackness of his veins had faded in the least, even after that massive release of dark energy. "You?" he asked Thalrok.

"That punch was nothing, this thing picked the wrong guy to hit, that's all." Thalrok chuckled and clapped Lotus on the back.

Lotus looked back over at the creature and got a few steps closer. He placed his hand on one of its limbs and closed his eyes. There was only the faintest of sensations, but Lotus could still feel a tiny spark of life left in it, even after it was blasted with dark energy. Maybe this being had been cursed by some outside force, and had been made to take the form of this odd wild monster...

"The rain looks like it might be slowing down. We should probably look for those thugs again." Thalrok suggested, checking around the woods.

Lotus had just used the last small bit of his dark abilities, there was no way he would be able to get close to sensing them now. That's always how it has been since...

Let me try one more thing, he thought. Lotus took a few steps away from the monster and sat on the ground just in front of it. He crossed his legs, placed his arms in his lap, straightened his back, and then took a deep breath in. He repeatedly inhaled and exhaled, slowly and deeply, trying his hardest to focus his mind and concentrate on the life around him.

There was nothing.

He focused on the people in his own life, his family, and friends. Everything that had happened to him in his life. *Who knows what happened to them? They probably fear you now, just like everyone else.* His own thoughts echoed in his head. He remembered the times he trained with his master and all of his friends in Petalbrooke.

They all think you murdered Din. Everyone does. These words clouded his mind. Lotus tightened his closed eyes. He tried to think of something calming that he could focus on, maybe like the people that took him in even when he destroyed part of the town to save Belle.

They all learned the truth about you, monster, more echoing voices chanted. It was hopeless.

Lotus opened his eyes after sensing nothing at all. All of his training seemed to have left him after those years of living alone in a harsh reality.

"Let's go," Lotus muttered, as he plodded off in a random direction.

"But Ronin, you..." Thalrok began.

"I have no idea what direction they went. Just... please, let's go." Lotus interrupted, sulking as he had failed his master once again. Those years of training were all for nothing.

Thalrok stood staring at the fallen beast behind Lotus as he walked away from it. For a second, he admired the creature in its singular beauty. He turned around and saw Lotus still walking away, not looking back.

Thalrok took one more glance, then hurried to join his ally in their search. Never in his life had he seen such incredible power contained in one person. This guy had just defeated a towering, rampaging forest monster. His ability to transform the terrifying creature into a thing of beauty in mere seconds was truly awe-inspiring.

The two young men left the giant to rest with the forest once more, now entirely covered in newly-blooming wildflowers.

* * *

"I can't believe those two took down a Timerackil! What the hell are those two made of!?" one of the thugs raged in panic, as he paced back and forth. Another grunt stood guard at the entrance of the cave they took refuge in, keeping an eye out for the two young warriors.

Their leader sat on the floor of the cave with his head in his hands, struggling to see a way out of this mess. Never did he think that some little village would find anyone this powerful to come and find their missing children—much less *two* of them.

"Boss, we really should leave while we can. We should load up the carriage and get out before it's too late. The heavy rain is starting to die down; we can make our escape before it totally clears out," one of the thugs suggested.

Everyone's heads turned to stare at their boss, who still sat there as if he was frozen in anxiety and disbelief.

"Fine, but we need to hurry before they find us," he finally agreed.

As a group, they immediately started preparing for a quick retreat, and hurried to load up their carriage. They all ran back and forth across the cave like a bunch of wild animals, wet feet pattering on the rocky floor, as they carried boxes of stolen goods and money.

"Hey! We still have to keep a lookout; we need to know whether or not they are getting close!" one of the bandits shouted at another.

"Both of you idiots keep quiet! I'll stay on watch while you all finish up," the boss growled as he headed for the entrance to the cave. His fists were clenched tightly at his sides, his teeth were clamped together, and his jaw was tense. Anger filled him to the core. His plan had gone all to hell after these two strangers showed up. Now he had to find a way to bring this plan back on course, or figure out a new plan.

The boss poked his head out of the entrance to see if there was any sign of those two showing up. He peered both left and right, until he was calmed by the reassuring sight of only the trees soaking in the heavy rainfall.

Looks like we still have time. Thank goodness. The thug's leader sighed in relief.

"I'm sorry..." a voice spoke from somewhere just above him.

The boss's head flew up and his eyes were met by a whole different beast, as the swift hammer of revenge dropped down and punched him in the stomach. He keeled over on impact, wheezing from the shock.

"But I don't think you answered my question back there." Thalrok sounded perturbed.

The other thugs had heard the commotion. They gathered around and now trembled in their shoes at seeing their boss subdued by a single punch to the gut. Some of them stepped toward him but were immediately stopped, as Lotus dropped in from above to block their way. Thalrok watched the broken bandit, down on all fours, coughing and gasping for air as he struggled to breathe.

"I'm only going to ask this one more time. Where. Are. Those. Kids?!" Thalrok growled. He grabbed the boss by his hair and lifted his head. Bloody spittle flew from the miserable man's mouth as he struggled to stammer out any words.

"They're in the back! Five of 'em, they're in the back!" one of his lackeys shouted out, hoping to save his boss from any more pain.

Thalrok's head slowly turned to the one who spoke, then dropped the man's head. Standing tall over the pathetic, beaten man, Thalrok reached back and unlatched his sword from its fasteners.

"You are now useless to me," he said coldly, as he began lifting his sword high into the air. The boss could tell that his life was in its final moments and would soon be ended by this giant of a man. He closed his eyes and accepted that this would be his end, this is where he would die.

"What are you doing?" Thalrok asked.

The bandit carefully lifted his head just enough to see Lotus standing between Thalrok and himself.

"W-what? What is he doing?" the boss wheezed.

Lotus stared at Thalrok most seriously, and calmly said, "You and I both know what they did is unforgivable. Even *they* know that what they've done is cruel, wrong, and would easily justify them all a lifetime in prison. But by the looks on their faces, they have learned their lesson here. You don't have to kill them."

"They are humans," Lotus continued, "and only have this one life to live. Whether or not someone is raised to be good or evil, a life is a life and we should never take that from someone. We have found all five of the missing children and have completed our mission. Let's just go back to the village and return them to their parents, please." Lotus suggested earnestly.

Even with the helmet covering his face, Lotus could see that Thalrok was not amused in the least by this idea. His sword was still raised high into the air, and he hadn't budged a bit.

These monsters stole innocent children from their homes and families. How low could someone be to do such a thing and still be spared? How can we just let them live? Thalrok angrily took a deep breath.

"I guess I can work with that, but don't cry to *me* when that mindset gets ya killed," Thalrok responded as he lowered his sword.

Relieved to see that the bounty hunter had agreed to his plan, Lotus knelt next to the thug and stared at him dead in the eyes.

"If you move at all, I'll let him kill you this time," Lotus promised in a steely low voice. Chills of fear ran down the boss's spine and he slowly nodded.

"All of you, wall—now!" Lotus demanded sharply, as he and Thalrok walked towards the back of the cave.

Without a second thought, the thugs all jumped at the sound of his voice, and hurried to line up along the nearest wall to stand still and stay out of the way. Their eyes followed the two young men as they made their way farther into the cave. Thalrok and Lotus could at last hear the small sobs and sniffles of crying up ahead, the voices of scared children whimpering in fear.

As the young men turned the corner, there they were, all five missing

95

children, three boys and two girls, bunched up together and scared for their lives. Seeing the two newcomers, the kids squeezed even closer to one another, thinking that more bandits were coming to terrorize them.

"Hey, hey, you don't have to worry anymore. We're here to take you back home." Thalrok said soothingly from under his helmet. He was trying to be gentle and comforting, but to the children, looming over them was a menacing giant with no visible face.

The kids stayed huddled together with panic on their upturned faces. They shivered with fear, and shrank back even farther towards the wall. Lotus gestured silently for Thalrok to lower his formidable-looking self. The two knelt on the ground at child-level, about ten feet away, so as to seem less intimidating.

"Please, I *promise* that you can trust us. We really are here to take you back home. Your families are worried sick and have been trying to find you." Lotus told them.

It took a few seconds for the children to truly believe him. These past several days they had lost all hope that anyone would ever find and rescue them. Fear at last turned to relief, then to joy. The children burst into grateful tears, rushed over to the two kneeling before them, and held onto them for dear life. They all clung to one another for some moments, hugging tightly.

"Oh no, Ronin! They are too strong!" Thalrok shouted, as he collapsed backward and pretended that the children had taken him down. "Ow! My back, how could these kids know my only weak spot!? Spare me, please!" Thalrok playfully cried out, as he rolled around the floor.

The children began to laugh at this immense, goofy stranger in a helmet trying so hard to cheer them up. Lotus enjoyed Thalrok's silly ploy as well, and saw that the children found comfort and distraction in his playful good humor.

Part of the mission, the hardest part, had been completed. Now the only thing left to do was to get these scared kids home.

7

Mark of the Past

"Please dear, stop crying. I *know* those gentlemen will bring back our Fedris. Please, night is almost here and you haven't slept a wink since he's been gone. You *need* to rest," Marak said, trying to comfort his wife as she sat under the gates of the town. "We should head back home."

Valla stared listlessly out at the distant horizon hoping to see those two young men returning with their child. It hadn't even been a full day since they left, but she felt like she'd already been waiting forever for their return. "Maybe you're right," she said bleakly, reaching for his arm. He helped her up from her stone seat and they began trudging cheerlessly back to their house. Both dragged their feet and splashed wearily through puddles, once more returning home without their child. It was too painful to bear.

All of Linbud was overwhelmed with dread and sorrow. The sounds of children playing were no longer heard, since none of their parents dared to let them out on their own anymore, lest they be taken. What they could hear, coming from a nearby house, was the Brittel woman crying and wailing for her own child, Orvis. She, too, had gone without food or sleep since his taking.

The rain had stopped a bit ago, but Valla's face was still wet from the tears running down her cheeks. She sniffled as her bottom lip quivered, and she tried to hold back her sobs. Marak supported her and rubbed her arm gently, as he too tried to keep his emotions in check.

Please boys, bring back our Fedris. I don't know what I'll do without him...

Suddenly, Valla felt her husband's arm release its hold on hers. She stumbled trying to keep herself upright, then collapsed to her knees. Her emotions couldn't be contained any longer, and she began sobbing loudly all over again. She knelt there in the damp street with her head in her hands, feeling a complete loss of hope. "Please, please, I just want Fedris back!" she cried, tightly balling the skirt of her dress in both hands, begging to the world over and over again for things to go back to the way they were just a week ago.

"Honey ..." Marak softly mumbled.

Valla just wailed even harder. She reached up to grab onto her husband, but he wasn't there. She turned around and saw that he was now a few steps behind her, looking back towards the gates of the town. He stood as still as a statue, barely breathing.

"Honey..." Marak's voice sounded a little louder, as he stared off into the distance. Valla struggled to her feet and shuffled to his side. Wiping her eyes, she looked out to see what he was staring at. Those once-teary eyes widened and her heart skipped a beat, as she looked down that dreary street and focused on the road and fields beyond. She stood quietly beside her husband, hope rising steadily. Then Valla clutched Marak's arm, staring intently ahead at what she'd been waiting for.

There they were. The advancing figures of a large man wearing a metal helmet and another smaller man with a bandana wrapped around his forehead were slowly pulling a large cart towards town. Along its sides seemed to be excited little children whose cries of happiness floated across the distance.

A woman passing by also stopped when she saw the small procession. She shrieked and waved her arms wildly, screaming out to the whole town that their children were back. It took only a matter of seconds for people to rush out of their homes and hurry over to see for themselves.

Lo and behold, there were all five children, now out of the cart and running ahead of Lotus and Thalrok, desperate to scramble back into the arms of their families.

"Mama! Papa!" they squealed as their parents ran to meet them, wanting to hold onto these precious children and never let them go. One by one, each child was swooped up into their parents' arms and comforted after their terrifying past several days.

As Lotus and Thalrok drew closer, the villagers cheered and applauded. "The heroes have returned!" "They saved the children!" the townspeople shouted. Sounds of joyous celebration—whistles, laughter, whoops and hollers—filled the air.

When the two rescuers entered the gates of Linbud, they were immediately surrounded by a mob of *very* thankful people trying to show their immense gratitude.

Lotus lifted his hand and shook his head. "Please, everybody, *we* are not the heroes. We were simply the ones who were able to get the kids back from harm. We couldn't have done it without the *real* hero." Lotus stopped, then pointed over at Baxion, the boy who had given them the lead about the strange noises to the north.

Everyone turned to look at Nethel's teenage older brother, who had supplied Lotus and Thalrok with their one and only clue, and then everyone began cheering for Baxion, who looked more than a little embarrassed at all of the attention. They lifted him high into the air and began chanting his name, like he was some great hero of legend.

Seeing the townsfolk rejoicing together as one big family brought great joy to Lotus, and he was filled with a deep satisfaction.

Then someone called out, "Hey! Who are those guys tied up in the cart?"

The happy chatter simmered down as the people noticed a group of men restrained and sitting silently in the middle of the cart with their heads hung low.

"Are those the dirtbags that stole our children?" another snarled.

The townsfolk had put two and two together, and rage burst from inside them. They turned toward the men in the cart, imagining all the pain and suffering that these bandits had put their children through, and how they would be repaying that with added measure. However, Lotus positioned himself in front of them and held his arms out to stop them from getting closer.

"What are you doing? Why are you defending them?!" a stocky man asked in disbelief.

Lotus took a deep breath in and realized just how hard this part was going to be.

"Please, I understand what you're feeling right now," he said. "I know how angry you all must be at them for the horrible things they did. However, they know damn well that what they did was wrong. I truly don't think they will ever try anything like that ever again. You probably all want to end their lives and dispose of these men who took away from you what you loved most, but please, reconsider. My only request is to look through their wrongdoing and see their humanity. All in all, they are living beings, just like us."

The crowd began to murmur and rumble with disgust. "You expect us to just let what they did go?! To let them free to be criminals again?" someone shouted angrily. The townsfolk remained unconvinced. How *could* they let these monsters go after what they did?

Lotus couldn't think of anything else to say. He simply drew a blank on how he could possibly persuade these people to do what he believed was right.

Then Thalrok chimed in, "Oh, we aren't letting them go. But, we can let *you* decide how to deal with them. If you want to put them to work, put them to work. If you want to send out a request for some City of Light guards from a nearby spire to come take these boys in, go ahead. However, as my friend said, they are just like us, only cursed with a bad upbringing in this chaotic world." Thalrok walked over and stood beside Lotus.

Somehow, the roar of the town got even louder as the people rallied together in anger at these criminals. No way would they be holding back on these kidnapping bandits.

Damn, I guess they have their minds set. What're you gonna do now, Ronin? Thalrok thought. As he turned to look at him, he saw that Lotus was no

100

longer standing. He was kneeling, silently bowing his head toward the ground, hoping to move these people to his way of thinking.

The uproar of the crowd began to die down as they saw what Lotus was doing. They grew quieter when they saw that Thalrok too, lowered himself to his knees and joined his friend. Slowly but surely, silence won out.

No one spoke a word now, as they saw these heroes of their town plead without speaking for their principled, if unpopular, request.

"Stand up, boys," an older, gray-bearded man said from beside them. They lifted their heads and saw a few villagers kneeling in front of them.

"If anyone's heads should be bowed, it should be ours," the village elder continued. "We are all complete strangers to you boys, and yet you went out of your way to help us save our children. From the look of it, you went through quite a fight. Shedding your blood for strangers, what a crazy lot you two are." He gave them a subtle smile. "We will follow your request, and we'll let the City of Light take care of these men. That is the least we can do for you," the elder announced, as he, along with all of the other villagers, deeply bowed their heads.

Lotus and Thalrok stood to see the waves of people filling the street all bowing down respectfully. It was incredible to believe how this had come about, but Lotus felt that warmth inside of himself again—the selfless joy of helping others, of making a difference.

"Take these thugs to the holding cells! We will wait for the City of Light to send a carriage to haul them off to the nearest Guardian Spire. A message will be sent tomorrow morning," the town elder shouted, as a few men grabbed onto the cart and began pulling it down the street.

The bandits inside slunk down even lower with their faces turned to the bottom of the cart. Their tremendous fear of facing these people they had so wronged was about over, and somehow they'd been given a chance to *not* be beaten to death by an entire town of angry families. Somehow, they would live another day, thanks to two young men who had seen their humanity through their wrongdoings. How... rare.

* * *

Nightfall arrived, with many stars and a waxing gibbous moon glimmering down from the sky. Everyone had returned to their homes, families happily intact and in for the night. Random drops of water splashed from the rooftops onto puddles below. The sound of crickets and tree frogs harmonized softly throughout the peaceful town. Lotus and Thalrok were offered a place to stay by the same couple whose cause they'd taken up after first meeting them back in Mellowtin, Marak and Valla.

"This place should hopefully help you two out for the night. I wish it was more accommodating, but it's all I have to offer." Marak said.

Lotus and Thalrok walked into the smallish barn, which would be bare of any livestock for a few months. Large stacks of hay and grass were everywhere, so while it wasn't exactly fancy or homelike, it was still a reasonable place to sleep.

"What are you talkin' about? People would pay good money for a place like this. It's got everything, some walls, a door. This roof is mostly a, uh, roof. Not to mention all the... the... uh, flooring." Thalrok chuckled.

Marak smiled at his good-natured banter, then told the two, "If there's anything else you need, just name it."

"Thank you, but this is plenty. We wouldn't want to intrude." Lotus replied, as he took a deeper look around the small barn. The two young men began to prepare themselves for the night, then realized that their host hadn't left the doorway. He stood there looking a little concerned, not about the two of them, but about something else that seemed to be on his mind.

"I have a question... I know it's getting late and all, but something occurred to me when you two brought those bandits back here." Marak began hesitantly.

Lotus and Thalrok stared at him silhouetted in the doorway.

"Did those men use any strange abilities at all? Anything curious that seemed to be somewhat, uh, poisonous or would maybe hinder you?" he asked earnestly, holding his breath.

The two turned to one another. They couldn't recall the men using any special powers at all. They'd just used some simple bladed weapons along with a few laced projectiles, nothing that was out of place for a run-of-the-mill group of thugs.

"They didn't use any special powers to our knowledge. They're just a few low-life thugs that were trying to cause some trouble." Thalrok replied.

They could feel Marak's great relief as he whooshed audibly through pursed lips. He placed one hand on the doorway, leaned over slightly and put the other hand over his heart. "Thank goodness," he said gratefully. "There are rumors going around that a big gang with very strange abilities has been going around pillaging and taking over some of the smaller towns. I'm just glad to hear it wasn't them."

Lotus and Thalrok were curious about this gang he was talking about; they hadn't heard of them. Lotus did recall a similar encounter he'd had with a group that sounded similar to what Marak described, but that had been years ago. All he could remember now about that day was how they all had some very strange power that had something to do with a poison.

"Excuse me, but what group are you talking about?" Lotus asked.

"All I know is that multiple villages and small towns have been attacked, and even totally leveled, by this group." Marak continued. "Sometimes they take a village over, and keep the people as hostages. I've also heard that they kidnap some of the villagers, destroy everything, and leave the town in total ruin. The remains of one of those towns are just west of here. It's been abandoned for years now, ever since *that* bunch came along."

Lotus thought back to his childhood, back when he was still living in Petalbrooke. While he and his friends were on a delivery mission, the village of Perksy had been under attack. Those ravagers had used some unusual power that poisoned the very air around their bodies, which made their adversaries fight for breath and be unable to move.

"Wait," Lotus murmured as something else clicked in his brain. He remembered another story he'd been told a few years ago. A story about a small town that was attacked by a group of people who came into town and caused mass chaos. They took supplies, livestock, and many lives. They left the people who still remained in the town miserable and scarred, and left a grandmother to care for her crying young granddaughter whose parents had lost their lives in the encounter.

"Where is this town?" Thalrok asked.

"If you leave from the west gates and keep going straight in that direction for about half a day, you'll end up finding a broken-down village that's been taken by the elements after years of abandonment. That's the one." Marak told them.

The two young men thanked him for the information, and were at last left alone to rest up after a considerably long day. They each found a pile of hay to lie on, and glanced up through the holes in the roof to the stars.

"Hey, Thalrok."

"Yeah, what's up?"

"Before we head back to Mellowtin. I want to check out that village he talked about. There's something about those rumors that reminds me of something." Lotus told him.

"I'm right there with you. We'll head out tomorrow to give it a look." Thalrok replied, as he rolled over, closing his eyes.

The big man still always kept his helmet on in front of others, which to Lotus, was a strange thing indeed. *How could that be comfortable?* Lotus thought. He too closed his eyes and rested his tired muscles from the events of the day. Though it had been a while, Lotus again found himself in a position where he was sleeping while surrounded by other people— even though he was just lying on some hay in a small barn with holes in the roof. It made him feel like he was a part of a village again. He was sleeping here in a town full of other folks who were actually grateful for him being there. *Let's keep it that way*, whirled through his mind, just before he drifted off.

The next morning, everyone in the village woke up an hour early so they'd be able to give the heroes who brought back their children a grand send-off. The townsfolk patiently waited outside the barn, chattering amongst themselves until Marak finally went inside to wake them up.

After a few short seconds, he exited the barn appearing dumbfounded, and said simply, "They're gone."

The villagers began to disperse in disappointment. They'd wanted so badly to thank those heroic young men one last time before they headed off on their next venture. Why would they leave without a goodbye?

* * *

"Why *did* we leave without saying goodbye?" Thalrok asked, stumbling around, still trying to keep his eyes open.

The two of them were now far from the village, heading west toward the abandoned town they'd been told about. Lotus led the charge, and he certainly didn't want to stop moving now.

"We got up so *early*. Ugh. Couldn't we have slept for just a few more hours?" Thalrok whined from under his helmet.

"I'm sorry. But you have to remember, I'm a wanted man." Lotus explained. "I couldn't stay in that village long enough for them to find out. Then I'd be leaving another town on a bad note and I wouldn't want their perfectly good day to be ruined by someone who's cursed. The capital guards would recognize me too if they showed up anytime soon. It's just safer this way."

Thalrok groaned, but did understand where his friend was coming from, even though he would *never* agree with getting up quite this early in the morning. At least the weather was much cooler now than yesterday. It was the perfect condition for traveling, no rain, not too much humidity, and a clear path ahead.

Just as Marak had told them, the village was indeed half a day away to the west. They found themselves at their destination far before the sun dropped toward the horizon. It hadn't been a short walk, but it was worth it.

Later that day...

"Wow. Marak was not kidding when he said this place was run-down." Thalrok commented as they walked over to a small, crumbling stone wall along the damaged road leading to the town.

Weeds grew from every crack in the ground, while vines climbed up to cover anything they could reach. Houses had shattered windows or no panes left at all, many of the walls had been smashed, and some of the broad-shingled roofs were caved in. It was hard to believe that anyone could have lived in this place.

As they were passing the entrance to the town, Lotus stopped and saw a tattered wooden sign covered in dirt and moss. He brushed it off gently and saw the words "Ashveil" in faded black letters on the wooden board.

"Ashveil?" Lotus whispered, as he left the sign where it was propped, and continued to look around.

As they explored deeper into the ruined town, things just got worse. Besides the houses being nowhere near living condition, there was a big crater in the ground surrounded with debris that was scattered in a large radius. Whatever went on here those years ago definitely looked like it had been a planned attack. The only question was, who or what caused this destruction?

"What the hell happened to this place?" Thalrok asked.

"I don't know, but whatever it was, was ruthless." Lotus noted, shaking his head.

It was terrifying to believe that this town once had thriving people living in it and then one day, something came along to cause this chaos and destruction—something or some*one*.

"I'm gonna go check over here." Thalrok pointed left, as he split away from Lotus and headed off to explore down one of the streets. Lotus went off in another direction to poke around and look for any clues left as to how this all could have happened. He passed by house after house, seeing the remains of what were once probably happy lives.

As he maneuvered around the rubble of one house, another one seemed to stand out a bit. There was a large symbol tagged on the side of this home with slashes of deep blood-red paint, faded now by years of direct sunlight. It was hard to picture exactly what the symbol was supposed to be. He walked through the front doorway and noticed that it seemed to be just another simple home where a family had lived. Broken picture frames hung precariously on the walls, and dust covered everything. Shattered glass crunched beneath his feet as he went farther inside.

There was nothing out of the ordinary so far. He didn't expect much, but thought checking it out was still worth a shot. As he continued on, peering at the past life of this home, he noticed some books on a shelf. Lotus dusted them off and placed what counted out to be eight books on a dirty nearby table. He examined the front cover of each. Out of all of those books, he noticed one of them didn't have a title. The eighth had just a blank cover which appeared worn, as if it had been used a lot. He picked it up and opened the first few pages to see if it contained anything of interest. The pages were handwritten, every one of them. It seemed to be a journal. Lotus's eyes widened with interest as he scanned from page to page to read the very similar words at the top of each one—"Day one since our town has been taken over..." he read out loud.

As he read each page, he followed the story of a young man by the name of Harath who was just barely surviving in this town with his wife, Marnia. Numbered days were logged on every page as he briefly described how the ones who took over his town were brutal monsters. They would force the townsfolk to work for their cause and punish them if they refused. Some of the people were being taken from the town to some unknown place or places. Others were killed outright for insolence or refusing to take orders. It wasn't until Lotus got to day 274 of the journal, that he was left speechless at what this poor man had gone through. He read:

It has been three days since I last wrote in this journal. Why am I even writing this? What's the point anymore? Who's gonna see it? This town is doomed. My beautiful wife, Marnia and I came here to start our life's journey together, and to create memories and traditions that we could pass on to our children. But these monsters, they took everything from us—our freedom, our possessions, our reasons to live. We are just worthless slaves to them. They took control to use our town as a base or hideout, or whatever they want to call it. They have brought nothing but pain to me and my friends and my family. A week ago, my wife told me great news— she was pregnant, and I was gonna be a dad. Was. Because of them, I lost my beautiful Marnia! She is gone forever! I have lost everything because of them. Everything! These assholes have no humanity left in them. They are pure evil in this world. It's heartless devils like these that show that our world is far from healing. I have no wife now, no child, and no more hope—none! Others from the village and I are going to rally together to fight back against these cruel monsters. We intend to fight till this town crumbles to the ground. No longer will we live in fear for our lives. No longer will our children be used for slave labor or be taken away from us. This day marks when we take back what is ours. Today is the day we of Ashveil curse these people. Death to the Infected...

The handwritten words stopped there. Lotus flipped the page to see what was next, but no, there was nothing. He kept swiping through all the rest of the pages to see if there was even a word or sentence written somewhere. But everything after was blank.

"Ronin!" Thalrok hollered through the doorway. Lotus was startled, then looked over towards the crooked doorway. Thalrok was poking his head in and peeking around.

"You're gonna wanna see this," Thalrok said grimly, and signaled for him to follow. Lotus snapped himself out of the book's spell and walked over to the front door.

He placed the journal down on a table on his way out and noticed a small picture frame there. It must be the man in the book standing next to his wife. Lotus stared at it for a second and felt a lingering pain fill his chest. He picked up the picture in its frame, dusted it off, and placed it softly back on the table. He slid the journal over beside it, then left the house to its silent and somber rest.

"Where'd you go, Thalrok!" Lotus shouted as he walked out into the street.

"Over here!" the bounty hunter yelled back, as he waved his hand from outside a larger building nearby.

This house stood tall above all the others and was tagged with a faded symbol similar to the one on the house that Lotus had just explored. Thalrok walked through a gaping hole in its wall. He saw that this room was full of old papers littered on the floor, and also various pieces of rusted weaponry, some hanging on the wall and others just strewn about. The house had apparently been converted into a stronghold by whoever these invaders were. The swords and weapons wore dulled red stains and the metal was riddled with rust. All of the scattered books and writings were discolored and falling to pieces from years of lying around unprotected.

"I'm in here!" Thalrok called. He used both of his burly arms to push over a large bookshelf which had been jutting out at an odd angle from the back wall of this room. The decaying wood shattered as it hit the ground, revealing a hidden stairwell. Without hesitation, Thalrok headed down the rickety wooden stairs, and Lotus followed right behind him, their every step punctuated with a loud crack or creak.

The twisted stairway to the basement was very dark, so Thalrok reached into his pouch and grabbed a match to light their way. Then he spotted a rusty lantern hanging partway down the stairwell which, luckily, still contained enough oil to provide a soft glow to light their way. When they reached the bottom of the stairs, they easily pushed open a wobbly door which led to a small room. It was like a bunker, with a massive old table made of dark wood in the center. A mild, but pervasive, stench of death lingered here.

Thalrok lifted the lantern high, then walked around methodically lighting each of the dirty fat candles in wall sconces to light the room. Lotus strolled over to the table in the center of the room and looked down to see an immense map.

"Thalrok, look at this," Lotus whispered in amazement.

The bounty hunter finished lighting the last candle and made his way over to the map. He placed the lantern down by it, and looked closely at all of the markings. Roads, rivers, mountains, forests- the map showed all of the nearby landmarks and towns for miles.

"Look, this town has an 'x' over it." Lotus pointed out. He brushed his hand across the map, stopping at the 'x' drawn in black ink over that town. As they continued to inspect it, they noticed multiple towns had that same black 'x' mark over them.

"Those must be the towns they'd been to and took over," Thalrok concluded.

"You're probably right, but what does a circle mean?" Lotus asked, as he slid his finger over to another town, named Thristle, circled with red ink.

"How far is that town from here?" Thalrok asked.

"I don't know, but it isn't a straight shot. It looks like some mountains and rivers might be in the way." Lotus replied.

Thalrok scanned the room and began shuffling about, looking for something. While the bounty hunter scoured the room, Lotus kept checking the map for any more clues.

"Infected Ones," he breathed softly.

"What?" Thalrok asked.

"Right at the bottom corner of the map. It says the words 'Infected Ones.'" I saw those words written in a few other spots around the town. That must be the group that Harath was talking about in his journal." Lotus replied.

"Got it," Thalrok announced, as he pulled a smaller map from a nearby shelf.

"Looks like this will help us find our way to Thristle." Thalrok placed the second map on the table. With his finger and soot from a candle, he marked where they currently were and where Thristle was. Now, by using both maps, they could navigate around the land of Prosper without getting lost.

"You still want to learn more about these 'Infected Ones'?" Thalrok inquired.

"Do you even have to ask?" Lotus replied, as they headed upstairs, ready to press forward once again.

With a new lead in hand, the two young men felt even closer to the scourge of these lands, those who caused terror and destruction from village to village, town to town. Without a doubt in his mind, these had to be the evil men who were in Ashveil, and also who had attacked his friend's village years ago. They could have even been the ones who—

Maybe...

8

The Cursed and the Infected

"Look, Mommy! I haven't fallen off any of the stones yet!" A little girl called out to her mother as she hopped from one large cobblestone to another. She skipped and jumped around the street, avoiding the little divots between each smooth rock.

"Great job sweetheart!" her mother, Kirra, praised her six-year-old daughter, Momo. Kirra's hands gripped two baskets filled with food for her family after a long day of shopping. The two of them had taken time on this warm day to roam about their small town, Thristle, for some precious mother-daughter time.

"Don't get too far ahead now!" she shouted out to her daughter, as the little girl got farther away. It was good that Momo could still manage to be in high spirits, after all, these past days had been hell on earth. This past *year* had been hell on earth, ever since *they* showed up. The mother brooded silently as she watched her carefree daughter prancing around.

Oh no...

Kirra nearly dropped her food baskets. Just beyond her daughter, she'd noticed three men, turning down their street. These men immediately locked their eyes onto her and her daughter. Momo paused in her tracks before turning on her heel and running speedily back to her mother.

"Well-well-well, what do we have in the basket, ladies?" the biggest, paunchy one asked, pointing at one of the baskets with a pudgy finger.

The three of them, smirking, were approaching ever closer. Momo hid behind her mother, grabbed her skirts and held onto her leg.

"Th-this is just some food for my family." Kirra stuttered. She didn't want to seem too scared in front of her daughter; Momo was already terrified. But no matter how tough she wanted to be, her deep fear betrayed her, and her voice was far shakier than she would have liked.

"Some food, aww, you shouldn't have. It would be an absolute pleasure to accept this kind offer and donation to the cause. Right boys?" the portly one said mockingly. He hulked over Kirra, and peered into the basket looking for his next snack. The two men standing beside him, one lanky and unkempt, the other nearly as large as the first but much more muscular, only laughed as they shook their heads.

"Please, we barely have any money because of..." She paused mid-sentence, and her eyes opened wide.

"Because of *what*? What were you going to say?" the paunchy foot soldier asked menacingly. As he leaned in closer, the foul stench of his sweat was overwhelming.

Kirra's legs wouldn't stop shaking, her hands, white-knuckled, clenched the baskets of food, and the pit of her stomach burned like fire. She trembled and swayed in fear, as she stared into the eyes of her waking nightmare-this monster of a human being who toyed with her, demanding that his words were law.

"I don't care who this food is for or how much money you don't have. *We* are the ones in control of this town, and as far as I know, you do what we say!" he bellowed. As he violently ripped the baskets from her hands, the filthy, skinny lackey backhanded her solidly in the face. She collapsed to her knees, crying.

"Mama!" Momo bawled. She hugged Kirra tightly, and buried her face in her mother's shoulder.

The three men stood over them, sneering.

"Listen here, little girl. You don't want to end up like your mommy. *You* will listen to us the first time," advised the huge, heavy-set man grimly. With one last scornful look back, they swaggered off with the baskets of food in their hands.

"Mama," Momo sniffled.

Her mother was unable to do anything at all. She couldn't fight back. She couldn't even talk back. Whatever Kirra might do would end up putting her family in more danger. All she could do was sit on the ground and weep, as her young daughter clung to her.

The next morning, and for the rest of the week, Kirra and Momo stayed inside their house, trying to keep a low profile. The small amount of food they had left dwindled. Poor Kirra found herself struggling to keep her own hopes up, let alone her daughter's.

Kirra's husband, Alfin, went out early in the morning to work, hoping his boss would give him a bit of overtime. Now that they had lost an entire week's supply of food, he had to work even more to get a little extra cash.

"Mama, can't we go outside?" Momo finally asked, late one afternoon, just before dinner.

Her mother put down the book that she'd been too distracted to read anyway, and her long, melancholy sigh filled the room. Kirra's breath trembled, and she looked over at her daughter, who was peering out of the window.

"No, my dear... It would be best for us to stay inside," she said softly.

"Oh... Okay," the little girl groaned, disappointed, as she ran back through the house.

When will this horrible nightmare end? When will our lives go back to the way it was before? Kirra thought mournfully as she picked up her book from the table, only to lay it back down again in her lap. Everyone in the village was suffering together. They'd become slaves of this powerful group of criminals.

"I just wish—" Kirra began to say, when out of nowhere, a violent banging sound erupted from the front door, making the sorrowing woman jump in her seat. She quickly stood up and hurried to the door, her heart in her throat. Opening the door nervously, she let out a scream of horror when she saw her husband lying there. She saw several bad cuts, fresh bruises, and the blood staining his clothes. He wheezed in pain with his eyes closed. She quickly ran to him and knelt at his side. Only then did she notice the foot soldiers out in the street. She shook her husband gently as she hissed, "Alfin! What happened? Please, say something!" But he could only groan.

"Your husband is a tough one, I must say, but he's gotta know his place." A deep-voiced grunt boomed from the street. His four pals laughed and smirked from alongside him.

When Alfin heard their voices, he growled furiously and tried to lift himself from the ground.

"Please dear, don't move. You'll hurt yourself or even worse!" Kirra told him.

Alfin struggled to bring himself up onto his knees, and at once balled up his fists. His lips pressed together into a grim line and blood dripped off of his chin from a nasty cut on his forehead.

"A whole year... of these monsters... these 'Infected Ones'... taking over our village, our home!" Alfin panted.

Apparently, he'd talked back to those men in some way and they lashed out in return. A five-on-one fight that was settled the second it began. He was out-manned and easily outmatched. Even when he had been knocked to the ground, they showed no mercy.

Kirra finally got Alfin into the house and onto the bed. She tended his wounds as best she could. The little family ate a meager dinner of potatoes and old bread. Later, as she lay next to her battered, broken husband, she looked up at the ceiling and clasped her hands over her chest. The curtains swayed slightly in the wind, and she felt her tears drying from the cool night breeze.

"Please, make this stop. Make all of this horror end. I can't bear to see my family suffer any more than they already have," she implored to the darkness, as her sleepless night dragged on for the too-many hours of lying in bed until dawn.

The evil chains imprisoning Thristle only got tighter as time passed. Although every villager wished and begged that these criminals would leave them for good, nothing had changed since when they'd first been invaded. How would anything ever change? People were taken from their homes and never seen again. Others were beaten for any perception of insolence or falling out of line. All was as it had been for months. There was no hope left.

Some days later, a restless Kirra stepped back outside once more, only for the sake of her daughter. Momo could no longer be confined to their tiny home and needed to run free, if only for just an hour.

The energetic little girl skipped across the whole town. With her mother always nearby, she played and amused herself as much as she could to make up for the past days of being kept inside. Her father had to stay home to fully recover, and was without work anyway. It wasn't easy, but they were still alive, barely surviving.

Kirra, still very fearful, could see her daughter's enthusiasm and smiling face which brought her one small bit of joy after these past weeks. She was glad to see that her little girl could find some happiness, even if the world around them was broken.

They began to move toward the central plaza of the town, where the roads met and opened up to a large public square. Many of the townsfolk strolled around there during midday, so it seemed like a perfect opportunity for them to be out, but not be noticed. All were careful to avoid those brutes, who seemed to tolerate this gathering, but only under their watchful eyes.

As Kirra and Momo entered through one of the side streets, they could see the usual large number of people wandering around and talking in small groups.

"Be careful not to get in anyone's way. Watch where you're going, okay?" Kirra reminded her lively daughter.

"Yes ma'am," Momo replied earnestly. 'Round and 'round she went in the big open road, looking at all of the people and into all of the shops. It had only been a few days, but how refreshing it was to be back out in the open again.

They were halfway around the plaza and the girl still showed no signs of being the least bit tired. Kirra could only smile while watching her little girl acting like a normal child again.

Momo twirled and twirled, holding her arms out as she danced around the street. After one final spin, Momo's eyes locked onto her mother's, expecting to see her smiling face. But she didn't see that happy face she'd seen before. Instead, Kirra wore a horrified expression, and her eyes were wide with fear.

Why does Mama look like that?

The little girl stepped back and spun around one more time, turning her head to see what her mother saw. Then, she collided with someone mid-spin. Momo's entire small body bumped directly into them, and she instantly dropped to the ground. The rattled little girl stood herself up quickly and began to murmur an apology, but as she looked up from the ground, her eyes widened too.

"No, no please! Don't touch her!" Kirra shrieked, as she quickly reached out to grab her daughter and pull her away.

Before she could get to Momo, two sinewy arms wrapped around her waist and yanked her back. Kirra wriggled and squirmed to be released but couldn't get out of this tall man's wiry grip. She screamed again and again, but could only watch helplessly as those same men who'd beaten Alfin now closed in on her small daughter.

The commotion first gained attention only nearby, but soon everyone in the plaza took notice.

"*You* bumped into me..." the biggest one of them said as he hunched over, looming over the little girl.

"I... I'm sorry." Momo mumbled, frozen in fear.

The hulking grunt paused. "Wait a second. Ain't this the daughter of that guy who bad-mouthed us a few days ago?" Squinting his dark eyes at her, he immediately knew that this was in fact that man's daughter.

"Your daddy said some pretty mean things to us, y'know," the grim-looking man said as he took a step closer.

Momo began to stumble backward. She could hear her mother screaming and pleading for them to stay away from her daughter. But however much Kirra screamed, no one could hear her that could help her.

It was hopeless.

"Looks like this whole family needs to learn some manners!" the brute bellowed in a deep voice as he loomed forward. He wore an ugly smirk on his face as he cocked back his fist.

Horrified, the townsfolk all around them simply could not do a thing. Their world turned very slowly now, time nearly stopped. All they could focus on was this helpless little girl in front of a fiend from hell. Kirra still screamed, but only silence filled their ears. Paralyzed with fear, they watched the horror that was now a part of their daily existence unfold before them.

"Please stop him!" Kirra bawled.

The burly man's huge fist began flying forward, and she had to close her eyes. She heard people gasp, and then some small murmurings. She knew that when she opened her eyes, her heart would break.

As Kirra squinted and slowly peered up through her lashes, she was shocked to see her daughter still standing, unharmed. Eyes wide open and staring now, she noticed an unfamiliar young man standing next to the horrid thug, holding onto his still-cocked fist.

The stranger's face was stained with anger. There was a visible thick aura of dark power steaming from his body, surrounding him; it was powerful enough to warp the air.

"Who do you think *you* are?" the grunt snarled as he fought to free his hand. But he couldn't budge it at all. He glared back at the stranger, who quickly spun and delivered a sudden, powerful kick that sank deep into his chest. It sent him soaring through the air and into a wooden cart, smashing it to pieces. His four cronies watched in surprise as their burly buddy got knocked across the street, and with only one single kick.

"What the hell?!" one of them roared. Shocked by what they'd just seen, they tried to take a step back, but felt some kind of a wall that stopped them.

Turning around, they were startled to see one mighty titan of a man standing calmly behind them, blocking their path. Lifting their gazes higher, they watched in surprise as his immense fists rained down from above like hammers of death, crashing directly onto their thick skulls. In no time, all four of them were knocked out cold.

"Ronin, the girl!" Thalrok shouted, as he noticed the first big thug, now recovered from his flight into the cart, going straight for Momo.

The beefy thug was moving fast for his size, but Lotus zipped by like a flash of light and swept the little girl off her feet. Without stopping, he carefully placed her back down out of harm's way. The beefy thug went straight for Lotus as his back was turned, but the young man swung his foot around and clocked him with a single well-aimed kick to his throat, then charged head-first back at the one holding Kirra. That man, a lanky, wiry-looking one, began to panic, and stumbled backward, holding onto her even tighter.

"Drop your weight!" Lotus shouted, and continued racing toward them.

Kirra snapped back to reality and lifted her legs as if to drop herself to the ground. The skinny brute tried to lift her back up but found himself off-balance. He saw the stranger reaching for his sword and moving in like a flash. The thug couldn't hold on to the woman *and* reach for his weapon, so he released Kirra in a big hurry, and she thumped to the ground.

The gangly foot soldier kept tripping backward while trying to reach for his own weapon, until suddenly, it was too late. The stranger had taken out some kind of broken sword and was now swinging it at his face. The thug's wide scared eyes focused on the oddly fragmented sword that passed right by his face—without making any contact.

It was a fake attack; Lotus quickly used his unarmed left hand to punch him squarely in the jaw. Down he went. The plan worked exactly as he hoped.

The six thugs who had terrorized Kirra and Momo had dwindled to a mere one. The brawny one who had been poised to hit Momo was back, but now he moved slightly away from the action, and stared in at this stranger in disbelief.

"Mama, mama!" The little girl ran over to her mother, crying loudly and calling for her.

"I'm right here, sweetheart!" Kirra knelt and held out her open arms.

Momo jumped right into them. The first thing any parent would want to do in this circumstance would be to comfort their child, but Kirra was distracted. She was awestruck by these two incredible, but highly unusual, gentlemen who had just rescued her daughter.

"Who *are* you?" she asked them softly, amazed at what had just had happened.

Lotus looked down and saw her, luckily unharmed. He bent down and said in a gentle voice, "We are here to save you."

She thought she hadn't heard him correctly. The words he spoke were simply inconceivable.

"Save us?" she whispered confusedly, and hugged Momo even tighter.

Lotus stood back up and stared intensely at the last of the six thugs. He was sure that this group of ruffians had to be part of those "Infected Ones" who were taking over towns throughout the lands of Perlaria. There weren't any actual signs yet, but this was the town marked on the map.

The sole thug still standing was rattled. He needed reinforcements, and frantically rifled through his pockets until he found a small metal whistle, which he immediately blew into long and hard. As the piercing vibrations shrilled through the town, more and more of the Infected Ones popped in from out of nowhere. They were all dressed head to toe in black and held bladed weapons in their hands. Some concealed their faces with masks, while others proudly flaunted their devilish and menacing expressions.

"Who did this? What happened to our men?" one of the newly arrived foot soldiers shouted out.

"Aw, don't worry about them. They're just napping." Thalrok chuckled, as he not-too-gently poked the nearest one on the ground with his foot.

The uniformed foot soldiers spent no time with any more questioning, or waiting for any signal; they immediately began to rush the two interfering young men.

By now the townspeople began to catch on to the air of danger in this area. They quietly backed off. A few fled for home as quickly as they could, Kirra and Momo, though grateful, among them. But many were very curious to see what these unexpected and rather unique young men were all about, so they remained to watch, but at a safe distance.

Thalrok brought out his gargantuan sword, then held it point down and high up in front of him. "Get ready for a little shakin'!" he shouted. The powerful blade struck the ground. The earth beneath their feet began to rock and quiver like a strong earthquake was rolling through the plaza. With his enemies thrown for a loop and off-kilter, Thalrok rushed in with a barrage of fast and effective punches all around.

Lotus tried to join in on the fight but was blocked by a crowd of Infected Ones. So, he put his sword away, securing the saya's fastenings. There was no point in using it right now. Instead, Lotus picked up the sword of the last thug he'd knocked out and pointed it at the ones now standing before him. Glancing at his extended forearms, he noticed the creeping stains of black crawling up his arms a bit more. Some of the anger had lingered inside of him from before, but he felt the dark energy inside flowing through him even more right now than when he'd stopped that asshole from attacking the little girl.

"Together—attack!" a tall, masked Infected One ordered. Four foot soldiers charged at Lotus, two with swords drawn ran across the street, and two with clenched fists, who jumped high into the air to get the drop on him.

Seeing their plan, Lotus closed his eyes, took a deep breath in, then exhaled slowly, feeling his powers build. He pushed off from his back foot and soared underneath the airborne Ones, who landed awkwardly in a large drainage ditch. He continued gliding through the air towards the armed Ones, and as the first blade slashed horizontally toward Lotus's stomach, he used his own to parry it into the sky.

"Nice try, you fool!" The second snarling grunt boasted as he swung right for him, but slashed mere inches past Lotus. The blade just missed cutting him, and Lotus grabbed onto his arm and twisted his wrist, which released the thug's grip on his sword. They both watched it fall uselessly to the ground. Lotus still held on tightly to this One's arm as they landed, pivoting his own body while dropping his stance low to the ground. Lotus's leg shot beneath the One's body as he lifted his shoulder against the grunt's solid chest. With one quick motion, the man was thrown high over Lotus's shoulder, then fell headfirst to the ground.

Darting his eyes immediately to the left, Lotus shifted his grip on the grunt's sword he had retrieved and threw it like a spear straight for the other incoming foot soldier. It was a concealed move, and the blade pierced deep into his thigh. A loud cry of pain burst from this Infected One, but that was abruptly silenced as Lotus grabbed him by the jaw while running by him, forcing his head across the ground.

Now, the two foot soldiers who had hauled themselves out of the drainage ditch stood before Lotus. Keeping his guard up, he bobbed and weaved around every kick and punch they threw. He was an untouchable force that appeared to only get faster the harder the Infected Ones tried to hit him. The shorter of the two advanced while the other held back to wait for an opening. Lotus took advantage without delay, throwing his own powerful punches. As the shorter One threw another punch, Lotus palmed his fist straight up into the air using his right hand, and dove underneath that arm to reach around the grunt's body. His left shoulder pressed into the One's armpit, then Lotus's left forearm snaked across his chest, and planted firmly around his neck. Once Lotus grasped his own left hand with his right, just behind the thug's right shoulder, circulation to the unfortunate thug's brain was cut off. Lotus squatted down, so that the flailing man unable to reach him. The goon could feel himself about to blackout, so he tried to reach his pocket to grab a dagger, but failed, as great weakness soon overcame him.

The second, taller One saw with great displeasure that his associate had been easily disabled in mere moments. But, since Lotus seemed to be occupied with keeping his partner contained, he chose this time to attack. He grabbed a plank of wood from the ground and swung it upwards, aiming for Lotus's back.

"I see you," Lotus said bluntly, as he squatted down a little more, pulling the enemy in his grasp down with him. Lotus twisted to face the path of the oncoming wooden plank. Instead of it hitting Lotus squarely in the chest, the shorter One he was holding took the blow to his midsection, and Lotus dropped him in a heap. The misfire from his ally had knocked the wind out of him, and left the other One standing there holding the plank, speechless.

"It was mean to do that to your buddy." Lotus then jabbed the taller One three times where he stood. Two sharp blows to the stomach, then one in the face, leaving him to stumble backward in pain.

When Lotus looked to the other side of the plaza, he saw Thalrok still standing, and with a large hostile group surrounding him. It was like watching a bunch of people try to corral a bull. They shouted, jumped on him, punched and kicked at him, but couldn't seem to make him budge. Thalrok slashed his sword around, and the crowd of Infected Ones backed away hastily. It was a death wish to try and stop that thing when it was moving.

As Thalrok warded off his own personal horde of enemies, he decided that he needed a little more room to breathe. He lifted his sword up, then plunged it straight into the ground, leaving it in an upright position. Thalrok, trained by titans, clenched his hands together and lifted them high above his head, then crashed them straight down onto the butt end of his sword's hilt. The sound was deafening. Nearby cobblestone streets split and crumbled. Jagged spits of land remained as other portions cracked from beneath the surrounding Infected Ones. The flattened terrain was extremely uneven now, and filled with fissures. Only about half of their enemies remained standing, but they were not about to quit the fight.

"Good to see you're still in one piece." Lotus panted, running over to join Thalrok.

"I can say the same for you." The titan-man pulled his sword from the ground. Lotus and Thalrok stood there together, watching each other's blind spots, waiting for what kind of attack would come next. They saw the circle of Infected Ones surrounding them slowly close in.

"Hold!" a clear voice commanded from across the plaza. All heads turned in the direction of that imperious voice, searching for the person responsible.

Lotus and Thalrok watched as one of the grunts led a group of even more thugs toward them. There had to be at least twenty more of these newcomers, more Infected Ones, following him, and there was a short man at the head of that pack. Something was in the leader's hand; it looked like a large piece of paper of some sort. He held it up high in the air and strutted over, smirking arrogantly. The circle surrounding the two young men opened up, and what appeared to be the head honcho breezily approached them. Murmurs of "It's Captain Mordo!" spread through the crowd, their attention now focused on the newcomer.

The person they beheld was somewhat shorter than average, and probably at least forty years old. He had a potbelly and stubby, bowed legs. Nonetheless, he exuded total confidence, authority, and a strength that his appearance certainly misrepresented. To a man, the Infected Ones showed him respect and reverence. By the looks on their faces, they also felt considerable fear.

"Stand down men! We have a guest of honor in our presence." Captain Mordo announced sarcastically. Thalrok and Lotus were confused about what he was saying—"guest of honor"? The stubby man flipped his hands around and revealed the haunting image that made Lotus cringe every time he saw it. His wanted poster was firmly gripped in the man's large hands, and he turned in a small circle to make sure that the entire crowd got a good look at it.

"Murderer of a Grand Sage, Ronin the Banished." Mordo began. "It is quite an honor to meet you; I've heard *so* much about you." Mordo continued snarkily. "Now, if you'd be so kind as to come with us. This reward money will help our cause a great deal. Plus, I know someone who would love to meet the man who took down the Gardener of Perlaria," he snickered. The lackeys he brought with him all laughed too, like it was some sort of joke.

Every time Lotus saw that poster he trembled to the bone. It rocked him to his very core, overwhelming him with self-hatred, and he again felt the twin burn of anger and frustration. Being called a murderer never got old to him. The label was a brand, a permanent stain on his reputation.

The sting of its disgrace was as fresh and bitter as the moment it was first given to him. He could hear the townspeople begin to chatter in the distance. They were probably all talking about him.

"Pfft, get a look at this fatass." Thalrok laughed, as he bumped his elbow against Lotus. The laughter slowed, then stopped when he saw Captain Mordo's face turn menacingly sour with annoyance.

Lotus couldn't let himself drown in their words, or the thoughts and feelings in his head; he had to focus on what was in front of him. Right now, there were dozens of enemies surrounding them.

"So that's how you wanna play it?" Mordo snarled. He lifted his hand into the air, and with one snap of his fingers every single one of his lackeys began to charge full speed at the two young men. The Infected One's furious battle cry sank into their ears as Lotus and Thalrok darted their eyes at each of the attackers coming for them. Back to back, they stood waiting for the right moment to charge in headfirst.

"Here we go, Ronin!" Thalrok yelled as he stomped the ground and ran straight ahead. Thalrok took on the Infected Ones' foot soldiers, goons, and any other clan members who joined in the fight, one by one. He was unmovable; their feeble arms couldn't even dent this giant man's skin. It was like a child's game to the titan, as he reached back for his sword and swung the blunted edge at these thugs. Even when the Ones put up their own weapons to block, Thalrok's sword broke through and pounded on their heads and bodies.

Meanwhile, Lotus was managing to fend off of his share of Infected Ones on his own. They were quick with their movements and synchronized in their attacks, yet they were unable to touch this nimble young man, who barely threw one punch. He could see them grow irritated and weary as he constantly avoided their strikes. They rotated positions, continuing this perpetual game of cat and mouse. Jumping, ducking, and diving around, Lotus was as swift as he was totally aware of his surroundings.

"There," Lotus whispered, as he dashed out of the way of an incoming sword-slash, then put one of the goons in a full nelson. Lotus stood directly behind him pinning his arms up in the air leaving him immobile.

"Get him offa me!" the One howled, but his fellow foot soldiers couldn't make a move. Lotus kept rotating any time he saw someone take a step forward. Maybe this was an unfair tactic, but it left him time to breathe, for now. Finally, an unarmed One came barreling in to save his associate. Lotus released his hold, and forcefully kicked the now-liberated goon toward his charging ally.

"Watch out!" the thug yelled to the other as they crashed into each other. Lotus immediately went for the next off-guard One, intently focused on the task at hand. Punches and kicks flew as Lotus went from one to the next, marking and enlarging his territory by giving each thug a proper thrashing.

The two young warriors seemed to be keeping up with the Infected Ones even though they were totally outnumbered. However, they wouldn't be able to survive for long at these odds, and the head honcho appeared to be a lot tougher than the grunts; his demeanor exuded smug superiority.

Lotus finished up with his last aggressor, then began a charge directly for the one who called the shots. Captain Mordo was watching Thalrok, which left him a clean opening.

Just keep your eyes on the big guy. Lotus sped up and lunged forward for a heavy strike to the boss-man's head. However, just before he could make contact, Mordo pulled his head to the right and dodged the attack. Lotus was astounded that he could react without even looking, and had no thought or time to protect his own body. Unbalanced and taken by surprise, the wanted man took one hard blow to the gut and was grabbed up by his collar. This Captain Mordo was far stronger than he looked. Lotus's body was still buckled over from the gut-punch, and Mordo threw him down hard.

Tumbling on the ground, he quickly rolled back up to his feet, reassessed, and pressed back in for another attack. As Lotus stepped forward, his vision went blurry and his head began to spin uncontrollably. His balance was gone, and he couldn't keep himself fully upright anymore.

What is going on?!

His whole body moved as if he was immersed in water. He slowly stumbled in circles. It was as if his feet couldn't connect to any stable ground. Captain Mordo began with a nasty snicker before he busted out into full and hearty laughter.

"Ronin!" Thalrok shouted, as he saw his friend weakened and struggling to stand. Seeing him distracted, Thalrok's foes began attacking more intensely, jumping on his back and trying to bring this titan to the ground.

"It seems you're a little dizzy, m'boy. Is my little party trick taking effect now?" Mordo taunted. "You know, this little contest was over the second you picked a fight with a Captain of the Infected Ones. Once I make contact with someone, they become completely off-balance, and their vision gets, hmm, just a bit cloudy. Ha! Right now you wouldn't know your own face in a mirror! Oh, thank you, my wise and powerful Master, for making me an unstoppable force!" he gloated, then snapped his fingers and pointed at Lotus.

One by one, dozens of foot soldiers struck at Lotus, again and again. His jaw, ribs, and legs all took heavy blows. Even though he couldn't bring himself to fight back, he tried his hardest to fend off the strikes and protect his body as much as he could. When he was able to dodge one attack, another shortly followed, and he was totally unaware of where it might come from.

I... can't stay up... anymore. I feel like my head is gonna fall off. Lotus panted, as one last punch to the stomach took him to the ground. He sprawled there, flattened from pain.

"Ronin, get up!" Thalrok bellowed full force. He tried his best to run to his friend's side, but was now effectively blocked off. With any advance he took in Lotus's direction, he was stopped by Infected Ones engaging him in battle. The titan roared out in frustration, and slammed his hands on the ground. The earth trembled beneath him once more, leaving his enemies teetering and unable to attack. Even with that small window of opportunity open, Thalrok was still too far away to be of any help.

"I can't believe a weakling like you lasted this long without being killed. Either you got lucky all those years, or I'm just too strong." Captain Mordo chuckled. He grimly loomed over Lotus with a menacing tilt to his head.

Slowly, he reached behind him and pulled a dagger from its sheath. He grabbed Lotus by the hair and lifted him up, forcing the pain-stricken boy to look directly into his eyes. "Do you have any last words, murderer?" the Captain asked.

Lotus simply couldn't do anything. His body was numb and bruised from the barrage of attacks he took. His head spun, he couldn't see, and he couldn't even feel his arms. His physical senses were all out of sorts; it was hopeless.

"You bastard! Let go of him! Come on, my friend, you have to snap out of it!" Thalrok shouted out to Lotus one last time. The faint words Lotus heard from the distance rattled in his head over and over.

"Friend." The word played on repeat one time after another.

How long has it been since someone called me that?

Lotus shut his eyes and dropped into a pool of his memories from Petalbrooke. The sounds of his closest friends calling up to him in his room to come outside and play. The time they spent together running around the fields and training. It was paradise on earth, and nothing seemed to be better than that. Unfortunately, fate was not on the young man's side now, as he awaited the sudden end of his life.

Wait a minute... I can... feel it?

He felt the warmth of life all around him for a moment. Something triggered inside, and he could slowly begin to feel each and every living thing in the plaza.

How is this happening?

Lotus wondered, then he realized that these moments he remembered, were blocking out the dark energy. Now, he could feel the light energy buried deep within.

"Time's up kid!" Mordo yelled, as he raised his dagger, ready to thrust it straight into Lotus's heart.

The world went silent, and Lotus's eyes were shut. The only sound he heard was the deep inhale of his breath and the slow exhale to follow. His body felt as warm and light as the air itself. It had been a very long time, yet he knew exactly how to keep this energy flowing.

"Roniiin!" Thalrok shouted one last time. He saw the dagger descend toward Lotus's chest and then... there was a blinding flash of light, as though a lightning bolt had burst out of thin air.

The plaza was suddenly quiet. Captain Mordo and everyone nearby stood motionless, puzzled. No one knew what exactly had happened until the silence was broken by the sound of a severed arm thudding to the ground, still gripping a dagger.

Mordo looked back at Lotus, who was holding up a broken sword in one hand. Blood dripped from the damaged blade as he lowered it. Captain Mordo suddenly screamed out in pain, and his remaining left hand released its grip on Lotus's hair. Mordo stumbled backwards, writhing in agony, holding onto a small bloody stub where his right arm had once been. The only thing the other Infected Ones could do was watch in horror. Their invincible general had been disabled and defeated by some freak of nature.

"Deja vu." Lotus huffed.

"How was he that fast after being poisoned?" the Infected Ones thought. Some of them began to back away as they watched Lotus rise to full height, his eyes still closed.

"Kill him, you morons! I don't want to see anything left of him!" the Captain cried, an insane anger fueling his brain.

Without taking a moment to question their orders, the Infected Ones charged back in on attack. The wanted man stood before them all, motionless, eyes closed.

Three on the left. Four on the right.

Waiting patiently, he felt them approaching. The energy he felt was clear, so clear; he could tell exactly where the thugs were and how they were going to attack.

"You're done now!" a hefty grunt yelled, as he swung for the young man's head. Without even opening his eyes, Lotus smoothly ducked out of the way. One after another, they leapt at him in a steady flow of countless attacks.

The Infected Ones filled the streets, and with each step Lotus took he was up against yet another enemy. Still, he was untouchable. And impossibly, with his eyes shut, he seemed to be even faster than before.

Thalrok, along with his own band of foes, actually ceased their fighting, just to witness this spectacle as it moved around the plaza. "This guy is something special." Thalrok smiled as he began cheering his friend on, wanting to somehow join in on his battle. Then he lifted his sword from the ground and smashed the earth beneath his feet, challenging anyone to come at him with all they had.

"Somebody stop him!" some of Thalrok's attackers shouted out, since none of the ones chasing after Lotus at this moment could manage to do it. Lotus moved around the streets and plaza in a relaxed, effortless flow with his eyes gently closed. Everyone there noticed the faint pale luminous energy that surrounded him like a bubble. Lotus was emanating pure energy from within his very being, and he shone like a low-lit white flame.

Keep breathing. Stay focused on the energy. Then, use it! Lotus abruptly opened his eyes, holding tightly onto this warm flow of energy. The few thugs still coming at him all charged in at once. The time for offense was now, and Lotus patiently waited for these goons to make a mistake and give him an opening.

* * *

"Move slowly, Captain, we're about done patching you up," one of the foot soldiers said as he helped his boss to his feet.

"How the hell did that bastard move so quickly? I had him incapacitated with my powers," the Captain panted, his teeth clenched in pain. He looked up slowly, seeing that one by one his men were quickly being foiled; that boy countered anything they threw at him. He was an untouchable monster weaving in and out of every single attack thrown at him. Punch, kick, or slashing of a sword, nothing seemed able to connect to this boy who was radiating a faint pearly light.

"We are slowly losing more and more of our troops. We need to call in for reinforcements or they will surely stop our campaigns and conquest," one of the foot soldiers suggested. The Captain glanced over at his lackey and grabbed him by the throat, glowering with anger.

"You think I can't handle something as simple as this on my own? I am your superior! Chosen by the master himself! I will not call for reinforcements and I will see to it that this boy is stopped." Mordo barked as he turned his head, seeing Lotus along with his gigantic friend continue to halt any and all aggressors.

For his part, Thalrok was energized as well, and delighted in piling his enemies up one by one while he hammered them with nothing but his strongest, most effective moves.

"Damn it." Captain Mordo whispered. He slowly began stumbling his way towards the wanted man, watching his own men drop one after the other, just like the weaklings that they were.

"How could they be such fools as to let this boy defeat them?" he growled, teeth pressing harder together. It was humiliating to the powerful clan of the Infected Ones. It was a mockery to the cause they all worked so hard for. He closed in on Lotus without seeming to be noticed.

"I'm gonna put this kid in his place. I know what must be done." Mordo murmured, as he stood only a few steps away from the shining young man. He reached for another dagger, but as his hand moved for the blade, Lotus zipped over and appeared right in front of him. Mordo was startled, and had no choice but to use his only arm to throw out one last punch.

"You weak scum!" the captain screamed out. Of course his hand was nowhere quick enough to land on this boy. Lotus grabbed his fist, stopping his punch like a brick wall.

"Damn it." Mordo sank his head on his chest, defeat washing over him. Lotus glared at this pathetic last attempt to win and planned to end this confrontation quickly. The boy pulled back his hand, channeling all of his energy into it.

"Ha ha ha-" the captain began to chuckle softly.

Lotus caught a glimpse of his face and saw that he was smiling to himself, with a kind of satisfaction. *Why is he laughing?*

Unexpectedly, Captain Mordo quickly lifted his head and, loud enough for all the world to hear, shouted out, "Realm of the Nightmare!" Suddenly, from the shoulder-flesh of his missing arm, shadowy black whips shot out from between the bandages, thrashing and writhing. The general laughed, and stared wickedly into this mere boy's eyes.

What is that?! Lotus had to move fast to throw that last punch before it was too late. But before he could connect it, whatever darkness was coming from Mordo's shoulder blocked his fist, then crawled up Lotus's arm like snakes. He backed away, trying to detach himself before it was too late. But within moments, the shadowy tentacles crept up his arm and wrapped around his whole head until it was completely sealed off. From the neck up, Lotus's face was covered with what looked like a pitch-black, fluid shadow.

"You foolish boy! You forced me to use my final and most painful move!" Captain Mordo shouted. Lotus stood swaying on his feet; his head was sheathed in blackness and still attached to Captain Mordo by the strong, whip-like, black tentacles.

Thalrok looked over and saw that his friend was once again trapped by some strange trick from that maniac of a captain.

"Damn it. I have to get over there!" Thalrok lifted up his leg, and slammed it in Lotus's direction, clearing a way out from behind this wall of troops. He dashed forward, barreling over any of the shaken enemies still able to keep their feet who were in front of him. He had to hurry before it was too late.

"By now it's already kicked in. You are experiencing immense pain, and your worst nightmares are flooding throughout your brain." Captain Mordo informed Lotus smugly. "Your mind will race while you experience the horror of nightmares that you cannot control." Mordo began laughing maniacally. As soon as this little exercise was finished, he would have broken the body, mind, and spirit of this boy and rendered him harmless. He watched as that faint light around the boy faded until it was no more. Lotus's body was cold, limp, and seemed lifeless. He was trapped inside his head, forced to suffer through the most terrible memories of his life playing on repeat—every single one of them.

"This will show you to never mess with the Infected Ones …" The captain slowly stopped talking. He had noticed Lotus beginning to twitch and shake every so often. The boy's hands began to shake more vigorously by the second, and now his whole body was fighting to get out of Mordo's firm hold.

What is going on? He should be completely immobile! Mordo thought as he watched Lotus's hands grab at his head. He scratched at the inky shadow surrounding his head, then clawed violently until it came off. The captain had never seen someone move at all after he put them in this trap.

How is this happening?! Mordo released his tentacle-like hold on the boy's arm and backed away quickly. As soon as his shadow appendages disappeared, he lifted his gaze and found himself looking into the eyes of something surely not from this world. Lotus's eyes were bright red with hatred, and anger seeped from every part of his body. The black staining on his arms darkened in color and rose higher.

The young man suddenly dropped to his knees and clutched his head in his hands as he curled into a ball. He screamed so loudly in pain, that the whole plaza could hear his cries. Drops of blood dripped from his eyes as he dug his fingers into his head. The captain never expected this kind of result from his attack. His foes would usually drop to the ground like a sack of lifeless flesh. This was unheard of.

Thalrok stopped in his tracks and sadly watched Lotus suffering all alone in his head as his friend's agonized screams got louder. The ground beneath them all began to shake and tremble. A black and malicious aura of dark energy erupted from Lotus reaching high into the air. Black lightning bolted out from his body, cracking the streets anywhere it struck.

"Oh no …" Thalrok whispered. He knew what was about to happen.

Lotus was unable to control his anger. The dark energy forced itself into every cell of his body. Even though he was trapped in that shadowy hold for only a few seconds, those bad memories played over and over in his head. Lotus's head snapped up, his teeth bared in a snarl as he glared wild-eyed at the one who'd caused this pain.

Captain Mordo took another step back, and realized that he had just awakened some great beast hidden inside of this young man. "Quick! Stop him—now!" he shouted, frantically pointing at Lotus.

"Boss, get down!" one of Mordo's lackeys yelled, quickly pulling him away. The captain stumbled and fell, so that Lotus, pouncing for his head, missed him by millimeters. The captain was overcome with fear. He had only experienced this feeling once before, and never wanted to endure it again.

"Get out of here, captain! We'll hold him off," his clansmen shouted, forming a human shield around their leader. Captain Mordo struggled to get back on his feet, then ran as quickly as he could to get away from that demon. The Infected Ones all packed tightly together, blocking the path between Mordo and this savage-looking wanted man. They watched as the dark energy swarmed and circled around the young man like a tornado. This energy he created transformed his hands into gigantic, beast-like claws of pure dark power.

The Infected Ones stood stock-still, readying for any attack to come their way. No matter what, they were not going to let him get through them to the captain.

Lotus shrieked like an enraged animal, then charged right for them. He swiped his monstrous black hands at their swords and shattered them to pieces. Any hit he took was absorbed like it was nothing, and any blow the Ones landed fueled his rampage even more. Lotus's claws slashed fiercely at his enemies, easily piercing straight through their armor and into their flesh. This merciless warrior didn't take any time to stop and think, he just kept moving forward to the next One who got in his way.

Captain Mordo kept running as fast as his short bowed legs could carry him toward the village stronghold. Dodging the fissures in the earth, compliments of a certain titan, he gasped for breath, huffing and puffing, with sweat dripping from his face. Yet he kept moving, trembling with fear. *What the hell is this guy?*

Lotus's rampage kept on until through the thinned-out crowd of remaining foes, he saw the fleeing man who had caused his pain. He stopped his assault on the Ones, and forced his hands down into the earth. His claws tore through the ground, where the dark energy flowing from him began to form a pool which eddied and swirled, spreading outward. Lotus gripped the earth at the bottom of the shallow but widening pool as his power nearly overwhelmed him.

Eyes never wavering from his target, the ferocity of Lotus's dark energy escalated. Shadowy tendrils rose into the air around Lotus and swirled violently. Black lightning erupted furiously from every corner of the dark pool in a violent and terrifying display. He swiped his hands through the dirt, sending the dark energy racing across the ground. The Infected Ones still in the fight recoiled and slowly retreated in terror, their eyes locked on the chaos and destruction before them.

"I am not a murderer!" Lotus roared, his voice raw with defiance. As he shouted, he thrust his hands forward. A torrent of pitch-black energy erupted, surging out across the ground like a flood. Dozens of jagged spikes of pure darkness shot up in their path, piercing through the remaining wall of enemies in a single, brutal strike. Captain Mordo, in his hasty departure, never looked back, but he could hear the chaos behind him that rattled the ground. By the time he did take a peek, he could only see a cloud of debris blooming in the air. It caught up to him, enveloped him, and then at last he emerged from it, still running.

Lotus had his eyes locked on his prey once again, and he wasn't planning on stopping.

The captain panicked as soon as he saw the monster, and frantically tried to scramble away even faster. He could hear the shrieks of the wanted man, and knew for certain that this would be the end of him. He could feel the power of this boy creeping closer to him by the second.

When the ground beneath his feet shook like a shockwave he lost his footing, and fell to the ground. This was it, death was here. The young man had to be right behind him at this very moment, ready to pounce and brutally end his life. As Mordo got to his knees and turned slowly to face his doom, he saw some kind of wall directly in front of him.

Thalrok reeled back his fist and struck Lotus hard across the jaw, using the momentum of Lotus's own attack against him. This hit had more force and power than any he'd ever felt before. Lotus was knocked completely off of his murderous path, and he tumbled across the rocky street.

"Ronin, snap out of it! This is not what you would want to do! Your anger has taken over and you have to calm down!" Thalrok shouted.

The demon-man stood back up and charged right back at Thalrok. The bounty hunter grabbed Lotus's wrists behind those fearsome claws and pushed him backward. The two were in a deadlock, and stood, feet planted firmly in the ground, each trying to push the other back. Thalrok was an extremely strong man, but he was struggling to keep Lotus's savage power in check.

"Ronin, you have to relax! Those memories of your past are gone! You are safe now, trust me!" Thalrok shouted, trying urgently to get through to his friend and change his mindset. Lotus just yelled out even louder, as the ground cracked and crumbled beneath their feet. Thalrok was running out of options, he would surely be overpowered if he wasn't able to stop his friend's loss of control. He had one final idea.

"Ronin, look at yourself! Is this what your master would want!?" Thalrok yelled, just as he felt his feet start to slip.

In that instant, Lotus actually heard those words over all of the noise in his head. In that moment, he felt his control coming back. The dark energy began to drain from his body and diminish. He could feel his eyes slowly regain focus. He was no longer trapped in his head with the nightmarish rage and memories, but the amount of energy he'd used was too much. His eyelids immediately fell shut and he crumpled to the ground.

"It's all right my friend, you rest up." Thalrok positioned Lotus on his side, and let him just lie still for now.

After ensuring that his friend was comfortable, he stood up and walked over to Captain Mordo, who still kneeled there panting in shock, eyes wide. Thalrok knelt in front of him, and through his helmet, stared Mordo dead in the eye. "I didn't *have* to stop him, you know? So you best listen to me carefully before *I* kill you." Thalrok said firmly.

* * *

The sounds of a horse-drawn cart being pulled across a bumpy road clattered in the Lotus's ears. Slowly, he opened his eyes and watched air currents pushing the clouds around in the sky. He felt his exhausted body aching with pain and overcome with weakness; even moving an inch was a challenge. His head bumped up and down on the floor of the large wooden wagon, as the rocky uneven road woke him up more and more. Bandaged and incredibly sore, Lotus lifted himself up carefully and rested his back on the side of the cart. "Where are we?" he asked.

Thalrok, who sat towards the front of the cart to look ahead, turned back and noticed that his friend was finally awake. "We're on our way back to Mellowtin," Thalrok informed him.

"What happened to Thristle?" Lotus wondered aloud.

"Everyone is safe. You did it, you saved the town. As of right now, the capital guards will be taking away the last of those Infected Ones, Mordo included. I'm not sure we got 'em all, but a good majority were disabled and stopped. They are probably at a Guardian Spire right now, locked up and taken care of."

Lotus looked toward the back of the cart, and watched them steadily distancing themselves from the opposing horizon. Then he dropped his head and checked on his various injuries. He noticed that his arms were still stained with faint dark markings as before.

"I lost control... didn't I?" Lotus asked. The bounty hunter didn't respond right away, and kept his eyes focused straight ahead.

"Yes." Thalrok finally answered. "Even though you did, no one was killed in the process. I made sure of it."

The bruised young man clenched his fists together and squeezed his eyes shut. He had been forced to look into and relive his darkest memories and again had been unable to stop that flow of rage and sorrow from overtaking him. He was still too weak.

"Don't stress yourself out. Because of your power, we were able to stop that clan, and save the town." Thalrok said in a more comforting voice.

"True, but if you weren't there, who knows what I would have done?" Lotus rubbed his face slowly, and felt the swollen knot on his jaw from Thalrok's massive punch. It had been a necessary action needed for the situation at the time.

"Thank you," Lotus added, glancing over at his friend.

"Don't mention it," Thalrok replied.

The cart rumbled onward and the rocky terrain showed no sign of smoothing out. The driver of the cart kept up a steady pace. For a long while they sat in silence there in the back, just rattling along and glancing ahead every once in a while. At last, near dusk, they caught sight of Mellowtin rising up before them. For the time being, adventure was on pause, and the two of them could rest up from their exertions of the past few days.

"Did you happen to learn anything about the Infected Ones when I was out?" Lotus asked.

"I was able to ask around to see what the townsfolk knew. Apparently, Thristle had been under their control for the past year. They told me that the Infected Ones used it as a stronghold, sort of a middle ground where they stored weapons and goods. They stole money and resources from the town daily. The Ones also enslaved the townspeople by force to make weaponry, harvest crops, and make sure their own troops were well-fed. They brutalized the townspeople. Some of them were taken away from their families and never seen again. Unfortunately, we don't know what happened to them. As we know, this wasn't the first town they took over. I think they are slowly trying to take over more villages until they have a foot in every portion of the world. They told me that the captain kept barking on and on about how their leader would change the world." Thalrok answered, shaking his helmeted head sadly.

It was a lot to take in. Over these past few days, they went from not even knowing the name of this group, to saving an entire town from these "Infected Ones" and learning so much more through the process. Each moment Lotus thought about it, it reminded him so much of the brutes who ambushed him and his friends years ago, especially the one who took away the one man he respected most of all.

It couldn't be...

Lotus sighed in exhaustion. That a group of people were seizing power and taking over small villages and towns was starting to sound too familiar. Who knew exactly what their ultimate goal might be?

"We've stepped into very dangerous territory, you know?" Lotus said thoughtfully. Thalrok only nodded his head and kept his eyes forward. He appeared to be thinking to himself this whole time, as if he too was putting together pieces of a puzzle. Thalrok rarely shared much he thought about, yet now he seemed to be acting even more withdrawn and brooding than usual.

"Ronin, I have a personal question." Thalrok finally said, staring down at his feet.

"What is it?" Lotus asked, thinking that maybe now Thalrok would finally tell him what was on his mind. He'd obviously been concentrating deeply on *something*.

"Do you think I should start naming some of my moves? Like, what if I yelled '*Earth Tremble!*' right before I did a big smash onto the ground? That would sound so cool, right? I'm thinking about making that my signature move." Thalrok said proudly, and he quickly turned his head for Lotus's approval.

Lotus, taken completely by surprise, chuckled to himself before replying, "I think it sounds pretty badass."

"Right?! See, I knew it was a good idea." Thalrok smiled and nodded to himself.

There he was, this was the Thalrok that Lotus had come to know. It was good to see that he still had some of himself left, that the traumas of these past days hadn't changed him too much. They laughed together as the town of Mellowtin grew closer, the lights of the town warm and welcoming. Their wild exploits had come to an end, for now.

"Thank you for the ride. You saved us from a long journey back." Thalrok bowed his head to the man from Thristle who had donated his time, cart, and horses to return them to Mellowtin.

"Are you kidding me? It's the least I could have done for you boys! This one right here is the strongest piece of work I have ever seen!" The driver gestured toward Lotus. "We can finally go back to living normal lives. We can hardly begin to tell you how appreciative we are, and I speak for the whole town of Thristle. We thank you so very much for putting your own lives on the line for us. A year of heartache can now finally be healed, thanks to you two. We are eternally grateful," he replied, as he bowed his head even lower in return.

The two young men, warriors really, felt incredibly honored by the words he spoke. The only thing they could do was smile modestly and relish in the relief of surviving these past few days.

I'm doing it, master, I'm helping the world, however I can.

They walked silently through the softly lit streets. By now, the whole town was asleep. All was quiet and they seemed to be the only ones still awake. That was until they got halfway up the stairs leading to their rooms and were abruptly stopped by a firm and irritated female voice.

"It's late, you know." Leyla's simple declaration challenged them. The two froze in place on the stairwell and turned toward the bottom of the stairwell. They saw one of the innkeepers standing there with her arms folded, watching them with a sour glare. Neither of them could think of a thing to say to her; how could a person explain everything that had transpired in the past few days?

"I'm just pullin' your chain, boys! Leyla said, eyes twinkling. Then she laughed and slapped her thigh with glee. The two sighed in relief as they shook their heads at her prank.

"You helped that poor mother find her child, didn't you?" Leyla asked.

"Yes ma'am," they replied in unison.

A big smile grew on Leyla's face, and she placed her hands over her heart.

"Wonderful, you two were so kind to go out of your way like that for her. Now, go upstairs and please rest up. Your rooms are exactly the way you left them," she said graciously. Still looking quite pleased, she started towards her own room for the night.

The two of them continued up the stairs and down the hallway to their joint living area. Without a single word spoken, each went straight into their room, then crashed in exhaustion on their beds. Thalrok had been restless and unsettled the last few days, watching over Lotus, who'd been unconscious far longer than he was comfortable with. Meanwhile, the wanted man, who'd been out cold for quite some time, found himself totally drained of energy. He needed some real rest himself.

As Lotus lay on his bed, he lifted his arms and looked at his hands. His veins were still somewhat dark and the skin tinted black from when the dark energy took over. He thought he'd be able to use light energy a bit longer, yet in reality, he seemed to be right back to square one.

"Maybe I can try again tomorrow," Lotus whispered. He shut his eyes to fall into a peaceful slumber in this place that still seemed too good for him to be able to call "home".

9

Home

"Good morning, Ronin," Thalrok said, not looking up.

"Mornin' Thalrok." Lotus carefully closed his door, stretching his arms high over his head. The bounty hunter sat quietly on the couch in the combined living area, casually reading Mellowtin's weekly bulletin. Lotus decided to have a seat as well, and rubbed his eyes to help wake himself up and focus on the day to come.

"Looks like I was right after all," Layla said in greeting, as she came down the hall with two cups in her hands. She walked over and handed Thalrok one cup, then gave Lotus the other.

"What's this?" Lotus asked.

"Well, it's morning, and I just assumed you boys would want a morning wake-up, am I right? I heard Mr. Titan moving around, and thought you would be getting up soon too. Looks like I'm correct, which of course, I always am," she giggled as she went back down the hall.

"Aw, that was nice of her." Thalrok brightened, and lifted his helmet just enough to take a sip.

Lotus looked into his cup and felt the warm steam hit his nose as he sampled the hot amber liquid. *Wow, this is delicious. It's been a while since I've had homemade tea.* He carefully set down his cup as Thalrok hummed in agreement, shaking his head up and down.

Surprisingly, it seemed like life was going along normally now. About a week had passed since their adventures in this small part of Perlaria had come to an end. The two had made Mellowtin a part of their lives. They had learned the layout of the village, and even became known in some of the local restaurants and taverns. Every night, Thalrok went to grab a drink at the Fork and Sword, where, due to his fun-loving nature, he always found some lively drinking buddies. Lotus would go for a run each morning, and he always greeted the locals who were setting up shop around that same time. Now and then he lent them a hand moving things, or later, cleaning up. With each passing day, the wanted man grew more connected to this town, and yet he still feared the worst for any of the people that he associated with. As his history had shown him, he could never feel safe somewhere without it all eventually blowing up in his face. Daily, he tried to cherish his present reality, should any signs appear that it was time to face the sad facts and leave forever.

"I'm off, need me to pick up anything for you while I'm out?" Lotus asked. Thalrok just shook his bowed head in a voiceless response. It was strange to see him like this again, brooding and silent.

What is going through that man's mind? Lotus thought. He made his way down to the lobby of the inn, waved goodbye to Leyla and Layla in passing, and closed the front doors quietly behind him after going out. Lotus took his time treading down the wide stoop, then broke into a light jog to head across town. A wash of damp air brushed across his face, and he felt the remains of drying puddles squish beneath his feet. He could smell the moistened grass still bathed in yesterday's rain. One would say it was a normal day in Mellowtin, yet to him, no day went on feeling normal. Any day, the unknown could be lurking around the corner.

Pressing forth, Lotus took a southbound route, body refreshed and well rested after that latest adventure. *Has it really been a full week?* He wondered. An animal placed in an unfamiliar world is prone to be on guard and anxious as it tries to survive. That same feeling swept over Lotus. Despite beginning to fit in and meager roots sprouting, he felt like he didn't really belong here in Mellowtin. It was hard to fall back into trust after being hunted so many times before.

As he surveyed the town, taking in the day, he could already hear the sounds and voices coming from everyone's favorite tavern, the Fork and Sword Canteen. While strolling past, he noticed that Stritan was sitting outside on a bench, kicking his feet distractedly. *I wonder why he's not inside?* Lotus mused, and as if his mind had transmitted that thought telepathically, Stritan lifted his head up and looked right at him. Without hesitation the boy stood up and ran over to Lotus, waving his hands. The young man waved back, marvelling again at how realistically Stritan's metallic arm and hand moved.

"G'morning Stritan, don't you work today?" Lotus said in greeting.

"Today is my day of rest, unfortunately. Dad says if I keep working every day, I'll overdo it," the boy replied with a touch of sadness.

"Your father is wise. Sometimes too much work can do more harm than good. I've been told that myself many times before." Lotus remembered the countless days practicing in Petalbrooke and hearing those exact words.

He waved to the boy again and stepped away to continue his errands across town, when he heard Stritan shout, "Wait a second! Since I have the day off, I have a request."

Lotus paused, dragged himself to a halt and dropped his head. "I told you, my sword is off limits," he groaned.

"No, no—not that again!" Stritan said, then huffed loudly with embarrassment. Lotus turned around and looked back at the boy, who seemed hesitant to ask his question, but had a twinkle in his eye just the same.

"Could you teach me how to fight?" Stritan asked eagerly. Lotus was shocked to hear *that* request but could tell that he spoke with great passion.

"I saw you practicing a few days ago, and I would love to learn from you. I can tell you're a real strong warrior—you have all those scars from what must have been some intense battles. Please-please-please?!" Stritan begged.

The wanted man would have been quite content to give his answer immediately. He could only see that agreeing would be digging a deeper hole for himself in this town. Day by day, he was getting closer to some of the people here, building connections, and Mellowtin felt like more of a real home. He just couldn't risk becoming a victim of his curse again, and yet...

This kid won't stop bothering me unless I say yes.

He turned away from Stritan and headed off to continue southward. After only a few steps, he suddenly stopped and lifted his hand up in surrender. "Sure thing kid, I'll teach you how to fight." Lotus surprised himself by saying.

Stritan, eyes wide with excitement, immediately began jumping up and down, his metal fist pumping wildly in celebration.

"Meet me at the small plot of grass on the west side of town, and we can start right away," Lotus said, as he walked away. Stritan wasted no time, and went back inside to grab what he needed to begin training.

As the dirt from the ground was kicked up from Stritan's enthusiastic retreat, Lotus couldn't help but feel some excitement of his own. Now for the first time, he was going to be in the shoes of the man he honored most.

Changing his original route, Lotus jogged through town toward the west side of the Mellowtin. The day was a lot busier than he expected, and the plaza seemed to be a little more crowded than usual. The sound of shop owners calling out to passersby chimed down the entire street. He carefully weaved between the clusters of people huddled around each stand, making sure to apologize to anyone he bumped into. Each day that he spent in Mellowtin, he used all the time he could to walk amongst people again. The feeling of not being watched all the time or hunted down was quite pleasant. Lotus took it in as much as he could for now. But even though he walked beside and with these people, he still felt as if he was just an outsider, just an unknown, just a wanted man hiding in plain sight. "Damn," he sighed.

Stritan, legs pumping, quickly turned a corner, kicking up more dirt as he sprinted toward the small field. Lotus watched as the boy, finally dressed in something other than work clothes, barreled down the path to meet him. He came to a screeching halt, then bent and placed his hands on his knees as he panted, gasping for air. Why he had sprinted full-speed Lotus did not know, but he could understand that the boy's bottled-up zeal was untamable.

"Ok… I'm ready…" Stritan wheezed.

Lotus chuckled to himself as he backed up a few steps away from the boy, and stared up into the sky. "The key to being a strong warrior is being able to understand *why* you want to fight, who or what you want to protect, or who you want to become. So, what drives you to become a strong fighter?" Lotus asked, as he slowly lowered his head and looked over at Stritan.

Stritan stood up straight, then glanced over to his missing arm. He slowly rubbed the metal arm and clenched its metallic fist before speaking. "I want to protect the ones I love. I want to be able to take care of those around me in case the time comes when danger returns. I wasn't able to help anyone years ago, and I lost my arm. I don't want anyone else to have to go through something like that." Stritan spoke with deep resolve, and focused intently on Lotus.

It wasn't much of a surprise to him, but Lotus could tell from the moment that he asked and was answered that this boy was pure of heart. "Good, it's important to understand why you begin training, because when at any point you find yourself lacking motivation, you must remind yourself about why you started," Lotus said, and then began rotating his head and loosening his shoulders.

"Now, come at me with everything you've got," he commanded, as he pointed straight at the boy's chest.

Stritan seemed extremely confused as to why Lotus would start off by saying that. "Wait, like, *fight* you?" The boy tilted his head.

Lotus only gestured with his hand for Stritan to come forward. "I need to know what you can do right now. From there, I can hone your skills to suit you best." Lotus explained.

The boy began to understand, but hesitated to lift his hands up to begin. He stared at Lotus who stood there calmly, like the undeniable presence of a thunderstorm looming in the near distance.

Here I go. Stritan charged forward and began swinging his fists left and right at Lotus, trying hard to hit him. But, every time he swung, his hands would pass right through nothingness, missing completely. As Stritan stomped around on the grass, chasing down his target, Lotus swiftly weaved and sidestepped, avoiding all contact and keeping his own hands at his sides. The young blacksmith grew more and more exhausted as he found himself to be on the losing side of this match. Even if he created an opening, Lotus was too fast. Finally, Stritan had to stop and catch his breath. He placed his hands back on his knees, huffing and puffing as he softly mumbled complete gibberish.

"Not too bad. I'll give you another shot, except this time, I won't move at all." Lotus said, placing his hands on his hips.

Stritan nodded his head, which drooped toward the ground. Then he stood straight up again, and walked over to his teacher. With hands protecting his face, he shuffled in closer to make his move. *Does he really expect to not get hit if he stands still?* He was embarrassed to have to be given a handicap, yet he was willing to do anything to learn how to fight. Stritan swung a swift right hook and let out a powerful yell.

Lotus smiled to himself, then lifted his arm and easily stopped the punch with his forearm. As the young student felt the recoil shake him to the core, he saw Lotus grab onto his wrist with one hand, his shoulder with the other, and suddenly he was smoothly tossed off to one side. Like a rock skipping across the water, Stritan tumbled through the grass.

This boy was a live one though, and Stritan got right back up to try it again. Punches, kicks, even fake outs, he tried his hardest to get in a hit, any hit. The fierce barrage of his own attacks eventually tired Stritan, and he had to pause for a moment. He planted his rump on the ground and panted heavily, sweat dripping from his face.

Lotus looked at his own forearms and noticed that each time Stritan had used his metal arm to strike, it left quite a red mark. "I best keep dodging those attacks," he said to himself.

"How the heck can you dodge and counter all of my attacks?!" Stritan struggled to spit out.

"I was just following the pattern," Lotus told him. "You seem to know a lot of basic strikes, and I could read which one you were gonna throw. After moving around and seeing what you would do after each move, I had a pretty good understanding of your fighting style."

Stritan flopped onto his back and stared up at the sky the moment he heard that answer. He knew it was hopeless for him to land any hit at this rate.

Lotus chuckled and walked over beside him. "It wasn't easy for me to learn that, you know. My master taught me day after day all that he knew, and how to make sure I could read all of my opponents' moves." Lotus explained. "To be honest, I was way worse than you—by a mile."

Stritan lifted his head and saw that Lotus was offering to help him up. He grabbed his hand and hoisted himself up from the ground.

"Your master taught you well then, he must be very proud," Stritan remarked, as he brushed dirt and grass from himself. Lotus paused, then stared off into the distance, thinking to himself, *I hope he is...*

"Wait a second. You said to come at you with everything I got, right?" Stritan asked.

"Y-yes of course you should. Give me everything you've got." Lotus replied.

"Gotcha, gotcha," Stritan mumbled, and he walked back to his starting spot.

Lotus seemed confused as to why he had to ask that question again. *Was the kid holding back? Does he have another attack he wants to try, or what?* Regardless, Lotus headed back to the center of the field and prepared himself.

The boy held himself a little differently now than the first time he sparred. He seemed to look a bit more comfortable. Stritan dashed forward, leading with his real arm and keeping his metal one screened from view. Lotus lifted his hands and expected another punch from his metallic fist. As Stritan stopped right in front of his teacher, just as Lotus predicted, he began twisting his body to strike with his other arm.

Just gotta parry it so it doesn't hit me. He expected the attack to come jabbing right at him, but for some reason, the boy was lifting his arm up as if he were to swing straight down.

"Don't get cut!" Stritan shouted, as his metal arm slashed straight down, just missing Lotus's arm. As Lotus saw the metallic arm cut through the air, he realized it wasn't an arm anymore.

It's a double-bladed ax?! Lotus panicked as he watched the sharp blade slash down on the grass.

Stritan immediately cut back upwards now that his teacher was off balance. The second slash just missed too, which left Stritan's back wide open.

I can grapple him now. Lotus realized, and he planted his feet, pressing in to lock his arms to keep Stritan from moving. As he reached out, Stritan spun his body around, and swung his metal arm horizontally. Lotus saw his arm moving through the air, noticing that it was no longer an ax; now it was a giant mallet! The metal slammed heavily into Lotus's shoulder and knocked him back a few feet. He rolled backward, gracefully pushing himself back onto his feet.

"I got a hit!" Stritan cheered with his arms in the air, bouncing up and down.

"What was that?!" Lotus yelled.

"Didn't I tell you? I can change the form of my metal arm to whatever I want. My power allows me to augment and shape materials, it's how I can use this arm like a real arm." Stritan explained, easily changing the mallet back to a hand once more.

Lotus had never in his life seen anything like *that* during any of the fights he'd ever taken part in. This kind of superpower was unheard of, and was totally unique to Stritan. "Well, I'll be damned," he chuckled, rubbing his shoulder. He was impressed that this kid could adapt so quickly to a fighting style that suited his particular ability. *He's a walking arsenal of weaponry, the walking war machine himself, Stritan the Blacksmith.* Lotus thought, with more than a little amusement, and also pride, in his first-ever apprentice.

"Are you ready to keep going then?" Lotus asked, his enthusiasm growing.

"Yes sir!" Stritan hollered back, as he switched his hand to the shape of a battle axe.

Lotus could only smile inwardly as he prepared for the next round. He found himself experiencing a familiar warm sensation again—the feeling of sparring with a partner, not to do harm, but to grow.

* * *

"I guess we can call it for today." Lotus huffed a few hours later, as he wiped the sweat from his cheek. He glanced off to the west and saw that the sun was about to kiss the horizon, ready to give in to the night.

Stritan was lying on the grass, staring up at the darkening blue sky, and gasping with exhaustion. As he looked up he saw Lotus standing over him, offering a hand. The boy groaned as he reached out and heaved himself up once again.

"Let's get you back home before your family wonders where you've been the last few hours," Lotus said, as they began walking back to the canteen. Stritan lagged a little bit behind him, with tired legs and a sore arm. They watched as shop owners began closing up for the day and lighting the street lights. The flickering torches sparked in the air and shed a warm glow across the cobblestone roads. The lively town slowly wound down.

"So, how long did it take you to master this stuff?" Stritan asked.

"I wouldn't say I've mastered the art of combat, but I trained very hard for a long part of my life. My master was a wise man who always made sure all of his students worked to the best of their own special abilities. All of us were completely different, and yet, we all worked hard together." Lotus replied.

"If you're this strong, then I'd be terrified to spar with your master." Stritan chuckled.

"In all my years I was never able to beat him, not even once," Lotus stated.

"Really? He must be some powerful guy!" Stritan's eyes were wide.

"Yeah ..." Lotus said softly, as the two boys turned the corner and saw Thalrok walking on the other side of the street in their direction.

"Hey, Mr. Titan!" Stritan hollered. Thalrok stopped and turned his head toward the two, then crossed over to meet them.

"For the last time, my name is Thalrok, little blacksmith." Thalrok sighed, as he tussled the kid's hair. Stritan laughed to himself and swatted Thalrok's huge hand away.

"What are you doing out and about?" Lotus asked.

"I was actually looking for you. I'd like to talk if you have time." Thalrok replied. Lotus was caught off guard, and wondered what was the matter.

"Yeah, sure. I just finished up what I was doing. Why don't you head home then, Stritan? And don't forget to practice what we worked on." Lotus said.

Without hesitation, the boy waved his goodbyes and started toward home for the night. The two watched Stritan leave, then Thalrok began to walk down the street. Lotus followed just behind him, but said nothing. Before long, they turned a corner and entered a small pub.

"Thalrok!" everyone shouted as he walked inside. He lifted his hands and greeted all the regulars as the bartender shook his head, laughing to himself.

"I'll get your regular, boss," the bartender said, smiling with a knowing wink.

The two of them sat down at the bar and rested in silence for a bit until the bounty hunter's drink came out. The pub was booming at this time of the day; seats were filled and conversations flew. Lotus just sat quietly next to his friend and waited to hear what Thalrok was going to say. The bartender slid his mug of ale across the counter, then proceeded to tend to the next customer.

Thalrok lifted his helmet just enough to take in a big sip. He slammed the large mug back on the counter and let out a sigh of enjoyment. Then, after a brief pause, he said, "Ronin, I gotta tell you something."

"What's wrong?" Lotus asked, concerned at Thalrok's solemn manner.

"I'll be leaving town tomorrow," Thalrok answered bluntly, keeping his eyes focused on the bar in front of him.

Lotus turned his head and saw that a cool detachment had washed over the bounty hunter. "Oh. Is everything alright?" Lotus inquired, concerned at this unusual behavior.

"Yes, it's just... after all this running across Prosper Valley, I can't help but wonder if this group, these Infected Ones, had anything to do with my hometown years ago. I have so many questions about what really happened to my family, and how, why, or if I was actually abandoned. Ever since I was taken in by the titans I've wondered to myself, what happened to them? My foster mother believed that they were under attack and fled, trying to save me in the process. I just need answers so I can keep... going." Thalrok declared.

The titan lifted his drink and took another big sip. After swallowing loudly, he continued, "I've heard that there's a seer that lives atop Mount Axi. He is said to be able to answer any question of this world. Apparently he is filled with knowledge of the past, present, some say the future. I plan to make my way there and ask him what happened myself." Thalrok said matter-of-factly. His voice was firm and determined.

Lotus was left without words at this moment; he really couldn't wrap his head around this news. The feeling of wanting to find what had been lost to you haunted him each and every night too. His own family, friends, and hometown still called out to him in his head, even though for these many years, Lotus had just been struggling to find peace and a place where he didn't have to run anymore. Now he felt something else that outweighed the constant yearning inside him. It was the feeling that he was going to lose something that he'd become rather attached to.

He didn't want Thalrok to leave.

Thalrok slid his empty mug across the counter. He reached into his pouch and placed two silver coins on the counter. He stood up from his stool and headed out the door without another word. The regulars all shouted out their goodbyes as the door swung shut behind him. Lotus could only sit there, feeling his—friend—grow more distant from him with every second that passed.

Thalrok quietly walked up the torch-lit streets with his eyes locked on the ground in front of him. He'd waited all day to tell Lotus the news, knowing that it wouldn't be easy. Yet, he was done waking up another day with those burning questions blistering the inside of his head. The bounty hunter looked up and saw he had reached the Lie-Inn, and climbed the steps up to the front door.

"When are we going?" a familiar voice inquired.

Thalrok stopped, still as a statue, at the top of the stairs. He slowly turned around to see Lotus standing at the bottom of the steps. " 'We'?" he said, tilting his helmeted head.

"Yeah. *We*," Lotus said, his voice was firm and unwavering.

"You're coming too?" Thalrok had a hard time masking his surprise, despite the helmet.

"Of course. You helped me, I think it's my turn to help you now. Plus, we both have unanswered questions. Maybe we'll get a few more answers than we're hoping for." Lotus replied, shrugging his shoulders.

"You're going to leave this village, a town full of people who *aren't* hunting you, to come with me across Perlaria and potentially encounter people who will try and stop you—something you've had to deal with for years. Just to help me get my questions answered?" Thalrok asked once more.

Lotus just nodded his head with a little smirk.

Thalrok stood atop the short flight of stairs above the man he now respected most, the man who was proving to him, once again, why he would follow him to the depths of hell and back. "You are one strange guy, Ronin," Thalrok said, looking intently at Lotus. Then he suddenly burst out laughing, slapping his leg and holding onto his stomach. Lotus couldn't help but smile at his friend's raucous laughter, and felt more than a twinge of both happiness and relief.

"We leave tomorrow morning. Rest up, and get ready for a trip to the northwest!" Thalrok shouted as he opened the door to the inn and stepped inside. Lotus nodded his head and hurried in with him. Both young men stopped suddenly when they were greeted by the identical frowning faces of the twin innkeepers.

"Do you two know what time it is?! Any louder and you would have gotten a solid kick in the pants." Layla said sternly, as Leyla nodded. Both looked quite annoyed.

Thalrok chuckled nervously, apologized nicely, then raced up to his room for the night. Lotus apologized as well, and returned more slowly to his room. He looked around, and saw that through these past seven days, it felt like he had made this room a bit of his own. However, now, whether he liked it or not, he found himself leaving town once again. The open world was vast and unknown, yet it seemed like the place where Lotus felt the most at home and comfortable. He laid himself down on the bed, wanting to get as much rest as he could for the mysterious new journey ahead of him.

"Let's see how this goes," Lotus whispered to himself. Then he drifted off to sleep for what might be the last time in this town that actually treated him like a person, not a monster.

10

Mount Axi

"Looks like he's sleeping in. Again," a child's voice noted with disgust.

"Is he ever gonna learn to get up on time?" another asked, sighing.

"*We'll* be the ones getting in trouble if he doesn't show up on time. Let's knock on his door again," added another.

Three children groaned in annoyance as they approached the fourth child's house. He was surely still sound asleep, snug in his room with the shutters closed and the sunlight barely able to sneak in. The three friends began to bang on his front door and toss small stones up to his shuttered window, but it was hopeless, the boy did not show his face or make any sound.

"Forget it, we tried," the three agreed. Then they turned to hurry along to the temple to begin training as they did every day. Their sleeping friend would likely be in trouble for being late to class again, but, hey, what else was new?

"What... what is picking at me?" the fourteen-year-old boy mumbled sleepily, as something hard and blunt hit his forehead time and time again. His eyes opened slowly, and realization kicked in as he looked up and saw his pet Koolic, a creature with an owl-like head and the body of a feline, trying to wake him up.

"Dang it! I'm gonna be late again!" He jumped up from his bed with incredible speed and rushed for his wardrobe.

"Come on Reggio, I thought I told you to wake me earlier!" he shouted, as he bounced around his room, frantically pulling on one piece of clothing at a time. "Now I'm gonna get yelled at again for being late, and I'll have to clean up after class again. It is just *not* fair that everyone else has parents to wake them up every morning, and I have to rely on you! Ugh, and it doesn't help that you like to sleep in too," the boy complained bitterly.

With only a few seconds to wake himself up, he was fully clothed and racing out of the front door. "I'll see you after class, Reggio—be good!" His little pet watched from the window as he raced up the broad curved road to the temple at the topmost part of his village.

The boy's village, Wisphire, rested atop Mount Axi, a prominent mountain in northern Perlaria near the coast. This extremely steep and windy mountain split at the summit into two peaks, and at the base of those peaks sat the village that was as old as time. Wisphire had been kept in pristine shape over the centuries thanks to the care of the seer's disciples, who had sealed themselves at the top of Mount Axi since the end of the Calamity. They created and maintained harmony amongst one another. No one would ever abandon their clan and village, and no one was ever allowed to enter. They had all the resources required to live in isolation atop the mountain, and would never have any need to leave. The disciples grew special foods and had a fresh reservoir of water that came up through a cave in the mountain. All this time had passed with no contact from anyone but their own kind, and they seemed to be doing all right for themselves. Yet they remained vigilant, knowing that fate and human nature often repeated themselves.

"Please don't be mad, please don't be mad, please don't be mad," the well-rested boy chanted under his breath, as he scrambled to reach the wide arches of the entrance to the temple. With the morning sun at his back, his shadow spread across the floor before him as he entered with hasty footsteps. Everyone's eyes turned in his direction. The boy slowed his pace. All of his fellow students and the elders watched him walk in shame to his spot on the temple floor.

"Oa! This is the fifth time I've seen you come in late. What do I have to do to get this through your head? You *must* be here on time." Today's teacher was one of the most senior of the elders, and he spoke in a stern voice, looking at him sharply.

"Sorry sir, it won't happen again." Oa sighed. He smoothly sank to the floor with his legs crossed. He stilled his body and quieted his mind, beginning his silent meditation. The mind was supposed to be at peace during meditation, yet all Oa could do was feel the eyes of the elders assessing him. Their scrutiny was a weighty distraction. He knew that they wouldn't let his being late again slide, and he would surely be told to stay after school to do some kind of chores, or who knew what, as punishment.

With no surprise at all, after class was dismissed for the late-morning break he was called over by the elder who was teaching today. Everyone else went home now, then returned to the temple after lunch. Oa dragged his feet across the smooth stone flooring and stood in front of the elder, who looked down at him, firmly disappointed. Usually, at this point, he was told what his punishment would be. He'd then head home to eat before coming back for the three-hour afternoon class, after which he would complete his assigned chores.

"The Grand Sage would like to speak with you," the elder said, and pointed to gigantic double doors on the far side of the meditation room. Oa was spooked out of his mind as he gazed across the large room at those foreboding doors. He could hear his heartbeat thrumming rapidly in his ears. Never once had he been called to speak with the Grand Sage after being late. Maybe it was because now he'd been late multiple times, and the elders had a duty to inform him. He put on a brave face and walked to the other end of the room. Swallowing his fear, the tall doors opened and he entered to speak with Grand Sage Gou, the village elder highest in rank over all of the villagers—the true seer of Mount Axi.

The doors creaked as they shut behind Oa, then abruptly there was silence. Sitting on his throne, which was created through a natural formation in the mountain, Gou opened his eyes.

"Young Oa. Please step forward, child," the Grand Sage said in a deep, slow voice. The boy did as he was told, and walked closer to the elder. He knelt before him, rested his head on the floor in respect, and dutifully awaited his punishment.

"What are you feeling right now, my son?" Gou asked.

Oa lifted his head from the ground, confused, yet answered honestly after a bit of thought, "I'm feeling kind of guilty, not to mention, also angry at myself."

"I know that you are a good child. When does a good sleep not get the best of us from time to time? Especially if there's also a wonderful dream," the Grand Sage said with a short laugh.

The corners of Oa's mouth turned up just a little bit at those words as he felt the fear of being scolded fading slightly.

The eldest of elders then pointed at the young boy and asked, "What do you dream of?"

Oa was taken off guard for a moment. He didn't exactly know how to answer this question. Did he mean his dreams in his sleep, or the ones he hoped for in the future?

"I would have to say, that I dream to one day be able to see my parents again. I think about that every single day." Oa paused. Nothing had been the same in the past two years since they were gone.

"I've also wondered what it's like outside of our village." Oa continued. "What is beyond the gates of Wisphire here on Mount Axi, and who lives in all of the lands of Prosper, of Perlaria? I know it's forbidden for anyone to leave, but I've always wanted to know what it's like out there," replied Oa, speaking with great passion.

The Grand Sage looked with some fondness at this young student, and couldn't help but smile. It wasn't every day a young boy would speak honestly of his curiosity about things beyond the village. Who would want to leave the safety of their home to venture into the vast unknown of the world? Was it a fool's fancy, or an adventurer's gift?

"You have quite the outlook for a child who sleeps half the day away," the elder chuckled. He looked around the room, contemplating a large tapestry hanging from the ceiling. Its cloth had become more deteriorated and faded as the years stretched on and on. Gou himself had been sitting in this temple for generations now, and couldn't remember the last time anyone had wanted to leave the village. Could this be a sign? Or maybe, it was a warning...

"I believe your dreams stray not too far from your future. The choice of the people to stay within our walls is the path all have always taken, but it is not law. Your purpose and destiny will come soon, child, just be patient," he said, and then reassured Oa that he would find a peace beyond his youthful years.

"Thank you, sir." Oa bowed his head. After those words, his heart, finally released from its rapid fluttering, slowed to a normal and steady rhythm.

"Now, go relax before your duties after class," the Grand Sage said, as Oa was not to be let off the hook quite so easily. Oa did as he was told, trying not to sulk. He went back home to eat, relax, and prepare for evening classes, just as all of the children of Wisphire had all been doing for centuries.

* * *

"There it is." Lotus pointed, and the two looked upward to see the gigantic wooden gates which were the only entrance to Wisphire, village of the seer's disciples of Mount Axi. The mere trace of a trail had been steep and rocky, and had no sympathy for outsiders. Their energy had been drained on the demanding journey to the peaks.

As they banked the last turn to the top, they could see just how naturally beautiful the architecture was. The disciples built everything around the natural shape of the mountains without harming or disturbing any of the curves or rough surfaces. The large wooden gates blended seamlessly into the mountainside, and were carved with what appeared to be symbols and scriptures of the seers from each generation. Many of those markings were old and worn, untouched since they'd first been etched into the wood so very long ago.

"What's the plan?" Lotus asked, as they got closer to the securely sealed, sole access to the village.

"No idea. I just hope they let me take a quick visit to the one who can 'see all of the world' and then I'm on my way." Thalrok huffed, still catching his breath from the endless climbing.

Though he appreciated Thalrok's optimistic point of view, Lotus couldn't help but sigh at the fact that this was his only plan to engage a group of people who had totally forbidden outsiders for the last several centuries.

Their long trek across Prosper Valley and the difficult venture up Mount Axi now concluded, they stepped up and stood side-by-side in front of the immense gates to the village. Thalrok cracked his knuckles, then slammed his big fist on the huge wooden double doors four times. There was no response. He tried again, but to his surprise, there was still no response at all. Thalrok glanced over at Lotus, who was giving him a stern look that screamed, *Don't do it!*

"Too late," Thalrok said, shrugging. Lotus threw up his hands and yielded, backing away from the doors to let Thalrok do his thing.

The bounty hunter loosened up his arms, then twisted his hips as he took a deep breath in and out. With both hands, he reached back, unlatched and then grasped the hilt of his titan-sized sword. He removed it from his back and looked at it fondly. Then, planting his feet and stabilizing his stance, he extended the sword backward and behind him, its tip touching the ground. Taking in another deep breath, Thalrok roared and swung it over his head, driving the huge sword straight into the massive door on the right. The wood split with a loud crack as it punched through to the other side. A big enough hole appeared when he pulled his sword back out of the fractured wood, which was flung everywhere. Thalrok clipped the sword back into its holster and cleared a path as he led the way for the two of them to enter Wisphire.

Within just a few steps, the young men were met by the frozen figure of a man standing near the gates. His face was painted with pure terror. It was as if he had just seen a ghost, or something even worse.

Thalrok had begun to brush off some wooden remnants of the gate from himself when he noticed the man staring at him. "Oh, hello there," he said casually, with a friendly wave of his huge hand.

Sweat dripped from the disciple's forehead. He simply could not believe what he was seeing and couldn't move. Someone had just broken into his village for the first time in, well... ever.

When not one, but two, intruders stepped forward, he overcame his paralysis and charged up the street toward the village proper to warn the others.

"That would be expected," Thalrok remarked, flicking splinters of wood from his chest.

"'Ya think?" Lotus scoffed, then shook his head as they slowly followed after the alarmed man on the wide spiral of a path.

There was just one main road in Wisphire, which started at the entrance gate. It wound upwards, around and through the whole village, then ended up at the temple. As for Lotus and Thalrok, they were a walking advertisement letting everyone know that, for the first time ever, visitors had indeed arrived. They passed house after house following the curved and stony road, watching as the people of Wisphire reacted to the unprecedented appearance of strangers.

All of the villagers were totally caught off guard. Most simply fled in fear for their lives. Some called out to warn everyone to seek shelter and hide themselves before they could be seen. The disciples of Mt. Axi were known as a group of pacifists who sought harmony and cooperation rather than war. It would be a rare sight to see anyone engage in any conflict. Now though, the village was in an unforeseen chaotic state, its frenzied people in a panic as two invaders approaching their most sacred temple. Still, no one even thought to face them.

The two invaders, for their part, showed no signs of hostility at all. They just continued to quietly walk farther up the path toward the peaks, barely registering the disciples' shock and distress.

"Wow, d'ya see that?!" Thalrok asked in excitement, as they finally rounded the last turn. The giant temple, an architectural masterpiece, rested compatibly in the space between the two uppermost peaks of Mount Axi.

"He must be in there. Let's keep going." Lotus murmured, and they made their way up the last bit of the path to the steps of the temple. As they got closer to the wide entrance, they could hear nothing but the wind. It howled through the dips and crevices of the mountain, singing the sounds of nature with each step they took up the broad stone staircase. Lotus felt a bit uneasy, as though something was off, or was subtly stirring in their blind spots. Staring up at the large arches at the entrance, they walked into the spacious main room of the temple. Their footsteps echoed across the walls.

"Hellooo!" Thalrok called out. His voice reverberated throughout the room. No response followed. The room seemed completely empty, as though it had been abandoned and vacant for years and years.

Was it all just a rumor? Is there really not someone in this world who can see all? Lotus wondered, rubbing his chin and admiring the simple but grand room. As they walked toward the center of it, an uneasy feeling flooded Lotus's chest.

"Halt!" a voice shouted from above. Both of them quickly looked up toward the sound of the voice. At that same time, a dozen disciples dropped down from somewhere above them, surrounding them in a circle. Once their feet touched the floor of the temple, large gusts of wind blew from all directions. The two intruders lifted their hands to block the dust in their air and pivoted to stand back-to-back, preparing to defend themselves.

"Please, we mean you no harm," Lotus said, as he spread his palms in a peaceful gesture.

"No harm?! You two broke through the gates of our village. You brought fear and panic to our peaceful people. How could you mean no harm in that?!" a disembodied voice asked, as the disciples began to slowly move closer.

"Told ya," Lotus whispered to Thalrok. The two observed the disciples around them, noticing that they were unarmed, but perfectly synchronized in their movements. They'd been told that the disciples here weren't hostile as a group, yet these here in the temple acted and handled themselves as though they were experienced fighters.

"I'm sorry. I just needed to get a question answered. Yes, this may not have been the best way. I... well, I just had nowhere else to go. I heard there was a man here at Mt. Axi who 'knew all', or something like that, and I had to find him." Thalrok confessed, trying to explain himself.

His words didn't seem to get through to them. The disciples just kept closing in. They were all older men, with mature, lined faces. They had bright eyes, and every one of them focused on these unwelcome intruders, glaring intently. Lotus and Thalrok knew they were going to have to fight their way through this, even though a fight would probably not help their cause.

"Now!" one of the disciples signalled, as he and three others pressed forward, pushing their palms in front of them. As they fully extended their arms, a giant gust of wind sent the two young men flying backward. Thalrok managed to stay mostly erect, but his feet slid across the smooth stone floor into a stretching stop. Lotus tumbled even farther away, back behind his companion.

"Ronin!" Thalrok yelled out, and he turned back to see if Lotus was all right. As his head turned back toward where Lotus had landed, it was met with the bottom of a foot that stomped the front of his metal helmet. The kick clocked him square in the face, and he was knocked backward from the impact.

"They can control the *wind*?!" Lotus panicked, rising to his feet and watching as two other disciples charged at him with incredible speed. They were nimble and swift-moving, as if they were the wind itself. The young intruder picked up his foot, about to lunge forward to dash away before it was too late. As his foot was only inches above the floor, a powerful gust of wind swept under it and pushed him backward. He crashed down on the floor, looking up only to receive a swift kick to the side of the face. Lotus's head rocked hard to the side as the broad top of the disciple's foot made contact. The ringing in his ear was louder than any sound in the room. Before any other attack could land, he rolled out of the way and sprang back up to his feet.

"Damn, that hurts!" Lotus growled, as he held the side of his face.

Now, the disciples split up evenly amongst the two interlopers, six and six. Lotus glanced over and saw that Thalrok was struggling just as much as he was. He had to think of some way to counter this power they possessed.

I can't fight and try to reason with them, Lotus thought. Then he glanced at the floor and saw a few rocks lying there that were just big enough to throw. *I've gotta try something, right?*

Dashing forward, he charged at one of the disciples in the direction of those small natural weapons. As expected, the man pushed his palms forward and sent a gust of wind directly at Lotus. He was prepared this time, and dove onto the floor of the temple, rolling below the wind to pick up one of the stones. As his body slowed from its gyrations, he rolled fluidly to his feet and instantly chucked the stone at another disciple. It rocketed through the air on a direct path to hit its target. But, with a swift, short blast of wind, the other disciple simply caught the stone inside a condensed ball of air. Then he jumped high in the air, and twisting his body, released the stone, flinging it right back at Lotus.

"You've got to be kidding me!" Lotus yelled, as he jumped out of the way, successfully dodging the rock that was aimed lethally at his head.

"You're useless in the air," one of the disciples shouted as he shot himself upward using currents of air exiting through the soles of his feet. He was right, Lotus was completely useless in the air, and he watched as the man pulled back his leg to deliver a strong kick aimed at his ribs. The airborne disciple used another rush of air to propel the flow of his kicking leg even faster. Lotus lowered his arm to brace for the attack, tightening his muscles for the impact. The sound of the blow rattled across the walls of the temple, and he felt his whole body shake.

"I'm really sorry for this." Lotus groaned, as he grabbed the man's leg before it could recoil, and pulled him in close, just before being sent flying from the kick. The disciple was caught completely by surprise, and joined Lotus in a quick descent to the temple floor. While falling, Lotus held on tightly to his opponent, twisting his body and pinning him neatly on the ground.

"Let go of me!" the disciple bellowed, as he tried to strike at Lotus's neck. Lotus was ready this time, and grabbed the disciple's wrist before he could make contact. The thwarted disciple couldn't get his feet under him, and stayed pinned to the hard surface of the temple floor.

Another disciple immediately rushed over. He was able to push Lotus back with powerful gusts of wind. The young man stumbled backward, and found himself closer to Thalrok. He could hear Thalrok's breath grow more ragged, as the titan was far too slow to match the speed of these disciples. It wasn't possible to see his face due to the mask, but right about now he would be baring his teeth, looking like a seething beast before it rampaged.

"I am sorry, but this is really starting to piss me off," Thalrok grunted; anger seemed to steam out from the slits of his mask. He lifted his arms up high into the air, let out an enraged roar, and slammed both of his hands down hard on the floor of the temple. Suddenly, the ground trembled, then quaked vigorously beneath them. Pebbles and stones from above rained down as the entire mountain top quaked. The smooth stone floor cracked and split with such force that all of the disciples resorted to their wind-control abilities to levitate up into the air. They looked like a flock of geese in an autumn sky, and the bounty hunter had an open shot.

"Take this!" Thalrok shouted. He had worked the fingers of both hands around a huge chunk of the destroyed temple floor, and now threw it with all of his strength directly at two of the closest floating disciples. In total shock, they were unable to avoid this giant rock soaring rapidly in their direction and the massive stone missile hit both of them head-on. The big piece of stone continued flying through the air, barely changing its trajectory after the apparently minor impact of the disciples' heads, until finally, it struck the far wall, rattling the whole temple as rocky debris washed across the room. Several disciples flew to the injured ones' aid, while the others kept their gaze fixed on these now-aggressive intruders.

Neither Thalrok nor Lotus had ever fought anyone who could use a power like these people, these supposedly peace-loving disciples, could. They were masters of the wind, and could use it to soar in the air, move or push people or objects, and even add power to their strikes; it was hard to tell what they might do next.

"How are you holding up, Ronin?" Thalrok gasped out, trying to catch his breath.

"I'm holding it together for now; don't know how much longer though. This whole thing isn't working out in our favor, you know?" The conflict was at a standstill. They found themselves surrounded again as they stood back to back near the center of the room. Two of the twelve warrior-disciples were now injured and unconscious, which meant that their chances of getting any answers seemed to be dwindling.

Concentrate Lotus, come on! I have to somehow get through to them that we aren't a threat and just need to ask someone a question. Easier said than done though. Lotus took a slow deep breath in, held it, then exhaled slowly. Focusing all of his energy on staying relaxed, he tried to once again pull forth the light-energy from around him to guide his way.

"Here it comes!" Thalrok shouted, as the disciples began to close in on them just like before. Lotus maintained his concentration and closed his eyes, trying to bring out even the slightest bit of light-energy. The disciples raised their arms and then began to wave them slowly side to side in unison, as they circled around the two young men. The wind that they created beneath their feet began to blow faster, in a circular motion. It grew larger and larger, blowing around Lotus and Thalrok like a tornado, surrounding them both. The disciples moved their arms faster and faster. The gusty winds picked up speed, flinging debris into the air.

"This wind is too strong, I can't see or move!" Thalrok shouted.

"Keep your footing! Don't let the wind push you!" Lotus yelled back, and he felt the pinch of rage click inside of him. He couldn't focus enough to generate any light-energy, but the second his thoughts turned negative, the dark-energy quickly lit a small spark inside of him.

"We just need to stop this tornado, we don't need to hurt them! On my mark, slam your hands into the ground again!" shouted Lotus, as he clenched his fists and pulled forth what little power from himself that he could. The wind was getting too forceful to handle, and they needed to act quickly. Pushing back against the wind, Thalrok reached his hands into the air slowly and readied himself. Lotus tried to look around at each one of the disciples, squinting to see through the dust in case any one of them might push in to stop them.

"Faster!" the disciples shouted in unison, as they stepped forward to tighten the circle.

"Now!" Lotus yelled, and Thalrok let out powerful roar, throwing his fists down. A rattling earthquake followed, and Lotus could feel the whole temple shaking. Suddenly the rushing wind around them came to a screeching halt—no breeze, no dust, nothing at all was moving in the air. It was absolutely quiet and still.

It worked! Lotus wanted to turn his head to look around, but realized that his neck wouldn't move. He tried moving every part of his body, but found that he was completely frozen. He started to call out for Thalrok, until he realized that he couldn't breathe either. As he hungered for air, frozen in place, he could see that all of the disciples before him and those in his peripheral vision seemed to be completely paralyzed.

What is happening?! Lotus panicked, but was unable to speak. He could feel his lungs aching, starving for air. He couldn't see Thalrok behind him, and had no idea what had happened to him after his attack.

"Enough." A slow, deep voice resonated throughout the whole temple. This voice sank deep into their ears as they struggled to breathe.

Within a fraction of a second, everyone gasped and took in a breath all at the same time, then fell abruptly to their knees. Lotus and Thalrok sucked in several deep breaths, immensely relieved that they could finally move their bodies again.

As Lotus turned around to see who or what was calling out to them, he realized that Thalrok's strike had never happened. The floor was the same as before; his hands had never made contact with it. Lotus looked up and saw that the giant double doors across the room were now wide open. Through the door he saw a gigantic and very old man sitting on a lofty throne. The man's hand was lifted from his lap, reaching out toward the two intruders. He appeared as though he'd been around since the beginning of time, and yet...

Was he the one who stopped us? The wanted man stood up, then helped Thalrok back onto his feet.

"The second I went to slam my fists onto the ground, my whole body was stopped right before impact. I don't know how he did it," the bounty hunter whispered. It was like a slap in the face, the amount of power that was in that old man's hands. He had barely lifted just one of them, yet he could stop someone from moving, even breathing.

"These boys... speak the truth," the old man said clearly, in his deep melodious voice. All of the other disciples' heads quickly turned in unison to their leader, more puzzled now than ever.

"But, sir, why would these outsiders break into our domain for just a foolish request? Surely they know that it is forbidden for any foreigner to ever set foot in our home here on Mt. Axi," one of the disciples challenged, with obvious suspicion.

Thalrok stood and raised his hand. "I did knock," the bounty hunter said in his defense. Lotus simply sighed, and signaled for Thalrok to kneel on the ground in respect, which, after a brief pause, he did.

The two intruders knelt down before this unknown entity, and placed their foreheads on the floor in apology for their disrespect. With this sacred temple now broken and desecrated by two outsiders, what would one feel after such insolence?

"My eyes may be old... but I can certainly see when a man is holding back his power," the man on the throne declared. The disciples turned their gazes back to the young men kneeling and bowing their heads, their noses still touching the floor.

"Holding back, Grand Sage?" one disciple asked.

Lotus's ears rang from the sound of those words; two of them were words he heard and had seen written many times about his old master.

"He's a Grand Sage?!" Lotus whispered.

The two young men looked up, but remained kneeling in respect, awaiting what was next. They could see the other disciples backing off to either side, allowing a fully open space between themselves and the Grand Sage. With each second that went by, this plan of theirs to enter a forbidden city looking for answers seemed to be the worst idea to ever come out of their heads. What had they *expected* to happen?

"Please, my children, stand," one of the elders told them. Without question, they followed orders and rose to their feet with haste. Thalrok glanced over at Lotus and noticed that he seemed a little shaken up.

"Tell me boys... No one has set foot on our sacred land for hundreds of years now... Why is it that you barged into our home... bringing fear to my people?" the Grand Sage asked.

Lotus hoped to make light of this situation, but before he could say a word, Thalrok stepped forward and took charge.

"It was my doing, sir," Thalrok said. "I am the reason that we came here today."

The elder squinted his eyes and tilted his head, hoping to hear a better explanation for this intrusion.

Acknowledging the unspoken question, the bounty hunter took a deep breath, then spoke his truth. "My name is Thalrok. I am a human raised by the mighty titans of Perlaria. I lived my whole life in the ways of the titans before I was forced to leave that village due to their customs. I was, and am, ever grateful to my titan foster mother for taking me in and making me who I am today. However, due to recent events, I came to realize that my real home probably went through some violent times, just as we have found other villages and towns who have experienced the same over the past years. I came here in search of the man who can answer any question of this world to help me return home to my family, my real family." Thalrok explained.

The room was silent as his final words echoed off the temple walls, utterly silent. The visualization of him and Lotus causing such chaos in these disciples' own private village dominated Thalrok's thoughts. And their temple—it was ruined because of him and his friend. The fact that he would now dare to expect an answer to any question after what he had done, well, that was just hilarious. But, even though the cards were not in his favor, Thalrok still put his faith in the basic humanity of these cloistered people.

The Grand Sage closed his eyes and wore a little smile, "Of course, my child."

The other disciples turned in unison to their master, completely and utterly baffled to hear those four words come from his lips. This titan-man, and his friend, had broken into their village, and had just destroyed parts of their sacred temple, and even injured some of their people. Yet, unbelievably, Grand Sage Gou was showing sympathy towards these intruders.

"Sir, you must be joking!" one elder cried out in disbelief.

"Did you not see what they did to us?" another asked in amazement.

"This can't be!" they all shouted, as they rushed to their leader.

Without saying a single word, Gou raised his right hand up ever so slightly, signaling them to stop speaking. In the same instant that his hand rose, the disciples immediately closed their mouths and all conversation ceased. He then signaled for Thalrok to step forward and stand beside his throne.

"I am the man you speak of… the one to know all of this land and its past, present, and future," Gou affirmed. Even with a helmet obscuring most of his face, anyone could see the bounty hunter's great surprise, as he came to stand in awe before this legend in the flesh.

"Listen to my words… Due to my many years in this world, I no longer have the strength I used to… Because of that, I can answer only one question, and then… I must wait quite a while to use my power again… In return for using my power now, I ask that when the time comes… You boys will return this favor with a request of my own… Do you two accept?" the Grand Sage offered solemnly.

Thalrok turned back to look at Lotus, wondering what he would say to this deal. The wanted man instantly nodded his head; he had no thought of keeping Thalrok from his deepest desire. The bounty hunter felt forever grateful for his friend's support.

"Yes sir!" Thalrok replied heartily, for them both. He was excited and prepared now for this momentous opportunity.

"Thalrok, the human titan, born and raised by the powerful titans of Titanos... One who controls the very ground beneath our feet and wielder of ancient traditions... What question do you ask of me?" Grand Sage Gou asked, looking intently, but kindly, at Thalrok.

After the countless days, journeys, and adventures leading up to this very instant, the bounty hunter would finally be able to get the answer he yearned for. Good or bad, this was what had always occupied his thoughts; and now, this was his time.

"I wish to know where the town I was born in is located," the bounty hunter asked earnestly, with deep emotion in his voice.

The Grand Sage moved his left hand from his lap and reached over to place it directly on top of Thalrok's head. Winds began to swirl around Thalrok, and a glowing light radiated from his body. The gusts of wind picked up speed as the Grand Sage closed his eyes and allowed the answer to come to him. It wasn't long until the wind died down and the light dwindled away, leaving them all waiting in anticipation. Lifting his hand from Thalrok's head, Gou opened his eyes and peered down at him.

"Far southeast of Mount Axi, you will find the mountains of the titans... then just south, in the high foothills... is a small town called Harthfield... That is your hometown." Grand Sage Gou declared in his halting deep voice.

There it was, the short but simple answer he so needed and craved. Thalrok could feel a swell of emotions swirling around in his head, like a twister of great joy. He couldn't help but shout out, "Yes! Finally, yes!" in celebration, as he clenched and raised his fists up in the air, ecstatic.

This reaction even brought out a chuckle from the Grand Sage himself. "In all my years... I never expected to meet such strange young men," he murmured, smiling to himself.

Thalrok began to thank him over and over again as he stepped back from the Grand Sage's throne. His words just streamed out all at once, without a breath taken in between. While walking back past the other disciples, he apologized to them profusely, one by one, for hurting them and for making a mess of their beautiful, sacred temple. The disciples stood there stoically with expressionless faces, still quite upset by the outsiders' actions. The fact that these strangers could break into their cloistered village, disrespect and destroy their temple, and then ask their leader to use his now-limited power angered them greatly. After all of that, seeing the huge muscular titan-man being so humble and kind toward them now, well, that was difficult to endure.

"I hate to cause any more trouble, so please, we will be off now. Again, thank you so much for your generosity." Thalrok expressed his thanks again, possibly for the hundredth time. Hoping to be respectful, he and Lotus began to walk toward the entrance of the temple planning to simply leave before they could do any more harm to Wisphire and its people. They discreetly avoided any cracks in the floor and the rocks that were now strewn about from the fracas.

"Just a moment boys." the Grand Sage said, stopping them. They paused abruptly, and turned around to see what was wrong. "I would like to use that favor of mine," he added.

The two stared at one another silently, both realizing that this was indeed the best time to use it, since who knew if or when they would return here to Wisphire. They began to walk back towards the Grand Sage, wondering what his request might be. Maybe it would be to help repair the temple or to help around town, to ensure a delivery of some sort, or maybe even to do a search-and-retrieve kind of task. They had no clue what would be expected of them.

"For my request... I would like you boys... to allow my student, young Oa... to join you on your journey... across our world of Perlaria," the Grand Sage stated. The whole room was speechless; the two young men, all of the temple disciples, and even little Oa, who, taking a break from his punishment of cleaning the temple, had hidden himself behind the Grand Sage's throne when he heard all the commotion.

"WHAT?!" the disciples yelled. They ran to Gou and surrounded their leader, all talking at once—mostly to forbid his request and ask why he would even propose such a rash and dangerous idea.

Thalrok and Ronin turned to one another with the same uncomfortable feeling, both wishing to be nowhere near *this* conversation.

"Sir, you have got to be insane!" "Have you any sense at all?" "No one is allowed to leave Wisphire!" The disciples all continued to rant, raving on and on, stating what truly would be expected reactions to this shocking plan. After all, this meant putting aside all of their beliefs, from generation upon generation, to let one of their own children roam this broken world with some random outsiders. The same random outsiders who had broken into their town and wreaked havoc. The disciples were all thinking about the laws of the village. They ignored the fact that any one of them might actually want to experience the world at large and branch out from Wisphire.

The Grand Sage could only smile and shake his head over the ruckus his disciples were making. Meanwhile, be it dangerous or not, young Oa slowly emerged from behind the throne.

Suddenly, Lotus shouted, "Yes, sir!" His voice rang out loud and clear, over and above all of the uproar. The great hall of the temple was silenced once more. Heads turned to the intruders, all hearts sinking in their chests—except for one young boy's. The young disciple, Oa, stared at Thalrok and Lotus as if they were superheroes. He had only seen them for these few seconds, but he knew that he was staring at his future.

"Absolutely not! No outsider is to break into our domain and leave with one of our people!" an angry disciple spat out.

The Grand Sage found all this shouting no longer amusing, and he again subtly gestured with his hand for all to be silent. Even though strong words ached to burst from their throats, his followers held their tongues. But still, they seethed with anger.

"Then it is settled... As of today, Oa, you are free to leave Wisphire... and follow along with these gentlemen on their journey." Grand Sage Gou peered down at his young disciple standing there unannounced by his throne—his young disciple, whose face, who at this moment, wore an expression that no one had seen on this child for quite a while.

Oa appeared genuinely excited for the first time in years. He had lost everything he loved two years ago, and the boy had never been the same since. He was late to class most days, daydreamed during his studies, seldom played with friends, and was eating less and less as the days went on.

Now, seeing Oa's eager and delighted face, the disciples swallowed their stifled angry words. Miraculously, they were witnessing a child's life being given back to him.

"Would you like to go with these boys, Oa?" the Grand Sage asked. The young disciple looked at the two outsiders one more time. What he saw was hope, hope that his remaining days still could offer him a time of joy, adventure, and dreams. His life, his very life, was there right in front of him, calling out for him to reach out and take it. He could see it clear as day.

"Yes, please!" Oa shouted, beaming with excitement.

Grand Sage Gou's eyes crinkled at the corners as he smiled down at Oa. Many of the other disciples gasped softly in wonder, as they watched this once-hollow boy genuinely smiling and truly happy again.

11

A Boy and his Dream

"**N**ow listen here... I want you to remember all that you've learned in the temple... and keep an eye out for yourself, *and* your new friends... Wisphire will always be here for you when you want to come home..." The Grand Sage spoke seriously but kindly, as he watched his young student struggle to keep his feet planted on the ground.

With the wind against his back, and hope in his heart, Oa's hand gripped his bo tightly. The entire village had turned out to wish him well on this wild adventure, which not one person before him had ever even considered. For everyone else, this was just another normal day—a day that would repeat endlessly, bringing a future beyond change. Oa was leaving that repetitive certainty, and safety, behind. Most of the village disciples fully trusted their wise Grand Sage's decision, plus, the joyful glow that now surrounded Oa also helped them to push aside any concern or worry that they might have.

Oa looked up at the Grand Sage and the elders, his teachers, for the last time in what could be many years. Then he gazed past everyone, visualizing himself, a lone boy, making his way down toward the gates of the village where his new friends, no, new *family*, awaited him. No one had set foot beyond those gates for centuries, and now it was time for him to see what called to him with such power. He had already said goodbye to little Reggio, who would stay in his home to be cared for by a new family. Only a very few of his belongings went with him.

Just as the sun could not be stopped from its journey across the sky, there was no stopping this boy and his dream. Oa set out down the path. As he neared the gates of Wisphire, all of the temple's elders watched him grow further from staying. It would be a hopeless effort to stop him, and an even more hopeless effort not to trust their most wise leader.

"Why? Why did you let him go, sir?" one of Oa's teachers asked. There was no response. The elders turned around to face the Grand Sage, who seemed lost in thought. They called to him, asking what was wrong. But Gou simply ran his fingers down his chin, then exhaled through his nose slowly, staring up at the ceiling of the temple.

"That man that was with the bounty hunter... He is a broken soul with the flower of life blooming from inside him... He is a wanted man... haunted by people whom he cares so much for." Gou said thoughtfully. When they heard the words "wanted man", the elders began to worry for their young student, and wondered even more why Oa had been allowed to leave with those two strangers.

"Please compose yourselves... Through time, and because of that wanted man... our young Oa will play a big part... in the future of our entire world." Grand Sage Gou reassured his elders.

In the last few hours, these disciples, the elders of their temple, had fought their first battle since time beyond memory, and they had lost a member of their tribe to outsiders— just not in a way any of them expected. In the distance, they saw Oa taking his final steps in the village of Wisphire, then walk out through the gates of their village, making history.

* * *

"So your name is Oa, right?" Lotus asked, as the jagged, steep way to the plains below tortured their feet and legs.

"Yes, sir! What's your name?" Oa asked. Unbounded curiosity about everything was coursing through his veins. With each step they took outside the village, the energetic boy's eyes darted all around. It was a side of the world he had simply never experienced; everything was fresh and new to him. The only thing with him that was familiar was the bo staff that his father and mother gave him a year before they left him.

"You can call me Thalrok, and this one, goes by Lotus." The bounty hunter introduced them both by name as he led the way down the mountain.

"You mean, like the flower?" Oa asked, tilting his head. Thalrok couldn't help but snicker the moment the boy asked. Lotus reached down, picked up a rock, and tossed it at Thalrok's helmet, sharply ringing his ears. Thalrok flinched the instant it hit him, then let out his barely contained laughter in huge guffaws.

"I'm sorry, I deserved that," he apologized, trying to stop laughing and look remorseful.

Lotus shook his head while exhaling slowly through his mouth. Like a little brother might, Oa laughed as he watched the two tease and banter with one another like old friends. He was hoping that they could all get that close as their journey went on.

"So, why is your name Lotus? Did your parents just like that flower?" Oa asked, not knowing anything about his past, or the part about him being wanted.

Lotus skipped a step, and hesitated before putting another food forward. An important realization struck him; he understood that if there was to be any trust created within this group, he would have to be totally honest, starting now. Thalrok could sense troubled feelings brewing in Lotus, and turned around to see if he was all right.

"Oa, what I'm about to tell you might discourage you from continuing with us across Perlaria. If you want to turn back, I understand, but it would be best that you know this now." Lotus spoke calmly to prepare the boy as they continued picking their way down the mountain. He took the lead now, and Thalrok held the rear as they got closer to the plains. The boy was a bit confused about what Lotus was going on about, but being curious, kept his ears open.

"My name is not Lotus. My real name is Ronin. I was banished from my hometown years ago for a crime I would commit in the future." Lotus began. "They decided to tie me up, secretly cart me out of the town, and abandon me in the wilderness to die all alone." The prevailing mood abruptly dropped to a level as low as hell itself. Oa's mouth gaped open, and his hand suddenly tightened on his staff.

Lotus continued candidly, "I was only eight years old when I was left for dead, until, after a few days in the wild, I was found by my master, Din, the elder of Petalbrooke. He took me in and raised me as his son. He taught me how to fight, and how to harness a special ability that is all my own. It wasn't till I was twelve years old that a stranger came into town, and murdered Master Din right in front of my eyes. I went into a fit of rage and confronted him before he could leave. I fought my hardest, but it wasn't enough; the murderer destroyed himself right before my eyes and my beloved master's life had been ended. Everyone in Petalbrooke thought I had killed him. A few weeks later, the wanted posters with my name and my likeness on them were put out for all to see. I was wanted for murdering a Grand Sage, one like your master. Ever since those posters went out, I shed my name and became the last Lotus flower my master planted for this world."

Three sets of footsteps crunched the dirt and rocks as they continued to descend Mount Axi in silence. The wind picked up with a melancholy moaning, as it weaved between the rocks, scrub trees, and around the three travelers. Already, the hopeful expectations of a boy who had been isolated from the wide world were being threatened, only hours after he left his home.

Finally, Lotus said, "I have no idea what happened to my parents after I was taken and then left to die. Their faces were shocked and horrified when our town seer told my future, and that's the last thing I remember of them. To this day, I am too afraid to go back and see them have that same look. Whether or not they miss me, I became only a curse to them." Lotus finished his tale and stared off ahead, letting the hypnosis of following a path let his mind roll on freely.

Oa's eyes flickered with his own painful memories that he too had faced in his life, and not too long ago.

Then Lotus said, "This brings a person to wonder, what do your parents think about you leaving?"

The sound of three sets of footsteps turned into two when Oa abruptly stopped walking. The sound of two sets turned to one when Thalrok stopped just behind him. Lotus turned around to see what was happening, then also stopped when he saw the boy with his head down and eyes staring blankly at the ground. This was a completely different side of the excited child gifted with life outside the walls that they had left Wisphire with.

"My parents passed away two years ago. They both were really sick, and... they didn't make it." Oa looked at Lotus, briefly meeting his eyes.

Two years earlier, this fourteen-year-old boy's whole world was brought to a halt when his beloved mother and father were taken from him too soon. The whole village had tried its best to heal and save them, but they were too far gone. After their death, many days went by, but Oa refused to leave his home and move into another; he wanted to stay in the one place he remembered being happy with his family. That was, until this new home, a home outside of his village, with new friends who would be like family, opened its doors to him.

The boy wiped his hand across his face, his damp eyes had settled back to contemplate his feet. Lotus could tell that Oa was brooding, swimming alone inside of his head, like he himself used to do. He walked over to the boy, and gently rested a hand on Oa's shoulder.

"It's tough to lose someone, isn't it?" Lotus said kindly. The boy's head lifted, and he stared into the wanted man's hollow eyes.

"Don't worry, you'll fit in with us just fine," Lotus assured him. Then he patted Oa's back just once, and continued on down the hill.

The boy was speechless. He stood there and watched Lotus continue down the path. Thalrok passed by him and tousled his hair. Every day since his parents had passed on, people showed him great sympathy and felt sorry for his loss. These were kind gestures from the village folk, but it only drove him deeper into depression. For some reason, the words Lotus spoke struck him differently. Here was someone he could relate to, someone who could truly understand his pain. Here was someone who had also been through grief, and even worse agonies, but who had still survived all of these years out in the world at large. Maybe there was hope after all. So, Oa shook his head to clear his mind, then called out "Wait up!" to his new friends while he hurried to catch up.

Mom, Dad, I can't wait to tell you about all the adventures I'm gonna have. Oa sang in his head.

* * *

The three of them finally reached the bottom of Mount Axi. Lotus and Thalrok legs felt their legs burning like fire after the long journey both up and down the mountain. Right now, the hard boulders partly sunken into the ground felt more comfortable than any seat in the world.

Even as tired as he was, Oa was still amazed and appreciative of the immense forest that they had entered. Through someone else's eyes, it was a simple forest at the base of a mountain range. However, there were more trees here than this boy had ever seen in his young life.

"I swear… If I have to climb a mountain like that again… I'm gonna lose it!" Thalrok complained, as he let himself slide down from his rocky chair and planted his back flat on the ground, heels in the air. Climbing, though, was far from being off the table in this long trek across Perlaria going southwest to the village of Harthfield.

Oa stood up from the fallen tree he'd been sitting on, surveying the area. He stepped across a small stream banked by small pebbles and sandy loam. He glanced up at the treetops, neck tilted all the way back to watch the birds flying above them. He looked back down, jammed his staff into the dirt, and squatted down low to stretch his legs.

Thalrok and Lotus turned to see where their new companion went and saw him doing a bit of stretching by the stream. Suddenly, with a quick extension of his legs, and hands held parallel to the ground at his sides,

Oa shot himself up into the air like a rocket, reaching the top of the trees in the blink of an eye. The bursts of wind he created from his feet and hands blew past his comrades, flinging leaves everywhere. They were completely shocked to see him shoot up into the high canopy above them so unexpectedly. Out of nowhere, this boy had just showed them what a unique power he had at his disposal.

Oa soared up to the top of the tree line and grabbed a high branch to hold onto, steadying himself to get a better view. He could see the whole horizon in all directions as he turned in the air—hills, trees, and plains as far as the eye could see.

This is what it was like in the lands of Prosper Valley. The boy let go of the branch, and as he descended he released small bursts of air from his feet so as to land softly. He retrieved his bo staff, and returned to where Lotus and Thalrok were watching him the whole time.

"What?" Oa asked, looking at them, one eyebrow raised.

"I didn't think *you* knew how to use those crazy wind-control abilities," Thalrok remarked with a grin.

"Oh yeah! After practicing in the temple for years, I learned to create and use bursts of air from both my hands and my feet," Oa told them, showing just a hint of pride. The boy lifted one hand up and let out a light current of air towards a nearby bush. As he pushed his hand forward, the soft wind he created started to shake the bush enough so that any loose leaves were sent flying. The first time the bounty hunter and Lotus had ever seen someone with this type of power was only a few hours ago, so it was still a very new concept for them.

"How much power can you release?" Thalrok asked eagerly.

Without a second thought, Oa smirked, and asked, "Well, d'ya wanna see?"

He faced away from them, rubbed his hands together, and planted his feet hip-distance apart on the ground, lowering his stance for stability. He began to breathe more slowly and rhythmically, concentrating. He pulled both of his hands back against his ribcage and felt the swell of energy building up inside of him. As his palms thrust forward, a strong rush of wind shot out of his hands, blowing a tunneling explosion of air directly in front of him. The trees and shrubby bushes shook and rattled, as the speed of that blast bent branches, stripped leaves, and pushed small rocks through the dirt. Even the ground shook from the shockwave of force that he had produced from his hands.

"Whoa!" Thalrok shouted as he jumped to his feet in amazement. He laughed out loud at just how incredible it was to witness such an impressive ability, and in one so young. Oa was smiling from ear to ear at Thalrok's reaction, and couldn't help but blush. Lotus was without words, recognizing the great potential of this very special student.

"Ok, ok—so how *high* can you spring yourself up in the air?!" Thalrok asked excitedly, as a follow-up.

Oa fed right into his excitement, and exclaimed, "Hey, I don't really know, let me try that!"

The young disciple of Gou backed up to find a spot where he wouldn't hit anything on his way up. He knew he could keep pushing himself up into the air with multiple bursts, but he didn't know how high he could go with just a single burst. He squatted and placed his palms on the ground on either side of himself, then lifted them up vertically about eighteen inches, palms still facing down. With another deep, concentrating breath, he felt the surge grow inside of him again. He pushed his hands toward the ground and released all of the energy from both his feet and hands. Oa zipped up to the sky in no time; he was high above the trees and then some. When his upward motion slowed to a stop, he looked to be the size of a hawk scouting for prey.

Thalrok cheered and hollered as he watched the young boy reach the peak of his jump and begin descending. Oa again stopped himself from slamming into the ground by using controlled bursts of wind from his feet.

Thalrok ran over to him as he touched down, shouting, "That was incredible! I wish *I* could launch myself up to the sky like that." He gave the kid a high-five, and slapped him on the shoulder.

"I love this kid! He is somethin' special, right, Ronin?" Thalrok laughed.

Lotus stood up from his seat and walked over to the kid, nodding his head. "I will say, you've got some crazy potential, Oa." He smiled thoughtfully as he handed Oa his bo. As the boy took back his weapon, he was a bit puzzled at what Thalrok just said to Lotus, but let it rest for the time being.

It was time to begin moving again if they planned to get across Prosper Valley to Thalrok's hometown of Harthfield in good time. This was going to be a very long walk. They realized that the sun was already hiding itself away for the day, and it was time to prepare for sleep.

The three travelers found a safe spot outdoors beneath the night sky. They ate sparingly, then got as comfortable as possible while sleeping rough, and relaxed their tired muscles.

It was Oa's very first night sleeping outside of Wisphire, so it wasn't a surprise that he had a hard time falling asleep. He looked up and saw thousands of bright, twinkling stars shining above him. He was just feeling himself begin to drift off, when he heard some rustling next to him. He turned his head and watched as Lotus got up and walked over to a large tree standing alone atop a nearby hillock. He sat at the tree's base, crossed his legs, and closed his eyes. Oa wondered why Lotus couldn't sleep either, so he got himself up and walked over.

"Feeling homesick?" Lotus asked, without opening his eyes.

"A little, but I'll be alright," Oa responded, as he sat next to Lotus, leaning his back on the tree as well. The two of then sat there in silence, in the middle of the night under the blanket of stars. Oa peeked over every now and then, trying to see if Lotus was really trying to sleep or if he was maybe concentrating or meditating.

"Could I ask you something?" Oa asked quietly, after some minutes had passed.

"Sure, what's up?" Lotus responded, eyes still serenely closed.

"I know you go by Lotus, but... I was wondering why Thalrok still calls you by your old name?" Oa asked hesitantly.

Lotus slowly opened his eyes to glance over at the sleeping bounty hunter. Thalrok was sprawled on the grass with his helmet still on his head, as always. "Thalrok refuses to call me the name of a flower. It's as simple as that." He chuckled a little under his breath, and closed his eyes again.

"Doesn't that make you upset?" Oa wondered.

"I trust Thalrok. I know he is calling me by that name just for me, and it doesn't sound the same as how my name used to sound when other people said it," the wanted man answered.

Oa then looked over at Thalrok and saw the sparkle of stars shine off his helmet, which prompted him to ask, "And what's with the helmet thing?"

"That's just a titan thing that his tribe does. It would be better to ask him in the morning." Lotus answered, and then fell silent.

Oa felt that maybe he had asked too many questions and that maybe he was interrupting Lotus from something at this point. So, he stood up from his resting spot by the tree, and stepped back towards their campsite in hopes of getting some sleep.

"Hey, Oa." Lotus softly called out. The boy stopped in his tracks and turned back toward the tree.

Then Lotus said, "As we travel across the world, you're gonna see a lot of things and people you've never seen or heard of before. The hardest part is learning that not all of them are kind, like you are." Oa felt that nervous feeling filling in his chest again.

"But no matter what happens," Lotus continued, "don't be afraid to ask as many questions as you like. Never be afraid." The corners of his mouth turned up in the hint of a smile.

The tight feeling in Oa's chest flushed from his body at those words, and he smiled back at his new friend. He went back over to the campsite and lay down on the thick, weedy grass. His muscles felt overused, but his mind was at ease, and the thrill for adventure still flowed freely inside of him. He found himself having a hard time sleeping again, except this time it was because he was too excited for tomorrow.

* * *

"Come on, Thalrok, I know you wanna sleep, but we've gotta go." Oa heard Lotus's voice making its way into his ears as he slowly awakened. He opened his eyes to not a dark, star-filled sky, but now a bright blue lake of one. He sat up, rubbing his eyes, as he watched Lotus shaking Thalrok to get him up. Thalrok only groaned, tossing and turning on the ground, until his slurred words slowly became recognizable—"No… no, it's not time, not yet."

"Good morning," greeted Oa, as he stood up and stretched his arms up high over his head.

"G'morning Oa. Do you mind helping me out?" Lotus asked, still struggling to roust the beast on the ground, who was trying very hard to ignore him. The boy giggled as he watched Lotus prod and shake the bounty hunter with his foot. Walking over to his side, Oa glimpsed the tree from last night and noticed something different.

Were there always flowers on that hill?

* * *

Dawn broke once more, and after many days of trekking through the lands of Perlaria, the three travelers at last saw their goal before them. The roaring sounds of many waterfalls, whose source came from cliffs high above and behind Harthfield, created a backdrop of pleasing white noise. Several separate waterfalls cascaded over lofty cliffs, then a series of smaller ones, until the icy, clear streams came together and at last flowed through the town proper as a river. Bridges over some of the smaller waterfalls and streams connected all sectors of Harthfield. Several larger bridges spanned the river as well. There were homes securely planted on every accessible hill, slope, and cliff, with more homes crammed between the businesses in the downtown market area, which was near the river.

The three friends had stopped on one of the bridges near the base of a smallish waterfall in a more isolated area of town. They stared down at the splashing water below, resting their arms on the chiseled-stone parapet. The rising mist dampened their faces.

"Is it uncomfortable?" Oa asked.

"Nothing I haven't had to do before." Lotus sighed, as he stood up and readjusted the hood of his cloak. His face was now completely concealed to hide his identity. Only moments after they arrived in Harthfield, they saw a "Wanted" poster with his face on it, displayed on a public information board for all the world to see. Lotus held back those thoughts that were best kept bottled up inside, and his clenched teeth kept in the words he must not say. They had traveled all this way; he couldn't ruin things for Thalrok.

"We've been here for about 30 minutes," Oa reminded them, as he walked across the top of the bridge's parapet, balancing himself on the narrow capstones, "What's the next step?"

Thalrok leaned against the edge of the stones and watched the waves of water flow more deeply into the lower, busier part of town. His journey, his quest, was coming to an end. Here he was, in the town he had left without choice far before his memory could even register how it had happened. He brushed his hands across the flat capstones and felt the moist grit on his palms. Feeling the mist of the rushing water here was refreshing, but it awakened no memories.

"This is my real home," Thalrok said matter-of-factly. Slapping a hand on the parapet, he turned around and casually leaned back on it, looking up stoically toward the very top of the cliffs behind Harthfield.

Lotus sensed more than a little inner strife behind that tough facade he wore, and said, "Oa's right, what's next?"

Each time either of them asked that question, a knife pushed farther into the bounty hunter's heart. It was like bringing a horse to water who didn't know how to drink it. Thalrok knew just what had to be done, but found it too hard to even begin to try.

"Do you think I'd survive jumping into the water from here?" Oa asked, as he leaned a bit farther out over the edge, staring down at the falls.

"Please don't bring any more attention our way than we already have," Lotus responded, letting out a small sigh of exhaustion.

"That wasn't really a no," Oa commented, but he jumped down from the wall with a flourish and came to stand next to them. They both glanced at Thalrok, who seemed locked into his own head.

The battle in his mind was at a stalemate, "do I or don't I", and the bounty hunter just couldn't take another swing against his own self. Thalrok felt the bottled-up fear inside of him swell; he couldn't really allow his life-defining question to simply fall into a grave and be buried unanswered, could he? He felt a hand placed on his shoulder, and startled in shock. Coming back to reality, he found Lotus standing next to him.

"It might not be the answer you want to hear, but you will want to hear it." Lotus counseled his friend, comforting him with his calm and rational presence.

Thalrok took a deep breath and shook off the anxious feelings lurking in his gut. He stood up tall and took the lead, striding purposefully back toward the more populated parts of Harthfield.

During the prior thirty minutes of wandering covertly around this unfamiliar place, they had seen much of the town from atop the waterfalls and bridges. It was just like a normal town, but with streets branching across both the natural land and many bridges. Now, the trio of tourists, with Thalrok leading the charge, found themselves approaching a crowd of people who seemed to be gathering around a large stone placed in the center of a bridge at the base of the town.

"What's all that about?" Oa asked.

"I don't know, let's go check it out," Thalrok replied, as they followed the road alongside the river to another bridge. This bridge was the largest one in Harthfield. It was wide enough for many people, or even several wagons side by side, to cross at once. In the very center of it was a large slab of stone placed vertically, surrounded by a bed of flowers and small pebbles. The trio stopped in front of it, peering past the others gathered there. One by one, folks were dropping off flowers and placing them at the base of this monolith, some even crying as they walked away.

It's some sort of gravestone. Lotus noticed the many names engraved on both sides of the tall standing stone. The print was too small to read from where they stood, but he could tell that a line of words, or some verse, was etched above all of the names. As people paid their respects one by one at this monument of the lost, they departed and the crowd dwindled. The three were able to get a little closer to read the words at the top, which said: "To honor those who lost their lives after the darkest day in Harthfield."

"Darkest day…" Thalrok whispered.

"You boys must not be from here, am I right?" a slender, elderly man standing by them asked. He did not turn his head from the memorial as he spoke. Thalrok looked over. He could see that this old man's tears of pain flowed as freely as the water flowing over any of the falls in town.

"Yes, sir. We are travelers, and just happened across this place." Thalrok lied.

The man wiped tears of sorrow from his face, and turned to the bounty hunter. "This stone is engraved with the names of our fallen people, all of the ones who didn't survive the terrible attack on our village many years ago," he told them. His words were heavy with grief, his face deeply lined.

More pieces began coming together in Thalrok's head. "How many years ago was that?" he asked.

"It happened about 21 years ago," the somber man replied.

The bounty hunter's eyes glanced over each and every word etched on that stone. Not one name seemed familiar, or called out to him in any way. The only thing he could see was a catalog of hundreds of strangers' names carved there in remembrance. All of a sudden, Thalrok buckled at the knees and dropped to the ground on all fours.

"Thalrok!" Oa cried, as he hurried to go to Thalrok's side and help him. A hand suddenly jerked his shoulder back, keeping him from the downed man. The boy turned to see Lotus shaking his head, signalling for him to let Thalrok be. There was nothing was to be done for the man who was trapped inside his own head. This was the curse of a stolen past, something that many a man would fear to even think about. Yet here Thalrok was, facing it head-on and trudging back through his shattered memories.

After several moments, Thalrok raised his head. He asked the old man, who was looking at him with a puzzled look on his face, "Please, sir, would

188

you be so kind as to tell me everything you know about what happened here all those years ago?"

It seemed to be an unusual request; why would this traveler care about the long-ago attack so much that he collapsed and crumpled to the ground? Then again, the old-timer, who had lived his entire life in Harthfield, didn't know that Thalrok was originally born here as well.

"I can do that," the old man answered. "My name is Gordell. Follow me, young man. I will read to you the tales of the past." He stepped away to cross to the other side of the bridge.

Thalrok looked back at his two friends, who vigorously gestured for him to follow along with them. Quickly rising to his feet, he caught up and walked along with Gordel. He was hoping to hear everything that he needed to know about the tragedy that had happened back when he was too young for any memories to be formed and embedded.

"He was crying," Oa whispered softly.

Lotus turned his head from watching his friend follow the path to the answers he sought, and saw that Oa was watching carefully as well. The boy was quite sensitive, and could see through their friend's metal mask as easily as if he were reading a book.

* * *

"Keep your footing a bit farther apart. Then you can keep your balance better as you let out the air bursts." Lotus suggested, as he watched Oa deepen his stance and push his hand forward, palm out. This created a quick burst of wind that hit a nearby tree.

Satisfyingly, the branches rattled, and leaves twirled through the air. While waiting for Thalrok, they had gone off to the edge of the town to practice in a nearby forest. This, Lotus hoped, would not to stir up any extra attention.

"How was that?" Oa asked eagerly.

"Much better. Now, do that same attack on me." Lotus instructed.

Oa wore the same surprised expression that Stritan had when he'd been

189

told to strike his teacher. Oa turned to face Lotus and took a deep breath in. He sprang up and down on his feet, then jumped back and forth with small hops from one foot to the other as his fingers clenched tightly and then straightened as he pushed out both palms.

Lotus watched Oa's feet follow the same order and rhythm over and over again. "Left, right, left, right," he observed, as he waited for those agile movements to work their magic. As Lotus predicted, the boy let out a snappy gust of air from his right foot and flew straight at him. Oa was quick as a flash, but his moves were readable, so Lotus twisted his body out of the way to let Oa breeze right past him. Feeling the wind sweep by his face, he watched the kid use small gusts from hands and feet to push himself off from a non-existent wall and rebound right back towards him. With another twist and step, Lotus barely dodged that one. Like a ball bouncing around a room, Oa used bursts of air to keep pressing back at his opponent with a wide range of attacks.

"Gotcha!" Oa shouted, as he came soaring in straight for Lotus's lower back. Feeling that the flattened top of his foot was about to make contact with his back, Oa swung his leg through the air to land the strike. But suddenly Lotus jumped up, dodging and letting Oa's foot and leg sail on past him. Startled and confused, Oa unraveled himself, but he began to lose his balance in the air. Lotus grabbed him by the arm and then tossed him over his shoulder, all while staying airborne. Oa was nearly flung into a tree, but he quickly stopped himself with a burst of wind. As he planted his feet on the ground, he turned back to his opponent with a smile on his face.

"I'll get you this time." Oa chuckled.

Lotus froze in place for a moment. His eyes glazed over. He saw the walls of Petalbrooke's dojo close around him with the feeling of that smooth floor beneath his feet with sunlight coming in through the open back door. "I'll get you this time!" young Ronin yelled, as he chased down his master, desperately wanting to land just one hit after all these days of trying. The smell of the flowers filled his nose, and he felt that same breeze go through his hair just as it had on those warm summer days.

The breeze got stronger, and as he snapped back to reality, the force of a solid punch crashed into his chest and pushed him, stumbling, back on his rump.

"Gotcha! I gotcha! Finally, I landed a hit!" Oa cheered in triumph, jumping up and down.

Lotus sat on the ground, coughing and wheezing as he tried to catch his breath from the sudden shock to his system. He'd been totally distracted and caught off guard, resulting in him taking a pretty darn hard wallop.

"Nice one, kid," he gasped, as he stood up and brushed himself off. Oa was still celebrating to himself, as Lotus looked toward the town again. It had been a while since Thalrok went with that kind old man from the village; who knew how long he'd be gone.

"Why did we let him go by himself?" Oa asked, now also peering over toward the town. Lotus paused, wondering what answer would make the most sense.

"This part of the journey is Thalrok's, not ours. It would be wrong for us to intrude on his path to discover the truth of his own life." Lotus answered.

Oa jumped to grab a branch, then pulled himself up to get a seat atop it. He watched the people walking around Harthfield, looking as if they had been doing the same thing for years. No matter how different the land, people, or time, they looked the same as the people where he came from who lived a predictable, routine life. It was all so different and yet so similar.

Oa piped up, "The elders taught me something similar to what you said."

Lotus looked at the young boy, kicking his legs in the air as he sat on the swaying branch.

"Others cannot journey alongside a man when his destination can only be reached by that man's own resolve." Oa recited sagely, "That's what they taught us." Then he leaned back, flipped over onto his feet, and asked, "Can we keep training?"

Without hesitation, Lotus detached his gaze from Harthfield, and readied himself for round two. Sharp gusts of wind flew across the forest as they kept one another on their toes. Oa had always trained with basically the same students and under the same teachers day after day. Never once had he trained with someone who fought like Lotus before. Lotus's style was unique and unpredictable. Sometimes, he was extremely quick and surprising with his strikes; other times, he was stable, and sturdy like a wall. But, however he was moving, or from whatever stance he took, he struck hard. Their training session soon ran into the late afternoon, and the bounty hunter was still in town, learning, they hoped, all that he needed to know about his true home.

It was near dusk when Oa quickly jumped up from where he'd fallen after their last skirmish, pointed, and cried out, "He's back!" Lotus wiped the sweat from his face and saw Thalrok approaching. He seemed to be walking normally, without dragging his feet or slumping his shoulders. That seemed to be a good sign.

"So, did you find what you came here for?" Lotus asked. Thalrok walked over and sat on a nearby stump, resting his arms on his knees. He stared intensely at the ground, feeling relieved from the strain of the past hours of questions, talking, and sharing information. It felt a little like the tiredness he experienced after physical exertions. Letting his body or mind relax after overusing it sometimes left him feeling both restful and restless, like now.

"I didn't recognize any name on that stone, not a single one. One of them was certainly my family's, maybe even my own name was there. I have no way of knowing at this point." Thalrok was still locked into this spiraling twister of a mystery as to where his family might be if they still lived. They could be here in Harthfield, relocated to who-knew-where, or maybe they had passed away during, or even after, that raid years ago.

What can I say to help? Lotus knew all too well that Thalrok's feelings weren't easy for him to bear.

"But you know what?" Thalrok suddenly spoke, "Gordell, the old man I talked to, was shocked to find out that I was born here in Harthfield all those years ago. He was surprised that I was able to somehow live on after what happened here to these people. I explained to him how I was taken in by the Titans, how they took care of me and taught me their ways until I had to leave and could live on my own. He didn't know who my parents were, and the list of names and scanty information was too broad make any assumptions. But then Gordell told me… he told me that he knows, alive or dead, my parents would be proud to see how their son had turned out, and that he had finally come home."

The three travelers sat together quietly in the lush greenery, the wind whistling lightly through the trees. They felt one with nature here, and already quite close in their connection with each other despite the relatively short time they'd been together.

Some minutes later, Thalrok spoke again. "I know that this wasn't the big answer I hoped to get, but it was good. It helped me so much, and I'm glad I came here after all this time. Thank you very much, both of you." Thalrok stood up from the stump and bowed his helmeted head to his friends.

Oa smiled as he jogged over to pat Thalrok on the shoulder, and told him to knock it off with that serious stuff. Lotus walked over to him too, relieved to once again see the same bounty hunter he had fought with all those weeks ago, now with a lot of that lingering pressure off his shoulders.

Night was creeping in, and it was too late to travel anywhere. So the trio decided to get a room at an inn in Harthfield, and then head out in the morning once Thalrok was ready. They had no reason to rush to leave, but the bounty hunter for one, knew that Lotus couldn't stay here for very long. At some point, someone would have questions about the cloaked man who stayed here among them but never showed his face. All three wanted to avoid any more commotion in a town that had gone through so much grief in the past, but they figured that staying just a night or two shouldn't arouse too much suspicion.

That night...

"Someone—help!" a voice shouted from outside.

Lotus's eyes shot open. He flew out of bed and raced over to the nearest window. The torches lighting the streets seemed to burn brighter than usual and the streets were shiny with the presence of fear once again. He pushed the window open and stuck the top half of his body outside, looking down the alley toward the main streets that ran alongside the streaming water. He couldn't see what was going on, but noticed several people hurrying in one direction.

"What's happening?!" Lotus yelled in alarm. He threw his clothes on without a second to waste, and ran straight for the door. It felt like his pounding heart was trying to leap out of his chest; panic coursed through him. Throwing the door wide open, he dashed straight out of his room. Like a pebble flung against a large wall, Lotus slammed right into Thalrok, who was waiting just outside his doorway.

"You heard the screaming, right?! Come on, we gotta see what's going on!" Lotus panted, as he took a step to lead the way. Thalrok grabbed the back of his collar and pulled him up quickly. Coughing from the sudden tightening around his throat, Lotus turned around, his face full of confusion.

"What are you doing? We need to go!" Lotus cried out frantically.

"No, *you* have to stay," Thalrok explained calmly. He let go of Lotus, then placed a hand on his shoulder to soothe his friend's heroic heart. "You are a wanted man. Whatever happens, you will be exposed, and then hunted regardless of anything else. Please stay here, and let me and the kid handle this one." Thalrok spoke softly, placing his fist on Lotus's chest and pressing gently.

Unable to speak, Lotus saw the bounty hunter turn to run out of the inn with Oa, who had appeared beside him, bo in hand. He went back to his room and watched from his window until his friends were out of sight. Gripping the scarred wooden windowsill tightly, he stood motionless in anger and frustration. Though bad feelings surged through his mind, he was finally able to stop himself from leaving to follow after Thalrok and Oa.

"It looks like there's something going on at the lower part of the town, a little past the main entrance!" Oa shouted from the rooftops as he hopped lightly from the ridge of one roof to another. With the power of the wind from his feet, and well-placed jets from the palms of his hands for balance, he could move swiftly across the top of the houses, getting closer to the action.

"Go ahead without me!" Thalrok shouted back, as he ran down the streets behind young Oa. The voices got louder, as now people were running back in the opposite direction, rushing toward and by Thalrok with fear contorting their faces.

Oa was searching for the source of the disturbance from the rooftops, when finally, he saw a group of differently dressed people along with some of the townsfolk standing in a circle around them. Someone near the center was yelling out to everyone. The people of Harthfield were cowering in fear, with every eye locked onto one of their own, a girl of maybe sixteen years, being held around the neck by some ruffian's arms.

I... I have to do something. Oa took in a deep breath and placed one foot on the ridge of the rooftop and then pushed forward, leaping towards the edge. With a burst of speed, he released a whirlwind of air from his feet and flew straight into the center of the ruckus.

"I'll give you all five more seconds! Five... Four..!" the vicious man shouted, counting down as he tightened his grip on the girl's throat with his forearm. Kicking and crying, she squirmed around as the breath left her body.

"Three!... Two!..." the man continued.

A sudden rush of wind blew past them all as the rocketing heel of a foot smashed into and across the aggressor's face. Everyone's eyes went wide with surprise, as they watched this child of the wind knock down a grown man with one kick. The ruffian's arm came unwrapped from the innocent girl's neck and he fell backward onto the ground, clutching his face. She fell to her knees, freed, and quickly crawled away to her family, sobbing with fright.

The other oddly dressed strangers yelled out in alarm, "Captain!" as they watched, horrified, as their leader slammed down hard onto the stony road. The townspeople now focused on this boy who had just flattened the captain of these bullying strangers. The boy stood with his gaze locked on the fallen captain, pointing at him with his staff.

"Stand up. Explain yourself, right now!" Oa spoke with a firm tone. His words came out sounding like a mighty warrior might, not some sheltered sixteen-year-old kid.

The two other strangers stood beside Oa in disbelief, unable to move at all from the shock of his drop-in attack. Oa swung his bo smoothly over the closest one's head, then in an arc parallel to the ground, sweeping him off his feet. As he toppled, Oa pushed his palm toward the side of his ribs and released a dense gust of air, which sent him flying across the street and into a wall. With Oa's back turned, the other stranger swung his sword at the boy's neck, but just in time, Oa twirled his bo around his body and ducked underneath the blade as it sliced through the air.

"You missed," the boy mocked, slapping the bo hard against his opponent's stomach. The sound of the hit pinged in the man's ear as his body hunched over from the stinging strike. Then Oa pulled back the staff and jabbed it into the ground, holding it tightly with both hands. Spinning around the wooden weapon, he lifted himself off the ground and kicked his foot out as he swung back around. He landed a solid heel strike to the back of the man's head, and the second opponent was out of the fight.

Oa landed gracefully on the stone road. This was just the beginning of his assault on these thugs, and he stared intently at his next target.

"You son of a—!" one of the grunts yelled, as he charged at this young disciple of Gou. He took only one step forward before being abruptly grabbed by the shoulder and yanked back. Falling to the ground, he looked up to see what had stopped him. The first thing to enter his field of vision was a fist the size of a dinner plate. Thalrok's mighty punch crashed into his face with no time for any reaction on his part.

Rage burned inside the bounty hunter as he locked eyes with the next thug and reached for his sword. With a quick yank, the straps unlatched, freeing the immense metal blade. Thalrok took the sword in both hands and slapped the flat side against the stomach of the grunt next to him.

The man's body folded forward, wrapping around the sword as Thalrok pushed through, sending him flying into the nearest building. The wall shook and crumbled inward as the man crashed into it.

"Cease your attack, or else!" a commanding voice called out. Both Oa and Thalrok looked over to see seven villagers being held at knifepoint, totally at the mercy of the dark blades pressed to their throats. Thalrok's blood boiled even more as he gripped his sword tightly.

"If any of you move, I'll make the call, and these innocent people will all die," the firm voice informed them, and a tall, slender man strode coolly past the other thugs into the bright torchlight. He had an evil smirk on his smug, angular face, and piercing, cold blue eyes which missed nothing of the scene before him. Long fingers flicked ashes casually from the cigarette between his thin lips, all the while his katana pointed right at Thalrok.

"Is this the metal-headed meathead that was with the brat who took your arm?" the katana-wielding man asked.

From somewhere in the back of the crowd, a short man stumbled out on bowed legs, holding onto his right shoulder where an arm would normally have been attached. The pot-bellied man's eyes flared at Thalrok even though he cowered in fear before his humorless commander.

"Th-that's him! It was him and th-the other one who took my arm," he stuttered, pointing with his remaining hand.

At first, Thalrok couldn't see it; it took him a bit to recognize the stubby man's face. But yes, it really was Mordo, who had been the commanding general of the small group of Infected Ones that took over Thristle, the town where he and Lotus had fought together.

"How the hell did he escape?" Thalrok wondered, as he watched the once-arrogant and powerful man tremble before his eyes. Then he thought, "So then, these guys are Infected Ones too? Figures, since they play so dirty." He gritted his teeth and slowly stood up straight.

Oa watched the panicked hostages crying softly, hands over their mouths. At present, more than twenty of the townspeople were being surrounded by other Infected Ones wielding weapons. Most of the other townsfolk knew what was going on by now, and they either hid or watched from what they hoped was a safe distance.

"My name is General Speral. I am here to clean up a mess that one of my equals…" he paused to glare at Mordo, "…failed to do. So before you think about hurting any more of my men, I need some answers from you. Now!" Speral demanded, as he pointed his razor-sharp katana blade towards the captured villagers.

Oa slowly began to lower his hands, palms facing the ground. His feet shuffled slowly into a better stance to hopefully get the jump on them, until suddenly that blade was pointed directly at him.

"I suggest not doing that, boy. You move, and my men will not hesitate to take action," Speral cautioned callously, glaring down at Oa.

"I have not yet seen a person with such abilities as yours. Still, a child and his stick will not put me to shame," the general added scornfully, as he'd had enough of this nonsense.

Seeing their defenders being neutralized made the townspeople worry again; the fading light of hope was ready to flicker out.

"I will ask but one time. I have no need to waste any more of my breath on you pathetic sheep. You will tell me where the man who took my cowherd's arm is. Where is Ronin?" He asked, his demeanor stern and stone cold.

Oa looked over to Thalrok, who stood frozen in place. "He's not here," the bounty hunter replied immediately.

Speral was not amused by this answer. He lowered his sword and his head, saying merely, "Hand." At that, one of the thugs restraining a hostage pulled back his arm and with one slash of his blade cut the man's right hand off. The man screamed out in pain as he dropped to the ground, blood spurting as he curled up in agony, cradling his injury.

"Stop!" Oa shouted as he went to help the man.

"Don't move!" Speral roared. Only his eyes moved back over to the kid, glaring icily. Oa stopped midstep.

The rough fingernails of Thalrok's hands dug into his palms, drawing blood. He watched angrily, but was unable to do anything without bringing on dire consequences.

"I've given you clear indication of what I'm here for. Tell me where he is, or you'll watch as each one of these people dies, slowly and very painfully." Speral warned the two.

Oa fell to his knees; he couldn't take his eyes off the poor man bleeding and crying out for help.

"Damn it," Thalrok whispered through clenched teeth. He couldn't let another one of these people get hurt. The Infected Ones would lie, cheat, steal and kill; humanity meant nothing to them when it came to advancing their cause. The titan had to either watch these people die painfully right in front of his eyes, or, turn in his friend. The clock was ticking, and he could see the look in the general's eyes grow more impatient the longer he waited.

What should I do?! At this rate there is no way to save them, and I can't just turn in Ronin! Damn it all, what do I do?! The voice in his head thundered and echoed, intensifying the frustration throbbing from within.

The general rubbed one eye tiredly and shook his head, upset at the number of times he had to explain this simple concept. "Leg." Speral barked, while he gestured with his hand to demonstrate once more that there would be severe punishment for making him wait.

A hostage was immediately tossed to the ground and grabbed by one foot. This one, another young woman, wriggled and squirmed to get away. She cried out piteously, begging them to let her go, while a jagged-edged blade began to swing upwards. All eyes were focused on them; everything and everybody else went silent. Oa felt ready to explode, his emotions a raging inferno, a typhoon of fury threatening to burst out of him. Thalrok, gasping for breath, couldn't produce any words. It was too late; he was trapped and helpless in this ruthless web of the Infected Ones' vicious infestation.

"Please, someone help me!!" the unfortunate young woman shrieked in desperation, as the dark blade began to descend.

"Enough!" a clear voice rang out, over and above all else. The blade stopped abruptly just before it could make contact with the young woman's leg. All heads turned toward that voice, which was coming from behind Thalrok. And Thalrok, whose heart had already sunk deep in his chest, knew immediately who was standing behind him. When he finally did look over his shoulder, he was the last of those present to lay eyes on the man who had put a stop to this carnage—the man who stood tall in the torchlit street.

"I'm Ronin," that man announced.

12

No Words Left to Speak

"What are you doing?" Thalrok hissed out through clenched teeth.

Lotus did not answer his question, he just walked past the titan, eyes locked on the scene ahead. Before he could get out of reach, Thalrok grabbed his arm and abruptly stopped him in his tracks.

"You don't have to do this. You don't have to throw your life away." Thalrok babbled; his loyalty for his friend knew no bounds.

Without looking the bounty hunter in the eyes, Lotus pulled his arm out of Thalrok's grip and continued on his way, saying, "Please take care of it for me." Thalrok, a bit puzzled over that request, watched as Lotus stepped farther and farther away toward his inevitable end.

As Lotus got nearer to Oa, he saw the young disciple's face frozen in horror after what he had just witnessed. The wanted man whispered a few words to the boy, patted him on the shoulder, and then made his way to the general, who stood there with a proud smirk, basking in his triumph.

"So this is the man who made our once-cocky Captain Mordo tremble in fear for days when *he* was the one made to experience those nightmares. I can't say that I'm scared. I'm only disappointed that my comrade lost to such a weak-looking man." Speral snarled, spitting on the ground in disgust. Face to face, they stood, one with a wicked smirk and the other emotionless and stoic.

"I have a deal to propose to you," Lotus said, in a calm, unwavering voice, as he held Speral's gaze.

"Oh, do you now?" Spiral laughed, looking around smugly at the obvious advantage he had over them and the other villagers. "Please, enlighten me on this deal you have for me."

"You obviously came to Harthfield because you were tracking me down. You have no quarrels with these people, so I offer this to you; if you leave these people alone, I will go with you, no struggle and no resistance." Lotus proposed.

The offer was set. The next move was now in the hands of the aggressor.

The smile on Speral's face dimmed like the flickering light of an oil-starved lampwick; his earlier amusement subsided. He seemed to be even more aggravated at the thought of someone telling him what to do. But momentarily, his smile grew twice as big as it was before. It was a cruel and devious grin, as if some monster hiding inside of him was pushing its way to the surface.

"Fine, fine. I'll take that offer," the general chuckled, as he placed his weapon back in its sheath.

Lotus's heart, lodged in his throat, began to ease back into his chest in relief. He began to feel himself breathing again after holding his breath in dread.

"However, just in case you want to try anything funny, these folks are coming with us on our little trip." Speral pointed at the hostages, who began to cry softly once again, after believing only moments ago that they were finally saved.

Lotus had no choice; he had gotten Speral to agree to his offer, but the man didn't seem like the one to negotiate any more than he already had.

"Alright." Lotus presented his wrists forward to be shackled together. A grunt pulled some rope from his belt and tied Lotus's arms together. One by one, the hostages were tied up and moved as a group to the carts that the Infected Ones had come in on. The convoy was made up of at least sixteen horses pulling eight carts, some of which were open and others closed and more carriage-like.

The remaining people of Harthfield who'd been surrounded by the thugs were freed. They were left to run back to their homes and hide with their families while the raiders finished packing up to leave. Thalrok and Oa, however, didn't move a muscle; they just stood still, staring at the ground in defeat. Every Infected One, whether injured or not, prepared for their trip back to wherever they had come from, taking along the wanted man of Perlaria and the innocent villagers, who wondered if this journey would be their last.

The moon graced the travelers with a cold aura of light from the sky, casting soft shadows below. The soft crackling of the torches in the streets could be heard under the chattering and crying of the townspeople as they tried to process what had just happened. Those who knew the hostages watched helplessly as the last of them faded off into the distance. They cried loudly and mourned the loss of their loved ones.

Thalrok and Oa finally walked back to their rooms, no words left to speak. Both boys passed Lotus's room, then Thalrok stopped. He reached for the doorknob, hesitating for a heartbeat, before turning the handle and walking inside. The room was in good order, with just the bed sheets tossed around from Lotus springing out of bed. The cloak he wore hung up on the back of the chair and…

"His sword." Thalrok's eyes widened, as he noticed that the sword that Lotus so lovingly protected was sitting out openly on top of the desk. It was then that Thalrok remembered the last words Lotus spoke to him, "Please take care of it for me." The bounty hunter reached out and ever so gently picked up the fragmented sword in its saya, looking at the intricate design of the lotus petals etched so carefully with the words "Our Hero" inscribed near the bottom. He turned around with the sword in his hands and saw Oa standing in the doorway with a serious look.

"Lotus told me something before he turned himself in," the boy relayed.

* * *

The inside of the locked carriage shook and rattled on its journey across the bumpy surface of Perlaria. These sensations were all too familiar to the wanted man; he found himself tied up and being taken away once again. Yet, he seemed to be calmer now than the last time. Some of the cracks of this moving wooden cell let in the moonlight, which gleamed on the inner walls when the clouds allowed. The undercurrent of moans and cries from the people locked inside with Lotus was background noise that continued on even as they grew farther from Harthfield. Their carriage led the procession, with all of the others following behind. If anyone were to escape, it would be easy to notice and to catch them, despite the darkness. General Speral had taken it upon himself to ensure that this package would get back safely along with the hostages. Lotus could hear their voices above them; it was the general and that one-armed captain, Mordo, who he and Thalrok had fought against at Thristle.

"Th-Thank you, Speral," said a tremulous voice.

"If you speak another word about this, I will report what happened in the village you were stationed in. I will report how you lost far too easily to this "wanted man's" curse. You're lucky this news was never brought back up to the others. Suppose the master had known that you had lost so many of our men. He would have ended you on the spot. Just be happy I was able to rescue you out of that cell." Lotus could hear them rambling on about the next few steps of this mission now that everything so far had gone according to plan.

Meanwhile, at the back of the caravan, all seemed quiet. "Looks like we're stuck on caboose duty again," an Infected One complained to his colleague. The other grunt just sighed and shook his head. These two were responsible for the safety and maintenance of the carriage full of supplies for the trip, which was positioned last in line. The caravan had been traveling around long enough prior to reaching Harthfield to use up half of their rations already.

"I'm glad we're going back already. This long journey has bored me out of my mind; we've been the ones holding down the back of the line every time. Are ya ready to get back to—" He turned to look at his partner, who wasn't there. A second later, the realization kicked in.

"What the—?" He jerked his head around to see if his partner had just fallen back or even completely off the cart, but he was nowhere to be seen. The now lone One immediately reached for the horn which would signal to those in front that something was wrong. Then, all of a sudden, something zipped past him in a blur. Spooked out of his mind, he took a deep breath and was ready to blow into the horn when a giant hand completely covered his mouth. All he could hear from behind him was a soft shushing sound as he was pulled into the back of the cart.

"What was that?" someone in the carriage just ahead of them asked.

"Probably just the horses," another said, just as the two of them felt a swift brush of wind blow over their necks, giving them both chills down their spines. The moonlight had dimmed.

"Damn, where did this wind come from? I hope it doesn't start to rai—" In the same moment the grunt tried to finish his sentence, that same blur tackled his partner, then disappeared into the shadows. His traveling companion was gone instantly, without a sound or any sign at all of what had happened.

"What the hell?!" Just as fear began to close in on him, the fourth thug was dragged from his post and consumed by the night.

"Hey," a man whispered. He called out again until Lotus opened his eyes and looked at him. The man sat on the opposite end of the carriage, checking to make sure no one above them could overhear him.

"You're the guy on that wanted poster they keep putting up, right? How are you so calm? These guys are gonna kill you, y'know," he whispered.

All eyes turned to the man sitting with his back against the wooden wall of their cell, staring serenely up at the ceiling. The carriage bounced around aggressively as Lotus closed his eyes once again, letting his head sink as if he were resting.

"Don't worry about me. All is safe," Lotus replied, his whispered reply barely audible under the sounds of the horses' hooves clopping on the rocky ground. The hostages began to look around at each other, their questions unanswered, and quite confused as to why this young man, who was sure to be killed, was still so relaxed.

It shouldn't be too long now.

All Lotus had to do was wait for the—

"General Speral!" a voice shouted from what sounded like a few carts back. The blaring of a horn blasted through the air, and the carts and carriages all came to an abrupt stop. The hostages tumbled into one another on the floor of the carriage, wondering what was going on.

"They're here," Lotus whispered, opening his eyes and turning to the door of the carriage.

"What is going on back there?!" General Speral shouted, peering blindly out into the darkness. A lone grunt ran up to the front of the line, gasping for air as he tried to warn the general.

"Please, sir… It's an ambush… We've been—" Before he could finish his sentence, another blur came from out of the shadows and, in a flash, abducted the man. Now, the general was spooked. He had just witnessed his man abruptly taken by something or someone that was lurking there in the darkness.

"So, the fools came back." Speral groaned and rolled his eyes. He rose from his seat and stood atop the carriage.

"W-what's going on?!" Mordo stuttered, cowering in fear. The hostages heard someone walk on the carriage roof above them and stop near its center. Speral felt another swift breeze brush past him. The general turned around quickly, only to see that his spineless cowherd was gone.

"That fool." Speral scowled. He took a deep breath and closed his eyes, letting his ears decipher each and every sound they picked up. Turning his head left, then right, he was waiting for that quick-moving monster to go right for him, the big boss. He felt his arms grow heavier as the nerves inside his arms began to wiggle and squirm under his skin. Speral chuckled; the attack coming at him was easier to read than a child's book. "I don't think they know who they are dealing with," Speral said, as both of his arms peeled into three parts, each one coated in swirling, dark energy. The general's arms whipped around his body like tentacles, all covered in pitch-black malice.

The one who danced around in the darkness came very close to landing his final strike, when he witnessed Speral's terrifying transformation. Oa was too fast to stop himself and had charged full speed into the general's back. He was grabbed by the throat and stopped dead in his tracks by dark tentacles that reached out for him and wrapped tightly around his neck, squeezing harder and harder.

"I caught you, little birdie. No more flying around for you, kid. It would have been best if you'd stayed back in Harthfield. Now, where's the meathead?" Speral asked Oa, while the boy scratched at the horrible tentacles, trying to free himself. Oa's legs kicked wildly as he pushed air from his hands and feet, trying to escape somehow, but, it was useless.

"I'm right here!" Thalrok yelled.

Speral turned his head toward the voice coming from the other side of the carriage and saw the titan's mighty sword flying like a javelin directly at him. The tentacles of his other arm wrapped around the blade, stopping it only inches from his face. He chuckled at their childish attempt to save their friend, and looked past the immobilized sword, but he saw no bounty hunter in that direction. Then, the carriage began to shake violently, and it was suddenly knocked over on its side, making the general stumble to keep his balance. The tentacles' grip on Oa's neck loosened enough for him to wriggle free, and he dashed away before they could grab him again.

The general jumped down from the overturned carriage and saw Thalrok holding two of its wheels which he tossed like frisbees at his head. The powerful thrashing tentacles immediately shattered them into pieces.

"You two came back; how heartwarming," he chuckled sarcastically. Oa came out of the shadows and stood beside Thalrok, blocking Speral off from the hostages still inside the cart.

"It looks like you two decided you want to take drastic measures here. Fine by me." Speral snarled, as the tentacles of his arms and hands began to stretch farther from his body, whipping the ground and slicing anything they touched.

Thalrok and Oa prepared themselves for battle. They would refuse to let anything pass them. "Bring it on!" they yelled in unison.

The crooked smile grew on Speral's face as he felt a manic drive to slaughter these enemies kickstart and grow inside. His pupils dilated and his feet dug into the earth; he charged right for the two of them, laughing out loud. As the general's foot first stepped forward, Thalrok slammed his own foot onto the ground, which then jolted and quaked. Even though the earth was shaking beneath their feet, Speral kept running straight for them, eyes locked on his targets. His black tentacle-arms thrashed around him, slicing and whipping anything in his way. Speral paused as he neared them. He pulled all of his tentacles back to either side of himself, then swiped them horizontally in toward each another. Oa quickly jumped high into the air to get out of the way, and Thalrok held firmly held onto his sword vertically, keeping it between himself and the attack. The slithery tentacles coiled around the blade and attached snugly to its metal frame. The bounty hunter couldn't actually see Speral because his sword was blocking his view, but he could hear him laughing to himself with the cackle of a devil. That smug smirk, and the haughty, cold look Speral always wore was just a ploy, a decoy even. Hiding behind that face was a psychopath who was ready and just waiting for the signal to be given for him to let loose and destroy anything or anyone in his way.

"These things are so strong!" Thalrok yelled, and he struggled to hold onto his sword as it was being pulled away. He lifted one leg up and crashed his heel into the ground, causing another massive shockwave beneath their feet. While Speral was trying to keep his balance, Thalrok grunted and used his incredible strength to swing his sword straight back, lifting the general off his feet and into the air. Speral's tentacles still gripped the sword as he was hurled upwards. Thalrok yanked his sword back down, which flung the general into a rapid arc directly toward him, much like playing with a child's paddleball toy. The bounty hunter pulled his arm back and launched a solid left hook at Speral's face as he came crashing down. Thalrok's fist slammed against that face hard, like a meteor smashing into a planet's surface. As Thalrok watched his massive strike land, he saw that Speral's head twisted with the punch, but not his eyes. Speral's eyes never looked away from Thalrok's. Chills ran down the titan's spine, and for a brief moment, the general's fixed glare made his muscles feel frozen in place.

"You call that an attack?!" Speral's voice was muffled as his lower face was full of fist. The general let go of the sword with half his tentacles and wrapped them around Thalrok's left arm, which had just punched him so effectively. The general then simply let himself fall back from the punch, and swung underneath the titan's arm. Thalrok was wide open on that side. He saw Speral quickly unwrap the other tentacles from his sword and tangle them together to form one giant fist. This fist was the size of Thalrok's head, and it came smashing into his helmet, knocking it, and him, forcefully down into the dirt.

"Just like I said, pathetic!" the general laughed even louder as he felt the ground tremble.

Thalrok's head rattled inside his helmet as it sunk halfway into the earth. His whole head ached, and he cried out as he blindly reached for his blade. Speral stood over him, kicking him in the ribs and telling him to get back up and fight.

"You heard me! Get up, weakling! Show me all that spirit you had a second ago!" the general roared. Then he felt a gust of wind at his neck, which brought an even bigger smile to his face. Speral slowly peered over his shoulder and locked eyes with that jumpy kid who could dart around in the sky. "Oh, there you are," he whispered maliciously.

Oa was behind the general, with both arms pulled back to his sides, his palms up and directed at his target. "Take this!" The disciple yelled as he forced his palms forward, releasing a powerful burst of wind straight at Speral. Just before the gust could send him flying backward, the general speared every tentacle into the ground. The pressure of the wind struck him hard, and he was pushed backwards with great power, but the pitch-black tentacles anchored him in place.

Surprised at this last-second defense, Oa ran around in the grass, bobbing and weaving in closer to sneak in a hit. As Oa approached, Speral's icy blue gaze never left his prey. He kept a close watch on each move, turn, step, and gust of wind that the kid released from his body.

Oa's maneuvers were like a book just begging to be read. At last, Oa found an opening, and he made a beeline for the general.

"You're making this too easy, kid!" Speral yelled, pulling his tentacles from the dirt, ready to slice them through the air. Oa was only a few feet from his target, whose freed arms, he now realized, were too fast to get through. At this rate, each thrashing tentacle would hit him by the time his foot hit the ground.

"Wallop him, Oa!" Thalrok shouted, as he snaked his arms underneath Speral's and locked him into a full nelson. The general was caught entirely off guard with no means of escaping the giant arms of the hurly titan.

When did that oaf get back up?

"Looks like you forgot to finish your first fight." Thalrok chuckled, and held on even tighter.

Pushing off from one foot, Oa, leaped forward, and using his unique wind-assist, kicked his leg into the midsection of the crazed monster. Speral buckled forward on impact, wheezing as he felt each molecule of air fleeing from his lungs.

"I got him!" Oa cheered. But, it was as if Oa had flipped a switch inside of Speral, because suddenly those tentacles went into overdrive and began to reach out farther, swinging faster by the second.

Thalrok could feel the general's rage bubbling out of him as if he were a pot of boiling oil. His grip was getting looser; he could barely hold onto this wickedly thrashing general. "Get out, Oa! Run!" Thalrok yelled, as he struggled to hold Speral back. The tentacles reached backward now, grabbed Thalrok by the waist, and threw the bounty hunter up and across the field. Oa, still in midair, weaved out of the way of the barreling titan, who soared like a comet. Thalrok crashed into an unlucky tree which snapped fully in half as he made contact with it and then crumpled to the ground.

"Thalrok!" Oa shouted, as he ran over to help his friend. The titan didn't appear to be too severely injured, just bruised up and gasping for air.

"I'm fine, I'm fine. This tree just got in my way." Thalrok said, shaking leaves and dirt from himself. While Thalrok sat up, the two boys noticed that for once Speral was no longer staring at them. Now, he was glaring directly at the cart. The general stood before the carriage full of his hostages, huffing and puffing with anger. His mind was a whirlpool of rage and bloodlust; he knew what must be done next.

"This fight grows more annoying as we go on. I want to see carnage! I want to see pain! I want to see blooooood!" Speral howled, now with all of his tentacles extended as far as they could reach in each direction. Laughing like a madman, he swung his arms wildly and sliced effortlessly through the wooden carriage. The wood cracked and shredded into splintery fragments as he stood in front to admire the mass carnage that he'd created.

Speral inhaled deeply through his nose to get a whiff of blood he so craved, but, there was none.

Hmm?

Surprised and flushing with anger, Speral checked beneath the rubble and saw no signs that anyone at all had been inside.

"No..." he growled, as he looked down the line of carriages, his troops nowhere in sight. He turned slightly and saw one man, spotlighted by the now bright moonlight, calmly walking through the woods. "You..." Speral growled even louder, "Of course, *you* would do this."

Thalrok and Oa looked off in the distance, sighing in relief, witnessing that their plan had worked. They had distracted Speral long enough for one particular hostage to get the others to safety, right under his nose. "Thank goodness you were fast enough, Ronin," Thalrok murmured, as he stood up.

Speral's anger reached new heights in these last few moments, and he could barely keep himself composed enough to even speak. His clenched teeth were on the verge of shattering from his jaw's pressure. The very earth below his feet trembled as his inferno of rage reached out through his skin into a thick aura of raw power.

"You defeated all my men, ruined my plans, and made me look foolish! I was hand-chosen, *hand-chosen*, by my master for this mission. I will see to it that I return with you! You have interfered for the last time!" Spiral screamed. Now, his arm-tentacles all split, doubling in number. Each one slowly reached around to a different part of his clothes and pulled out a knife. Now, every thrashing tentacle wielded a small dagger in each hand, whipping even faster than before.

"I will not return unless your severed head is with me!" Speral bellowed. He ran full speed at Lotus with tentacles and blades slashing through any branch, bush, or tree in his path.

Lotus didn't move a muscle; he just kept his own blue eyes locked onto Speral's bloodshot, icy-blue, savage ones. He waited patiently for his moment to react, that split second where he would find his mark.

"Not yet…not yet…" Lotus saw the space between the two dwindle while the general's raging only got louder and louder. Then, as the madman was about to swing every blade right for him, Lotus swiftly turned and dashed away, speeding in the opposite direction. The daggers cut through the air, their target in the wind.

Speral stared down at the ground, no blood had been spilled, again! He bared his teeth like a rabid dog, seething. As his eyes darted to the left, he saw Lotus running away.

"Get back here, you coward!" the general cried out, chasing after him. He was nowhere near as fast as Lotus and began losing ground to him in the forest.

"You bastard!" Speral roared. Kicking things up a notch, the general used half of his tentacles to swing from branch to branch above the forest floor below him. The evil smile on his face reemerged as he quickly swung through the semi-darkness, getting ever closer to his prey. Even with Lotus darting or pivoting off in different directions, Speral was closing the distance.

I've got you now.

The general swung forward, pouncing for the kill. As his last tentacle left the branch, Lotus did a quick 180-degree turn and wrapped his arms around every single tentacle of Speral's left arm.

General Speral was caught off guard and had no time to dodge this trick. "Ha! You forget, I have a whole *other* side of arms!" He laughed triumphantly, and positioned his right-side tentacles to thrust their blades and stab into Lotus's back. He felt a jerk on his multiple right arms. They were abruptly stopped dead in their tracks and were... stuck? He turned his head in surprise, seeing that it was that cursed bounty hunter who was holding them back.

When the hell did he get here?!

That sneaky coward must have zig-zagged back toward his titan buddy without him noticing. With the little room he had left for his tentacles to move, he swung them around, trying to pierce through his captors' skin. Some of the blades were able to wiggle enough in their hold and cut into Lotus and Thalrok, but they refused to let go or fall back.

"What do you two plan to do now, huh?!" the general cackled, knowing they would have to let go soon.

"Two?" Thalrok questioned, as he tightened his grip.

At first confused by the bounty hunter's response, the general then realized that indeed there was still one more tyrant to deal with, and he could be seen a short distance away. Through a gap between the trees, moonlight revealed that the third tyrant's feet were planted firmly on a grassy patch with his hands drawn back behind him. He could feel the eyes of the boy locked onto him.

"You think your weak little wind-attacks can hurt me?! You are one hilarious fool! I implore you, go right ahead and try your best to get me. These two can't hold on much longer; you'd better hurry!" the general challenged Oa, mocking him from afar.

Keeping a cool head, the boy felt the familiar swirl of wind around his forearms as the pressure coming from within himself grew. He knew that his friends would hold that monster until he was ready.

Speral's arms swelled and grew a little larger as his ego inflated. Thalrok and Lotus were struggling to hold on, and he taunted, "Too scared to move now, huh? That's what I expected from a weak—". Just as his last words were about to come out of his mouth, the force of two palms striking hard into his chest took them from him.

General Speral's eyes gazed off into the distance where he saw an empty patch of grass with no boy standing there on it. As his head lolled and eyes slowly closed, he glimpsed that same boy in front of him, butterfly-palming him squarely in the chest.

How is he... that fast...

Speral moaned aloud as his body went limp. His tentacled arms withered and shrank back together to form normal arms again. Thalrok and Lotus simply let go. Speral fell to the ground, out cold and defeated.

For a few seconds, huffing and puffing was the only conversation they were able to have with one another as they caught their breath. They had endured blades and punches, and were bruised and bleeding. They took this time to accept that their plan was a success, surprisingly with very little actual planning involved.

"Here ya go. I did what you said and made sure it was safe." Thalrok reached behind him, sighed, and held out Lotus's sword, safe and sound in its saya.

The wanted man looked at his master's sword now in the hands of this giant bounty hunter, who only weeks ago had fought him and tried to take him in for the reward. Lotus's gasping breaths turned into a little chuckle as he took back his sword.

"Thank you, both of you," Lotus said, smiling warmly at his companions.

Oa turned to Thalrok and held out his hand for a high-five. "That's what I'm talkin' about!" Oa boasted, as he felt the mighty titan's large hand slap into his still-tingling palms. While the young warrior flung his hand around from the extra stinging of the slap, Thalrok laughed out loud at his reaction.

These two are something else! Lotus watched Oa bounce around, waving and flailing his sore hand, his actual pain probably greatly exaggerated.

Once Oa had settled himself down, Lotus told him, "I'm impressed that you had such quick-thinking skills in combat. I know all this was not very pleasant to see, especially for somebody who's only been out in the real world for a little while. But, I am proud of you, kid." Lotus said this quite sincerely to Oa, who broke into a big smile even as he tried to hide his embarrassment from the praise he'd been given.

"Yeah, good work, buddy." Thalrok gave Oa a friendly little shove on the shoulder. Even though it was only a tiny push from the titan's point of view, the boy stumbled backward two steps.

"Stop calling me kid!" Oa laughed, then threw a punch at Thalrok's upper arm. He was immediately met with pain in his hand, as though he'd just hit a tree trunk. The two laughed and carried on while Lotus just watched in amusement. Suddenly, an awful smell filled their nostrils.

"What is *that*?" Thalrok asked, waving his hand in front of his face. Next, they saw some particles of dust form small clouds which rose up from the ground and drifted into the air. They all looked down at the fallen general and saw that he was beginning to decay and disappear into nothingness.

"No... No way..." Lotus whispered as a flash from the past shook him to the core. The chill ran down his spine, at this unnerving, terrifying memory that flashed through his head. He felt his heart begin to race and his heart sink deeper into his chest while his throat seemed to close. He snapped himself back to reality, then turned to run back to find the other Infected Ones that Thalrok and Oa had captured. Those thugs had left bound and tied together in the forest nearer the caravan. "No, no, no..." flew through Lotus's mind.

"Ronin?" Thalrok and Oa started after him to ask what was happening, But all three of them stopped in their tracks when they heard faint laughter coming from behind them. They slowly turned around.

"You can not stop... what is already infected." Speral's voice coughed out, and he disappeared from this world and into the air in a cloud of ash-like dust.

"Please, no..." Lotus continued his way back to where the other Infected Ones from the caravan had been held. He could see a plume of grayish dust, a big one, drifting skyward in the distance.

"What's happening?" Oa asked, as neither he nor Thalrok understood what was going on.

Lotus didn't respond at first, he just let his chin drop as he held his sword tightly to his chest. He could feel the memories brush onto his hands from his head and his heart. "It was... These had to be the ones..."

215

he muttered, watching the dust vanish into the air. His friends glanced at one another, confused about what he meant.

Lotus took a deep breath, then turned around to say, "We saved the people of Harthfield. Let's get them home before the townsfolk worry anymore."

"Right!" Oa replied. He ran off to let the hostages know that they were safe and would all be going back home now. Thalrok started after Oa, but stopped as he came up beside Lotus, whose face was smeared with sorrow and pent-up anger like war paint. "Ronin?" Thalrok said, concerned.

"It was them, these Infected Ones. This group—*they* were the ones who took my master from me. I am sure of it." Lotus declared grimly.

13

The Land Skipper

ugs, tears, joyous reunions—each one of the villagers who'd been taken hostage was now safely home and surrounded by the arms of loved ones. This was becoming a recurrent theme for the wanted man of Perlaria. He helped innocent people and brought missing ones safely back to their families in all the places he stumbled upon. Yet afterward, every time he watched them crying happily and hugging one another, he knew that his curse had been the cause of their initial pain and misfortune. None of these people would ever have gotten hurt if he hadn't come to their town. A man's curse never truly leaves him. It simply lies dormant, waiting for life's circumstances to provide the opportunity for its return.

"Are you hurt?" Thalrok asked.

"Nothing too bad. You? Lotus replied as he stood beside him, watching the town rejoice and celebrate the return of their loved ones.

"Nah, that stuff just tickled," Thalrok said, with a dismissive wave.

"We really should get going." Lotus began to walk back to the inn to grab his things so he could shove off, and let Harthfield be relieved of its burden. Thalrok and Oa followed. The two of them watched the man who had just saved these people and safely returned them to their homes brood to himself as he walked, lost in his tormented mind. They passed crowds of people who roamed the streets this chilly night who were holding close to one another, their soft chatter filling the streets. Lotus passed by them, barely noticing anyone or anything.

"Wait!" a nearby voice shouted to Lotus. He stopped in his tracks but didn't lift his head or look toward the voice. Why look at someone when you already know what to expect?

"Those bad people, they came here looking for you, right?" a man called out as he stepped into the torchlight behind Lotus. Guilt began to swell even more inside Lotus's chest; it felt like the heavy hand of judgment was closing over his heart.

"From what I can tell, you must be that wanted man, Ronin, who ended the life of a Grand Sage." The words continued to jab into the cursed man's back as the sound of coarse paper unfolding came from behind him. The man who had spoken was an elder of Harthfield, and he held out the wanted poster with Lotus's face on it.

The people of the town gasped and started whispering amongst themselves. They thought they were being very quiet, but Lotus heard every word they spoke—"It really *was* him!", "I thought I knew that name when he asked!", "He's that wanted man?", and more of the same reached his ears.

Times up.

Lotus braced for the moment when he would be glared at and vilified, seen as the monster he'd been made out to be.

"Your silence must mean we are correct. If that is so, then there is something that must be done!" the elder proclaimed for all to hear.

Maybe this was the time he should call it quits. What was the point anymore, when he would always just be perceived as a murderer? A curse is a curse, and there's no helping the hopeless. Lotus let the flow of familiar thoughts take its course, then closed his eyes, just wanting all of this to end.

The sound of thick paper being ripped in two somehow lifted above all the noise in the town. People's voices, the rushing of the water as it hit the river from the falls, everything, all went silent with the tearing of that single piece of paper. Lotus's eyes opened in shock and he slowly peered over his shoulder. There he saw the elder of Harthfield destroying the very paper that condemned the name of the man who had just saved their people.

"You are no murderer. You are a hero. You and your friends are true heroes. The Guardians made a mistake; they cannot see the heroic soul that shines so clearly from you— from all three of you boys. Ronin, you are not 'wanted' in this town," the elder said earnestly. Then, with a grand gesture, he tossed the torn pieces of the wanted poster up in the air, and smiled.

Time slowed as Lotus watched the tiny bits of his past drift off in the breeze and out of sight. His eyes lowered, and he stood there among the smiling faces of the townsfolk, who continued to thank him and his two companions heartily for making the sacrifices they had.

See, Ronin, in your actions, you are *a hero. No burden from the past can stop you from becoming just what your master trained you to be.* Thalrok thought to himself, as he watched his friend being shown that despite his years of pain, brighter times can blossom.

"The man of days gone by is a ghost, a memory. Only the man of today is truly present, and it is he who truly matters." Oa said knowingly, coming to stand beside Thalrok.

"Is that another… 'thing' you disciples say?" Thalrok asked, tilting his head quizzically.

"Yep, but the rest of it is the upsetting part," Oa replied. He continued, "The man of today is truly present only through the eyes of the noble, compassionate, and forgiving."

It was, unfortunately, so. Most people judge their fellow man on their past actions and what they've been told by others, so most would only see Lotus for what he had been seen as and labeled in the past—a monster.

Together the three travelers moved along back to their inn. What surely had to be the longest night ever in Harthfield ended at last, just as it had begun. Again, they rested in their rooms, recovering from yet another encounter with the parasites of Perlaria that crept and plotted in the shadows.

* * *

The town elder met Lotus, Thalrok, and Oa as they prepared to leave. "We can't thank you enough for what you boys did. Whether or not these people were hunting for you, you still put yourselves last to protect our village. You saved our people! Thank you, boys, thank you very much," he told them with great warmth and sincerity. Many of the townspeople had gathered to see them off, and the trio bowed their heads in appreciation for their kind words.

An elderly man said to Thalrok, "As for you, young man, please remember, if there ever comes a time you need a home, we will always have a place here for you." It was Gordell, the man who had been kind enough to show Thalrok around Harthfield and tell him of its history and scars from the past. That good deed in itself had done so much for the three young men, of course most of all Thalrok, on this journey.

Townsfolk lined the main roads and bridges that ran around the waterfalls high above the downtown river area to watch them depart for whatever was next on their journey. While they walked down one of the stone-paved streets, Lotus glimpsed a bulletin board and saw that his wanted poster was no longer pinned up there. To most, removing the poster would seem like a small, trivial action, but it was a most significant gift to this young man who had lost it all and then some.

Lotus, Thalrok, and Oa neared the end of the street, where the stone paving turned to dirt and the sound of the waterfalls faded farther into the distance with each step. From behind them they heard a voice call out, "Wait a minute, boys!" They turned around to see that Gordell was hurrying along as best he could to catch up to them.

"Everything alright?" Thalrok asked.

Gordell said nothing, but as the three of them backtracked to meet him, he stopped and signalled for them to follow him. He took them down a somewhat hidden and barely-used path that led around the eastern outskirts of town to a large barn. Once they got to the front of it, Gordell asked the bounty hunter to help him open the gigantic doors.

Thalrok grabbed one of the huge wooden handles and with some effort slid it open. The wood creaked, and tangled overgrowth and vines were torn off, for it hadn't been opened in quite a while.

Oa eagerly peeked inside as soon as any light began to break in through the doorway. "What *is* that thing?" he asked, his eyes wide with surprise. Thalrok got both doors fully open, and there before them was something both totally unfamiliar and astonishing.

"I call her the *'Land Skipper'*!" Gordell said with obvious pride, as he patted the side of "her" and then brushed off the dust from his hands.

The three gazed with wonder upon a strange boat-like structure. It had two forward bows similar to a catamaran, but was designed to move over the land like a carriage. There was one immense sail. On the lower deck they saw a small cabin and the helm atop it, which displayed a row of rods and levers probably used to brake or steer. There were three large wheels made of some kind of light but strong metal on either side, which allowed it to roll over even rough terrain. The odd craft seemed to be in a sorry condition, covered in dust and with tears in the sail.

Lotus tilted his head, looking at it. *"Land Skipper?"* he asked skeptically.

"Yes, sir. It was many years ago when I found this thing abandoned in the middle of Prosper Valley, broken and busted up. I had no idea how a *boat* could get into the middle of the grasslands without any water nearby. It puzzled me, so I managed to get it towed back here. Then, I tinkered with its design to create the mighty ride it is today." Gordell boasted.

The three were mesmerized by this incredible creation before them. Oa had never seen any type of boat at all before. As for the other two, they had never seen any boat quite like this one.

"Sadly, I haven't been able to take her out for a ride in years. Getting old has left me unable to work on her like I used to." Gordell added, with true disappointment in his voice.

Thalrok walked alongside it and brushed his hands across the grainy wood, watching the thick dust fall from the touch of his hands. It was a remarkable invention, a way to get across the grasslands with ease— no need to walk across the vast plains of Perlaria on foot with this contraption.

"How long have you been working on this?" Lotus asked, as he and Oa climbed on deck, disregarding the plentiful dirt and debris.

"Oh, I wish I knew. It's been for quite some time now, many years. That's why I think she deserves a new home." Gordell smiled.

All six of their eyes simultaneously flashed to focus sharply on Gordell, their faces filled with curiosity. They watched him chuckle to himself at their reaction, then laugh when he saw that the shock of what he really meant finally sank into their heads.

"Wait… you're giving this to us?" Oa asked.

"If you boys would like. She can help you on your journey." Gordell offered.

The three darted eyes at one another with the same expressions on their faces; surprise at first, then eagerness took over as they began to ask the man if he was truly serious.

Gordell could only laugh again as he continued to insist that she was theirs now. "It'll be a rough ride since she's not been taken out for even a test run lately. Plus, she's been cooped up here for a long, long while, but I'm sure you boys will have fun with her." He turned, then added, "If you'd like, I'll help make sure she's in working order before you leave. How does that sound?"

"Yes please!" Oa cried out in excitement, before Thalrok or Lotus could even begin to respond.

Some hours later, with all of them working together, the sail was patched, moving parts oiled and working, and any structural repairs completed. Lotus, Thalrok, and Oa expressed their many thanks, as Gordell, satisfied with his decision, slowly headed back to town, leaving the three of them to figure out this new member of their crew, the *Land Skipper*.

"Okay, right there should be fine!" Oa shouted, as Lotus and Thalrok pulled the craft from the barn. The wheels rubbed against the axles, creaking as loud as the barn doors until the oil Gordell had applied worked its way into all of the bearings. Seeing sunlight for the first time in many years, the *Land Skipper,* in all her glory, was brought out into the world once again. The three of them brushed off some remaining grit and dust from her rails as they further explored the small vessel in the light of day. At the back of the boat the little cabin had a single bed in case anyone needed to rest. Newer-looking shelves and cabinets lined one of the small room's walls, but they were empty. The windows on the sides and back were covered with moss and leafy growth, barely letting in light. There was a lantern with some oil still inside hanging from the ceiling at a most convenient spot for anyone's head to bump into. In front of the cabin was the helm with all of the control levers that were probably for steering and braking. The single sail, newly repaired, flapped in the wind as a breeze began to push against the huge thick cloth.

"Uh, I guess this..." Lotus pulled one of the levers as he pushed the others and saw the wheels shift directions. Reversing his motions, he turned the levers in the other direction. Just then, as he moved the wheels to the left, a gust of wind pushed against the sail and nudged the boat forward.

"Whoa!" Oa stumbled as the sudden movement caught him off guard.

Thalrok came out from the cabin and went ahead to see them moving forward ever-so-slightly. "Looks like she wants to get going." Thalrok laughed, and walked to the end of the front left walkway to sit down on the bow and relax for the ride.

"Let's hope I can steer this thing," Lotus mumbled to himself. The wind kept pushing them forward at a snail's pace, inch by inch across the grassy earth. The creaking of the wheels lessened. If they reached a slope they would pick up a bit of speed, but for now, they were on a steady, slow ride.

Oa tapped his foot on the wooden floor as he stood on the boat's first level. He leaned against the wall below Lotus on the control rods, growing impatient. "Why don't I give this thing a little boost, huh?" he smirked gleefully, rubbing his hands together. Thalrok and Lotus looked at Oa skeptically as he planted his feet on the decking, faced his palms up toward the sail, and shouted, "Get ready, you two!"

With the burst of wind released from Oa's hands, the sail immediately billowed out and the *Land Skipper* darted forward. Thalrok was thrown on his back from the jolt, and hung on to the nearest rail for dear life. Lotus gripped tightly to the steering rods so as not to get thrown off. The rolling wheels were kicked into overdrive, and the three of them felt the wind blowing in their faces.

"Now that's what I'm talking about!" Oa cheered and laughed, as he sent another burst of air into the sail to keep the *Land Skipper's* momentum going. Lotus tried to focus and keep his concentration on steering their wild ride. He could hear panicked yelps coming from the bounty hunter below, but they were being drowned out by the boy's robust laughter.

"Off we go!" Oa shouted.

* * *

"How much longer till we get back to Mellowtin?" Thalrok asked as he pulled himself up onto the upper level of the *Land Skipper.*

Lotus still stared ahead, watching the terrain bend and lift in many curves and arches. He had nearly dozed off for a moment, tunnel-vision making him unaware of anything except the landscape before him. The three of them had been land-sailing for half a day now and had yet to catch any sight of Mellowtin.

"Helloooo, Ronin!" Thalrok called out once more.

Snapping out of his daze, Lotus glanced over to see Thalrok looking at him, his helmeted head atilt. "I'm sorry. We're about halfway there by now, I'm sure," he replied, then looked down at Oa, who was staring off into the distance from the lower level of the *Land Skipper.* Thalrok stood beside Lotus and looked off in the distance alongside his friend—just the wind blowing between them and the sounds the large sail made as it flapped softly above. The sun painted the mountain ranges and forests with light, and a beautiful portrait of Perlaria lay there before their eyes.

"What's that?" Oa called out to them as he pointed off the port side.

Thalrok and Lotus turned to see where he was pointing and saw the silhouette of a large, towering city far off in the distance. The wanted man's eyes widened, thinking that it might be the largest city he had ever seen.

"That's Cannon-Gulf. The city of stone and power." Thalrok informed them.

"You've been there before?" Lotus asked.

"It's been a bit, but I used to journey there pretty regularly. Beneath the city are underground markets where bounty hunters get jobs, and sketchy merchants sell their products. It's a good place for groups of criminals to take refuge and run their clans." Thalrok spoke as he sat down with his back to the city. Lotus and Oa kept their eyes on the city way off in the distance as they both wondered what it was like.

Hmm, maybe...

"Can we go check it out?" Oa asked with an eager look in his eyes. Lotus peered down at the boy, then back over to the city. If what Thalrok said was true, he would surely be noticed as the wanted man he was. Yet, curiosity nagged at him, for during all of these years on the run, he had never seen this place before.

"Thalrok?" Lotus asked, one eyebrow raised.

"It's your call, captain," Thalrok replied.

Looking down at his hands holding onto the steering rods, he thought to himself for a moment, questioning a theory he'd formed based on what Thalrok had just said. Taking in a deep breath, he pulled the left steering rods back until the mighty Land Skipper turned port-side and was heading straight for the city of secrets, Cannon-Gulf.

"Give us a little boost, Oa?" Lotus asked.

With a smile, Oa nodded, and moved himself right where he needed to be to send this ship sailing. "Here we go!" he shouted, as he released a large blast of air from his palms and the *Land Skipper* leapt forward again.

14

Cannon-Gulf

The faraway silhouettes of the city were no longer silhouettes. The metropolis of Cannon-Gulf lay right before them, alive with noisy activity.

Lotus looked around and saw a small lever next to the steering controls etched with the word "brakes." He grasped it and pulled it back to help the *Land Skipper* slow down as they neared the city. The tension on the wooden rod resisted as he pulled it, so he grabbed it with two hands and pulled even harder, with no result. Lotus put his whole back into it, and felt the lever release from something as it suddenly snapped back. The *Land Skipper* showed no sign of slowing down, and the buildings were only getting closer.

"What's wrong?" Oa asked, as he walked up beside Lotus.

"I think our only way of stopping just broke," he replied calmly, while just staring dead ahead. Oa noticed that they were maybe a hundred yards away from crashing into some decrepit stone buildings that were outside of the city.

"Alrighty—hold on!" Oa said, as he hastily dropped down to the lower level. He pushed his hands through the center rails between the double bows, and building up as much air pressure as he could, quickly released strong gusts from both palms. The *Land Skipper* was countered with a hard jolt and skidded roughly to a stop on the grassy plains.

226

"Ow!" Thalrok yelled. He opened the cabin door to see that they had come to a complete stop. "A warning would have been nice, kid," he said with some annoyance. He rubbed his neck in pain as he looked out at the city he had left behind some months ago.

"Sorry, Thalrok." Oa grinned. He took no time before hopping off, ready to explore outside the city.

It was as if Cannon-Gulf was too large for its own good and needed to expand past its high stone walls to grow even more. Numerous market stalls of various small businesses were scattered in a sprawling bazaar here outside the city walls. Vendors called out to anyone and everyone passing by to stop in and try their goods. Plainly, some of them were quite frantic to make a sale. At no time was there a lull in the hubbub of voices, even with the setting sun nearly below the horizon. Lotus wondered how hectic the inside of the town must be if it was this lively outside of its walls.

"You coming, Ronin?" Thalrok asked, as he looked at the streets filled with swarms of people.

They had hidden the *Land Skipper* in a small copse of trees. Putting on his cloak and snapping out of his thoughts, Lotus locked the sail up in the *Skipper's* cabin and joined up with the others, his hood up and securely in place.

Thalrok took the lead as they approached this bustling merchant district just outside of Cannon-Gulf, and prepared to swim through the crowds to explore it. "Listen, you two, if you want to survive in this city, you have to stay by me the whole time. Do *not* get too far from our little group, got it?" he warned, "And no matter what you hear, ignore it and keep walking until we get through the walls and into the city." It wasn't dangerous; these people just wanted to scam them out of their money, of which they had little left.

"Why do these people seem so desperate for business?" Oa asked.

"People all around Perlaria think that if they move to Cannon-Gulf, they will be able to start a new life and their business will prosper. The hard part to swallow is that they can't make it inside the walls without any start-up money, so they have to settle for shops outside here. They have to work hard every day, and compete to get customers so they can turn a profit. Some make it out pretty well while others, well, don't." The bounty hunter scratched his neck below his helmet and pressed on ahead.

Together, the three companions weaved through crowds of people, trying not to call any attention to themselves. They approached the city's wall, then looked up as they passed through the entrance, a massive stone archway that loomed over their heads. People standing on the top stared down as they walked through.

Once inside, Lotus and Oa noticed that the architecture here was incredibly unique and complex. Bridges connected walkways to other walkways coming from different levels above their heads. Streets twisted and turned across the floor of the city, with smaller streets branching off in all directions out of nowhere. Small streams of water flowed underneath city bridges, outlining some small-town districts. It was a phenomenal sight for the two outsiders, for one had never left his small, isolated village, and the other had never been to a city quite so grand. It was both mesmerizing and terrifying, all at once.

This has got to be the most people I've ever seen in one place before. Lotus's eyes scanned across every inch of this complex city as he followed Thalrok closely. Cannon-Gulf was a city like no other, in many ways.

"Thalrok, I have a question," Oa spoke up rather loudly, so as to be heard.

"What's up, kid?" the bounty hunter replied. He turned his head so he could hear what Oa had to say above the noise of the crowd..

"This place is called Cannon-Gulf, and yet, this isn't a gulf at all. So, why is it called that?" Oa asked.

Thalrok stopped moving abruptly and looked all around them, leaving Oa to bump right into his back. He surveyed the streets as if he were trying to find something. "Over here, this way," he finally said, as he headed for a fork in the road. As they followed Thalrok, Lotus, who held up the rear, stopped momentarily. He turned around and glanced slowly at the throngs of people in the streets. He'd felt an unease, a prickly feeling go down his neck just a second ago, as if someone or something unseen was watching him.

Oa called out, "Hurry up, Lotus! Like Thalrok said, you don't wanna get separated!"

Releasing his irrational fears, Lotus followed a few steps behind them. Something still felt off, but maybe it was just the crowded streets making him feel a bit claustrophobic.

"Here, this should answer your question." Thalrok pointed ahead at a large wooden sign in the center of where several roads met. The sign was a giant map showing you where you were in the city at that moment. He got closer and pointed at a body of water, much smaller than the city but big enough to be visible on the map.

"It is said that this spot of land was once all water, a part of the ocean, but it was destroyed in the chaos of the Calamity ages ago," Thalrok said. "This small lake is all that remains of the once large gulf that connected this city to the Coralic sea hundreds of years ago."

"Seriously?" Oa asked.

"I can't say for certain, but it's what I hear from most people." The bounty hunter replied with a shrug of one shoulder.

His two companions checked out the map a little longer. Lotus noticed the flickering lanterns beside the map, illuminating the large diagram with their light. He glanced up at the sky and saw that it was no longer a bright shade of yellow-orange, but far darker, and realized it was getting pretty late. They hadn't eaten much of anything since they left Harthfield. Lotus and Oa followed closely behind Thalrok again as the number of people filling the streets never lessened. It was as if the city itself never took time to rest.

"We should probably find somewhere to eat, Thalrok. Do you know a place?" Lotus asked.

Confidently leading the charge, the bounty hunter chuckled to himself and told them, "Oh yeah, already got that planned."

"Oh, thank goodness." Oa sighed as he dropped his head to his chest in relief.

Thalrok explained that they were about to come up on one of the city's several food districts, but this one had the very best selection of food and places to eat. It was only a short distance away, and soon they'd be able to smell the food cooking on the streets. Shortly after he said that, the air filled their nostrils with the delectable smell of hot food being cooked somewhere nearby.

"I thought that since the kid was so eager to visit this place, he can pick where we eat." Thalrok turned back and pointed to Oa. The boy's eyes widened and his smile grew even wider. Oa hurried ahead to Thalrok's side to get a better look at all the eateries there were to choose from.

Lotus was left in the back to follow them, and with each step he took, he felt that same odd feeling. *Someone is following me*, he thought, as he slowly peered around the hood of his cloak which still covered his head. He didn't want to make it apparent that he was trying to find out who was following, but he couldn't be caught by surprise either. His heart rate began to speed up gradually as he hoped to pick out the watchful eyes that he felt at his back.

"Lotus!" Oa called out from ahead.

Lotus snapped out of his thoughts and saw the two waving him down. Hurrying to their side, he found them standing outside of one restaurant that didn't appear to have too many people inside.

"The kid picked this one—you okay with that?" Thalrok asked.

"Of course," Lotus replied, and the three of them headed inside to get something to eat.

This restaurant was much like any other, with a big open floor plan and tiered levels so that people could enjoy their food and chat. Circular wooden tables lined the floor with big windows in the front so people passing by could look in and admire the look of both the food and the hopefully satisfied customers. Waiters moved quickly from table to table, taking orders and delivering food to their hungry guests.

"Outstanding! I have *never* been to a place like *this*! How do we get our food?" Oa wondered out loud. He was scoping out the big place in amazement—everyone was dining with everyone else! All the seers and disciples of Mount Axi would eat meals in their homes with their families using the crops they grew together as a community. Oa had dined alone for two years and missed those days when he had dined together with his parents.

"So this is really your first time eating in any kind of restaurant?" Thalrok asked as they were seated and offered refreshments.

"Yeah, this is all new to me. What do I do now?" Oa asked, looking around the table.

"It's pretty easy. Someone will come over and ask what you would like to eat, and you'll just... tell them." Thalrok began to chuckle at having to explain this very simple process.

Oa shrugged his shoulders and thought, "Well, that should be easy enough to do."

When the waiter arrived, Lotus and Thalrok went first, ordering what they wanted. Oa copied them, sounding as though he'd ordered food at a restaurant every day of his young life.

"How was *that?*" Oa asked proudly as the waiter walked away with their orders. As soon as he asked, Thalrok erupted with laughter and slammed his hand on the table.

"You did great. Just like a pro." Lotus replied, as he darted a look back over at the entrance to the restaurant. The whole time they were seated, his eyes never left it for long. Something felt off since he entered this city, and it didn't sit well with him. The uneasy feeling that someone was following him had weighed on his mind for some time now, but he had no real evidence.

This might not have been the best idea.

Every few seconds that went by, he would check the door to make sure nothing out of the ordinary came up. He watched many people enter and leave as if it was a normal day for them, showing no signs of suspicion. Really, the only suspicious one here was Lotus in his cloak with a hood over his head.

When the boy's food finally arrived, the expression on Oa's face was priceless. Thalrok and Lotus watched how shocked and delighted he was to see a giant plate of food delivered to him by a stranger who had asked what he would like to eat just minutes ago. It brought a smile to their faces to see their unworldly companion finally experiencing a bit of joy and wonder since leaving home.

While watching Oa, Lotus was briefly taken away from his constant state of worry. He was quite self-conscious and uneasy being in a place where so many people would know of his reputed status and his bounty. When he grabbed for his fork he noticed the hairs on his arm were sticking straight up. Lotus glanced over at his other arm and saw that those hairs were raised, too. The deep feeling of dread in his chest surged through his body. Hastily, he looked at the door and saw the silhouettes in the window.

"Crap," he murmured softly, as the sound of glass shattering filled the room.

At the sound of the breaking glass and sudden panic, Thalrok shot to his feet. He turned to look at the restaurant's shattered front windows, now broken wide open. He saw everyone in the dining area began to scream and run for safety, pushing tables, chairs and other people out of their way.

"Lotus!" Oa shouted.

Thalrok saw that his wanted partner was already charging full speed at one of the windows where several thugs were coming in. They wore masks covering their faces, had hoods over their heads, and were dressed in all black with many types of weaponry attached to them. Knives, daggers, kunai, and small metal darts were strapped in place across their arms, legs, and bodies. These were men accustomed to fighting.

Lotus rushed straight for one of the thugs and dove at him without leaving a moment for him to react. The man reached for his hip, grabbed the handle of his dagger, and got ready to swing it at his target. Before he could move his arm even an inch, Lotus grabbed his wrist and stopped his frenzied slash. The thug's arm was immobilized and he felt a hand grab the top of his head and squeeze. With a quick thrust, Lotus leaped forward and slammed his opponent's head hard into his knee. The thug collapsed on the floor as Lotus pushed past him and ran out into the city.

"Lotus!" Oa shouted again, as he watched him jump out of the window and dash down the street.

"After him!" one of the other intruders shouted, as they threw down smokebombs and scrambled off to pursue their target. The exits filled up with smoke and any people remaining inside cowered in corners and under the tables, huddling together, coughing.

"Damn it! We gotta help him. Come on, kid!" Thalrok gritted his teeth as he saw the smoke billowing through the room.

Oa picked his staff up from near their table and ran for the front door. He took a deep breath and forced a giant burst of air toward the entrance, blowing the smoke out of his way.

"I'm going after him, Thalrok!" Oa shouted, as he swiftly cleared the doorway and ran into the street.

The bounty hunter was left behind, armed and ready, but unable to help due to his lack of speed. Thalrok could overpower any opponent, but when it came to speed, he was out of luck. He punched the table in frustration, muttering angrily as it shattered beneath his fist. Thalrok went for the front door, hurrying to follow the others and catch up.

"I have to get rid of these guys somehow." Lotus panted to himself. He darted down the busy streets of Cannon-Gulf, jumping from level to level, moving up and down rooftops and alleyways. None of his maneuvers shook off these aggressors; if anything, they were only getting closer. They called out to one another, spotting him after each turn or move he made. It was like a pride of lions chasing a gazelle through a maze of trees on a plain, except the lions knew every path.

Lotus dug his feet into the ground, trying to create the most unpredictable patterns he could while navigating through an unfamiliar place. The sounds of projectiles being thrown at him began to get louder, and their accuracy was increasing as they closed in.

"I won't be able to run forever. I need a plan." Lotus worried. The heaviness in his legs began to worry him. He turned his head to check just how far he still had between himself and those thugs. He noticed many figures, too many, spread out across the rooftops, streets, and walls behind him. His doom was closing in, and he could feel the struggle of the constant chase wearing him down.

I just need an opening to make a move or something. Damn it, think!

He pushed on with the fleeting amount of energy he had left inside of him. Along with the zinging of the many knives and thick metal needles being thrown at him, Lotus also detected a slight pressure of wind that hit the nape of his neck. His eyes widened, his body turned abruptly, and for a moment it seemed that his heart had stopped.

No! Why did you follow me?!

Lotus panicked as he watched Oa drop one of the aggressors to the ground.

Along the rooftop Oa ran, and behind him another thug fell to the streets from his sneak attack. Half of the attackers' attention now turned to the young disciple of Gou, and they were signaled to go after him. Several of them even broke off from chasing Lotus and went after the boy.

"No!" Lotus shouted as he pumped on the brakes and ran toward Oa, who was trying to catch up to him.

"Lotus!" Oa shrieked.

"Duck!" Lotus yelled out, hoping it was not too late.

Without question, Oa immediately dropped down flat and heard the air being sliced in two just above his head. Glancing up, he saw his reflection beaming off the polished blade of a katana just above him. While in this low-prone stance, he was in a perfect position to shoot ahead with a burst of wind from the soles of his feet. Releasing a strong gust, he lunged forward to get away from whoever was behind him. But when Oa had just begun to move forward, his body was jolted backward by a strong hand, which had grabbed him by his shirttail. He found himself yanked back onto his bottom with a muscular forearm wrapped tightly around his neck. Oa grabbed onto the beefy arm, struggling to pry it from his throat.

The thug's eyes narrowed. His katana blade was facing his victim and he was ready to strike. Oa could feel his young heart pounding and his breathing becoming harder by the second.

"Let him go!" Lotus shouted as he landed atop the roof. With his feet firmly planted on the topmost ridge of the house, he heard the sounds of other feet landing around him. He was not alone. These persistent goons were quick and moved extremely well around the city. This situation was going to be a pain to deal with.

"You move, and the kid gets it, buddy," the thug with the katana growled, pulling the blade closer to Oa. The boy squirmed and kicked his legs to free himself but was far outmatched in strength. Lotus could see his struggle and lifted his hands slowly into the air to reason with him.

"I'm cooperating. Just don't hurt the kid." Lotus said calmly.

Oa's captor cackled at that request, laughing at how his target thought he had any authority at this moment. "You—tie him up," the thug said dismissively, pointing his blade to someone behind Lotus and then to Lotus himself.

The wanted man couldn't see who was behind him, but he heard the footsteps approaching. His eyes were locked onto Oa's the whole time, trying to let him know with just his gaze that it was going to be all right. Lotus heard the steps stop behind him and felt hands roughly pull his arm behind his back. He glanced over to his side and saw the man's waist from the corner of his eye. There it was.

Lotus twisted his body and, with his free hand, grabbed for the man's waist and pulled off a set of small pellets. Ripping his other hand free, he hurled them all at the rooftop, sending big clouds of smoke erupting and billowing from around his feet. It only took seconds for the whole area around him to be completely shrouded in smoke and concealed from view.

The thug holding Oa hostage held onto him even tighter than before while sounds of fighting echoed out from the smoke. There was no telling who was winning. There was only moonlight to see by, and the thick fog covered any signs of victory or defeat. It wasn't until he saw the first of several bodies fly out from the murky smoke off the edge of the roof and down to the street below that he knew what was happening.

"Idiots!" the man holding onto Oa grunted, shaking his head. Then he felt the boy suddenly drop his weight forward, pulling himself closer to the ground. The thug refused to let go and pulled in the opposite direction, picking him back up. As Oa felt him tugging in the other direction, he planted his feet on the ground and pushed off in the same direction aided by a small burst of wind from his feet. Stumbling backward, the man's grip loosened as he struggled to keep his balance. It was just enough for Oa to wiggle his way out.

"Damn it!" the angry thug yelled, as he watched the kid immediately dive headfirst into the smoke. Grunting angrily, he knew he had to get in there himself and fight through the blind chaos. He had only taken a few steps forward when someone emerged from the murky haze. Tendrils of smoke swirled out in different directions as the compact body of Oa came launching back out of cover and straight for the man who'd held him hostage only moments ago. He was moving too quickly to be dodged, and landed three direct kicks to the thug's right knee, quadricep, and neck. Using his instincts, Oa released an even bigger burst of wind from his foot into the man's chest and sent him flying backward. The thug hurtled across the rooftop until he slid off the edge and down to the street below, joining his companions.

"Oa, you alright?" Lotus panted, as he ran out from the smoky cloud which was starting to slowly disintegrate.

"I'm fine, just still catching my breath," the boy panted, as he glanced around for any other nearby enemies.

Lotus grabbed his cloak, ripped it off, and tossed it down. He let out a large exhale. "Not much good this thing did," he sighed as he walked over to the roof's edge to peek down at the street. The attackers who had fallen were still unconscious on the ground, being recovered by others of their clan.

"Where's Thalrok?" Lotus asked, beginning to run in the opposite direction of the remaining thugs.

"I have no idea. Last time I—" Oa was interrupted by a loud crash rattling the ground behind them. With the tremors beneath their feet, and spooked by the sudden crashing, they looked back to see a large boulder smashed into the roof of the house behind them. They stared at each other with wide eyes; what if something had thrown that at them but missed?

"You have nowhere else to go!" a rugged voice from somewhere below the rooftops bellowed.

Lotus and Oa looked down at the streets and saw a huge, burly man wearing a sandogasa slamming his foot on the ground, which shattered the stone street into chunks. They witnessed him lift two large pieces of rubble and crash them together to form one giant projectile. Except, he had never touched any of the stones, boulders or rubble. He appeared to have an earth-wielding type of ability, and knew very well how to use it.

"Did he just...?" Oa asked in shock.

"Yes, he did. And if he's anything like other earth-wielders, we're in for some trouble." Lotus answered, as he dashed away and motioned for Oa to follow closely behind. They heard the loud crashing of the boulders hitting other buildings as they zig-zagged across the irregular slopes of the rooftops. Lotus realized that they were an easy target if they stayed this high above ground. They would have to sneak in the shadows of the streets and keep out of sight.

"Lotus, watch out!" Oa screamed, as he watched another masked bandit sneak in from the side and tackle Lotus completely off the rooftop. The wanted man went flying across a narrow alley, then down and into the side of a house, where he slid down the wooden siding until he crumpled on the ground.

"Lotus! No!" Oa cried out again. He quickly dropped down to ground level too, and was running hard toward his friend to save him. As he watched Lotus struggle to stand, Oa saw him lift one hand out to him, palm forward.

"Don't do it, kid!" Lotus yelled, just as a flying chunk of the street crashed into the boy's side. Oa was launched into another building, breaking through its wall as the ground rumbled.

Lotus felt his weakening body pulse angrily as he saw some gloating goliath strutting down the street toward him. Dressed in black, loose-fitting clothes, the husky man first took off his sandogasa and then removed the mask from his face. "Geez, it's annoying tryin' to see with this thing on. Good thing the boss isn't here to yell at me. Not like anyone's gonna be able to tell him anyway," he sniggered to himself, tossing his hat to the ground and cracking his knuckles.

Oa...

Wild-eyed and furious, Lotus was ready to simply charge recklessly into this beast, who was now only a short way down the street. Just as Lotus stumbled to charge forward, the twang of metal rang out. Without needing to look, he kicked off from his right foot to evade the oncoming arrows flying at him. They thudded and stuck into the rubble where he had just been standing. His teeth were clenched as he stared up at the rooftops to see several archers locked in on his position and positioning to fire again. "There isn't an end to this, is there?" Lotus panted. He didn't want to do it, but he started to reach for his hip, his hand slowly getting closer to his sword. Lotus hesitated, trying to think of what else he could do.

The archers above will keep me from being able to take direct paths to that brute in front of me. As for him, I can't see myself getting close without getting smashed by a boulder or two. I have to see if Oa is alright, but I can't go near him, or I will create more chances for him to get hit. Lotus ran the play-by-play in his head.

"This is the part where you realize how you are in a pinch, am I right?" the earth-wielder shouted with satisfaction.

"Who are you? And why are you after me?" Lotus called back. The faint laugh grew louder and deeper, and he watched the big man buckle at the knees, roaring in delight.

"Maybe I could tell you that… but then where's all the fun!" he bellowed. "I guess you can call me Rohm, if you last long enough," the man smirked. He thrust both his hands down toward the stony surface of the street, lifted a giant chunk of it above his head, then hurled it straight at his prey.

Lotus was readying himself to jump out of the way when the fateful sound of bowstrings being pulled tighter touched his ears. Time slowed, and Lotus could see his windows of escape close tighter and tighter. *Crap!*

What can I do? he thought in a panic, with his hand ever nearer to the hilt of his sword. That boulder was getting closer by the moment, coming in for a direct hit. Lotus felt sweat from his forehead run down his face until it dripped on the ground.

"Ronin!" a voice shouted, as a large figure slid right in front of him, and all thoughts ceased.

"Thalrok?!" Lotus gasped.

The bounty hunter crossed his arms, flexed his knees, and stabilized his body. The boulder crashed right into him, shattering into pieces. Various sizes of stones and rocky debris were scattered across the street and hit the walls, leaving a sort of clear tunnel outlined behind Thalrok and Lotus. When the dust settled, all eyes saw the two of them still standing there, unharmed. The rooftop archers, for now, held their fire, awaiting a signal from Rohm.

"You think a little rock like that'll hurt *me?*" Thalrok laughed. Even from this distance, the torchlight showed a large vein popping out on the earth-wielder's wide forehead.

Lotus took a deep breath in relief. The bounty hunter had jumped in to rescue him just in time. "Thank you, Th—" Lotus started to say.

"If you *ever* make me run that much again, I will hit you so hard you won't remember how to remember!" Thalrok thundered, as he turned around abruptly, pointing his finger no more than an inch away from Lotus's nose.

The wanted man could only respond with a small nod of his head. He could hear how hard the bounty hunter was breathing from all the running around and searching that he'd had to do just to find him, and then he'd stopped a flying boulder to save him. But, now that Thalrok was here, Lotus had a chance to help Oa. "The kid got hit pretty bad. Can you keep me covered while I go check on him?" Lotus asked.

"Like you really need to ask," Thalrok smirked beneath his helmet. He slowly reached back, unfastened and pulled his gigantic sword from his back. Lotus headed off towards the hole in the building to make sure that Oa was all right as Thalrok approached the enemy before him. His mighty sword rested on his shoulder as though it weighed nothing.

"Look at you, big guy! Just because you stopped one of my attacks doesn't mean you're hot stuff." Rohm taunted, as the titan slowly advanced.

"It does mean, however, that you throw lousy attacks. That guy you tried to hit, my buddy, he's punched me harder than that puny pebble did." Thalrok fired back. This only made the brute even more enraged, which Thalrok found quite funny, and he had to chuckle a little to himself.

"I don't want to see a single arrow fire at this one. You just keep an eye on the target and the kid. This one is mine!" the earth-wielder shouted up to the archers.

"This isn't part of his plan. We must fight as one—" the nearest archer called back.

"Did I *stutter?!*" Rohm interrupted with a shout. He was furious, and glanced up at the archers, glowering.

Thalrok's fingers curled around the hilt of his huge sword, preparing for the challenge before him. A man blessed with the ability to control the earth itself—here was a match, and one that might turn into a real struggle.

Rohm raised his hands and the rocky debris from behind him levitated high in the air. Then he swiped his hands forward, sending stony chunks and all soaring right at Thalrok.

Switching his grip, the bounty hunter grabbed onto his titan-forged sword with both hands and struck each and every piece of rubble coming at him. The swarm of projectiles was no match for the force of his blade, which smashed them into ever smaller pieces. One after another, the earth-wielder sent more chunks of the earth, debris, and street-stone flying at the titan. But the bounty hunter didn't break a sweat; his blade glided through the air, crushing whatever was in its path.

This guy's got some serious power behind his swing. Looks like I'll need to take it up a notch. Letting out a gargantuan yell, Rohm slammed his foot to the ground and lifted up a giant boulder, one larger than his own body. Using his special abilities, he floated it off the ground with ease, positioning it between himself and the bounty hunter.

Thalrok couldn't see his enemy past the big rock, but suddenly it flew at him on a direct collision course. "This one's gonna hurt," he sighed as he quickly lifted his sword hilt above his head. With a firm thrust downward, Thalrok slashed at the incoming boulder to smash it to pieces. But just as his sword was about to strike the rock, the rock stopped short right in front of him. His counter-attack had missed completely. His sword sliced deep into the ground, which then shook beneath Thalrok's feet.

What?!

The figure of a large man appeared from atop the large chunk of rock in front of him. Rohm had followed after the boulder, abruptly stopped it, and quickly hopped on top. He knew this would both shock the titan and give himself a satisfying close-up and personal view of his foe's upcoming destruction. With a smug smile, Rohm jumped over the first boulder with another firmly in his grasp, high above his head.

"You missed, fool!" the earth-wielder jeered wickedly, as he swung his hands towards the bounty hunter.

The boulder collided with Thalrok and then continued on into the ground, burrowing Thalrok beneath it. Nearby buildings shook and tremors could be felt for miles.

Rohm stood atop his colossal rock, arrogant and triumphant after his final attack. "I told you I didn't need you twigs to help me!" he crowed, pointing up at the archers on the rooftops. He hopped onto the boulder, crushing Thalrok, and gawked down from above. With his spirits high and guard down, the earth-wielder was astounded when he felt the boulder he so proudly stood on tremble beneath his feet. It shook and quaked; all the while he was being lifted slowly upwards. "What the hell?!" he shouted.

Thalrok grunted loudly with his feet planted firmly on the stony ground below while his hands dug into the solid rock above him. His powerful legs pushed hard as he lifted the boulder higher and higher into the air. "Nice try, ya punk." Thalrok gasped, as he gritted his teeth and tossed the boulder off to one side.

Rohm jumped down before he could lose his balance, and observed this beast before him who had countered his attack without getting even a scratch. He couldn't see the bounty hunter's face, but he could tell this was all a joke to him. He was probably smirking under that helmet, mocking him. Rohm's irritation grew, anger boiling from his very core. "You wanna play games then, huh? How about this!" the earth-wielder shouted, as he stomped his feet into the ground, lifting smaller rocks up from it. With a roar, he sent them flying one by one at Thalrok with incredible speed. The bounty hunter kicked his huge sword up from the ground, gripped it tightly, and with ease, swatted away Rohm's feeble attack.

The earth-wielder had had enough. Seeing the unyielding stamina of this tenacious enemy, he resorted to his greatest weapon, the one that was right on the mark. Rohm reached his hands out toward Thalrok, then curled his fingers and pulled them right back, tightening his grip in the air.

Thalrok didn't know what Rohm was doing until the ground shook again, and he saw that the boulder he had just thrown off of himself was being pulled back toward him, and at full speed.

Crap! He panicked, and quickly turned around while pulling his sword closer to his body. With one precise thrust forward, the titan sliced through the big boulder with one clean cut, splitting it perfectly. The two pieces came to a sliding halt on either side of him. He turned back around to find Rohm closing in on him with an evil grin.

"That was just a dee-coy!" the earth-wielder taunted in a singsong voice.

Thalrok was rattled now, and found himself completely open to three blunt strikes to the body. He felt the brute's knuckles collide with his stomach and ribs as Rohm pushed him back with each blow. Feet stumbling on the street, he tried to collect himself. His chance for counterattack was now; he had to stop Rohm from doing any more damage. But, before he could take a step forward, he noticed that the earth wielder had become quite still, his face a mask of evil intent.

Rohm's arms reached out sideways in opposite directions at chest-level with his hands forming claws in the air. "Crush!" he shouted, as he pulled his arms together. The two pieces of the split boulder followed his hands' movements and slammed together into one another, crushing Thalrok between them. The solid clapping sound of the surfaces colliding echoed down the streets and into the night sky.

Rohm panted, huffing victoriously as he stood over his defeated opponent. "I warned you, this is what happens when you mess with the..."

The earth-wielder was interrupted by more small tremors beneath his feet. Like a heartbeat they pulsed, the tempo getting faster and faster. It was coming from inside the boulder, which seemed to be cracking from the inside.

No way...

The increasing vibrations suddenly shattered the rock into pieces, scattering fragments across the street. Thalrok bellowed out loud and long, then he slowly turned his helmeted head toward his prey.

"I think I've had enough of this." Thalrok sighed, as he gasped for air.

Rohm froze in place. Seeing such raw strength and power from a human being was truly terrifying. *Who is this guy?*

Thalrok lifted his sword up from the ground one last time and drove it into the remains of the street between him and his target. He clasped his hands together and lifted them above his head, then slammed them down onto its thick pommel. The jolt of impact sent shockwaves in all directions of the street, with large cracks breaking out below both of them. Fissures began to fan out even farther across the street as Thalrok rushed head-on at the off-balance earth-wielder.

"Your turn now!" Thalrok shouted, as he pummeled his foe with an onslaught of punches. One after the other, he socked him hard in the face and stomach, giving him not one moment to react. Maybe Thalrok couldn't manipulate the earth, but he could certainly break through anything in his path.

This guy is really starting to piss me off! Rohm dug in his heels in and briefly caught both of Thalrok's hands in his own. That collision rattled the very bones in his body, and he wheezed from the onslaught. "I... have never... failed a job..." he panted, jumping backward to get as far from this beast as he could. Then the earth-wielder dropped low to the ground.

Using all of his concentration, he slowly lifted another huge boulder which he kept levitated just above his head. The vein in Rohm's forehead pulsed with anger and his eyes bulged as he stared the titan down.

Thalrok was ready to shatter this hunk of rock just like the other. He pulled his fist back and waved it around like a batter at the plate egging on the pitcher.

"The job was to deal with the target, and if I can't deal with *you* properly, I'll just go for the *real* target!" Rohm shouted, as he looked over at the hole in the building where Lotus had run in to help Oa.

Thalrok looked over his shoulder and realized what he was now aiming for. "Don't you dare!" he roared. But it was too late. The boulder was already soaring through the air at the targeted building. The titan watched as it passed closely by him, then a foot away, then a few feet, and then out of reach. It smashed through the wall with ease. The walls collapsed, crumbling into a giant pile of rubble at the base of where the hole in the wall had been.

"Ronin! Oa!" Thalrok shouted, as he ran over and stood above the messy remains of the wall. He knelt down to push away the debris but stopped when he heard laughter behind him. His muscles froze, stopping him from moving at all; they ached in rage, hungry for revenge. He glared back over his shoulder to see Rohm holding his big gut and shaking with laughter.

"You fool of a man! Did you forget to keep an eye out for your buddies? Such a shame they had to go out that way, unaware and not able to do a thing about it." Rohm taunted.

Steam, like smoke from a dragon's mouth, billowed from the small slits in Thalrok's helmet with every breath he exhaled. He stood up slowly and took one heavy step towards the earth-wielding thug, barely containing his adrenaline rush of battle mode.

"Aww, looks like I made the big guy mad. Don't worry, you'll be with your friends shortly," the earth-wielder chuckled, as he lifted three smallish boulders from the ground. He launched them at the titan without even touching them. The bounty hunter didn't flinch as the jagged rocks slammed into his muscles and broke on impact. Thalrok kept on walking.

A nip of fear marked Rohm's face when he saw that his attack had no effect whatsoever. "There's no point in trying anymore, the end of your pitiful life will only be put off for a few seconds longer," Rohm called out. Again, he slammed his foot to the ground and lifted larger boulders into the air. They were sent soaring at the bounty, much faster this time than the first round. But they, too, smashed against Thalrok's body and crumbled to pieces with an incredible sound.

Thalrok remained unmoved and kept on walking. He was still upright, unharmed, and resolutely getting closer by the second as he stormed down the ruined street.

"You've got to be kidding me," the earth-wielder panicked. He began sending as many boulders as he possibly could at this terrifying menace. Each one of them broke on contact with Thalrok, without leaving a scratch on him or slowing him down one bit.

"Stay back!" Rohm yelled, as he stumbled backward, finding himself mesmerized by the piercing amber eyes showing through the tiny slits of the monster's helmet. Sweat dripped from Rohm's forehead as he saw the bounty hunter speed up, so that now only a too-short distance remained between them.

Thalrok planted one foot firmly on the ground, mere inches from his foe. As he reeled back his mighty fist, Rohm grabbed a hidden knife and jabbed it directly at Thalrok's heart. Pieces of metal clanged onto the ground as Thalrok grabbed the blade and shattered it with his bare hand. The earth-wielder was unable to move; time in his world slowed. He saw the bounty hunter grab his shirt with one hand and pull back his other in a fist. There was only one thing left to do.

"Fire you idiots, FIRE!" he shouted into the air. As he gazed past the beast before him, he looked up to see where the archers were keeping an eye out from the rooftops. He smiled then, knowing that his life would be safe for another day—until no arrows were fired. His smile faded as he saw something even scarier than the beast before him.

No... Rohm trembled in horror.

The archers were downed, unconscious. And who *was* standing there watching from above?—none other than Lotus and Oa, safe and sound.

The earth-wielder's terrified eyes turned back to Thalrok, whose fist was only inches away from walloping him through the ground. With devastating impact, Thalrok's fist slammed into Rohm's face. He was driven down into the rubble-filled streets by the hammer of righteous revenge. Debris flew, and the tremors from the force of collision rolled to a slow halt. Pebbles and crumbs of stone plunked on the ground as they fell from the titan's hand. He huffed and puffed as he stared at his now unconscious foe.

"You all right, Thalrok?" Lotus asked, as he nimbly jumped down from the rooftops. Oa, who was only a little shaken up, landed beside him.

"I'll be alright. Fighting someone with the earth on their side is quite a pain. Luckily, I can smash right through his little pebbles." Thalrok chuckled, brushing off small pieces of rubble from his arms. The trio stood above the earth wielder, knocked out cold now with his smug look wiped clean off.

"How long do you think they were following us?" Oa asked.

"I sensed someone watching us since we got here. It's only a matter of time now till more come our way." Lotus answered.

They all looked around at the large area of chaos and destruction from their battle. During the fight, people had stayed far away from the uproar. But now, they were beginning to make their way back down the street and had of course noticed the disruption. So much for keeping a low profile now.

"Hey guys, I hate to say it, but Ronin was right." Thalrok pointed out, as he pointed up at the rooftops. The two others looked up as well, and saw more masked men there. They supported their knocked-out comrades in their arms as they peered down from above.

Suddenly, Lotus noticed movement in his peripheral vision. Without a sound to be heard, they saw a tall brawny man there in the moonlight heaving Rohm's limp form onto a flatbed cart. "Get ready, you two." he whispered.

Thalrok gripped his sword tightly and pulled Oa behind him. Lotus kept his eyes on the foes above them who stood on the eaves and ridges of the nearby roofs. They were once again outnumbered.

One of the rooftop thugs whispered to the others, "Let us retreat for now. We will tell the boss of our discovery." He gave the signal for all to retreat, which was passed along from one to the other. Several of them tossed smoke bombs to cover their exit, and in an instant they all had vanished.

"Crap, they got away." Thalrok groaned, when the smoke cleared to reveal that their attackers had disappeared. He kicked a stone across the street in disappointment.

"We need to do the same and start heading back to the *Skipper* before they bring more company," Lotus said, and he began to hurry back the way they had come. His companions followed closely behind him as they passed through crowds of people who still filled the streets, even this late into the night.

Finding our way out of this maze by moonlight isn't gonna be easy. But it being long past sunset sure didn't stop whoever was after us.

* * *

"How'd you like your first time in the big city, boys?" Thalrok asked.

Luckily, they had gotten themselves back onto the *Land Skipper* without incident and were setting off to get as far from Cannon-Gulf as quickly as they could. Their adventures there would be left behind them.

"Eventful," Lotus answered.

"Could have been worse," Oa added.

Belching out loud, Thalrok laughed wildly. Then he took another swig from his flask to help him decompress from what had been, as Lotus said, an "eventful" day.

The wanted man only shook his head. He was just happy that they'd been able to escape this time. Someone was definitely after him there, and he didn't want his friends to be harmed any more than they already had been. It wasn't easy for him to see people getting hurt because of his issues; he had seen quite enough of that.

"Fellas, it looks like we are almost fresh out of money. We gotta head back to Mellowtin to get our elbows dirty for some dough." Thalrok burped from inside his helmet.

"Good idea. It'd be best to lay low for a bit to ensure we aren't followed either." Lotus added as he turned the *Skipper* due north toward Mellowtin.

"Or…" Oa began. The two looked over at the young boy when he paused. Oa seemed to have something to say, but instead was silently holding onto something in his hands.

"When we were leaving the city, I snagged this from a notice board while I was trying to take Lotus's wanted poster down. Check it out." Oa said, and he held a piece of paper up to Thalrok, who walked over to take a look.

"Says here that some Hemridge archer challenges anyone who thinks they can beat him. The winner gets a huge reward!" Thalrok shouted, as he stepped up to Lotus's post at the helm to show him the poster too. It looked undamaged, as though someone had put it up not so very long ago, and even included a rudimentary map.

Lotus looked over at Oa and saw that look of curiosity on his face again. Their last adventure based on that look had ended up being an unfortunate battle and lucky escape. This was the least he could do.

"All right, next stop Hemridge," Lotus announced, as he turned the *Skipper* a bit to starboard. Thalrok and Oa both cheered loudly and pumped their fists in celebration. Out in the depths of the Evercrest forest was their next destination, the wooded village of Hemridge.

* * *

"What's his condition?" one of the masked thugs asked as he leaned against the wall.

"Rohm is just knocked out. He will be pissed when he wakes up, but he's in stable condition," the other responded.

All was quiet as the lanterns flickered and snapped in the windowless room. The dozen masked thugs who had just encountered a surprise, "wanted" visitor to Cannon-Gulf had brought in more unconscious comrades than expected. Wounded archers and foot soldiers were patching themselves up too as they awaited their next order.

When the sound of footsteps began to echo from the other side of the door, their faces fell, heart rates began to rise, and breathing tightened, as the steady, firm thudding of them got closer. Whatever lay beyond that door was somewhat of a mystery, but experience had shown them that it was never anything good.

The door opened slowly as an older man walked inside, his dark eyes turning immediately towards those lying there on the floor. His face showed great displeasure, and he turned his gaze to the others, searching for an explanation.

"We have good news sir, we—" one of the grunts tried to say.

"Good news? You call *this* good news?" Their boss spoke, his sarcastic tone amused, yet definitely unhappy.

"Yes, sir. Even though they overpowered us, we—"

"Overpowered?" His aggravation grew by the second. His voice got louder. "You want me to believe that my men were overpowered? By what? Capital guards? Another feeble tyrant trying to cause a stir around the city? What could *possibly* overpower *us*?"

His men cowered in silence. Their all-powerful boss glared at them with irritation at the result of this latest engagement. One eyebrow flared upward as he awaited any sort of answer. Looking pointedly at each of them from left to right, his frustration at this absurd delay soared.

"Well?!" he shouted, his deep voice bouncing off the walls of the room.

At that, one grunt dared to speak. "We tracked a group coming into the city and Rohm took over the charge, but was defeated. We didn't stand a chance so we thought it'd be best to retreat and—"

"*Retreat?*" the angered boss interrupted, reaching out a hand, palm up, stopping the man from continuing.

"Y-yes, sir."

"You outnumbered those fools and yet you decided to *flee* instead of fighting to your bitter end for that witless tyrant!?" his voice got louder and the room shook from the sound of it.

Any foot soldier who was able to move backed away, fearing now that their mistake was going to bring them unwelcome consequences.

"You two, take Rohm to the infirmary," the boss commanded as he stuck his head out of the doorway. Two of his men came running in, picked up the brute and slowly carried him out. The older man simply shook his head as he watched them leave.

"There is still good news in this, sir. We—"

"Enough." The boss could not bear to hear this man speak anymore. He rubbed an eye with one hand as he held out the other. He sighed heavily, then said, "I do not want to hear another word from any of you. Ever." The room began to fill with black smoke.

The thugs immediately knew what was happening. They began pleading with him, begging to be spared.

"I will not waste my time with you fools anymore. You have stained the name we so proudly wear. You are a disgrace." The boss's final words were spoken firmly as he closed and then locked the door. Black smoke continued to rise relentlessly, filling the room.

The thugs banged on the door as he slowly walked back down the hall, his eyes hardened with anger and his fists balled up. He heard their screams from behind him as he allowed the weak to be purged, dispelling them from his domain.

"I will not let weaklings ruin my plans for this world. Only the strong will prevail. That's why *I* will be the one to change this world." The old man's frown turned crookedly upwards into a maniacal smile. His pace quickened as his evil laughter clicked off the walls of the hallway.

"Our master was wrong to pick you. I will prove that once I dispose of one final pest," the boss scoffed. "Now… where is your feeble student hiding, Din?"

15

Where I am weak, I am strong

"Get up, you two. It looks like we're almost at the start of the woods."

Thalrok and Oa slowly sat up from the deck, rubbed their eyes, and looked ahead as the *Land Skipper* closed in on the great forest of Evercrest.

After that troubling brawl, which had been forced on them in the big city, the easy ride through Prosper Valley had soothed them on their journey. Lotus stayed alert the whole way, keeping course on their voyage to the forest.

Now awake, Thalrok climbed up to the top deck with Lotus and readied himself at the stern to help stop the ship before she collided with the first of the trees. Lotus called out the signal, and he hopped off the back with a rope in each hand that was tied to the *Skipper's* stern. The titan of a man dug his heels into the ground and pulled hard so that she slowed gradually to a serene halt.

Standing before the tall trees of Evercrest was somewhat intimidating. The three stared blankly into the immense wooded area where the sunlight poked through the canopy of leaves and onto the grassy forest floor like bright constellations.

"These trees are soooo big. It looks like they go on for miles." Oa murmured in awe, as he launched himself up and onto a low-hanging branch. Even though this branch was the lowest to the ground, it was still plenty high in the air.

"Are we planning to leave the *Skipper* here? It might be tough going to bring it through these trees with the terrain and all, even though there's prob'ly room enough between 'em." Thalrok said, looking into the wooded depths.

"True, but we have supplies and a safe place to sleep when it's with us. Let's take the risk and bring it along." Lotus suggested.

"I can see a break in the woods ahead. It looks like a path might be only a little bit north from here!" Oa shouted from somewhere atop the large trees.

Thalrok and Lotus shrugged, then hopped back on the *Land Skipper* to set off once again. They watched as Oa carefully dropped back down from his perch high up in the treetops.

"Did you guys hear that noise too?" Oa asked as the *Skipper* shook from his landing on the deck.

"What kind of noise?" Lotus asked.

"It was like a bunch of voices off in the distance. I think it might be the village we are looking for! The poster did say Hemridge was towards the outskirts of the forest." Oa replied, his excitement at this new adventure starting to show. He gave the *Skipper* a little burst of wind to get them back on their way to the village in the forest, while Lotus navigated the forest floor with great care. They reached the wider path to the north shortly and continued on. Gradually the sounds of cheerful revelry grew louder, and soon they were approaching the entrance gates of a very different type of village.

"Ah, hello, travelers! I offer you a warm welcome to our most hospitable village, Hemridge!" a gray-haired man by the gates greeted them congenially. The lively community inside radiated with music and chatter as the people of Hemridge mixed and mingled in good cheer.

This was a village that took full advantage of its unique environment. Their dwellings coated the ground below and were stacked up into the treetops above. Lanterns were strung from rooftop to rooftop. Hefty ropes crept up the large supporting trees which connected one house to the others with wooden plank bridges. Small ponds below glistened in the sunlight that peeked in from above the canopy. Happy voices and laughter coming from every direction filled the air as the three companions hopped out of the *Land Skipper*.

"This is quite the turnaround, huh?" Thalrok chuckled.

"You're telling me!" replied Lotus.

After dropping the sail and locking up their quarters on the *Skipper*, they headed inside to enjoy the festivities. Cheering came from all directions and the music only got louder the farther they went. Not a single soul was in sorrow. Robust positivity nearly burst from the trees themselves. Lotus looked over at Oa, seeing the big smile on his face as he observed all of the homes that scaled the trees.

"Wow! Do you guys smell that?!" Thalrok shouted, as he pumped the brakes. His head darted from left to right. Lotus could hear him sniffing deeply through his nose even through his big helmet. Finally, his eyes snapped over to a food stand selling a variety of meats from all across Perlaria. "Oh, thank you, world, you have answered my prayers!" Thalrok actually giggled, and he ran straight for it.

Oa laughed at his giddy reaction and started to follow him. He paused, then turned to Lotus, and asked, "Can I go with him? I wanna get some food, too."

"Oh, of course. Here, this is the very last of our money, so make sure to get something that'll last you the rest of the day." Lotus told him. He was shocked that Oa had asked for his permission to go, but, in reality, this was still all new for the kid. He saw Lotus as a leader and respected him, which was not a bad thing.

While Thalrok and Oa went off to get some food, Lotus continued to stroll through the village. This whole place fascinated him, even if he had seen places that felt somewhat similar. Hemridge wasn't as big as Petalbrooke had been, but it was booming just like it. The streets were filled with people happily running around, grabbing some food and drink, dancing, and just celebrating in general. There must be a festival of some sort going on.

As Lotus rounded a nearby corner, he was stopped by a sudden burst of loud cheering that shattered the air. When he turned to look that way, all he could see was the backs of a large group of people. They were all looking in the same direction with their hands raised and waving in the air, still cheering. Other folks ran past him to get a look, trying to peek through the crowd. Lotus wanted to see for himself, but as he got closer, he could see even less; a wall of people's backs and shoulders blocked his view.

"What is going on?" Lotus asked himself, as he walked around the crowd, trying to get even a glimpse of what was happening. He finally found a small opening and swam his way through to check it out. Peering between the other spectators, he finally saw what everyone was here to see. In a clearing there was a large archery field, with targets lined up side by side at one end and archers firing their arrows into them from the other.

This must be the contest that Oa was talking about. He looked at the row of archers as they prepared for their shots. Then they shot their arrows one by one, some hitting close to the bullseye and others farther off.

But which one is the challenger that the poster talked about? Lotus couldn't pick out who it was since there hadn't been anyone's likeness drawn on the poster. He just had to wait and see which archer was the most skilled. One particular man stood out to him. He wore his hood up and stood there in total calm, not like the others who had more of a nervous energy about them. Somehow, this guy stood out like a sore thumb, but not exactly in the way that a champion would. It seemed strange, so Lotus watched to see what would happen.

"Ladies and Gentlemen, it's time for the final arrow!" an announcer shouted, as the crowd cheered on. One by one, every archer nocked an arrow and got ready to fire at their target. Each in turn then took their shot until it was finally the hooded man's time to shoot. Everything quieted down as competitors and spectators alike went silent. The man in the hood drew back his bow evenly, steadied his aim, and took a deep breath in. Then, he turned his head slowly away from the target, in the opposite direction, toward where Lotus stood.

Is he doing it without looking?

Lotus felt a bit of anticipation himself. He observed carefully, trying to get a better look at this champion's face. The hooded archer's head was now turned fully toward Lotus, and not his target, so that the Lotus could see something he'd never expected.

Is that a blindfold?!

And then, the arrow was fired, soaring through the air until it reached the target, piercing through the exact center of the bullseye. The crowd exploded with applause and celebrated the victory of their beloved hometown archer.

"Ladies and Gentlemen! Our undefeated champion, Blind Shot Nyloc Inngan!" the announcer shouted, struggling to be heard over the roaring crowd.

Did he just say blind?! Now, Lotus was truly shocked.

The winning archer lowered his bow and waved to the crowd of people as he removed his hood, but not the blindfold. He walked over to the other competitors, shook their hands, and thanked them for competing before heading over to the sidelines.

"No way that guy is blind," Thalrok spoke through a mouthful of food. Lotus turned around to see him and Oa, who had also watched the last shot.

"How did he do that?" Oa asked, as he tore into his own meal. None of them had any idea what kind of trick the archer could have played. Maybe it wasn't even a trick at all. Maybe, it was real.

"So, which one of us is gonna give it a go?" Thalrok asked, pausing briefly between bites. "That's why we came here, isn't it, to see if we could win the prize money?"

They all stared blankly at one another to see who would volunteer to go, except it looked like one was already picked. Lotus saw the food in their hands, both of them chomping down like starving wolves.

"Okaaay... I'll give it a shot then," the wanted man replied, as he adjusted the hood of his cloak and headed over to the registration area. Oa and

Thalrok followed behind him, still fully enjoying their meal.

"I'm sure glad he said that, 'cause I've never shot an arrow in my life," Thalrok whispered.

"I've actually done it a few times before, back in my village," Oa replied.

"Oh yeah, were ya good?" Thalrok said, smacking his lips.

"Nope," Oa admitted, wiping his chin with his hand.

The two kept eating, but stopped talking, as they followed behind Lotus, who had gotten in line with all of the others who wanted to defeat the undefeated champion. They slowly moved up the line as each individual gave their name to claim a spot on the list of entrants.

"Sorry, sir. We're out of entry slots for today, it's all filled up. This is the last match of the festival, too, so you'll have to wait until next year," the clerk registering names said, when Lotus at last reached him.

"Damn, is there any way I could participate? I traveled all this way." Lotus asked.

"I'm sorry, sir. We just don't have room," the registrar told him, shaking his head.

Lotus was just staring in disbelief at the man who denied his entry when the blind archer himself stepped up and intervened.

"Excuse me for a moment, but what's your name, sir?" Nyloc asked.

"Me? My name is Lotus," he replied.

Nyloc was confused by Lotus's response, feeling as though his own instincts must be wrong. He shook it off quickly, then patted the registrar on the shoulder. "I think we can let this man participate. What's the harm, huh?" he said, and smiled as he headed off to prepare himself for the final competition.

Lotus sighed with relief as the registrar shrugged one shoulder, then deferred to the champion and wrote down his name below the other competitors on the list. Lotus headed for the archery field.

"Do you think Lotus is gonna win?" Oa asked.

With a mouth full of mutton, Thalrok mumbled to the young boy, "You know, I've never seen him fire an arrow, but I bet he can pull something off."

Oa nodded in agreement, as he settled in to watch Lotus who was now stretching his arms and testing out the feel of his bow.

"This your first time in Hemridge?" Nyloc asked Lotus.

"It is, and might I say you have such a lovely village," Lotus replied. It was still strange for Lotus to see a blindfolded man act as if he wasn't blind at all. He walked and seemed to look around as if he had two working eyes. It was the strangest thing. He had long, dirty blonde hair pulled into a low ponytail with some loose strands flowing down his shoulders. His dark green hooded jacket matched the colors of the village and his bow rested on his back. Beneath his jacket, and undetectable from any great distance, small daggers and pointy projectiles were barely concealed. He was definitely a prepared warrior when it came to combat. The two stood beside one another as ten other men lined up next to them in position for the competition to begin.

The announcer stood in the center of the archery range and shouted out to all the spectators, "For this final round, all archers will fire at their targets together at my signal. Do you think any of these eleven men have what it takes to defeat the reigning champion in a battle of accuracy? Let's give it up for the final match of the festival!" The crowd cheered loudly, chanting Nyloc's name as they pumped their fists into the air. Oa and Thalrok sat in the front row and softly cheered on their friend, watching as Lotus held tightly to his bow and picked up his first arrow.

Lotus glanced over and watched Nyloc reach back at his quiver and grab an arrow with practiced ease. He was the first to draw his arrow back and wait for the signal to fire.

I know I'm competing, but I just wanna watch him fire this arrow. Lotus readied for his own shot.

With a sudden shout, the announcer yelled out, "Fire!" Then there came the whistling of twelve arrows soaring through the air. The pattering of arrows pierced the painted wooden targets as each one of them landed in a marked circular zone. Nyloc's arrow was right in the center of the bullseye.

"There you have it! The first arrow has been fired, and it looks like

Nyloc is already in the lead," the announcer hollered. Each competitor was scored on how close they got to the center of the target. The closer to the bullseye, the more points the archer would get. With every round of this final match, the archer with the fewest points would be eliminated from the competition.

"Not a bad shot, Lotus." Nyloc praised, as he nodded his head to his rival.

"Thank you. You're not a bad shot yourself." Lotus replied. He was suspicious as to why Nyloc seemed to be so personally interested in him. Even if he was only being respectful, it just seemed very odd.

Arrow after arrow was fired across the range until the remaining contestants with the most points dwindled down to the two standing beside one another, Lotus and Nyloc.

"Well, folks, it looks like we have the final arrow ready to go! Nyloc is in first place by ten points, leaving Lotus to need a bullseye to take the lead. That is, *if* Nyloc were to miss," the announcer called out with an amused smile. The crowd laughed loudly at that ridiculous scenario before going completely silent as they awaited this last and most important shot. Oa and Thalrok sat on the edge of their seats, hoping for a miracle.

"Please, take the first shot," Nyloc suggested.

Lotus still felt that something was off about this guy, but he took the offer. He picked up his last arrow, shuffled his feet into place, and began to draw back on the bow.

"How about we make this a little interesting?" Nyloc proposed.

"What do you mean?" Lotus replied, as he lowered his bow and looked at his opponent.

"If you can hit the target, just hit it. Then you win the competition. It can land anywhere on the target as long as you hit it." The hint of a smirk on Nyloc's face was easy to read; he had something up his sleeve. Lotus glanced down and saw that Nyloc's bow was lowered, and his stance was nonthreatening.

"What is he planning?" Thalrok whispered to Oa. Even from where they were watching, he too could tell that something was dodgy about the situation.

"Sure, I'll take your offer," Lotus said with a slight nod.

The announcer immediately reported this new information, and shouted, "Ladies and gentlemen, it looks like we have a surprising change of events! Nyloc has challenged Lotus that if he can just hit the target anywhere on it, he will win the competition!" Gasps filled the air, and chatter moved in waves through the crowd. The spectators were wondering why Nyloc was giving his opponent such a huge advantage. Was he that confident that Lotus would miss the target entirely? Did he have a plan?

Lotus tightened his grip on the bow and lifted it once more. He stared down the range at the target he had hit many times already. "Just a normal shot now, nothing crazy," Lotus whispered to himself, and he took a deep breath in. The complete silence of the crowd was heavy enough to feel, like a dense fog. With a quick release of his fingers, Lotus's arrow shot through the air. Its path was smooth and directed straight at the target. All eyes watched as it took flight and flew closer to the target by the millisecond. Just as it was a few feet from hitting it, some swiftly moving object crashed into it, knocking it completely off-course.

What!?

What just hit his arrow? He turned his head to look at Nyloc, whose bow was still up, its bowstring vibrating from the recently fired arrow. As Lotus realized what had just happened, he knew that Nyloc had been staring his way the whole time, and with that same little smirk on his face.

"Incredible!! Nyloc has just shot Lotus's arrow with his *own* arrow, stopping it from hitting the target!" the announcer screamed. The crowd erupted in cheers as they jumped up and down in celebration for their undefeated champion. Oa and Thalrok's jaws dropped to the ground in disbelief at what had just happened.

Nyloc, blindfolded ever in place, lowered his bow and went over to shake Lotus's hand, expecting him to be angry or at least a bit peeved. Holding his hand out, he awaited total rejection, or maybe a lousy handshake with either a dirty look or no eye contact at all.

However, Lotus smiled, looked directly at where his eyes would be beneath the blindfold, and shook his hand right back, and with just the polite amount of firmness. "That was unbelievable. Great work, Nyloc." He smiled as he patted Nyloc's shoulder. Lotus then calmly walked back to his friends, his head held high despite having claimed no victory and, more importantly, no prize money.

Nyloc, who had just stunned the entire crowd, was now the one left speechless. He was confused when Lotus simply returned to his pals, and the three of them headed back through the village, not the least bit upset. This reaction was quite unexpected, but Nyloc couldn't let that distract him for now. So, he walked around to thank the other competitors as he always did, and was slapped on the back and congratulated by many of his fellow villagers as he passed by.

The festival days were coming to an end, but music and laughter still echoed in the streets. Hemridge residents and visitors alike roamed around playing games, dancing, enjoying food, drinks, and camaraderie. As for Lotus, Thalrok, and Oa, they headed back to the *Land Skipper* to figure out a plan to make some money. Their best bet would be to head back to Mellowtin and help folks around town with any jobs they could find while they saved up a nest egg. For now, it was too late in the day to shove off in the *Skipper*, plus they had taken all this time to make their way here. So, the three of them decided that they might as well stay for a bit, at least for the night.

When nightfall arrived, the many lanterns strung across all of Hemridge brightened the forest from within even more than the sun had during daylight hours. Music still meandered through the trees as midnight saw continued cheer and revelry. While Oa and Lotus rested in their bedrolls on the foredeck of the Skipper, Thalrok decided to return to the village. He wandered around for a bit until something caught his eye.

"Ah, now we're talkin'!" he laughed and clapped his hands together. Off he headed for the first bar he saw to have himself a drink for the night. Walking through the double doors, he made straight for the counter and grabbed a seat. Music was playing, talking and laughter filled the room with cheer. It was still very lively for this time of night.

"Bartender, if you'd please pour me something for a person who's never been to this part of Perlaria, I'd be most appreciative," Thalrok asked.

"That would be our Green Woven Whiskey, made from the roots of the trees that grow here in Evercrest," the bartender replied.

Thalrok reached into his pouch, and realized then and there that they were completely out of money. "Damn, never—" he began to say, but the bar suddenly erupted with cheering. Thalrok turned his head and saw that the champ himself had wandered into the bar.

Nyloc noticed the titan that Lotus had been with was sitting there at the bar and made his way over.

"Good evening, may I sit?" the blindfolded man asked.

"I should be asking you that, champ." Thalrok chuckled and offered the seat next to his. The archer thanked him and sat down.

"Ale for my friend and me, please," Nyloc told the bartender. The smile on Thalrok's face grew, as he saw that his night was about to change. The busy barkeeper brought them their drinks, and Nyloc respectfully paid the man in advance for the rest of the night.

"I noticed that you were with that Lotus fellow, but I never got your name." Nyloc said, looking over at his new drinking buddy.

"My name is Thalrok," he replied, lifting his helmet just enough to take a chug of his ale.

"Pleasure to meet you." Nyloc tilted his head up at the titan, and took a small sip of his own drink.

They chatted with one another and drank together through the night as time rolled on. "So, how did you and Lotus meet?" Nyloc eventually asked, signaling for another refill.

Thalrok slammed his mug down on the table and belched loudly. At that question, he let out a short hearty laugh. He told Nyloc all about how long and hard they had fought one another the first time they met, then flashed forward to now when they were traveling across Perlaria together. Nyloc let out a little chuckle himself at the titan's tale as the barkeeper brought their fresh drinks.

"So, it's true then. You're traveling with a wanted criminal, right?" Nyloc asked in a serious tone.

Thalrok stopped as he was about to take another sip of his drink, the mug halfway to his lips. Even in his woozy state of mind, he sobered quickly. He placed his mug down carefully before murmuring, "How many of you have noticed him?"

"Only myself. Luckily for him, probably because of the festival, nobody has even batted an eye. But *I* have noticed. Now, can you please answer my question?" Nyloc asked once again.

Thalrok balled his hands into tight fists. In a few moments, after he was able to calm himself down, he responded with, "First, I have a question for you." He slowly turned toward Nyloc, then asked, "Is a man's worth solely determined by ink on paper or by the man he really is inside?" The two of them went silent. Even though the music and chatter in the bar could be heard from outside, they paid no attention to any of it.

Eventually, Nyloc said, "I noticed him immediately, and couldn't trust him to be here in my village. Yet, after I tried to bring out some evidence of the wanted man in him with that dirty trick I pulled, he was unexpectedly very kind. Still, I don't trust it." Nyloc continued to ponder over Lotus's reputation versus his own recent perception of the young man.

Thalrok chuckled and took another sip of his drink before saying, "For someone without eyes, you've seen Ronin for who he really is, which is far, far better than how over half of this world thinks of him."

Nyloc was surprised to hear such respect and sincerity in Thalrok's voice when he spoke so highly of his friend.

"You are sure that this man you travel across Perlaria with, the one posted as 'wanted for murder' across every village, town, and city, isn't who he's written about and shown to be?" Nyloc asked.

"You should see for yourself," the bounty hunter replied, and burped heartily. Nyloc scratched his chin in curiosity, and realized that he felt a tingling in his feet.

"Now, let's get loose before this night ends!" Thalrok shouted, as he raised his drink high. After those several mugs of ale, he was a tad bit tipsy and ready to go. Not "go" as in leave, but "go" as in get the night really going.

"It's time to party everyone! Your champion is in the building!" he shouted, as he pointed at Nyloc. Without hesitation, the room cheered Nyloc's name again and again, jumping up and down, fists pumping. Embarrassed at the attention and a little tipsy himself, the archer just sat and waved back to them all.

"Now let's get this festival started for real!" Thalrok shouted, as he put his arm around Nyloc's shoulders. The two lifted their cups and downed their drinks; surely this would not be their last night as comrades.

The next morning...

"Come on, Thalrok, get up!" Oa shouted as he nudged the titan with his foot.

Thalrok groaned. His eyelids felt heavier than usual and he struggled to lift them. Piercing sunlight peeked through the slits in his helmet, making him squint. He felt the floor of the deck moving beneath him. "What time is it? Is there an earthquake going on?" he mumbled, as he tried to sit up.

"No, we are just outside of Evercrest, and it's a few hours past sunrise. You've been asleep this whole time." Oa answered. The severely hungover bounty hunter could make himself sit up just enough to see that the *Land Skipper* was skimming across the plains of Prosper Valley.

"Are you feeling alright?" Lotus asked from above.

Thalrok grabbed the sides of his helmet as the throbbing pain of yesterday's mistakes caught up to him. He had no idea as to what had happened last night, or even how he'd gotten back to the *Skipper*.

"I might have gotten a little, uh, drunk... last night," Thalrok confessed, as he propped himself up against the wall.

Oa laughed as he gave the Skipper another burst of air to speed their journey. "A *little*?!" he giggled.

Thalrok rubbed his helmeted head some more, trying to remember anything at all from last night.

"Oa, you keep an eye ahead. I'm gonna see if we have anything to help Thalrok with his headache." Lotus said, then hopped down from the top deck.

"Yes sir!" Oa shouted, as he hopped up to take over at the steering rods.

"Thanks." Thalrok sighed, as he tried to piece together a few parts from the previous night. He remembered drinking with Nyloc and some of the locals. They partied and danced to the music in the bar. *What did we do after that?* Thalrok tried his best to remember.

Meanwhile, Lotus went into the cabin to look around for anything that might help Thalrok.

"Oh wait, I know   I left with Nyloc. He was stumbling around a lot. Right! He helped me back to the *Skipper* last night, because I had a little trouble, y'know… uh, getting around." Thalrok remembered.

"What did you guys talk about?" Oa asked.

"I don't even remember at this point…" Thalrok replied. He was thinking hard.

"Thalrok!" Lotus shouted.

The bounty hunter's eyes squinted as he heard Lotus's voice coming from inside the cabin of the *Skipper*. He heard more clearly as Lotus poked his head through the doorway, and suddenly Thalrok remembered one small detail of what had happened last night.

"You wanna tell me why Nyloc is in the bed of the *Skipper*, passed out?" Lotus asked.

16

Trust

"You *what?!*" Lotus asked in surprise.

Nyloc sat, arms crossed, leaning against the back railing of the *Land Skipper.* "I want to come with you."

Lotus was still trying to understand what had happened in these last few minutes. He remembered going to look for something in the *Skipper* when he noticed a man-sized lump under the blankets on the bed. When he checked it out, there was Nyloc.

"You want to come with us?" Oa echoed.

"Did the first time I said it not make sense?" the champion archer replied tartly.

"But why?" Lotus asked.

Nyloc turned toward the very hungover bounty hunter and pointed a finger at him. "Your buddy there invited me."

Lotus and Oa turned to look at Thalrok, who was still cradling his helmeted head with both big hands; it was throbbing painfully.

"I did? Oh…yeah, I guess I did." Thalrok recalled. He was remembering more of last night—how, at the bar, he had said, "You should see for yourself," in regards to talking about Lotus. And then, how, many drinks later, he'd stumbled through the village with Nyloc holding onto him to help him get back to the *Skipper.*

"I knew the instant I saw you in my village that you were the wanted man on the posters pinned up in our town. Your friend though, he speaks very highly of you. The whole night, he told me about all the noble things you've done." Nyloc told the wanted man.

"All my life, I stayed in Hemridge. I mean, why would I need to leave, right?" Nyloc continued. "When those posters went up, all I thought was that this is a wanted man, born and raised a criminal, a murderer even. Yet, only several hours ago, I was told that I was absolutely wrong." He brushed his hand over the smooth wooden bow that he always carried with him.

"So, I had to know for myself." Nyloc went on. "I've always thought about venturing out into the plains of Prosper Valley before. I just needed a sign. I guess my curiosity about *you* was that sign." He stood up, adjusted his blindfold, and rested his bow on his back. "As of now, I am joining your little crew. I want to see what is out there and what else I have been blinded by. You will please take me with you on this journey—alright, Captain?" Nyloc requested, not really allowing for much in the way of argument.

Oa and Thalrok turned to Lotus, whose face stayed emotionless, his body still. Lotus didn't know how to respond. His goal was to keep himself away from others to keep them from harm, and yet, somehow they kept being drawn to him.

Lotus at last said, "Y'know this isn't going to be some happy joyride. There is no sign of what the future holds. If you are to journey with me, you may well be doomed."

Nyloc scoffed, "You will come to see that I am no damsel in distress. The comforts of my home have not made me soft. This is what my master has trained me for, to one day leave my home, seek out adventure, and not be shackled by my own curse as well."

"Curse?" Oa asked.

"It appears that you are the blind ones. Have you not noticed that I was not gifted with sight like all of you are?" Nyloc gestured toward his blindfold with a smirk.

"Obviously, we know you are blind, but how can you uh... see, I guess?"

Thalrok asked.

Nyloc carefully felt at the blindfold over his eyes, and then he smiled. "May I share, captain?" he asked.

"Please, go right ahead," Lotus said. He had been wondering about that himself.

The archer took a deep breath in. A good many years had gone by since he last shared the story of his past, which was not, in truth, a sad story. It brought him joy to share the tale of how a man without sight reached farther in life than any in his village had before.

"So... it took my parents a month or so after I was born to realize that I was completely blind." Nyloc began. "The village of Hemridge has always been best known for our skilled archers, so to have a child who had lost an archer's only source of success would be heartbreaking. My mother and father were both crack shots with their bows, so finding this out about their son was awfully disappointing, but, they never gave up on me. Even when I got a little older, I still needed somebody with me just to get around the house and town. I eventually heard about bows and archery when I was about eight, and I was instantly hooked! But I couldn't see a thing, or even walk around much on my lonesome, much less aim a bow at any target. My parents tried their all, but my dream of being an archer was simply not to be. They tried to point me in different directions, different interests, hoping to find something that would bring me happiness. But nothing at all brought me joy in those dark days."

Nyloc paused momentarily, smiling when he thought about a very specific day. "Then one day, a knock came at our door. My parents had no idea who the man was, but right away he asked, 'Where is the one who does not see?' At first my parents were a little nervous about some stranger who just showed up out of nowhere, but in the end they decided to introduce me to this man who was so curious about my condition. The very first thing he asked me was, 'Do you want to be an archer?' In a heartbeat, I smiled and shouted 'yes!' So, he and my parents took me outside to a plot in the woods where there were no houses around. He told me to stand there by myself and tell him what I heard—which was rustling leaves and bushes, the wind, and some voices off in the distance. He told me to keep listening, every day, to keep listening and listening. After a while, I memorized the route to where I stood and sometimes I even went out on my own. It scared my parents, but I learned to get back home as well.

Nyloc stopped again, remembering. "I knew nothing about my master, not a single thing. I've never even seen the guy, literally. All I knew at the time was that his name was Sango."

"Finally, after over a year of just listening and listening, I got really impatient," the archer went on. "Then my master told me to stop listening. I was completely confused. I was even more confused when he poked me in the forehead and said, 'You cannot leave this spot until you can tell me what is in front of you.' I was speechless, and even more so when he gave me plugs to put in my ears. Blind and deaf, there I stood in the middle of the woods. The day dragged on and on. Finally, Sango grabbed my shoulder, removed the earplugs, and asked me what was in front of me. I couldn't tell him—I didn't know! So he told me to walk around the next day. Blind and deaf, I walked in the woods, never knowing what I'd run into. He made me do this for a year, a whole year! Again, he poked me in the forehead and asked, 'What is in front of you?', and I still couldn't think of anything. I wondered how long this process would take, this meaningless walking around, listening, not listening, and hopeless training. For what? At last, all I could think of to say to him was, 'The whole world.' My parents told me that when he heard that answer, Sango smiled and beamed with joy." Nyloc shook his head, and the smile on his face brightened as well.

"So how did that make you see?" Oa asked.

"My master, Sango, told me that if I could focus all of my energy, all of my might from the inside of my body, on what I heard, sensed or felt, tasted, and smelled, my vision would become clear, and the whole world would be known to me. But it would happen only if I focused with my mind, not my eyes. Sure enough, as the months turned to years, I focused really hard and finally 'saw' the blurry images of two people standing near me, my mom and dad. They cried when I called for them, not knowing how I knew they were there. After that, I trained night and day, using my other senses and the entire focus of my mind to visualize everything around me. It took me until I was fifteen years old to not see with my eyes, but with my mind, where all became clear as day. And, unlike when you use your eyes, I can perceive everything that is happening 360 degrees all around me."

"No way! Turn around, tell me how many fingers I'm holding up!" an astonished voice called out.

"Not now, Thalrok, let him finish." Lotus scolded.

Nyloc gave a little half-smile and went on, "My master never saw me again once I'd begun to see with my mind. I was truly distraught; I wanted him to see me succeeding with this *so* much! But the craziest thing about the whole situation was something that my parents were told never to speak of until I was eighteen years old. Sango, my master, was completely blind as well! Destiny must have brought him to my village to find me. So, yeah, that's about it." Nyloc finished.

It was hard to believe that someone could lack sight in their eyes yet see anything with such clarity. Here was a man who had learned to navigate the world with an acute awareness—he could sense the subtle vibrations in the air, the shifts in sound that revealed his surroundings, and the warmth of beings nearby. He had trained his mind to perceive far more than what others could see, piecing together a vivid mental map from the hum of life around him. Then again, this world did hold many more mysteries than one could even imagine. The three, now four, companions would come to discover that this was just the tip of the iceberg as far as mysteries were concerned.

"That's incredible! You are one freaky guy, but I'm glad you're ridin' with us now." Thalrok laughed, then grabbed his helmeted head from the pain of it.

I guess I have a little more in common with him after all. Lotus returned his full attention to the steering rods and kept them on course.

"How does your family feel about you leaving the village?" Oa asked.

"Oh, they don't know that I've left—no one does," the blindfolded man said.

"What?!" Lotus shouted, as he turned around abruptly.

"Hey, hey, I'm an adult! I can make my own decisions." Nyloc lifted his hands in the air, indicating that he could certainly manage his life independently.

"Won't your family be worried about your sudden disappearance?" Lotus asked.

"My family stopped worrying about me a long time ago. Not that they don't love me, but they rest easy knowing I have two feet to walk on and the whole world in front of me." Nyloc replied.

This response didn't settle well with Lotus. Not that he didn't understand where the archer was coming from. He just felt like he was stealing someone away without a proper goodbye.

"Ronin, are we there yet—at Mellowtin?" Thalrok asked, not unlike a whiny child.

"I will tell you when we get there," Lotus told him.

"Why does the bounty hunter still call him Ronin?" Nyloc asked

"Ooh, ooh! I want to explain it this time!" Oa shouted.

*　*　*

"That is a lot to take in... I didn't expect your life story to be anything like that, captain." Nyloc shook his head then lifted it, as he could sense the town getting closer by the second.

"Yeah, welcome to the club." Thalrok chuckled, as the *Land Skipper* slowly came to a complete stop just outside of Mellowtin. The four of them hopped out, planting their feet in the soft grass. The long journey across Prosper Valley was finally over. A few random stops had made the trip a little longer for Lotus and Thalrok, but finally here they were, home again.

"Damn, it's good to be back." Thalrok stretched robustly, then he headed toward town.

"A lot of detours along the way," Lotus added, falling into step behind Thalrok.

Oa and Nyloc walked side by side, following after them. "This seems like quite a nice place. What's it like here?" Nyloc asked Oa.

The boy shrugged and said, "You're asking the wrong guy, I've never even been here."

Thalrok and Lotus stopped for a moment, looked at each other, and realized he was right.

"Oh yeah, this isn't just the champ's first time. The kid's never been here yet either." Thalrok acknowledged.

"Like I said, there were a lot of detours." Lotus chuckled. "Come on, we can show you around," he said, as he and Thalrok led the charge through town to their first destination. Their brief stay in Mellowtin felt like it had been an eternity ago. But now both of them had the same unspoken feeling that they had to let someone know they were back—two someones, as a matter of fact—the two ladies who were almost like mothers to them, always helpful, warm, and caring.

"Ms. Leyla! Ms. Layla!" Thalrok shouted, as he pushed open the double doors to the inn and burst into the foyer.

"The Lie-Inn?" Oa whispered skeptically.

"Interesting name," Nyloc replied, as they followed along into the peaceful lodging house.

"Oh no, please don't tell me all that racket is… it is." Leyla rolled her eyes in mock annoyance and stern disapproval when she turned to see the bounty hunter and the wanted man returned safely from their adventures.

"Oh now, don't act like you didn't miss me," Thalrok said, tilting his head, his chin lifted, and with what he considered his most charming smile plastered on his face, which was barely visible under the helmet.

Then Layla came out from the back, beaming at the sight of them. "We are *so* glad to see you two back here in one piece. How was it?" she asked.

"It was a long journey, but we survived, sometimes just barely. Please, may we introduce our two new fellow travelers?" Lotus said, then moved aside and signalled for the young disciple of Gou and the champion archer to step forward. Both of them approached the counter and received the same intense looks from the twins that the others had when they'd first arrived.

"Don't worry, they aren't like 'headband' over there," Thalrok smirked and pointed at Lotus.

"What's your name, young one?" Leyla asked.

"My name is Oa. I'm from the village Wisphire that lies on top of Mount Axi. Very nice to meet you," the boy said with a tenuous smile. But soon his grin lit up the room when the twins placed their hands on their hearts and warmly smiled back. They were quite charmed by his innocent appearance and sweet, polite nature.

"It is an absolute pleasure to meet you, young one. And you?" The twins turned their attention to the archer.

"I am Nyloc from Hemridge in Evercrest. Happy to meet you. To be honest, I don't think I've met twins before," the man wearing a blindfold told them.

The twin innkeepers slowly waved their hands in front of Nyloc's face, wondering just how he could see them and know that.

"I know I may appear to be blind, but actually, I can see quite well," the archer chuckled.

The innkeepers looked impressed when he gently touched Leyla's fingers mid-wave. "It's nice to meet you too. Will you be staying with your friends?" Layla asked.

Thalrok and Lotus glanced at each other, both realizing that they had no money to afford rooms for Oa and Nyloc. Lotus was also certain that their old rooms were occupied by now, and that they'd have to pay to get other rooms for themselves as well.

"I'm sorry to say, but unfortunately we won't—" Lotus began.

"Do you not remember what I told you two before you left?" Layla interrupted.

All they could do was stand quietly with their hands folded while Layla's kind smile rested on them. With all of the goings on and as they'd been away for a little while, Lotus and Thalrok had both momentarily forgotten that the two of them always had a place here whenever they needed. Now, it began to come back to them.

"You were told that your rooms will be ready for you when you get back. Remember?" Layla reminded them.

The two bowed their heads, unable to find a way to properly thank the twins for the kindness that they continued to offer.

"For us?" Oa asked. Lotus and Thalrok lifted their heads to see Leyla and Layla holding out two keys, one for the young disciple of Gou, and the other for the blind archer.

"Their rooms will be at the end of the hall, right next to both of yours," Leyla explained.

"Wait, wait, but we can't pay!" Thalrok blurted out.

"Who said anything about paying?" Layla asked. Speechless, the four of them stood as the twins tossed Oa and Nyloc their keys. "Why don't you show them their rooms?" Leyla suggested.

Thalrok shook his head and chuckled in relieved disbelief at their compassion as he headed up the stairs with their two newest companions right behind him. Lotus had to process this for a moment. Such hospitality seemed unreasonable, but why?

The twin innkeepers had returned to their duties when they noticed Lotus still standing there. "You all right, sweetheart?" Layla asked with concern.

"Yeah.. yeah, I'm all right," Lotus mumbled, as he headed up after the others. He'd gotten lost in his mind for a moment, but then walked up each of those steps and down the familiar hall to see that the door to his room was still there. It wasn't a dream.

"Whoa! I get my own room? This is pretty cool. I like how small it is." Oa hopped around and checked out all his room had to offer.

"This is very kind of them just to let us stay here for free. Not to mention, this is a very nice inn." Nyloc said, nodding as he placed his few things down in his room, across from Oa's.

At the end of the hall their four doorways opened to a small central living area, which contained a sofa, two chairs, a small table, and a large window. In Room 26, the first room on the left, was young Oa, who'd been offered the chance to leave his cloistered village and join in on this adventure to scratch his itch of wanderlust. Next door in room 27 was where the wanted criminal, known throughout Perlaria as the one who struck down a Grand Sage, resided. He'd been hunted for years and was said to be a curse incarnate who brought only pain for others in his footsteps. Across the common area from Lotus in room 29 was the bounty hunter, a titan-man just trying to survive in this world, who had found someone he wholly respected and wanted to follow. And next to Thalrok, in Room 28, the first room on the right, was the blind archer, who hoped to learn more about the wide world without being distracted by what was said by others, and to find the truth for himself. Four completely different people, yet so very much the same.

"You alright, Ronin?" Thalrok asked as he slowly opened his door.

"I'm alright, just thinking," Lotus replied.

"Okay, just don't think too hard. You'll pop a blood vessel." Thalrok said, smiling.

"Very funny." Lotus shook his head, scoffing at the titan's joke.

"You ready to take these two around town some more?" Thalrok asked.

Lotus didn't answer right away, he just peered through the window, told Thalrok to go ahead, and said that he would meet up with them in a bit.

The bounty hunter was slightly concerned, but thought Ronin might just need a little time alone. Much had happened since the last time they were here. It was a lot to take in. "We'll be at the canteen when you're ready to join up, okay?" he told Lotus.

"I'll see you guys there," Lotus called out, as he stood up. He just stood in the middle of his room and let his vision blur and his mind run.

Right or left. Up or down. Hot or cold. Heads or tails. One way or another. Whether he would be shown unreasonable kindness or handed unrelenting pain was always a gamble. It hadn't even been a month since he met Thalrok, and now Oa and Nyloc had joined their little crew. It scared him. So many more people to get hurt. So many more chances to lose a life he was building.

The wanted man headed out of his room to catch up with the others. He galloped down the stairs, across the foyer, and grabbed the door handle. Just as he was about to pull it forward, he froze in place. Releasing it, he turned around and headed back to the counter.

"Excuse me," Lotus said softly.

"Yes, dear. Is everything alright?" Layla asked.

"Why did you trust me? *Me*. Why are you two being so kind to me, even though all of Perlaria, the whole world, is out to get me and have my head, all because I was the one they thought killed a Grand Sage? I am the face posted below the name. I am the one who was there. I am the one who was called "cursed", "a monster", "murderer". Bruised, cut and hurt, I was on the run for so long, and still I show no signs of stopping. Yet you both trusted me completely after I said just a few words." Lotus spoke openly and with no anger.

The innkeepers had stopped what they were doing and now walked over to the counter in front of him. Their faces looked as if they'd heard news that a family member had passed away, stricken with grief and hollow with sadness. The two reached out and each took one of his hands in their own, holding them gently as Lotus bowed his head.

"My sweet child, we have seen hundreds of faces come into this inn. Every day, we risk our lives by letting people stay here. Early on, we had our fair share of bad tenants. But, the longer we worked here, the more we learned how to know whether someone was lying to our faces or not. It took some time," Layla recalled, "but we are pretty good at it now."

"The look in your eyes, the tremble in your voice, everything about you showed the signs of an innocent child. How would we be able to live with ourselves knowing the most notorious criminal in all of Perlaria was at our doorsteps, innocent and without a home? We had no choice but to trust you. You did nothing wrong, after all." Leyla added.

Lotus felt their warm hands holding his, and the calming sound of their voices resonated deep in his head, soothing his taut nerves with every passing second.

"You want to cry, don't you?" they both asked at once with the softest of voices.

The wanted man slowly lifted his head.

"It's okay," the twins said. "You have been through a lot, after all."

17

The Calm

The air was cold. There was a sensation of soft pillows of tall grasses that lightly prickled Lotus's back as he slowly opened his eyes. The clear blue sky above was so pleasant with its vibrant hue and cloudless void. With a slight push of both hands, he sat up, feeling the grass beneath him supporting his weight.

"Hello?" he asked, hearing his voice echo over the open grassy plains which went on for as far as he could see. He folded his legs and sat there on the ground, brushing his hand across the grass.

"I've been here before," the wanted man realized, as he looked around a bit more. It had been a while, but he remembered being in this exact same place. Lotus stood up, then took a few slow steps forward to see if there was anything to this mysterious place.

"How did I get here?" he wondered, his eyes darting everywhere to see what else might be in this empty world. Suddenly, he heard screams and shrieks coming from somewhere behind him. Immediately his skin crawled, and a feeling of dread overcame him as he turned around. Distant screams of pain echoed one after another. He saw, off in the distance, a large dark mountain range, and a terrifyingly blood-red sky behind it.

"Lotus!" "Lotus, where are you?!" "Ronin!" Lotus heard several different voices screaming in agony and calling for him by name. He took a step back. The red sky bled into the bright blueness above him, its darkness spreading out toward and over him.

"Where are you?!" Lotus shouted, as he began to run, fleeing the dark red sky. He watched as the mountains grew, reaching higher into the air, while the grass beneath his feet darkened and rotted away as it turned to ash.

What's going on?!

Lotus's heart began to race, faster and faster. He gasped for air. His feet felt like they weren't even connecting to the ground, and his body felt limp and numb. Taking a peek behind himself, he saw that the mountains were coming in to surround him, and the sky was all blood-red. The remaining air left his lungs in one last terrifying breath. He could hear all of the screams reverberating from the mountains, calling his name in distress. Then, one single voice rose above all of the others.

"I found you," the deep voice rumbled.

Lotus abruptly sprang out of bed and thumped onto the floor, his heart racing and beads of sweat dotting his face. His legs shook as he grabbed onto a chair to stand and get his bearings. His room was completely silent. He was the only one in it. It was just him there, along with the little bit of sunlight shining in from between the curtains.

A dream... it was just a dream. Lotus calmed himself down and swiped both hands across his face. He took some slow, controlled, deep breaths as he glanced outside, noticing that he'd slept in a bit.

"Excuse me? Is everything alright?" one of the innkeepers asked from the hallway. The young man made his way to the door and cracked it open a little, poking his head out.

"I'm sorry, I... I fell out of bed." Lotus apologized.

"Well, are you alright, sweetheart?" Layla asked, mildly concerned.

"Yes, yes, I'll be fine. I hope I wasn't too loud." Lotus quickly answered.

"Not at all. I heard a noise and wanted to make sure everything was as it should be. Have a good day then, m'dear." Layla smiled and made her way back down the hall. Lotus closed the door and slowly slid his back down it until he sat on the floor. His arms lay limply beside him, his chin on his chest.

"One week," he whispered.

It had been one week now since they came back to Mellowtin. Every time he thought about staying another night, he felt like he was holding a bomb, not knowing when it would go off. He still felt that life here was too good to be true, especially after all the commotion and running about they'd done in those other villages.

In the past week, Lotus and Thalrok had introduced newcomers Oa and Nyloc to the town, and most notably, to Stritan. When they met Stritan, they both enjoyed his cleverness and his enthusiastic nature. To Nyloc's great satisfaction, Stritan was able to properly tune up his bow. He also enhanced Oa's staff by installing a thin sheet of metal at each end which wrapped around to give the tips a little more punch. Of course, Oa was thrilled, and couldn't wait to try it out. Stritan was even able to help out with fixing up the *Land Skipper*. The kid had been left speechless when they showed him the *Skipper* the day after they returned. He begged and pleaded to get a chance to work on it, promising over and over that it would be worth it. They saw no risk, so Stritan had been allowed to tinker with it as much as he liked.

Putting his thoughts aside, Lotus stood up, dressed, and headed out to find work. Making his way down the inn's stairs, he waved goodbye to the twins and headed out. Today was cool with a light breeze. Some rain had fallen yesterday and left a fresh smell in the air.

"Morning." Lotus waved to a woman sweeping as he passed by the local bakery. He slowed long enough to ask, "Do you need any help today?"

"Not today, Lotus, but thank you!" she replied. The young man returned to his run and continued on, asking folks at the local restaurants, shops, or anyone anywhere who he could help out and also keep himself busy. Each day, he went to a different part of Mellowtin to help around until they said they were all good for the day. In return, they'd pay him for how hard and generously he had worked. He'd insist on not taking the money they offered, but they would never let him leave without it.

"Ay! Mornin' Lotus," an elderly man called in passing.

"Good morning, sir. Have you seen Thalrok today?" Lotus asked.

"I think he's helping out at Gayle's today," the older man replied. Lotus thanked him for letting him know and went on his way.

The bounty hunter had been doing his share of labor as well. One of the sweetest ladies in the town ran a small lumberyard, and he had been working there since they came back. He'd been splitting wood, stacking the woodpiles, and also did much of the delivery work.

"Speaking of… g'morning, Thalrok," Lotus said, happy to see the titan out and on the job.

"Oh, mornin' Ronin." The bounty hunter carefully placed down the immense bundle of wood he was carrying and wiped the sweat from his forehead. "You're starting out a little late. You alright?" he asked.

"Yeah, I'm fine. I just slept in today." Lotus told him.

"'Sleeping in' isn't in your vocabulary." Thalrok pointed out, tilting his head.

"Okay, I accidentally slept in. Happy?" Lotus rolled his eyes.

"Yes. Yes, I am." Thalrok chuckled, as he picked up the bundle again to be on his way. Then he turned to ask, "Hey, d'ya know where Nyloc and Oa are?"

"I think Oa is definitely still asleep. As for Nyloc, I'm sure he's training again out by the *Skipper*." Lotus reasoned.

"Alright, just wanted to check. See you tonight." Thalrok shouted, and he pressed on.

Lotus watched him march down the stone street and ease his cargo around the corner. He had asked Thalrok if they could meet up tonight to talk about something important. Of course, the bounty hunter agreed, but was curious as to why it had to wait until later. Lotus just assured him that it would be better that way.

This last week, he'd been thinking a lot. Each day that went by, he wondered about every interaction he'd had so far with that group of thugs and bandits. They all seemed the same. He thought back further to when he and Thalrok had reached the town of Ashveil. They'd found it in shambles and with no sign of life, only remnants of lives that were since gone.

"Infected Ones," Lotus whispered. That was the name written in many places in the destroyed village. He recalled the symbols they'd marked the buildings with, and then the map in that basement. After following it, he and Thalrok had found another village invaded and in distress. Even when they left the Infected One's leader there in Thristle with one less arm and in the hands of the City of Light guards, he had somehow escaped. Then because of that skirmish, they, the Infected Ones, started to go after him with more focus. In Harthfield, General Speral had called out specifically for "Ronin" and wanted to take him somewhere.

Where?

Then, the most surprising thing had happened while rescuing the hostages of Harthfield. He'd seen Speral, and all of his other thugs, turn to ash just like that monster did all those years ago; it had sent chills down his spine. His whole body had gone cold, and his eyes couldn't believe what they saw. Nothing had been left of them, not a trace.

It has to be.

When they had detoured into Cannon-Gulf, even in that huge metropolis, Lotus stood out like a sore thumb. Somehow, the masked clan there immediately spotted him and knew exactly where to find him. "Tell the boss about our discovery." That's what they'd said before they retreated. Every time, and with everyone who identified him, it wasn't like they knew him from his likeness on the poster. It was like they knew exactly who he was.

Later that day...

"Alrighty, that should be all for today. Again, thank you so much, Lotus. This was very kind of you," the shopkeeper said, bowing to the young man.

"Truly, it's nothing. If I can ever help out again, please let me know." Lotus bowed in return before leaving for the day. The sun had somehow already made its way across the sky and let the night creep in. The bell on the door above him rang on his way out, signaling that work time was over, and the end of the day lay in front of him.

One jingle after another, the bell above the door of the Fork and Sword chimed as hungry and thirsty patrons entered. Thalrok peered over his shoulder and saw Lotus walking towards him, where he grabbed a seat.

"Who did you help out today?" Thalrok asked.

"I helped out Mr. Currin at his shop. Got to help set up the store since he had to close for a little while when his wife was sick." Lotus told him.

"Nice, nice. Thanks to the cooler weather, I was able to get a lot of work done. Just give it a day, and it'll be humid again, ugh." Thalrok shook his head.

The two sat at the bar and just looked off in silence. When the barkeep arrived, Thalrok ordered his favorite ale, and Lotus just got some tea. Then they didn't say anything at all. It was like they were complete strangers on an awkward date. One drink after another, the silence was only broken by their exhales after taking a sip.

"You wanted to talk?" Thalrok finally broke the silence.

"Yeah, I want to discuss something with you," Lotus murmured. The surrounding noise of the busy bar began to fade away. Despite all the chatter and hubbub, the two of them could hear nothing but their own voices.

"I need to leave," Lotus muttered, staring into his tea and speaking as if he had no connections with anyone or anything. It was as though he were talking to a stranger, not his friend the titan, with whom he had a very good relationship. "Every time we went to a different place, even Cannon-Gulf, those people knew who I was." Lotus continued, gripping his cup tightly.

"Everyone knows who you are, you're the 'most wanted' man." Thalrok snorted.

"No, they knew who *I* was," Lotus said with great intensity, then turned to Thalrok. The air was still, and they locked eyes with one another. This was a side to Lotus that Thalrok never wanted to see. This was the face of a man distancing himself in order to do something drastic, something that would change everything.

282

"So, what now?" Thalrok asked.

"I'm going to go find the Infected Ones. I think, no, I know, these thugs had to be the ones that took away the man who changed my life years ago. They are moving around in the shadows destroying and taking lives. I need to find where they are hiding and stop them before it worsens. I'm sorry, but this is something I need to do, or I will never rest knowing they are out hurting people just to find me, like at Harthfield." Lotus slammed his hand on the counter. The impact shook the whole bar, rattling the cups and glasses all across the counter. Everyone looked around to see what was going on, but no one had any idea.

"Please, help Oa and Nyloc see the world and do what they want. I just can't stay here any longer. I know this will all end poorly because of me. I need to seek out the Infected Ones before they hurt anyone else. Or worse, before I hurt anyone else." Lotus stood up from his seat, put some money on the counter, and headed back toward the inn. He felt the heavy pressure on his shoulders releasing slowly. He'd thought this talk would put his mind at ease, but instead he just felt worse. It felt like his moments surrounded by familiar company were seconds from ending. The roots he'd dug into this town were being ripped right out of the dirt. It *was* too good to be true, after all.

"I'm coming with you." A firm voice split the night air.

Lotus stopped walking, then slowly turned around. "No, you're not. I can't—"

"You can't what?" Thalrok interrupted. "You can't bear to lose anyone else? You think I can't handle myself even after all we've been through? Ronin, listen. You know how important this is to me too. I saw the mark of the Infected Ones on a barn in Harthfield. I was too scared for it to be true in the moment, so I didn't say anything. But I know in my heart that these Infected Ones are the villains that took my family too." Thalrok stood tall before the wanted man.

After a beat, Thalrok added, "Plus, I think I might know where they could be hiding."

"You do?" Lotus quirked an eyebrow.

"It's a hunch, but I think that they might be somewhere in the underground city beneath Cannon-Gulf. It's not a fun journey, but I'm almost ninety percent sure they are there." Thalrok replied.

Lotus stood there, contemplating whether or not this was a good idea. He heard the many voices calling out different opinions in his head. *Should he let Thalrok come too? Should he just go on his own?*

"You've been trying to protect me and the others this whole time. You forget, we are trying to protect *you* too." Thalrok reached over and placed his big knuckles on Lotus's forehead.

Thalrok's words and actions resonated louder than all of the other conflicting voices in his mind. Now, everything was clear.

"All right. Let's go," Lotus said, no longer looking at Thalrok as some stranger, but now seeing him as the loyal friend that he truly was. "Oa and Nyloc have to stay here. This isn't their battle, and I can't afford to lose them in the chaos that might unfold," he added.

"Of course, I just hope they take it well. That poor kid will be so upset when we say good—" Thalrok paused abruptly and looked over at Lotus, his amber eyes narrowed. "Don't tell me..."

"Yep, we're leaving before they wake up," Lotus replied.

"You have got to be *the* expert at leaving without a goodbye, you know that." Thalrok sighed, and they got up to head back to the Lie-Inn.

Even with all this serious talk, Lotus allowed himself a little smirk at the titan's displeasure. With a new plan in effect, he was ready to leave Mellowtin behind and take on the Ones who had hidden in the shadows for all these years. Finally, he would face the man behind all this chaos, whoever he was.

The next day...

"You ready?" Thalrok asked.

"More than ready," Lotus said, as he hopped aboard the *Land Skipper*. As his feet touched the wooden deck of their ship, his body tingled, and his heart skipped a beat. It was a weird feeling, almost like he really didn't want to leave, like he didn't want to just abandon the twins, the town, and especially Oa and Nyloc. *Really, it's for the best,* he thought.

With the help of Stritan and his clever craftsmanship, the *Skipper* had gotten a complete tune-up. He'd refashioned the metal of the wheels, fine-tuned the brakes and steering controls, and provided any other touch-ups as needed as well as a few extras. She looked almost brand new and was ready to take on Prosper Valley once again.

"Last chance to change your mind." Lotus reminded Thalrok.

"Not a chance in the world," Thalrok replied. The two nodded their heads, and Thalrok grabbed the newly installed controls. Stritan had taken into account times when Oa wouldn't be able to give them a push with his wind-assist, and had installed something of his own design. On the main deck of the small ship, a thick metal rod poked out from the floor with a vertical bar across the top. If you were to pull it, the axles would turn and make the wheels move the ship forward, just to give it a start for the wind to then take over. Thalrok pulled and pulled, over and over, and the *Land Skipper* began to propel herself forward. Lotus took a deep breath and looked behind to see Mellowtin slowly getting farther and farther away. No one was awake besides them; there had been no goodbyes, no controversy, no nothing.

It'll be worth it.

"Is this gonna be enough speed?" Thalrok asked, grunting with effort as he continued pulling the bar back and forth.

"That should be good for now. The wind will do the rest." Lotus shouted down, as he grabbed the steering controls himself. The sun finally decided to wake up and peeked just above the horizon, lighting the way for the two adventurers on their journey back to Cannon-Gulf.

"We should be able to get there in about a day's time if we keep going through the night. You gonna be all right with that, Ronin?" Thalrok asked.

No response. He looked back from the front of the ship's starboard deck and called back up, "Ronin!"

The wanted man snapped out of his daze and looked around. "Oh. Yeah,

I'm good with that!" he called back.

"You thinkin' about something?" the bounty hunter enquired.

"I just hope Oa and Nyloc aren't mad at us for abandoning them. It's for the best. I just hope they understand." Lotus fretted, as a little voice in his head said that they really should have said goodbye. Thalrok, too, thought they should have had a chance to at least say goodbye or something. But, the mission was already too far in motion, and there was no turning back now. What had happened, happened, and they would proceed as planned.

"Did you hear that?" Lotus asked.

"Hear what?" Thalrok looked puzzled.

"I don't know, I thought I heard some thumping noise somewhere on the ship. Maybe something is loose?" Lotus and Thalrok looked around the sides of the ship and didn't see anything out of the ordinary. The wanted man had just gotten his hands back on the controls when he heard it again.

"Thalrok, I know I hear something. Check inside for me?" Lotus asked.

The bounty hunter again stood up from the starboard bow and headed for the door to the cabin. Lotus turned to the back of the ship and stared ahead. Then he let go of the steering levers, deciding to see for himself.

As he approached the stern, he saw something. "*What*?!" he and Thalrok shouted at the same time, jaws dropped and eyes wide. To their great surprise, they had discovered stowaways.

"Ok, let me get this straight. You overheard Thalrok and me talking about leaving for Cannon-Gulf to plunge ourselves into a very dangerous and life-threatening mission. So, you just decided to come with us?" Lotus asked Nyloc and Oa, who had successfully gotten caught doing exactly that.

"Let me get *this* straight. You were gonna leave us in Mellowtin to wonder and worry where you were this whole time?" Oa said, giving them a look that screamed, *how could you do that to me!*

Lotus and Thalrok looked at each other, both feeling somewhat guilty.

"It was his idea." Thalrok pointed at Lotus.

The wanted man sighed in annoyance, then punched Thalrok's shoulder.

"Hey! I'm just telling them the truth!" the titan shouted in his defense.

"Listen, you two, what you did was very noble. But you're forgetting something really important. The young disciple and I *chose* to follow you two." Nyloc said bluntly. "We knew what we were getting into by following a wanted man. This was our choice, and we intend to stick to it." Nyloc stood on the deck facing them, his arms crossed.

"Nyloc is right. I left my village to follow you two, and I don't care where that leads. I will be right by your side." Oa said, and smiled.

Lotus felt a warm feeling in his heart. However, it was promptly cooled by the thought of them getting hurt because of his own curse. But, that couldn't matter now; they were here, and plans had to be adjusted. "Fine, just *please* be careful. This isn't going to be a fun trip." Lotus told them, and he headed back to the controls.

"Yes, sir!" Oa shouted.

"Yes, Captain!" Nyloc affirmed.

Oa and Thalrok took their usual spots on either side of the ship's bow, while Nyloc sat on the top deck near Lotus. They all felt fired up and ready to plunge into whatever hell might lay before them. Their future was a great unknown, with no signs of what was to come—uncharted territories and probably unknown enemies.

"Infected Ones," Lotus whispered. He inhaled deeply, trying to relax from the constant thought of that evil man taking his master from him, leaving the blame to fall on his own young shoulders. Over five years had passed since then, but it felt like it had happened yesterday every time he woke from sleep. He was finally going to get some answers or die trying. This truly was the calm, right before the storm.

18

The Storm

"This is your last chance, you two. Are you sure you want to come with us, even though we don't know what to expect?" Lotus asked the two stowaways.

"I'd be lying if I said I wasn't scared, but my gut tells me to go," Oa replied, holding tightly to his bo.

"What about you, Nyloc? You've only been along for the ride for about a week now. Do you even know what you're throwing yourself into?"

The champion archer stood up and flipped his hood over his head, blindfold ever in place. "Just because I never left my village doesn't mean I'm weak or gutless. I fully understand what I'm getting into. This is what I've trained so long for." Nyloc replied. He stood there resolutely, bow on his back and ready to go.

Lotus finally turned to the last of the crew. "Take the lead, Thalrok."

The titan nodded his head, cracked his neck, and hopped down from the *Land Skipper*. They'd been spotted quickly when in this city the last time, so they'd waited until now, when the sky was pitch-black, with the moon casting faint beams of light across the ground. The plan was to move stealthily in the shadows as best and quickly as they could. Despite it being well past nightfall, people still roamed the streets en masse as if it were high noon, just like on their last visit.

"This way," Thalrok whispered, as he led the others down a small walkway through the walls of the outer city. They followed Thalrok carefully and quietly. Checking every corner and peeking down alleyways, they cautiously made their way to one of the inner districts of the city. It wasn't exactly the center of the town, but it was close enough.

"Oa, hop up to the roof and tell me what you see," Thalrok whispered. The young disciple used subtle air-bursts to move up beside a building until he could grab onto the edge and look out over the city. "Do you see anyone posted up on the other levels?" Thalrok kept his voice low.

"No, just people walking around like before," Oa said in a loud whisper, as he hopped back down.

"Then we should be good for now. There's only a little bit of a walk to go." Thalrok sighed.

"Someone's coming." Nyloc interrupted. Everyone quickly turned to him, wondering what he saw. "I can sense someone walking behind us down the alleyway. We need to move." Nyloc told them.

The four of them hurried out onto the main road, trying their best to walk as nonchalantly as possible. Continuing on up and down on other levels, they covertly scouted out each corner, rooftop, or person they passed. They didn't want to risk losing this opportunity to move around the city undetected.

"You feel anything, Ronin?" Thalrok whispered.

"Nothing. We should be in the clear." Lotus assured him.

"Are we close yet?" Nyloc asked.

"We are very close, we'll walk just a little farther." Thalrok pressed on, retracing the footsteps he had taken a while ago. Memories started returning to him, this road, these buildings. The distance to his goal grew shorter as they crept in the shadows.

"Get inside," Thalrok said suddenly, and waved them in individually as they all entered the small ramen shop. Only a couple of people were inside, and neither of them even turned their heads when these new customers came in.

The owner stood up from his stool and watched as a man in a cloak, a kid, a guy wearing a blindfold, and lastly a titan-sized man in a helmet entered his eatery. "Welcome to the—" he began. Then he paused, recognizing one of them in the group. "Ah, I see that you enjoyed my food so much ya had to bring yer friends," the owner said.

"Of course. Long time no see, Fulross." Thalrok greeted.

They all took seats at the counter, and the owner placed a menu in front of each of them. Lotus kept his head low to conceal his face while the others acted as naturally as they could. The two other people in the place sat quietly eating their noodles, still showing no interest at all in the newcomers.

"I'm guessing you four would like what you had last time, is that correct?" the owner asked the bounty hunter.

"Yes, please, and make it quick." Thalrok nodded.

"We're closing for the night, everybody! Get out, I'm tired." Fulross shouted. The two diners groaned as they left their seats and exited, leaving their payment and two nearly empty ramen bowls behind. "Geez, Fulross, thanks for nothin'," the taller of the two said under his breath on their way out.

The group of four sat in their seats, patiently waiting. Lotus could feel his heart rate revving up as he tapped his foot on the ground. *It'll be alright, it's gonna be alright.*

"Ok, they're gone, come on back." Fulross gestured for them to follow him toward the kitchen. Thalrok stood up first, leading the way. One by one, they followed him past the kitchen and to the very back of the shop.

"How long has it been, maybe about a few month or so? Didn't think I'd see "Guillotine Titan Tytler" again." Fulross chuckled, as he pulled the metal door open. "Quite the unique posse you have with you. Never expected you to be one to surround yourself with company."

Lotus and the others squinted, confused as to why he called Thalrok that name. Did he make a mistake, or was Thalrok hiding something? They couldn't focus on it just yet, they weren't in the clear.

"Well, maybe I've changed," Thalrok replied, as he started down the long stairwell. One by one, they followed behind him with Lotus holding the rear. He was the last one to tread on that first step down when he felt a hand grab his shoulder. His heart stopped, and everyone immediately turned around when they heard Lotus gasp in surprise.

Crap! Lotus panicked.

He turned his head only slightly to one side to ask what the matter was, only to hear the owner say, "Hey, have fun down there, y'all." Fulross grinned knowingly, then released his grip on Lotus's shoulder and closed the door, latching it behind them. The four of them let out the breath they didn't realize they'd been holding, then continued down the torchlit stairs and into, for three of them, uncharted territory.

"How do you know about this place?" Nyloc asked.

"I used to come down here sometimes early on in my prime bounty-hunting days. This is a world hidden from all eyes, an underground city. This place is crawling with sketchy people, so don't talk to anyone." Thalrok replied.

They descended even deeper down the long, dank stairwell and paused briefly at the bottom to regroup. Once gathered there, it was Nyloc who asked the obvious question, "Why did he call you Tytler instead of Thalrok?"

The titan explained. "When I was spending most of my time in the city, I began to become a recognizable person. I racked on bounty after bounty, and they would ask me who I was. They gave me the 'Guillotine Titan' name because of my sword, and I just told them that my foster mother's last name was Tytler. I may have been one of them, but I didn't trust them. They didn't need to know my real name."

It made sense for Thalrok not to use his first name, but still, a weird concern formed in the pits of their stomachs. They approached the door now, the only way available to go forward.

"You all right, Oa?" Thalrok looked at the boy.

"Yeah, I'll be okay. It's just a little, uh, ominous, that's all." Oa muttered, looking ahead. The door was now only a few steps away. Thalrok was the only one who had seen any place like this before; it was a complete mystery to the others.

"Everybody ready?" Thalrok asked, as he grabbed the handle on the door. When he pulled it open, the metal hinges swung freely, and the door slammed into the stone wall behind it. A burst of heat came back at them. They walked out onto a bridge, high above level upon level of other torch-lit walkways and bridges. Lotus and Oa gasped as they stared out into the deep, dark underground. The drop from the bridge seemed endless, with sharp stalagmites piercing the darkness, reaching upward. There was just enough light to see that this was like a man-made hell. Pillars, thick as fifty tree trunks, shot up from the ground with platforms wrapped around them. Some tunnels were dug into the giant walls surrounding the area. It was a labyrinth where even veteran travelers could go astray; one wrong turn, and you were lost for good.

"Like I said, keep close, talk to no one, and don't stand out." Thalrok spelled it out for them. He took another deep breath to calm his own nerves. He'd never come down to this place feeling so on edge. It was a new experience for him, and not a pleasant one.

"You getting all of this Nyloc?" Lotus asked.

"More than you think, Captain," he replied, as he held onto the railing.

After reaching the end of the bridge, the chaos began. Shouts of anger, jabber from bargaining shoppers and merchants, the banter of oddly dressed men and women bombarded them as they kept on the move—"You stay off my territory next time, or I'll make sure it won't happen again!" and, "You can't get weapons like this, people. The surface is too scared to sell stuff like this!" and, "Hey, cutie, what's someone like you doing all the way down here?" They heard hundreds of conversations going on all at once. But, like a train on the tracks, they stayed close together, trying not to bump into the wrong guy. They could be done for if they did.

"Do my eyes deceive me?" A sultry female voice called out from somewhere nearby.

Oh no... Thalrok stopped, turning toward a small crowd of people. Everyone's heart skipped a beat. Oa held tighter to his staff. Nyloc slowly moved his hand closer to the dagger at his side. Lotus stood stock still, his head down and face concealed by his hood.

"What are the odds I'm running into you after... how long has it been? Geez, but I could spot you anywhere, ya big lug," the voice called out as a provocative-looking woman approached Thalrok.

"Do I know—oh right. It's been a bit. How are you?" Thalrok said, feigning friendliness but carefully shielding his true thoughts.

"How's your hunt for the big rabbit going? Any luck?" she asked, looking up into his face with wide eyes.

"Nah, no luck at all. That guy has got to have the best hiding spots ever to keep on the run for this long." Thalrok said, discreetly gesturing behind his back for the others to keep walking and find somewhere to lay low before this got bad. Lotus took the lead, and the three melted into a low-lit alleyway nearby. Lurking there, they anxiously listened to Thalrok's conversation.

"Were those three a part of your clan?" the woman asked, looking around for where they had gone.

"No, they just happened to be heading off in the same direction as I was." Thalrok was trying his best to seem normal and then get away from her so they could keep moving. He had no idea what the next step was anyway. He hoped to find a sign or even someone who looked like the Infected Ones they'd come across before.

"I'd love to stay and chat, but I really must be going." He waved goodbye and turned to find his companions.

"Hey, wait a second," she said.

Thalrok froze, gritting his teeth, just wanting to move along. "What's up?" he said, as pleasantly as he could manage.

"You got plans to get another bounty soon?" she asked, seeming very interested in how much money he may have or be getting.

The others watched from the shadows, their hearts beating frantically, hoping that this little chat would end soon. "Hey, you guys, look." Oa whispered. Lotus and Nyloc turned to where he was pointing. In the center of the street was a convoy of six hooded, masked brutes surrounding a small group of men with their hands shackled and their backs prodded cruelly if they walked too slowly. Some of the men were

293

sobbing, all looked crushed and miserable.

"Where are they taking them?" Oa asked.

"The real question is, why did they bring them here?" Nyloc added.

Lotus watched closely as the group moved down the street. "The weaponry on their hips, the masks on their face. It looked—just like the others..." he whispered.

"What others?" Nyloc asked.

"Oa and I have seen those masks before. They look like the same bunch that came after us the first time we came here. Which means..." Lotus turned back to get a better look. It was only a hunch, but he wanted to see where they were going. "Let's go," he whispered as he headed out from the alley.

"Wait, what about Thalrok?" Oa was concerned.

"He'll be fine. He knows his way around here, and he'll find us soon enough." Lotus told him.

The three of them stealthily left their hiding spot and followed their quarry from a safe distance. The prisoner convoy went deeper and deeper into the underground until they came to a bridge. This was the only bridge that led to a smaller pillar out in the open.

"Crap, hold on, you guys," Lotus whispered, as they watched the group walking further away.

"What should we do, Captain?" Nyloc asked.

Lotus had to think. They couldn't really just stop. This could be the only shot they had to find out if these guys actually were connected to the Infected Ones. "As soon as they go through that door, we hurry across and go inside too. We've gotta be ready 'cause we don't know what to expect," he said, gauging their distance from the door.

For a few seconds, they stood there holding their breath and hoping that no one would bat an eye at them crossing this particular bridge. The masked thug in the front of the group finally got to the door and opened it, pushing the prisoners in one by one until the last thug in line shut it.

"Now." Lotus headed straight for the bridge. As quickly and as carefully as they could, they started across, feeling it bob and sway from the old ropes holding it up.

Oa peeked back to see if anyone was noticing them. "We seem to be alright for now. But what about Thalrok? He's still not here." Oa whispered.

"It'll be okay. We have to keep moving." Now Lotus himself began to worry. He had no idea what was behind this door. Maybe Thalrok knew, and he would have stopped them. Maybe it would be precisely what they're looking for, or maybe it would be a trap. Hurrying ahead for what felt like ages, Lotus grabbed the door handle, turned to the others, nodded his head, and swung it open.

"Empty?" Nyloc said, confused.

"Uhh, let's just get in for now." Lotus decided, and they all dashed inside. The smallish room was circular, with no visible ceiling and several torches on the walls. The natural stone floor had no cracks, no trapdoors, no chips. It seemed completely sealed from inside and out.

"Where did they go?" Oa asked quietly, his voice echoing in this strange room.

"I have no idea." Lotus began to feel along the walls and floor for any sign of a hidden switch, but noticed nothing out of the ordinary.

"Guys, do you hear that?" Nyloc asked as he turned to the door. They all turned to the metal door that sealed this stone room. Their hearts pounded, and they backed away slowly. They heard the ropes from the bridge groaning and the wood creaking from heavy footsteps.

"Get ready." Lotus began to calm himself as he moved in front of the other two. This was something that he was familiar with. He knew what to do and how to do it, but he needed to be out in front and center.

The footsteps grew louder until they heard the door handle jiggling. Oa held his bo, ready to burst into action. Nyloc, who's sensing ability ended just where his comrades field of vision did, at the stone wall and metal door, nocked an arrow and drew it back. Lotus reached through his cloak and grabbed onto the hilt of his sword, just in case. They held their breath as the door swung open.

"You're in *here*?!" a voice hissed.

They were all startled, but quickly lowered their guard and their weapons when they saw the bounty hunter glance inside and then barrel in.

"Whew... It's just Thalrok." Oa sighed in relief.

"I'm sorry if I scared you guys. I couldn't get away from her. What a gold digger! She is a *parasite*." Thalrok shook his head.

"So the bounty hunter must have made a few friends down here." Nyloc quipped as he smoothly and methodically returned the bow to his back and the arrow into its quiver.

"Trust me, no one is your friend down here," Thalrok replied.

"Hey, hey, we can make small talk later. We have to figure out what to do from here." Lotus interrupted, as he looked around some more.

"I'm guessing you were following the group of shackled men being taken by those masked ones, right?" The bounty hunter asked as he checked out the room.

"Yeah, and they came in here, but I don't know where they went," Lotus said with a sigh.

"Hey guys, what's this symbol?" Oa asked. Thalrok grabbed a torch and brought it over. As fire illuminated the wall, Lotus and Thalrok's eyes widened in shock. Here was the exact same symbol that they'd seen so many places in the ruins of that abandoned town, Ashveil.

"It's them," Lotus muttered grimly.

"It *is* the Infected Ones," Thalrok added. He was downright certain now. "So, those masked bandits that ambushed us here—that was them! Rohm, the archers, and those goons—they were all hunting for you, just like Speral! The thugs that took over Thristle with Mordo, same thing—they all *have* to be connected!"

Lotus put his hand over the symbol and he leaned on it, his head down. As his hand pushed on the rough surface of the cave, the portion under the symbol sank in. The floor began to shake and rumble beneath their feet as they tried to keep their balance.

"What's happening?" Nyloc shouted.

"I don't know, but get ready for anything," Lotus warned.

* * *

"Would you stop crying! You try and pull any of that crap in here, and you're as good as dead. We spared you all to give you a second chance. A chance for a new life with the leadership of someone who will actually change this world. So quit it, and shut up!" the thug in charge growled, turning back to glare at the shackled men one last time.

"Sir—excuse me. Do you hear that?" one of the masked men asked. The leader stopped their advance down the hallway. He looked around but didn't seem to hear anything. Glancing to the floor, he saw the pebbles on the ground begin to jump and rattle around like the earth was shaking.

"Is that... the elevator?" he asked. They turned around and heard the opening at the end of the hall vibrate; the elevator was indeed moving down to their level.

"You two stay here and watch these rookies. Everyone else, follow me. Pretty sure there shouldn't be anybody else comin' down yet," he muttered as he grabbed his knife and led his cronies toward the lift. They readied their weapons, surrounded the doorway, and squinted in concentration, prepared to drop who or whatever was about to show its face. The doors began to open.

"What?" They gaped at each other in surprise. The elevator was dark, and seemed to be empty. There wasn't a sign of anyone in it.

"Go check it out," their leader suggested, pushing one of them forward.

"Don't *push* me," the skinny lackey growled as he carefully approached the open doors. He peeked in, looked left and right, but couldn't see anyone there in the darkness.

"Looks like it was a false alarm," he said with a sigh, then stepped fully inside to check one last time. He peered straight up to stare into the dark void above him, where, by the light from the doorway, he saw the whites of six eyes looking back. His skin crawled in shock as he saw four strangers clinging like spiders onto the extinguished torches above and on either side of the doorway.

"It's an att—" he started to yell, but Oa burst off the wall, slammed down

297

on top of him, and pummeled him flat. Oa then zipped toward the next closest grunt, taking him down with a single kick to the head.

"Where did *they* come from?!" a burly thug shouted in confusion. He could barely keep his eyes on fast-moving Oa. They were caught completely off guard and had no plan.

Lotus and Thalrok dropped to the floor too, and ran through the doorway for the others.

"Run! Go! Tell them we're being attacked in—!" the burly grunt shouted, just as Thalrok's gargantuan hand grabbed him by the face.

"I don't think he should do that." Thalrok interrupted the hefty one, picking him up and slamming him into the wall. His back crashed through the cave wall's hardened crust before he was pulled back again in one smooth motion. Then Thalrok threw him at the grunt, trying to get up, and knocked both of them to the ground.

The two thugs farthest in the back with the shackled men stood fixed in place having no idea what to do. When they did snap back to reality they decided to go alert everyone before it was too late. But it *was* too late. As they turned their backs to run, they heard a faint whistling. In moments, each felt the painful jolt and stab of an arrow; one was pierced in the back, the other in the calf. Collapsing to the ground and peering over their shoulder in fear, they saw a blindfolded archer readying another arrow.

"Get up, we have to—!" one of them began to scream, then noticed a hooded man right above them both. He had his fist pulled back, and sucker punched the screaming man, knocking him out cold while the other watched. "Y-you're..." he mumbled. But before he could finish, Oa hurled his staff at the back of his head. The staff's cold metal butt end jabbed into his skull and slammed his head forward, cleanly knocking him out.

The hostages stood in disbelief, shaking and mouths agape. "Unbelievable," one of them murmured. They watched their heroes brush themselves off without a scratch on any of them.

"Nice work, Captain. Your idea worked out pretty well. Is everyone all right?" Nyloc asked, as he joined the others.

"Who are you?" asked one of the younger hostages.

"That doesn't matter. What matters is that you all are safe and need to get out of here." Lotus replied, as he went over to help remove their shackles. Even as they were being freed from their chains they simply couldn't believe it.

"Can you tell me how you got here?" Thalrok asked.

"Well, we were in our village when these men in black with hoods and masks all showed up. They threatened that if we didn't do what they said, they would kill us. They took over our village. And we're not the first group of people they've taken from our homeland. We didn't know what they did with the others, and we still don't know," explained a tall man, as the last one of them was freed from his restraints.

"Don't worry, we are gonna get you out alive," Thalrok promised, looking around the room.

"Nyloc, you take these chains and lock their wrists together so they have a hard time moving if they wake up." He indicated the unconscious thugs. "Oa, you make sure these men all get back on the lift," Lotus instructed, as he kept glancing down the hallway to make sure no one else had been alerted.

"Yes, sir." They replied, and they went right to it. Oa guided the hostages back onto the elevator as Thalrok helped Nyloc move the unconscious bandits and shackle them to each other.

"Listen, you aren't safe just yet. You will have to make your way back up to the surface. We can't go with you, but I know you can make it back up if you remain calm. Okay?" Lotus said to the newly freed men.

"We can do that. Thank you, thank you so much for saving us." one of them, still trembling, mumbled.

"Don't mention it. Now go!" Lotus signaled for them to leave.

The floor shook, and tiny chips of stone fell from the ceiling as the lift slowly rose back up to the top. The hall became silent again once it stopped one long floor ride up.

"Ok, first part's done. Now, we just got what's at the end of this hall." Thalrok huffed, as he straightened up, and stared into the unknown. They all gathered there the hallway, looking at the faintly lit doorway at the end.

"Hey, I have an idea." They all turned to Oa, who was standing over the downed thugs.

"It'll be a risk, but what if we wear their cloaks and masks? Anyone who sees us will think we are one of them." Oa proposed.

"That's not a terrible idea," Nyloc commented.

"Good thinking, kid. Ronin, what do you think?" Thalrok asked.

Lotus considered it. The fact that they would practically be in plain sight was terrifying. But, it was the only plan they had. "Let's do it," he replied.

So, they all wrapped the dark cloaks around their backs and placed the masks over their faces. Thalrok's face was already concealed because of his helmet, so he was covered. They marched down the halls watchfully in case they came upon any unusual activity.

"Just follow my lead and stay with me, alright?" Lotus told them.

"Right," his three companions replied.

Now the next doorway was right before them. Lotus took a deep breath, grabbed the handle and pulled it toward them. As the metal door swung open, they all looked inside to see a rounded room with tunnels branching out in several directions. The surfaces here were no longer like the other roughly hewn tunnels and hallways. Giant blocks of carved stone laid out the floor of the cavern. The walls and archways were uniquely chiseled, and had lanterns held in bronze sconces. Stone pillars up against the walls were smooth and evenly placed around the room. They no longer were crawling around a rat's tunnel; this place was created to be here.

"Well, this is a change," Thalrok observed, checking the room out.

"Which way do we go now?" Nyloc asked, feeling the etching on the stone walls. This round room had three walkways, one in front and two to the side of them. They could see some more light ahead, maybe with a bigger room opening up. Since the walkway curved, they couldn't be seen by anyone up ahead where they were standing right now.

"Let's go this way," Lotus suggested, and he led the way ahead. They strode down the walkway, trying to blend in as much as possible. They hadn't run into anyone yet and, as far as they could tell, were the only ones here.

"I can sense something ahead," Nyloc whispered.

"It's fine. They shouldn't be able to tell we aren't one of them, dressed like this." Lotus reassured them, as they kept walking. Shortly, they saw the room ahead open up.

"Cells?" Oa muttered. He saw little rooms blocked off with metal bars like a jail. After entering the room, they noticed dozens of small holding cells there. They slowed their pace and surveyed them, checking if anyone was inside. Thankfully, they were all empty. "Maybe this is where they were taking those men," Oa murmured, and he pushed open one of the barred doors to get a closer look.

"Captain," Nyloc called out.

Lotus turned around and headed in his direction. "What's wrong?" he asked.

All Nyloc did was point at the cell with blood tainting its back wall. The stain appeared to have been there for some time.

"Not a good sign," Thalrok added, as he walked over next to them.

"Let's keep moving." Lotus began to head down another arched hallway branching off from this room. Everyone carefully followed, not knowing what might pop up out of nowhere. They expected this place to be swarming with bandits and thugs, outnumbering them by the dozen, but so far they hadn't encountered a single person on any path or with any turn they'd taken.

"This seems strange, right?" Oa asked in a low voice.

"The young disciple is right. We should have at least seen one or two people by now." Nyloc added.

Lotus rubbed his chin, thinking over what was going on down here. Were the other masked and hooded men all on the surface doing something? Or is this an ambush, and are they falling into a trap? There were too many questions to ponder.

"What's that?" Thalrok pointed out, as they came to an intersection. A small slab was pressed into the wall ahead with arrows pointing in two directions. One arrow pointed down the stairs on their left, which bent around the corner as it descended. The other curved up and to the right, as those stairs climbed upward.

"Coliseum?" Oa furrowed his brow as he spoke.

"What's a coliseum doing this deep in the underground?" Thalrok, too, was confused.

"Which way should we go?" Nyloc asked the obvious question.

Lotus looked to his right, then his left. He felt uneasy about descending farther into this hell, so he headed for the stairs on the right. The four of them cautiously went up the stairs, hearing muffled sounds that got louder as they went up each step.

"You all hear that, right?" Thalrok asked.

"Yeah, something's up here for sure," Lotus whispered as he kept close to the wall. The top step was finally visible, and the sound they heard was as clear as day—the roaring of a crowd, cheering and chanting at the top of their lungs. Lotus slowly peeked around one corner and saw a small balcony. He crept over for a closer look, peering through spaces in the carved stone balustrade down into the giant pit below it all. "Holy..." he muttered.

"What is it?" Thalrok asked from two steps behind him.

"What do you see?" they all whispered.

"It's definitely a coliseum, and now we know where everyone is," Lotus replied as he straightened up and walked farther out onto the balcony, where he stood above hundreds of frenzied people who were waving their hands high and cheering. The room was gigantic, lit by torches and lanterns scattered across its entirety, and had stone bleachers below with a pit of some sort even farther below them.

"This is unreal," the bounty hunter said, grabbing onto the thick stone handrail and glancing down.

"Why are they all here?" Nyloc wondered aloud, as he could sense everything around him.

All of a sudden, Lotus's body felt cold, but not the type of cold one feels when the weather outside is wintery. Deep inside his core, he had a frigid sensation like no other. The hair on his arms stood up, bristling, and chills ran down his spine.

"Get down!" he hissed, pulling everyone to duck down behind the balustrade.

"What's the matter?" Thalrok asked.

"I don't know, but something is coming," Lotus answered.

The four noticed that the cheering had gotten even louder, and all eyes in the crowd were now focused on the balcony directly across from theirs. Those below wore expectant smiles on their faces as they waited, but for what? Finally, two men in black walked out onto the balcony and stood there above those gathered below. The crowd erupted in even louder cheers as they awaited their message of salvation.

"Who are they?" Nyloc asked.

"More importantly, who's coming next?" Thalrok added, just before a third dark figure emerged from the depths of the shadows. He wore a stone-cold expression on his lined face as he walked out with purpose yet not with impatience. The chanting had reached a new height, shaking the very floor beneath their feet as the followers jumped up and down in their zeal.

Lotus felt a severe unease deep within his chest, a bitter feeling that made him feel almost sick to his stomach at the sight of this man. He watched the man place both of his hands on the balustrade and survey his men, the raucous horde below. Lotus saw an icy smile creep onto his face as he observed their ravenous energy.

"Silence!" he commanded. The crowd's cheering died in an instant. He slowly raised one hand into the air, balled it into a fist, and reached out toward his rapt audience.

"For many years, I have spent my days building the ultimate weapon to change this world," the leader began, standing tall, both hands now at his side. "I work night and day to spread our reach through the shadows, and to tear open the very earth with our own bare hands. I've grown impatient with too many days passing. I feel there is a need for change now! No longer shall the Infected of this world go on without recognition. We have slipped into the cracks of this broken world and changed the very meaning of what power is. You, my chosen disciples, have done well in helping me with my cause. Now I will show this world what it is like to feel power. Now I will show them what it's like to feel pure strength!"

The words he spoke with such passion rattled in the heads of his audience. They could feel the full force of his charisma and inspiration which radiated throughout the underground. As for the four outsiders, they could only feel the dark pressure of an energy that grew more ominous with each word he spoke.

"Order. Order is not what this world needs. Years ago, it was proven that the strong survive and the weak die. It is time for us to show this world that we, *we*, are the ones who will create a world so wondrous that there will be no one to stop us," the man said passionately, the white streaks in his black hair catching the torchlight. He lifted both hands high and gazed up into the black sky of this underworld.

"Who *is* this guy?" Thalrok asked.

No one responded. They turned to one another, except for Lotus, who was still staring ahead.

"Ronin?" Thalrok lightly nudged him. Lotus still didn't take his eyes off of the man who was speaking.

"The time for change is now. You have the power to be among the few who survive to enjoy this grand future we will bring. Soon we will have to suffer no more. You have worked hard under me to become someone worthy of a life in this future that we hold in our hands. This is the only way I will prove it to them—to him! That this is, and always was, the way!" the leader shouted fervently.

The crowd roared again, erupting with cheers. He stood above them, smiling, then laughing, his voice lifting over the hubbub below.

Lotus could feel his heart racing faster and faster by the second, his fingers digging into the stone ledge.

"I will lead you all through the charge. I will be the one to command it all, as we triumph through the hell we will bring into this world. We will fight to the death to bring forth our future. There is no room for the weak in our palace anymore. *I* am this world's hero! *I* am this world's savior! *I* am your master!" At this, Lotus's heart sank, his mouth fell open, and his blood surged.

"*I!*" the speaker went on, his voice at full volume. Lotus's mind began to race, remembering his legs shaking and trembling as it finally hit him.

"*Am!*" the speaker shouted, and Lotus could feel memories of the past punching the inside of his skull, a barrage of nightmares. A name so tainted he could never forget his master warning him.

"*Delus!*" The man proclaimed.

19

Through Hate comes Anger

"Ronin? Ronin, are you alright?" Thalrok hissed, elbowing him ever so slightly. As his arm made contact with the wanted man, a cold and bitter feeling zapped him like a static shock. Reflexively, he pulled his arm back, and all three of them stared at Lotus.

"Hey, Lotus…" Oa said softly, seeing the horror on his friend's face.

"Captain?" Nyloc whispered.

"Delus…" Lotus replied. The lone word spilled out of his open mouth, dropping like a stone. The way he spoke it showed the deepest emotion he had expressed in quite some time. His quiet, petrified voice worried the others.

"Ronin, do you know him?" Thalrok asked softly, leaning in closer.

The wanted man couldn't look away; it was impossible. He was locked in a daze, unable to get out of this nightmare before him. "My master… he…" Lotus mumbled..

"What are you saying?" Thalrok was getting truly concerned for his friend.

"It was him… *he* was the one… the one my master told me about years ago." Lotus stared ahead in utter disbelief. He never thought he would be standing in the same room as his master's former classmate. He could hear Din saying that name all those years ago, telling the story of how that man destroyed everything Din loved and got away. Now, there the scoundrel was, in the flesh, standing right in front of him.

"What does this mean?" Nyloc asked.

Lotus could feel everything falling into place as he connected the dots. This man, he is the reason this world is falling apart. He is the reason all of those villages are living in fear and despair. These were the ones who attacked them when they first came to Cannon-Gulf. He was behind the attack back in Perksy. He was the reason Belle… everything—that was all him. He… he, *Delus*, is the reason that his master is gone.

Lotus's three companions felt the icy coldness that surrounded him. They saw the dark look in his eyes as his thousand-yard stare pierced the distance to glare at the man.

"Are you sure it's him?" Oa asked.

"I could never forget that name. *That's* him." Lotus growled, as he felt his blood boil from deep within his core. His fingers dug into and through the stone rail, crumbling it. There was no stopping the flow of dark energy from inside him. He welcomed it; it fueled his hatred as the memory of his master's end played out repeatedly in his head. Lotus slowly stood up, his cloak fell from his shoulders as he dropped his mask to the floor.

"Sir?" one of the men next to Delus whispered.

"Yes, I feel it too. But what—?" Delus scanned the coliseum below, feeling some type of strange energy building to incredible heights.

"Master, over there." The other pointed.

Delus gazed out over the room at the balcony straight across from him. He saw four people behind the balustrade, all staring at him. The three wearing black cloaks and masks were crouched down. But one, one of them, was standing straight up. That man instantly caught his attention. When the identity of the person before him clicked into place, he could only respond with a maniacal smile.

"This is quite a pleasant surprise. I thought today couldn't get any better, but now, he's appeared right at my doorstep." Delus muttered, then chuckled. His laughter grew, and the stadium slowly silenced when they all saw him laughing in triumph above them. Delus felt that his days of waiting were coming to a close.

"My disciples, today… *Today* is a wondrous day." Delus smiled down at his ardent followers. "For many years, I've been searching for the last mistake I—no, the mistake that the weakness of the past—had let live. I can't believe my eyes. After these many years, I finally get to meet the man I've been searching for." He paused then, and lifted his gaze to the balcony across from his own.

"Oh no…" Thalrok realized that they were spotted. The three of them tried to pull Lotus down and out of sight, but he was unmovable.

"It feels *so* good to finally put an end to this chapter. You got away those many years ago through a fluke, but now—now, I will not let you escape." Delus said malevolently. He pointed directly at the balcony, where Lotus stood tall. "Here we have the world's most wanted criminal! Ronin the Banished, I welcome you!" he shouted, and all eyes locked on the wanted man.

Lotus felt the swell of anger inside him building and growing. This wasn't like a last-minute adrenaline rush; this was him. He stepped up onto the balcony's wide railing and watched them all turn in his direction. His fists balled at his side as murmurs of shock rumbled across the crowd below.

"Behold, the one we have been searching for all this time now presents himself before us!" Delus cackled.

Lotus had just met this man, and yet he hated hearing anything that came out of his filthy mouth. The words stung his ears. He could only stare back at Delus with clenched teeth.

"Ronin, there are too many, we have to leave now," Thalrok warned, reaching out to pull him down from the stone handrail.

By now, the aura of dark energy around Lotus was thick enough to feel. It was as if the gravity around him was more robust than the earth's. Tendrils of black hazy smoke swirled around him as his immense dark power built up and intensified.

Thalrok was inches away from grabbing onto him, but as he was about to make contact, Lotus simply vanished. "What?!" the bounty hunter yelped in shock.

"Thalrok, over there!" Oa shouted as he pointed ahead to Lotus, who was already across the wide space, heading straight for Delus.

That foul man only scoffed at this lazy attempt at an attack. "Kenji. Ogan," he commanded. Without a moment of hesitation, the two young men at his side readied their weapons and stepped up, prepared to meet the fast-approaching target.

Only a few feet from striking the man who took everything from him, Lotus found himself soaring into new opposition. His words burned through his lips, "Get out of my way."

Kenji slashed one of his blades at the wanted man. It phased through him. "What?!" he mouthed, then froze as he watched the figure that was once in front of him fade completely away. Kenji turned to his left and saw that now the enemy was behind them.

"Master!" Ogan shouted, but Delus didn't move at all. He only exhaled in disappointment at his underlings.

"So pathetic," Delus said, shaking his head sadly. He stepped back with his right leg and lowered his upper body far backward toward the floor while the distance from Lotus to his target grew shorter by the second as he flew to strike down this foe. Delus balled his right hand into a tight fist, and bared his teeth in a vicious smile. Then, he swung that fist forward.

"Pathetic!" he shouted, as every bony knuckle smashed into the side of Lotus's face. The wanted man could feel his head snap hard to the right as his body soared back through the air and down into the pit.

"Lotus!" "Ronin!" "Captain!" his three companions yelled in unison from their places on the opposite balcony. They stood up in horror, watching their friend fall into the chaos below.

"Let's go!" Thalrok shouted, as he immediately jumped off the stone railing of the balcony. Without hesitation, Oa and Nyloc followed, plunging down into the deadly chaos.

Lotus's body was limp, and he could barely think straight. That punch felt... unreal. The amount of raw power behind it was unbelievable. He snapped out of his daze midair and prepared himself to land below. As his feet touched the stony floor, he noticed just how outnumbered he really was. Glancing to his left and right, he saw that Delus's followers, these "Infected Ones", surrounded him. They wore malicious smiles and looked hungry for a bloodbath.

"I have to get back up there." Lotus lifted his head to see the villainous Delus staring down from above, smug and triumphant... and alone. He prepared himself to jump back up but felt a sudden pressure behind him. Without turning to look, Lotus quickly ducked as a blade swung across where his head had just been. Planting his hands on the ground, he kicked his leg backward and struck Ogan right across the chest. The first of Delus's two main men fell back from the kick to stand beside the other, Kenji.

"Together," Kenji said calmly.

"Right," Ogan replied, as they began to step forward.

Suddenly, the entire underground shook and trembled. All eyes turned to the source as Thalrok barreled down onto the floor of the coliseum, hammering his sword into the stone. He waited not another second and swung his fearsome blade into the nearest enemy. One after another, his huge sword smashed into them and sent them flying.

"Roniiiin!" Thalrok shouted, as he saw just how far he was from his friend. "Nyloc, go help him!" the bounty hunter yelled, as he grabbed the archer by the collar as tightly as he could.

"What... what are you doing?!" Nyloc panicked; he had no idea what was going on. Thalrok planted his foot, lurched back and then threw his shoulder and arm forward, effectively launching Nyloc across the entire stadium toward Lotus.

"I don't like this!" Nyloc shouted, as he headed straight for the target zone. He soared through the air, trying his best not to thrash while flying across the open room. As gracefully as possible, he crashed into one of the thugs and somehow managed to get up unscathed, bow intact. "Ugh, that was... completely unnecessary." Nyloc moaned, as he stood beside Lotus.

"My disciples!" Delus shouted. Everyone looked back up at their master. "I have been blessed with closure. I no longer have to search day and night for the weakest and most pitiful of them all in the world. I have prayed for this day to come, and my prayer has been answered." His face went from joyful to severe in a brief moment as he stood there on the balcony before them all. "Kill them. Now," he commanded curtly.

The four of them felt genuine fear at that moment. Delus's blunt order was followed by complete silence. They could feel their adrenaline kicking in. Even a dozen Infected Ones would outnumber them, and these louts wouldn't be holding back.

All eyes slowly moved back down from Delus to the intruders there among them. Quiet ripples of contemptuous laughter began to flow around them.

"Oa, stay by my side, alright?" Thalrok instructed, preparing himself for quite a battle.

"I might be y-younger, but I won't go down that easily." Oa stuttered, trying to sound confident as his legs shook.

Thalrok grasped the hilt of his mighty sword, watching as the Ones surrounding them crept in closer. "I don't know why, but this is getting me really pumped up," Thalrok smirked as he lifted his blade high into the air. "You wanna fight?!" he called out to them, "Then come at me!" His blade slammed into the ground and cracked the stone blocks below. The tremors and quaking that came next had the thugs struggling to keep their balance.

"Now, Oa!" Thalrok shouted, and the young boy jumped up and sent an immense burst of air out in front of him. The group of Ones facing them flew backward, and Thalrok charged head-first at them while they were still off-balance.

"All alone now, kid!" a voice jeered from behind Oa. The young disciple quickly turned around to see a brute swinging a mace down onto his head. Reacting as fast as he could, he thrust his bo up just in time to block it. The wooden staff flexed and bowed, barely holding, but the spiked head of the mace finally bounced off. Oa hopped up a few inches front he ground and leaned back. When his feet faced his foe, he sent a quick burst of air at him. The man let out a grunt and flew wildly backward as he felt that gust of air hit his chest like a cannonball.

"Oa, look out!" Thalrok shouted. It was too late; someone snuck behind Oa and wrapped an arm around his neck. The young disciple struggled for breath as the tightness around his neck increased.

"This just... pisses me off... I hate... when this happens." Oa gasped, as he reached for the dagger on his attacker's hip. The One who had Oa in a chokehold cried out as his own blade was thrust deeply into his thigh. Oa forced the grimacing thug's arm from his neck, took a big step forward, and twisted his body with a wind-assist pushing his leg as he swung it. The laces of his foot smashed into the side of the brute's face and his head snapped to one side.

"Thalrok!" Oa shouted, as he placed his palms directly on the man's chest.

Thalrok turned around and saw that the boy had launched his foe directly toward him. All the bounty hunter could do was smile at seeing just how tough this kid was. Thalrok, clashing blades with multiple enemies at once, took a step to one side and let the soaring man crash right into the others. All of them toppled to the ground, and before they could catch their bearings, Thalrok took the flat end of his colossal blade and slapped it down on their heads.

"Come on! You call this a fight?! Give me more, you cowards!" Thalrok bellowed. He laughed to see them all shrink back from his terrifying rampage. "Aw, too scaaared?" he sang, smirking and sarcastic. Then with a sudden shout of, "I'm not!", he charged for the next bunch of Infected Ones. Like some mythological beast, he broke through anything they threw at him. He laughed in their faces and stomped his feet across the ground, swinging his weapon and breaking through the weak metal of their blades.

Oa could see just how powerful this titan of a man really was. He was just thinking how lucky he was to have him on their side when he heard a cruel deep voice say, "Well, well, well. Looks like I get my chance to squash you again."

Chills sped down Oa's spine.

Thalrok immediately stopped what he was doing. He'd recognize that arrogant voice anywhere.

"You!" Oa's voice shook as he watched Rohm, the earth-wielder, pushing through the crowd until he stood there in front of Oa with a malicious grin.

"Oa!" Thalrok shouted, as he stormed towards the two of them. He'd taken only a few steps forward when he felt a tightness around his ankles. He peered over his shoulder and saw a tall man, armored in all metal, holding him back with whips.

"Your fight is with me," the masked man said.

Thalrok looked back and saw Oa, frozen in fear.

Damn it. Thalrok knew that he couldn't do anything for the kid at this moment. He needed to deal with this problem, and was going to have to trust that Oa could take care of his own. Thalrok slowly turned around and cracked his knuckles, whips still coiled around his lower legs.

"You gonna try and move me? Good luck." Thalrok boasted. He rested his mighty blade on his shoulder and tilted his head.

"*Pull* you? Oh no, no, no. I have another trick up my sleeve," the masked man scoffed, shaking his head. The smug tone of that smooth voice gave the bounty hunter an uneasy feeling. Then the armored man pulled both whips back and cracked them forward, sending black lightning bolts down the metallic thongs. Thalrok was instantly stunned by the stinging pain that shot into his body. He twitched, screamed out, and was dropped to his knees in a matter of seconds. Falling face-first on the ground, Thalrok's muscles spasmed. He could barely move.

"So, you may have raw strength and all, but what I lack in power, I make up for in technique. Rohm was too much of a meathead, just like you. Now you have to deal with me, Nevol!" The armored One pulled his whips back, releasing their grip on Thalrok.

The bounty hunter moaned in pain as he tried to lift himself. He was barely able to plant one arm on the ground before falling again, with the stinging pain of a metal whip slapping his shoulder.

"Oh, I don't suggest trying to move. I wouldn't know personally, but I hear my paralysis volts hurt... a lot." Nevol wore a vain smile as he casually strolled closer to the titan, who lay there twitching in pain.

I have to... get up. Thalrok struggled to make any voluntary movement at all. The stinging pain of the poison ran through his body and hurt everywhere. This Nevol had one of those really irritating types of special skills. To be able to use metal whips and produce a paralysis shock was a new one. How many more of these guys know how to use abilities like this?

"You ready to calm down now, and accept your death, ya poor brute?" Nevol asked. His voice was definitely smug, but his tone was almost... comforting.

Thalrok could hear Nevol getting closer with each step of his heavy boots. There was only one thing the bounty hunter had to do.

"Answer me, you imbecile!" the armored man shouted, bringing one arm back and readying his whip to thrash the pitiful beast lying there before him.

"Shut up!" Thalrok shouted as he quickly slammed his fist into the ground. The earth quaked around them, and he took this chance to get up and grab for his weapon. Thalrok swung his sword in a wide arc for Nevol's waist, but his reach was just short and missed by a foot.

The wiry armored man leapt back a safe distance away wearing an extremely puzzled look. "Are you holding back?" Nevol asked mockingly.

"What?!" Thalrok was infuriated. This was truly the biggest insult that he'd heard in a long time. It made him wanna smash that metal mask right off his face.

"You swung the blunt end of your weapon at me. Why? Are you trying to spare my life?" the armored man asked with contempt.

Thalrok lowered his head and shook his head, smiling through the pain. "It's because of that guy you're all after, that's why I'm doing this. So, yeah."

The bounty hunter took a step forward and was immediately met with the two whips, one wrapped itself around his blade while the other coiled around his forearm. Thalrok grabbed both whips instantly and pulled forward as hard as he could. Nevol sprang forward, stumbling, but all the while sending his paralysis volts down the whips' metal coils. Thalrok felt every zap jolt through his entire body. Yet, he remained standing. He endured every bit of energy this Infected One put into his attack, no matter how much it hurt.

"I guess you could maybe say I'm holding back," Thalrok said, tilting his head.

Even with a helmet covering nearly all of the bounty hunter's face, Nevol could tell that Thalrok was laughing at him. "This guy," he growled, and he swiftly pulled back his whips before the titan could latch on any tighter.

At this point, even though he was surrounded by his fellow clan members, Nevol felt very alone here in the thick of it all. The amber eyes of this bounty hunter stared at him through the slits in his metal helmet and sent a cold chill down his spine. *I didn't think anyone could be this stubborn,* he thought to himself.

Thrashing his whips from side to side, little sparks shot out of each end as they cracked through the air. "It's time I show you the full extent of the power of the Infected!" the armored man shouted, as both whips entangled and joined with each other.

"Wow, you have a bigger weapon now. What, are you compensating for something?" Thalrok mocked, egging him on.

Nevol's expression grew sour as he held onto his whip with two hands. "Enough out of you!" he yelled. The whips flicked through the air as one, crackling in unison as they extended. Though it was not very close to the bounty hunter, a single thick bolt shot out from the tip and flew at him. Thalrok was stunned and unable to do anything as the poison struck his chest. He fell to his knees, eyes rolled back, and clutched his chest, where the skin had been singed and blackened by the strike.

"You still don't understand how foolish you are for being here, do you? This is what you get when you test your skills with those who will soon rule this world." Nevol turned on his heel to walk away from the downed titan. Unamused by this waste of his time, he abandoned his victory. "Have at the remains. I grow tired of this pathetic buffoon," he said to the Ones nearby.

Thalrok could hear Nevol's footsteps echo across the stone floor and fade away as he knelt there in pain. He could hear the Infected Ones rushing in. They got straight to it, jumping on him, punching and kicking him as he was brutally laid low, face down. Heels stomped on him, hands grabbed, choked, and punched. Thalrok lay there and took it all. He could feel himself growing weaker by the second. His eyelids began to close.

"I'm sorry, Ronin... looks like this might be the end," he mumbled, as his eyes finally shut completely. Thalrok could hear his attackers cursing him out as they beat him down. One after another, they crowed about how the mighty titan had lost his battle and there was no hope left for his cronies. How this was his final moment, and how they would deal with the kid next.

"Oa," Thalrok mumbled. The bounty hunter opened his eyes, *Where's Oa?* Between blows, he slowly turned his head left, then right. The boy wasn't in his sight, he didn't know where Oa was. "I can't let him get hurt. I made a promise." Thalrok grunted, placing one meaty hand down on the stone floor and pushing himself up.

"Oh no, ya don't, big guy!" an Infected One shouted, as he swung a fist for Thalrok's throat. Thalrok grabbed onto his forearm as he stood up, and the arm was stopped midswing. As the titan firmly clenched his fist around it, the One's forearm was crushed, bones shattered. He howled out in pain, then writhed on the floor, whimpering. Suddenly, as though a switch had been flipped to maximum power, Thalrok kicked into overdrive, moving with the ferocity of a wild beast on a ravenous rampage.

The armored man turned around to see Thalrok striking down every foe in his way. It was like watching a bear in a fight with baby ducks. "Unbelievable." Nevol sighed through his teeth, watching.

With nothing but his bare hands, Thalrok destroyed anything in his path. He refused to let this be the end of his days. He refused to let anyone else put him down. He had a duty to uphold and he intended to see it through. Thalrok finally locked eyes with the paralysis freak, who he'd been searching for as he fought. "Found you!" he shouted, barreling towards him.

"This again." Nevol sighed in boredom, as he readied his whip. The train that was Thalrok headed right for him, and was only picking up speed as it rolled through anything and anyone that stood between them. Nevol knew that it was all about timing, waiting for that exact moment to strike down the titan for good. He thrashed the whip around, building up a current of power.

Thalrok could see the black bolts reaching out as the whip cracked through the air. It didn't slow him down a bit. He kept barreling toward it, ready to go.

"I'm honored that you would want to go down by my hand. I will take that helmet of yours and reward myself with it as a victory trophy for defeating such a brute as yourself." Nevol said arrogantly. Then he saw his opportunity and thrashed his whip forward, inches away from zapping Thalrok directly. Anyone would be expected to dodge such an attack, but not the titan; he reached out for it.

"What?!" Nevol was astounded. He watched Thalrok's massive arm absorb the hundreds of volts coming from his whip. The titan coiled the end of the metal whip around his hand and yanked it forward. Nevol was jerked completely off his feet and flew at Thalrok, totally out of control. When close enough, the bounty hunter grabbed him by the mask covering his face. He dug his fingers into the metal, ripped it angrily off of his head, and smashed it to the ground.

"You don't have the right to wear this mask!" Thalrok bellowed. He let go of the whip and took a step forward. Using that momentum, he punched Nevol squarely in the face. He kept on punching hard until his foe was pushed through and down into the stone floor below, his whip dangling above him like a ribbon in the breeze.

"Do you *hear* me?!" the bounty hunter roared. Panting and hurting, Thalrok stood above the fully defeated Nevol. He glanced down at his stinging arms and saw whip's burning red marks seared into his skin. When he looked back up, dozens more of the Infected Ones surrounding him began to close in, making him realize just how outnumbered they really were. There wasn't another second to waste, but before he could advance—*Wait, where's Oa?!*

20

Through Anger comes Suffering

"The little pest I squashed before wants another go, huh?" the squat and burly earth-wielder, Rohm, chuckled as he cracked his neck. Oa couldn't help but feel uneasy standing before Rohm. During their last encounter, he'd been faced with a giant boulder smashing him into a building.

Calm down, Oa. Just relax. He told himself, trying to do just that. He held tighter to his staff, pointing it right at the thug.

"Aw, you think that little toothpick will do anything to me?" Rohm of the Infected Ones lifted his foot into the air and stomped. On impact, three chunks of stone levitated effortlessly and floated in front of him. He reeled back his fists and punched them one by one at the young boy. Oa jumped and weaved out of their path, launching himself quickly to dodge the rocky projectiles.

"Still as quick as a fly, I see. Hmm... no matter," the earth-wielder muttered, unperturbed. He twisted his feet, burying his ankles into the stone below as though it were soft sand. With an arrogant grin on his face, Rohm forced his tensed hands out at Oa and launched himself on a direct path. He flew through the air with the stony earth latched on behind him like the body of a snake, which helped propel him quickly forward.

"What!?" Oa was caught off guard and dodged to the side to get out of his way.

319

Slithering and sinuous, Rohm's course changed as he moved his arms and weaved back and forth targeting the boy. He was much faster now. "I gotcha, kid!" he shouted, as he was just barely able to grab Oa's ankle.

Oa was jolted to a stop. "Crap!" he shouted in panic, as Rohm whipped his snakelike body and propelled him down to the ground. Oa's back plowed into the stone first, and his head shortly after. The boy's vision went white for a moment; all he could hear was his name being shouted out all around him. His eyes shot open as he gasped for air in a frenzy. Immediately Oa saw the meteor high above him closing in to strike, and despite the pain, he scrambled to his feet and got himself out of the way.

Missing his target by a hair, Rohm shook the coliseum as he struck its floor. His serpentine boulder-body slithered upright and he stared dead ahead at the young disciple.

"Y'know, all ya got on you is your speed, kid, nothing more. It's sad, really." The earth-wielder shook his head in disappointment, then headed right for him.

"You know what..." Oa lowered his head, closing his eyes as he took a deep breath. He'd had enough of this guy and of him underestimating him. The constant gloating about how tough he was and how weak Oa was. He felt a swelling force of power building up from deep within. Oa closed his fists, feeling the energy of the wind grow with each second. He had finally reached his breaking point.

"I've had enough of being called a *kid!*" Oa shouted, and then he lifted his head, opened his eyes, and forced his palms forward. The immense burst of wind was so powerful that everything, every single rock, no matter how big, was blown halfway across the coliseum. Even Rohm was blown back through a crowd of Infected Ones.

"I'm sick and tired of everyone calling me 'kid'. 'Kid' this, 'kid' that. You know what?! You wanna treat me like a kid, go ahead! I'll show you just how much of a 'kid' I am!" Oa yelled.

Sitting up from the ground, Rohm glared across the empty tunnel between them. "Looks like I hit a nerve," he mumbled, brushing debris from his shoulders. Then, in a mocking tone, he called, "Aw, I'm sorry

I hurt your feelings. You wanna cry, or should I just put you down now?" After which Rohm chuckled to himself, expecting the brat to be intimidated.

"Try me," Oa replied, even more stern than before.

The earth-wielder was beginning to get really pissed off by this kid's attitude. Rohm lived to see the fear in his enemies' eyes as he overpowered them. *But,* he thought, *this little fly won't play my games anymore. I wanna crush him and feel his bones crumble in my hands.*

Hurling his squat body straight at the impudent pup, he roared, "Be careful what you wish for!"

Oa held his place, and began concentrating as he built up the wind pressure in his palms. The earth-wielder was only a short distance away, reeling his fist up over his head to strike Oa down. The young disciple quickly threw both of his palms forward at chest-level to blow him back and away with an intense gust of wind. Yet, Rohm didn't budge.

"Weak!" Rohm shouted, as his fist descended.

Oa was surprised that his counterattack hadn't knocked Rhom back, not even a little. He scooted out of the way just in time, as the brute's fist smashed into the ground. Oa looked over his shoulder and saw that Rohm was right there, anchored in place as his foot was sunk halfway into the ground.

"I am *not* letting you run!" the earth-wielder yelled, as he swung his fists at this little fly.

Oa, exhausted now from the overuse of his wind-control ability, dashed away on foot as the hammering fists behind him just missed. No matter how fast he was, this guy was always right behind him, smiling and ready to destroy. He was like an unstoppable train, fueled by blood-lust and earth-power.

"Stop running, you coward! Where's all that confidence you just had?" Rohm taunted, trying to get a reaction.

Oa could feel himself wanting to prove this guy wrong, wanting to shut him up. As he ran, he took a little leap forward with both feet and managed to force small gusts of air from his soles. Oa gazed down as he rose into the air. He watched the figures below get smaller and saw Rohm crash into where he had just been. The young disciple of Gou lifted his arms above his head. He forced as much wind as he could from his up-turned palms, driving his heels down to slam into the earth-wielder's spine and smash him into the ground. It didn't seem to matter how hard he hit this brute; he only got angrier with each one. Oa quickly jumped off of Rohm and ran, then watched from a distance as the stocky bruiser promptly flipped himself back over.

"Nice try!" the earth-wielder shouted, as he dug his hand into the floor and flung several smallish rocks at Oa. The boy covered his face to avoid as many of the projectiles as possible, but when he lowered his hands, there was Rohm. The brute was already up and after him, his arms now covered in rocks like armor, and swinging toward him.

"No way!" Oa panicked, as the encroaching fist closed in. There was nothing he could do. Oa held his arms up to block, but still suffered a blunt, jagged punch to the body and was knocked across the room. His body hit the ground and bowled through a small crowd before coming to a slow screeching stop. His adrenaline just wasn't kicking in, but he got back up to be ready.

"What..." Oa mumbled, as he saw the impossible. There was no way; he had been sent flying so far. *How?* He saw Rohm coming at him from a too-short distance away. The earth-wielder had barreled his way through the chaos to reach him.

Feeling exhausted, Oa saw no way to avoid his attack again. He was going to just keep getting punched until he was nothing. That smile... that smug smile on Rohm's face was getting so annoying. He wanted to wipe it off, right here, right now. Oa felt his heart beating in his head, his hands moving on their own, palms out, as they lifted toward his approaching doom.

What would Lotus do?

Time slid to a stop. He remembered how Lotus looked when he was staring at Delus, how he appeared to be in so much pain, suffering from deep inside himself. Oa had wanted to help him so much at that moment.

He wanted Lotus's pain to go away, and Oa knew that he wouldn't be able to help anyone if he was dead. The earth-wielder's fist was moments from hitting him. This was it. But... he wasn't done.

"Get away from me!" Oa shouted at the top of his lungs, as tremendous blasts of wind shot out from his palms. Both of them were sent flying backward in opposite directions. The stones clinging to Rohm's arms snapped off when he awkwardly tumbled backward a few feet. As for Oa, he was launched backward across the arena, creating a tunnel between the two of them.

"I really hate this kid!" Rohm bellowed, as he slammed one fist on the ground. The brute then started to laugh hysterically and grabbed his head with both hands. He realized how hard he was struggling, truly struggling, to destroy this little insect that had made its way into their base. Rohm flung himself around, hopping mad, laughing like a lunatic. Then he raged at the top of his lungs, "I'm the strongest, *me*! I am stronger than you ever will be. Do you hear that? You think that since you are so quick and can run, you win. You are wrong! You just can't face the fact that I am stronger than you. Me! ME!" he raved, as he dug his hands deep into the stone beneath his feet. The floor began to shake and tremble. Rohm's veins popped and his eyes bulged with effort.

"You are kidding me." Oa gasped, as he watched this brute break far down through the very earth to lift a gigantic chunk of the coliseum's stony floor. He held it high above his head, almost twenty times the size of his body. This power was unbelievable.

"You see now? You see how foolish you are for challenging me! I was hand-picked by Master Delus! You will be crushed like the little bug you are, kid!" the earth wielder roared. He was preparing to throw it at Oa and instantly finish him.

Oa couldn't move. He could only watch as the Infected Ones nearby ran for their lives. He knew this was the end. There was no escape now. That was, until he lowered his head and saw his saving grace.

"Die, you puny insect!" Rohm shouted, preparing to hurl his masterpiece. He looked up at his marvelous creation, ready to prove he was the strongest. As he lowered his eyes, he noticed that Oa was standing strangely; he was hunched forward, holding onto something.

"It doesn't matter what you try to do! You will just end up—." Suddenly, Rohm felt the soft caress of a breeze brushing past his ears, and the cold, brisk chill as it flowed over his skin. That initial soft touch was accompanied by an agonizing stabbing pain, compliments of the blunt metal end of a staff ramming hard into his gut. Oa had used as much wind force as he could to jet himself forward, staff held firmly out in front, flying like a javelin into its target.

Rohm never saw it coming. Even when exhausted, this kid was just too fast. He fell to one knee with his eyes rolling back in his head and consciousness fading. He was going to lose.

But then, abruptly, his eyes snapped open, his adrenaline-fueled frenzy revived. "I told you being fast didn't matter!" the earth-wielder shouted, as he forced the gargantuan boulder toward that pesky fly.

"No way!" Oa shouted, moments away from being crushed. He'd been sure that a pointed strike to the abdomen at that speed would have worked, but he'd been wrong.

This, indeed, was the end. He couldn't stop or escape something this massive moving so very fast at this short a distance. Only someone as strong as Rohm could do that. Oa closed his eyes and braced for the inevitable.

After a moment or two, Oa opened one eye, thinking he certainly should have been crushed into nothingness by now. He opened both eyes, glanced at Rohm, and saw the sour look on his fleshy face.

"You all right, Oa?" Thalrok asked, as he stood over him holding onto the immense chunk of stony earth, stopping it from crushing him.

"Thalrok!?" Oa cried out in relief, now seeing just what was happening. Both Rohm and Thalrok held the boulder in the air. One was using his power and trying to crush them, the other was using simple brute force to try to save them.

"Oa—his other knee!" the bounty hunter yelled. Oa snapped back into the moment, looked down to see the earth-wielder's one leg still supporting him. Rohm tried to stand back up on both legs, but before he could, Oa swiftly zipped behind him and kicked out his main support.

"Damn it!" Rohm shouted, and collapsed to both knees. Thalrok immediately let go of the giant chunk of earth and dashed forward. He clotheslined the brute with his brawny forearm, then forced him backward flat onto the ground. Losing control, Rohm tossed his most massive boulder backwards at the topmost corner of the coliseum, where it stuck, making the people above-ground wonder what was happening. As the Infected earth-wielder flopped onto his back, he saw his worst nightmare. That agile kid, that insect, was above him in the air, descending as fast as he could.

"I refuse to let you win!" Rohm shouted, trying to scramble to his feet. It was too late. Oa drove both heels into Rohm's chest, effectively draining the last drop of adrenaline he had left. The earth-wielder's eyes closed, his head fell back; he was knocked out cold. Oa jumped off of Rohm's chest, panting and exhausted from his latest exertions and stress.

"You alright?" Thalrok looked at Oa.

"I'm fine. Everything just hurts."

"I'm sorry to say, but we can't relax now. We've got more inbound." Thalrok said, tilting his helmeted head toward the hoard of Infected Ones closing in.

"What about Lotus?" Oa asked.

21

Through Suffering comes Pain

"You alright, Nyloc?" Lotus asked.

"Yeah, I'll be alright, Captain," Nyloc replied, carefully keeping tabs on the two Infected Ones before him.

Kenji and Ogan, Delus's main lieutenants, had finally come face to face with the man their master had been searching for all these years. Both stood there at the ready, red hooded cloaks up and glaring ahead. Kenji held his two long cleavers poised for action, their irregularly saw-toothed blades razor-sharp. Ogan's elegantly curved and deadly dagger, now free of its sheath, gleamed wickedly. They glared at Lotus and Nyloc, waiting for the right moment to strike.

"What are we gonna do?" Nyloc asked under his breath, "We are completely surrounded and have no way of escaping."

Lotus peered left and then right, seeing the vicious expressions the Infected Ones wore as they stared them down. Usually, he would try to assess the situation and think of a careful way to get out safely. However, the wanted man couldn't think straight, not after seeing... him.

"We just have to deal with this, one step at a time." Lotus exhaled, as he reached for his sword. As the two of them went for their weapons, Kenji and Ogan lowered their stance, ready to pounce before their prey could get any more prepared.

"Now!" Kenji shouted, as he dashed forward. Their coordinated attack was on, and each ran at their target. Kenji went straight for the archer, blades drawn, ready to cut right through him.

"Good luck dodging with that blindfold on," Kenji commented. He crossed his arms and pulled his long cleavers close to his body before slashing them away from one another to slice forward at Nyloc's chest. Quickly pushing off from one foot, the archer leaped into the air, avoiding both blades. He pressed his other foot on the top of Kenji's head and sprang off, landing some distance behind him.

Kenji's head was forced downward, and he stumbled blindly. A flame of rage burned deep inside him, and he turned around, screaming out, "Asshole!" He dashed for Nyloc, who stood calmly upright, not even facing his direction. Kenji pulled one of his jagged cleavers back, ready to slash a lethal blow down through the archer's shoulder and chest.

"I see you," Nyloc whispered, angling his bow into sight and firing backward at Kenji without even turning around.

The Infected lieutenant was caught entirely off guard and couldn't dodge the arrow that swiftly closed in. Kenji watched it thwack into his left shoulder, then screamed out as it pierced through skin, muscle, and nerves, stunning his whole arm. "You annoying—"

But before Kenji could even finish his insult, Nyloc immediately took advantage of this change, keeping up the offensive by kicking Kenji's useless hand which sent one wickedly sharp cleaver flying across the room.

"Looks like you only have one blade now," the archer observed as he planted one foot forward and reeled back his fist.

Still unprepared and wide open, Kenji was clocked hard across the jaw with a right hook. Just as his head snapped to the right, Nyloc delivered a hearty uppercut to his exposed chin. Kenji's head whipped back on impact and he felt pain flooding in.

I hate this guy! Kenji jumped backward, holding onto the one blade he had left. He gently rubbed his face where he'd been hit, feeling the stinging pain of those two solid punches.

"You wanna try again?" Nyloc gestured for him to come back at him.

"You want some more? Fine. I'll give you more." Kenji took in a deep breath and stood up straight.

Nyloc didn't know what he was up to now, but felt quite uneasy. He sensed that those surrounding him were backing away, distancing themselves from Kenji. "That can't be good," he whispered to himself.

Suddenly, clouds of dark-maroon smoke poured out from Kenji's mouth and body which surrounded him, then spread horizontally. It just kept on coming, layer after layer, blocking everything from sight.

"Smoke?" Nyloc wondered, as it crept closer to him, blurring his senses. He took in a shallow breath and immediately felt burning in his lungs which made him cough in pain. "Toxic smoke?!" he gasped, as he moved his hood to cover his nose and mouth.

"What's the matter? Don't like my poison?" Nyloc could hear Kenji's mocking voice, but couldn't tell where the man was. He thought he sensed him to the right, but found himself terribly mistaken when a hammering punch struck him hard across the face.

"Dammit, *focus*, man!" Nyloc scolded himself. He jumped backward just in time to dodge the blade that followed right after the punch. The metal blade rang out as it struck the stone floor, stinging the archer's ears.

He can see even in this haze?! But Kenji wouldn't let that stop him. Wincing, he pulled the arrow from his shoulder, staunched the blood, and prepared to continue the fight.

So... I haven't trained like this in a while. Should be a good refresher, right? Nyloc waited and listened carefully. He expected to hear one man's footsteps rushing toward him. But, it was far worse. He could hear footsteps coming at him from multiple directions.

Three to my left and only one on the right. Hm, shouldn't be that much trouble. Nyloc determined as he reached for his hip. His bow rested on his back; for now he was fully dependent on his close combat skills. With a swift twisting of his hips, he flung a shuriken at the Infected One on his right. Through the haze it flew, and into the chest of the hidden foe, who cried out as it pierced him through his clothes.

"Right there," Nyloc whispered, dashing towards the voice.

The surprised Infected One was trying to pull the small flat throwing blade out of his chest while wincing in pain. When he looked up from his wound, he found Nyloc there in front of him. The thug fumbled to react before being attacked, but it was too late. The blind archer jabbed him hard in the nose. His head snapped back just as a swinging hook demolished his ribs. Nyloc had just heaped an abundance of pain on this Infected One, and finished it off by twisting his body and thrusting the heel of his foot into those same injured ribs with a vigorous side kick.

"One down," he whispered, hustling over to find his next victims.

"Kenji said he was right around here. Keep looking, he couldn't have gotten far," a wary thug whispered, as they searched for the blind archer through the clouds of poisonous haze. Nearly all of the Infected Ones had been desensitized to the special abilities of their comrades-in-arms, so these two were able to continue to tiptoe unaffected through the toxic fog. Cautiously, they checked in every direction for the intruder.

Hearing the softest of whistling sounds, the One in front shouted, "Look out!" and they dropped flat. Another set of shurikens soared through the air just where their upper bodies had been a split second before.

"He's that way! Get him!" The two Infected Ones shouted and ran toward where the projectiles must have originated, weapons drawn and ready to strike. They still couldn't see anyone through the thick layers of smoke, which was one downfall of this unique power.

"Nothing here. Where did he go now?" the One in the lead asked, as he looked around for his partner. Peering left and right, he couldn't see him anywhere. He called out for him but got no reply. What he did get was a painful pinching feeling after the thud of something hitting his upper back. He turned his head to see an arrow deeply embedded in his shoulder. His skin crawled in shock as he turned back, only to run into a sharp elbow to the temple. Nyloc knocked him out cold and was ready for the next one.

Two more down.

Nyloc coughed as the smoke's poison was slowly slipping through the layers of his hood. He could feel himself getting lightheaded. His body felt sluggish. If he stayed in this haze any longer, he might not make it out.

Hmm, now where is that last one? He listened carefully, determined to go on. The surrounding chaos drowned out any small sounds nearby. There was nothing. It had been some time since he'd felt this blind before. The haze was making his foresight somewhat less clear, and it was hard to get a good sense of anything.

A breath? Nyloc suddenly heard the faintest exhale. He jumped forward to avoid the slash of a blade from Kenji, who had dropped down on him from above.

"I can't believe you're still standing in my smoke. You're tough, I'll give you that." Kenji said with a tinge of grudging admiration, as he pointed his blade at the archer.

"Well, I can't believe your clan mates don't know how to be stealthy," Nyloc said, his voice muffled under his hood.

"You won't be able to breathe under that much longer. It's only a matter of time." Kenji informed him, then grunted as he dashed forward. He ran straight at Nyloc, blade drawn and ready to slash through him. The archer stood as still as he could, listening. Kenji's blade crossed the air, right for his neck, but Nyloc moved just in time. Slash after slash, Kenji danced through his haze, missing every strike he took at that blind man. He swung his terrifying cleaver of a blade time after time, and his heavy panting turned into loud grunts. Nyloc could hear each movement he made and was sensing every swing of his blade as it traveled through the air. This countless dodging was getting tiresome to the archer, so he swiftly sprang high into the air, above the layers of smoke. Kenji, angry at being taken for a fool, jumped up after him. As he exited his layers of poisonous smoke, he saw it—Nyloc, in the air, with his bow drawn and pointed right at him.

Noooo! I fell for his trap! Kenji panicked as he watched the archer pull his arrow back just far enough.

Nyloc was a split second away from firing when he heard a loud shout coming from his left saying, "Nyloc, switch!" With no hesitation, Nyloc immediately turned his bow away from Kenji and fired his arrow toward the voice.

* * *

While Kenji rushed at Nyloc, Ogan ran straight for Ronin, ready to face the man he'd heard so much about. This wanted man was both a mystery and someone he knew all too well. Ogan pulled back his curved dagger, watching Ronin carefully wrapping each finger around the hilt of his sword.

I'm not gonna give him a chance to draw it! Ogan pushed off from his back leg, putting all of his energy into it, and thrust his lethal dagger at the heart of his foe. Lotus quickly drew his sword from its saya and swung it vertically to clash paths with the dagger.

Ogan was shocked when he saw the shortened fragment of a blade shimmer. *It's broken?!* Who would ever expect this *legend* to bring a faulty weapon into battle? Ogan backed off for a moment, collecting himself.

"That sword? Why do you use it if it's broken?" he asked his opponent, even though they were in the heat of battle.

"Wouldn't you like to know?" Lotus scoffed, as he pressed in to fight.

Ogan kept his guard up, unsure of what to expect in a fight with a blade like that. The Infected lieutenant closed the distance between them. He cut and slashed for Lotus, trying to kill him with each thrust of his razor-sharp curved blade. Even though he jabbed his dagger with great force and skill, Lotus would deflect or dodge it every time. The sounds of clashing metal rang and echoed as they battled across the underground coliseum.

I won't be able to keep up at this rate. Ogan waited for an opportunity to strike. He could see that with every second they fought, the wanted man became increasingly angrier, and worse than that, increasingly stronger.

"There it is." Ogan planted one leg forward, thrusting the blade upwards at Lotus's ribs. Just as Lotus was about to deflect the blade, Ogan pulled it back. The broken blade swung freely upward, and Ogan grabbed Lotus's arm to stop him from bringing it back down. Lotus locked eyes with Ogan, staring angrily. As he peered deep into Ogan's blue eyes, he felt all of the anger and dark energy drain from inside of him and begin to fade away.

"What... the... ?" Lotus stammered. He felt weak all of a sudden, like his body had been physically drained of strength and stamina.

"What are you... " Lotus felt his arms grow heavy and his eyelids droop. He felt extremely tired, as if he was seconds away from falling into a deep sleep.

"Aw, Ronin, you're getting tired? Don't take a nap on me now." Ogan whispered wickedly.

The sudden pain of a dagger slicing into the side of his ribs woke Lotus right back up. Lotus grabbed Ogan's arm, and holding his wrist, pulled it forward and kicked him in the stomach. Ogan stumbled backward, and Lotus held pressure on his wound. He still felt dead-tired. Every drop of dark energy was completely gone, and he had no adrenaline now to keep him going. "This isn't good. I've gotta keep my eyes open." Lotus said, panting softly with his face upturned.

"Careful where you look, though. If you keep looking into *my* eyes, you just might fall asleep... and for good." Ogan said with a smirk. He wasn't going to let this chance get away from him, and hustled back to his prey.

Lotus was at a standstill; he felt like he wasn't ready to defend anything. Even as death came charging in at him, he couldn't generate a bit of energy. Finally, his eyes closed all the way, and his legs buckled.

Ogan scoffed as he pulled back his dagger, aiming for his opponent's throat.

As though his body was immersed in very deep water, all Lotus could feel was the heavy weight of his muscles. He saw, as if in a dream, a faint light there in front of him. *Wait... what?*

As the dagger was inches away from piercing his throat, Lotus dodged out of the way.

"What?!" Ogan shouted, as he watched his blade miss its target.

Lotus opened his eyes slightly and used all of what little energy he had to grab Ogan's shoulder and thrust his knee against Ogan's chest as he fell forward. He could hear the sound of the air wheezing out of his lungs as the knee thudded into him.

I can see his energy, Lotus thought, as he swung his fist toward the source

332

of life he was sensing. His fist barely missed Ogan, who had backed away just in time.

How can he still move? Ogan wondered, as he watched Lotus, his eyes closed again but stumbling to stand.

Since the Infected One's power had drained all of Lotus's dark energy from his body, light was the only thing left for him to feel in this physically tranquil state. It was faint, but he could feel it, and feel it growing.

"I have to… control it!" Lotus murmured, as he forced his eyes open and let small bursts of energy radiate from his body. Ogan covered his face as he watched the tiny bits of light shimmering from his prey.

"He really broke past my ability, huh? Oh, I will change that." Ogan vowed, as he adjusted his grip on his dagger's elegantly curved handle.

Delus was watching over all from above. His expression grew bitter when he saw that type of power coming from Lotus. It reminded him of a man he had hated more than anyone else in this world. The one he couldn't stand to see overpower him.

I- I did it. I can still control the light! Lotus thought in relief as he felt that warm energy pulsing once more through his body. He looked at his hands and saw the black veins fading a bit. Clenching his fists, he glared ahead at Ogan.

"You think your little trick will stop you from being put to sleep? Try me." Ogan said as he dashed back at Lotus, fully committed to the fight. Delus's lieutenant bared his teeth, his eyes wide and staring into Lotus's. He watched the wanted man move slowly, placing his blade back into its saya and calmly closing his eyes.

"Damn it, open your eyes!" Ogan shouted, as he rushed in to cut the wanted man down. His blade sliced through the air, passion and fury pushing the blade faster. As the metal touched Lotus's shoulder, it just phased through.

"Again!?" Ogan panicked as he saw Lotus's afterimage fade completely away. He turned to his right and saw the wanted man standing there with his palm cocked back and aiming a clear shot to his head.

Damn it! Ogan was unable to do anything. He was moments away from a world of pain.

Lotus could feel the warm power inside himself growing slightly as he forgot all about where he was. He was just overjoyed that this power of light was still inside of him. He refocused himself, forcing his palm at Ogan's head.

"Pathetic," Delus spoke scornfully from his vantage point high above them.

Even at that distance, Lotus heard that voice. He heard it clear as day. Just the sound of Delus's voice immediately sapped every bit of light energy from his body. He felt his limbs weaken, his hand dropped, and he buckled at the knees.

"Perfect," Ogan smirked, then grabbed Lotus's shoulders and stared him in the eyes.

Lotus, who was losing control and filled with dread and anger after hearing Delus's voice, accidentally locked eyes with Ogan. He couldn't help it, nor could he disengage from Ogan's piercing cobalt gaze. Lotus felt himself seconds away from falling asleep.

His body felt numb. His mind was nearly emptied of thought, and the blackness around his field of vision was taking it over. He was helpless; the light inside him was gone, and he was going to die. If only he didn't have to look into those eyes...

With every bit of energy he still had left, he called out, "Nyloc, switch!"

22

Through Pain comes Death

The immediate shock and pain of the arrow that was fired into Ogan's shoulder encouraged him to release his grip on Lotus. His concentration was broken, and he held onto the embedded arrow to stabilize it. Nyloc, still high in the air, turned back to Kenji, who was closing in on him following the arcing path of his jump.

He could switch targets and fire that quick? No matter, he's open now. Kenji observed. He readied his wicked-looking cleaver to slice into Nyloc's midsection, but before he could swing his blade horizontally, Nyloc flung his last shuriken at Kenji's wrist. It cut into his forearm and shocked the nerves in his arm. Kenji winced in pain, his weapon now useless and drooping, as he watched the archer descend.

Nyloc planted his feet on the paved floor and instantly ran in Lotus's direction, another arrow already nocked. He heard Ogan scream out as he pulled the arrow from his shoulder and threw it off to one side. Then the Infected lieutenant reached for his dagger, which had fallen beside his foot. As he did, another arrow hit it, and as a clash of metal on metal rang out, the dagger was pushed noisily across the stony surface, far out of reach. Ogan's hand closed on nothing, and he glared in the direction of the oncoming archer.

"That son of a—" Ogan began, but was interrupted by something pulling his shirt. He turned his head and watched as Lotus, eyes closed and swaying on his feet, clocked him in the temple. Ogan concentrated on keeping himself standing.

"Captain, look out!" Nyloc shouted as he saw Ogan swinging his fist at Lotus. Lotus couldn't really tell where it was coming from, so he guessed and ducked. Through a stroke of luck, the punch passed his head, and he shoved at Ogan, who stumbled far away from him.

"Thanks for the heads up, Nyloc." Lotus panted, as he could finally open his eyes a bit. Nyloc made his way over to where Lotus was and helped him regain stable footing.

"Please forgive me." Nyloc apologized just before he raised his hand and slapped his captain hard across the face.

Lotus's eyes shot open as he stood up straight and felt the stinging on his cheek. "Whoa!... what was... oh... oh, thanks." Lotus stammered, realizing what Nyloc was doing as he finally felt a little more awake.

"Nothing a little slap won't help." Nyloc sighed, as he readied himself for the next round.

Ogan was already back in front of the two of them and Kenji was racing towards them from across the way.

"You said switch, right?" Nyloc asked.

"I did, and thanks. Now, whatever you do, do not look in this guy's eyes." Lotus told him.

"I think I'll have an easy time with that," Nyloc smirked to himself just a little while he adjusted his blindfold.

Lotus, now mostly awake, ran toward Kenji, who was getting closer to them.

Ogan stood in place, watching as the blind archer drew another arrow. "This could be a problem," he muttered, backing away and snapping his fingers. Nyloc didn't know what Ogan was planning until he sensed a group surrounding him again.

"Twelve of them? Yikes..." He sighed, and swiftly fired an arrow at the closest one. They charged at him one after another. Nyloc could sense each one of them, every punch, every kick, every swing of their weapons. He could see it coming a mile away. Their movements were a lot slower than Ogan's or Kenji's; these grunts were just inferior pawns.

Ogan watched as every lackey who tried couldn't land a single hit on the archer, who just danced in and out of every measly attack they threw.

Those idiots. Whatever... At least I can help Kenji now. Ogan glanced over and saw Kenji and Lotus in an all-out brawl. As he started to take a step toward them, an arrow passed right by his face. He turned in the direction it had come from and saw Nyloc, still busy in his own fight, facing him.

"I hate this guy," Ogan murmured. He ran for the archer, noticing that the ground below his feet was shaking.

* * *

"Die!" Kenji yelled, poised to slash Lotus across the neck. The wanted man, his hands in fists, and the Infected One, weapon at the ready, ran towards one another. Lotus watched slowly as Kenji's cleaver cut through the air with enough force to slice cleanly through his neck.

He looks just like m— Lotus's thought went unfinished as he felt the raging anger inside of him grow. The dark energy whirlpool was once again freely taking residence. There was no fighting it, and it had indeed already taken some control.

As Kenji's cleaver reached out, Lotus ducked underneath the instant before he was struck. The blade crossed through the air, leaving Kenji wide open. Lotus thought he had the advantage until he felt a bony kneecap being driven into his jaw. Kenji had known that his first attack wouldn't work, so he'd baited his foe with it, then drove his knee hard into Lotus's chin as he ran right into it. Lotus's teeth slammed together and his head rang from the blow.

"I will show you what real power is!" Kenji shouted, as he planted his leg back down and twisted his hips. With his empty left hand, he swung his fist and hooked Lotus across the face.

The wanted man's head snapped hard to the left from the impact, which also moved him back a few feet. Kenji watched Lotus stumble, fall, and then lie there motionless. He just scoffed, and took a step forward to end

337

this. As his foot touched the ground, he felt a wave of pressure burst out from Lotus. The surge of power easily pushed his foot back, and Kenji watched as a pitch black aura issued from the wanted man. It grew, and circled around him.

"What is that?!" Kenji murmured. He hesitated to even try to take another step. He watched Lotus plant one hand on the ground, lifting himself slightly. Kenji felt his skin crawl as he locked eyes with Lotus. The eyes of a monster stared steadily back.

This... this feels just like master's power.

Kenji panicked when he saw his foe rise and stand up straight. Within the blink of an eye, Lotus was in front of him, with one clenched fist inches from his face.

What!? Kenji couldn't do anything. He felt the hammering power of Lotus's punch strike him squarely. It sent him flying into the thugs watching nearby, where he was quickly helped back up. Feeling for his cleaver, he noticed that it wasn't anywhere near him. Kenji looked back and saw it in Lotus's hands, where he held it by the blade and squeezed until it shattered.

"That little trick won't save you." Kenji panted. He ran head-first at Lotus, who had the same idea. They ran straight at each other, with no weapons in hand, just bare knuckles. Time after time they swung their fists. With each blow, things only got more complicated as they maneuvered across the floor, layering move after move, each trying to strike the other down. Kenji realized that every time the wanted man attacked—*He's getting stronger and faster!* His time at this stalemate was slowly coming to an end. He had to make one good last-minute move right now, or he would lose. As Lotus took one big swing at him, he quickly dashed backward. Lotus's fist found only empty air, and he watched as Kenji retreated a short distance away and took in a deep breath.

"Time's up!" Kenji shouted, as he discharged an explosion of maroon colored smoke around them.

Lotus covered his face as the haze expanded. He took a little breath and coughed immediately after.

Poison? Great... he mused.

Then, Lotus's mind went quiet. He hadn't realized it at first, but now he noticed it the moment he took a breath. *This smoke... It's the same...* he thought, feeling his heart pound faster. *It's the same as... Perksy!*

Years ago, his friends had encountered this type of toxic smoke with some thugs in Perksy. *So it really was them, the Infected Ones, way back then... They were the ones who...* and all thought ceased as Lotus felt a great release of dark energy coming from within. He was too frozen in shock to stop it.

Kenji felt the force of dark energy that his foe had created quickly building up, and stopped his smoke attack. He stood stock still, terrified about what was hiding there with him inside his fog.

Lotus felt his fingernails dig into the palms of his clenched his fists. He was seconds away from running amok; he felt the black energy seeking to go on a rampage and urging him to go berserk. He bared his teeth in a snarl and began to take a single step forward when a voice shouted— "Lotus!" and suddenly, an immense blast of wind came through, blowing at the cloud of smoke.

"Oa?" Lotus snapped out of his rage, and saw the toxic haze quickly dissipating. He turned to see the young disciple dropping down from above, checking in to see if he was all right. "You okay, Oa?" Lotus asked. The dark energy seemed at bay, for now.

"I'm fine, I'm fine. Thalrok headed over to help Nyloc." Oa informed him.

"Thank goodness." Lotus was relieved to hear that they were safe.

"Lotus, where did the guy you were fighting get to?" Both looked around the now smoke-free area around them, but Kenji was nowhere to be found.

* * *

"Master." Kenji panted, as he clambered up the final ledge to reach the high balcony where Delus stood. Delus gave no reply, just sliding his gaze over sideways at his young lieutenant.

"Sir, I believe it's best we retreat. I don't know what it is, but—" Kenji blurted out.

"Retreat? Did I hear you correctly?" his master interrupted, in a scornful voice.

"Yes sir..." Kenji mumbled.

Delus clenched his fists at those words. "You think we need to retreat? You really are still that weak and foolish child I took in all those years ago. You believe our army of the Infected can't stop a single pest here in our own domain. This is the most naive thing I have ever heard you say. We do *not* retreat from a fight. We either win, or *you* all die trying!" Delus roared, each word angrier than the last.

Kenji was too scared to even attempt to reply. He just stood there, staring into the demonic eyes of his master, who then yelled emphatically, "*I* will be the one who makes these decisions. Do you hear me?!"

"Yes, sir," Kenji said softly, as he headed back down.

Delus watched with judgmental eyes as his long-time disciple returned to the battle below.

"I think it's time," Delus murmured. He climbed up to stand on the wide stone railing of the balcony from where he'd been watching everything. "Infected! Hear me!" he shouted down into the coliseum. All eyes turned upward to look at their master as he stood there with his arms out, smiling.

"I have been blessed with a chance to avenge what I have lost. I have endured many years of sleepless nights wondering if I would ever be graced with the chance to see the man who took what I loved most from me." Delus paused and pointed right at Lotus. "*He* is the one!"

Everyone's eyes turned to Lotus. They all stared at him. Some were confused, but others realized precisely what was going on.

"*This* is the man who killed my son!" Delus raged. "He is the one who struck him down. Five years ago, I lost my son to this man."

Lotus had no idea what he was talking about. He had never killed...

"Ah, but now, I have been blessed! I am face-to-face with this man who took my son from me. My boy was a hero! My son *slayed* the pathetic man who took what was mine when I was young." Delus smiled evilly.

Even from far away, he could see the complete and total horror on Lotus's face. "It's only fair, right, boy?" he tilted his head with a smirk. "*You* took the life of *my* son. *He* took the life of your so-called master!"

23

Through Death comes Hate

Many people say there's a calm before the storm—a moment when all is clear and still. No disturbances exist; there is no tumult. A stillness, a brief point in time occurs, when one can look around and feel just how tranquil and motionless everything is.

"Ronin!"

The calm before the storm. The word calm is such an unjustified word. It should be called the moment before disaster. Nothing can be calm before a storm, oh no. If anything, it's like the spark right before the match bursts into flame and then burns brightly.

"Lotus! Please, answer!"

The calm before the storm. The moment before disaster. Two different beginnings. One identical ending. What's after that, you might ask? What *does* come after that?

"Ronin!"

The wanted man sat on his knees, his white-knuckled hands tightly gripped his head as a stinging pain rang in his ears. Eyes wide open and mouth agape, he couldn't hear them shout for him. Their calling out was a hopeless effort on their part.

"Look at his arms!"

"Is he going to be alright? Lotus... Lotus!"

They saw the black stain slowly creeping higher up his arms. Tiny bolts of dark lightning were snapping from his body. The floor below them began to tremble and shake.

"Move!" There was a crashing sound as Thalrok forced his way through to Lotus's side. He knelt next to him and very gently put a hand on his shoulder.

"Ronin. Ronin, you gotta calm down. Please, I know exactly what's going on in your head, but you gotta breathe. This isn't the Ronin, no, the Lotus, you want to be. Fight against it, and let's get out of here." Thalrok tried to comfort him, reason with him.

The poor man didn't stir. They could see his back heaving up and down, faster and faster. His breathing became so intense that they could see steam coming out of his mouth. Thalrok pulled back his hand.

"Din..." Lotus could barely say the name.

Thalrok's fists clenched tightly at the sound of his friend's voice. The pain, the absolute pain, that he heard come out of his mouth, was unbearable. Thalrok dropped his head, thinking of what he could do next.

"Thal... Thalrok?" Oa stuttered. The bounty hunter looked over his shoulder and saw Oa pointing at Lotus. Turning back, he saw the side of Lotus that he had only seen once before. His eyes widened behind the helmet he wore as he saw that the creeping black stain on Lotus's arms now reached up to his shoulders. Lotus's entire arms were now coated in black, coal black veins bulging, and a low dark flame flickered up from his skin. His fingers were like claws digging into his head.

"Not again..." Thalrok mumbled sadly as he felt the ground begin shaking harder.

Suddenly, lightning bolts shot out from Lotus in every direction. The Infected Ones closest to the four companions started backing away, their cocky smiles replaced by expressions of fear and alarm. They could feel the surging energy that pulsed out of Lotus intensifying.

"*They* did it..." The creaking sound of his voice no longer sounded in pain. It was... different.

"What? What's wrong?" Thalrok asked.

"*They* did it… They killed…" Lotus's voice got louder, but he was unable to complete his thought out loud.

Thalrok reached out to him, trying to think of something to calm him down. "Ronin… " he began.

"They need to… pay…" Lotus finally said, then took a deep breath.

Thalrok's hand was inches away from grabbing Lotus's arm, but in the blink of an eye, Lotus was gone, and the screeching howl of a man crying out in boundless rage pierced the ears of every being there in the underground coliseum.

The unlucky Infected One nearest the four of them found himself staring deeply into Lotus's blood-red eyes. "What the—?!" he shouted, as Lotus swung and struck him down with a single punch. Before his body could even collapse to the ground, Lotus was already on to the next One. He pinballed through the crowd of the Infected, knocking them out one after another. There was no stopping him.

"What's going on?" Oa asked, a little worried.

"This is the true power Lotus holds inside of himself. This is his curse." Thalrok said, watching as all the eyes were fixed on his rampaging friend. The three of them stood in place and felt the ground rattle as Lotus punched his opponents through the very earth with each strike he threw.

"We have to stop him. Come on, let's go!" Thalrok shouted.

"Wait, wait!" Nyloc grabbed Thalrok's arm and pulled him back. "Why are we stopping him? He's wiping them out even quicker than before."

Thalrok turned and watched as Lotus obliterated everyone in his path, sending men flying as he kicked and punched his way through them. It was a fearsome sight.

"Do you hear that?" Thalrok asked. "Do you hear him screaming? He's suffering."

Nyloc listened carefully. He could easily hear the Infected Ones shrieking and shouting as Lotus soared across the coliseum in a frenzy, their numbers dropping faster and faster. Then he did hear it—Lotus shouting wildly and crying out as though he was stuck in some nightmarish trance.

"I've seen him like this before. He was in pain, crying out just like this, and hoping this pain would end. The power inside Ronin is overtaking him, and we have to help him before he does something he regrets." Thalrok told them.

Oa and Nyloc could tell just how serious Thalrok was. They too, felt unnerved seeing Lotus like this. As powerfully as he was fighting, this just wasn't right.

"How can we stop him?" Oa asked.

"I don't know. I can't help him like I did last time. We just have to get to him and show him it's all alright or something." Thalrok began running off in his direction.

"You think that'll work?" Nyloc said skeptically.

"No idea," Thalrok replied, then reeled back and clocked the Ones in his way as he rushed over to Lotus's aid.

Meanwhile, Lotus was running amok and could not stop his savage frenzy. He felt the overwhelming flow of energy forcing its way through each limb of his body. His legs felt like they could run forever; they forced themselves into the ground as he pushed off. His arms were still coated all in black and the sharp claws of his demon-like hands cut through whatever weapon was used to block his strikes. Like an unstoppable train on a track that went on forever, in Lotus's chaotic mind only one mantra repeated—*Destroy them all! Make them pay!* It was a painful cycle. He saw the Infected Ones in their masks and could only think of that night, the night he lost his master. These were the villains behind it all. They were the thugs who went after Belle's village all those years ago. They were the outlaws who attacked Perksy. They were the evil-doers who killed... "Din," Lotus muttered, and he only moved faster. Another and another One fell. The rocky ceiling above their heads trembled as he rampaged on and on.

"Ronin!" Thalrok shouted. The titan jumped forward, arms reaching wide as he tried to bear hug Lotus before he could dash away. But his arms wrapped around nothing as Lotus disappeared just before he could grab him.

"Oa, now!" Thalrok called out, as Lotus was headed in the young disciple's direction.

"I'm sorry, Lotus," Oa whispered, as he sent an immense burst of wind in his direction. The colossal force blew everyone in its way soaring backward, except for Lotus, who was utterly unaffected. The boy was shocked to see Lotus's momentum remain constant. Suddenly, Lotus jumped forward, right in Oa's direction. He reeled his first back and was flying directly at him.

"Ronin, don't do it!" Thalrok shouted.

"Lotus, it's *me*!" Oa yelled, as he threw his arms up to protect his head and ducked.

Lotus, bursting with dark energy, swung his fist right at Oa as the boy cried out, "NO!" The fist flew inches past Oa's head, missing him entirely—but it did strike the earth-wielder, Rohm, hard in the gut as he loomed over Oa. The young disciple opened his eyes to look behind him. Rohm of the Infected had dropped to the ground, instantly unconscious, and Lotus was already off to take care of the next One.

"Right about... now!" Nyloc waited carefully to fire his arrow into Lotus's path. The arrow went through all the chaos, and the smoke bomb on the arrowhead exploded as it hit him in the chest. A small cloud of smoke surrounded Lotus's head, blocking his vision as he ran forward. He rubbed his eyes to get the haze out of his way. As his vision cleared, a human wall crashed into him.

"Gotcha!" Thalrok gasped, as he held tightly onto Lotus. His strong arms wrapped around him as the raging Lotus kicked and squirmed to get away. He cried out, shouting in frustration as he tried his best to free himself. Thalrok could feel the burning energy radiating from inside him. Being so close to this dark power was disturbing, and though Thalrok felt quite uneasy, he refused to let go. His skin was physically burning as he held onto his friend, but he still refused to let him go.

"Ronin! You have to calm down! I know they did an unforgivable thing to you! I want nothing more than to get back at them. But I can't let you suffer like this. This isn't how you would want to do this! This isn't how Din would want you to either!" The instant Thalrok said that name, the power inside of Lotus grew twice as strong. The ground quaked and rumbled as Thalrok struggled to keep his friend contained.

"Master?" Kenji and Ogan had both gotten themselves back up to the balcony above all the mayhem.

"This. This is the exact reason why that man was a fool. Look at how weak this boy is; he can't even control this power." Delus scoffed and then shook his head in disappointment.

"What is your next request, sir?" Ogan asked.

"I have no need to be here anymore. I will leave the rest to you." Delus turned away from the ledge and took a single step forward. At that, Lotus's body stopped battling Thalrok. He had felt the dark pressure of Delus's movement. His eyes darted up to the balcony, where he saw Delus walking away.

"I'm sorry about this!" Thalrok shouted in Lotus's ear. The bounty hunter positioned himself to headbutt Lotus and knock him out. For some reason, Lotus was still for a moment, and this was the only shot he had to calm him down. His head jolted forward and passed through nothingness, and he felt his now-empty arms fold into his own body.

"What...?!" Thalrok was stymied.

"Thalrok!" Nyloc shouted, pointing up at the balcony. Lotus had teleported up to the high balcony without skipping a beat. Kenji and Ogan jumped backward, as the wanted man appeared from out of nowhere to perch on the wide stone handrail of the balustrade.

Time slowed. Lotus was a mere three steps from the man who had directed it all, the man who'd given the order to take his master's life. He could feel the dark power overflow and rise to even higher levels; his blood surged and his anger took complete control.

"Deluuus!" Lotus cried out, as he jumped down and swung a fist at him. The slow-motion movement of that swinging fist went on for what felt like hours. The wanted man watched Delus slowly turn around, peer over his shoulder and glare at him. Just as he was about to be struck down, Delus raised his palm and effortlessly stopped Lotus's fist. The pressure of the punch whooshed back at Ogan and Kenji, who watched their master scowl.

Lotus felt his heart drop. He was so close to him.

Death.

The look of death was what he saw. The physical embodiment of death was standing before him.

"This… *this* is what true power is, boy." Delus grabbed onto Lotus's fist and reeled back his other hand. Using his entire body, he twisted his hips and drove his fist into the ribs of this weakling. Lotus's body collapsed as he shot backward like a bullet. Through the air he soared, flying across the coliseum faster than ever.

"Oa?!" Thalrok yelled.

"I've got him!" Oa shouted back, as he shot into the air and hovered directly in the path of the missile that was Lotus. Lotus's limp body crashed into Oa, who grabbed him by the waist, then stabilized their collision and made a quick descent as only he could. Using small bursts of air, Oa got them both safely down to the stony floor, where he carefully placed Lotus.

"Lotus!" Oa shook him.

No response.

Thalrok and Nyloc quickly hurried to his side and knelt beside him.

"Is he gonna be alright?"

"He will be fine. It seems like he's just knocked out for now." Nyloc reassured them.

Though Lotus's rampage had been quite effective, now that it had stopped there were still dozens of Infected Ones left standing throughout the coliseum.

"Nyloc, get Ronin," Thalrok spoke sternly. Being as careful as he could, Nyloc picked Lotus up and held him securely over his shoulders.

"Oa, get ready to send out another burst of air when I say," Thalrok said, looking Oa in the eye.

Thalrok reached back, unlatched and took his massive sword in hand. He curled his fingers around the grip and held it tightly. Looking down, he bowed his head and said to himself, "We *are* getting out of this—alive." Then he turned his gaze to his companions.

"Are you ready?" Thalrok stated.

"Right," they both replied, nodding.

The bounty hunter slowly pulled his blade over his head, higher and higher. He channeled all of the energy he had left into his arms. He could hear the remaining Infected Ones stampeding toward them. This was his last effort, or they were goners. With the bellow of some great beast, he smashed his blade into the ground and shook the entire underworld surrounding them with that one strike. Stalactites fell from the ceiling. The Infected Ones could barely stay upright.

"Now!" As Thalrok's signal was called, Oa shot a giant force of wind forward, which sent the already unbalanced Ones nearest to them flying backward.

"Let's go! We have to get Ronin out of here!" Thalrok shouted.

The three of them, with Nyloc carrying Lotus, ran for the way they'd come in. They could hear the Infected Ones yelling, and, as they recovered, running after them. Up the stairs they flew, as arrows and other projectiles were hitting all around them. After reaching the top, they hurried through the hallways.

At regular intervals, Thalrok punched the stone walls and pillars to collapse the ceilings and walls to cover their exit. At last, he cried, "Come on, you two! We're almost there!"

24

I need to go…

A soft breeze brushed over the broken man lying there. His fingers twitched, feeling small twigs and leathery leaves beneath his hands. Lotus opened his eyes slowly and saw gently swaying treetops high above him.

I'm here again? he thought, cautiously sitting up. He looked first to his left, then to his right. A feeling of nostalgia flushed through him. He stood, and as he took a few tentative steps around this place, a little part of his mind was telling him he had been there before. *But when?*

Strolling through the towering forest, he tripped over a root poking out of the ground and stumbled forward. Lotus kept himself from falling flat on his face and then stopped abruptly. *I gotta keep a better eye on my footing…*

As his eyes more thoroughly explored his surroundings, he noticed someone lying on the ground several yards in front of him. *A kid?* he speculated, and without a second thought, he rushed closer. The young boy was lying on his back and not moving. When Lotus could finally get a good look at this boy, he froze in place. His heart sank, and his head couldn't wrap around what he was seeing. *Is that…?*

All of a sudden, the young boy woke up. He rubbed his face with both hands and then stood up, brushing himself off. Lotus could only stand motionless and watch. The boy glanced around until he finally noticed

Lotus. He didn't say a word; he just looked at him, expressionless.

Lotus did not know what to say. He tried to mumble some words, but only little noises came out of his mouth.

The kid spoke. "I wanna go home," he said. That was it. He just stood there without moving and said that he wanted to go home.

"What?" Lotus asked.

"I wanna go home," the boy said, in the same way as before.

Lotus took a step forward and reached out to the kid. "Are you—"

"I wanna go home." Again, that was all the boy said. He didn't sound worried. He didn't sound sad. He just sounded... maybe a little bit stoic.

"You're me, aren't you?" Lotus asked.

The kid didn't respond. He just tilted his head and gazed at Lotus. Finally, the kid asked, "Do *you* wanna go home, Ronin?"

"What?" Lotus was shocked as the edges of his vision faded into a bright white light. He reached out for his younger self, calling out, "Wait, please wait!" Then the white light turned to black, everything went black, and he could feel incredible pain flooding through his entire body. His face twisted into a grimace as he opened his eyes.

"Another dream..." the wanted man mumbled, and looked up at the ceiling. It took about three seconds for him to realize that he was not only alive, but was back in his room in Mellowtin. Like a flash, he shot upright in the bed, ignoring all the pain, and darted his eyes around the room. In a panic, he thought, *What happened?! How did I get here?!* Heart racing, he threw off the blankets and jumped out of bed. But as soon as his feet hit the floor, his legs buckled, and he crumpled down in a heap. While forcing himself to stand, Lotus noticed his forearms and stopped to stare at them. He could hear himself panting heavily at seeing that the black-tinted veins were darker, and now they reached up past his elbows.

"Damn," he sighed as he relaxed. Gingerly, he walked over to the window. Flicking the latch, he pushed the double windows out and let the wind push against his body. He saw the many bandages wrapped around him, most with blood staining the nubby tan cloth.

"Where's my—" Before he could finish his sentence, he saw that his

351

sword was safely resting against the wall, saya intact. The panic attack was diverted, but he still had no idea how they escaped.

The last thing I remember was... Delus. He could picture Delus standing above them all, telling Lotus that he had given the order to kill Lotus's master. After that, everything was a blur.

So, where are the others? Are they alright? He hobbled to the door. Bandaged up and barely clothed, he left his room to find out where everyone was.

As his door closed, he saw Oa sitting outside his room. The boy had fallen fast asleep while waiting for Lotus to wake up. The wanted man watched Oa's head bob up and down with each breath; he could barely keep it upright.

"Oa." Lotus tapped the boy's shoulder. Oa jumped, startling himself awake. His words were mumbled nonsense as he rubbed his eyes and looked around.

"Lotus!" he shouted as he sprang to his feet. Without hesitation, Oa wrapped his arms around his friend and hugged him. Lotus stiffened and winced, as the boy's arms squeezed him tightly with heartfelt enthusiasm. Oa immediately realized this was probably hurting him and let go.

"I'm so sorry, I just—I'm so happy that you're alright." Oa stuttered, trying to hold back his tears.

"It's okay. I'm glad to see that you're safe too. How did we escape?" Lotus asked.

Oa carefully escorted Lotus over to the couch in their common area, and they both sat down. The boy seemed hesitant to talk. He didn't want Lotus to feel bad for his frenzied outburst of dark power.

Oa began in a soft voice, "After you heard the man watching from above say all that stuff about his son and your master, you lost control. You went on this crazy rampage, wiping out anything in your path. You took out more than half of their troops in a matter of minutes," he explained. "It was incredible to see someone with that kind of power. It was a little terrifying, too."

"So, I lost control?" Lotus asked, glancing over at the boy.

"Yeah…" Oa said in a small voice.

Lotus sat forward and placed his head in his hands. He realized that his violent rage must have been how the veins of his arms had gotten even darker.

"After you tried to strike down their leader, he sent you flying through the air with a single punch." Oa went on. "That hit knocked you out cold, and then Thalrok created a huge shockwave for us to escape, and—"

"Is everyone else alright?!" Lotus shot back up to his feet, interrupting Oa and staring at him in distress.

"Yes! Yes, everyone else is okay! We are all just a little beat up." The boy stood and placed his hand on Lotus's shoulder to calm him down. Oa saw that right now, anything and everything got the wanted man on edge; he was entirely out of it and had just gone through quite a lot. They all had.

"Thalrok is trying to distract himself and is training on the outskirts of Mellowtin. I'm almost certain Nyloc is, too." Oa tried his best to reassure Lotus that everything was all right. Even though they'd barely gotten out of the Infected One's lair, they were all still alive.

Lotus noticed the bandages on Oa's arms and felt guilty about himself all over again. "It's my fault," he mumbled.

"Lotus…" Oa began.

Lotus turned to the boy and stared toward the floor. "All of this was my fault because I pulled all of you into it—then I lost control! I was too weak. This is all my doing. I am the reason you all got hurt; I should never have brought you there. I just—"

"You did nothing wrong," said a firm voice. Lotus's head lifted back up, watching Thalrok walking into the room, interrupting his tirade of self-condemnation.

"Ronin, you did nothing wrong. If it wasn't for your incredible strength, we surely would have died," the titan told him.

"Thalrok, your arms…" Lotus noticed the angry-looking burn marks covering Thalrok's arms that looked like they'd scar pretty severely.

"They are fine. Ronin, you need to remember that we—" Thalrok tried to continue.

"I do… I remember. You tried calming me down, and my dark energy… burned your arms." Lotus cut in, his eyes staring off into the distance as even more guilt washed over his face. Thalrok didn't know what to do now. His friend was spiraling, and he couldn't stop him.

"Captain, please listen to the titan, he is right." Nyloc chimed in, appearing from down the hall.

Lotus sat on the couch, head in hands, and Oa rubbed his back, hoping to soothe him.

"Ronin, we told you while we were on the way there. You are our leader. We will follow you to hell and back. All you have to do is say it, and we will do it. Whatever the foe in front of us, it doesn't matter. We will always fight alongside you." Thalrok spoke gently, yet made the powerful meaning behind his words very clear.

Lotus didn't lift his head this time. He kept shaking his head, letting the pain he caused burn in his head. "I… I need to go." Lotus softly panted.

"What?!" his companions blurted out in surprise. They watched the wanted man steady himself to stand up and head back to his room, then followed him as he hobbled across the floor.

"Ronin, you can't be serious?!" Thalrok shot back.

"You really should be resting right now," Nyloc suggested, but Lotus wasn't listening.

"Where are you going?" Oa asked. They watched him frantically get dressed, ignoring his physical pain. He tried to hurry out of his room, but before he could, they blocked his path.

"Please move. I need to go—" Lotus said hastily, looking at the floor.

"No! You can't just leave us, Ronin. We are in this together to the very end. No matter what, we will stick together." Thalrok objected, refusing to move.

"Please! I just… I need to figure this out by myself! I don't know what to do! I can't even process what happened." Lotus spoke with a mixture of confusion, fear, and great anguish. This was the most emotion he had ever exposed to them. He really didn't want them to get hurt anymore. The wanted man refused to make eye contact with his friends as he tried to get through their barricade at his doorway.

Thalrok suddenly realized just how painful this must be for his friend. Without wasting words, he said, "Fine," and promptly stepped out of Lotus's way.

"WHAT?!" Nyloc and Oa yelled, both very confused as to how Thalrok could just let him leave.

The bounty hunter didn't reply.

Lotus stood in the doorway, also confused and not knowing why Thalrok had suddenly changed his mind. But, snapping back into the moment, he hobbled down the hallway and down the stairs.

The three of them stood in place until they heard the front door close behind Lotus, unable to watch him leave or even say goodbye.

Oa lowered his head and began to cry. Nyloc put an arm over his shoulder, tried to comfort him, and told him not to worry. Then he turned to Thalrok, asking, "Why did you let him go?"

Thalrok turned to look at Lotus's sword, which still rested against the wall where they'd placed it. "He just needs some time alone, but I know he will return. He plans on it."

* * *

Anger. Fear. Confusion. Pain. Guilt.

With every step the wanted man took away from Mellowtin, the noise bombarding his mind never stopped. The pain from his wounds was nothing compared to the pain inside his head.

Left foot, right foot. Blank eyes stared at the grassy plains below his feet as he pressed on into an unknown direction.

Left foot, right foot. His hands brushed past his legs, swaying in the air. His head was low and his heart was heavy.

Left foot, right foot. Lotus continued marching through the fields of Prosper Valley, the unknown before him, regrets behind him.

Left foot, right foot. A single second and an hour felt identical to the other. How long had he been walking? How many steps had he taken?

Left foot, right foot. This is all his body was programmed to do now—to walk forward and not worry about what was in front of him.

You lost control. You could have killed someone. You put everyone else in danger. You are too weak, and your master chose wrong. Whose voice was saying all of this in his head? His own? Was reality having its say in all this chaos?

Left foot, right foot. His life replayed in his mind. All of Lotus's regrets and failures flashed back repeatedly, haunting him. His eyes kept watch in front of him but registered nothing. All he could see was the cursed movie that streamed unbidden in his head, replaying over and over.

Left foot, right foot. He could feel the pain in his legs growing as he walked on for however far he'd come.

I am Delus! Lotus's pace got faster.

Pathetic. The sound of that voice blotted out everything else in his head and got louder. Left foot, right foot.

It's only fair, right, boy? You took the life of my son, and he took the life of your so-called master. Lotus's eyes burned a hole in the ground as his breath pumped in and out of his lungs.

Left foot, right foot. The singular moment of Delus standing there above the Infected. That image was burned into his brain. He could not get it out. There he was, that was him. The man his master had trained with. The one who took his master's family, friends, and teacher. The one who had him killed...

"Din..." Lotus whispered.

Ronin. The faint sound of his master's voice echoed in his head.

Left foot... he stopped.

It had been quite a while since he'd heard Din's voice so clearly in his head. Why was it so clear now? Lotus lifted his head, realizing just how long he'd been walking. As he turned around and checked where he was, Mellowtin was nowhere to be seen. The sky was barely lit, and now the day was completely over.

"Have I been walking for that long?" Lotus wondered. He surveyed the terrain and noticed there wasn't anything of much notice to be found around him. It was just a normal spot in Prosper Valley with the faraway mountains and hills surrounding the grasslands which stretched for miles. He had managed to get far away from Mellowtin, who knew how far.

What am I doing? Lotus wondered, as he felt a drop of rain hit his nose. The wanted man lifted his head and noticed the dark clouds crawling farther across the sky.

A storm? A giant crash of thunder boomed in the distance.

"Yep," he said to himself, realizing that to be true, as the pattering roar of pouring rain became louder and louder. Lotus saw the wall of rain creeping closer. Quickly, and trying to ignore his many pains and sore muscles, he ran in the opposite direction to find some cover. Lightning flashed and thunder rumbled all around him as the rain splashed down on his back. Soaked and hurrying across the wet grassland, he hoped for some shelter.

He ran on, searching for something, anything, to shield him. The sky had now fully blackened over the setting sun. The only light available came from the intermittent and unpredictable lightning.

Lotus could barely hear his own voice over the roar of the rain. When one intense flash of lightning illuminated the sky, he saw what appeared to be the silhouette of a house. He kept running in the same direction, waiting for another flash to confirm what he saw. When the lightning again lit up the sky, followed quickly by a sharp boom of thunder, he saw that he was right.

"Just my luck," he murmured as he changed course and headed for the house. Between the storm and nightfall, the entire plains were completely dark, and he used the very little light created by the storm to judge his distance from the house. After a little bit of blind running, he made his way to it. He stood on the covered porch, catching his breath as he dripped head to toe with water. Wiping the rain from his face, he looked at the house, hoping that there wasn't some angry resident inside ready to kick him out. Cautiously peeking in the window, it appeared to be empty, utterly and forsakenly empty. He made his way to the door, noticing that it was quite old, and already cracked open. When he pushed against the door's worn wooden panel, it creaked and swung in slowly against the wall.

"Hello?" Lotus called out.

No response.

Still dripping head to toe, he felt the rush of pain kick back in from both his battle and this long journey across the plains of Prosper. Since the house seemed to be completely abandoned, he walked in, felt his way to a wall, and slid down to the floor with his back against it. Having come to a rest there, he stretched out his legs and sat alone once again. No one was around, just his own self here in an empty house. He didn't have to worry about anyone else getting hurt. It was just like when he started out this past five years, when he was just a lone boy who had to run from others. They were either hunting him down, or he was getting them hurt in the process.

"I wish you could help me master," Lotus muttered as his lip quivered, and tears began dropping as fast as the rain.

Ronin.

He heard his master's voice again. He didn't move. He just stared blankly ahead as the tears kept coming. He moved his legs closer to his body and crossed them, placing his hands in his lap. Lotus took slower breaths as he let his heavy eyelids close carefully.

Ronin. Do you remember...

The closer he was to dozing off, the more the wanted man could hear his master's voice.

Ronin. Do you remember what I told you before? The voice continued in his head.

"Yes, sir... I remember." He mumbled, moments from falling asleep. The memory of his master was becoming more apparent, stronger, as his head bobbed up and down with each sleepy breath.

You have to think of this power as a part of your very spirit. Keep your composure and remember what you fight for. Only then will you be able... the voice died away and the faint memory vanished as he dropped his head and fell asleep.

He was a young man in a house all by himself again, his grim goal met. No one around to get hurt. No one around to hurt him. The drumming of the rain was the only sound to be heard. No friends here, no family. Just a wanted man with tears staining his face, sitting in an abandoned house. And even though he knew that the others were finally safe...

He missed them.

* * *

The storm had passed, and from it, a new and brighter day was born. Barely a single cloud moved in the sky, and the sun gave the morning dew a sweet warmth. Birds soared and little critters raced across the ground as a lonesome man opened his eyes. Waking up in an unfamiliar room brought Lotus a dreadful feeling. Then he remembered coming in here to take shelter from the storm.

The young man stood up from the floor and brushed himself off. He stretched his arms into the air and looked around. There wasn't anything joyful about this day. Just like before, he had nothing to wake up for anymore. What was the point? He headed over to the back door and pushed it open. It wasn't the same feeling as the other villages. Lotus wanted it to all be a dream, and that he was still in Mellowtin. He wished he were still in Petalbrooke. Heck, he even wished he was still in—

Souder?!

Standing in the door frame, Lotus stared blankly at the town he'd been banished from years ago, and was completely baffled at what lay there before him. This town was entirely abandoned. Not a single soul was walking the streets, but he knew exactly where he was.

This is... this is Souder. This is my home. He paused, mouth agape, his brain unable to process what was going on. It had been many years since he'd been banished, yet he knew that this was his home. Lotus took a few steps from the doorway and looked around some more.

"It *is* Souder, " he whispered to himself, heading down the street. Unbelievable. He had to be dreaming again; this couldn't be real. He brushed his hand over the side of a neighboring house and felt the mossy wall damp from yesterday's rain. Peering around the corner of it, his eyes locked onto a familiar building—the school where he'd been taught. Lotus headed over to it. He did not run wildly through the streets to quickly see it all once again; he just walked around alertly and took it all in.

Where is everyone? he wondered as he walked inside the school. It was bare of students, appearing as though they'd all just gotten up and left. A few books and scattered debris remained, but not a single soul had been in here for a while. Lotus left the school and immediately knew where to go next. Though years had passed, muscle memory took him back along the once familiar route.

My house.

There he stood, right outside his childhood home. Oh, how long had it been since he set foot in *this* place? Lotus hesitated to open the front door, stopping his hand inches away from the latch. He took a deep breath, then grabbed the handle and pushed the door open. His heart raced as the open door cleared the way to his past life. A few chairs, a table, a couch, and no family. It was almost entirely empty. He didn't expect to find anything special; he just wanted to check. He walked through all of the rooms. The kitchen, living room, dining room, and, of course, his old bedroom. It was incredible to see it all again, a huge blast from the past.

He left the house and wandered around, still in awe that he'd stumbled upon Souder after all these years.

Wow. It's all the same...

Lotus turned the corner of one of the empty streets and saw one more familiar place. This place brought a cold chill down his spine. Here was the village temple. The very spot in the street where it all started—where everyone had stared at him, terrified. He took a deep breath and headed for the temple doors. It was like a nightmare seeing this place again, yet he wanted to see it. Lotus grabbed onto the two handles and pushed forward. They wouldn't move, so he pushed harder, feeling them budge only slightly.

"Just a little more," he groaned as he forced them wide open. They slammed back and into the walls, and the sound echoed through the room. Lotus looked around the wide-open room and noticed it was like every other building here—barely anything was in it. His eyes scanned the large room until he noticed something unusual. There was a single chair, way in the back, with the form of something on it.

His heart stopped beating for a second.

"Is that?" He took a step forward and saw the slumped figure move. "Oracle?" Lotus whispered.

"Unbelievable…" the old wavery voice sounded muffled, "Is that you, Ronin?"

25

The New Peace

Silence.

The town, the temple, the room, the two of them. Nothing but silence. Neither of them knew what to say. It had been so long since the last time they had been face-to-face. The last time they'd been anywhere near one another, the Oracle had been watching a cart take the young boy away.

"I... I can't believe it's you." The young man once known as Ronin was baffled and in shock. He could barely speak. He took a step forward to get closer to the old man. That look on his face—was it fear? Was this all a dream?

The Oracle appeared to have seen a ghost for the very first time. His skin was ashen, and his sunken eyes stared forward. Lotus stopped after his first step.

The Oracle's surprised expression turned to confusion, and then Lotus realized. *He still sees me as a monster. I guess that makes sense.*

Lotus watched as the Oracle's lips trembled; he was unable to muster a single word. Then the old man's hand slowly lifted from his side, shaking as he pointed right at Lotus.

All this time. All these years. It seemed like nothing had changed. After so very many years, he was *still* seen as a monster. Even if the Oracle was the only soul left in this town, "Ronin" was still forbidden.

"I guess I should just…" Lotus's voice trailed off.

"It's my fault." The Oracle finally said. His rarely-used voice was like a croak. He coughed to clear his throat.

Lotus stood still, unable to understand what the old man was talking about. He started to speak but was interrupted.

"All of this is my fault. You… you are like this because of *me*." The Oracle confessed.

"What do you mean?" Lotus asked.

The Oracle, in his old and weakened state, slowly picked himself up from his chair. He reached down and scooped up one of the dozens of large thick papers from the floor near his feet. The old man straightened and held it up into the light. "You are who you are, because of *my* doing," he muttered, his head lowered.

Lotus stared at the wanted poster the old man held out in his trembling hands. Glancing at the others on the floor, he saw that they were all wanted posters. Each one of them had Lotus's face on it. The young man looked back up, seeing that The Oracle's face was masked with horror, just like it had been all those years ago.

He thinks I'm finally coming back for revenge, I guess.

Lotus's face glazed over with shame and disappointment. Nothing had changed. Different name, same story. It didn't matter how long he waited, it would all end the same.

"Ronin." The Oracle mumbled, taking a hobbling step forward.

Lotus just stood still, not moving from his spot. He was ready for the earful of hate he was about to hear. The words would sting, but he knew this was the only way to honestly know what the old man was thinking after all this time. The Oracle shuffled closer, his shaky finger pointed at the wanted man. He stopped a few steps away from Lotus, his eyes wide and mouth agape. Lotus focused his eyes on the floor, not trying to look. All of a sudden, he heard a thud and looked up.

"I am so, so, so sorry, my child. Because of my misjudgment, you became the man you are today—a wanted man. I… I am to blame for it all—the village, its people, and you. I am *so* sorry." The Oracle had dropped to his knees with his gnarled hands supporting him and his forehead bowed down to the floor. Tears dropped from his eyes and his rasping breath was too easy to hear.

"You're... sorry?" Lotus asked.

"I am terribly sorry, my child. You were just a boy, and... and I... I can't believe I could do such a thing. I deserve whatever you have planned for me. I must atone." There was no fear in his voice; there was only regret. All through these years, he had been haunted by his past actions and had lived in shame with the reality of his mistake. He had seen the posters about Ronin and realized that it was all his fault. If he had just dealt with the situation differently, who knows what could have happened?

"Sir—" Lotus began.

"Please, curse me out. Beat me up, even kill me if you must! I deserve it all!" The Oracle interrupted fiercely. "My foolishness has cost me my people, my village, myself, and my honor as a human being. Please, do what you must."

Those last few words were spoken softly, with great sorrow and sincerity. He was truly suffering from his mistakes and wanted to leave this world without this burden.

"Oracle..." Lotus paused. He didn't know what to say. Here was the Oracle, the man responsible for his banishment from Souder. The man responsible for him being tied up and dropped off in the middle of the woods to die. He'd been a scared child left to try to free himself, fend for himself, and to most likely be killed by whatever the land held. Here was the reason he'd been found in those woods, started a new life and then lost it—the reason he is now seen as a criminal and must constantly be on the run. It all came back to him. His current life was all because this man had trusted a vision over reality.

"I'm sorry." The Oracle kept mumbling as tears flowed down his face. He did not hear one word spoken by the wanted man; all that he heard was a little shuffling and a soft thump. The old man lifted his head and saw the young man sitting cross-legged in front of him.

"Please, sit up, sir," Lotus said.

"What?" the old man sniffled out, thinking he had misheard. Lotus nodded his head, indicating that he had indeed heard him correctly. The old man slowly sat up, puzzled about what was happening.

Lotus spoke calmly and with great empathy, "Are you alright?"

"Y-yes, I'm fine," came the hesitant response.

"What happened to Souder? Where is everyone?" Lotus asked.

The Oracle looked around the room, a man without his people, his life broken as a result of his own actions. He took a deep sigh and lowered his head. "They left because of me. It was about a year after you were..." he paused. "The whole town became, uh, different. People started to second-guess my abilities. They came to fear me as an executioner, not a leader. The children were scared to see their future, afraid that it would be like yours. The people began to push back from tradition, and family by family, they left. Finally, I woke up one day, looked around and... they were all gone."

Lotus had no idea about the truth of what had happened. They hadn't been attacked. They didn't have to flee. These people all chose to leave. "How long has it been this empty?" he inquired.

"A few years now, I think. It's been so long that I can barely remember. I just sit here, waiting for what the future will bring to my door. It looks like I know now," he said sadly.

Lotus saw a dejected old man sitting there in front of him, his heart broken and his soul barely alive in his body. He was genuinely suffering from his mistake.

"Ronin, please, I don't know what you have been through since you were taken from your home here. But I understand what you have to do. The man you killed was a good man, wise and powerful. His death is on my shoulders for turning such a kind boy into..." Again, he paused. "Please, do what you must." The Oracle said in a soft voice, bowing his head.

The wanted man just sat and stared for a moment. The man who had ruined his life sat right there in front of him. He was permitting, even asking, Lotus to kill him. It was almost poetic and yet...

"When I was banished, I was terrified," Lotus told him. "After freeing myself, I stood there in the lands of Prosper Valley in a void of terror. After somehow surviving for what felt like months in the wild, I was taken in and saved by a single man. He gave me food, clothes, and a home. He taught me how to fight, how to protect, how to live. I admired him *so* much, and I was willing to follow him to the ends of the world. I made friends while I was there. It was a new life, a new family, a new home. After only five years of that new life, I was reminded of the curse I bear." The Oracle lifted his head at this, and listened carefully to the young man's words.

"That day. It was one of the worst days of my life." Lotus continued, trying not to become too absorbed in this particular memory. "I came home from a morning run and saw him. He was lying on the ground, bleeding out, as a man stood over him. I tried to stop the stranger, but it was too late. My master Din had been killed, and the man who did it vanished into dust. They all thought it was me, that I had killed him. I was chased from my new home. A few days later, the wanted posters came in." Lotus clenched his hands tightly together.

The Oracle felt guilt piling on even heavier than before. He thought this child had become a ruthless murderer because of his decision. This appeared far worse. He had just toppled the first domino that began the cascade of an endless life of pain for this boy. "So, you didn't kill him?"

"No, sir. I respected him greatly and was entrusted with his final request." Lotus said solemnly. Taking a deep breath in, he added, "You probably think I hate you, and I want nothing but pain for you and the rest of your life, but I don't."

"Wha… what?" The Oracle had not expected to hear those words.

Lotus stood up and turned back to the doorway. He took a few steps toward it and stared out at the deserted village. "If I had stayed here in this village, I wouldn't have met Din. I wouldn't have made the friends I have along the way. I wouldn't have been able to see Perlaria for the vast world it is. Maybe it wasn't the fulfilling life I could have lived, but I was happy to be able to meet the people I did and to help the ones I could."

Lotus's words, though practical, were spoken with heartfelt emotion.

The Oracle stood up from the floor slowly, not looking away from the boy—no, the man—in front of him. He was certainly not the scared kid that he had been, not anymore. Now, he was a man who had faced the realities of the world, the real world, and dealt with them.

"Thank you," the Oracle mumbled. Lotus turned around and saw the old man covering his face with his hands. He mumbled, "Thank you so much, my child. You don't know how many nights, over and over, I had nightmares of that future that I'd seen–you, raging and bloodied, standing there in the middle of death and destruction. It made me question my decision and second-guess myself each time. Maybe it wasn't even Souder in that fiery ruin, maybe it was somewhere else... Maybe it wasn't even real. You have grown so much, and you cannot know how very happy I am to see you today. I was a fool and made a mistake..." The Oracle couldn't stop his tears. He would wonder no more, and could now be at peace, knowing that the boy whose life he was sure he had ruined had indeed forgiven him.

"Oh, and your family, they—"

Lotus held his hand up and stopped the Oracle before he could continue, and quickly said, "Please, sir, I ask you not to finish that sentence. I can't bear to hear what you might say next."

It seemed like an impossible request, but the Oracle did not speak another word. Instead, his heart still pounding from all that had just happened, he made his way to Lotus's side and stared out at the desolate village once more.

"The day is quiet, and the air is still." The Oracle spoke calmly.

"Yes, it is, sir," Lotus replied as they both took in the village, empty and devoid of its past life. The wanted man started down the stairs, ready to head out.

"Wait! Wait!" The Oracle stopped him before he could reach the bottom. Lotus halted mid-step and turned around. "You're just going to leave?"

"Yes, sir. It was good to see my old home, and Souder, again, but I really must get going." Lotus said, again treading lightly down the stairs.

"Wait. Please." The Oracle begged, stopping him once more before Lotus could get any further. He seemed nervous, even scared, to say his next words. "If I may, I need to know that you have a future. A real future that you can be happy in. A future where you are not a cursed man."

Lotus looked up at the frail old man above him, pleading for help one last time in regards to that boy from the past. Lotus scoffed to himself and nodded his head. Then he turned around to stand before the Oracle once again.

The old man shakily descended the stairs, then stopped so that he was standing a few steps above the young man. Gently, he placed his hand on Lotus's head and closed his eyes. After a few seconds, he slowly put his hand back down at his side and then smiled. "Thank you." The Oracle said, looking into Lotus's eyes meaningfully before bowing his head.

"Of course, sir," Lotus replied, as he bowed in return and headed off.

The old man saw Lotus make his way down the street with his back straight and head held high. He was really not the same boy as before; he was indeed a whole new man. The Oracle watched that man until he faded completely out of sight. Then, taking one last deep breath of fresh air, he returned inside and walked towards his chair. He labored to pick up each wanted poster and put it in a pile as he went. When that was done, he ripped them up one by one until they were nothing but tatters. When The Oracle finally sat down, the bits and pieces coated the floor next to his chair.

As he sagged against the backrest, fatigued from his efforts, he sighed and felt like the weight of the world was taken from his shoulders. What he had done long ago wasn't right, and he knew that well. But in those last few moments of coming face-to-face with Ronin, he found release from his pain, guilt, regret, and years of nightmares. Maybe it was lucky that things had ended up this way.

With a serene smile and a final whisper—"One last vision… thank you, Ronin…"—the Oracle closed his eyes for the last time.

26

Beyond the Clouds

The wanted man's long journey had come to an end. During the mindless strolling, his mind had been allowed to race with memories of the past, one of which then unexpectedly and literally appeared right in front of him. While away from Mellowtin, he'd had the time to climb out of the pit he'd been slowly falling into. It hadn't exactly been a time to relax, but a time to breathe and to gain distance and perspective.

The cool air whistled as Lotus walked through the gates of the village, and he took a deep, welcoming breath. It felt as if he'd been gone for quite a while, but surely nothing had changed in his absence.

"Thank the heavens." Layla sighed, as she saw the wanted man standing in the doorway.

"Hello." Lotus greeted her and then nodded to her twin sister, who immediately appeared from around the corner. He carefully shut the front door behind him.

"Your friends were worried sick, y' know. Leaving them wondering if you were ever going to come back." Leyla scolded, shaking her head and looking sharply at Lotus.

"I'm sorry. I just needed to get away from it all for a bit. I apologize." Lotus replied.

"Don't go apologizing to us. You'd better let *them* know you're back."

Layla pointed toward the stairwell.

Lotus slowly nodded in agreement, then headed up the stairs for his room. With each step that he took, he didn't know what he expected to find. *Would they all be here still? Did they resent him a little for leaving? What would they say? What would he say?* Totally lost in thought, he walked up the stairs and turned the corner, where he bumped into something solid.

"Oh! I'm sorry!" Lotus lifted his head to see who or what he had bumped into.

"Ronin?" a surprised familiar voice asked.

"Thalrok…" Lotus didn't know what else to say, he had no words. They both stood there for a long moment.

"I knew you'd be back." Thalrok finally spoke, placing his hand on his friend's shoulder.

Lotus didn't expect the titan to have such a simple response to his return. He had seemed so hesitant to let him leave before, but now…

"Happy to be back," Lotus replied.

"We didn't think we'd see you this soon. We were actually just—" The bounty hunter suddenly stopped talking.

Lotus tilted his head, waiting to see if this sentence had an end to it, but Thalrok was frozen in place like a statue.

"Thalrok?" Lotus asked in confusion, but his friend didn't reply.

"Speaking of the others, where are they?" Lotus asked.

"Uh… they're on the rooftop lounge." Thalrok hesitantly answered him. The bounty hunter then brushed past Lotus and headed for the stairwell, which led to the top level.

Puzzled by his response, Lotus followed him. No other words were spoken. Lotus was still confused about why Thalrok acted so strangely when he asked about the others.

As they turned onto the last short staircase leading to the roof, Thalrok finally spoke up. "So, here's the funny thing…" In a moment, he had reached the top, and he shuffled off to one side to let Lotus go through the doorway first.

The wanted man slowly climbed the last of the stairs and stepped out onto the patio. Blinding late afternoon sunlight beamed across his face. All eyes were immediately on him. As he squinted from the brightness, he heard their gasps of surprise. He used one hand to shield his face and opened his eyes. He saw that Thalrok was now there at his side, and sitting in front of them, there they were—Oa, Nyloc, and… Lotus's eyes widened. He couldn't believe what he was seeing.

"Lotus!" and "Captain!" his friends shouted. They quickly stood to rush over and greet him. In their haste, they left the strange visitor sitting there alone.

"Thalrok…" Lotus began, perplexed.

"Yes, Ronin?"

"Is that?" Lotus asked, shocked at what he thought he was seeing.

"Yep, that's an angel," Thalrok confirmed, taking in the look of astonishment on Lotus's face.

* * *

"Hey, you wanna take a walk?" Nyloc asked, as he noticed Oa still sitting in the common area of the inn.

The melancholy expression on Oa's face was painted on thickly. He could not stop thinking about what would or might happen next. Lotus had just left, and he didn't know when, or even if, he would return.

"Sure." Oa replied glumly. He stood up and followed Nyloc outside. They casually strolled around the village, taking in the day and just enjoying being outdoors. Nyloc could sense that Oa's head hung low, and his downcast eyes gazed only at his feet as they walked.

"Don't worry, you heard Thalrok. The captain will return. It's only a waiting game now." Nyloc reassured the boy.

"Yeah, but what if he doesn't?" Oa said sadly.

"He will. He's not the type of man to up and leave when things get tough," the archer replied confidently.

"Nyloc, I have a question," Oa asked, stopping for a moment. "You started following us around Perlaria, not knowing anything about us or even trusting us when you first met us. Yet you're still here. Why?" Oa asked. He didn't come off as disrespectful or rude. The boy was just confused about what made Nyloc want to follow along to such a hellish place as the underworld of Cannon-Gulf.

"As foolish as it may sound, I know that fate shows me the path I must take," the archer replied with a childlike smile on his face.

"Fate?" Oa asked.

"Correct. I had no idea my life would play out the way it did until fate came knocking at my door. Now, I can truly live my life without fear. Waking up in your ship was just the next chapter for me. I never thought it would include following a falsely accused murderer, but here I am. I know my next chapter will come to me eventually, and I have time. I respect Lotus very much and I intend to see him through his own story and help however I can."

Oa had never really had a deep conversation with Nyloc before. This was somewhat therapeutic for him.

Several seconds went by, then Nyloc asked, "Why do you follow the captain?"

Oa was caught off guard; that question had never occurred to him. Lotus had been his way out of Mount Axi and a way for him to see the world. Nothing continued to bind them together, so why did he keep following him?

"I never really thought about that before." Oa began. "Grand Sage Gou was the one who asked Lotus to take me with him on his journey across the lands. I was never actually instructed to stay by his side the whole time, yet I don't want to leave. He started teaching me about this world, and some fighting skills too. I thought he was trustworthy, and I thought of him like he was…" Oa stopped, lowering his head, remembering that he may not see Lotus again. The young disciple felt his back being patted softly.

"It'll all be alright in the end. You must trust that fate will point you in the right direction." Nyloc advised, as he turned back toward the inn. Oa felt those words cut deeply into his soul.

"Trust that fate will point you in the right direction, Oa," Nyloc repeated from several steps away.

Taking these words to heart, Oa made his way around the village, thinking about everything that had happened. The past couldn't be changed, the present was confusing, and the future was one big mystery.

What is going to happen next? Will Lotus ever return? What would Grand Sage Gou say? His young brain churned.

"Dang it," Oa grunted and flopped down on the grass. The boy looked up at the overcast sky above, then dreamily watched the clouds form and reform as he let his racing mind relax.

Suddenly, he sat up. *What is that?* Oa thought to himself. He swore he saw something way up in the clouds. Blinking a few times, he looked up again. *I swear I see something.* The boy looked over to his side, wanting to tell Lotus that he had seen something odd, but at once realized that Lotus was still gone to who knew where. Oa felt the looming depression creeping back again. He stood, then lifted his chin and whispered, "Fate will point me in the right direction."

With a quick burst of air from his feet, he shot up into the sky. One wasn't nearly enough, so he continued letting out burst after burst from his feet and his hands, pushing himself upward higher and higher. The layers of clouds hindered his vision as his altitude increased, but still he trusted that he would see something. In time, his special ability to create wind power was reaching its limit and he could barely maintain his upward flight.

"Just a little more," he murmured, when suddenly he felt gusts of wind blowing hard against his face, one after another. He felt that his time was about to be up and surely he would start falling soon. Heavy gray clouds blocked his vision, but he forced out one more burst and reached up above his head. As the arc of his descent began, his hand touched something. Without thinking, he curled his fingers and grabbed onto it.

What am I touching?

Still unable to see through the dense clouds, he grabbed onto what seemed to be a ledge with both hands. He hoisted himself up, lifting his entire body and looking like a prairie dog poking out of its hole in the desert. Oa struggled to get a leg up and stand, then, emerging from the clouds, he stared in awe at a golden paradise which had remained hidden for ages.

What the... "

Before the boy was something out of a legend, or some epic tale, that people spoke of but no one could see. Except that now, Oa had stumbled upon this place, this land of the angels, which was called Nimbusara.

Different-sized islands of Earth floated here, all with beautifully manicured emerald green lawns, gardens, and hedges. Billowy opaque clouds surrounded nearly everything. Chiseled to perfection, smooth white stone bridges stretched across the many islands as they drifted in the air as one. The snowy white buildings that Oa could see had elegant hints of shimmering gold decoration everywhere. Angels flew around from one place to another. It was a living paradise above the land far below.

Oa was utterly speechless as his eyes panned from left to right. He took in all that he could see as he stood there in place, watching the angels soar gracefully about. Turning his head to follow one's flight, he locked eyes with a girl who stood there only a few feet away. Her dark, wavy hair curled down her back, and her large, white wings glowed warmly in the sun. The flowy white dress that she wore was decorated in bits of delicate gold trim at the bodice and waist. More tiny flecks of gold sparkled from the gossamer layers of the calf-length skirt as it swayed in the breeze. Oa, dumbfounded, just stared.

"Hello, I'm—" he began automatically.

"How did you get up here?!" she shouted in a whisper, her eyes darting everywhere.

Oa mumbled incomprehensibly, unprepared for that kind of response.

"Come here!" she hissed as she grabbed his arm and pulled him inside what looked to be a simple yet elegant home. She quickly closed the door and locked it, panting as she turned and braced her back against it. She stared at Oa, who was standing there in the foyer glancing distractedly around the room.

"This can't be happening," the angel mumbled, as she caught her breath.

"This place is so beautiful, so unique! Everything is tidy and pristine." Oa commented, looking around and taking a few steps farther inside.

"Stop!" the girl shouted, quickly thrusting her hand out.

Oa froze in place. The angel peeked out of the nearest window and made sure no one was coming. She ran over to the opposite window and checked that one as well. Apparently, the coast was clear.

"How many more of you are there?" she turned to the intruder and asked in alarm.

"How many? Like, how many people came with me?" Oa was puzzled.

"Yes, yes! How many?!" she repeated, clearly in panic mode.

"I'm all by myself. I just saw something up in the clouds and decided to check it out. Never thought I'd see *this* place." Oa said, still checking out the room though he kept his feet quite still.

Knowing now that it was just this boy alone, the angel felt a bit of relief. She glanced at his back, noticing that there were no wings. *How strange.*

Then she shook her head and reined in her curiosity to focus on the task at hand. "You need to leave right now," she said firmly.

"Leave? Oh, I'm sorry. Did I do something wrong?" Oa asked.

"You are a *land*-dweller! This is Nimbusara, the Kingdom of Angels. You are forbidden from being here. Don't you know that?" she replied, as if this was common knowledge.

"Forbidden? I—okay, I'll leave. I'm terribly sorry for coming all the way up here." Oa said, just a little disappointed as he headed for the door.

"Wait!" She suddenly stopped him. Oa paused with his hand only inches from the door handle. The angel had no idea why she stopped him. Was it her curiosity or the fact that she was still in shock?

"You're the first human to set foot in Nimbusara for hundreds of years. You know that, right?" she asked.

"I do know that, now," Oa replied as he lowered his hand. "Am I in trouble?"

"No, but if you get caught, you will be." The angel sighed as she checked outside of the two front windows one more time.

"I tried to introduce myself before. My name is Oa. What's yours?" Oa asked politely.

"My name is Rina."

"Rina, I like it," Oa replied with a smile.

The angel was both confused and troubled about what was happening. Not just a few seconds ago, she'd been going home as usual, only to run into a land-dweller who had somehow made his way this far up into the clouds. This boy was the first human to set foot on their sacred lands for time out of mind, and now, who *knew* what might happen?

"So, why are you here? How did you get up here?" Rina asked, her thoughts tumbling over one another.

"I was lying in the grass, staring up above, when I saw something in the clouds. So I used my air abilities and jetted myself up here." Oa explained.

"Ah, so you are a Disciple of Gou then?" Rina believed that she had guessed correctly.

"Yes! How did you know?" Oa was shocked that she knew about Grand Sage Gou.

Rina finally relaxed and took a seat, saying, "We have a library with all of the vast knowledge of the world collected there. I remember reading about the Disciples of Gou the Seer and their ability to harness the energy of the wind." She was still trying to process this strange situation.

"That's right!" Oa sent a gentle burst of air from his palm toward her. Her dark hair was brushed back from her face and she closed her eyes.

"I probably should go now. I don't wanna get in trouble for being here." Oa reached back for the door handle and started to pull it open.

"Oa, wait!" the angel called out once again. She still had so many questions that she wanted to ask him. When would she ever be able to come face to face with a human again?

"What's wrong?" Oa asked.

"I... I have a few questions... about the land below." Rina mumbled under her breath. She was nervous about asking. If he stayed, it would risk him getting caught, but if he left she would never get her answers.

"Go ahead, ask away," Oa replied, as he closed the door and went over to have a seat.

* * *

"That's about all I know, I guess." Oa exhaled as he sat back on the couch. Their conversation had lasted for a whole hour, and Oa answered all of Rina's questions. What were the terrain, food, people, and places like? She wanted to know everything. He told her about how he left Mount Axi, what Perlaria was like, and about everything up until he came here to Nimbusara..

"Wow... that was a lot. I never knew anything about what's been happening below the clouds this whole time. Is it scary?" Rina asked when he had finished his tale.

"There were a few times when I was scared for my life, but I knew I'd be safe with the people I was with." Oa smiled.

"You traveled with others?" The angel seemed surprised.

"Oh yeah, I guess I didn't mention the others. There's Lotus, Thalrok, and Nyloc. Nyloc is this archer who is blind but can also see, I guess. I forget how it works and all. Then there's Thalrok. He is this super tough guy with huge muscles who was raised by the titans! I don't know anyone stronger than him. Lastly, there's Lotus; he... he was the one we all followed across Perlaria." Oa had lowered his head and slowed his speech.

"What's the matter?" Rina could tell that her surprise-guest was troubled over something.

"Nothing—it's just that Lotus left earlier today, and I don't know if he's coming back. A lot has happened to him, and I just... I just hope I get to see him again." Oa stared down at the floor.

"I'm sorry, Oa." Rina said softly.

The two sat there silently until Oa took in a deep breath. Trying to take his mind off his concerns about Lotus, he asked, "Any other questions?"

"Of course! Let's see... Oh! What is it like to—"

"Hold on, Rina. I have an idea." Oa interrupted. He stood up and walked over to the door.

"Why don't I just show you? You can come down and see for yourself."

Rina hadn't seen that coming. She was shocked, and almost a little excited. Then reality kicked in. Her eyes lowered and a mask of sadness came over her face.

"What's wrong?" Oa asked.

"I can't leave here. It's forbidden. No one can leave, and no one can enter." Rina told him.

Oa knew this rule very well. The Disciples of Mount Axi had also refused to let others enter their domain or leave it. They had created a life of peace and refused to allow any outsiders to ruin that.

"You're lucky. You were given the blessing to leave your village. I would be seen as a traitor if I ever left Nimbusara." Rina plopped her head in her hands.

Oa felt terrible for her. It was like looking at a mirror image of himself in another life. With some hesitation, he made his way over and sat down next to her. "I'm sorry, Rina, I know that kind of thing is tough to bear." Oa tried to offer some comfort, even if they were strangers. "Do you have any more questions?"

"No, it's okay. You should probably get going. My family will be home soon." Rina stood up to go and peek out the front door. She didn't even turn back around to look at him anymore. Oa knew it was time for him to go.

"I'll head out now. Thanks for letting me stay a little while." Oa grabbed the handle of the back door and pulled it open, taking one last look inside before he left.

"See ya," he said, closing the door quietly and then heading down the path. Oa found the approximate place where he had clambered up, took one more glance around at Nimbusara, the Kingdom of Angels, with its beautiful islands in the sky, and then simply hopped off the edge. He felt the rapid pressure of air against his face as he dove headfirst towards the ground. Once he shot out from the clouds that had blocked his view, he could see the vast open lands below him.

"Whoa!" he shouted, as he took it all in. It was so pretty to see from this high up—the hills, plains, and valleys, the town of Mellowtin far below and the endless horizon ahead. It was breathtaking. Oa had to prepare himself as the ground got closer by the second. He was planning to drop down just below the Lie-Inn, and got ready to counter his long fall to earth using his own special air-control.

"Oh, there's Thalrok and Nyloc!" he shouted happily, mere seconds away from hitting the ground. Just in time, he let out strong bursts of air from his palms which slowed his speed tremendously. After only a few more bursts from his feet, he calmly planted them on the ground.

"Hey, sorry, I was taking a little trip." Oa apologized, as he headed over to them.

"No worries—" Thalrok said, then froze. Nyloc, too, didn't speak.

Oa stood in front of his friends, wondering what that same look on both of their faces meant. "You guys, alright?" he asked. Oa then noticed that they were staring behind him.

He slowly turned around and was thrown for a loop himself.

"Rina?!"

"I guess I'm a traitor now," she grinned, adding a little nervous chuckle.

* * *

"Hopefully, that catches you up a little," Nyloc said, as they all sat together on the rooftop lounge.

"So, you just illegally left your home to come down here? Why?" Lotus asked.

"Well, Oa explained to me how he'd been in a similar situation to mine. Both of our homelands forbid anyone to leave or to enter. He told me how his elder encouraged and blessed him to leave his village and follow you all on your journey. I know I'm leaving a lot differently than he did, but... I can't let my people dictate what I want for myself." Rina spoke with great resolve. Even though she could possibly fall into some kind of death trap here, she wanted to see these lands for herself.

"I'm sorry, but you can't come with us," Lotus said firmly.

"What! Why not?!" Oa shouted, rocketing to his feet.

"*She* will stick out more than *I* do. Does she know who I am and what's going on?" Lotus countered.

"We filled her in on everything, and the townspeople of Mellowtin got used to seeing her around all that time you were gone. Sure, nobody could believe it at first, but pretty soon they all moved on from it. Lotus, you let *me* come with you. What's the difference now?" Oa was confused about what had changed in Lotus. What had happened over the last few weeks?

"The situation is different now. Before, I was just trying to find a place to live and not be constantly hunted and in fear for my life." Lotus explained. "Now, I found the man who took everything from me—the man who had my master's life taken. My master, who gave me a life worth living, is gone because of him. I have to be the one to stop him. I can't keep living easy when I know this evil man is out there hurting people. Before, we were just on a journey around Perlaria, but now, we'd be walking into a hive of cold-blooded killers, and I am not putting you all at risk again." Lotus's fists clenched as he spoke. He whooshed out a breath and looked each of them straight in the eyes.

This was a different Lotus. Time and time again, he told them how he would cause nothing but pain to the ones surrounding him. Time and time again, they refused to back down, believing in him through and through. They knew what kind of person he was, and they didn't want to let him live alone and lonely, no matter what he said.

"Captain," Nyloc said soberly. "The whole time that you were gone Oa spoke very highly of you. He told the angel of your journey, your struggle, and your life. Even before you returned, she, too, said she would follow alongside you in your fight." Nyloc walked over and sat next to Lotus.

"It's true." Rina chimed in. "I've heard it all. Please, I know you may think this is an outrageous request, but truly, I am no weakling myself. Let me aid you in your battle and help you bring peace to your soul. I want to travel this world with you all and learn of what this world has to offer." Rina pleaded earnestly, holding her hands together as though in prayer.

"Ronin." The wanted man turned to Thalrok as he heard him speak his name. "We all chose to stay here after what happened. Any of us could have left and never returned, but we all stayed. If you told us we were returning to Cannon-Gulf the second you woke up this morning, we'd have been back on the *Skipper* right then and there. We *choose* to follow you, and that's that." Then Thalrok reached behind his back, drew Lotus's sword from its saya, and held it out to him.

Lotus stared at it, watching it glow softly and flicker in the golden hour sunlight. He reached out and gently took his broken blade from the bounty hunter's huge hands. Lotus looked at each of their faces in turn. They all looked back at him in perfect faith, waiting for his next order. This feeling. This trust they had in him... it felt familiar. It felt like being with his good friends back in Petalbrooke...

Breaking Lotus's reverie and capturing everyone's attention, Thalrok announced, "I have good news, too. I did a little digging when you were gone and found out where the Infected Ones might be hiding out. We'd have to return to Cannon-Gulf and plunge ourselves back into *that* hell, but, it's your call."

Everyone again stared at Lotus. The wanted man looked at his friends, who now wore serious expressions on their faces, ready to finish what they had started. He glanced at the latest addition to their crew, who looked ready to go right then and there. Lotus lowered his head and took in a deep breath. Slowly, he lifted it back up to say, "Let's finish this."

27

No More Running

The sound of a door slamming shut echoed through the corridors of the catacombs. Heavy footsteps followed one after another, and shortly afterward, the faint sound of an exasperated grunt followed.

"Weak! They're all weaklings!" Delus shouted, storming off and descending deeper into his domain. He was finished dealing with insubordinate lackeys who questioned everything he said. "They don't know what true loyalty is. They don't know what it's like to be loyal to their master. I *do* know. I know! If only you were here right now..."

Delus paused for a moment and a grin grew on his face. "Soon, very soon, you will be here. Then, this world will know what true power is. Right, master?" he said to himself, chuckling as he continued down the hallway to his quarters.

* * *

The mighty Infected Ones stood together in their underground world, feeling uplifted and inspired after their master's last speech. They awaited their next orders, eagerly expecting to demonstrate their power to the world very soon. The room they filled was another underground-type coliseum. This one funneled upwards and had a wide spiral walkway along the outside walls with hallways stretching out from each level to a different part of the underworld. It was massive, like a crater underneath the very crust of the earth. Hundreds of Infected Ones covered every inch of the big room like bees in a hive. It was only a matter of time before they would swarm out and create chaos in this world again.

"Did you feel that?" one of the many hundreds of Infected Ones asked.

"Feel what?" His companion had apparently felt nothing.

"There it is again." Many of them began to quiet down, wondering what that constant thrumming sound they were hearing could be.

"It sounds like... shaking?" One of them looked down at the floor. He felt the very ground beginning to shake beneath his feet and saw small bits of stone tremble and jiggle around them.

"An earthquake?" he wondered.

Suddenly, from above came the crashing sound of the earth rupturing and caving in on itself. The entire coliseum trembled and shook as chunks of the stony earthen crust came thundering down. The underground ceiling was destroyed. Debris demolished portions of the spiral walkway and blew into many of the hallways. The newly made hole allowed sunlight to peek in through the dust, exposing the now-ruined lair. Most of the Infected Ones ran for their lives into any unblocked tunnels they could find, as the chaos from above rained down. A few of them still watched through the dust while the ceiling above them crumbled like raindrops, and suddenly... There they were.

Thalrok, leading the charge, had smashed his way through the surface to come crashing down into their base. "Found them!" he shouted with satisfaction, as three more figures came down into the mayhem and landed shortly behind him.

"It's an ambush! Everyone—attack!" several of the Infected Ones shouted. Their cronies, those who remained standing, turned to focus on the intruders.

With three of their company now safely on the ground and ready to fight, they watched the circle of thugs closing in on them. "Rina is up there keeping watch. It looks like Thalrok's attack plan worked out pretty well." Nyloc noted, as he readied his bow.

"Thank goodness I trained for this." Thalrok boasted wryly, a cheeky grin on his face.

"Let's stop this here and now." Lotus clenched his fists as he stared intently ahead. Oa was at his side, staff in hand.

"Right!" they shouted, and charged headfirst into battle.

Singly, in pairs, or in small groups, more adversaries came flooding in. The bottom level of the underworld was now crawling with the Infected, and they swarmed the four companions. Shouts rang upward toward the gaping hole in the ceiling as the fighting commenced. Thalrok took his mighty blade and smashed it onto the ground—severe quaking deterred any and all grunts that came after him. Those who managed to stay upright would try to jump on his back and strike him down with their foolish little attacks, but all Thalrok did was brush them off and smack them far across the room, where they fell, unconscious.

Oa zipped around everywhere, untouched and on to the next once he finished off an opponent. Whenever the Infected Ones tried to surround him, he sent them flying against each other with huge bursts of air.

Nyloc stayed by Lotus's side, firing off arrows at whoever was in his blind spot. He covered Lotus as he fought against the unending chain of Infected attackers, taking some of the attention off of him while they held their ground. With two extra-large quivers full of arrows, Nyloc was fully prepared.

Lotus, continually weaving around and putting down any of the Ones attacking him, kept an eye out for Delus. He knew this commotion would cause Delus to show up in person; he simply had to.

"Lotus!" Oa shouted. The crew glanced in Oa's direction and saw him in the air, pointing.

Taking a quick look in that direction, they saw Ogan and Kenji dropping in to join the fight. Lotus turned back to the One, swiping his blade at him and ducking out of harm's way. As he swung the blade back through again, Lotus struck the thug's wrist with his left palm, stopping his arm. He then swung his right fist straight down, which shattered the blade into pieces. As the thug watched his blade's remains drop pitifully to the ground, Lotus kicked him across the face with a swift roundhouse and sent him tumbling.

"Ok, Nyloc! Let's go!" Lotus shouted, heading towards Kenji and Ogan.

"Right behind you!" Nyloc shouted back. He fired off one last arrow at the man directly behind him without even turning around, then joined Lotus, retrieving spent arrows along the way.

"How did they manage to find us?! Where is the master?" Ogan shouted.

"I don't know, but we have to stop them from taking out any more of our troops!" Kenji replied, and he planted his feet on the ground. The two of them had dropped from one of the open tunnels above. They saw Lotus and Nyloc fighting their way towards them. Clearly, they had planned this out.

"For the future." Kenji pledged.

"For the future," came Ogan's vow in return. They sighed as they readied their blades.

Emerging from the crowd, Nyloc and Lotus jumped up and over anyone in their way and went head-first at Delus's two lieutenants. Lotus could see the ferocity in their eyes, the anger that they held deep within was seeping out.

"Kenji now!" Ogan cried, and immediately Kenji let out a gigantic cloud of poisonous smoke, which quickly surrounded them. Their vision was completely obscured as they hid in the maroon haze.

"Good luck getting through this again," Kenji smirked. Then he winced, feeling a sudden thud and pinch in his upper arm. A stinging pain kicked in as he saw that there was an arrow embedded in it. Wincing, he yanked it out. Then he heard Ogan, too, yelp in pain. Looking down, Ogan found two arrows firmly lodged in his lower leg.

"Ogan!" Kenji called out, and he took one step towards his brother. His foot barely hit the ground when another arrow flew into and through his calf. He grimaced as the leg gave out and he fell to one knee. Kenji grabbed the arrow, broke off the fletching, and pulled it out. He struggled to push himself up to get to Ogan. Once again, he'd taken just one step when this time, the full force of a hammering fist struck him in the face.

"Damn it!" Kenji spat blood. After the punch to the face, he felt a knee forced hard into his chest. His body bent over, and next, Lotus's heel slammed down onto his back. Kenji hit the ground, yelling in pain.

"Kenji!" Ogan cried out, limping with all the speed he could muster towards Kenji. Somehow, no other arrows found Ogan as he ran through the toxic haze to his brother.

How can they move like this through my smoke?! How can they see us?

Kenji grunted as he tried to sit up. Wildly, he swiped his new cleaver-blade upward. He missed Lotus completely, since Lotus wasn't even there. Kenji knew that now he must go after Ogan. "Watch out!" Kenji called out, but it was too late.

Lotus, using the smokescreen to his benefit, was able to roundhouse Ogan across the belly and curl him over. Planting his foot back down, he twisted his hips and swung a fist for the side of the Infected lieutenant's head.

"Enough of this!" Ogan shouted. He thrust out an arm and stopped the punch with his bare hand. Lotus, caught off guard, felt Ogan's other hand grab his collar. Ogan swiftly pulled him in close and wrapped an arm around his neck, choking him with his forearm. Lotus pried at the forearm, trying to release his grip, but it wouldn't budge.

I have to get away! I can't breathe! Lotus could feel his body becoming limp as the choke-hold effects of Ogan's power kicked in.

"I got him, Kenji!" Ogan shouted, squeezing tighter. He felt Lotus wiggle and squirm, trying to free himself, but it was hopeless. His struggles got slower and slower as seconds ticked by, and Ogan knew that Lotus was about to pass out.

"Time to rest now," Ogan whispered, as he felt Lotus's body go completely limp and his head fall forward.

"Finally, he's d—" As Ogan slowly released his grip, Lotus's limp head flung back and smashed directly into his nose. Ogan's eyes immediately began to water. He grabbed his nose and hunched over, dripping blood.

Exhausted from taking poison into his lungs for so long, Lotus used the remaining strength he had to jump straight up and completely out of the cloud of smoke. As he broke through the thick dark-maroon layer, he took in a giant breath of clean air before falling back down. Then, like a man swimming in water, he held his breath and plunged through the haze.

"Ogan, where are you?!" Kenji shouted as he ran, limping, through the clouds of his own smoke. Arrows kept flying in his direction. First from one way, then from another, just seconds later. Each time he just barely evaded one, another came out of nowhere. "Where *is* that damn archer?" he hissed in alarm.

"You mean me?" Nyloc whispered playfully into Kenji's ear.

Kenji quickly swung his blades behind him, but the blind archer had already jumped out of the way. Kenji held his two new cleavers, swinging them back and forth. He rushed at Nyloc, or where he thought Nyloc would be, in the dense dark-maroon haze. His blades dug into the air, cutting through the fog but missing Nyloc every time. Kenji slashed with increasing furor while Nyloc danced around in the haze.

Finally, Nyloc nocked an arrow and pulled back his bow. Kenji was close enough to see this one coming and quickly covered his face with his cleavers. But he didn't feel the arrow strike the blades; it hadn't hit him anywhere at all.

Did he miss? Kenji wondered, lowering his cleavers just a bit to peer ahead into the haze. Nyloc was gone.

Damn it, now where did he go?! Kenji panicked. He turned around and there was Nyloc, now with a dagger in hand. Before the blind archer could jab at him, Kenji simply leaped backward and the menacing vision of the blindfolded archer faded away in the haze.

Kenji landed on the ground, wounded arm and calf aching. He took in a deep breath, thinking, *I just have to keep this smoke up and I'll be able to keep my distance.* However, timing could never have been worse for this lieutenant of the Infected. A moment after finishing his thought, a big gust of wind blew the entire cloud of his dense smoke away in just seconds. Now Kenji could easily see Nyloc, who was standing a few yards ahead of him, smirking.

No way...

Then, Kenji felt some sort of unholy pressure behind him. He slowly turned his head to see Thalrok towering over him with his huge fist cocked back.

"It's over!" Thalrok yelled, as he swung his fist toward the ground. Kenji barely scrambled out of its path as the ground trembled beneath their feet. If that punch had hit him, it would have been lights out. Instinctively, Kenji discharged as much smoke as he could, shielding himself from their sight and covering his blind spots.

Panting and exhausted, he hid in his smoke-clouds. He had no idea what to do. "Who *are* these people? How have they gotten this much stronger?" Kenji asked no one in particular, his voice barely wheezing from his mouth. He poked his head out from one side of the smoke cloud and saw the four intruders continuing to take down man after man. The number of Infected Ones still upright and able to fight was decreasing by the minute.

Where's Ogan? came to Kenji's mind. He glanced around and saw him going toe-to-toe with Lotus. Ogan had his curved dagger and Lotus had his broken sword. They slashed at each other mercilessly.

Kenji had a bad feeling about this whole thing. Once again, his Infected Ones still outnumbered these four busybodies, yet all four of *them* were still standing.

Then Kenji finally saw him. *Master!*

He created a trail of smoke to cover him as he made for the wall. Struggling painfully to hop up, ledge after ledge, Kenji made it to the platform where Delus stood. Delus never turned his head. He just glared down at the battlefield which had once been their hidden underground coliseum. His eyes scolded them all with the utmost contempt and disgust.

"Master, I don't know how they found us, but... this is bad. I don't know what happened, but they somehow—"

Delus held his hand up, signaling the boy to stop talking. "Are they still set?" he asked calmly.

"Yes… Yes, sir, does that mean I should signal for us to retreat?" Kenji asked.

"Us?" Delus now turned his dark eyes toward the boy.

"Yes, sir, we should retreat now. This invasion plan of theirs has dropped our numbers. We are losing men left and right. We have to leave before they take any more." Kenji insisted.

At las,t Delus turned, giving Kenji his full attention. He lowered his head, eyes still locked on his young lieutenant, and said, "I still don't know what you're getting at, boy. You say that we should retreat, yet *I* don't remember saying that *you* can come along."

"Master, are you saying that… Sir, we still have hundreds of our own men down there. We will kill them all if we do that!" Kenji shouted, pleading with his master to reconsider.

Delus took a step forward and loomed over Kenji with his eyes wide and anger steaming from his body. "You will do as I say, Kenji. When I tell you to, you will give the signal for the arrow to be fired to ignite the bombs."

"But master, Ogan is down there! He'll be—" Kenji was horrified.

"If you do not do as I say, then you are disobeying a direct order!" Delus interrupted forcefully. "I don't care how many troops we lose. These pathetic weaklings will be destroyed here and now!" The aura of anger surrounding Delus seemed to be actually smoking as he bared his teeth and glared at his lieutenant.

Kenji was frozen, his heart pounding. He didn't know what to do. He couldn't bring himself to destroy Ogan and the others.

"Sir…" Kenji's voice trembled as he watched his master standing here above it all and watching in disgust.

"Make the call, boy. Or do you want to die down there like the rest?" Delus muttered, waiting for his disciple to respond. Delus had had enough of this, and was ready to end it all.

Kenji could barely move. He stared down and saw the Infected Ones fighting against these invaders. Ogan was just barely holding on against Lotus.

He couldn't do it; he couldn't be the one to make the call.

"Make the call now!" Delus commanded.

"I…" Kenji mumbled. He wished that he could just disappear.

"This is an order! I am telling you to make the call!" Delus bellowed one last time, the floor shaking beneath his feet.

The orphan who long ago was taken in by this master simply couldn't do it; he could not muster the strength to sentence the only brother he ever knew to certain death. He tried to appeal once more, "I have to go down there and get Ogan out. We have time. I can get him—"

"FIRE!" Delus's thunderous voice rang out.

Kenji's eyes widened in horror as he heard his master's voice echo across the ruined coliseum. He watched as a man perched on one of the levels opposite them fired an arrow. His ears went deaf, and all he could see was the arrow, flame at its tip, soaring through the air toward a pile of exposed explosives. He knew that beneath the entire floor were more barrels filled with explosive powder, all just waiting to be ignited.

"No…" Kenji's voice trailed off as the arrow hit its target.

Below him, the explosion erupted across the entire coliseum as if the world were ending. One after another, explosions discharged left, right, and center. Far beneath the ledge where he stood there was a fiery inferno, brightly ablaze. Kenji saw the rubble, debris, and yes, those were the bodies of men, shooting up in the air.

Delus watched it all happen with a displeased scowl on his face. What was to be a sweet moment for him had been soiled by the weaklings he'd surrounded himself with. He observed the endless fireworks of destruction and watched coldly as the limp figures of Infected Ones were sent flying while even more explosions covered their screams.

Finally, the last blast went off.

Ashy residue drifted down to cover the remains of the coliseum. Kenji's ears still rang from the eruptions as the dust settled. The poor young man's eyes widened even further, and tears formed at the sight of what was below. Kenji dropped to his knees when his eyes locked onto…

"Ogan!" he shouted. Oblivious to his injuries, Kenji hurried to the bottom to see if his brother was all right. Hastily picking his way across the rubble, he dropped down at Ogan's side.

"Ogan... Ogan! Please, wake up! *Please!*" the young man cried as he held his dearest friend's body. But Ogan could not respond; he was already gone.

Kenji dropped his head and sobbed, his tears flowing freely. The pain he felt was unbearable. Those years they'd spent together—training, living, and getting stronger—always together. They did it as a team. Both had been orphans who became like brothers, and they'd promised to always be there for each other. But now...

"Ogan..." Kenji cried, as he carefully lowered his brother's head to the ground.

"Pathetic." Delus scoffed from above, "Each and every one of them was a pathetic weakling. No matter, I have no use for them now. The world's rebirth is near; the Dark Empire will see to that."

Delus began slowly walking down the now dusty hallway. His followers' numbers had just been reduced by the hundreds, and by his own hand. A malevolent grin shone below the twisted man's evil eyes. He thought smugly, *After all these years, any remains of that fool are finally gone. Our master chose wrong, Din. Looks like you did, too.* Delus cackled, knowing that he'd finally killed the last person who could possibly get in his way. Still smiling, he closed his eyes and chuckled to himself, ever so pleased with his victory. When his eyes opened, he found himself face to face with an unexpected sight.

"What?!" Delus shouted in surprise.

The young disciple of Gou stood before him. Oa's wrists were pressed together, fingers curled back, and palms facing directly at his chest. With a sudden burst of air, Delus was sent flying backward. He was hurled down the tunnel, and shot out of the ruined entrance. At first his body thrashed around in the air, but he quickly centered himself as he dropped and landed on his feet atop the wreckage.

"One of them lived?!" Delus was truly puzzled; he had no idea how any of them could have survived those explosions. Then, he felt a wave of disgusting energy coming from afar.

"Well, well, well. That's how," he smirked, seeing the others off in the distance.

Lotus, Nyloc, and Thalrok stood there together, surrounded by a warm golden light. "They found an angel. How wondrous." Delus grinned wryly.

Rina had quickly made her way down just in time to help them.

"Healing powers, huh? It would have been nice to know you could do this earlier." Thalrok panted as he felt the pain in his body slowly fading away.

"Try not to move, I'm almost done." Rina remained serene and focused. She concentrated, eyes closed, held her hands over each of them in turn, and gently healed their wounds.

"Thank you for this. If you weren't here, we would've been dead for sure." Lotus huffed as he stared ahead to where Delus was climbing up a large pile of rubble on the ruined coliseum floor.

I guess this battle isn't over then. Delus thought. *A rematch of old rivals in new forms. I wish you could see this, Din. You could watch me beat your pathetic little student into the ground just like all the others.*

Delus turned his body to fully face the five companions, his pitiful adversaries. He stood with his arms crossed over his chest, looking down on them in contempt from afar.

"Entertain me," he demanded arrogantly. His words echoed in the void.

"You alright, Ronin?" Thalrok asked.

Without taking his eyes off his enemy, Lotus took a deep breath, then said, "Yeah. I'm ready to finish this."

28

I will...

The stage was set. The sun was a spotlight above the underworld shining down on the main event. Lotus, Thalrok, Oa, Nyloc, and Rina stood staring at the man before them—Delus, leader of the Infected Ones, murderer of countless beings, and the man who had taken everything from Din. This moment didn't feel real.

They watched Delus standing calmly atop the rubble some distance away, his head lifted and his eyes staring down at them. They felt a cold, sickening aura of energy radiating from him. The five of them stood next to one another, weapons at the ready and hearts pounding.

"We just have to stay together. Fight as one, and we will stop him here and now." Lotus reassured the others, and himself.

He paused, the blackening shutters of his eyelids closed for a brief moment. The split second they lifted back up, he stared out at... no one.

Immediately to his right, he felt a bone-chilling wind of dark energy press against his body. His head shot in that direction, where he saw Delus grabbing Thalrok's helmet and pushing him backward.

"Thalrok!" Nyloc shouted, pointing his bow at Delus.

"Nyloc, wait!" Lotus cried out, but he wasn't quick enough, and the leader of the Infected grabbed Nyloc's arrow the second it left his bow. Crushing the shaft in his hands, he took the remaining arrowhead and jabbed it into Thalrok's upper chest. The titan howled out in pain.

Delus, wearing the usual disappointed look and still holding onto Thalrok's helmet, pulled him in closer and slammed a knee into his midsection. Thalrok gasped for breath as Delus released his grip. He then grabbed the back of Thalrok's head and smashed it not just on, but through, the cavern floor. Pieces of stony debris and dust flew up from the huge crater that formed on impact.

"You bastard!" Oa shouted, dashing headfirst into the dust cloud.

Delus couldn't see much from inside the debris, but when Oa swung straight down with his staff, it suddenly stopped mid-swing. He then used Oa's bo to force air downward, pushing the dust out.

"No way..." Oa stuttered.

Delus didn't even look away from Thalrok, lying on the ground. "That weak little trick won't work on me," his deep voice muttered as he pulled the staff in toward himself. Oa didn't let go and was yanked in.

A deep purple fire began to flicker around Delus's hand as he drew back his fist and swung. Oa had to think fast, and inhaled a deep breath. Blowing as hard as he could, he forced a burst of air from his mouth which jetted him backward just in time. Delus barely missed punching him in the face and watched him soar to safety.

"Pathetic," he scoffed as he tossed the staff away. Delus then stared down at the bounty hunter, who was still not moving a muscle. "How pitiful. To call yourself a titan is such a joke," he jeered, then suddenly reached out and grabbed an arrow inches before it struck his head. He turned in Nyloc's direction, and scowled. "Wasn't it obvious the first time that arrows won't work here?"

Nyloc angrily gritted his teeth and fired arrow after arrow. Each time, Delus grabbed them out of the air, slowly advancing on Nyloc. He held seven of Nyloc's arrows bundled in one hand, and they began to glow a deep purple. When he released them, the arrows levitated around him, each burning with an intense purple flame.

Sensing all that was happening, Nyloc backed away with his bow drawn and sweat beading his face. *Aw crap, this isn't good!* When the arrows turned in perfect unison toward his direction, Nyloc panicked. Delus slowly pointed his finger towards the archer, ready to fire them.

"Don't you dare!" Oa shouted, launching himself back into the fight.

"Foolish child," Delus whispered, and, with a flick his finger, the arrows swiftly turned and fired themselves at the flying Oa.

The boy stopped mid-air. Seven arrows were flying right at him at high velocity and from too close of a distance. He was unable to do anything to move himself in time. Oa covered his face and awaited the painful barrage of arrows to strike.

Suddenly, the young disciple felt his body being jolted. As his eyes flew open, he saw Lotus holding onto him, safe from the arrows passing by.

How did he...? Oa thought in wonder as he saw Lotus panting with effort.

"You alright?" Lotus asked.

"Uh... fine, yeah. Wow... close one." Oa mumbled as he planted his feet on the ground.

Delus watched the arrows miss their target and embed themselves in the solid rock wall across the cavern. Then he tilted his head. "You know..." he began thoughtfully, and then vanished. "I never had the pleasure of seeing a real angel before," he finished saying, suddenly reappearing behind Rina, who was kneeling over Thalrok and trying to heal him without being noticed. She stiffened, eyes wide, as she felt the creeping pressure of doom and darkness upon her.

"Rina!" Lotus shouted, planting his foot on the ground. He saw multiple jagged spikes shoot out from Delus's forearm, then stab Rina in the back. The girl screamed, feeling the intense pain race through her body.

A little grin grew on Delus's face as he watched her body fall to the ground. Then he felt an uneasy presence, and looked up to find Lotus there in front of him. The young man punched him hard in the face and sent him sliding backward. Delus remained upright, his feet digging into the ground.

"Damn it, he blocked it." Lotus exhaled, seeing Delus's arms up in front of his face.

In the meantime, Oa ran over beside Rina to check if she was all right. There were black wounds where the spikes had stabbed her, and now veins of darkness spread out from them, curling like the tendrils of vines. "Oh no—what's happening?!" he asked, shocked.

"I feel... so weak, and I... I can't use my power." Rina cried helplessly.

"You can't use your power?" he gasped. Oa knew exactly what that meant. He then looked over at Lotus and saw him standing between them and Delus.

"You have quite a lot of strength inside of you," Delus spoke, lowering his arms. "You are filled with such hate and anguish. I can feel it so clearly. It's sad to say, but that stolen power of yours will go to waste now." Delus sneered.

Lotus could feel a great fear inside of himself that broke past every other feeling he had. Seeing such fearsome power close up and in person was intimidating. Lotus then glanced behind him and saw the four of them, his steadfast companions who had chosen to stand with him against anything.

Thalrok was on the ground, out cold. Nyloc stood there, legs shaking, but with an arrow drawn and ready. Rina was sitting on her knees, crying from the pain, Oa by her side.

"Oa..." Lotus whispered. He saw the brave face Oa was putting on, and even though he could see that he was scared, the boy held onto the tears in his eyes as best he could.

I have to do... something. Lotus took one single deep breath in. He looked the boy right in the eyes. "Oa. It'll be alright. I've got this," he said firmly.

Though the boy kept on a brave face, his tears couldn't hold anymore and trickled down his cheeks. "I know you can, Lotus," Oa said with great sincerity, then bent back to tend to Rina.

The words that the boy spoke to him, his demeanor, felt so... warm. Even in this moment, with fear taking over, and muscles too frozen to move, Lotus felt this warm feeling inside. Each of them put their trust in him even as death loomed right before their eyes. He wanted to protect them. He wanted to help them.

Delus squinted, he felt a change coming over Lotus, and that made him uneasy.

"I will protect them," Lotus whispered to himself, turning to Delus.

"This feeling..." Delus grunted, growing angrier by the second. He had enough of waiting and was ready to end this all right now. Intense purple flames erupted around his hands along with the dark energy that leaked from his body and mingled with them. Charging full speed, he reeled back to force his fist at Lotus.

The wanted man saw the evil smile on Delus's face grow as he swung at him. Purple fire erupted in every direction as he hit Lotus. The burning energy was so powerful it stretched far out to each side with just a single strike. "Pathet—"

"I'm not." A simple statement interrupted him.

Delus's body shook at the sound of that voice. Through the black and purple flames, he caught a glimpse of its owner. A translucent yellow wall was in front of Lotus's face, shielding him. Delus could see through it clearly, and he saw the wanted man's bright blue eyes focused intently on his own. The leader of the Infected stared back, then heard him speak in a very familiar way.

"I'm not letting you hurt them," Lotus spoke ever so calmly.

"What? How can you be so..." Delus's words trailed off. He felt powerful energies forming all around him and saw arrows of light spawning in Lotus's blind spots.

I have to back up now or— A sudden hard punch to the stomach stopped that thought. Surprise, and then pain, registered. He lifted his head to see Lotus unloading a heavy strike aimed at his chest.

"The brat!" Delus wheezed. His insolent smirk had faded and turned into an angry scowl. Another punch to the chest landed right after the first, which pushed him back a few feet. The evil man slid to a halt, planting one foot behind him to charge back in, except...

I forgot!

In his peripheral vision, Delus saw the arrows of light zinging toward him. His figure vanished. The arrows went through the empty space he had just inhabited. Delus's afterimage faded away as the arrows of light struck the ground. He rematerialized some distance away, and saw Lotus looking right at him. The punk had known exactly where Delus was going to be.

The older man huffed as he saw the expression on the Lotus's face. It was the very same expression Din had worn all those years ago. Lotus didn't seem angry; he looked oddly blank, with just a vague look of concentration in his eyes as he focused on his foe.

"You want to see power? Fine." Delus grunted as he slammed his palms together. Slowly pulling them apart, that same deep purple fire erupted around his hands as a sword made of pure dark energy was being created between them. As Delus's arms spread as wide apart as possible, the blade was finished. He grabbed the handle, pointing the tip at Lotus. The coal-black blade burned with purple flames coming from every inch of it. "Careful what you wish for," Delus murmured, and a wicked smile crept up the sides of his mouth.

"I will protect them." Each time Lotus said these words, he felt the warm energy inside of himself glow brighter. He reached for his hip and slowly pulled out his sword. As the broken blade was completely freed from its hand-decorated saya, Delus watched. It took a moment, but then, in surprise, he recognized it.

"You still carry around that man's broken blade? Even after all this time? Hilarious!" Delus mocked. "I can see it now. It must have broken when my dear son came to your little town and struck him down. Ah, how proud I am. I so wish that I could have seen it." Delus lifted his head, closed his eyes, and began laughing hysterically, taunting the young man. He was trying to get on his nerves, poke the bear, bring him to his breaking point. Then, he would be able to truly infect and destroy him.

Suddenly, Delus felt that uneasy feeling in front of him again. His laughter stopped and he glanced down to see Lotus in front of him, blade drawn back, ready to slash through him.

"Still weak!" he shouted, as their blades clashed. Metallic clatter rang through the underworld as the young man used what was left of Din's sword to fight. Lotus swung at Delus over and over, battering him with quick jabs and slices from his broken sword while dodging Delus's longer swinging arc.

Their eyes locked; Lotus's expression was still blank. Delus could feel the young man's power increasing each time he struck. Rage bubbled up from his core, as he felt himself being pushed around the rubble by this mere child.

"He reminds me so much of... him!" Delus growled, and the purple fire from his blade rose higher from the black metal.

Back and forth the two of them went, zipping across the entire coliseum floor and slamming into one another. The others could barely keep them in sight as they flew across the room, their speed increasing every time their blades clashed. The power flowing out from each of them was so thick that they could feel it in their chests.

"Enough!" Delus shouted, as their blades crashed together for the umpteenth time. The metal ran and screeched as they pushed into one another. All this is running around, going toe to toe with a weakling like this boy; it only pissed him off all the more.

Lotus watched as the smile on Delus's face suddenly returned. Then the wanted man felt the black blade move forward so rapidly that it was like his own blade wasn't even there. Glancing down, he saw that his broken sword had phased through it but missed its target because it was too short. But, the single slash of Delus's blade cut deeply into Lotus's shoulder. It stuck down into his body, burning him, as he lowered his head and then himself to the ground.

"I warned you, boy." Delus exhaled, and chuckled evilly to himself. One more strike and this child would be no more.

Lotus's head slowly lifted, he stared serenely into Delus's eyes.

"What?" The leader of the Infected was confused. That boy should be lying in agonizing pain right now. But why was he...

"I will not let you hurt them," Lotus whispered.

At those words, Delus finally felt it, felt the change in energy. He glanced down and saw the broken blade of Din now glowing white. Light energy stretched out from the fragmented metal and pierced his midsection. The evil man gritted his teeth, pulled his sword back and swung it for his foe's neck. As the fiery blade was inches away from striking Lotus, another light barrier popped into existence and stopped it from hitting its mark. Delus turned his gaze back to Lotus's face, noticing that his hand was right in front of his face and contained a small ball of light.

"Protect them," Lotus muttered. The ball of pure light exploded and Delus was hurled across the room.

After landing, his body rolled a few feet before he could quickly push himself up and slide smoothly to his feet. Now, Delus's entire being focused on Lotus.

"I'm gonna destroy this kid!" Delus shouted. He was about to charge headfirst into battle again when he felt the stinging thud of three arrows hitting his left hip and torso. He turned to see Nyloc running at him, firing more arrows as he barreled in from across the room.

The Infected leader tightened his fist, and the arrows turned to ash; those wounding him fell from his body. He then turned back towards Lotus only to find Oa in front of him. The young disciple's palms were already thrust out, about to expel a huge burst of air. Delus shielded himself before it could hit, but Oa knew that this would happen. The boy let out a small gust from his feet and flew above him. Once in place, he forced out all of the air he possibly could, all at the same time, his palms trembling with the effort. Delus could neither stop nor escape that all-powerful wind, and was pushed flat onto the ground.

"Another foolish attempt!" Delus yelled, scoffing as he rose to his feet. He grabbed an arrow that was swishing toward his head, lit it with purple flames, and launched it right back at Nyloc. The blind archer dodged the fiery arrow and kept on with his aggressive attack. His arrows didn't really faze Delus, and some were turned to ash, but distraction, too, can be a worthwhile weapon.

Delus's rage was building up to new heights as he once again turned in Lotus's direction, wondering, *Where did he go?!*

The brat was not there. The spot where he'd stood was empty. Then, Delus felt a powerful rise in energy, a pressure, behind him. He instinctively jumped out of the way as a thunderous punch slammed into where he had been standing. Thalrok was healed enough to be back on his feet and back in the fight. Again and again, Thalrok sent a barrage of punches at Delus, following him as he sidestepped and dodged. None of them connected, but as they hit the ground, they shattered it.

"I will put you down again, you weakling!" Delus taunted. He drew back his evilly forged sword and the black blade again erupted with deep violet fire. Delus swung at Thalrok's throat.

The bounty hunter firmly planted his feet and watched the formidable sword grow closer. "Oh no ya don't! I am not goin' down like before!" Thalrok shouted back, and he grabbed the blade with both hands as it swung for him. The sharp metal cut into his hands, but Thalrok held on just the same. "Now!" Thalrok roared.

Right on cue, Oa zipped through the air feet first, his arms over his head and the heel of one foot out in front. Aided by wind power from his palms, he smashed the black blade, shattering it. Delus watched, irate, as the pieces fell to the ground and the purple flames flickered and died.

Thalrok, black shards still in his hand, cocked his fist. Delus hopped back as soon as his fist got close to him, easily evading the punch. It was just another foolish attempt to hit him. That was, until he felt... something.

No... Delus froze.

He looked over his shoulder and saw Lotus. There he was, with his whole body brightly luminous and his eyes dazzling white and glowing. No longer was his face a blank slate; it was rage-fueled and ready to finish this.

The wanted man's fist hit him squarely in the back which launched him straight into the wall of his ruined underworld. Rocky debris and grit flew as he broke through and into the solid stone. All anyone could hear was the faint sound of broken stones skittering down the wall.

"Ronin, you alright?" Thalrok asked, blood dripping from his hands.

"I'm fine. What about you guys?" Lotus responded.

"We're alright. Rina is still in pain, but she is managing for now." Oa replied, as they gathered and stood there together. They all stared at Lotus, who was radiating with a bright, warm energy.

"Is this—?" Oa began to ask, when a sudden explosion came from the fractured wall, interrupting him.

Together, they turned to see Delus firing out from it. He slammed onto the ground in front of them and knelt there, staring ominously at them. Dark energy flowed from his entire body as he got to his feet. They stood warily on guard, ready to go again. The whole room was overflowing with the dark energy he was creating. They had awakened the beast inside, and it was angry.

"Your master, he took everything from me!" Delus pointed at Lotus. "I dedicated years and years of my life to our master, and he chose *Din*?! What an old fool! Our master chose the wrong man—it should have been *me* who inherited the power. Me!" he spat out. "I could have changed the world, brought it down the right path, but no; I was too weak." Delus stared down at his hands, feeling the power inside of him increase by the second. To the others, the power he created felt like a disease infecting the very air; the heaviness of it made breathing alone feel tiring.

"I was denied my destiny." Delus went on. "But... I found a new master. One who knows the true meaning of power. One who acknowledged me for my strength. He knew that *I* was the one who would change this world. He knew that *I* would be the one to follow beside him and create a new world—a world where the strong surpass everyone. He gave me my own power—the power to destroy whatever I want!!" Delus shouted, and the force of his raw power pushed them all backward. They shielded their faces as they saw the swarms of black energy, like thousands of tiny starlings, forming and reforming in dark clouds that flew around the entire ruined coliseum. Black lightning bolts shot out from them in all directions, and the earth trembled.

"I will show you, master! The Dark Empire will arise and destroy all who are weak!" Delus chanted as the dark energy continued to pour out from him.

"What's happening?!" Oa shouted, as he pointed ahead. Peering through the shadowy dark energy surrounding them, they could see that Delus's appearance was changing. His body was morphing, mutating, and he grabbed and tore at his head, shrieking. His muscles bulged, then ripped through his shirt, showing skin which had turned a deep red. Fearsome horns grew, one large one from each side of his head, and curled toward his jaw. His fingers reformed, and wicked-looking claws, sharper than any blade, crept out. In time, the painful screams of transformation slowly turned into laughter, cruel laughter which revealed teeth that were jagged and uneven. His figure looked quite a few inches taller too, as he stood up tall and stretched, then howled loudly and victoriously.

"He..." "No way..." "How can..." the companions stuttered out in turn.

"A demon..." Lotus whispered, as they all laid eyes on this leader of the Infected Ones, now present in this monstrous form.

Now the metamorphosis of Delus was complete, and one last surge of dark energy was forced out of his body. They covered their faces again, then peeked out to see him standing there in the midst of all the rubble.

"I will show you. I will show the *world* what true power is." Delus smiled savagely as he slowly turned his horned head to glare at his prey.

29

True Power

"Delus… He was a terrible man, yet he was one of the strongest people I have ever known." Din stared into the sky, watching the sun lying on the horizon.

"I think that's enough for today." Din brushed off his hands and then began to head back to the village.

"Have you seen him since, uh, you know?" Ronin asked, being careful with his words.

"I have not, but I know he's out there. It's only a matter of time until he shows up again." Din pondered as he stroked his beard.

"How do you know?" Ronin asked.

"Delus would train harder than any of the other students. Night and day, he would break his body down until it would repair itself and become stronger. Knowing him, he is out there training, planning to use his power to destroy this world." Din stopped walking and lowered his head.

"Master?" Ronin tilted his head.

"I fear the day that I have to come face-to-face with that monster again. I fear how strong he has grown over these years."

* * *

Oa stared at the ground. His hand felt the craggy stone debris there as drops of blood fell from his face and stained the ground. He rested there for a moment, one knee on the ground, barely able to stay upright. He could feel his lungs ache as he took a deep breath. Using what energy he had left, he lifted his head up and watched Lotus, still in battle with that beast.

"Lotus…" The single word wheezed from his mouth as he watched with one open eye.

The sound of Delus's scornful cackling bounced across the underworld as the Infected leader and the cursed man went at each other. Delus's speed had doubled, and his power had increased beyond comprehension. He was truly a demon now.

"We have to keep going. He won't be able to keep this up much longer." Oa panted as he rose from the rubble.

"Do you understand now?!" Delus sneered. He battered Lotus with his fists, again and again.

Weaving and dodging out of the way took all of Lotus's effort. He could barely keep up with Delus's speed now, even though the light was flowing through him more than it ever had before. This devilish transformation was an unexpected turn of events. Lotus had no chance to throw an attack; it took all of his effort to avoid those of the rampaging demon before him. He could see the savage beast's sharp teeth as Delus laughed wickedly. He had knocked down any and every attack the others threw at him like it was nothing. Lotus was the only one still standing now, and it was all up to him.

"I have to… protect them," he gasped, trying his best to keep up.

"I applaud you for getting this far, boy. But now it's time for you to truly understand that you chose the wrong master to follow!" Delus shouted as he reeled back his fist.

"I have to stop this one!" Lotus held his palms out, creating a light barrier in front of him. Delus didn't bat an eye, he just swung his fist and broke through it like it was nothing. The shield of light shattered, and Lotus was sent soaring across the room. His limp body smacked into the wall, sliding down onto the ground.

"You monster!" Thalrok yelled, as he swung his mighty blade at Delus's back. With a twist of his hips, the demon turned and easily swatted the blade from his hands. Thalrok watched it fly across the room and embed itself into a stone wall. He didn't hesitate to take the next step and stomped his foot on the ground, shaking the floor below them. Delus stumbled only slightly from the tremors as Thalrok swung a huge fist in an uppercut to his jaw.

"You are so amusing." Delus snickered, as he looked up, letting the punch just scratch his jaw. Thalrok had missed and now felt the hammering force of a roundhouse kick in the back. The titan was launched across the room, slammed into and through the very stone.

"Delus!" Lotus shouted.

The demon turned to the sound of his voice and saw him standing there, body hunched and breath barely in his lungs.

"Ah, perhaps you've reached your limits, boy?" Delus slowly shook his head in contempt.

The light surrounding Lotus had began to flicker, fading like a dying candle. He was so exhausted, he was running on nothing but adrenaline and he simply couldn't go on for much longer.

I have to keep going. I need to use what I have left to end this.

Lotus stood up straight, took a deep breath, and concentrated on keeping this energy flowing. It was like riding a bike and trying to write with your nondominant hand at the same time. He wasn't used to doing all this at once again. Then the aura around him grew brighter than before, his eyes locked on Delus. The demon stood in his place and watched Lotus focusing all his power to take him down.

"Pathetic." Delus chuckled as he prepared for this weak attack to come. He watched Lotus lower his body, gathering himself to charge.

A head-on attack? No surprise there. Delus thought, and remained quite still, his eyes completely focused on the boy in front of him.

"It's about time I—" A sudden jolt of pain shot down Delus's spine. He felt his skin crawl and his entire body go numb with shock. The excruciating sensation of a single blade that had pierced deeply into his back caused his knees to buckle.

"What the...?!" he shouted, as he turned to swat at whatever was behind him. Black blood poured out of the wound. When he ripped the blade from his back, he noticed it was *Ogan's* dagger?! Yet, he saw nothing or no one behind him. "Who did—"

"Delus!" a voice shouted, interrupting him as he lifted his head.

"You." Delus snarled.

"You *monster!*" Kenji shouted as he dove straight down from one of the many ledges high above with his cleavers pulled back. Anger flooded his face and tears dropped from his eyes.

"Your insubordination will cost you your life, boy." Delus scolded.

Kenji was coming down from right above Delus, and he was wide open. It was a death trap; he would be an easy target to put down. But, before Kenji was anywhere close to striking his master, he swung his cleavers out, one to each side, and simply tossed them away.

"What?" Delus was confused.

That was when Kenji put out both palms and shouted at the top of his lungs,

"Poisonous haze!" The dark-maroon smoke shot streaming from his hands, and in no time, Delus was surrounded by it and blinded.

"You come at me with this pitiful attack, what a shame. Your poison will do nothing to me." Delus sneered. "I will dispose of you, you traitor. You can join your weak companion in death." Delus, disappointed in his prior lieutenant, exhaled as he awaited Kenji's attack. Just as the second he thought the boy would appear, he did not. Waiting there in the fog, he wondered where Kenji was. Delus's felt a shiver creep down his spine, then his head quickly darted to the right. He had been distracted from his biggest problem.

"No!" Delus shouted as he saw *him* flying through the haze with a blade in his hand. Lotus had taken that brief break to rest and recharge. He used Kenji's attack as a decoy, and jumped in to fight while the demon's thoughts were elsewhere.

Delus lifted an arm up to stop him, but Lotus cut right through it. Delus felt an immediate stinging from the pure blade of light as it cut a third of the way through his forearm. Lotus saw Delus's other arm swing back to punch him while he was airborne. Before his fist could land, he pointed the blade in its direction, stabbing through his knuckles.

The demon howled as Lotus pulled the blade out and dropped to the ground. As his feet connected with the debris, he pushed off of it to slash at Delus's ankle.

"You weakling!" Delus shouted, punching the ground with both hands. The fog dissipated and his vision was cleared.

"Where are you…" He growled as he glanced from left to right.

"Right here!" Lotus shouted back. Delus turned around and saw him standing there, blade returned to its saya.

"Let's go! You and me!" Lotus called out, as he held up his fists and the bright aura around him grew.

Delus hated this sight, it was just like before. "Damn you, Din. You took this power from me. Now it's about time I—"

Lotus charged in full force, swinging his fists at the demon. Back and forth they went again, every strike hitting harder than the last. The others watched from afar, feeling the pressure of winds created by the opposing energies pushing against them.

I have to keep going!

Over and over he swung his leg and slammed it against Delus's body. Every now and then he created a barrier of light to block the demon's attacks.

I'm going to stop him!

His last bit of adrenaline kicked him into high gear and he generated the most light energy he ever had. His speed was unmatched as he teleported around the room, striking Delus when he couldn't even be seen.

I can do this, Din!

He had the advantage and was hitting his targets each time and with greater power every time. Everyone there watched and shouted out Lotus's name, telling him to end this, to finish it now.

This is it!

Lotus saw it. Delus had dropped to one knee and wasn't even watching him. Standing right in front of him, Lotus pulled back his fist, ready for the final blow.

Digging his feet into the dirt, as his fist cocked backward, the dark veins in his arm faded completely away. The scars on his arms which were always tainted with the dark energy, were totally gone. Fireflies of light began to spawn around him, glowing as bright as the sun. The energy around him shimmered brightly, and he felt the warmth inside of him comfort his mind.

There it was. His fist shot forward and his vision went white. He heard a ringing in his ears. Lotus's body went numb and it felt like he was taken from his physical form.

Suddenly, he became aware of his feet, then his hands and back. His heavy eyelids opened up to see a familiar ceiling above his head.

"What... ?" He rubbed his eyes and felt blankets on top of his body. Blinking a few times to adjust his vision, he realized, "I'm in my room!?"

Lotus shot up out of the bed and looked around frantically. He touched the bed, the window, and every part of the room to make sure it was all real. Then he quickly ran to the mirror to see... "It's not there..." The scar on his face wasn't there, and he was a kid again.

"What is going on?" Lotus wondered as he backed away slowly. He opened the door and slowly made his way down the hall. He turned the corner and then headed downstairs, treading carefully. The young boy felt his bare feet touching the wood floor, which creaked with every step he took. The sight of the dojo was too good to be true.

"It's just like how I remember it." Lotus smiled. The young boy was walking around the living area when he heard whistling coming from the back garden. His head darted in that direction and saw that the doors to the garden were cracked open.

"No..." He ran for the doors and forcefully pushed them open. Bright light blinded his eyes as the blazing sun beat against him.

"Ah, it looks like you're finally awake," spoke a voice from outside.

"Din!" Lotus shouted as he ran over to his beloved master and wrapped his arms around him.

"Whoa, whoa, what's wrong? Are you alright, son?" he asked kindly.

"I'm okay. I just had a really bad dream." Lotus told him, happy now in the embrace of his master.

30

The Dark Empire

A huge, terrible nightmare. Every part of it had to have been. Everything that had happened was just one big, horrible dream. It couldn't have been real. It can't be real. It can't be...

"It can't be real..." Oa mumbled, as he stared at Lotus, who stood there frozen in place with Delus's hand against his cheek.

"Lotus..." Oa's lips trembled in fear. He watched as a thin plume of sinuous dark smoke leaked from his palm, then rested on the wanted man's face.

Delus's panting slowly turned into uncontrollable laughter. The cackling of their doom echoed around them. There they all stood, feet glued to the ground, hoping that this was all just a bad dream. That's all it was. A nightmare. Soon they would all wake up and be back in their beds in Mellowtin, right?

"I warned you about this, boy! This is what happens to the weak when they think they can stand up to someone of real power. They crumble! You and all your other friends will spend your last day in this hell. Your master was weak! I proved it to the whole world, and now, it's your turn." Delus slowly stood up, the trails of murky smoke still hovering around Lotus's face.

"What did you do?!" Thalrok shouted.

Delus just laughed wickedly. "I put him in his worst nightmare. The day he lost it all replays in his head as we speak. Except this time, *I* control the story." He snickered again.

"His worst nightmare?" Thalrok now realized exactly what Delus had done. He glanced over and saw Lotus's motionless body.

"His arms... " Thalrok saw the blackened veins creeping back up his arms like vines up a tree.

"Oh no... Not again." The titan knew what was about to happen. His skin crawled, heart pounded, and beads of sweat appeared on his forehead.

"Everyone, run! *Now!*" he shouted as he ran toward Rina. The others had no idea what was happening. They were sure that they'd have no chance of escaping and would be destroyed on the spot.

"We need to get out—right now!" Thalrok shouted, as he picked up Rina and ran as far as he could from Lotus and Delus. Oa and Nyloc hustled to Thalrok's side without question.

"You too, let's *go!*" Thalrok yelled at Kenji. Even though they were enemies, Thalrok was trying to warn him. Kenji, having no clue as to what was happening, saw the frantic look on Thalrok's face and ran off in a different direction.

"Trying to escape, are you? It doesn't matter how far you go. I will..." Delus stopped talking. He felt strangely uneasy, a malignancy tainted the air. He turned back to Lotus and saw that he was still standing there, frozen in place. Except there were coal black veins on his arms that stretched to his shoulders and up his neck. Lotus's arms began to tremble, black lightning shooting out aggressively as seconds ticked by.

"What is this?" Delus, concerned, wanted a closer look. He knew that now playing inside Lotus's mind was the day he lost his master, but this time, things were a little different. Lotus couldn't jump off the cliffside to escape, and had to fight against his friends and family. All of Petalbrooke and the people in it were destroyed, burned into a fiery inferno as they all shouted at him, calling him a monster, a murderer. It truly was his worst nightmare.

"He can't break out of this. It's impossible." Delus murmured, as he reached out to make sure that his mental trap remained in place. His hand was inches from the wanted man's face when Lotus's black-veined hand grabbed onto his. Delus, startled from the sudden movement, yanked his hand out of Lotus's grip.

Then, the dark smoke in front of Lotus's face disappeared, and an explosion of dark energy burst out from the wanted man's chest. Delus was sent flying backward from the amount of sheer power, and Lotus fell to his knees, grabbing at his head. The whole of the coliseum had become like the heart of a storm. Wind was forced in all directions, thunder rolled, and lightning flashed as it shot from Lotus's body. His wretched screams of pain could be heard over everything else. He was being forced to witness the worst moment of his life on replay in his mind, this time with an even more horrific outcome.

"Where did this power come from?!" Delus shouted, as he watched the young man shriek in anguish.

Lotus could not control the energy inside of him. The dark power permeated his entire being, surged and then overflowed like a monster, and he could not stop it. He held his head with both hands as the pain inside of him took control of his body. Lotus's screams and wails continued as everyone watched from a distance. Tears flowed down his face as the pain wouldn't go away. The vision of Petalbrooke burning to the ground, its people slaughtered, was scarring. He wanted it to stop. He wanted the pain to go away. He wanted...

"Ronin!" Thalrok shouted, as he grabbed onto his friend. The bounty hunter had managed to fight his way through the wind, bolts of lightning, and pulsing energy to reach his friend's side. Each time this had happened to Lotus before, Thalrok would try to calm him down, but not this time.

"Ronin, look!" Thalrok grabbed Lotus's hands and pulled them off his head. Lifting Lotus's head, Thalrok tilted it in Delus's direction, yelling, "It wasn't your fault this happened! It's his! He did this, Ronin! *He* did it!"

Though in a frenzy of torment, Lotus heard Thalrok's words very clearly. His suffering, miserable expression turned angry and menacing. He gritted his teeth and charged headfirst at the man who caused him such unbearable pain.

"DELUS!!" Lotus bellowed, as he flew over and struck Delus across the face. The dark energy inside fueled him like an unstoppable train.

Delus felt that this punch struck differently than the others had. This one hurt. Still, he shouted out, "You weakling!" and readied to swing his own fists. But, before Delus could move another inch, Lotus grabbed his arm and effortlessly tossed him across the room. As Delus's body went flying, Lotus leapt after him. In mid-flight, the Infected leader turned and positioned himself towards the rampaging Lotus, watching him close in.

"You think your power is greater than mine?! Come at me!" Delus taunted. He heard Lotus's cries of anger getting closer and focused on the wanted man's enraged face.

"Head's up!" Thalrok shouted from above.

Delus glanced over his shoulder and saw the titan just above him.

How did he get there? Delus panicked.

The bounty hunter whacked the demon on top of the head hard enough to shove him right towards the ground. As he crashed through the floor, even Delus's bones rattled from the power behind Thalrok's swing.

Feeling a raging anger inside, he shot back onto his feet and screamed out in disgust,

"I've had enough of this!" Demonic energy flooded the body of the leader of the Infected Ones, and soon began to burst. He glared ahead at Lotus running at him.

"I am tired of these weaklings getting in my way. Such pathetic humans will *not* destroy the Dark Empire!" Delus clenched his fists and went toe-to-toe with Lotus.

They battled each other once more, now darkness to darkness. Each strike cracked the rubble below their feet. They had no means or desire to stop. The two of them dashed and hurtled around the room, throwing each other into the walls with punches and kicks. Anyone watching could barely keep up; they were almost too fast to be seen with the naked eye.

"DELUS!!" Lotus shouted as he swung his leg at the beast's ribs.

"*You* will suffer another *nightmare!*" Delus howled, reaching out to grab the wanted man's face. As his hand was inches away, a mighty gust of wind pushed it off course.

"That pest!" Delus growled, as he noticed Oa beside them in the corner of his eye.

"Get him Lotus!" The young disciple got out of the way as Lotus's kick struck hard against Delus's ribs. Delus cringed as he felt that leg connect, but was back on the offense in a split second.

They struck one another with everything they had. One fought to prove his power and superiority, the other to protect his friends and avenge the man he trusted most.

"It's only a matter of time before your luck runs out, boy!" Delus smirked as he struck Lotus across the face. His fist landed a direct hit, and Lotus's head began to turn to the side as he pushed through. But then, Delus felt his fist being slowly forced back. His eyes locked onto Lotus, whose face seemed to be repelling his fist.

"This guy..." Delus huffed, as he saw the true power inside of Lotus steaming out of his entire body.

Lotus pushed his hand out of the way and charged right back in. There was no end to it. Regardless of how many times they hit each other, neither would show any signs of slowing down. Delus had to finish this now before...

"You know, boy. Your master was a fool. He let me live because he was weak! He didn't know anything about strength. That's why your pathetic master is dead!" Delus said scornfully.

Time came to a stop.

The last word Delus spoke repeated over and over in Lotus's head. His mind couldn't concentrate on anything else at that moment. His anger was pushed to its very limit. Nothing could stop him from the outburst that was about to come.

Lotus shouted out at the top of his lungs. His power increased even more. The earth split beneath his feet, and black lightning shot out of his body.

"This is it." Delus smiled as he readied to finish this boy off here and now. He lowered his stance and held his palms close together. Charged with as much dark energy as he possibly could, a ball of it appeared between his hands. He drew his palms apart, then lifted his arms above his head and watched the sphere grow and grow. Delus smiled at the sight of it, watching as its majestic power increased. He lowered his head and stared at Lotus. "Do you think you can stop me now!?" Delus sneered.

Just after he finished his sentence, Delus felt a painful thump at his left eye. Surprised, he dropped one of his arms and grabbed at it, feeling an arrow jabbed into it. He calmly yanked the arrow out. Nyloc was off in the distance, watching him with a smirk.

"Pathetic," he grumbled, then realized that his sphere of dark energy was shrinking. He repositioned his arm and glared at Lotus with one good eye and the remains of the other to find him glaring right back.

"Delus, you took everything from me; you caused so many people great pain, and I will *never* forgive you for that." Lotus panted, ready to launch himself forward.

"Those people were weak, just like your master! Those who are strong survive, and those who are weak die in the process! I am doing this world a favor by creating one where only the strong remain standing!" Delus retorted. It didn't matter what Delus said at this point, anything he said now would only make Lotus even angrier.

"Deluuus!" Lotus shouted one last time and launched himself towards the demon. At the same time, the Infected leader lowered the ball of pure dark energy, held it out in Lotus's direction, and fired it at the wanted man. Delus grinned, excited to see him die by his very hands, when…

Suddenly, a familiar maroon cloud of smoke totally obscured Delus's vision. Kenji, dropping in from out of nowhere, had struck again. "I hate you! You will know my pain!" he shouted.

"That little trick is useless to me now." Delus swatted the dense smoke away in annoyance, eagerly anticipating the sight of that pathetic wanted man's death. As his arm pushed the last of it away, there he was, but… Delus's heart sank deep into his chest. He wouldn't have expected *this* sight in a million years. There in front of him stood Lotus, and nestled in his hand was the energy that he himself had created.

"Unbelievable... " Delus whispered, as the mighty hand of revenge, fueled by his own power, struck him right in the face. The ball of energy exploded on impact.

Everyone ducked and tried to shield themselves as the underground trembled and rattled all around them. The entire place erupted as if many more explosives had gone off. Their ears were ringing and their eyes were blinded by the dazzling bright light.

Finally, as the shockwave came to a slow rolling end, rocks and rubble fell to the ground. No one could see anything, and when the dust finally settled the four companions were afraid of what they *would* see when they looked back. Slowly, they turned around.

And there he was. Lotus stood over Delus as he lay limply on the ground. The wanted man's gaze was intense as Delus remained motionless. Now back in familiar human form, the older man wheezed and gasped for breath as he stared back at Lotus.

Delus, through his ragged breathing, began to laugh. "This brings me back. This is exactly how it was all those years ago with your... weak... master."

"This time is different. You're not getting away." Lotus sternly replied.

"Oh, but that's where you're wrong. I knew your master; you won't kill me." Delus's arrogance remained intact.

Lotus closed his eyes, took in a deep breath and then exhaled slowly. He tilted his head, and with the barest hint of a wry smile said, "You're right, I won't kill you... But *he* will." Lotus's expression turned serious.

Delus turned his head to the right. With one swift strike, Thalrok's blade dropped onto his neck, severing it instantly.

Lotus looked up and saw the bounty hunter holding his mighty sword in one hand, the blade embedded in the neck of Delus, once-leader of the Infected Ones.

It was all over.

Not a word was spoken.

What was to be a moment of victory was overshadowed by thoughts of the dire consequences that would have happened had Delus triumphed.

Lotus stood there, his body completely drained of energy, staring at the blackened veins that now reached his neck.

"Lotus!" Rina and Oa cried, and "Captain!" Nyloc shouted, as the three of them ran to his side. Oa jumped up on Lotus's back and hugged him, overjoyed that Lotus was alive and seemed to be back to normal.

"Thank goodness you guys are alright! Rina, are you still hurt?" Lotus asked.

"No, no—the one with the smoke, uh, kind of a smoky breath, helped me somehow. He had some special balm and put it on my wounds," she replied.

"Smoky breath? Is she talking about...?" Thalrok questioned, as he glanced around.

Where did he go? Lotus wondered, as he'd hoped to thank Kenji for his help. It must have been hard for him to betray his master like that. Lotus was just happy they'd all made it out alive.

He stared down at the fallen leader of the Infected Ones. Delus remained there, motionless and gray, his head separated from his neck, an unholy sight to see. He'd had no chance to disappear into ashes, as his life had been so abruptly taken from him. No matter how this ended though, nothing could rewrite the past.

"Come on, we have to get out of here. We aren't safe just yet." Lotus said, as he began to head for the nearest way out. The others quickly followed behind him.

Thalrok was holding up the rear, but noticed that Oa had fallen behind. "Oa, let's go," he urged, but the young disciple stayed there where he'd stopped, staring at Delus's lifeless body.

"He said that 'The time for the Dark Empire to bring the rebirth of this world is near.' What do you think he meant by that?" Oa asked, slightly concerned.

Thalrok walked back to his side and placed his big hand on Oa's shoulder. "It doesn't matter what it means. Whatever comes our way, we will stop it. No matter what." Thalrok spoke in all seriousness. Then they quickly evacuated this underworld battleground before anyone else could arrive.

Delus, leader of the Infected Ones—the man who had led legions of troops, and who, under the shadows of the world, had ravaged countless villages and towns, enslaving, torturing, and killing the inhabitants. This man, who was the cause of Din's death, was no more.

Even though they'd all managed to come out alive, they were not unscathed. This battle had shown them just how powerful some people are in this world.

As Lotus and his companions made their way back to Mellowtin, he asked himself.

Who is this new master Delus spoke of?

31

It's not our fight

Today, the sun seemed to kiss the tops of the trees with an extra radiance, as if the world itself was awakening to something new. A calming breeze swept away all things gloomy, and the people of Mellowtin filled the streets. Men, women, and children all went about their day, enjoying each other's company with the soft hum of chatter heard everywhere. Seen from above, the village seemed so peaceful. This day could bring forth only good cheer and happiness; no worry, no fear could possibly be anywhere to be found. Right?

"There you are." Oa found Lotus sitting in the rooftop lounge area of The Lie-Inn. Stritan followed along behind the young disciple.

"Afternoon, you two." Lotus waved as he stood up from his seat.

"Are you alright? You seem a lot quieter lately. You should be happy!" Oa grinned brightly as he gently shoved Lotus's shoulder.

The young disciple was right; he should feel happy, but something kept eating at his mind. "It's fine. I've just been thinking, that's all." Lotus replied, "Why don't you two head down, and we can continue where we left off yesterday."

"Right!" The boys took the stairs down two at a time, eager to start today's training. Lotus stayed behind for just a moment.

About a month had passed since they'd invaded the underworld and managed to survive. Even though they won in the end, it was still a terrifying thing to remember. But something just didn't feel right. Even though they had taken down Delus, that powerful demonic leader, nothing would change what had already transpired.

Lotus looked down at his arms and saw the veins still blackened from his outburst. *The Dark Empire. What did he mean by that?* Exhaling deeply, he finally went on his way, heading downstairs to go train with Oa and Stritan.

Since their time back in Mellowtin, all five of them had begun to fall into a routine. Lotus trained with Oa daily, and Stritan was happy to be included. Thalrok had been visiting his hometown of Harthfield recently to check in on how those folks were doing. Nyloc took this time to meditate, train, and from time to time chat with Lotus late into the night. As for Rina, she volunteered at the local care center in Mellowtin, healing those who were sick. Rina became the talk of the town. She was the first angel to visit the lands below in, well, no one could even remember how long or if ever, and everyone was in awe of her beautiful white wings.

Each of the companions was just happy to be alive after escaping that hellhole at Cannon-Gulf. No one had heard any news of that kind of commotion happening anywhere since. None of them understood how the Infected One's activities hadn't been noticed by the people of Cannon-Gulf back in those days, but then again, that was a dodgy and dangerous place anyway.

So, a time of peace was upon them, knowing they had prevented a future where a corrupt man destroyed others' lives. They all believed that, except for Lotus and Thalrok, who couldn't stop thinking about what Delus had said.

* * *

"I think that'll be enough for today." Lotus panted as they came to a heavy stop. They had just finished sprinting around the town, which ended their training for today.

"Thank... goodness." Oa gasped, falling onto the ground.

"Everything hurts… so much." Stritan dropped to his knees and stared up at the sky. Even Lotus rested his hands on his hips, huffing and puffing from the exertion. "If you two want to get stronger, combat training alone won't be enough. You have to break down the body and rebuild it to grow stronger. Endurance, strength, and stamina are all important parts of an excellent warrior." Lotus told them, panting as he took a seat.

They rested now and allowed their breathing to return to normal, having finished today's workout. Both of the boys had grown a lot stronger in these last few weeks. It had been some time since Stritan had trained with Lotus, but Lotus could tell that he had been working out on his own while he was gone.

"Looks like you guys could use a drink." Nyloc chuckled, heading toward them with a water pitcher and some cups.

"Oh, thank goodness!" "My hero!" the boys gasped, as they crawled over to him. They each grabbed a cup, chugged every last drop of water in it, then smacked their lips and sighed loudly in satisfaction. Lotus could only stand and watch, shaking his head as he chuckled at their exaggerated behavior.

"How are you feeling?" Rina asked, as she glided over to join them.

"We are definitely tired, but we're all feeling better. How about you?" Lotus asked.

"I'm feeling alright. The marks on my back are still there, but I don't have any pain." Rina turned around and moved her wings to show them the scars down the middle of her back.

"Glad to hear." Lotus sighed and took another deep breath to relax.

Nyloc came over with a cup of water and handed it to Lotus. The five of them sat down in the grass together, taking a break. The day was still in full bloom. The two boys finally caught their breath and could speak whole sentences again. Lotus just sat and listened as they all talked to one another. Even though he didn't join the conversation, it was nice to be a part of this. It gave him a familiar feeling—the same feeling of sitting underneath that tree in Petalbrooke with all of his friends after a long day of training.

He gazed out at the Lands of Prosper and saw the grasses blowing in the breeze. As he stared off, he noticed a large figure approaching.

"Thalrok?" He tilted his head. Everyone looked in the same direction. There he was.

"Hey! Thalrok's back!" Stritan shouted, as everyone stood up and waved. The boys ran out to meet him and welcome him back.

Lotus was glad to see him returning, and still in one piece. It had been several days since he'd departed for Harthfield. He hoped Thalrok had accomplished everything he'd wanted.

"Welcome back, Thalrok." "How was your trip?" "Did you enjoy Harthfield?" The questions flew at him as soon as he was within earshot.

"Thank you. Yes, I did, in fact, enjoy it all. The townspeople were very kind to me, and I hope to visit them again." the bounty hunter replied.

Lotus joined the group and held out his fist, "Welcome back," he smiled.

Under his helmet, Thalrok smiled in return as he bumped knuckles with his friend. Then, sounding serious, he said, "Ronin, we need to talk." At that, the mood suddenly shifted, and everyone was puzzled as to why this happy return now felt so ominous.

"What's wrong?" Lotus asked.

"On my way back, I had a lot of time to think. I know it's been going through your mind, too." Thalrok began.

Lotus knew exactly what he was going to talk about, and he was right. He had known this time would come. But for some reason, after these last few and *very* pleasant weeks in Mellowtin, Lotus felt that maybe he could start living a normal life now, and he didn't really want to risk losing that.

"The Dark Empire." Thalrok continued. "Delus said those words many times when we were in that hellish underworld. I don't know what he was talking about, but it's time we find out. As far as I know, we are the only ones who know of this 'empire', and it's time we discuss how we're going to handle it. This has to be our responsibility, now that we know."

The air felt heavy, and everyone's eyes were on Lotus. The silence was deafening, and the wanted man couldn't seem to reply. He didn't know what to say, yet it seemed so clear. At last Lotus said carefully,

"We… can't…" His words were calm, but quite firm.

"What?!" Thalrok's tone shifted. It was still serious, but was now tinged with anger.

"We did what we needed to do. We went from village to village, stopping their forces and taking down the man behind it all. Without Delus, their army will crumble slowly but surely. If any more show up, we can stop them. For now… this isn't our fight anymore." Lotus stated flatly.

Nyloc, Oa, Rina, and Stritan too, all stood there quietly, a cold, uncomfortable feeling began in their chests and rose up into their throats as they watched this argument unfold.

Thalrok was astounded. "Not our fight?! This is *absolutely* our fight! We were told of this 'empire' or whatever it is that will destroy the world, and *you* don't want to stop it?" Thalrok shouted and threw up his hands in anger. He took a step closer to Lotus.

Lotus stood still, trying not to make eye contact. "The City of Light can take care of this now," he said. "The Infected Ones moved in the shadows; their actions were hidden. If this 'empire' does become a problem, the Guardians will be able to handle it now. We don't stand a chance. We did all we could." Lotus took in a slow, deep breath, hoping his words would—

"Are you *kidding* me?!" Thalrok burst out. "You plan to just sit around and hope that the City of Light—ugh! Might I remind you that *you* will have done *nothing* about this looming threat at all—you will sit back and *pray* that the City of Light will know what to do if and when this comes! Ronin, *what* are you saying?" Thalrok took another step closer.

"Please, I know this is hard to handle… but we barely stood a chance in that underworld. None of us will come out alive if we fight someone stronger than Delus." Lotus's voice was almost pleading for understanding from his friend, while Thalrok was getting even more upset.

"Hey, why don't we—" Oa tried to interject.

"You stopped him with the power your master trusted you with. We just have to keep training, and surely we can do this!" Thalrok blurted out.

"It doesn't matter if I have this power or not. We got out on a fluke, and that won't happen again. No matter how strong we all get, I'm not sure that we'll have the same lucky outcome." Lotus insisted.

Everyone went silent. Lotus and Thalrok were just standing in the center of them all, arguing back and forth, with Thalrok becoming more heated by the second and Lotus trying hard to deflect.

"I'm sorry, but this *isn't* our fight." Lotus spun around and started to walk back into town.

Thalrok watched him in disbelief as Lotus turned his back on them. He clenched his fists, his anger overflowing. "Do you *really* think that this is what your master would want you to do?!"

Lotus stopped midstep the moment Thalrok finished *that* sentence. He slowly turned to face the titan, and now his forced composure was gone. "You have *no* idea what my master would want me to do." Lotus hissed.

"Whoa, whoa… everyone, just take a deep breath." Nyloc positioned himself between Thalrok and Lotus, holding his hands out to keep them separate for a moment. Thalrok immediately brushed him aside as he and Lotus stepped forward to face one another.

"I know that he wouldn't have watched as the whole world gets destroyed. I know that he wouldn't want his student to sit back and let others get hurt." Thalrok reasoned, poking at Lotus with his words, trying to make him understand that he was wrong.

"Thalrok, you have to realize I am doing this for *us*! I can't take the pain of anyone else getting hurt anymore!" Lotus shouted, his face turned up to glare at Thalrok's helmeted one.

Thalrok leaned down, their faces now only inches apart. "I *refuse* to sit back and let people *die* when I know I could have done something!" he spat back.

"Me neither, but this is no longer our fight," Lotus argued.

For a brief interval, everything went silent. Lotus and Thalrok stood glowering at one another. The others couldn't think of anything to say that would help. Thalrok's huge fists were balled up and he squeezed them ever tighter as he loomed over Lotus.

"You know... maybe Delus was right..." Thalrok spoke through clenched teeth. "You *are* weak," he hissed, then suddenly he punched Lotus square in the jaw.

Everyone gasped as they watched Lotus's head snap to the side. Lotus didn't even realize what had happened at first; the shock of it stunned him. Then a switch went off in his head. He snapped his head back and struck Thalrok hard in the chest. Nyloc, Oa, Rina, and Stritan immediately jumped in to pull them apart. "Calm down, you two!"; "Stop fighting!"; "Both of you, take a breath!" they shouted, struggling to separate them as Thalrok and Lotus continued trying to swing at each other. Once they finally managed to get them far enough apart, they tried to calm them down, but by this point, their words meant nothing.

"I respected you, Ronin! But this 'not our fight' business—that is something I *never* thought I'd hear from *you*!" Thalrok bellowed, shaking Nyloc and Stritan off of him.

"I'm doing this for everyone's safety! I care about your lives, Thalrok!" Lotus shouted, not in anger, but more from a place of suffering. He truly did not want to see his companions go through what they had, or worse, again.

"I'm *sick* of this!" Thalrok threw up his hands in frustration.

Both of them stormed off in different directions. Lotus strode angrily back toward Mellowtin to be alone. Thalrok stomped across the grass into a small wooded area just ahead. The others stood there like statues, watching them walk away from each other.

"What just happened?" Oa asked, astonished and not knowing what to do next.

"I... I don't know..." Rina responded, looking back and forth at them.

"It'll be alright. Why don't Oa and I follow Thalrok? Rina, you go see where Lotus is going. Stritan, I guess you might as well head back to the smithy. Somehow, we'll get this worked out." Nyloc assured them as he headed off to where the bounty hunter was pacing furiously among the trees.

"Make sure Lotus doesn't try to leave town, okay?" Oa asked Rina before he joined Nyloc.

"I'll do my best," she promised, and flew off toward Lotus, who was already at the edge of town.

"Please, just let me be," Lotus said moodily when he heard Rina drop softly down behind him.

"I'm sorry, but what you need right now is to talk this through. Keeping those feelings all bottled up inside of you isn't going to help." Rina told him.

Lotus didn't stop walking; he marched on, following some aimless meandering path through town. It didn't matter which direction he was going; he was really just trying to escape this intense anger that he didn't want to feel.

"Hey, why don't we just grab some food? I might help get your mind off things. What do you say? You were training pretty hard, after all." Rina suggested, hoping this would get through to him.

Hearing that, Lotus finally stopped. She was right. Walking all over the place wouldn't solve anything. He did have to let these thoughts and feelings out.

"You're right, Rina, I'm sorry. Let's grab something to eat." Lotus apologized, and they headed for the nearest eatery.

When they found some seats, Lotus let out an exhausted sigh and dropped into his chair.

"Go ahead. Talk. I'm all ears." Rina sat with her back straight, wings relaxed and ready to actively listen.

"I... I don't understand why he can't see things my way. You were there. You saw what we all had to go through, what we had to fight against. We barely got out alive. If there really were any other threats out there, I'm not sure we'd be able to stop them like we did before." Lotus sat up and placed his head in his hands.

"You're just looking after what's best for us, right?" Rina reflected.

"Exactly. I know we went through this before, but now things are different. We could all get seriously hurt, or even worse! I just think we should trust the City of Light with this one." Lotus exhaled.

The waitress finally came over, took their order, and returned with some water moments later.

Lotus felt a burning in the back of his head. It was probably related to the feeling that he had said the wrong things to Thalrok. Thalrok, who had been with him from the very start of this mess and stuck with him the whole time. Thalrok was the perfect right-hand man for him, but now he may have ruined that for himself.

"Rina, I don't know what's going to happen to me. I know in due time, my curse will show its face again. That's just how it goes. Is it selfish to say that I just want to enjoy this time? I only have a *little* more time before word gets out from travelers that I'm here. Then all hell will break loose again. If this threat really *is* something to worry about, I know for a fact that the City of Light and the Guardians are ready." Lotus looked up from the table and noticed the look on Rina's face. She looked totally shocked.

"What's wrong?" he asked. She was staring past and right behind him. She opened her mouth to speak, but before she could say a word, she was interrupted.

"But they *aren't* ready," a mysterious male voice broke into their conversation. Lotus had no idea who was sitting behind him. He began to turn around, but the voice instructed him not to move.

"You're talking about the Dark Empire, right?" the voice inquired.

It was then that Lotus realized who was behind him. It had taken a moment, but this voice was indeed familiar. "Yeah… yes. What do you know?" he asked, looking straight ahead at Rina.

"I don't know much about it. All I have heard is that there is a castle deep within the forbidden world that holds some kind of 'key' to the future," said Kenji, the former right hand of the leader of the Infected Ones and a traitor to his former master. He sat at the table behind them, observing the back of Lotus's head.

"A castle in the forbidden world?" Lotus was puzzled.

"All I can remember was the old man talking about how he stumbled upon it many years ago. He said that it was there where he was shown the potential that the future can hold, the 'grand future' that the Dark Empire will bring." Kenji answered.

Lotus rubbed his chin, wondering what castle, and what key, Delus could have found in the forbidden world. Whatever it was, that was the source of it all. Here was a start, at least. He replied, "Th-thank you. That helps a lot. I also need to thank you for... you know—"

"No need." Kenji interrupted. "If anything, I should be thanking you. For once, I finally feel in control of my life. I still have many questions, but for now, I'm just trying to survive." Kenji sighed with relief. He was finally able to get that off of his chest.

"I hope you get all the answers you seek," Lotus told him. He was grateful to hear Kenji's voice. It was the same man behind that voice, and yet, he sounded very different from their first meeting.

"And by the way," Kenji continued, "You don't have to worry about me or any more of the Infected Ones. A group of them and I have taken refuge in an abandoned town, which we are slowly rebuilding. Some of us will go to any villages still under the Infected Ones' control and tell them to fall back, their master is gone. If they refuse to side with us, they will be put down, as are any others who we find still trying to keep that monster's legacy alive. You have my word that I will take care of any other mess that Delus brought to Perlaria." Kenji spoke earnestly. At last, his life had become his own.

Lotus was honestly happy to hear this. Kenji had played a big part in their last battle, and knowing that he was doing good work for this world brought a warm feeling to his heart. He hoped to see him again. The sound of a chair shuffling across the floor registered in Lotus's ear. He turned around to stop Kenji, but he was already gone.

"That's incredible," Rina said, still surprised.

"I know. I can't believe he is putting in that much effort to undo what his master had done." Lotus said appreciatively.

"No, no, not that. It's incredible how much better he looks. His eyes don't seem to be filled with fear and hate anymore. He looked... at peace." Rina commented.

Lotus and Rina finished their meal, paid, and prepared to leave. Lotus had been able to spill out his emotions as he scarfed down his food. Rina only sat and listened the whole time, letting the young man vent. Lotus wasn't the type to ramble on and on, talking for no good reason. That much was obvious after their time spent together. So, this had been a much-needed session.

"Thank you again, Rina. You did help a lot. Now I just need some alone time." Lotus said, then held the door open to let her through.

"I'm always here to help. I'm so glad that you were able to express yourself and let out this negativity. Also on the plus side, we heard from Kenji and were able to thank him for what he did." Rina reminded him with a joyful grin.

"You're right. I just hope that's all the surprise visits we get today." Lotus said, then he closed the door behind him as she exited. When he turned back around to follow Rina, he bumped right into her wings.

"Oh! Sorry, Rina, I—" He froze. She was facing away from him, standing stock still and silent. Lotus, too, was now left without words; he had just jinxed himself.

"Lady Rina Ellerath, you have been summoned back to Nimbusara per Lord Vortigon's request. You have broken the sacred law of the Kingdom of Angels and are under restraint, effective immediately. You and your accompanying land dweller are to come peacefully. Now," the tall male angel demanded. The four other foot soldiers with him held the points of their spears inches from their faces.

"Oh no..." Rina mumbled.

32

The Watcher

The wind howled as the ground below shrank in the distance. Rina, hands tied together in front of her, sulked. She glanced over at Lotus, who was also effectively restrained. Before they could even think of what to do or say, their wrists had been bound and they were soaring miles up into the sky. Lotus was tied up in this mess, too; the angels had seen him speaking with Rina and, of course, came to the conclusion that he must be a part of her offense.

With an angel firmly gripping each of his upper arms, Lotus instinctively shielded his face by dropping his head to his chest as they shot up headfirst into some dense cloud cover. The world around him vanished into a churning sea of white, the wind howled in his ears as they rocketed up through the vaporous bog. The air was thick and damp, and moisture clung to his skin and clothes like a second layer. Flashes of light and shadow flickered within the clouds, as if they were flying through a living storm.

Then, just as suddenly as it had swallowed them, the fog began to thin. The oppressive whiteness peeled away, revealing the breathtaking expanse beyond.

Before him stretched the sky islands of Nimbusara, the legendary Kingdom of Angels in the heavens. Enormous landmasses floated effortlessly among golden shafts of sunlight, suspended in the sky like ancient jewels. Waterfalls spilled from their edges into the misty abyss below, vanishing into nothingness. Towering spires of crystal and gold rose up from the islands, their tips glinting in the light of the sun. Bridges of light and clouds connected the islands in impossible arcs, and winged figures glided gracefully between them, their feathers catching the sunlight like fire.

Lotus could only gape in awe as the angels descended, carrying him into a realm that felt like a dream painted across the sky.

"…Unbelievable," he muttered, as he was finally setting eyes on the one mythic region of Perlaria that he'd never thought he would see. Radiant white and gold gleamed from every inch of this city. The unique architecture was breathtaking. The wanted man had never expected to be a part of *this* mysterious world.

"Lotus, I'm so sorry you have to—" Rina started to say.

"Enough! Silence, both of you! " one of the guards demanded as he planted his feet onto the grounded plateau.

They all gently landed on their feet, then began traveling over the giant chunks of land via the curved pathways that led from one to another. Each angel who passed by on fluttering wings above their heads gave them a passing glance and then let out a gentle gasp, as they saw that their lost angel was being brought back to the palace, accompanied by some bare-backed land dweller.

What are we gonna do? Rina panicked, feeling her decisions coming back to bite her. She had known leaving her home could result in a dilemma like this. Now, she'd gotten Lotus into it, too.

What is he thinking right now? She wondered, glancing backward. She could see him showing no fear or worry as their eyes met. Lotus appeared calm, and even curious. His eyes couldn't stop bouncing from one part of this city to the next.

Are you not even worried about what's going on?! She cried out in her mind, becoming even more uneasy.

"Eyes forward," the guard escorting her commanded, and then said under his breath, "He isn't happy, you know. It has been hell up here because of your childish decision."

Rina could feel guilt weighing heavily on her shoulders as she saw the palace up ahead.

Now before their eyes floated the biggest island of earth in the sky; it stretched for miles across the heavens, with lush trees growing throughout. Long vines crept down over the thick crust-like edges, while the grass growing there was a deeper shade of green than below. A long white-bricked bridge in front of them stretched down and over the long gap between the two islands.

Lotus peered down and could see the faintest image of Perlaria painted in pastels far below him. He had never been up this high before, and under normal circumstances, he would have greatly enjoyed this view.

At the heart of the island stood a castle adorned entirely in gold. It resembled a scene from a fantasy tale. Lotus struggled to keep his mouth closed as he walked past the initial battlements. Walking down a meticulously crafted covered walkway, he caught a glimpse of brightness up ahead. Soon they swerved down a grand corridor which lead toward it.

"We're here," stated the tallest guard, halting them at the entrance to an enormous round room that towered skyward high into the air. Soaring open windows framed in shimmering gold stretched nearly entirely up the walls, which were decorated with beautiful pearl white and gold detailing intertwined with lush greenery. At the far end stood a window far wider than the others, and with even more ornate gold framing. As a whole, the lofty, tunnel-like room resembled a fenestrated telescope aimed up at the stars. Sunlight flowed through easily, fully illuminating the space.

"Into the center of the room, you two," a deep voice from behind them said brusquely, and they were shoved forward, stumbling. Side by side, they regained their composure and walked slowly to the center of the room.

"Lotus, do you know what's going on?" Rina whispered.

"Not really. I can tell this isn't good, obviously. What's going to happen?" he replied, still looking around. He noticed that outside of the dozens of windows in this room, many angels hovered and watched from above. There had to be a hundred of them. "It'll be alright though, don't worry." Lotus tried to be more reassuring than he felt.

"I don't know…" Rina spoke through her teeth, afraid of what he didn't know.

The chatter of the others watching bounced off the pearly walls as the tension built. Lotus, inspecting the room carefully, noticed everyone beginning to look at the giant window in front of them. He turned his own gaze to the front and saw angels in full armor gliding through it in pairs. Two, four, six, eight, ten of them all flew in and stood side by side, a short distance apart. Between the two lines of five was the throne before them, still empty.

"He's not gonna be happy." Rina shivered as she closed her eyes.

The guards slammed the butt end of their spears to the floor in unison eight times and chanted, "Kneel before the King of Nimbusara, Lord Vortigon!"

Everyone watching immediately fell to their knees. Rina, without question, hit her knees faster than a drop of rain falling from the clouds. "Get down!" she hissed, dragging Lotus down with her.

With their heads glued to the floor Lotus couldn't see a thing, but he had to take a peek. He glanced up at the throne ahead and saw an old man, an angel. His wings were decorated with golden feathers. The white sleeveless robe-like tunic that he wore was finely made, regal, and had elegant golden ornamentation. His white beard was neatly carved around his face, and his piercing blue eyes glistened more than any gold. He looked to be older, but from the look of his cannon-sized arms, his peak power was far from gone.

In a deep resonant voice, the king said, "Rise."

Everyone returned to their feet. Lord Vortigon, the King of Nimbusara, studied the mismatched pair standing before him, glancing back and forth from one to the other. The throne room was silent, the weight of the king's anger palpable. He stood tall, his regal presence filling all corners of the room as he stared at the two figures before him.

The king's voice, rich with authority and centuries of power, echoed from the white stone walls of the great room as he said, "So... it has come to this, then. You stand before me, having committed a crime that cannot be excused—a betrayal that cannot be overlooked." He stared directly at Rina, eyes slightly narrowed and intensely focused.

"You..." he paused, his gaze darkening, "You, of all people. Flesh of my flesh, blood of my blood. How *could* you do this?" He clenched his fists, but his voice remained steady and controlled, though anger still burned beneath it.

"How could you leave the protection of this realm? The laws of this kingdom, the laws of this land, have stood for centuries. For generations, they have been upheld, sacred and unbroken. And now, here you are. After all these years, after all of the warnings, you—" He gestured vaguely toward her, his voice rising. "*You* decide to fly beyond the veil. To leave the safety of what has kept us all from the horrors of the world outside."

The king stepped forward, glowering, his tone turning more demanding, insistent. "What possessed you? Was it some foolish curiosity? Did you think the world beyond the clouds was better than what we have built here? Did you not listen? Did you not learn from the stories of the elders about the dangers that lie just below our world, where the trees grow thin, and the shadows stretch longer?" He paused again, taking a deep breath as he calmed himself, though his eyes blazed furiously.

"You, of all people, should have known better. That rule is not just a rule; it's a safeguard. It is the reason we still breathe, the reason our lives have remained peaceful, protected, and uninterrupted by the madness of the outside world. Now I am forced to ask myself... what *else* did you leave behind? What else have you forgotten?"

The king turned sharply to the stranger now, his voice suddenly colder, sharp as a dagger's edge. "And you. Who are you to manipulate this child, this wayward soul, and tempt her away from my kingdom? What madness possessed you to walk with her? What were your intentions?" He stepped closer to the stranger, his imposing figure towering over Lotus as he spoke.

"Please, I—" Lotus tried to speak.

"Do you understand the danger you have brought upon yourself? Upon her? Upon *all* of us!?" The king's eyes flickered back toward Rina. "There are ways... There are consequences for what you've done..." He faltered, his voice growing low, almost pained, "But that's the crux of it, isn't it? It's not just the crime. It's not just the rule you broke. It's... It's the trust." He inhaled sharply, his expression softening momentarily, though his eyes remained stern. "To think I would be standing before my own *granddaughter*, seeing her break such deep trust before my eyes. The fruit of my bloodline. How... *could* you?" His voice caught for a moment.

Lotus's head turned ever so slowly, with his mouth slightly opened and eyes wider than the window before them

What did he just say...?

He looked over at Rina and saw the "Maybe I should have mentioned something..." face she was wearing.

You have got to be kidding me.

"Was it worth it? The king continued. "Was the world below really worth the price of your safety, your very place among us? Have we done nothing to make you feel whole here?"

He turned away from his granddaughter, pacing slowly, his voice lowering as he spoke more to himself than to the others. "Hundreds of years of peace, of security, built on wisdom and the bones of sacrifice. And for what? To have it undone in a single, foolish decision?"

The king stopped, his back to them, his voice cold and distant. "I wonder if you think this was an accident—that you didn't know the weight of what you were doing, but you must have known. You *had* to have known." At last, he turned back to face them both, his face unreadable.

"Tell me, what did you see beyond the clouds? What could possibly be more enticing than the peace we've fought so hard to maintain? What was it that pulled you from your path? Was it the call of the unknown? Or something more..."

The king eyed her once more, his tone softening just a touch, though still stern. "You were warned, child. We have *all* been warned. But in the end, we must face the consequences of our choices. And you..." His gaze flickered over her again, his words almost a whisper. "...will face them with me. Together. So long as you remain in this kingdom, your fate is mine to decide."

He turned to the stranger once more, the icy calm returning. "And *you*, whoever you are, will answer for your part in this too. I do not take kindly to those who walk into my land, whether with good intentions or bad." A long, cold pause followed. Lord Vortigon, King of Numbusara, looked at Lotus, sizing him up with narrowed eyes.

"M-my name is Lotus," the young man began to explain, "and I was the one looking after your granddaughter while she was down on the surface. I can assure you that she was safe and—"

"Safe?" the king interrupted, and scoffed. His face soured with displeasure. "Can you not see the scars on her back from whatever trials and horrors she withstood down there? To my eyes, they do not seem like the result of a happy venture."

The scars on Rina's back from the battle with the Infected Ones were in plain sight, there in the middle of her back.

"Please, grandfather. It was my own childish choice to leave the skies. I had no place to attempt something so foolish." Rina stepped forward, trying to reason with the king.

"More lies I see..." The king lowered his head and slowly shook it with disapproval. "After you went missing, it was later discovered that you'd been seen with a land dweller here in our domain. Someone had spotted you and this man leaving the skies together," he said, raising his head to see his granddaughter's reaction.

Rina knew he was talking about Oa. She thought that Oa hadn't been noticed, but it turned out that she was wrong. She began to explain, "This wasn't the same—"

"It's true, I did come up here." Lotus interrupted. Rina saw him walk past her, stopping her before she potentially put the others in danger too. He continued speaking as he stepped forward. "I came up here after seeing a glimpse of something in the sky. To my surprise, I never thought I'd find this place. Your granddaughter told me I needed to leave before I was caught. I didn't listen, and she hid me before I could venture out onto your land. I told her about the world below yours, and she must have wanted to come down and see for herself."

The king could not handle hearing another word spoken. He turned his back to them and huffed.

"Because of your daughter, I stand before you today. I owe my *life* to her!" Lotus declared. "Rina saved my life, and she helped me save what could be seen as the entire world we know. If not for her insubordination and curiosity, I don't know what would've happened." His words touched Rina deeply; he spoke with such sincerity and truth. But would it sound that way to the king?

Vortigon turned back to face them. "I am the one who sits above it all—the one who has been observing from above since time out of mind. 'The Watcher,' they call me. I have seen what remains below my domain, and there is no good reason to return *or* grant permission for others to set foot in Nimbusara. We destroyed all the sky-ships many years ago but it would seem we missed a vessel." The king shook his head, displeased by this error. "The ones you call 'Guardians' are the only feeble protection you have over your land, and I have a strange feeling about that dark presence in the east which is only growing. It's terrifying to even think of returning to what was below. Only time will tell for all of *you*." The king strode through the two lines of his guards and back to his throne.

"Wait—what do you mean—" Lotus begged.

"I am finished with this rubbish in my home," the king declared. "Take him to the holding chambers immediately. As for my granddaughter, I will deal with her later." Stone-faced, he gestured with one hand, summoning his guards to take them. The armored angels turned in unison and began to walk towards the two.

"Please, I need to know what you meant by that!" Lotus shouted, but the king favored him with neither a response nor even a backward glance of any kind as he turned to walk away.

"Lotus, stop! You will only make it worse!" Rina tried to grab his arm to pull him back.

I can't be taken away now; this... this could be it...

He saw the guards approaching him, and felt the adrenaline pumping. Sensing the strength in his arms building with dark energy, he quickly pulled them apart and snapped the strong braided filaments that bound his wrists.

Surprised to see the pieces of Lotus's broken restraints explode across the room, the guards immediately drew their spears and closed in, shouting for him to stand down.

"Please just answer me, Your Highness. I *need* to know!" Lotus begged, as he drew out his broken sword and backed away from the royal knights now surrounding him.

With the tips of their spears pointed at him from all angles, he didn't see a way out of this. He was grasping onto a hunch, one small chance that what the king was talking about was the evidence they needed. This could be the answer he was looking for. *This* could be—

"Drop your weapon *now!*" the guards shouted, surrounding him and closing in.

A decision had to be made right here. Lotus would either have to fight his way into their understanding, or he could hope they would hear him out if he stood down. Neither of those sounded reasonable, so what could he do?

Annoyed by this foolish shouting, the King of Nimbusara glanced over his shoulder and saw something... something unbelievable.

"Halt!" the king commanded. His guards, though confused, stopped their advance. They backed away from the land dweller and held their weaponry upright again, but at the ready.

"Sir?" his first general asked.

"What are you babbling about?" The king asked. He walked toward Lotus with his head lowered and piercing blue eyes focused intently on the interloper.

The young man was still fueled with adrenaline and had to get his bearings and prepare his question. Quickly shaking his head, he fumbled for words before asking his question. "I... uh, you... You spoke of a dark presence coming from the east, correct?"

"I did. What of it?" replied the king curtly.

"Please, tell me whatever you can about it. What exactly did you mean by dark presence?" Lotus remembered what Kenji had told them, how there was a castle deep in the forbidden world that held the "key to the future."

"I can't say for certain, but I have seen an unsightly structure off in the distant east. We keep our home far away from that part of the world," the king told Lotus, feeling uncomfortable at just the thought of it.

That's got to be it. That's what Kenji was talking about. Whatever the place is, it could be what is coming for Prosper Valley. Lotus realized, as his eyes widened with excitement at hearing this news. Except, what made the king want to answer his question now?

"Grandfather?" Rina mumbled under her breath.

The old king squinted his eyes at the young man and inspected him carefully. His guards were preparing their weapons to engage again as they saw the young man still holding onto his weapon. Looking back to their king, they saw him subtly gesture with his hands for them to fall back.

"Rina, I don't know why you left our home. I should be quite furious with you right now, and yet... I am not." With a wave of his hand, the king signalled for the release of her restraints. One of the guards immediately walked over and removed the bindings from her wrists.

What is happening? Lotus wondered.

"Take them away," the king demanded, an upset tone spilled from his mouth.

"Please, Grandfather!" Rina shouted as she covered her mouth with her hand, crushed.

"You chose to leave our home. You knew the consequences of your actions, and yet you did it anyway. Now, you must live out the rest of your days with this decision etched on your soul." Lord Vortigon, the King of Nimbusara, had spoken. He sat back on his throne and stared at them both.

A flow of tears began to run down the girl's face as she felt her heart shatter.

"Take them away, now," the king instructed. Two guards left their posts to escort the two young offenders from the throne room.

Lotus and Rina walked away in silence. Lotus could not understand the king's sudden change of heart. He peeked back and saw the king still staring at him, then tilted his head as he saw the royal one's eyes watching him most curiously.

Rina remained silent. She couldn't come to terms with what had just happened. Never did she believe that this would be the outcome of her decision. Lotus was right to warn her when they first met. She really hadn't thought it through.

Lotus tried to get her to speak on the way back to her home, but she refused to talk. Maybe it was still the shock from it all. Maybe it was the fact that she had done a quite disrespectful thing to her people, her family, and especially her grandfather who just happened to be the King of Nimbusara. Who knew what was going on in her head right now?

"Rina!" her mother's voice shouted from a short distance away.

Snapping out of her blank stare, Rina shouted out and ran for her mother. They held each other tightly as tears of both joy and sadness danced to the ground. Her father, standing with arms crossed and brows slanted, coolly watched the reunion of his daughter and wife.

"I'm so happy to see that you're back. You don't know how much we were worried!" Rina's mother mumbled through uncontrolled sobs.

"I am so sorry, Mom! I-I should have... I should have been more responsible... But now I... I..." Rina struggled to speak.

"Lana. Let's take her inside," Trint, Rina's father, spoke in a low voice as he headed into the house.

Lana's mother wiped tears from her face and stood beside her daughter, only now catching a glimpse of the man behind her. Gasping at the sight, she saw that his back was bare of wings. "The land-dweller..." she muttered.

"Mom! Mom, wait!" Rina tried to cut her mother off before she accused him, just as her grandfather had.

"You are the man who kept my daughter safe, aren't you?" Lana asked.

Lotus, a little surprised at this reply, answered her, "I... I was the one keeping an eye out for your daughter, yes."

"Thank you so so much! I was worried sick all this time, thinking she was out there getting hurt. I'm glad I can put a face to the man who kept her safe." Lana wiped a few more tears from her cheeks.

Lotus, smiling softly, bowed his head, thanking her for the compliment. "Trust me. I should be thanking you; without your daughter's help, I wouldn't be standing here today." Lotus stood back up and nodded towards Rina. Her proud mother rubbed her daughter's back as they headed inside.

"Grandfather?!" Rina shouted in surprise and froze in place when she saw her grandfather standing there in the middle of her living room.

"We have to talk, my dear," he said firmly.

"What's going on?" Lotus asked, staring at the king.

"I will explain everything. Please just listen to what I have to say." the king said respectfully. Lotus and Rina walked closer, ready to focus on whatever he had to say.

"My dearest granddaughter, you have broken the most sacred rule of our people. That, I cannot forgive," the king began. "However, following my intuition, I have decided to let you and this man return to the land below and continue with this quest that you're on." he paused, glancing over at Rina's father, who appeared somewhat displeased.

"I have an uneasy feeling, truly an ominous dread, about that odd structure far in the east. If you dare to delve into this mysterious source of energy, then by all means, proceed. I have no plans to stop you on your journey," the king said earnestly.

"Are you saying I... I'm forbidden to come home?" Rina asked, holding back more tears.

Her grandfather sighed, lowering his head. "Yes. From this moment, you cannot return home again. I must fulfill my duties as king, just as my father and grandfather did, and I cannot allow an exception," the king replied matter-of-factly, but sorrow tinged his words.

Rina once again broke down into tears. Her own actions had decided this fate. To her dismay, it was one thing she wished she could undo if given the choice. Yet, she did *not* regret being there for the others when they had needed her.

"Rina." Lotus took her arm, trying to comfort her.

"No, I'm fine." She wiped her face of their tears. "I made this decision, and now I have to live with it." The girl straightened her back, wings erect, and stood before her family.

"My dearest granddaughter, you have taken a path which will lead you on the journey of a lifetime. I do hope that you stay alert and trust your instincts appropriately when venturing out into the unknown," the king told Rina. Then, looking at both of them, he added, "I know not what lies ahead. However, I do know that it is not something of this world."

"We will use that information wisely, sir." Lotus bowed his head, thanking him for his generosity.

"Please, escort these two back down to the land below," the king asked one of the guards.

Rina hugged her parents quickly but meaningfully, her tears at bay. Then she and Lotus followed the armored angel. Lotus was stopped by a gentle hand on his shoulder before he could continue.

"Please, keep my granddaughter safe, child," the king looked into Lotus's eyes.

"Yes, sir," Lotus replied firmly, meeting his gaze. Then he nodded and continued through the doorway.

In a short while, the two of them were standing right where Oa and Rina had first met. They glanced down and saw the shafts of light and clouds shifting, and Perlaria far, far below them. The perspective from this high up was incredible. Now, all they had left to do was jump.

"You ready?" Rina asked.

Lotus nodded his head, ready to jump. Just as they were about to hop over the edge, Rina's name was called by someone behind them.

"Yes?" she said, turning around. One of the guards hurried over to her with a box in his hands. It was a thin but wide box, iridescent white and beautifully adorned with fine gold filigree.

"What's this?"

"Your family wanted you to take this with you on your journey. They intended to give it to you on your eighteenth birthday. However, they believe now would be a good time as ever." The guard then handed the box over to her. She carefully lifted the lid and was shocked to see what lay inside.

"B-but... I'm not sure... This is a cherished treasure that has been passed down for generations. Why am I being given this now, especially since I am leaving the kingdom?" Rina asked.

"I was not told. Your family entrusted you with it," the guard said.

Rina could feel a warm smile growing. Even though she had left her home and had broken a sacred rule, she was still a part of her family. "Thank you," she said, truly grateful.

"No need, ma'am. But I would be going now. I don't think your friend can land without wings," the guard noted.

"What do you—" Rina paused and looked back over to her left to see... no one. Lotus hadn't stopped when her name had been called.

"Oh no!" she shouted, and quickly leapt over the edge, box in hand, rushing downward to catch him before it was too late.

Her mother, watching from above, saw her daughter distancing herself farther and farther from her home; yet instead of sadness, her heart swelled with hope and pride.

"I can't believe you let her go again." Trint shook his head in full disapproval of what had transpired, his lips pressed together in a straight line.

"Trust me, " the king said as he rubbed his beard. He narrowed his eyes as he recalled memories from many years ago, "That boy is a lot stronger than you think he is."

"What makes you say that?" Lana asked.

The king walked back inside, still rubbing his beard as he remembered one face in particular so very clearly. "If that sword belonged to who I believe it did, then they will be perfectly fine," he told her. The King of Nimbusara, the Watcher, smiled to himself knowingly.

33

Decisions

"How do you think we can help him relax?" Nyloc inquired.

"I have no idea. Ever since I've known them, they have never fought like this. I don't know *how* we can calm them both down," Oa sighed as they walked.

Oa and Nyloc were traipsing through a forest, navigating through the trees and shrubbery, hoping to find Thalrok. Out of nowhere, a loud crash shook the ground, accompanied by a deep grunt. Then they heard it again, and the ground vibrated beneath their feet. The sequence went on relentlessly, each booming crash followed by a grunt, reverberating through the trees.

"I think I might know where he is," Nyloc remarked sarcastically.

Trenching across the ridged forest floor, they weaved between the trees to an opening ahead. Then both halted abruptly. Before their very eyes they saw the angry titan in the center of thunderous chaos.

"Whoa..." Oa muttered, watching as the bounty hunter ruthlessly smashed one tree after another. With each strike of his knuckles, the trees split apart, shattering into fragments as the remnants cascaded to the ground. Tree by tree, the human chainsaw was methodically decimating the forest, clearing the land from the center outward.

"Thalrok, hold on!" Oa yelled.

The bounty hunter ceased his activity and sighed heavily before gradually turning toward the sound of Oa's voice. He had already destroyed nearly a dozen trees in his frenzy.

Oa pleaded, "Can we just talk?"

Thalrok remained silent, moving instead to sit against one of the fallen trees he had just toppled.

"This is a start," Nyloc said under his breath.

They headed over to his side and quietly sat next to him, allowing him a moment to breathe. Thalrok let out a loud exhale through his nose and stared at his outstretched feet, big fists clenched tightly.

"Thalrok, we don't—" Oa began.

"*How* can he just say that!?" Thalrok burst out. "Doesn't he know what we all have been through? We fought to our very end to stop Delus, and he just thinks we will roll over and let this 'Dark Empire' destroy the world. How can he say that?!" Thalrok couldn't wrap his head around it. He was taught his whole life to never back down from a fight, to fight to the very end, or die as a warrior doing it.

"We understand where you're coming from. Then again, Lotus does have a point," Nyloc added hesitantly.

"Ever since we left the underworld. Lotus seemed a bit less... stressed. He's obviously been thinking about this, too, but he's also thinking about us," Oa stated, attempting to reason with Thalrok.

"I know. I just... You two agree with me, right? We know this information. We can't just do nothing with it." Thalrok started to speak more calmly, relaxing both his fists and his overall attitude.

"I do agree. I think we should at least figure out what this empire really is and take action from there," Oa replied, looking over to Nyloc to see what he thought.

"I'm glad you two at least agree with me. I just wish Ronin would, too." Thalrok exhaled with a whoosh, releasing some of his stress.

"I believe you both should take some time to reflect on this. Try to understand each other's perspectives and have a conversation tomorrow. While it's true that it's not ideal to go to bed upset, maybe it's best for both of you to spend the rest of the day apart," Nyloc proposed.

"You're right. Thalrok gave them a sideways glance, then admitted, "I prob'ly overreacted a little, didn't I?"

"It's alright. We can't alter the scripture of the past, but it can shape our future actions," Oa said sagely, giving Thalrok a reassuring pat on the shoulder.

"It makes me mad that this little guy is the wisest of us all sometimes," Thalrok chuckled as he tussled Oa's hair.

"Not this again with the 'little' comments," Oa sighed, rolling his eyes as he sent a gentle breeze to push Thalrok's hand away from his head.

"I'm just joking. Hey, I didn't say 'kid'!" Thalrok laughed again. "Let's head back home; I could use a drink."

* * *

Back at the Lie-Inn, the morning sun crept in through their curtains, casting a soft, golden light into everyone's room. Lotus and Rina had returned late in the afternoon from their impromptu adventure, and stayed in their quarters. The others had retired after dinner.

Now, the silence of the early hours hung heavily in the air. The new day loomed before them like an uneasy truce. It had been twenty-four hours since the argument—the fight—that had left everyone a little shaken, confused, and unsure of how to move forward.

In the stillness of the inn, the air seemed to crackle with anticipation as the three of them loitered between their rooms and the common area just outside of them. Nyloc, Rina, and Oa all knew that *the* conversation was coming, and with it, there was an uncertain tension about what would happen next. Would they resolve things? Or was this the beginning of something much harder to fix? Time stretched on and on as they strained to hear signs of Thalrok and Lotus stirring from slumber.

Suddenly, both doorknobs turned with a synchronized creak, and like ghosts emerging from the shadows, they stepped out of their rooms in unison. A hush fell as Lotus and Thalrok exchanged glances, then watched as the others shut their own doors and approached them. Their hearts were beating so loudly that anyone could hear. They didn't say a word. They didn't move a muscle, and those few seconds felt like hours.

"…I'm sorry." Lotus and Thalrok both said, bowing their heads simultaneously.

Sighs wheezed from their friends, who were mightily relieved to hear them both apologize. "Thank goodness," Oa murmured, his head dropped, and his held breath whooshed out.

"Thalrok, I'm sorry that I came off like I thought your idea was impossible or even totally off the table. I completely understand where you're coming from. I could never let this world crumble while I'm on the sidelines, not now, not ever. I do have an idea. If you'll let me, could I please share it?" Lotus looked over at Rina.

"Absolutely. What've ya got?" Thalrok replied heartily, and everyone sat down.

"A lot of stuff was thrown at me yesterday. I found something out about this threat coming our way. Rina and I were graced with knowledge of a looming presence in the east. It's beyond the walls and in the depths of the forbidden world. Now, you think we should handle this. I say we should let the City of Light handle it. Let's do both," Lotus suggested.

"What do you mean?" Thalrok sounded open to this idea, but skeptical.

"We should go to the City of Light and warn them about the Dark Empire and how they could be a threat to this world. We use this information we know to alert the ones who could handle this better." Lotus said, then sat there quietly, hoping that Thalrok would agree with his proposal.

The bounty hunter leaned back in his seat, scratching his neck while the others watched him intently. After pausing to contemplate the idea, he straightened up to bluntly say, "No."

"Thalrok, please just—" Lotus tried to speak.

"I'm not finished. I don't think it's a good idea because you're a high-level target. Not to mention, we have an angel with us now. Who knows what they'll think when they see *her*? I'm taking a page out of your book; this puts your lives at stake, and I can't let you do that," Thalrok spoke with sincerity and a genuine concern for the safety of his friend and their

449

crew.

Lotus felt pleased to see him making an effort to consider what was best for all. "That's it, though; *that's* our ticket in," he said with a smirk.

"What do you mean, captain?" Nyloc asked.

"Oh, we aren't all going in as a group," Lotus said, standing up and holding his wrists out in front of him. "You guys will be turning me in."

34

Judgment

The *Land Skipper* glided over the fields of Prosper Valley, the wheels creating a melodic hum. With most of their crew onboard and a clear course set for the City of Light, their minds were filled with unease.

Regarding Rina, Lotus had instructed her not to accompany them. That was his last request before his upcoming capture, as he wanted to ensure her safety and avoid the possibility of her being taken in too. Consequently, hoping for the best, she watched the ship leave Mellowtin, carrying four of her friends away with only three to return.

"Lotus, you really can't be serious about this," Oa said. The worried look on his face was as clear as day. He couldn't understand why Lotus was so calm at the moment.

"I'm a hundred percent serious. If you guys turn me in, they will see you as someone on their side and they will trust your words. If we just show up and tell them about this Dark Empire, there's not a chance that they'll believe us," the wanted man replied, eyes forward.

"Sure, but are you honestly willing to risk your life for something we still understand so little about?" Nyloc chimed in, propping himself against the *Skipper's* railing.

"We don't have many other options here. This is the only way to get this info out and keep everyone safe. I don't know what will happen to me after you hand me over. I'll just know that you all will be safe," Lotus exhaled, having already come to terms with the possible consequences for him personally.

Thalrok, sitting near the front of the right hull, was still opposed to this idea. He knew that there had to be another way to solve this, but also knew that Lotus's mind was set.

"Trust me." Lotus continued, "No matter if this is the last moment we share, I believe deeply in the City of Light and its ability to rise against this foe. If this is my fate—helping this world and ensuring your safety—then I wouldn't choose any other way to go."

The remainder of the ride passed in silence. The three of them struggled to accept the concept of turning Lotus in to the authorities. It was not something they wanted to do. He was innocent and had done nothing wrong. The wanted man was helping this world by letting it see him for the monster he wasn't. Their long journey neared its end as Oa spotted the high walls of the City of Light out on the horizon.

With the entrance of the city approaching quickly, the time to prepare for their plan was now. Oa took the controls while Nyloc and Thalrok secured Lotus's hands. To ensure that it would appear convincing, they tied him up quite firmly to emphasize their intentions.

"This is your last chance. Are you sure you want to throw your life away?" Thalrok whispered.

"I know that this is something that'll help this world. That's all my master wanted, and I want it too." Lotus replied, a little smile on his face.

Thalrok thought this was all very noble, but he still hadn't accepted it yet, and already the archways of the main gate towered high overhead. Polished stone walls stretched dozens of feet toward the sky. This main entrance had enough room to fit a giant crowd of people through all at the same time. Cruising in on the *Skipper,* they gazed up at the people far above who watched them passing underneath. They also observed what appeared to be city guards staring down at them as they rode in on their unusual vehicle.

"They saw us. They should be sending someone soon. Hopefully, your plan goes accordingly." Thalrok muttered, and they stayed on course.

The City of Light was the world's largest city by far, and was where everyone felt safest. It was broken into several concentric sections. The first was the outer ring. These walls stretched all the way in a circle for miles and miles. This region served as the agricultural hub, where numerous small villages and fields cultivated food for the city. The middle ring was where small towns and suburbs formed; this was a closed-off area where people lived. Then there was the inner city. Like Cannon-Gulf, but bigger, it was a gigantic urban center packed with businesses and building after building. The land naturally lifted underneath the city, and atop the sloping hill was an enormous cathedral that housed the Guardians.

"Lotus…" Oa said quietly.

Lotus turned his head slightly and glanced sideways so as not to seem like he wasn't a prisoner. He saw Oa discreetly showing him his sword in its sheath.

"What do you want to do with this?" Oa, looking worried, tilted his head in question.

Before Lotus stood a troubled friend, Oa was struggling the most with this situation. The thought of losing him weighed heavily on Lotus, given all that they had endured together. Taking a deep breath, Lotus met Oa's gaze directly. "Take care of it, please." He smiled.

"I think it's time, everyone!" Thalrok shouted just loud enough for their crew to hear. He grabbed and held onto Lotus like he would some wily and dangerous prisoner. Lotus had instructed him to really sell this scheme and to not be nice to him no matter what.

The *Land Skipper* slowly came to a full stop. Five figures stood in their path. Everyone on board was in their place. The plan was in full action and it was go-time. The four of them hopped off the ship. Lotus's head was down, his face stone-cold as Thalrok callously hauled him across the field. Nyloc and Oa followed behind with their weapons drawn and pointed at the wanted man.

"All of you, *freeze!*" the slender dark-haired woman in front shouted. They did as told and halted, waiting to hear what she would say. The serious-looking young woman before them was the leader of the City of Light's elite fighters—Almira, chief of the Fifth Judgment.

"Tell me what you are doing here, now!" she said in a clear, authoritative voice.

"I'm a bounty hunter, and I am here to deliver 'Ronin the Banished' to the City of Light." The words came out of Thalrok's mouth, but left a sour taste. Every second he went through with this plan still stung his soul.

"The most wanted man in Perlaria, captured by a lonesome bounty hunter?" Han, Almira's right-hand man, said snarkily. He smirked and crossed his arms.

"You think I can't handle a puny criminal like him? Yeah, right! He put up a good fight, but in the end, all he could do was run!" Thalrok shouted back, kicking out Lotus's leg and buckling him to his knees.

"Hard to believe, but it really is him," Othas, another member of the Fifth Judgment, added.

Almira was unsure about this little scenario. Something seemed off; she just didn't know what. She stared at Lotus and saw the cold flat look in his eyes. Finally, she was face-to-face with the wanted man she had been searching for all this time.

"We also have information that the City of Light might want to hear," Thalrok added.

"Oh, really? What information?" Almira, though distrustful, was intrigued.

"Before we were able to detain him, he boasted about something called the 'Dark Empire', some big threat growing in the forbidden world that might be the root of something disastrous, another calamity, perhaps," Thalrok told them. "He hasn't spoken at all ever since he was captured. We wanted to let you know, hoping it could be useful information and maybe help you protectors—or whatever you call yourselves."

Everything was going according to plan. Thalrok had said his piece. The only thing they had to do now was hand over Lotus.

"The Dark Empire?" Almira squinted her eyes; something was suspicious about all of this. What does a bounty hunter care about this world for? They are money-hungry grunts that only care for themselves. And how was this wanted man on the run for years, and then so easily detained?

"Captain, I did a scan. There's nothing else of note on that ship," Agne, the fourth member of Fifth Judgment, whispered.

"Thank you," Almira replied as she turned her gaze back to the bounty hunter. She had one more hunch to follow to see if this was all a ploy of some sort. "We truly must thank you. Because of you three, we finally have this murderer in our hands. You must be expecting the reward money, am I right?"

"Trust me, another second with this man would be torture. He was a handful to deal with, and we are happy to give him up to be *your* problem. We just wanted to turn him in and give you this information," Thalrok boasted.

There it was. Almira knew something was up. Since when did a bounty hunter ever deny money? "He got to you then. Didn't he?" she asked.

"What?" Thalrok began to worry.

"All this time. All these years, we have been looking for this man. For him to be stopped by a low-life bounty hunter, a teenager, and what looks like a blindfolded bowman sounds awfully far-fetched. This criminal is known for corrupting the minds of those he surrounds himself with. We see through your lies and demand that you stand down before we use force." Almira and the other four began to close in on them.

What?! No, this was supposed to work. They need to trust them! Lotus began to panic, realizing that things had changed and the plan was failing.

"Please, believe us. We are here to turn him in," Thalrok attempted to convince them, but they seemed determined on their course of action.

Sora, the final member of Fifth Judgment, held her palm out. Frigid air swirled and created a spear of ice in her hand. Pulling it back, she hurled it at the bounty hunter. The moment before it could strike him in the chest, Lotus broke his restraint and reached out one arm, grabbing and shattering the ice-spear before it could hit Thalrok.

"What are you doing?!" Nyloc loudly whispered.

"It's all a ploy! Stop them now!" Almira shouted as they ran in.

Their plan had gone horribly wrong; they had placed themselves center stage inside the walls of the world's most powerful forces, and now… they had no way of escaping.

"Get back!" Oa shouted as he sent out a burst of wind, pushing all members of the Fifth Judgment a few feet backward. In no time they righted themselves, ready to run back on the attack.

"Be prepared. We don't know what they can do." Almira huffed as she cracked her knuckles.

"What do we do now?" Oa asked.

Lotus had fully removed his restraints and stared at the imminent threat ahead of them. "I don't know…" he replied, his heart racing a million miles an hour. They were all in danger now, no matter what they did. They would all become criminals after fighting against the Fifth Judgment of the City of Light.

"Stop them!" Almira commanded, as the Fifth Judgment charged in.

35

The Outer Ring

The Fifth Judgment was in a full sprint, their focus locked onto the enemy and their weapons drawn. Almira, leading the attack, was set on taking down Lotus herself. She planned to end his constant running once and for all.

"Spread out!" she shouted, and the army of five branched off. Almira, holding tightly onto her long, pure metal bo, twirled it over her head and swung it horizontally at Lotus's head.

"She's fast!" Lotus panicked, ducking out of its path before he could get hit. As his head weaved underneath the swinging metal, he noticed her leg following right after it. "Gotta dodge!" Lotus hesitated too long and felt the top of her foot roundhouse hard across his face. His vision went fuzzy, and stars flickered in his eyes as his jaw rattled.

"Everyone, we gotta—!" the wanted man shouted to the others. He wanted to warn them to stay together, to keep close, and to stay strong, but before he could give any direction, the ground beneath them erupted violently, propelling them into the air and sending them sprawling in various directions. As this chaotic upheaval unfolded, the earth raised towering stone pillars from its depths, scattering them indiscriminately across the landscape, transforming the scene into one of awe and confusion.

"Ronin!" Thalrok roared.

"Lotus!" Oa and Nyloc shouted as they were separated.

Crap, this isn't good! Lotus watched them all being driven farther apart. He looked around and saw Othas forcing his hands into the ground, sending more pillars of the earth and stone columns in his direction.

"He's the one doing this. Another one who can control the earth," Lotus huffed as he jumped off one monolith before more crashed against his platform. Landing off balance, he watched two others appear that slammed into it and shattered it to pieces. Before he could get his bearings, Almira was already dashing in his direction. Lotus's feet pressed into the earth as he sprinted directly toward her.

"I'm coming for you," Almira whispered. Gripping her staff with one hand, she thrust it forward. Swiftly sidestepping, Lotus evaded her jab and retaliated with a punch to her open side.

We have to get out of here. I can't have them getting caught as well. They're accomplices now, Lotus worried, as he watched his fist just miss Almira. He felt the cold metal of the bo brush across his shoulder as his fist passed her face. Their bodies closed in as both of their strikes missed. Before his fist could get any farther, he grabbed onto her shoulder with the punch that missed and pulled her in. He shot his knee upwards, slamming it into her stomach, but winced as he landed the shot, his leg shaking as it struck the armor she wore.

"Let go of me!" she shouted as she sent a sneaky left hook to his ribs. Lotus felt his leg give out once her fist struck his body. Before she could swing again, he jumped sideways out of the way and got back on his feet.

"That armor is gonna be a problem," Lotus panted, watching her spin her staff around, pointing it right at him.

"Enough of this running. Stand down. Now." Almira commanded sternly.

"Please, just listen to us. We are trying—."

Almira interrupted, "If I have to repeat myself, this will not end well for you and your cronies."

She refused to pay any attention to his words. It was hopeless, but Lotus didn't want to give up.

Almira came back in to attack, holding her weapon on her shoulder and running straight at Lotus.

There has to be a way to get them to listen. As Lotus ran and evaded, she continued her relentless assault with her staff, staying close behind him. Lotus jumped, dodged, and sprinted, trying to devise a plan—any plan—except to engage in a full-on fight.

"Enough running, you coward!" she yelled, and swung her metal bo straight down at his head.

Lotus was unable to move quickly enough to jump out of the way. He lifted his hands over his head and grabbed the thick metal as it crashed down, which sent a brutal recoil down his arms. His fingers curled around the metal staff as he pulled one knee to his chest and was ready to stomp hard enough into her armor to send her flying backward. He felt the dark energy inside of him beginning to bubble. It was only a little, but he could feel it pumping into his muscles. *Just a little kick.* The wanted man held his breath, moments away from launching his attack.

Suddenly, the muscles in his arms began tensing up, and a painful shock flowed across Lotus's whole body. His knees buckled as his hands spasmed and gripped the bo tighter. He howled out in pain, unable to release his grip. His body contorted and burned with each pain-filled second. When the zapping sensation finally stopped, a kick landed squarely on his chest, knocking him backward.

"What was *that!?*" Lotus coughed out, the tingling feeling still lingering in his hands. He looked down and saw that his palms were red and warm. He glanced up to find Almira glaring at him, her hands crackling with enormous sparks of lightning, resembling a fierce storm cloud.

"You have made a big mistake coming here," Almira warned, then thrust her staff into the ground. She curled her fingers, fists close to one another as bolts of lightning connected them. Cracks of thunder rumbled through the air as she pulled her hands apart. The static kept growing, reaching out from her arms now as she focused on her prey.

This isn't good! Lotus gasped for air and worked to stand and plant his feet on the ground. As he struggled to get his balance, Almira extended

459

her hands towards him, forcing out lightning bolts aimed directly at his location.

Lotus barely made it out of the way by diving and rolling across the grass, then hopping back up to his feet. The lightning struck exactly where he'd just been.

She's got a lot of power. The wanted man could still feel the tingling in his arms from the shock.

"I hope you and the others don't think you're escaping. This is the end of your running. You, Ronin, are guilty of the murder of Din, a Grand Sage. Stand down, or else." Almira pulled her bo from the ground. Lightning shot from her arms, electrifying her weapon as she spun it around.

Her words only fueled his flow of dark energy. *No, no, no. Calm down, I need to calm down. She's not an enemy, she just...*

But Lotus *had* to fight back, no matter what. She was, unfortunately, right. There was no running away for them. This was a failed plan that was turning out badly for them all.

The ground suddenly quaked with a familiar rattling sound. "Thalrok..." Lotus whispered.

The bounty hunter struck the ground again, with tremendous force which shattered the earth and the surrounding area. His breath steamed through his helmet as he grunted with the effort and seethed with anger at the man before him.

"You are starting to piss me off!" Thalrok growled as he lifted his head and saw one of the Fifth Judgment standing there, unscathed.

"I'm sorry, but you chose this for yourself. Stand down, and this will all be over," Han called back as he bounced on the balls of his feet, jabbing the air.

Thalrok straightened up to his full height and brushed debris from his shoulders. Taking his sword off his back, he jammed it into the ground. "Won't be needing this just yet," he grunted, then cracked his knuckles.

Han smiled as he stared ahead at his muscular opponent, ready for round two. Waving him on, Thalrok jeered, "Come on then, elbows. Bring it,"

The second in command of the Fifth Judgment planted his feet and reached his hands straight out. Bending his knees and dropping his weight low to the ground, he pulled his elbows back, fists tight to his sides. A steady stream of fire erupted from his elbows and flowed behind him. Like a human flamethrower, it intensified, ready to launch Han forward with its force.

"Let's go, big guy!" Han laughed as he jumped straight up and then jetted ahead to attack. Just as Oa could use the wind to move himself around the air, Han could create fire from within his body. Enough fire shot from his elbows to propel himself forward with incredible speed.

He can move even quicker?! Thalrok raised his arms to shield himself from Han's strike. The bounty hunter was just in time to shield himself, yet he felt nothing. Anticipating the block, Han had altered his trajectory at the final moment. Thalrok's head turned, revealing a smirking Han hovering just next to him.

"Too predictable!" Han sang out, then shot forward to punch Thalrok right in the face.

Thalrok's head bobbled around in his helmet as another punch struck him right in the chest.

How can he hit me that hard in the head and not feel a thing?! Thalrok fumed.

Each punch hit with the power of a dozen fists striking as one. Finally finding a small opening, he swung his own fist at Han.

"Too slow." Han jeered as Thalrok's strike missed him by a mile.

"I wasn't aiming for *you!*" Thalrok shouted as his fist kept going and punched hard into the ground. The ripple of the ensuing shockwave broke the earth and quickly spread toward Han.

"Didn't see that coming." Han raised one eyebrow and watched as the seismic wave closed in. Right before it could reach him, five giant columns of earth and stone shot up and blocked its way.

"What!?" Thalrok turned his head and saw Othas on the sidelines, dropping his hands.

"You want some too, boulder boy?" Thalrok taunted. He started to advance towards Othas.

461

The earth-wielder only shook his head slowly, saying, "You still have another problem to worry about." He was watching as Han burst through the wall of stony pillars, flying straight at Thalrok.

The bounty hunter wasn't expecting anyone to break through *that* wall and hadn't seen Han coming. *Who is this guy?!* Thalrok panicked, not able to move in time.

Propelled by blazing fire erupting from both elbows, Han was just inches away from landing his punch.

"Eat *this!*" Oa shouted, flying in as he dug his heels into the side of Han's jaw, launching him across the field.

"Oa!" Thalrok yelled, unharmed.

"I'll take care of this guy. You wanna deal with that earth-wielder?" Oa asked in a calm but assertive tone.

Thalrok looked at Oa and tilted his head. This Oa appeared to be much more mature and confident than ever before. "Yeah, I got it. Be careful, though. That one's a freak! He is totally unpredictable." Thalrok warned.

They parted ways as Oa chased down Han, and Thalrok charged at Othas.

"Another person who can control the earth... great." Thalrok groaned.

Othas stood his ground assured and without fear even at the sight of this titan barreling toward him. It left him unamused. As Thalrok began to close the distance, Othas flicked his fingers upwards causing pillars of the earth to shoot up in Thalrok's path.

"You think these punching bags will stop me?" Thalrok laughed and swung his giant fists right through them. Again and again, columns of stone and earth shot up from the ground in front of Thalrok, but he smashed through each one. These tree-sized pillars were nothing to the bounty hunter.

"Now what?!" Thalrok roared, as he smashed through the last obstructing pillar to find Othas standing in front of him.

The Fifth Judgment earth-mover still seemed unamused, not fearing the train of pure muscle who had charged at him. Pieces of stony debris still flew through the air. Thalrok's fist was already cocked back and ready to strike him down. Othas merely mumbled, "Sinkhole," and he dropped down into the ground. Thalrok's fist swung at… nothing; the man standing there before him was suddenly gone.

"What?!" Thalrok shouted, looking down at an Othas-sized hole. It appeared that Othas could not only create pillars of the earth, but he could also invert his ability to create open shafts or sinkholes in it.

"That little…" Before Thalrok could react, a small stony pillar shot up and punched into his stomach. As the bounty hunter buckled over, he stared down into the hole. Through the black emptiness appeared a faint image of something firing out.

Another pillar shot burst out and smashed into him, sending him flying across the field until he crash-landed in a heap on the ground.

Othas emerged from his subterranean refuge and stood with arms still crossed, seeming disappointed. "You have so much strength for the average human, and yet you waste all your time smashing things. You don't seem to think at all, do you?" Othas observed.

"You know… You talk a lot for a guy too scared… to get his hands dirty," Thalrok panted, brushing himself off. He glanced to his right and saw a familiar companion.

Ah… Now it's your turn, old friend, Thalrok thought to himself. He reached out, gripped the handle of his sword, and removed the massive blade from the dirt. Then, replying to his foe, he said, "Thinking during battle is weak! The strongest will always come out on top. It's just a matter of who is willing to keep getting up after getting knocked down." He took his first step towards Othas. As his foot hit the ground, he was immediately surrounded by giant columns of earth.

"I'm sad to say that I was once like you, but now—" Before Othas could finish his sentence, a giant hole was blown out beneath the trapped bounty hunter.

Thalrok materialized from out of the debris, still walking forward and now huffing aggressively, "I told you. It's all about the one who can get up no matter how many times they get knocked down."

"Let's hope your accomplices have the same mindset." Othas stepped towards the bounty hunter, ready to kick it up a notch.

Meanwhile, the young disciple of Grand Sage Gou was jetting and soaring like a bird through the air, swerving and dodging as quickly as possible. Han kept up the aggression, staying on Oa's tail despite his speed and agility.

"Thalrok wasn't lying. This guy is one strange opponent," Oa, breathing hard, placed his palms towards the ground and sent a burst of air downward. He quickly launched straight up and saw Han pass below, missing his attack.

"Now!" Oa then sent out another burst from his hands as he held them up to the sky. Plummeting downward, he drove his heels into Han's back. The Fifth Judgment's fire-wielder was smashed into the ground and the earth split beneath his body.

"Got him!" Oa gasped, finally getting in a good hit. As his legs buckled from the impact, he felt the air around him heat up. His eyes shifted to Han's arms, and he saw the flickering flames. Before the young disciple could take another breath, Han's elbows erupted with fire. Oa instinctively jumped back to avoid being burned. Although he escaped just in time, he still felt the intense heat.

"A smart plan, but you forgot something," Han muttered, "I'm not your average opponent." Standing back up, he turned only his head to the side to look coolly at Oa.

At that, a creeping chill ran down the Oa's spine. Han no longer had that smirk on his face, it was wiped clean off. Now, he appeared to be quite serious, as if he was done playing around. The flames on his elbows wafted in the breeze that brushed past them both. Sweat from Oa's forehead trickled from his face, his fingers trembled. When Oa's eyes closed to blink and then opened back up, Han was right there.

"What?!" the boy shouted.

Before he could react, he felt the forceful impact of Han's jet-propelled fist crash into his face. Oa was launched backward, twisting through the air. About to crash into the ground, he fired out a small burst of wind to stabilize himself. Coming to a hard stop, Oa rebalanced, found his bearings, and then planted his feet.

"He's much faster now," Oa panted as he looked up to find Han right in front of him once again.

Time slowed. Oa saw Han's fist creeping closer to his face, ready to clock him again. He felt unsure of what to do. Han was much faster and stronger than him. His fighting instincts, power, and overall skill were too much to handle. He was bound to lose.

Remember what Lotus taught you, Oa thought, as he felt one last chance open up.

Swiftly moving his head out of the way, he felt Han's fist sail right past him. Han's eyes widened; he was not expecting to miss.

Now that his opponent was caught off guard, Oa took this opportunity to strike. He continued to twist his body as he punched Han across the jaw. The hit was direct, but didn't have much power. Even so, Han's head was turned to one side from the impact.

"Just a scratch," Han sneered, as he darted his eyes sharply back around. Nothing was there. Where the boy had been standing was now empty air.

"What?!" Han shouted, just before he felt his left leg collapse. Oa had found his blind spot and kicked out his leg. The Fifth Judgment's fire-wielder fell to one knee.

Oa followed through, firmly planted his own leg, then forced as much air as he could out of the other heel. That leg whipped through the air for Han's neck.

"Not again!" Han shouted. He then fired a powerful jet of flame from his right elbow and spun around on his knee to face Oa. Han's arm blocked the kick just in time.

I can't get this pace slowed down! The young disciple pushed himself further. He pulled his other hand back and punched at Han. The fire-wielder's elbow exploded with flames and he threw his own punch. As their fists approached each other Han saw the weak boy's hand already surrender and release its balled grip. He smirked as he watched this poor excuse of an attack near him. But when he glanced back at the boy's eyes, he was unsettled. Oa did not look about to surrender, he was wearing a defiant and, yes, cocky expression. When Han realized what was happening, it was too late.

"Take *this*!" Oa shouted, as his hand fully opened up into a palm which emitted a massive amount of wind pressure. Before Han's fist could reach Oa, he was sent tumbling and skidding awkwardly across the field.

"Han!" Almira shouted, noticing him zip past. Distracted, she had dropped her guard, and was met with another heavy punch to the body. Her feet slid only slightly across the ground as Lotus shook his hand.

"I think... I'm starting to get used to hitting... that armor," he grunted, standing up straight.

Almira scowled at him, lightning sparking from her hands faster.

"You think you have a chance, don't you?"

"No, I don't. I just need you to listen to me," Lotus replied.

"I will not repeat myself! You will stand down *now* before it's too late!" Almira commanded, thunder erupting as she shouted.

36

The Outer Ring II

As the four of them became separated on the battlefield, Nyloc clung to the ground while it lifted him and pushed him upwards. The distance between the scattered companions was growing, and he could hear Lotus calling out to them. He could tell that he was being pushed in the direction of the *Land Skipper*.

"Guess I'll hold up the rear then," Nyloc huffed as he hopped off of the earthen pillar. Once his feet hit the ground, he immediately drew his bow. The blind archer stood before the *Skipper* and held his post, ready to defend it.

"Nyloc!" Oa shouted, rushing over to his side, "You alright?"

"Yes, quite all right. Yourself?" Nyloc asked.

"Just a little shaken up, but I'm okay." The two looked back over at Lotus and Thalrok battling the Fifth Judgment. The fight was well in progress and there was no going back.

"This isn't good." Nyloc sighed.

"You're right. His plan failed." Oa replied, exhaling deeply.

"I'll hold the rear and supply any assistance I can from here. You go in and help our friends." Nyloc suggested, pulling his bow back.

"Right!" Oa shouted, and took off without hesitation.

Nyloc watched the boy dash headfirst back into the fight, launching himself in Thalrok's direction. Then his senses alarmed him of an encroaching threat from the east.

"Hmm. It seems that I am faced with the one who stands out the most." Nyloc turned to one side and sensed her cool presence. It was Sora of the Fifth Judgment, now walking towards him.

Sylphlike, she walked with great poise and composure. Her skin was a faint bluish hue. Her hair consisted of two blue-green waterfalls that flowed down her body then turned to mist before hitting the ground at her feet. Sora was both elegant and intimidating.

Without skipping a beat, Nyloc nocked two more arrows, pulled back the bow, and fired all three. Sora watched them zip through the air as she gracefully waved her hand and changed the path of her flowing watery hair. It moved between her and the arrows then froze into solid ice. The arrows pierced through just enough to become stuck, but not close enough to touch her.

"A foolish attempt," she scowled, melting the ice and coming closer. The arrows dropped to the ground.

"Ice? Interesting," Nyloc pondered over his next move. He reached for another arrow, then stopped himself. "Might be a good time to switch it up, I suppose," He exhaled as he placed the bow on his back.

"Giving up so soon?" Sora asked. Her voice was other-worldly, mellow and hypnotic.

"No, ma'am, not at all," Nyloc replied as he ran toward her.

Seeing that her attacker's eyes were completely blindfolded, Sora believed this was nothing but a ruse, a trick to fool the enemy into a false sense of security. Even if he couldn't look, that didn't mean he couldn't see.

"Just like we practiced." Nyloc tried to psych himself up, knowing that Sora was only a few feet away.

Sora's watery locks flowed down to her hands and began to wrap around her arms, hardening into ice. The thick layer of frozen water gave her gauntlets of ice to protect her from any incoming attack.

"Try and hit me now." Sora invited, waving him on.

Quickly reaching to his side, Nyloc grabbed a kunai and swiftly threw it.

Sora lifted her gauntlets and covered her face before the projectile could strike. The kunai ricocheted off her icy shield with a *plink*, but as it did she felt a painful pinch in her leg. Her knee buckled and she saw that another kunai had stabbed in deeply just behind it.

"That clever—" She lowered her arms to find the archer coming at her head-first. His fist was cocked back, and he struck Sora across the face. The water around her head splashed with the impact. She felt another jab hit her in the shoulder, then a sucker punch connected with her stomach. Her teeth pressed together as streams of water rushed from her head.

"Enough!" Sora shouted as she clapped her hands together. The ice surrounding her hands thawed out, then whirled around Nyloc where it rapidly froze. The frozen ice grip held Nyloc in place from the waist up, his elbows stuck to his sides.

"Pardon me," the archer apologized in advance, then he kicked her hard just above the injured knee. Her leg buckled once again from the shock to the nerve and she felt the tingle of it radiate down to her foot.

Luckily for Nyloc, he could just barely reach a small dagger on his hip and he hurriedly chipped away at his icy restraint. Sora's gaze darted angrily from her throbbing knee back to the archer. Her watery hair flowed turbulently down as her blood boiled with rage. By now, Nyloc had worked at the ice just enough to create a crack that shattered some of it. He freed his arms.

"What?!" Sora panicked.

Nyloc took a larger dagger from his side. He took a big step forward, and slashed at Sora. Watching the blind archer closing in, Sora leaned back just far enough to evade his attack. The flow of her hair quickly changed directions to run down the front of her face where it froze just in time. Nyloc's dagger slid across the icy helmet, but he punched through his foiled strike with his other hand, hitting her mid-chest. Sora buckled over with the breath knocked out of her.

Nyloc was trying his best to be respectful, as he was fighting one who they hoped would become an ally. He sighed heavily, and began saying, "I apologize, miss, but I need for you and your people to lis—" but was interrupted by the infuriated Sora.

"You monster!" she screeched, lifting her head with the icy mask in place. Her wild sea-green eyes glared at him through the two small holes in it. Again her hair flowed down to her hands and formed frozen gauntlets, which were even bigger this time than before.

"You expect us to *listen* to you after you fight back like this!?" she shouted, charging like a wild beast at Nyloc.

"I'm sorry, miss. I just need you to hear what we have to say," he pleaded. It was no use. He knew that not one of the Fifth Judgment was about to stop and listen to anything.

Nyloc reached over to his side again and grabbed a few small balls from his pouch. "Thanks for the idea, you Infected fools," Nyloc muttered to himself as he hurled three smoke bombs to the ground at Sora's feet. Great billows of smoke erupted around them and Sora was caught inside and blinded.

"Smoke?!" she panicked as she waved her hands around to clear her view, but the haze was far too dense to be simply fanned away.

From across the field, Thalrok saw the large cloud of smoke. "Atta' boy Nyloc. Thalrok panted as his body slumped over. He turned back to look at Othas and panted even harder.

"You give up yet?" Thalrok asked.

Othas didn't even respond, he just grunted back at the bounty hunter, who continued on to say, "You thought you were dealing with a bunch of low-life weaklings. You have *no idea* what we have been through."

"I think *you* believe you're dealing with just the four of us." Othas said, shaking his head. Thalrok didn't understand what he meant by that—"just the *four*" of them? *What is he talking about?*

That was when he remembered… there's one more…

As Thalrok contemplated their overall situation, on the other side of the field Sora continued to swat her hands around in the haze, trying to get her bearings. Blind and disoriented, she shouted, "Han! Othas!" while floundering frantically. Just as she planted one foot on the ground, she felt a thud in her calf. Sora screamed out as an arrow pierced her skin and dove into the muscle underneath it. She began to hobble and bounce on her good leg as pain shot up the other with each step she took. Reaching for the embedded arrow, she felt three more thunk into her gauntlet of ice from a whole other direction.

"Where *is* he?" She began to panic, still unable to see.

Now, Nyloc was like a shark in the water. This was his domain. He was in full control without any way for his prey to escape him. After dealing with this kind of situation in the underworld, he found it to be to his own great advantage. "Hey!" Nyloc shouted out.

Sora looked off in the direction of the voice. As her body turned towards it, another arrow thudded into her back. She screamed again, feeling the stinging pain throughout her torso. At this point, Sora was handicapped and quite vulnerable. She had no help, couldn't see, and was being barraged with sharp projectiles. She had no other choice.

"*Agneeee!*" she shouted out with all her might.

"Agne?" Nyloc whispered in confusion as he dashed toward Sora.

Then, midstep, he was brought to a jolting stop. He felt his legs being pulled downward by something twining tightly around his ankles. The archer sensed that from beneath the ground something like the branches and supple twigs of a tree was holding onto him.

"What the—" Before he could move another inch, tree branches like tentacles shot out of the ground to lift him and thrash him around in the air. They thrust him above the clouds of smoke then hurled him far from it. His body tumbled across the field as he rolled to a painful stop.

"What was *that*?" Nyloc groaned as he stood up. He could sense the presence of two people now, Sora, finally emerging from the fog, and Agne, the last member of the Fifth Judgment to join the fight. Agne's bark-skinned body towered above them. She was a walking tree on sturdy trunklike legs. Her long arms stretched out like living tree branches, complete with patches of green leafy growth. Her hair was made up of leaves in many shades of green, and her bright yellow eyes were focused on Nyloc.

Ah, my hunch was correct—she really does have Druunai blood in her, Nyloc

471

noted to himself. The Druunai were a group of tree-like beings that roamed the earth nocturnally. They would root themselves in place to rest each day just before the sun came up which would feed them and replenish their power.

"No need to worry, Sora. Let *me* take over for you." Agne smiled. Her hands cracked and creaked as they formed balled up fists of wood. She had disrupted her daytime rest early at the sound of her comrades in battle.

Nyloc, still shaken up from the bumpy landing after being launched out of his smoky defense, wondered how he was going to get out of this situation.

I don't know how strong this one can be. If I was as brawny as the bounty hunter, I might not have any problem. Unfortunately, that's not the case. Nyloc reached back to grab his bow, and… it wasn't there.

"Looking for this?" Agne taunted, holding it in her now outstretched woody hands.

"Not good…" Nyloc sighed as he watched her snap it with ease. Without his weapon of choice, Nyloc felt himself to be outmatched. He watched as the Fifth Judgment's hidden weapon totally revealed herself and barreled toward him. He held his hands up and prepared to do what he could to survive whatever she had in store. He saw one large arm, covered in bark, reinforce the fist she made as it came crashing down at him.

"I-I don't know what to do…" the archer panicked. He watched, frozen in place, as the trunk-sized fist was moments from hammering into him.

"Nyloc!" a familiar voice shouted.

The now-bowless archer sensed Thalrok jump in between him and Agne.

"Thalrok?!" he shouted, as the bounty hunter held up his arms to stop Agne's fist. The impact shook the ground as Agne's punch met Thalrok's meaty hands. His whole body ached from the shock as he forced her fist back in her direction. Agne backed up just a little, assessing this new foe.

"You okay?" Thalrok asked.

"Y-yes. I apologize for the moment of weakness." Nyloc was somewhat flustered.

"Don't worry about it, we all get like that sometimes. Now let's go, we got ourselves a tree to chop down!" Thalrok observed with a little smile, ready to go toe to toe with Agne.

"Wait! What about the one you were fighting?" Nyloc asked.

"As soon as that waterfall girl screamed, he disappeared for a minute. I saw you were in trouble, so I came to help." Lifting the mighty sword from his back, Thalrok pointed it at Agne and met the giant's yellow gaze.

"Come on. I still got a whole lot left in me." Thalrok huffed, running into battle.

37

Scars

The bright blue of the sky above the battle of the Outer Ring began to decay and fade away. Cloudy overcast soon covered every inch of the sky, and dark cumulonimbus clouds rumbled with thunder. Sprinkling ever so lightly, the rain plucked at the ground, for now holding off the cloudburst to come. The once-pleasant day was now covered in a cast of dreariness and melancholy.

"I can see that you realize how foolish you were to even attempt this ploy. You mask yourself with a brave face, but inside, you're trembling," Almira stared Lotus down and exhaled forcefully.

The wanted man, kneeling on the ground, his eyes mere slits, couldn't breathe. His entire body stung every time one of her lightning bolts hit him. Each strike she threw was backed up with an incredible amount of force. She had to have been training for years to get to this combat level.

"I don't know what to do," Lotus panted, trying to just open his eyes. He could feel a few drops of rain patter on his skin, the precursor to a downpour. A storm was coming, not only above them but inside himself.

"Look around you," Almira said. Using what strength he had left, he slowly opened his eyes and looked around at the battlefield—the cracked and broken earth beneath them, the burnt grass and potholes from their fighting, and each of his friends, all tired and trying their hardest to stay toe-to-toe with these unyielding members of the Fifth Judgment.

"You and your gang of thugs have failed in whatever this pathetic attempt was. There is *no* chance that you will leave here. Have you gotten that through your dense skull?" Almira, her hands sparking with more lightning, closed in on Lotus. He could feel the energy of her presence getting closer, so he tried his best to stand up.

This whole time, he'd been holding back a built-up pressure of dark energy. His will was like a dam holding back an overflow of water. Yet the dam had cracks, and little bits of water could seep out, but it was only a matter of time until the dam broke.

"Please…" Lotus hoped she would give him just another minute.

"Enough! I am sick and tired of this charade. Be quiet and accept your fate!" Almira commanded. She ran at him, twirling her weapon high above her with outstretched arms, then fiercely swung her metal bo down at Lotus's head.

Just before her strike could land, Lotus rolled out of the way and stumbled back up to his feet. His muscles shrieked. Any movement was excruciating. The substantial amount of electricity he had endured was taking a toll on his body, and it was becoming unbearable.

"You've resorted to running once again, have you? Typical. That's all you did once you murdered him, didn't you? You just ran and ran and ran. Cowering away and corrupting even more innocent people's minds while you got away with murder. How many others have you toyed with, huh? How many more have you killed?" Almira shouted angrily as she swung her bo in lethal arcs over and over again at Lotus.

Using what little strength he had, Lotus was just trying to evade her attacks. To himself, he panted, "I didn't… "

"Over all these years of running, did you even stop to *think* about your actions—or how many lives you've ruined?" Almira kept yelling at him, trying to destroy him from the inside out.

"I didn't… do anything…" Lotus wheezed as he jumped away from a bolt of lightning striking where he'd been standing.

"You have endangered countless lives and brought only pain to the people of Perlaria. Your face and name are scattered across this whole land. Everyone knows who you *really* are— a heartless murderer who is too afraid to show his face and take accountability for what he has done. You cower and hide because you *know* how weak you really are." Almira's bo slammed into the ground, once again just missing her mark.

"Stop..." Lotus begged.

"Is that what Din, the Grand Sage, asked you? Did he beg you to stop before you—"

"*ENOUGH!*" Lotus bellowed, his voice thundered louder than ever before.

"You have *no* idea... *no idea!...* of what I have been through." Lotus could sense that the dam inside him that was holding back the dark energy was failing, allowing even more to spill over and through it. He felt his sore muscles begin to numb as that energy coated his body in a powerful aura. He took one step forward, ready to shut Almira up.

"Lotus!" Oa shouted weakly. The wanted man turned his gaze to Oa lying there helplessly a short distance away and his heart sank.

"Oa..." Lotus whispered.

The boy was lying on the ground, reaching out for Lotus, calling his name. Han was above him, the flames from his elbows burning brightly as he stomped on Oa's chest.

"No... please..." Lotus muttered.

"Captain!" Nyloc shouted. Lotus looked over and saw Nyloc frozen in place from the neck down. All that was free was his head.

"Shut it!" Sora yelled as she struck him across the face, knocking him out.

"Stop..." Lotus murmured, holding it back.

"Ronin! Don't give up!" Thalrok shouted.

Lotus saw Thalrok standing across from Agne, his legs shaking and his sword just barely held upright. He watched as Agne charged at him.

Thalrok, standing his ground, placed both his hands on his sword and gripped it tightly. The giantess reeled back her woody fist and swung it forward, extending her tree branch arm to reach toward Thalrok. The bounty hunter was ready to chop this tree in half and rescue the rest of his friends.

This isn't how it's gonna end. We can still come back from this. We're gonna be alright. Thalrok said to himself reassuringly, readying for his next move.

The fist-bearing branch was nearly in front of him. He lifted his sword high overhead and prepared to crush her attack.

"We can do this, Ronin!" he shouted, swinging his mighty blade down and shattering the wood into pieces. The cocky smirk he wore after landing his hit was clear as day through the mask.

"I won't be stopped that—" Thalrok's voice faltered.

He felt an incredible amount of pain coming from his chest. He slowly looked down to see that a branch had stabbed into it, and it was still stuck there.

His heart skipped a beat.

Thalrok looked back up and saw that Agne's arm was *not* shattered. When he swung his sword down, Agne split her arm into multiple branches and spread them to avoid his attack. Then, she redirected one of them at the titan's chest, impaling him. Afterward, Agne broke off that portion of wood from her arm and watched the bounty hunter stumble.

"What…" Thalrok dropped his blade and gently touched the tree branch piercing his chest. His legs buckled, blood began to drip from his wound. He then glanced over to Lotus, knowing that his friend had been watching the whole time.

"I'm sorry…" Thalrok mumbled, and the mighty titan fell flat on his back.

"Don't you see now? Your army has fallen." Almira scoffed, looking back at the empty lifeless stare in Lotus's eyes—the eyes that had just seen his friends' defeat.

"I guess you do," she sighed. Then she shouted, "Now!"

Out of nowhere, Othas shot out of the ground behind Lotus with a giant pillar of stony earth rising behind him. Lotus's body didn't even react.

"Han!" Othas shouted. Within the blink of an eye, Han fired himself at Lotus, forcing both of his fists into his chest and knocking him back into the stony column.

"Pin him, Sora!" Han yelled, elbows bright with flames.

"On it!" The water nymph's hair flowed across the ground and around the pillar, freezing to shackle Lotus's wrists to the stone.

Then the ground rumbled as Agne forced her arms into the ground and reached her branches to wrap around Lotus's legs from below, holding him into place.

The wanted man couldn't speak.

"Ronin," Almira called out.

His head didn't move. His body was pinned to a giant stone pillar with his arms frozen in place and his feet rooted into the ground.

"I, Almira, Captain of Fifth Judgment, hereby sentence you to death for the murder of the Grand Sage Din." She grabbed her bo, reeled back, and then threw it across the field. The bright metal rod soared through the air, flying directly on target. The bo struck like a javelin through the center of the wanted man's chest. Almira then curled her fingers toward each other, generating as much electricity as she could. When she reached her hands out, furious lighting sizzled and stretched all the way to the metal rod, electrocuting Lotus from the inside out. Lotus screamed in pain, howling out in agony with his last remaining breath.

Then... all was silent.

The wanted man's head hung low. Each of his companions lay motionless on the battlefield. As a group, the Fifth Judgment stood stock still, staring at what remained of an impossible task that had finally been completed. The rain that had been holding off for dear life commenced in earnest. The downpour of water began to wash away the battle that once was. Thunder rumbled in the distance as they stood together in victory.

"The wanted man is no more. Let's tie up the others and call for the cavalry to inform the Guardians," Almira instructed as they turned their backs to Lotus and began to move away.

"You..."

A voice was heard, but whose? Each of them froze in complete and absolute horror. They felt their skin crawl, prickling and tingling from their feet to the tops of their heads. Almira and the others turned around slowly. They watched as the water poured down Lotus's drooping head and splashed on the ground.

"will..."

Their eyes widened. They were staring at a real-life ghost. The surrounding air pressure thickened astronomically, and they couldn't seem to move. They watched as Lotus's head slowly lifted up and dark hollow eyes glared at them.

"fall..." Lotus stared intently at each of them in turn. Lightning illuminated the sky and thunder boomed overhead. In the blink of an eye, each blade of grass, tree, bush, or mound of dirt blackened as its life was drained instantly.

The Fifth Judgment felt the pressure and force of powerful energy overwhelm the surrounding area as they stared at this real demon.

"Who *is* this?" Almira managed to mutter, her voice strained and barely audible.

The dark energy inside Lotus could not be contained any longer.

The dam had broken.

38

On the Run

The *Land Skipper*, doing her best, pushed across the fields of Prosper Valley, over the hills and through the valleys. Like a mother gathering up her children as she ran to find help, she held the companions on board, trying her best to get them home before it was too late. The creaking wood sang the sorrowful song of a most weary ship. Her gears and bearings were barely holding, but day or night, she wouldn't stop. The *Skipper* would persevere over whatever terrain and weather she met. There wasn't much time left.

"Uhh…" Thalrok groaned, feeling himself slowly regaining consciousness. He could see the soft blue sky through the slits of his mask and feel the swaying and jiggling of the *Skipper* against his back as he rested on the deck. It didn't click at first, but the *Skipper* was indeed moving. His eyes flickered as he realized what was going on. Then Thalrok painfully propped himself up and darted his eyes across the deck. He saw Oa and Nyloc lying there near him. Both were banged up but still breathing, and little by little they stirred and woke up simultaneously.

"Where are we?" they muttered as they rubbed their aching heads. Before either of them could get another word out, the *Skipper* came to a slow rolling stop. They turned toward the bow and noticed…

"Mellowtin?" Thalrok mumbled in a raspy voice.

"How did… how are we back here?" Oa asked. From the back of the ship, they heard the sound of a soft thud as something fell to the ground behind the *Skipper*.

Their hearts stopped.

Their eyes widened.

Ignoring all pain, they got to their feet as fast as they could, dropped to the ground, and hurried to the stern of the *Skipper*.

"Lotus!" Oa shouted as they spotted their captain lying crumpled face down on the ground. Blood soaked his dirty clothes. He had extended himself beyond all physical limits to push the *Skipper* all the way back to Mellowtin. It was a miracle.

"Ronin!" Thalrok shouted and carefully turned him over. All gasped at the deep bloody hole in Ronin's chest.

Thalrok sat down beside his friend and held him as he lay there unconscious. Profound anguish poured through him.

"*Roniiiin!* Wake up... please, wake up!" he cried out. There was no response.

"Oh my goodness! What happened?!" Rina shouted as she came around the side of the *Land Skipper* and saw the horrific scene. She noticed they'd returned and hurried to meet them, never expecting to be greeted by a sight like *this*.

They all gaped in horror at the hole in his chest. The wound was bloodied both front and back. From the center of it, dark jagged marks from Almira's lightening scarred the skin. It was like looking at a drawing of a blood-red sun with charred flares radiating from it.

"Rina, please, you gotta start healing him!" Nyloc begged.

The angel didn't skip a beat. She quickly knelt beside him and placed her hands, open palms down, above his body. A green aura glowed from her hands and flooded over Lotus as it surrounded his whole body. Specks of light began to sparkle and flutter above him as her healing abilities slowly did their work.

"Come on, Lotus! *Please*, wake up!" Oa urged, tears running down his face.

"He *pushed* us all the way back here." Thalrok realized, as he glanced back over at the *Skipper* and saw the bloody handprints that stained the rear panel of their ship.

Suddenly, a familiar voice chimed out from around the other side of the *Skipper*, "You guys are back! How was the—" The young blacksmith's excited reception stopped abruptly.

"Stritan, don't—!" Thalrok shouted, but it was too late. He turned to see the boy's face go stark white when he caught sight of Lotus's bloody body.

Stritan stood frozen in place, unable to process what he was seeing. Nyloc immediately went to his side and physically turned him away from the gruesome sight.

"He'll be fine. He's going to be fine. Please, just go get help," Nyloc spoke in a calm yet urgent voice. He could sense the overwhelming emotions Stritan was feeling. The boy stood there, tense and wide-eyed.

"Stritan, please, we need your help!" Nyloc shook him a bit to snap him out of it.

"Ohhh... okay!" Stritan gathered his thoughts and then ran into town, shouting for people to come and help.

Thalrok held onto Lotus as gently as he could while Rina tried her best to heal him.

"You can't go now, Ronin. You can't leave before we all..." Thalrok got choked up. With great difficulty he stopped himself from letting a single tear fall. Lotus was going to live. Lotus would never die this easily.

"It's gonna be alright..." Thalrok said to himself.

* * *

The sound of a constant ringing in her ears, the overwhelming pain in her body, the feeling of a rough surface beneath her—all was a confusing and unpleasant haze, the same feeling as waking up from a nightmare.

"Almira... Almira!" Han shouted, nudging her aggressively. His captain's eyes opened painfully, and the muscles in her body screamed.

"Captain, are you alright?" Han asked one more time, shaking her more gently now.

"W-what happened?" Almira asked, slowly propping herself up. Her mind was muddled and blank, she couldn't remember anything of what had gone on here. She looked to one side and saw her other three companions lying on the ground, unconscious. They appeared to have been intentionally placed there, side by side, in a short row. Their bodies were covered in dirt, cuts, and bruises. Their wounds appeared to have been tended to, but who would...?

"I have no idea." Han shook his head.

"The last thing I remember was... Ronin." Almira wore a confused expression. They'd had him completely trapped, thought he was dead, and yet he was still able to get away. Their all-out efforts hadn't been enough to stop him. But somehow, *they* were all still alive, even after staring directly into that monster's eyes.

"Are you alright?" Almira asked, struggling to stand.

"I'm fine. It looks like the others are too." Han replied.

Almira gingerly rose to her feet and went over to check on the others. She wanted to make sure that they were all breathing, and luckily enough, they were. By now the sky was as black as ever; night was taking its turn to dance across the sky. What moonlight there was filtered through dense cloud cover. The faintly lit outer ring was as quiet as ever; only the low whistling of the wind could be heard over the fields.

"Come on, we have to get the others back to base. We have a lot to discuss." Almira ordered as she knelt by Agne, who was just waking up. She heard no reply from Han. Almira turned and saw him standing off on his own, perplexed and staring in the distance. "What's the matter?" she asked.

"He got away," Han said in a flat voice.

Almira supported Agne's branchlike arms so she could get to her feet, then walked over to Han's side. She patted his back gently, and trying to be of some comfort, told him, "As upsetting as it is to say... it's fine. We will always have another chance to—"

"No! No, that's not what I'm thinking about." Han interrupted. He looked over at the others, injured and weakened but alive, then back over to his captain. "He could have easily killed us... Why didn't he?"

39

Waiting

The slowest week of each of the crews' lives had reached its end. With each day that passed, their hopes had never faded, and they knew that Lotus would wake up soon. Rina used her strongest healing abilities and administered them to Lotus every day, in hopes that it would make a difference.

Each of the companions dealt with this situation in different ways. Thoughts of anger, regret, fear, and great sadness tormented their minds. Depression followed. They couldn't help but bear the burden of not being able to do anything for Lotus. He had fought that whole battle with the Fifth Judgment to the very end, and then *pushed* them in the *Land Skipper* all the way back to Mellowtin, where they would be safe.

Thalrok did the best he could in trying to cope with his strong emotions. The bounty hunter would go out to the wooded area near the village and get his frustrations out by training. For hours, he would be out there, training hard and overthinking recent events. In reality, he was not allowing himself enough time to heal either physically or mentally.

Nyloc was the opposite. He took this time to seclude himself and stayed in his room. The blind archer would meditate for hours, which also kept him from either facing or being there for the others.

As for Oa, the poor boy never left Lotus's side. He spent every day sitting in a chair by his bed, just waiting for him to wake up.

"Please…" Oa murmured, dropping his head to his knees. He sat and waited patiently, spending every second he could at Lotus's bedside. Sometimes he even spoke to Lotus, just to break the silence. He endured sleepless nights and painful mornings without any sign of his friend waking up. Yet, Oa never lost hope. He never stopped believing that soon Lotus would say something, *anything*. And then…

"Oa?" a hoarse voice croaked.

"Huh?!" The boy jerked his head up. Springing up, he spun around and noticed Lotus's arms subtly twitching. His eyelids were trembling a bit too, attempting to open.

"Lotus!!" Oa shouted. He couldn't figure out what to do next. He was overwhelmed with happiness and relief. As his head darted from right to left, he spotted the open window. Like a bolting rabbit, he hopped out of it and burst out onto the rooftop of the inn.

"He's awake!" Oa shouted to the world.

"What!?" Rina, sitting on a bench below reading, threw her book on the ground. She glided up and followed Oa back in through the window. Placing her hands on him lightly, Rina channeled all of the healing energy that she could summon to help him awaken. The wanted man felt his painfully sore body regaining sensation, and at last, his eyes finally opened.

"Oh my goodness… it worked." Rina dropped to her knees, so happy to see him awake again.

"Where am I?" Lotus asked.

"You're in your room right now. We're back in Mellowtin." Oa replied, tears still falling down his face.

Lotus stared up at the ceiling and began to remember all that had happened in the City of Light. Having to fight the Fifth Judgment, the overflowing, uncontrollable energy that had taken over, the hazy image of him pushing the *Skipper*—it all came back. Except, he didn't remember consciously making those decisions. It had just come to him… naturally, instinctively.

"Is he awake?!" Nyloc shouted as the door broke open and in he surged. "Captain!" he exclaimed, rushing to his bedside.

"Nyloc, are you alright?" Lotus asked.

"You're asking me?! I should be asking you that," the archer chuckled softly as he knelt beside him. For such a stoic person, Nyloc showed great pleasure at seeing his friend awake after an entire week of being unresponsive.

"I'm fine, I just—" Before Lotus could finish what he was saying. The sound of what felt like an earthquake rattled the inn. It rolled through the front door and up the stairs. Everyone's eyes turned to the doorway as Thalrok sharply turned the corner and surged into the room.

"Ronin!" The bounty hunter shook his head in relief as he rushed over to join the others by his friend's side.

"Good, you're all safe then." Lotus smiled softly, then closed his eyes and let out a grateful sigh.

"How do you feel?" Thalrok asked.

"I feel like I was dropped from the sky and crushed into the ground... a couple of hundred times," Lotus groaned as he tried to sit up and prop himself on one elbow. Everyone immediately jumped to stop him from any more movement.

"You need to stay as still as you can right now. You lost a lot of blood, Lotus." Rina told him as she carefully helped him lie down.

"Do you remember what happened?" Oa asked.

"I remember bits and pieces. It's all very hazy, but I remember losing control and my body moving purely by instinct." Lotus's arms twitched slightly as a stinging sensation coming from his chest caught his attention. As he touched the middle of his breastbone, he winced as a shock-like pain jolted through his body.

"Careful! I did what I could to help it heal, but it's not perfect." Rina carefully removed the blanket from his chest to reveal his large, unusual scar, the stab wound where Almira's metal bo had pierced his chest, and the burns from her lightning radiating out from around it.

"Wow..." Lotus finally saw the end result of his battle. He was left speechless for a moment. He didn't realize just how bad this could have been.

"Do you remember anything before you lost control?" Nyloc asked.

"I just remember seeing that woman with a tree for a body—" Lotus's eyes widened and shot over to Thalrok. Abruptly pushing himself up, he stared and said, "Thalrok! You were stabbed, too! Are *you* alright!?" Nyloc and Oa held him back from throwing his legs over the side of the bed to sit up on the edge of it.

"*Please* stop moving! I'm fine, see." Thalrok showed Lotus the scars on his own chest and shoulder from his scuffle with Agne. "I got lucky," he admitted. "Those tree limbs didn't go all the way through, and the branch broke off and kept the blood from pouring out too fast."

Lotus was very relieved to hear that Thalrok was safe from what could have been a fatal attack.

"Rina made sure to take care of all of us when we got back. *She* is the main reason you are still alive right now," Nyloc added.

"Truly, I can't thank you enough, Rina. Once again, we wouldn't be where we are now without you," Lotus winced as another jolt of pain went through his body.

"You are all too kind to me. Please, all I ask is that you all continue to rest." Rina replied. Then she added loudly, "Especially *you*, Thalrok!" and got right up in his face, brows raised.

"Okay, *okay*... I *will*," he groaned, and then headed out to lie down in his room. Rina followed to make sure he actually went to his room this time and didn't sneak out again.

"Thalrok has been taking this hit harder than most of us. He feels horribly guilty for this whole thing. He called himself weak and trained every day in spite of his injuries until his body shut down and he collapsed out in the woods," Nyloc said, head lowered.

"Really?" Lotus sighed.

"It's been hard for us all, to say the least." Nyloc sat down and rested his elbows on his knees.

"Did you really push the *Skipper* all the way back to Mellowtin?" Oa couldn't understand how he'd done it, and had to hear the words from Lotus's mouth.

"I guess I did." Lotus rubbed his head, "I have a terrible time remembering what exactly happened."

Nyloc and Oa both reminded him that his main goal for right now was to rest up and heal himself from his horrendous injuries. Then Nyloc said, "Oh, and uh, before we go—Stritan unfortunately saw you in your, uh, condition when we got back. It scared him pretty bad. Is it alright if he comes by to say hello now that you're awake again?"

"Of course he can," Lotus assured him. Now that he'd seen that big scar on his chest, he knew that he must have looked pretty rough when Stritan last saw him.

Nyloc and Oa left the wanted man alone to rest and recover. That he wasn't unconscious anymore gave them all great peace of mind.

Lotus noticed the pitcher of water by his bed and poured himself a glass of water. "Oh, that's good," he gasped as he took the first sip of water on his own for a week. In a matter of seconds, the whole pitcher was completely empty. He cautiously lay back down, then stared at the ceiling as his damaged body recovered from a fight that had nearly taken him out for good.

"Deja vu," he shook his head.

He could hear the people outside, busy as ever. Through the streets walked the lifeblood of the town, all of them enjoying a sunny afternoon. It didn't take very long for Lotus to grow tired of his room. He wanted very badly to go outside.

He peeked over to see that his door was closed, and that no one was watching. As painful as it was, he sat himself up and placed his feet on the floor as he sat on the edge of the bed. Huffing out in exhaustion, he stood up and shuffled over to the mirror. He saw the bandages on his arms and legs, and that huge mark on the center of his chest, a deep red circle with jagged burns stretching out from it. It really *was* like a blood moon.

"Another scar," he murmured, glancing out the window with a sigh. After getting dressed ever so slowly, he hobbled over to his door and opened it stealthily. Shimmying out and closing it slowly, he was met with a surprise.

"Going somewhere?" Oa asked.

Lotus jumped at the sound of Oa's voice as he closed the door behind him. "I just need some time out of my room," Lotus replied.

Oa shook his head. "Rina said you needed to rest. One wrong move and things could end badly." Oa reminded him.

"It's fine. I've had way worse times than this." Lotus confessed.

"Really?!" The young disciple appeared to be distraught now, troubled to know that this latest awful fight wasn't the worst he had gone through.

Lotus froze in place and strained in the distance. "Yeah... " he muttered, then walked unsteadily over to the seating area. He and Oa both settled on the couch and just sat together in silence for a moment.

Every time something happens like this, it always goes the same way. It's just fate on repeat. Just like before, Lotus realized.

Everything began to click into place. It always went the same way every time. Which meant it was only a matter of time until the City of Light came after him. They had seen how much more of a threat he was after fighting, and defeating, the Fifth Judgment, their elite team. The clock was ticking now. Soon, they could come breaking down their doors.

"Do you wanna talk about it?" Oa asked.

"I won't bore you with my life. Come on, I wanna take a walk." Lotus carefully stood up and made his way down the hall. Oa, watching closely, stayed by his side as they left the Lie-Inn and walked through the village.

"What have you all been up to while I was out?" Lotus asked.

"Well, Nyloc has been doing a lot of meditating. He hadn't come out of his room until you woke up. Rina was reading as much as she could, trying to figure out a better way to heal you. And you heard how Thalrok was training night and day in the woods. He really hasn't been coping with this very well," Oa replied.

"What about you?"

"I..." Oa hesitated to reply, "I couldn't think or really even sleep. So I just stayed by your side, hoping every day that you would wake up."

Lotus smiled and softly chuckled, "You know, I won't be around forever. Because of that, I want you to remember how strong *you* are. I managed to get a glimpse of how you fought against Han, and oh boy, you have come *so* far since you joined us on our journey." Lotus praised. The young disciple blushed, not knowing what to say.

"I really do appreciate the concern you all had for me. You all are too kind." Lotus tousled the boy's unruly brown hair.

"Hey, cut it out!" Oa grinned as he swatted his hands away. They laughed together as they made their way toward the Fork and Sword Canteen. They weren't able to get more than half a block before they heard a voice shouting, "Lotus! Lotus!" and there was Stritan, running over to meet them.

"Wow, I am *really* glad to see you're alright! I was worried sick after seeing you so... uh..." Stritan choked on his words. He couldn't bear to remember that horrible sight.

"I'm sorry I worried you. I'm much better now, and I'm happy to see that you're alright as well," Lotus reassured him as he patted the boy's shoulder.

"Stritan got some of the others from town to come and help us get you inside. He was a big help." Oa told Lotus.

"Thank you very much for what you did, Stritan." Lotus bowed his head to the young man.

Stritan couldn't help but leak a tear or two at the sight of his now-conscious instructor. Clasping his artificial hand inside of his real one, he asked eagerly, "Can we continue training again soon then?"

"Once I am back to full recovery, we most certainly can," Lotus replied, smiling.

"Yes! Yay!" Stritan cheered and jumped up and down.

"Stritaaan!" They heard his name being shouted from the direction of the canteen.

"Dang. I would love to talk more, but I gotta go! See you guys!" he shouted as he ran back to work, metallic hand glinting in the sun as he waved goodbye.

"That boy," Lotus smiled again as they headed out through town. Lotus and Oa got to spend some quality time together, chatting back and forth.

The one who'd been the most worried about his friend finally got to see him up walking and talking again, on the mend.

As they wandered through Mellowtin, Lotus had plenty of time to think. What was next? He had just fought against the City of Light, which surely made him the top priority on their agenda. That looming threat still brooded and grew in the forbidden world. There was a great deal to think of at once. So, what to do now?

Later that day...

"How are you feeling?" Rina asked.

"My whole body is still in a lot of pain, but I think moving around actually helped a lot," Lotus replied.

"That's good to hear. I'll still administer a bit more healing energy before we all call it a day." Rina decided. She, Oa, and Lotus all sat on the rooftop of the inn, lounging there watching the blue skies darkening and turning orange as daytime was closing up shop.

"There you are," Nyloc said as he headed up the last of the steps.

"We were wondering where you guys went," Thalrok added, following just behind.

"Lotus and I got some fresh air and walked around for a while. We wanted to stay outside and decided that up here would be a nice place to relax." Oa said, sliding over to give the others some room.

Just like before, the five of them sat together and just bantered about the day. It was as if nothing of note had happened a week ago. Was it that they didn't care? Or did they fear bringing up the elephant in the room?

"Ronin..." Thalrok spoke. All eyes turned to the bounty hunter.

"Yeah?" he replied.

Thalrok stared down at the floor. He took a deep breath in, then exhaled slowly. "We can't thank you enough for what you did. You were completely right before. I don't know what I was thinking. If we can't even handle a group of five elite warriors, then how can we handle what could be out there in the forbidden world?" Thalrok said bleakly. He held his head in his hands, still sulking over his own perceived weakness.

"We realize now just how dire this situation is, and to be honest…" Oa paused.

"We don't know what to do," Nyloc finished his sentence.

"We thought about it this whole week, and we truly have no idea where to go or what to do next," Rina explained.

"After all that we went through, all that *you* went through, we are at the point where, no matter what we do, we cannot see a brighter outcome." Thalrok stood up from his seat and looked into his leader's eyes. "Ronin, what do you want us to do?" he spoke sincerely and with respect.

Lotus glanced to his left, then his right. He saw that they all were looking at him, waiting for an answer. He'd known that another talk like this would come up. Luckily for him, having this whole day of peace had given him plenty of time to come up with an answer—one that would solve every problem and also bring hope.

Lotus stood up from his seat and looked around at all his friends. "I got to witness just how strong you all are. Each of you trained vigorously for the battles we went through," he began. "I believe wholeheartedly in everyone here. With all of us working together, there isn't a single thing that can stand in our way. No person, no army, no nothing! We are proud warriors. We can, and will, fight with whatever it takes to win." Lotus affirmed.

This was a sudden change in mood. Everyone started to feel their adrenaline surge and their hearts start to race. What shifted to make Lotus talk and act like this? They expected him to be the same as before, wanting them to be away from conflict, protected, and safe. But now, it was like he was rallying his troops for battle. What was going on?

"Two weeks," Lotus held up two fingers, emphasizing the urgency, "Two weeks. We will train, work, and prepare. Because when the sun rises on that fifteenth day, we will board that ship…" he paused, feeling the weight of anticipation as they all leaned forward, riveted by his words. With a triumphant smile, Lotus delivered his final statement, "And we will take down the Dark Empire."

40

The Red Sky

The sun hung low in the sky, casting long shadows over the barren land before them. Giant walls loomed on the horizon, their gray, crumbling edges cutting into the horizon like the rotting teeth of some ancient beast. The air was thick with unease. Even the wind, usually so careless and free, seemed to hesitate as it swept across the grassy fields, whispering as if it knew what was to come.

The *Land Skipper* had been tended to by Stritan a week before their departure and was again in fine working order. Now, she brought the five companions closer and closer to the one place no one from Perlaria had ever dared to tread—the forbidden world.

A silence had settled over her crew, deeper than the eerie stillness of the wilderness surrounding them. No one spoke as they rode onward, their eyes set on the destination ahead. Every breath felt heavy, as if the weight of the walls already pressed down on them, pushing the air from their lungs.

For two weeks, they had trained for this objective. Every morning, they'd pushed their bodies beyond limits they hadn't known existed—blisters, bruises, and exhaustion had become their constant companions. But this venture... this was going to be something else.

"No turning back, right?" Thalrok spoke in a steady tone. The question had been hanging in the air, unspoken, for days.

"No turning back," Lotus's answer was firm, but his eyes betrayed the doubts that lingered in the corners of his mind. He had always been the cautious one. But this mission was strangely different. No amount of planning and training could prepare them for the chaos that must lie behind those walls.

The others said nothing, their expressions fierce and ready. Each of them carried their own thoughts, their own fears, but their profound silence spoke volumes.

Ahead, the massive walls grew larger with every turn of the *Skipper's* wheels, ready to separate them from everything they had ever known. They were taller than any structure they had seen in their lives, their surfaces forbidding and cold, dark as the shadow of some ancient god. It was said that no one had ever gone to the other side of those walls, and that the world over there was a cursed place—wild, untamed, and full of dangers that defied comprehension.

"We've been through a lot together," Nyloc spoke, resting against the railing.

"We have," Oa added.

"Let us push through. We will not stop until we have discovered what threatens us beyond these walls," Rina announced, standing tall.

A shiver ran down Lotus's spine as they neared the base of the towering battlements that now cast a dense shadow over them. It felt to him as though the world itself was holding its breath, waiting. The air felt thick with the weight of all the stories, warnings, threats, promises, clashing against each other.

A small, shaky breath left Lotus's lips as he gazed up at the wall. "Once we step past this… we are in unknown territory. We can't just walk out when things get too hard."

Thalrok, Oa, Nyloc, and Rina nodded, the gravity of the moment sinking in. Everyone of them had known it from the start, but hearing those words spoken aloud somehow made it real in a way nothing else had.

The *Land Skipper* came to a slow, easing halt. They took this quiet, still moment to stare blankly at the gigantic barricade before them. It was a dry stone wall, made of huge megaliths and boulders, with no visible mortar. It had been standing for ages. Rooted in cracks, vines crept up the sides, and occasionally debris fell down from the top. Here was an ancient relic of the past that held back the nightmares of the future.

They began to inspect each dark portion of the rocks, looking for their entrance.

"There it is," Thalrok pointed out. They all turned their gaze to one crack at the base of the wall that looked big enough to squeeze through.

Then, one by one, they hopped down from the *Land Skipper* and made their way to the crevice. "This should get us to the other side. It's a tight squeeze, but it'll do," Lotus said, as he peered in and then began to wriggle his way through. The others followed behind him, except for Thalrok, who stayed to finish securing the *Skipper*. They all hoped she would still be there when they returned. *If* they returned...

Just like going through a tunnel, they all had seen the light at the end and crawled out to the other side.

"Mountains." Lotus squinted, peering out into the forbidden world.

Emerging from the dark passageway, they stood there blinking in awe. In front of them was a valley surrounded by mountains and hills that stretched far across this vast world they had yet to discover. In places, mountaintops even poked above the high dark walls.

"Incredible," Thalrok commented as he squirmed out of the crevice and walked out into the light.

"Our journey has just begun. Come on, we have to keep moving," Lotus reminded them as they started moving to the east.

He was not lying to them; the journey was far from being over. Even though the long trip to the wall had been a fairly simple one, the real adventure began now, which was to travel on foot through this unknown environment. The five of them were bound to the same task: to find the Dark Empire's stronghold here in the forbidden world and stop whatever threat was to come.

The five of them marched on for miles and miles, over hills, trenches, plateaus, and valleys. Hours went by with fresh terrain discovered as each cresting horizon shared new land to behold. The forbidden world appeared a lot more... normal than they expected. It just seemed to be like some other part of Perlaria. Maybe after all these years, the scars of the past *had* healed in this world.

The sky was becoming dimmer, and night was almost upon them. They were out in the unknown; who knew what would happen when the sun went down? They found what they hoped would be a safe place to spend the night.

As they began to set up camp, each claiming a spot to sleep, Lotus felt like something was off kilter. "Whoa. Do you guys feel that?" he asked. Everyone looked around, not feeling anything unusual.

"What is it?" Rina asked.

"I don't know. It just feels... uneasy, weird." He stared off into the east, senses tingling. He decided that it was just nervousness getting to him again, so he ignored it for now to continue organizing and setting up camp.

Their first day in the forbidden world was over, and as they rested under the stars, they could only wonder what lay ahead. From what they'd seen so far, this place seemed just like typical parts of Prosper Valley and Perlaria. Maybe tomorrow would bring something more...

The next day...

"Everybody packed up?" Nyloc asked, his own gear at the ready.

"All good," Thalrok announced as they headed off to start their second day of exploration.

Their tracks across the map of the forbidden world distanced them farther from the lands of Prosper, heading east to more unknown. As the sun moved across the sky throughout the morning and their expedition clocked on for hour after hour, Lotus began to feel even more uneasy.

"Ronin?" Thalrok asked. He had noticed an uncomfortable look on his friend's face.

"I don't know what it is, but the farther we go east... I keep feeling some kind of powerful energy, and it keeps growing." Lotus shook his head, unable to fully describe what he sensed.

"I'm starting to feel it, too," Oa added, looking around at the others.

"That's a *good* sign. It means we're heading in the right direction!" Thalrok clapped, ready to continue their trek.

"Hey, have you all noticed this?" Rina pointed straight into the sky. Above them, the serene blue sky that had been watching over them was turning to an orangish hue—almost as if it was sundown, yet the sun was directly above them.

"We're getting closer. Let's keep going," Lotus replied. He led the charge onward.

They all followed swiftly behind him. No questions. No replies. Just the stoic faces of a group of able warriors, ready to go.

The farther they traveled east, the darker the sky became. What was once a blue sky became eerie and red in color. What was once a calming walk around the unpopulated lands of Perlaria became a trek through a completely different world. The lush greenery gradually disappeared. They found themselves climbing dusty hills in a desolate wasteland. It was empty of all life, just powdery, barren soil and some debris from what could have been homes hundreds of years ago.

Time passed. The pressure, the disturbing energy that Lotus had felt earlier, was only growing. All of them felt it now. They all had a looming fear lurking in the back of their minds, but made sure to suppress it, hiding it away from their reality.

"I think we should call it for today," Lotus panted as he stopped atop the steep foothill they'd climbed. Everyone dropped to their knees as they reached the peak, resting and basking in the tainted moonlight.

"Check it out, a cave." Thalrok pointed off to the right and headed over to take a look.

The craggy hole in the adjacent mountain was small, but roomy enough for them to take refuge. At a higher altitude, the dead of night could be cold and harsh in this part of the world. A sheltered place to sleep would be helpful to both body and soul in a place like this. Setting up their gear and lighting a fire for warmth and cooking, they allowed themselves to rest and recharge as the night glided on.

The last few embers in the fire flickered. The soft howl of the wind whistled through the cave and over the sleeping companions. They lay there on the hard floor of the cave, getting as much sleep as they could. In the wee hours of the morning, Oa felt his heavy eyelids pop open. Awake now, he looked around to see if the others were asleep, but didn't see Lotus among them. He checked around more carefully, but still couldn't find him. Then Oa noticed him sitting just outside the mouth of the cave.

"You doing alright?" Oa asked as he walked out and stood beside Lotus.

"Oh, yeah, I'm alright. Did I accidentally wake you?" The wanted man spoke quietly.

"No, I'm just a little homesick. Having a hard time staying asleep, y' know?" Oa took a seat next to Lotus, and they stared at the thousands of stars. Each of them twinkled in the black sky like a performance of dancing lights.

"Do you miss your village?" Lotus asked.

"A little bit. I miss my friends back home, and Reggio too." The young disciple of Gou paused. He smiled, then lowered his head. "And even though it's only been a small part of my life, I think I miss Mellowtin."

"Really?" Lotus asked.

"I know it hasn't even been that long, yet, but I feel like that's where I can go to and call home. Ever since my family passed away, I haven't had a place that felt, y'know, warm, like a home should. After going to Mellowtin with you all, my life feels more… full, I guess." Oa wore a joyful smile on his face as he reminisced about his time with this crew. They had traveled across Perlaria and had been allies through countless battles, companions who always had each other's backs. Their time together had brought them closer as a team and really bonded them.

"I've been to a lot of villages in my life, but Mellowtin… it does have that special feel to it, doesn't it?" Lotus commented, leaning back to stare up at the stars.

"What about your home? Don't you miss it too?" Oa asked. The young disciple knew about the wanted man's past. He knew exactly what he had gone through and the trials he'd faced along the way. But none of that changed the fact that both Souder and Petalbrooke had been home to him, and he'd had a life there in each.

"I… I really do miss the two places that I've called home. I can't say there's a day that goes by when I don't think about going back to those times and places." Lotus fell onto his back, continuing to stare blankly skyward.

"I don't know what will happen next, but as of now, Mellowtin is my home. We have all become a part of each other's lives, and we have each started to forge our own path." Lotus paused. "Lately, though, my home no longer feels like a village or a town; it's where I feel the most at peace. And right now, I feel more at peace than I have in quite a while," Lotus exhaled deeply, letting out any and all leftover fears.

"And you," Lotus sat up, looking over at Oa, "You have become an amazing fighter. Your skill, courage, and overall power have grown so much since you joined Thalrok and me. I cannot tell you how proud I am of you," Lotus spoke earnestly, his words sinking deeply into Oa's ears.

"Really?" Oa asked excitedly.

"Of course. I can't say I've seen someone with your talent ever grow so fast in their training. I wish I could be as strong as you one day." Lotus tousled Oa's hair as he stood up.

Oa's heart beat faster with excitement; those positive words fueled both his body and his psyche. He couldn't remember being given praise like that ever before, and from someone he so respected. He was riding high. "Please! Keep training me; I want to grow more and get even stronger," Oa begged.

Lotus watched the boy fold his hands together and stare at him with wide eyes. The wanted man smiled to himself as he replied, "Of course."

Oa was *very* excited to hear *that* response. His legs twitched, and he wanted to jump around the whole cave, fist pumping. But, the others were sleeping there soundly after the long day of hiking, so Oa contained his delight and finally joined them in rest, as did Lotus.

The first full day here was over, their hopes were high, and the morning sun was preparing to bring them into tomorrow.

The next morning...

Dawn beckoned them into wakefulness early the next day. Lotus's eyes flickered open in the faintly lit cave. He tossed and turned, then at last hauled himself up and rubbed his eyes. Everyone else was waking up at the same time. The uneasy pressure from yesterday seemed to have grown overnight. As they broke camp, readying to shove off to the east, Rina looked around the cave searching for something.

"What's the matter?" Thalrok asked.

"Have any of you seen Nyloc?" she replied. They poked all around the nooks and crannies of the cave but couldn't find him. Then Oa caught a glimpse of him standing outside, staring off into the distance.

"Hey, Nyloc!" Thalrok called out.

No response.

"Is he alright?" Oa wondered. They all headed over to him to see what the matter was.

"Hey, Nyloc, are you alright?" Lotus asked.

Nyloc pointed off into the distance, far across the hills and mountains. Their eyes followed his finger as it indicated a place far across the land. In a concerned tone of voice, Nyloc said, "Did anyone notice that castle last night?"

41

Sirens of Fear

The sky overhead had become suffocatingly red, the air thick with the weight of despair. Beneath the warriors' feet, the once-dusty plains had transformed into a forsaken land of destruction—blackened ash crunched like brittle bone with their every step. Jagged spires of rock rose from the earth, twisted and deformed by some ancient and malevolent force. The ground beneath them trembled as if the very heart of this forsaken world pulsed with hatred.

Lava bubbled from cracks that split the earth open, sending orange glowing phantasms dancing like hellfire across the horizon. And looming above it all, on a jagged cliff of stone, stood the castle. Its silhouette was sharp and formidable against the sickly glow of a dying sun.

No breeze stirred the air. No birds cried from above. The land was silent, save for the distant roar of molten rivers and the steady, heavy footfalls of those who dared to walk into the very mouth of evil.

"What *is* this place?" Thalrok murmured.

"I have no idea," Lotus replied, eyes wandering and mouth agape.

This must be the structure the king was talking about. The wanted man concluded as he took a few slow steps forward.

The five of them made their way through the cursed domain. Eyes steely, senses sharp, they felt the desolate land's sinister gaze upon them, as if the very earth had awakened to challenge their presence. As they grew closer to the towering castle, which rose higher than any building they had yet seen, they noticed the rubble of what was an old city. Dust and ash covered a large area of age-old ruins as they passed through what had looked to have once been a populous, functioning metropolis. Any being that lived here, past or present, appeared no more; they saw not a single soul anywhere.

"Where is everyone?" Oa asked.

Nyloc paused to perceive any signs of life from the area of devastation around them, then said, "I don't think anyone has lived here in a very long time."

They followed the path over the foul dark grit below their feet. The pressure they felt before was now heavier than gravity itself; they felt like their shoulders were being pushed downward. Something seemed extremely off about this. They hadn't seen a single living thing since they got here, no wildlife or living beings at all. It was so strange. All they felt was this dark force. Surely they would have been spotted by now if someone were here. Right?

As the path began to rise, they could see the entrance to the castle ahead of them. Their mood became even more solemn.

Here we go. Lotus thought to himself, as they found themselves standing before hell's door.

"Is everyone ready?" Lotus asked quietly.

"Ready," they all whispered back, holding tightly onto their weapons. Thalrok and Lotus rested their shoulders on the giant doors in front of them. Lotus counted down from three and then they both quickly pushed the heavy doors open. A heavy creaking sound echoed through the castle as they hurried inside.

Nothing.

The foyer and adjoining room inside were completely empty, like everything else here. Discolored patches marked the walls after many years of decay. They noticed that grime and debris coated every inch of this place as they warily looked around.

"Hey, don't go too far off. We still don't know what this place is," Lotus whispered as he saw everyone going off in a different direction. They returned to regroup, then walked down a long hallway heading to its far end. But before they could reach the end—

"Lotus, check it out!" Rina called out, pointing over to a set of stairs that led higher in the castle, "Should we go up?"

"There doesn't seem to be anything down here. Let's go." Lotus was curious.

The rest followed him up the long, winding stairs. Floor after floor, they surveyed each and every room of this castle.

Nothing.

It didn't matter what floor, what room, or how far down any of the hallways they went; this castle was as empty as a dried-up lake. Confused and wondering what this place was all about, Lotus and the others made their way up the rest of the stairs.

"Whoa... you are all gonna want to see this," Thalrok called down from yet another set of stairs off to their left.

Everyone except Thalrok had taken a break from the relentless climbing, but now they stood back up again and followed the sound of his voice. When they reached the top of these stairs, they entered a huge, wide-open room which was, as per usual, vacant.

"What is *this*?" Oa wondered.

The room had no walls; there was only a floor and a ceiling. Tall, thick stone pillars stood evenly spaced around the room, supporting the weight of the floors above. Wide openings in between them looked out over great expanses of the forbidden land.

"What an incredible view!" Awed by the panorama, Rina moved closer to the edge for a better look. Everyone investigated a different area of the spacious open area, searching for anything meaningful. It seemed that they must be getting closer to the top of the castle.

Lotus noticed that beside one of the pillars was another staircase leading up to the next floor. *It must not be too much farther to the top.* A sour feeling was forming in his stomach from the ever-increasing dark force. It was clear as day to him now—whatever was causing that odd pressure or energy must be right above the castle.

They roamed the wide-open room for some time, checking out the view and taking in the odd light. The sky was still a blood-red color, with barely any clouds to block the crimson sun.

As Lotus's eyes panned across the horizon, he noticed the statues of strange beasts attached to the sides of many of the pillars. Two-legged winged monsters with huge talons gripped onto the exterior sides of the outer pillars, frozen in stone with faces turned upward. Their heads were grotesque, tube-like maws, consisting entirely of a large circular mouth with thousands of jagged teeth in rows that seemed to tunnel down into their throat. Apparently, they had no eyes whatsoever.

Lotus looked carefully at each one of them, checking out their structure and wondering if such odd creatures could have ever truly existed. He strolled across the floor, his eyes on the last statue.

He froze in place.

This one was different. This beast was in the exact same position as the others, except...

This one seemed to be looking right at him.

"Oh no..." A shivering feeling of unease trickled down Lotus's spine as his ears began to ring.

"RUN!!" Lotus shouted, as an ear-piercing screech burst out from the beast's mouth and shook the air around them. From the other areas of the room, Thalrok, Oa, Nyloc, and Rina immediately darted a quick look over to the source of that horrible sound. Their hearts cartwheeled in their chests. They watched as the beast that let out another skin-crawling shriek leapt from its pillar and dive-bombed Lotus.

Before it could crash into him, Lotus neatly dodged the attack. He watched the creature spin and slide backwards, dragging its sharp talons across the floor to slow and then come to a stop.

"Run for the stairs!" Lotus shouted as they all stampeded for the stairway to the next higher level. Lotus drew his blade and held a steady stance. His legs shook as he watched the winged demon pull its claws from the stone floor. It made a strange, high-pitched yawning sound and the many teeth in its throat clicked like big drops of water falling onto dry leaves.

"What *is* this thing?" Lotus panted as his heart continued to race.

The ravaging demon again launched itself at the wanted man, its mouth wide open. Lotus quickly hopped above its pounce and slashed at its wings. With four clean cuts across its back and gashed wings, the demon toppled over and thrashed around to get its bearings. Shrieking in fury, the beast again charged Lotus but was interrupted as a meaty hand wrapped entirely around its head from the back. With an abrupt change of direction, Thalrok forced the monster's head straight down, smashing it on and through the floor.

"You alright?" Thalrok asked, pulling back his hand with a look of revulsion.

"I'm fine, but we gotta—" Before Lotus could even finish his sentence, the floors and walls began to quake and tremble. It shook as if an entire army was marching at them to attack. Unfortunately for them, it was.

"Thalrok! Lotus!" Oa shouted from the stairwell.

They saw the young disciple pointing behind them. Both let their gaze follow his finger, turning to see a swarm of those freaks of nature all climbing onto their level. Drool dripped from their toothy mouths as they clawed their way up. A wall of death was closing in.

"Come on!" Thalrok shouted as he grabbed for Lotus's arm. The two of them ran toward the others, who were already scrambling up the stairs in a panic. Lotus peeked over his shoulder and saw that the entire room's outer edges were now lined with these creatures. The screeches of that unlucky beast who first attacked must have signaled the others.

"There are too many of them!" Nyloc yelled.

"We have to get to higher ground! There's no chance we can go back down now!" Thalrok bellowed out to Rina, who was at the front of their group.

"Just keep going!" Lotus shouted, as they could feel the stairway shake even more.

The windows of the castle looked out onto a bleak world as the many demons flicked their wings and smashed their way in. The horde began to close in on the companions as they fought to get past the ones who were creeping in through the windows.

Run.

Fight.

Run.

Fight.

They had no time to think or even breathe as the army of bloodthirsty monsters kept them moving. All five of them ran for their lives, closing in on the very top floor of the castle. Each stairwell grew steeper as they sprinted through the maze, desperately looking for a chance to escape. A chorus of guttural growls echoed up the stairwells as they found themselves stepping out into a hallway at the very top of the castle.

This hallway curved to the left and right around the rounded bulge of what looked to be a very large room, with the walls of it just in front of them. High ceilings stretched far above them, and there were several tall open windows in the hallway's outer wall where more of the demons could easily get in.

"Which way?!" Rina shouted. Lotus and the others looked both ways, heads darting back and forth.

"This way!" Lotus decided, then sprinted to the right. The others followed on his heels.

"Lotus, they're coming!" Nyloc informed everyone, as he sensed them diving in.

"Just keep running!" Lotus yelled.

They knew that the stairwell they'd come up was now overrun with monsters who were coming right for them. There was no turning back.

"It's a door!" Oa pointed out as they rounded the bend.

"Come on, we have to push it open!" Lotus and Thalrok sprinted ahead, charging full speed at the gigantic metal door ahead. They slammed their shoulders into the tall door, ramming it at full speed.

"It won't budge!" Lotus cried out.

"Oa, quick, we need a push!" Thalrok shouted.

The young disciple pulled both his hands back then forced his palms forward, driving as much air as he could into the door. Oa's barrage of wind smashed into the middle and upper portion while Thalrok and Lotus pushed as hard as they could, nearer to the bottom of it.

"It's moving!" Thalrok yelled.

"Let's go! Everyone, get inside!" Lotus shouted out as they funneled through. Watching anxiously as the swarm of monsters was only moments away, the last two dashed inside.

"Close it! Close it!" Rina shrieked.

Her four companions pushed with all of their might on the heavy door, feeling their muscles scream. It shifted barely an inch. Then Thalrok pulled back his hands and slammed his huge fists against it. Vibrating with the impact, the massive door moved and slammed shut. And with that sound, all other commotion ceased. The only noise left was the metal echoing as the doors remained safely closed.

"Is it over?" Thalrok asked. He tilted his head, listening.

"I don't know," Lotus panted and slowly turned around. From the time that the first "statue" moved, he'd had no time to process anything. He was relying totally on instinct to run and escape the swarm of demon-creatures.

Time slowed as Lotus eyed the room that they found themselves sheltered in. Here at the very top of this castle one side of the room faced to the west and presented the forbidden world stretching out before them. It was as if this entire wall was just gone. Lotus's eyes panned over until they rested upon the other side of the room.

Wordless dread overcame him.

His heart sank deep into his chest.

The fear in his body was more intense now than he had ever felt in this lifetime. The others, too, had all become overwhelmed with acute terror.

Their hearts stopped beating.

Their bodies stopped moving.

Their minds couldn't think.

In front of them was a vision so impossible, so unfathomable, that their terror was now complete and all-consuming.

"It... it can't be..." Thalrok's low voice trembled.

"Th-there's no way..." Oa thought to himself.

"Is that—?" Nyloc whispered.

"No..." Rina covered her mouth with both hands.

Lotus, standing in front of them, felt his hands shaking the same way they did when he had stood before his dying master. He was speechless and horrified. His gaping mouth closed, and he was finally able to hoarsely utter,

"The Demon King..."

42

The Lurking King

The air was thick with a heavy silence, one that pressed in from all sides like the weight of a thousand years. The room seemed to stretch beyond sight, its vastness swallowed by the deep shadows that clung to the castle walls. Here, in the silent heart of the Demon King's lofty sanctuary, the faintest echo of their breath felt like a sacrilege.

The five of them stood just inside the doorway, frozen. None of them had ever seen him before, and yet they all knew exactly who he was. He was the one whispered about in fear-soaked corners, the shadow in every nightmare, the name spoken in hushed tones in every broken village.

The Demon King.

The End of Ages.

The Lord of Despair. And here he sat before them.

The throne, a grotesque seat of blackened iron, was twisted into a shape that defied reason, as though it had been forged from the agony of a million souls. And there he was, resting easily upon it. A presence so profound, so consuming, that the room itself seemed to bend around him.

His figure eclipsed them all, towering, immense, as if the very concept of scale had been rewritten in his presence. He loomed above them, a monument to terror, an embodiment of nightmare and legend. Two sets of horns crowned his head, jagged and impossibly sharp, twisting upward into the air like the spires of some forgotten temple. Each horn seemed to pulse with an ancient, malevolent energy, casting ripples through the very fabric of the room.

A scar, pure and radiant as a shard of bone, marred his chest. It glowed with an eerie, unearthly light, as though the wound itself was not merely physical but was a scar on the world's very soul, a mark of some forgotten failure that had scarred both the Demon King and the earth beneath him. The light from it flickered and danced, casting sickly shadows across the darkened chamber.

His limbs were like carved stone, muscles taut and defined, as though chiseled from the very bedrock of the earth. His hands, his feet, each tipped with claws that gleamed like obsidian daggers. One could only imagine the potential damage from a single slash.

There was no softness in him, no flesh that would bend or break, only the unyielding, unforgiving strength of something that had existed beyond time and reason.

In the Demon King's presence, space itself seemed to warp around him, the room bending beneath the weight of his sheer, oppressive power. It was not just his size, nor his form that dwarfed them; it was the palpable, suffocating aura of dominance that radiated from him. The world itself seemed to quiver, as though it recognized him for what he truly was: the end of all things.

For a long moment, he said nothing.

There was no motion, no sound in this unsettling silence. None of them could look up into his face; they were caught up in a web of fear, dreading to meet his unblinking gaze. Had they done so, they would have found that there was no gaze to meet. The Demon King's eyes were closed.

The five stood there, immobilized by the sheer weight of his presence, knowing in the deepest corners of their hearts that there was no escape, no victory to be had. There was only the unfolding of the end, and they were standing in its path.

At last, Thalrok peeked up through the slits in his helmet and noticed that the Demon King appeared to be sleeping. He whispered, "Look," and pointed to alert the others, then breathed out, "What do we do?" as quietly as he could, trying not to wake the beast.

"I don't know," Lotus replied, hesitating to move even an inch, even though the Demon King's eyes were closed and he did seem to be asleep. The moment was something of a nightmare.

"Do my eyes deceive me?" a deep velvety voice slithered its way out from *behind* the throne, its tone dripping with malice. The five intruders flinched in surprise, their hands instinctively reaching for weapons as they looked around for its source.

"It's been quite a while since I've seen a human venture this far into our domain." A figure emerged from the shadows, moving with a terrifying, unnatural grace.

"Another demon?" Rina's voice cracked, her body trembling.

"This one is... different," Nyloc growled, nocking an arrow into place with a soft, dangerous sound.

"Oh, and an angelic companion, too? How quaint." The demon's cackle echoed off the walls, the cruel mockery in his voice thickening the air. He sauntered forward, casting a long shadow over the throne. As he passed it, another figure emerged, followed by two more. They formed a loose, but imposing, semicircle.

"*Four* of them?" Lotus whispered, dread crawling up his spine. His broken sword shook in his grip.

"Ah, you probably think your arrival will awaken our precious king, don't you?" The demon's nasty laugh punctuated the tension as his finger lazily gestured toward the slumbering form of the monarch above them.

For a brief moment, all eyes lifted to the king on his throne.

Still motionless.

Silent.

Safe... for now.

"No need to worry about that," a second demon chimed in. Her voice was soft and almost sweet, as if offering them some small comfort. Her eyes were neon pink, wide and innocent-looking as she surveyed them. "Our king has been in a deep slumber for quite some time. He's not going anywhere just yet. But..." she smiled crookedly, her pink eyes now glittering with dark promise, "The time is near. *Very* near."

Lotus swallowed hard, his throat dry, "Are you... The Dark Empire?" His voice barely rose above a murmur.

The demon who had spoken first chuckled, his voice low and mocking. "Ah, so we've made a name for ourselves already, have we? How quaint. Isn't this *wonderful*, Rozzameth?"

"This is a *real* honor, isn't it? I'm sure our king would be delighted to see you all here. What do you think, Thurkoroth, shall I wake him?" Rozzameth snickered.

The five of them stiffened with every muscle locked in fear as the demon's tone shifted to something dangerously close to a threat.

Rozzameth, the winged demon, let out an exaggerated sigh, her lips curving into a wide grin. "Oh, did you see their faces? Priceless!" she laughed—no, howled—with abandon, clutching her sides as if the sight of their terror was the funniest thing she had ever witnessed.

"Enough, Rozzameth!" A sharp voice from her left cut through her laughter, harsh and commanding, as the demon Zellmon backhanded her lightly, but with unmistakable authority.

"Enough from *all* of you," the final demon, Volvimor, growled, his voice thick with irritation. He stood on the far right, his posture rigid and gaze unflinching as he surveyed the intruders. His arms were crossed tightly, "You've had your fun. Now focus."

Rozzameth straightened, wiping tears from her eyes, but the cruel smile never left her face. "Sorry, Volvimor," she said, her voice still tinged with amusement. "But really, did you see them..."

The five companions now said nothing, their eyes locked on the group of demons there in front of them, a looming threat impossible to ignore. The air hung heavy with unspoken tension. The mocking laughter of these demons? That was the least of their problems.

"I can tell by the fear on your faces that you must know who we are," Volvimor called out, stepping forward. "I don't know why you have come here, but it was a mistake." A red aura began to glow in his veins. It reached all the way up to the horns on the sides of his head, one of which was broken off near the base. Then, thick steam emanated from his body.

"Our king will not be disturbed from his slumber. The time for reckoning is near, and we will *not* have some feeble intruders destroy the one who will be our savior!" Volvimor shouted as he dashed forward, zipping right in front of Lotus with his fist cocked back and quickly swinging forward.

"Ronin!" Thalrok shouted, jumping in front of him. The bounty hunter held up both forearms to block the demon's punch, which worked, but they rattled with pain and began to burn. "Crap, that hurts!" he winced as he hobbled backward.

"You came into our domain. What for, I do not know. But now you face the wrath of the Demon King's Four Pillars of Despair." Volvimor huffed as the red aura around him flared brighter.

This was it. There was no other choice now.

Lotus and the others were face-to-face with real demons, ready to destroy them at this very moment.

There was no escape.

There was no retreat.

This was their final battle... or it was the last war.

Lotus, who had been trembling more than anyone else in the room, straightened up and took a final deep breath. With calm eyes and a steady heart rate, he smiled and whispered to himself, "It's time."

43

It's Time

In the world of Perlaria, the dawn broke as it always had, casting its golden light over the land. The people rose from their slumber, moving through their daily rituals with the same quiet certainty as every other morning. They went to work, tended to the land, built their cities, and returned to the warmth of their home and families at day's end. To them, it was just another day. The sun climbed, its rays dancing across the sky before sinking quietly beneath the horizon. There were no signs of threat, no whispers of fear. The world was calm, and all in it were blissfully unaware of the storm brewing just beyond the edge of their world.

Far from the lush valley of Prosper, past the looming walls of the forbidden world, a different story unfolded. There, in the shadow of an ancient power, five souls—four humans and one angel—fought desperately against a force unlike any the world had ever known. On this day, the fate of Perlaria would be written in blood. And its echo would be felt across all time.

"Be gone with you!" Volvimor shouted as his fists crashed into the ground. Demonic energy inside of him overflowed and fueled him to escalate his rampage.

Thalrok, huffing and puffing from exhaustion, found himself at a loss. He couldn't keep up with this guy; he was too powerful.

"Come on, Thalrok!" Lotus shouted as he ran past him, charging at Volvimor. Lotus gripped his master's sword and slashed for the demon's chest, but with each effort, the monster weaved away before he could land an effective strike.

"Your foolish attempts to strike me with that puny blade are embarrassing," Volvimor jeered, as he thrust his heel into Lotus's ribs. The young man flew, tumbling across the ground, but rolled right back up on his feet. Without a second to breathe, he shot right back in to fight.

"Ronin?" Thalrok wheezed. He saw his friend charging grimly back in. He glanced over and saw how everyone was fighting with all of their heart to win.

"Watch out, Rina!" Nyloc shouted, as he fired five arrows in her direction.

Rina soared around the room, battling it out with Rozzameth. Seeing Nyloc's arrows approaching, she quickly dodged to the side to let the flying arrows strike the winged demon.

Before the arrows could pierce Rozzameth's body, she folded her dragon-like wings in front of herself to block them. The arrows penetrated the tough hide only slightly, and she immediately flung them off by whipping her wings wide open again.

"This one is annoying me," she scowled at Nyloc, who was down below with his full attention locked onto her.

Just as she looked away from Rina, the angel thrust her spear dead center into Rozzameth's chest. The demon buckled with the hit, folding her wings in as the impetus of the strike pushed her back. Rina flapped her own wings forward to push through until she slammed her foe's back solidly against the wall with a loud thud.

"Got her," Rina panted as she tried to pull back her spear. It refused to move.

"What?" She didn't understand what was going on. Rina looked back at the spot in the demon's chest that she had struck and then saw that Rozzameth was sneering.

"Pitiful! You humans, angels, and whatever *that* one is!" Rozzameth looked down at Thalrok in his helmet. "You and your foolish attempts to destroy us. When will you learn?" she shook her head and sneered.

In the spot where the arrow should have pierced the demon's chest was a glob of an odd pink goo. It was a shocking pink in color and writhed around to grip Rina's weapon. This is what had prevented her spear from impaling the demon.

"We are *far* superior!" Rozzameth shouted, and she swiped her sharp-tipped wings across her body at Rina. The angel quickly pulled herself back, successfully retrieving her weapon and just barely missing the razor sharp talons on the fingers of the demon's leathery wings.

"Gotta line this up," Nyloc spoke through his gritted teeth. Then he fired another series of arrows at Rozzameth. He had relocated, so that now his arrows approached from a different direction than before. He sensed them closing in on Rozzameth. The arrows were inches away from striking her neck when thick, bright pink sludge appeared and grabbed onto the arrows.

"What?!" Nyloc shouted. How had his arrows *not* hit and disabled his target?

Rozzameth slowly lowered herself to the ground, shaking her hands as if they were wet. From her arms oozed more of this shocking pink goo. The strange substance glowed and appeared translucent as it continued to seep out of her body and wings and follow her as she strutted closer.

"Good luck trying anything funny now," she smirked.

Suddenly, a strong gust of wind passed by them. Rina glanced over to see Oa zipping around the room.

Oa darted, dived, and dodged, flying for his life with three winged wraiths in close pursuit. These were totally black, shadowy creatures who somehow stayed right on Oa's tail. The boy, soaring through the air, turned his body around and held his palms straight out at them.

"Air Cannon!" Oa shouted, as his palms suddenly expelled a huge burst of air. When it struck the demons behind him, they rippled and faded away like dissipating clouds of smoke. Oa landed on his feet and slid backward, then locked eyes with Zellmon, the Shadow Manipulator.

"Having a fun time playing with my puppets?" the demon asked, standing there relaxed and unamused.

"You too scared to come fight me on your own?" Oa mocked as he lowered his stance.

Zellmon scoffed. He rubbed his face carefully with his taloned hands and shook his head, "You humans are all so predict—" Oa was right there when his hands uncovered his face. Firing forward, Oa planted his foot across Zellmon's face and launched him backward. The demon was caught completely off guard and crashed to the floor.

"You ignorant pest! You have no right—" His brief moments of rambling in outrage were enough to leave him wide open. Oa was already at his doorstep, throwing a punch.

Zellmon's yellow eyes went wide as this terrifying boy clocked him across the jaw. As his head flew to the side on impact, Oa grabbed the demon's shoulders and hurled him in the other direction. Zellmon went flying through the air in surprise, and saw Oa planting his feet to come right back at him.

One more burst. Oa panted as he took off, firing as much air as he could from his feet. He was closing in on the demon and readying himself for his next move—a roundhouse kick that would slam him onto the floor. "Vortex Spike!" Oa shouted as he twisted his body and fired a sharp kick on top of Zellmon's body to drive him straight down. His foot cut through the air perfectly on target, and… his leg phased right through the demon.

"What?!" Oa shouted as he watched the form of Zellmon fade away and disappear like dust in the wind. His eyes darted everywhere, trying to find where Zellmon had gone.

All of a sudden, Oa felt a painful thud on his back near his shoulder. He yelled out in pain and surprise as he fell to the ground. When he looked over his shoulder, he saw that a blackened arrow had struck him.

"That was an admirable attempt to best me, boy. But unfortunately, your efforts were in vain," a gritty voice said.

Oa turned around to see Zellmon standing a short distance away, unscathed, and with a shadow-figure standing beside him. A blindfolded figure who was holding a bow.

"Nyloc?" Oa mumbled, confused with what he was seeing.

"I think I did a pretty good job getting the features of your companion, yes? Now let's see how well you do against this one." Zellmon smirked as the shadow-figure morphed into someone else. Its pitch-black, colorless form shortened and transformed into a person Oa knew fairly well.

"It's... me." Oa huffed in annoyance as he realized what was about to happen.

"How about you have some fun fighting your own self, huh?" Zellmon crossed his arms, ready for the show to begin.

Staring at a mirror version of himself was terrifying. Oa saw a body double, a duplicate, but as a blackened figure with empty white eyes, motionless and emotionless.

"Go have fu-un!" Zellmon sang, and pointed at Oa, bidding his carbon copy to attack.

"Here we go." Oa prepared himself as the apparition leapt forward to strike. Oa froze in place, not knowing what would come next. Does this thing have abilities like him? Will he be able to use the power of the wind to fly and fight?

Before he could think any further, a flash soared right past him and struck through the shadow. Oa's duplicate disintegrated into nothingness.

"You alright?" Lotus shouted out to Oa, feet sliding across the floor. The young disciple snapped out of it and saw Lotus, blade in hand, looking towards him.

"I'm fine! Thank you!" he shouted back.

"Thurkoroth! What are you doing? Take care of this one, you oaf!" Zellmon yelled at his ally.

"Don't shout at me! This one is just a bit of a pain, is all," Thurkoroth growled as he gripped tighter to his blade.

"You can do this, Oa!" Lotus cheered Oa on, then bolted back over to his own opponent. He held tightly to his broken sword and swung upwards at the demon, right for his chest. Thurkoroth, wielding a long, thin blade that was the length of his own body, held it out before Lotus could strike.

"Do you not have any faith in your own team?" Thurkoroth laughed.

"I have plenty of faith in them," Lotus smiled as he pushed his blade upwards, flinging Thurkoroth's blade above his head. Then the wanted man balled up his left fist and struck the demon in the chest, pushing him back. The demon's feet slid to a halt as he grabbed his blade with both hands.

"You have a lot of confidence for someone who was shaking at the knees when they saw us." Thurkoroth tried to get under Lotus's skin.

"Say that again?" Lotus tilted his head. The demon grunted in annoyance at having to repeat himself.

"I said—"

Before he could speak another word, Lotus was right behind him. He'd phased and vanished from sight in that brief moment, then reappeared behind Thurkoroth.

"I heard you," Lotus whispered into the demon's pointed ear. He quickly swung his blade and slashed Thurkoroth's back four times.

The demon howled out as the jagged blade cut into his reptilian-like skin. He jumped forward, spinning his body and swiping his blade crosswise trying to reach Lotus, sure that it would slice him in two. Then he noticed that his prey had appeared underneath his arm.

"You putrid son of—" Thurkoroth began to rage, but was interrupted when Lotus slashed at his right hand and cut off four thick fingers. The demon lost his grip and released the long, thin blade, which rattled to the floor. Shouting out in pain, he immediately felt Lotus strike him across the chest with his foot. Thurkoroth tumbled awkwardly backward, trailing black blood.

"You pathetic human! I hate you!" Thurkoroth bellowed as he stood up. He stared angrily back at the wanted man, cradling his dripping, fingerless hand.

Lotus just stood there—calm, composed, and ready to go.

Nearby, Thalrok and Volvimor heard the demon shouting and cursing Lotus.

"That's our Ronin," Thalrok smiled as he saw the powerful man he'd once fought against all those years ago shine. It reminded him of all the reasons he had decided to follow Ronin on his journey. Yet, this wasn't the same man. This man was confident, without fear. By now, he would usually be fighting the urge to lose control of his power. What was different now?

Then Rozzameth shrieked, "Volvimor!"

Thalrok looked back over at Volvimor only to find that he was gone. "What?" The bounty hunter's head whipped around to find him. He glanced over at the winged demon who had cried out, and saw that she was being outnumbered.

Nyloc and Rina had somehow found a way to sneak past Rozzameth's guard and trap her. There she lay on the ground, Nyloc digging his knee into her back as her thrashing body was pressed into the floor. Her defense of pink sludge was exhausted and no longer helping. With Rina's spear pointed at her head, the angel was shouting for her to stop moving. Nyloc had taken his arrows and stepped them through her wings and into the stony floor, holding her there.

"Stop moving, or I'll fire another!" he commanded, as he drew his bow right behind her head. The demon squirmed and wiggled to get out of her restraint, but it was too much. The two of them outnumbered her. It was an unfair match.

"Nyloc!" Rina screamed.

The archer could sense everything around him in a complete 360-degree angle, which was a miraculous ability that he'd developed. However, sometimes distraction can undermine the best of abilities.

Nyloc had no time to spin around. He tried his hardest to point his bow behind him and fire at the incoming attack. It was too late.

Volvimor struck the archer across the back of his head and sent him flying across room. Nyloc crashed into a pillar headfirst and flopped awkwardly to the ground.

He didn't move.

His body lay still on the floor, his new bow, Stritan had made, snapped in two.

When Lotus's eyes locked onto Nyloc's motionless body, he felt his heart skip a beat. He felt his blood pumping and surging through his body. He felt the dark energy now beginning to show itself. Quickly, an overwhelming hatred began to build. He took in a deep breath, closed his eyes, and slowly whispered, "Let… it… out… "

Thurkoroth, pointing and laughing at the downed archer, felt a terrifying presence in front of him. He turned to see Lotus there, just to his left, black lightning sparking from his body.

"What the…?" He squinted as he felt a change, a completely different energy. Once again, in the blink of an eye. Lotus was gone.

"Where did he go?!" Thurkoroth panicked as he felt powerful knuckles smash into his face. In quick succession, Lotus punched Thurkoroth eight times before kicking him square in the back. The demon soared across the air from those attacks. His body bounced off the far wall.

"You little—" Thurkoroth wheezed. Using his own special ability, he clapped his hands together and pulled them apart, creating a blade twice the size and heft of Thalrok's. He stood, brandishing his heavy weapon. "You want some more?! Come on!" Thurkoroth thundered, angered beyond comparison.

Lotus, with the dark energy inside him rising, ran full speed at Thurkoroth. Both pulled back their blades to strike. One blade was taller than both of them combined, the other, barely the size of Thurkoroth's forearm. But, as the demon's huge and mighty blade struck Lotus's broken one, it didn't budge.

"How?!" Thurkoroth bellowed, as he pulled his weapon back to hammer down another blow.

The battle continued, both combatants fueled by rage in what, from afar, must have looked like a very uneven matchup. Lotus could feel the dark power surging as he concentrated deeply. He remembered how it felt to see his friends hurt; he remembered how it felt to see his master slaughtered before his eyes. He remembered all of it. Each memory stoked the furor inside of him, wanting him to let loose, wanting him to yield to his powers and finish this. There was no need to hold back.

Lotus's blade was in mid-thrust when he heard Rina scream his name.

He abruptly vanished from Thurkoroth's view.

"Where did he go?" the demon shouted in confusion as the huge arc of his swinging blade crossed through empty air. His eyes scanned the room but he couldn't find Lotus anywhere.

Rina had screamed for Lotus, then covered her face when she saw Volvimor's fist crashing down on her from above. As it did, Volvimor, who planned to crush Rina with all his might, felt something off.

Too late.

His fist flung debris into the air as it struck a surprisingly hard surface. When the dust settled, he found that his target was gone and the floor ruined.

"I *missed?*" Volvimor spat out in anger. He watched as far across the room as Lotus was carrying the angel and placing her down gently beside the unconscious archer.

"Help him please, Rina. I'll deal with this." Lotus told her. And in the blink of an eye, Lotus was gone.

Rina wasted no time, she began administering her healing powers to Nyloc right away. As she placed her hands above his body, she felt a cold presence over her shoulder. She darted her head to see that behind her was one of Zellmon's shadow-figures.

"It's... Thalrok?" she stared at the huge helmeted black wraith, panicked and was unable to move.

"Get away from her!" Oa shouted, zipping by and striking the shadowy likeness of Thalrok with his bo. It toppled, disintegrated into fine black smoke, and disappeared.

"Are you alright?" Oa asked.

"I'll be fine, just... can you keep them away from me for a bit?" Rina asked, panting nervously. Oa reassured her that he wouldn't let anything get to her, and then off he went, back into the heat of battle. She watched him go, hoping that he meant what he'd said, and returned her attention to Nyloc.

From the other side of the room, Volvimor saw Lotus charging for him with a speed never before seen. With his brute strength, Volvimor could bulldoze through any obstruction in his path; he had no fear of this weak human, however fast they might be. He felt the malevolent energy inside of him surging through his veins. The red glow it produced only flared brighter as his inner rage boiled and bubbled over.

"Bring it." he hissed, knowing that Lotus was already at his doorstep.

Lotus grabbed his sword and pulled it back to slash horizontally at the demon. Volvimor feared no blade and was ready to punch this puny broken one to kingdom come. He pulled his fist back and lunged forward to strike… and was suddenly stopped mid-step and jolted backward.

"Get him, Ronin!" Thalrok shouted, as he tightened his mighty arms around the demon's thick waist.

"Let me *go!*" Volvimor shouted, wildly thrashing his arms. But the titan's grip held.

Lotus swung his broken blade and cut across Volvimor's chest with one clean slice. With that deep and painful slash, adrenaline shot through the demon's body. He howled in fury and broke free from the bounty hunter's hold, whipping his arms around wildly.

Lotus, seeing the demon escape Thalrok's grasp, felt the dark energy inside of him overflow and fill the depths of his core. For some reason though, now, it was… different. By this time, he usually would have lost complete control of his mind and gone into a savage and animalistic state. He didn't have time to process that this *wasn't* happening, and simply used the dark force as a power-up to boost his fighting ability. He prepared to get in another quick slice to his opponent, but that opening, unfortunately, had closed. A fresh conflict was at hand.

"Die!" Thurkoroth shouted as his oversized hammering blade crashed into the ground, barely missing Lotus. The wanted man had instinctively leapt backwards just in time.

"Stop running, you weakling!" Rozzameth called out. Having escaped her bondage, she flew in from behind to cut him down. She slashed her sharp wings through his filmy afterimage, as Lotus had already phased out.

"Where did he go?" the demons panted, then noticed him standing a short distance behind them.

Lotus didn't move, he just held his broken blade in his arms and stared at them. Black lightning bolts shot out from his body in all directions. The veins on his arms looked pitch black as he stood there, impassive and silent.

"You think you can defeat *us*?!" Thurkoroth roared, as he picked up his giant sword, charged at Lotus, and swung it down in a huge arc.

The wanted man watched the sword falling on him from overhead. He didn't dodge it or even flinch. He placed his own sword in its saya and lowered his head. The immense blade was inches from him. That was when he clapped his palms together overhead at the perfect time. The sword, twice the size of Lotus, stopped precisely in between his hands as he swiftly pressed in with his palms at the perfect moment.

"How—" Rozzameth could not believe her eyes.

Thurkoroth, still holding onto the hilt, was speechless. He had just witnessed a true warrior's power.

A sharp crack of thunder erupted from the black lightning surrounding Lotus as he screamed out a battle cry and pressed his palms together. With the accumulated power inside of him, he unleashed even more energy and shattered the giant blade above his head.

The two demons watching the shower of metal rain down were wide-eyed with mouths agape. Thurkoroth turned to Rozzameth and saw that the wanted man was already just inches from striking her across the face.

"Rozz—" He wanted to warn her. In the next instant, she was hurtling across the room where she crashed to the floor in a heap, winded and coughing weakly.

"You piece of—" Thurkoroth felt the air around him suddenly grow cold and heavy, as Lotus's head and attention turned sharply in his direction. His skin crawled as, too slow to defend himself, he watched Lotus knee him in the chest. Then came a punch across the face, two to the chest, and finally a swift kick to the ribs. It had all happened in a mere instant, but would be felt for many days. Thurkoroth was brought to his knees, and Lotus pummeled him into the ground.

Thurkoroth lay on the floor in pain. Seeing Lotus about to throw one last strike, he shouted, "Volvimor, *do* something!" He managed to roll out of the way this time, so that Lotus's fist struck the ground, just missing him.

Volvimor, still going toe to toe with Thalrok, heard his name and glanced in that direction.

"Don't forget who you're fighting!" Thalrok shouted, as he threw a heavy blow at the demon.

Volvimor's hands were too quick. Before Thalrok could hit him, Volvimor grabbed Thalrok's helmet and pulled him in to knee him in the stomach. The bounty hunter had the wind completely knocked out of him. Before he could do anything else, he felt two feet being planted into his chest as he was drop-kicked and sent flying.

Then, Volvimor inhaled with all his might, filling his entire lungs with air. He cupped his hands around his mouth and shouted out for the entire castle and kingdom to hear, "Ravage the intruders!!" His voice reverberated across the room.

Everyone turned to stare at him. There was a moment of total silence, which shortly afterward, was filled with the sound of flapping wings and stampeding footsteps. Hearing Volvimor's command, the hundreds of winged, toothy monstrosities that they had barely escaped from earlier began bursting in through the doors. They seemed to relish their invitation to the throne room.

"Pillars! Return to the throne!" Volvimor shouted as he picked up Rozzameth and ran to rejoin their sleeping king.

Thalrok watched as the dozens of unnatural creatures poured in from the two doorways. He ran to Lotus's side, unlatched his fearsome sword, and readied himself to fight.

Oa saw as Zellmon, too, retreated quickly toward the throne, his shadow puppets already gone. "That's a lot of enemies," Oa huffed, looking at the slavering beasts.

"Looks like the battle has only just begun," Thalrok panted, watching the hoard close in.

"Looks that way." Lotus felt the energy inside him flowing ever so freely. No wall to break through, no holding back. He could feel his consciousness begin to fade the more he allowed it to consume him. If they were going to get out alive...

"Hey, Ronin." Thalrok nudged him with his elbow, "Let's finish this and get back to Mellowtin." Thalrok smiled, then let out a maniacal howl in the face of the challenge that lay ahead.

Lotus pulled out his sword once again and stared at the approaching stampede of foes. The dark energy inside him was overflowing, corrupting his entire body with hate, rage, and malice. He should be on a rampage right now, and yet, he could feel such a warm feeling in his heart as he stood there next to his friends. With a smile on his face, he simply said, "Right!"

44

Fate on Repeat

Foe after foe, one after another, the beasts just kept coming. Rina and Nyloc stayed hidden behind a pillar, one knocked out cold and the other trying to heal him. Meanwhile, Oa, Thalrok, and Lotus continued to fight tooth and nail as the relentless, infinite swarm of monsters kept coming for them. It seemed like a battle without end.

Thalrok swung his blade and batted at them, hurling them through the air or slicing them in two. They climbed on him, scratching and biting, but couldn't overcome his brute strength. He hammered his fists against them, and one after another, down they went. He crashed his blade into the ground and knocked them off their feet with the tremors, then clobbered anything in his path.

Oa was weaving and dodging his way out of anything the demon-creatures threw at him. He was untouchable. The boy soared and dove through the air above and raced across the ground below, striking down any enemy that pursued or confronted him with or without using his bo. Releasing huge bursts of air, he pushed each horde of monsters far enough back to clear the battlefield time and time again. It didn't matter what angle they were coming from; he sent them tumbling backward to land in a heap.

Lotus. It was like watching a master at work. He was unfazed by anything these ravaging beasts tried to do, as they scratched with their claws, gnashed their many rows of teeth, and ran crazily at their three targets. His body moved on its own as he felt the powerful rush of energy inside him push him beyond his limits. When Lotus looked to his left and then to his right he saw his two friends fighting there by his side. Seeing them gave him a bittersweet feeling, and he couldn't hold back a smile, remembering just how good it was to fight alongside the ones you were close to.

The power inside him grew even more. He felt as he had never before. The raging, uncontrollable power of the dark energy was being overtaken by something, something warm. But, the dark energy wasn't fighting it, or being taken over... it was flowing *with* it.

Then a deep, terrifying voice crackled and broke through the commotion, "That feeling..." It was not a voice born of flesh, nor of breath. It was ancient, otherworldly, the echo of a thousand forgotten years.

Everyone's hearts sank.

The four of them felt their stomachs turn inside out, realizing that they had forgotten the threat that loomed right there in plain sight.

"It can't be..." The voice got louder.

Lotus, Thalrok, and Oa turned their attention to the throne in the center of the room, and were overcome with nothing but total fear.

"That power..." the voice boomed, clearer now and full of deep hatred and anger. "I *know* that power..."

The Demon King was awake. His fire-red glowing eyes scanned the room. The Four Pillars knelt on the ground at the sight of their king alert and stirring.

"King Farous," they greeted him respectfully with heads lowered.

"No way..." Thalrok said under his breath.

"It has been hundreds of years since I first perceived that power." His fingers curled around the armrests of his throne, cracking it beneath his grip. "Now, to sense it again brings me nothing but pure *rage!*" the Demon King Farous bellowed. He gritted his teeth in a snarl as he leaned forward. He glared at Lotus, staring him up and down, then squinted his eyes and rested back on his throne.

"The power that put me *in* this state hundreds of years ago is right *here*, in *my* throne room…" Farous began to chuckle, then roared with laughter and howled in delight.

"I found you!" he crowed, "Finally! After all of these years, I can be rid of it! I, Demon King Farous, will take my rule as this world's god and I will vanquish the weak!" The air soured with those words.

Thalrok and Oa looked over to Lotus, surprised to see just how calm he was.

Is he… smiling? Thalrok wondered, sweat dripping down inside his helmet.

Lotus dashed over to the bounty hunter's side. "Thalrok! I need you to buy me some time! A minute tops!" he begged.

The bounty hunter had no idea what Lotus was talking about, but loved seeing this fearless side of his friend. "Right!" Thalrok replied, brandishing his mighty blade.

"Attack them, my loyal subjects!" Farous commanded as he gestured at the intruders with his taloned hands. Volvimor, Rozzamoth, Thurkurok, and Zellmon, along with the packs of fearsome monsters, rushed to obey their king, ready to tear the intruders apart piece by piece.

Lotus darted to Oa's side and pulled him behind a pillar so fast that no one even saw where they went.

"What's the matter?" Oa asked, having no clue what was going on.

"Listen to me very carefully." Lotus grabbed onto Oa's shoulders and began to speak.

Thalrok, standing alone at present, but feeling the will and strength of the titans flowing in his blood, shouted out, "Alrighty, who wants some!"

At this moment, there wasn't a thing in the world that was going to stop him. He felt invincible.

The winged and toothy creatures attacked first, one after another, and were simply swept aside. Again and again, they charged him, but at this moment, the bounty hunter who'd been raised by titans was unstoppable. Even though he was totally outnumbered, he unleashed all of his strength to bat away any monster or demon that came at him. He laughed in their faces; their puny attacks were no match for him. This could go on for a minute or even a whole day, it made no difference to Thalrok.

"I have to buy Lotus the time he needs," he panted, slamming his blade into the ground and shaking the stony floor with massive tremors. He saw the four demons readying themselves to make a move.

Hidden behind a pillar with Lotus, Oa was speechless. He knelt there with his mouth half open and his eyes staring blankly in the distance.

"Oa, can you do this for me?" Lotus asked.

"I…" Oa was bewildered by his request.

"Oa, *please*," the wanted man begged.

The young disciple, astonished, couldn't believe what he was hearing. His body froze, his mind raced, and fear rushed in.

Lotus glanced up and saw that Oa was bleeding. There was a deep wound on his head where he'd been cut pretty badly by one of Zellmon's shadows.

"Here." Lotus took off his bandana and wrapped it around Oa's head to staunch the blood and cover the gash.

"Lotus…" Oa mumbled, as his chin dropped to his chest.

"It'll be fine." Lotus smiled as he patted Oa's shoulder reassuringly and then dashed back to Thalrok's side.

The young disciple watched him run off to battle and just sat there, stunned and motionless. All he heard was Lotus's words repeating over and over in his head.

"Took you long enough!" the bounty hunter said jokingly as he saw Lotus return. He slammed his hands on the ground, flinging the swarm around him backward as Lotus joined him.

"You ready?" Thalrok asked.

"Ready," Lotus nodded.

The two of them stood side by side, watching their enemies come back to battle them. Lotus and Thalrok had been together in this from the very beginning. They'd found out about the Infected Ones together, which led them to meet the others who joined them, which eventually led them here.

They'd learned a lot about one another along their journey, which was a demanding one, for sure. Together was how they'd started, and that had to be how they ended it.

The Demon King now sat forward and boomed, "I *cannot* sit and let this go on. I will end it *myself*!"

"Sir, you shouldn't! Your wound hasn't fully healed!" Volvimor advised.

"It doesn't matter! I must see to it that I end what has done this to me!" Farous bellowed angrily, and then held his palms towards each other in front of him, chest-high.

The castle began to shake. Wind swirled around the room and spiraled its way to the Demon King. His hands were close together and in the hollow between them a small purple sphere of energy began to grow. Pulses of energy shot out of it, cracking like thunder as the tremors only got worse. The Demon King's evil laugh floated over the battle going on below his throne.

Thalrok and Lotus could feel the pressure of his building power. "That's gonna be a problem," Thalrok gasped, as he knocked down another of the endless enemies.

"Looks like it," Lotus huffed.

The two of them watched Farous' energy grow more powerful, and soon the entire place shook from its foundation up.

"It doesn't matter what he does! We can take it! Let's do this, Ronin! You and me! Let's finish this!" Thalrok declared, enthusiasm high as he readied to battle on with his friend by his side.

"Let's..." Lotus replied.

Thalrok had just turned away from Lotus when he felt two slender arms slide under his armpits, clench tightly, and pull him abruptly backward. Suddenly, he felt his whole body being lifted. Astonished, Thalrok found himself flying across the room.

"What!?" he shouted, totally confused about what had just happened. He looked up and saw Rina hanging onto him for dear life. Her arms could barely hold the heavy bounty hunter as she flapped her wings desperately to gain altitude. Oa hovered uneasily nearby with Nyloc slung across his shoulders.

"Rina?!" Thalrok looked back and saw Lotus facing that formidable horde all by himself. "Ronin! What are you doing?!" he shouted to Lotus.

The four of them stared down at him from their airborne perspective; he stood there alone, smiling up at them.

Lotus didn't say a word to his friends, and when he turned back toward his foes, his smile was still in place. "They're safe," he said, and exhaled in relief. That was when the surging light energy overflowed and bloomed from inside of him. His blackened veins disappeared as a luminescent warm glow surrounded his whole body.

"*That* power! I *will* destroy it!" Farous shouted, as his orb of energy grew.

The hordes of demons and monsters charged at Lotus, but their efforts were pointless. He moved even faster than ever before, zipping across the room, swinging his fractured blade and knocking them down faster than they could come at him.

"You *and* that power will fall by my hand!" The Demon King's voice roared above the chaos, his own power continuing to grow quickly.

Lotus couldn't remember the last time he fell this way. The intense power inside of him was not overrun with sadness; this time, there was… peace. He had no worries on his mind and could let himself breathe.

"Let me go! I need to help him!" Thalrok shouted, from their position close to the high ceiling. He wriggled a little, testing Rina's hold on him. The others said nothing.

Working hard, Rina flapped her wings to keep her weighty cargo above the fray. Oa, struggling for balance with Nyloc's limp body slipping off to one side, flew just behind her.

"Roniiiin!" Thalrok shouted. He watched as his friend knocked his foes down one after another with his radiant aura glowing brightly. He'd never doubted the whole time he knew him; *this,* was Ronin.

"*Get* 'em, Ronin! *That's* what I'm talking about!" the bounty hunter cheered.

Lotus moved faster and faster, almost too fast to follow, except by the trail of fallen enemies. He was knocking down one after another like it took no effort at all.

"What are you guys doing? We have to go help him!" Thalrok yelled, but got no single response. Even though the drop was now high enough that he might perish, Thalrok tried to free himself. Rina gripped him even tighter. She remained silent, laboring to fly far from this battle.

"*This* is your *end!*" the Demon King proclaimed. His moment had come.

Then Lotus could feel it, could feel the light energy calling for him to take it and run. The wanted man stopped where he was. He stood in front of the throne a short distance away and stared up at the Demon King.

The surge of energy Farous had created was ready to burst. Forcing both of his hands forward, he released a wide beam of dark demonic energy that fired out like a rocket.

Lotus, closing his eyes, held out his own hands. As the giant beam of darkness was about to destroy anything in its path, Lotus created a wall of pure light that towered far above him. The energy released from Farous crashed into that wall and pushed.

The Demon King pulsed his hands, forcing all the energy he could into this attack. Lotus could feel his hands shaking as he held back this unfathomable amount of power.

"You are a fool for bringing *that* power here. My time to come out of the shadows is near! I will *take* what is mine and *destroy* this world!" the Demon King bellowed. He spewed out even more energy, making his dark beam grow even larger.

Lotus stood his ground, feeling his feet slipping backward just a little. The mighty wall of pure light stood strong. He wasn't going to let anyone hurt his friends.

"That's what I'm talking about! That's the Ronin *I* know!" Thalrok cheered as they neared a window, and would soon be outside.

Lotus could feel his eyes closing and his power draining fast. He wasn't going to be able to maintain his wall for much longer. He had to think of something to do, anything to stop this attack. He felt his hands trembling, his arms aching, as the demon's power only grew. Then, Lotus's eyes shot open and he saw, right there between his hands—

"Come on, Ronin!" Thalrok cheered even louder. They were far outside of the castle walls now. "Rina, I am *serious,* take me back! Oa, you have to—" Thalrok looked over and saw Oa staring back at the castle with his eyes wide and his mouth agape. Tears were rolling down his face.

"Oa?" Thalrok didn't know what was going on. Then, the bounty hunter turned around.

Oa's eyes had seen it. No one looking that way could have missed it.

With the sound of a sonic boom, the gigantic beam of demonic energy broke through and demolished the entire wall of light in front of Lotus. It shattered in a crackling flash, splintering into shards of light that dissolved into the air. Even before the dust could settle, the roaring beam consumed the spot where Lotus stood, a blinding shaft of energy that swallowed everything in its path as it shot across the entire land. From the outside, there was no sign of him, only the searing dark energy, writhing and expanding, until the world itself seemed to vanish inside it.

The four companions, hundreds of feet away and flying to safety in the opposite direction, watched as the beam finally faded and trickled from the sky. They could barely see the top of the castle clearly, but it was obvious to them.

Lotus… wasn't there.

45

All is Lost

The wind was a cold, unfeeling thing that whipped past them, carrying with it the hollow sounds of a battlefield left behind. Their ears rang. Their bodies ached with the strain of their escape, but it was not a physical pain that consumed them, it was the emptiness that gnawed at their souls. The nightmare of events from moments ago scratched through their minds, unable to be forgotten.

They had fled.

They had escaped while one of their own had stayed behind, sacrificing himself to the darkness.

Rina's wings, which simply couldn't hold up anymore, buckled in exhaustion. Oa, still with Nyloc slumped on his back, couldn't produce another burst from his feet. They were able to glide awkwardly for a short way before crashing to the ground, where all of them tumbled and then came to rest like puppets suddenly parted from their strings. There they lay, beside one another, crumpled and defeated. The broken, sprawled on a patch of unfamiliar ground that offered no comfort, could find no refuge from the torment that pursued them.

Rina lay there, her chest heaving with labored breaths. She stared skyward, with nothing in her blue eyes but the dull shimmer of a soul lost in despair. She had been their hope, their healing savior, and now she was as broken as the rest of them.

The sky above was a shade of red so deep it felt as if it were pressing down on them, suffocating them with its oppressive weight. There was no sunlight to warm them, no light to reassure them. The world was a void, an abyss that echoed the gaping hole inside each of them.

They had abandoned him.

The sounds of the battle still rang in their ears, a symphony of destruction that played over and over in their minds. The final image of their friend, the one who had stood and fought alone, burned into their retinas. That flash of dark energy, so pure, so consuming, had torn him from their sight.

Had he felt it? Had he known the end was coming?

No words passed between them.

What could they possibly say after abandoning a friend, a brother, and then witnessing his cruel and merciless end? Guilt and sorrow wrapped around their hearts like an iron vice. Terror of the raw power of the Demon King, who effortlessly broke past their attempts.

The wind still howled.

The earth still turned.

But for them, everything had stopped.

And in that stillness, all was lost.

Finally, Thalrok stood up, rising from his pit of despair to get on with… something. Oa and Rina, tears on their faces, saw him stand. He stood staring off toward the castle with his fists balled up, squeezing tighter and tighter. In time, he relaxed his grip and let his hands dangle in the wind. Then, without saying a word, he walked over to Nyloc, who was still out cold, and picked him up.

Rina and Oa, faces covered in blood, sweat, and tears, saw Thalrok throw the archer over his shoulder and head west, back toward the wall. They got up and followed behind him, their heads hung low.

The three of them marched on, the last vision of their fallen friend miles behind them. They felt a flood of emotions as the sound of the dirt beneath their feet crunched in harmony.

Hours… Hours and more hours of mindless walking.

The three of them would not, could not, stop. They trod an unbearable path of pain, and moved as though in a trance.

Nothing about this was real.

None of it could be real.

It was all a nightmare. They were all going to wake up from this hell, and everything would be back to normal. So, on they went.

Finally, there it was, the part of the wall they had crossed through.

Five had gone in… only four came out.

Thalrok, emerging from the crevice through the wall, covered his eyes as the setting sun hit his face. Right where they had left it, the *Land Skipper* was ready to take them home. Even the ship, in its stillness, felt that something was missing, as though somehow its insentient self, too, knew it was leaving something behind.

Thalrok wrapped his fingers around the steering rods. He exhaled as he turned the ship around and let the gentle breezes take them home. Oa, Rina, and Thalrok hadn't said a single word to one another since their flight from the castle.

Then, Nyloc's unconscious body twitched. He sat up and rubbed his head, feeling the world moving around him. He had no idea how he got here or what had happened. He did, however, know that at least they'd escaped. Did they win? Did they lose? He didn't know what to ask. That's when he felt that something was terribly off, and asked, "Where's the captain?

* * *

The *Land Skipper* came to a slow stop. There was Mellowtin, just in front of them, going about business as usual. They were home. They made it out. They did it…

Following behind one another in single file, with heads down and bruised, bloody bodies, they headed back to the inn. Dragging their feet, the four of them stuck out like a sore thumb. People from the town walked past them, glancing at the blank looks of misery and pain on their faces.

"Hey, hey! They're back!" Stritan's dad shouted from inside his shop when he saw them walking up the road. Stritan ran outside to see them with his own eyes. He raced over to them, waving his hands and shouting out, "Welcome back!" Then his eyes bounced from one to the other.

One.

Two.

Three.

Four...

"Hey... Where's Lotus?" Stritan asked, his brow furrowed in confusion.

Not one of them stopped walking. The four passed right by Stritan, staring at the ground.

"Guys..." Stritan mumbled. He was worried and wanted to know what happened, but by the looks on their faces, he was afraid to know the answer.

No one responded, except for Nyloc, who was holding up the rear. Without a word, he placed his hand on Stritan's shoulder as he passed by, then let it drop and sway down by his side.

The boy was speechless. It couldn't be true...

When the doors of the inn creaked open, and they entered one behind the other. Leyla and Layla came out from the backroom and saw them looking battered and bruised. They both immediately noticed that there were four, not five, who had returned.

The twins had no chance to prepare themselves. They knew *exactly* what had happened from the hollow eyes and sad, dazed expressions they saw on the faces of their favorite guests. They held onto each other and cried softly, as the four dejected companions dragged themselves up the stairs.

The long hall seemed to stretch on for miles as they made their way to the common area connecting their rooms. Oa, Nyloc, and Rina stood quietly, lifting their heads to watch as Thalrok walked over and stared at Lotus's door. None of them knew what to say. Each of them felt an unbearable anguish and did not know what to do to ease it.

"It is said," Thalrok finally spoke in a broken, deep voice, "Years ago, if a titan were to return home after fleeing a battle, or leaving a man behind, he would be disgraced…" The bounty hunter turned and walked across the room. He sat down on a couch there and sat with his head in his hands.

"It's shameful for me to abandon my friend and still call myself a titan." Thalrok gripped his helmet, then carefully lifted it, removing it from his head. Everyone's eyes widened in shock. So stunned was Oa at his friend's actions, that he felt dizzy and swayed a little on his feet.

Thalrok placed his helmet on the table in front of him and looked briefly and directly at each of his friends in turn. This was the first time in many a year that he had shown his face to *anyone*.

"I… I can no longer call myself a true warrior…" He broke down.

His friends watched sadly as Thalrok's rugged face flooded with tears.

46

Grief

Days. Weeks. One month… an entire month passed. For a while, they stayed secluded in their own rooms, refusing to show their faces in the village. Countless sleepless nights exhausted them, and when they did manage to fall asleep, nightmares consumed their minds and woke them up in a panic. Leyla and Layla tried their best to bring them out of the hole they were in, bringing them food and checking on them discreetly.

It was hopeless. They would never be the same.

When Thalrok resurfaced, he spent his days at the bar drinking, and then drinking some more, to numb the pain. There wasn't a single moment that he *wasn't* at the Fork and Sword Tavern when it was open. And it was open sixteen hours every day. The barkeeps would sometimes suggest that this might not be the best for him right now, but he begged them each time to please just give him one more drink, and so they did.

Oa emerged a few days after Thalrok, and would stay outside training from morning until late at night. He broke his body down over and over, trying to fill the void inside of him. It didn't matter the weather. Scorching heat, raging storms or endless gusts of wind. He kept pushing himself further. It wasn't the same without Lotus; it was too… different, empty. He passed out more times than he could count from overexertion; he just couldn't stop. The more often he stopped, the more he obsessed over what had happened.

Rina couldn't help but feel as guilty as everyone else did. After about a week she made herself go out and then spent her time helping those around the town. She would be out at all hours, wherever and whenever she was needed. Using her healing abilities to help others who were sick and hurt was a way for her to numb the pain, to prove in her mind that she can still help others. She *can*...

Nyloc must have left Mellowtin after spending only two days there since they returned. They hadn't seen him at all the entire month. No letter, no sign, so goodbye. He had given no notice whatsoever to anyone about going, much less where he was going, or what he would be doing. It was hard to bear, but the others understood.

When the twenty-eighth day rolled around, late that night, Oa, Rina, and Thalrok all found themselves trudging back to their rooms at the same time. They couldn't even look at each other. They felt the guilt and pain flow as they stood miserably by one another in the common area between their rooms. Without a word, they moved to turn in for yet another sleepless night.

"Wait." Rina tried to stop them. The bounty hunter and disciple of Gou halted simultaneously and stood staring at the doors to their rooms.

"We can't keep living like this. We can't keep living in the same state of pain day after day," she pleaded softly.

Oa turned around from his doorway and saw the look of despair on Rina's face. The two of them then glanced over to Thalrok. He didn't acknowledge them at all; his drunken self just fumbled with the door handle, staggered inside his room, and closed the door behind him. He just couldn't bear to open that wound.

The two of them stood in silence, hanging their heads as Thalrok's door shut. They didn't know what to do. They didn't know what to say. Even though a whole month had passed, this wound still felt fresh. Rina sniffled. She was about to go back up to the roof and cry herself to sleep as always. Then, the sound of light footsteps echoed from down the hall. It must be Leyla or Layla bringing them some late-night tea. They turned to see—

"Nyloc?!" Rina cried.

There he was.

"You're back!" Rina rushed over and wrapped her arms around him. She could feel just how cold and thin his body was, his muscles felt weak and frail. Her eyes widened when she pulled back and saw his sunken cheeks and pale face. It seemed as if he hadn't eaten for a while. His clothes were dirty and the filth on his body coated him from head to toe.

"Where did you go?" Oa asked noticing the ragged appearance of his friend.

Rina guided him over to take a seat on the couch. His feet dragged across the floor as he fell into the chair with a plop, then put his head in his hands.

"I looked everywhere," Nyloc rasped.

"For what?" Rina asked, rubbing his back.

"I looked for him everywhere." His stoic voice strengthened, but sounded full of regret. "I checked village after village. Big, small, or broken. I checked the entire city of Cannon-Gulf. Villages far north, east, and west. Even a broken-off village in the south. I didn't find him anywhere," Nyloc sobbed.

"Is… Is that why you left? To look for Lotus?" Rina asked.

"I let my weakness create our defeat. This is all *my* fault!" Nyloc shouted, slamming his hands on his thin thighs.

"Nyloc, this isn't your fault. We…" Rina didn't know what to say. She had no idea how to comfort him right now. She felt the tears welling up in her eyes as she heard the pain in his voice resonate through the halls

"It's *my* fault," Oa spoke up.

"You're wrong! I am—" Nyloc was interrupted.

"Just *listen!*" Oa shouted.

Nyloc and Rina went silent. They had never heard him raise his voice like this. They looked across the table to him sitting in the chair, head low and hands in fists.

Oa's face was pinched with anger, not at the others, but at himself. He began by saying, "Lotus pulled me aside during the battle. He… he told me that he planned it this way from the very beginning. He knew that if there really *was* a real threat in the forbidden world, it would be too big for us to stop." Oa paused, wiping tears from his eyes.

"He told me that, no matter what happened, he would make sure we got out alive, and that he would take care of it. He said his power would take over, and he wanted us to escape safely." Tears streamed down Oa's face. He felt at his forehead, at the bandana that he hadn't taken off since the battle a month ago.

"I should have sworn to him that we would be by his side to the very end, but he... he was insistent and so at peace with his decision. He looked so happy to see us fly to safety. I... I didn't know what to do." Oa broke down completely, placing his head in his hands.

Rina and Nyloc hurried to his side to comfort him. The boy had lost a friend, truly a brother. He couldn't hold it in anymore. He trained hard every day to push back the pain and anguish, yet at some point, he was bound to break.

A creaking sound caught their attention. They lifted their heads to see a door slowly opening. Thalrok emerged from his room, eyes hollow, but body upright and steady.

"This is what Ronin wanted?" Thalrok asked. His voice was quite sober, and serious.

Oa, swiping tears from his face, nodded his head.

The bounty hunter walked over to sit across from his comrades. He took a deep breath in, exhaled through pursed lips, then lifted his head. Despite being most certainly more than a little drunk, his amber eyes were clear and he looked into each of their eyes in turn.

"There is something we have to do," he said sternly.

A week later...

"Are you all packed up?" Leyla and Layla asked the four companions.

"Yes, ma'am." they replied in unison.

"Alrighty then. We will keep the *Land Skipper* safe while you're gone.

And your rooms are here for you as usual, for when you return." The twins bowed their heads as the travelers waved goodbye and headed out.

Since the night that Nyloc returned, all four of them—Thalrok, the bounty hunter, Oa, disciple of the seer Gou, Nyloc, the blind archer, and Rina, the angel—joined together again as allies in battle, and fellow travelers. Now, they were off once more.

As they passed under the gates of the Mellowtin, they heard Stritan yelling, "Wait! Please, wait!" They stopped, and turned back to see him sprinting toward them.

"Please... *please* come back safe, alright?" he puffed. Stritan's bottom lip quivered in a face that was overcome with worry. He just wanted them to be okay, and to come back all together and in one piece.

Thalrok, who still would not wear his helmet, went to him and placed a big steadying hand on his shoulder. He looked Stritan in the eye and smiled, saying earnestly, "I promise."

Feeling somewhat reassured, Stritan waved as he watched them get farther and farther from Mellowtin. He felt as if another part of him was leaving, and too soon. There had been a lot for him to take in, but he was ready and willing to do his part. Stritan wiped his face and went back to work. They were all relying on him. The four of them all pressed on through the lands of Prosper Valley. The wind was at their backs and the path ahead was clear.

"This is what Ronin would want." Thalrok beamed, as the others followed behind him. Their long trek across Perlaria went more quickly than expected. With a powerful motive and a burning passion, the world was on their side.

"The City of Light," Oa whispered, as they crested the horizon and paused. They could see the city just ahead.

"We tried once and failed. Now, we *must* succeed." Thalrok took a first determined step forward, the others following along.

"We need to warn the City of Light of the terrible danger that is on its way. The people, the city, and the world, *everything* comes down to this moment!" Thalrok shouted. They marched on, ready to do what they

could before it was too late because—
    The fate of the world was on the line...

To be continued...

About the Author

For a large part of my life, I struggled to focus on anything. My ADHD was a lot to handle, and my mind was always racing to different places. I would often daydream, imagining myself in other worlds, creating childish stories in my head. I didn't realize it back then, but that would later spark my passion.

I remember feeling this strange sensation deep inside when watching movies, listening to music, and even reading books. I wanted to be that person on the other side, to craft stories that pulled people to the edge of their seats. Sparking their imagination and having them beg for more each time they experienced it. Even after the movie, book, or song was over, there was a lingering sensation of just wanting to feel it again. *That's* what I wanted to do.

When March 2020 came around, I found myself wanting to scratch the itch of creation. I always loved making things, whether it was music, videos, or even writing. Funny enough, this was the one thing I put last on my list, and now, it's the one that flourishes above them all.

I look forward to the moments I can sit down and write each day. If my younger self heard me say that… he would definitely think I was lying.

Never would I ever believe I would have to be typing something like this out, but damn, it feels good. I would not be where I am without the loving people I surround myself with: my family, friends, and my students. In the story of my life, *they* are my favorite characters.